The Sky Soldiers

A novel

By

Victor R. Beaver

Published in the United States of America

Copyright © 2000, 2001 by Victor R. Beaver
All rights reserved. No part of this book may be reproduced,
stored in a retrieval system, or transmitted by any means,
electronic, mechanical, photocopying, recording, or otherwise,
without written permission from the author.

ISBN: 0-75961-299-4

This book is printed on acid free paper.

1stBooks – rev. 4/24/01

With Earth's first Clay They did the last Man knead
And then of the Last Harvest sow'd the Seed:
Yea, the first Morning of Creation wrote
What the Last Dawn of Reckoning shall read.

The Rubaiyat of Omar Khayyam

Acknowledgements

Special Thanks

A very special thanks to my parents, Victor and Marcelene Beaver, who helped me, coddled me, nurtured me (and tried to feed me vitamins) throughout the final writing of this book. Had it not been for their unselfish support, this work might not have ever been completed.

Special Acknowledgements

Donald W. Jackson, former crewchief and Soc Trang Tiger, I salute you for being there during the final stages of this work. You never tired of giving that moral support so typical of an ex-comrade-in-arms.

Natalie Marie Beaver, who believes in me, who always believes in me, and who gave of her time to proofread and offer invaluable suggestions to improve the manuscript.

Acknowledgements

Over the years the following people have encouraged me or offered editorial assistance or advice: Mike & Trish Doyle, Laura L. Beaver, Mike Dash, Virginia O. Moebus, Marcelene L. Beaver, Marcia Graham Smenner, Jeanne Myers, Jay & Cleo Zarr, Sherry V. Beaver, and all the others, too many to mention. Thank you one and all.

Honorarium

There are two men I would like to honor...both of whom I served with in Vietnam. Had it not been for either of them, this book might not ever have been born.

CW2 Lawrence J. Babyak, killed in action late November 1969, vicinity of Quan Loi, Republic of Vietnam.

MSG Jeffrey G. Moebus, U.S. Army retired, who many years ago spoke a truth to me like no other man could.

I dedicate this book to

Laura,

Who gave me two very lovely

And precious daughters...

Natalie and Anjuli.

Author's Note

This is a work of fiction. It is neither history nor a personal account. Except for such historical names as then President-elect Richard M. Nixon and General William C. Westmoreland, any resemblance between any character and any person living or dead is purely coincidental. On the other hand, the 1968 Tet offensive did happen; the members of Warrant Officer Candidate Class 67-15 did graduate, but in September 1967; and any military unit mentioned by letter or number designation existed but not necessarily at its actual location or referred to by its actual unit callsign nor is the time frame that it performed at its actual location necessarily consistent with fact. The names of all hamlets, villages, towns, cities, geographical entities, etc., are real and are mentioned in exact relation to one another. But any military unit that resided at or performed at any particular location or any description of any location is drawn from my memory at the least and my imagination at best. Finally, any technical inconsistency (in fact, *any* inconsistency) is both intentional, depending on the dramatic effect it is attempting to elucidate, or an oversight (or lack of remembrance, or due to a complete and unintentional ignorance, but never intended to mislead or misrepresent), and I leave it to the reader to decide or speculate which.

—Victor R. Beaver

In Memory of the following Sky Soldiers

CW2 Griffin, Francis L.
CPT Bradley, Franklin S.
WO1 Hull, Ricky L.
SP5 Anzelone, Paul R.
SP4 Lynch, Michael J.
SP4 Catlin, Willie B.
WO1 Moncrief, William C.
CPT Hering, Robert H.
SGT Purtell, Robert B.
1LT Carmichael, Robert E.
WO1 Debner, Dennis C.
LTC Kvernes, Roger W.
SFC Spivey, Eddie L.
WO1 Luse, Kenneth A.
WO1 Boyter, Geddes C. Jr.
WO1 Chaney, Arthur F.
CW2 Creal, Carl M.
WOC Ammons, Charles R. Jr.
CW2 Crews, Robert

The Sky Soldiers

A Saga of Men in War

Part One

Sandy Adamson

War Demands Resolution, Firmness, And Staunchness

RESOLUTION is an act of courage in single instances, and if it becomes a characteristic trait, it is a habit of the mind. But here we do not mean courage in face of bodily danger but in the face of responsibility; therefore to a certain extent against moral danger...mere intelligence is still not courage, for we often see the clever devoid of resolution. The man must, therefore, first awaken the feeling of courage, and then be guided and supported by it because in momentary emergencies the man is swayed more by his feelings than his thoughts.

Firmness denotes the resistance of the will in relation to the force of a single blow. Staunchness in relation to a continuance of blows. Close as is the analogy between the two, and often as the one is used in the place of the other, still there is a notable difference between them which cannot be mistaken. Inasmuch as firmness against a single powerful impression may have its root in the mere strength of a feeling, but staunchness must be supported rather by the understanding, for the greater the duration of an action the more systematic the deliberation is connected with it, and from this staunchness partly derives its power.

Force of character leads us to a spurious variety of it—obstinacy.

From Ernest Hemingway's anthology *Men At War*.

Chapter 1

KEITH SLATER SUCKED DEEPLY as blasts of hot humid air swirled around him. The helicopter had slowed, rocked slightly as the ship's assigned crewchief and gunner moved to open and pin back the two large cabin doors, then steadied again as the aircraft picked up speed. He watched the crewchief, the doorgunner on the left side, swing his machine gun up to level, lock and load the belted M-60 ammunition from the feed can, then adjust his position on the nylon seat, he thought for a better angle to shoot. Peering at the land below, then a quick glance at the crewchief, Slater expected bullets to come flying up at them any minute. Instead, he saw the man lean back, yawn deeply, rub his eyes, and then stare off into space.

Slater felt the helicopter bank right...there was the sensation of slowing again...and then he could feel the ship bank left, back to an attitude level with the horizon. From the left cabin side he could see—surrounded by a vast domain of rice paddies and large isolated clusters of vegetation—an oval-shaped airfield perimeter with a long paved runway situated down the middle. On the west side of the runway stood a two-story, red-and-white-checkered, air traffic control tower. North of the tower were two large steel-topped hangars. And surrounding these were many smaller buildings, each seemingly engulfed by large clusters of banana trees. "We're on left downwind!" Slater shouted to the crewchief. Immediately, he felt foolish; he had blurted it out to impress the chief that he was a pilot.

"Soc Trang! Your new home!" the man came back.

Slater nodded. *Yeah, right, my new home, half a world away from Hutchinson, Kansas...* It seemed as if he had left there ages ago. Had it only been six days? He shook his head and remembered the drive with his father to Wichita. From there he flew to Kansas City and caught a direct flight to San Francisco. He spent three days at Oakland Army Depot waiting for his port-call date. The first two nights were spent in a drunken stupor as he and several other brand new warrant officer pilots toured Fisherman's Wharf and the strip-tease joints off Haight-Ashbury. Finally, on the third evening, everyone was packed in buses and driven to Travis Air Force Base to board a World Airways Boeing 707. There were no bands, no flag-waving, no speeches about honor and bravery and coming battlefield glories—just one hundred and sixty-seven officers and enlisted men ferreted away under the cloak of darkness, in the middle of the night.

The trip over took twenty-three hours. They refueled twice, in Hawaii and then at Clark Air Force Base in the Philippines. At last came the final descent, during which they felt the big jetliner bank sharply left and right every few moments until they were lined up on approach to Bien Hoa Air Force Base, Republic of Vietnam.

The humidity hit them like a ten-ton sauna.

They spent two days in-processing at Camp Alpha. On this morning he waited for a flight out of Tan Son Nhut to Can Tho, leaving at noon aboard a de Havilland CV-2B twin-engine Caribou. At Can Tho he endured the three-hour paper shuffle that processed him into the battalion. And now the helicopter ride from Can Tho. Slater checked his watch; he noted that it had taken eighteen minutes to fly to the Soc Trang Army Airfield traffic pattern. In four minutes, he would be officially in his unit and officially in the war.

At mid-downwind the crewchief tapped his shoulder; he pointed toward their left front at a cluster of trees and hootches that bordered the airfield perimeter at the south end. "VC Village!" he stated. "We got this gook who likes to take a pot-shot at us every now and then when we line up on the runway!"

"Oh yeah? Do you ever shoot back?"

"Not allowed to!" The man shrugged. "No one's taken any hits—yet!"

"Shit, why doesn't somebody go after him?"

"I think it's because we don't want him replaced by someone who can shoot straight!"

Slater looked again at the village. *That's just great. Today he'll get lucky and hit me right in the ass—!*

Well, it was the first tidbit about his new home and Keith Slater felt pleased that at last he was in real danger, something of consequence to write about in his journal. And then, suddenly, he felt very uncomfortable. He knew that his hands couldn't stop a bullet, but he cupped his groin area anyway and brought his legs into a semi-fetal position and wished like hell he was sitting up front, in one of the armor-plated cockpit seats.

The helicopter banked sharply left. Looking down, Slater saw the main POL (fuel storage) point and next to it a pool of oily water. There came another sharp bank to the left, so low to the trees and hootches of the village that he could almost reach out and touch them. Then the aircraft turned abruptly to level and he could see they were lined up on the runway. Within another second they passed over the south perimeter fence. "Mr. Oakerson is one nervous dude, man!" the crewchief said. The chief was referring to the ship's AC (aircraft commander). "He swears one day that damn gook is going to shoot us straight out of the sky!"

Slater finally breathed a sigh of relief when the helicopter slowed and came to a hover not far from a white, stucco-sided, tile-roofed building with a sign out front that read:

The Sky Soldiers

WELCOME TO SOC TRANG AAF
121ST ASSAULT HELICOPTER COMPANY
HOME OF THE
FAMED SOC TRANG TIGERS

WO1 Fred Oakerson, whom Slater had met and talked to briefly at Can Tho before boarding, was in the right seat on the controls. Oakerson kicked in left pedal, hovered to a square pad of PSP (perforated steel planking), kicked in right pedal and turned again, aiming the helicopter perpendicular to the runway. The helicopter swayed as it lowered; when the landing gear touched, there came a sudden violent jolt, as the aircraft became earthbound. "Mr. Oakerson can't land this thing worth a shit, either!" the crewchief shouted for the last time.

"God, I'll say," Slater muttered to himself. He rubbed his neck, relieved to find nothing jarred loose. He wondered, too, how the man made it through flight school...much less had become an aircraft commander.

The crewchief helped him off-load his baggage, placing the gear near a small cluster of banana trees, after which the man returned to the aircraft and got into his seat. Slater then watched as Oakerson lifted the ship off the pad. It wavered awkwardly then seemed to charge across the runway, coming to a halt just before hitting one of the high-walled, sandbag-filled, PSP aircraft protective revetments. Observing all this, Slater wondered if he was about to witness, for the first time in his young aviator life, the complete destruction of a perfectly good helicopter. He shook his head in disbelief as he saw the aircraft settle into its assigned revetment—intact.

His briefcase in hand, Slater turned and went into the stucco-walled building. A tall, dark-haired, rather gangly-looking man, standing behind a chest-high counter, looked up. "Ah, Mr. Slater. Welcome to Tiger operations. I've been expecting you. My name is Captain Slote. I'm the operations officer. If you have your flight records, you can hand them to me and I'll post your name on the flight status board." Slater shuffled through his personnel folder until he found the wanted records. He handed them to the captain who glanced through them momentarily, then turned and faced a large mission planning board covered by a sheet of clear plastic. Slater gazed at the board. Black horizontal and vertical lines crisscrossed the board against a white background, and marked in blocks, in grease pencil, were the names of aircraft commanders, co-pilots (termed peter-pilots in Vietnam), flight crewmembers, aircraft tail numbers, aircraft readiness status, and current missions being performed. Slote said, after he logged Slater's name and current flight time: "I take it the rest of your gear is outside?"

"Yes, of course, sir."

Slote called into the back room. "Mr. Henry, would you come out here please?" The gangly captain cocked an amused smile. "Mr. Henry's my assistant operations officer."

Slater took a moment to size the captain up. He noted that the company operations officer was sharply dressed—in spite of the heat and humidity—in a set of neatly pressed jungle fatigues. Perched at the tip of his hawk-like nose was a set of reading glasses, giving him the appearance of an Icabod Crane. His ears poked out from the side of his head like two opposing shark dorsal fins; and when he spoke, his high-toned voice made his Adam's apple bob up and down like a weight at the end of a spring. It was within that moment that Slater knew he disliked the man intensely.

"I'll have your in-country stan ride posted after Lieutenant Whitaker gets back from Vung Tau," Slote stated. "Should be some time in the next few days. He's the White Tiger platoon leader. It looks like you're going to be assigned to his platoon."

Slater nodded. "Okay, sir."

When Henry appeared Slater almost burst out laughing. Turquoise-colored paint was everywhere: in the man's hair, on his face, all over his fatigue pants and his OD T-shirt. Keith extended his hand. "My name is Slater, Keith Slater. But I like to be called Kip."

"Hi, I'm Robin Henry."

"Mr. Henry, would you help Mr. Slater with his luggage? I believe Lieutenant Whitaker wants him in the hootch next to the Tiger's Den."

"Yessir."

Slater followed Henry outside. "Been painting...as you can plainly see," spoke Henry. "Slote's kiss-ass idea, a jump-start on sucking up to the new CO we got coming in three weeks. Personally, I think the color stinks."

"Boy, I'll say."

Slater hoisted a duffel bag and small suitcase, while Henry picked up the new man's flight helmet bag, along with a bag containing his in-country clothing issue.

"Overall I think you'll like it here," Robin Henry said, as he guided Kip toward three stucco-walled hootches near a larger building on the far side. "We've got the best gun platoon in the Mekong Delta. They're called the Vikings. I've got my name in for a left-seat slot when one becomes available. They're real picky who they let fly with them."

They went past a tiny Quonset hut hidden among a cluster of banana trees. "The officers' barbershop," Henry said. "The little papa-san who works in there—I swear—will make a new man out of you. He gives a terrific neck and back massage." They continued past the Viking ready hootch. Through open shutters Slater saw several men inside shooting pool, each man wearing a black T-shirt, a trademark of the Vikings. Directly outside the hootch, parked between protective revetments, were two Huey gunships, heavy looking with rocket pods and machine guns mounted on their sides. A crewchief was on top the aircraft closest to them handling a grease rag, inspecting the main rotor system. Henry paused to watch. "The gunships are always set for a quick-start: main and start fuel on, throttle set just past the idle detent. I've seen them become airborne in less than a minute, consistently."

"Man, that's fast," Slater said.

"Got to be if we want to nail Charlie before he shuts down his mortar tubes."

"Mortars?"

"Yeah, we get hit about two to three times a week. Twelve to eighteen rounds. Funny thing is, it's been about a week since our last little event...Those little pricks must be saving up."

Henry turned toward a yellow-walled building fortified all around by sandbags packed as high as the shuttered windows. Slater saw that most of the sandbags were rotted open. "Your hootch," Henry commented, as he entered the building and guided Kip down a narrow, darkened hallway. "Built by the Japanese during World War Two. Practically all permanent structures here are left over from the Japanese occupation."

Slater nodded. "Is that why the paved runway?"

"Yep. We've had to do very little construction here. Places like Can Tho and Vinh Long, with all their helicopter activity, can be virtual dust bowls."

Henry turned left into a vacant room. "This is it. Ain't much, but with a little imagination, you could have some first-class living quarters."

Kip dumped his duffel bag on the cement floor. There was an army standard metal folding cot (minus a mattress) against the far wall; above the cot was a window with both shutters closed. In one corner was a small closet with a few hangers hung on a rod; in another a table and chair. Slater glanced up. Overhead he observed the ungainly rafters exposed to view. Overall the room appeared dark, dank and dingy.

"If you get chummy with the guy next door," Henry said, indicating the room adjacent to Kip's, "he just might invite you to share his air-conditioning."

"Air-conditioning?"

"Yeah. His name is Bronski. He's one of the gunpilots. He's got it sealed completely. I swear it's like an icebox."

"Are you kidding?"

"Another thing, when he leaves...in three months...he's going to sell that room. Bet he gets at least four hundred bucks."

"Four hundred dollars?"

"You got that much to blow on an eight-by-eight cubby hole?" Henry asked.

Just then someone appeared in the doorway. "Hey, Kip!"

Slater turned. "Leo!"

"Why I'll be a sonofabitch—what the hell you doing here?" The two gave each other a bone-crushing hug.

"Hey, I'm assigned to this unit."

"You're shittin' me."

"I ain't shittin' ya."

"It's obvious you two know each other," Robin Henry said.

"Of course," Kip Slater exclaimed, elated to see his friend. "Leo Tannah and I went through flight school together. We partied practically every weekend at Panama City Beach."

"So what the hell took you so long to get over here?" Leo said.

"Well, when they changed my orders, they issued me a new port-call date. It gave me an extra week at home."

"Lucky stiff. Hey, guess who else is here?—McNamara!"

"Mac! No shit—?" McNamara was also an ex-classmate.

Henry excused himself, leaving the pair to their reunion.

"Come over to my room," Leo said. "It's right across the hall from our resident polar bear. He keeps it cold as a deep-freeze. There are guys saving up to buy it from him before he leaves. It'll easily go for over four hundred dollars."

Kip frowned. "Yeah, Henry told me. How can he sell it? Isn't it assigned to the platoon?"

"Yeah, it's assigned all right, but a couple of weeks before he leaves, if he wants to get rid of it, and somebody wants to trade rooms, that trade ain't going for no chickenfeed—I guarantee."

Leo's room was lavishly furnished. In the company eight days, he had already acquired a small refrigerator, a Pioneer amplifier and tuner, two large Kenwood speakers, and an Akai reel-to-reel tape player. A fan whirred in one corner moving the air with a soft pleasant breeze. His cot was against the wall; a camouflage dust cover served as a bedspread. Overhead, hiding the rafters from view, hung a flare parachute. Leo invited Kip to be seated in a wicker chair, opened the refrigerator and presently handed him a beer. "Cheers," said Leo, as he raised his can. "Welcome to the Soc Trang Tigers. Best assault helicopter company in all of Vietnam—!"

Kip took two healthy swigs and felt the liquid warm through him. He stretched his legs. "Jesus, Leo, you got a great setup. Where'd you get everything?"

"Well, I've been to Saigon twice, to the Tan Son Nhut PX. That's where I bought all the stereo equipment and the refrigerator. The fan I got here at our little PX. They sell like hotcakes. You've got to be right there when they come in. I got the parachute the day I took my stan ride. It was with a guy named Justen. He's a CW2. He's been over here eighteen months. He and Lieutenant Whitaker are the company standardization pilots. When you take your ride, with either one, boy are you in for a treat. We did low-level, pop-up autorotations, over treelines—*to a touchdown!* That's how I got the parachute. We landed near one and Justen asked if I wanted it. So I jumped out and stuffed it in my flight helmet bag. They make neat ceilings, don't they?"

Kip nodded. He took another long swallow of beer. Leo turned his stereo equipment on. A Peter, Paul and Mary song began to play.

> *"Puff, the magic dragon*
> *lived by the sea*
> *And frolicked in the autumn mist*
> *in a land called Honah Lee..."*

"So how long does it take to make aircraft commander?" Kip asked.

"Two to three months."

"Is that all—?"

"Well, in that amount of time you'll have been everywhere and done everything—and you'll probably have over three hundred hours."

"No shit—three hundred hours?"

Leo nodded. "Christ, Kip—the first day I flew, after my stan ride, I logged nine point seven hours. The second day I logged ten point three. So far, in five straight days of flying, I've got over forty hours. This is my first day off."

Kip computed quickly. "Crap, at that rate you'll have over two hundred hours in a month's time. It took us nine months of flight training, minus the four weeks we spent in preflight, to get two hundred and eleven hours."

"I know, I know."

"You been on any combat assaults?" said Kip.

"Nope, not yet. Just re-supply—ash and trash. And the two courier runs to Saigon." Leo rubbed his hands together. "But I can't wait, Kip. With you and me here, we're going to kick Charlie's ass—!" Leo then stood, went to the refrigerator and drew two more beers. He said:

"I got a question."

"So shoot."

"You still doing your journal?"

"Yep, I've hardly missed a day. Why?"

"Well, I'll tell you," Leo said, the tone of his voice very somber, "there's a real story over here."

"Well, hell, I wouldn't doubt that."

"No, I'm serious, Kip. If you plan on writing a novel, what's taking place over here, no one will believe. Take lots of notes."

"Well, I plan to record everything," Kip said.

"That's good, that's good...It needs to be."

* * *

SECOND LIEUTENANT PAUL CHRISTIAN reached up and adjusted each of the six cockpit-light dimming switches until the instruments were bathed in a soft

11

red glow. He leaned forward. Peering into the darkness, he sought the slightest trace of a horizon: there was none. Their progress was marked by the slow passage of an occasional dim yellow light that would appear suddenly out of the gloom, seem to float toward them, then disappear beneath them...as if the light had motion and the helicopter had none.

Christian looked to their left front. He could just barely make out a large concentration of lights. He took his flashlight and turned it on. A red beam played over the map he held on his lap. He determined that the lights were those of Bac Lieu, a medium-size city near the coast of the South China Sea. Checking further he saw that a canal ran straight from Bac Lieu to their destination, Ca Mau, still seventy-five kilometers away. At a speed of ninety knots they would arrive within the half-hour.

He glanced at the ship's clock: 0315. They had been airborne for seven minutes. The lights of Soc Trang Army Airfield were now far behind them. As they flew along, enveloped like they were in the nearly empty blackness, it was not hard to imagine they were on some ill-begotten journey, going to some remote, far-off region, to a place no one knew, where gremlins lived and dragons roamed. Christian shuddered. He had been in-country a mere three weeks and was still unfamiliar with the AO (area of operations): To him, Ca Mau couldn't have been more remote had it been placed on the moon.

They were pulling the nightly medevac standby mission. They had been on the standby duty since eight o'clock that evening. On call from dusk to dawn, the crew and ship provided medical evacuation support for the ARVN (Army of the Republic of Vietnam; a person or persons in the Army of the Republic of Vietnam) for the lower half of the IV Corps tactical area. They had had only one call earlier, from Vinh Chau, a small outpost south of Soc Trang. The American advisor there radioed that one of the local RF/PF men was experiencing bad stomach pains and nausea. When they brought the man in he was taken and operated on immediately. (RF/PF, Regional Force/Popular Force, or South Vietnamese government local force militia.)

Christian looked left. The pilot in the left seat sat in stone-like silence. "Where are you from, Mr. Justen?" he asked. He spoke mainly to break the silence.

"Me?...Oklahoma."

"You married?"

"No."

"I understand you've been over here awhile."

Justen nodded. "Awhile."

Several awkward moments of quiet prevailed. Paul Christian sat back and sighed. He reflected on his first days in the unit. He had been assigned as a White Tiger section leader shortly after he arrived and it was then that Trent Whitaker told him all about Derek Justen. He learned that Justen was twenty-eight, that he was just now beginning his second six-month extension with the Tigers, that he kept pretty much to himself, and that he had a brother, actually a half-brother, listed as MIA, missing-in-action. Trent told Christian that Jake Cole, late in November 1965, was flying his O-1 Bird Dog "reconnaissance" aircraft around Bay Hap, a small village south of Ca Mau, when he reported having engine trouble. Soon after he put out a Mayday call and gave his position as three kilometers east of Bay Hap. No further radio reports followed. An air search conducted later that day located the wreckage, but when the ground team arrived, they found no trace of the ship's pilot. However they did see several sets of footprints around the crash site. It was therefore presumed that First Lieutenant Jacob Aaron Cole had survived the impact and was probably being held prisoner. At the time, Justen was in the United States attending flight school. When he arrived in Vietnam five months later, as a new pilot assigned to the 121st Assault Helicopter Company, his brother's actual status was still unknown.

    The helicopter slipped past Bac Lieu to the right. Christian continued his search for the horizon, but the darkness ahead pervaded. Still no demarcation between sky and Earth. Justen was flying by instruments and Christian noted that the aircraft commander was doing it expertly from the left seat. He had taken his in-country standardization check-flight with Justen two weeks before. Expecting a certain amount of animated conversation to put a new man at ease, Justen, instead, briefed him cordially, yet with noticeable detachment, on the flight maneuvers to be performed. Though Justen's silent manner calmed him, Christian still sensed a tremendous underlying tension about the chief warrant officer. Justen's mission, he further uncovered, was to remain in Vietnam however long it took to find or learn about his brother.

    Christian again splayed light over his map. They were now passing due north of Gia Rai, a small village still thirty-three kilometers from Ca Mau.

    Justen said, "Take the controls. Keep this heading and two thousand feet. I'll look up the Foxmike frequency."

    Christian acknowledged then placed his feet and hands on the controls.

    Justen withdrew a small booklet, called the SOI, signal operating instructions, from his left breast pocket. He adjusted his map light and quickly found the frequency along with the current callsign. He tuned the radio. "Digger Run Five Three, Digger Run Five Three, this is Tiger Nine Eight Six."

    There was no reply. Justen tried again. Finally, a tired voice came back. "Tiger aircraft...inbound...are you the medevac ship? Over."

    "That's affirmative," Justen answered. "ETE about seven minutes. We'll need fuel."

    "That's a rog...we'll be waiting. You'll also have two extra passengers to take to Can Tho."

    They flew several more minutes. Gradually, a collection of lights came into view, having the appearance of a large horseshoe on a black canvas.

"Ca Mau," Justen announced. "The airstrip runs east and west, almost splitting the city in two. Made of dirt and gravel, the runway parallels, on the south side, an elongated body of water."

Justen directed Christian to descend straight ahead to one thousand feet. As they lost altitude, the air became noticeably warmer. "Okay, slow back to sixty knots so we can open the doors." Once at the slower speed, Conrad and Finch, the ship's assigned crewchief and gunner, unlatched the cabin doors, slid them open, and secured them with stainless steel pins. The two doorgunners then readied their machine guns. "We're set in the back, sir."

Justen directed Christian to turn slightly left. "Okay now roll out. You're lined up on final. Start a five-hundred-foot-per-minute rate of descent."

Christian did as he was told. "Man, I sure hope you know where we're going...I can't make out a damn thing."

At three hundred feet above the ground Justen reached across the center console and flicked on the landing light and searchlight. Two white beams penetrated downward. The airstrip was directly in front of them. Justen rotated the searchlight until he found one of the large black fuel bladders near the water's edge. Justen said, "I have the controls."

Christian gave the controls over and fixed his eyes outside. Justen slowed the helicopter more, bringing the ship to a high hover fifty feet from where a nozzle attached to a black hose was perched on a metal rod sticking out of the ground. The aircraft commander then moved the helicopter toward the metal rod until it was abeam the ship on the right-hand side. "Are we clear down?" Justen asked.

"Clear down right," Finch responded.

"Clear left," said Conrad.

With the aircraft on the ground, Finch got out, closed the right cabin door, and released the fuel-tank cap. He lifted the fuel nozzle from the metal rod and squirted a small amount of fuel on the ground, to clear the hose of any moisture or stray contaminants. He then stuck the nozzle in the fuel-tank opening. After the refueling was done, Justen hovered the ship to the passenger pick-up pad in front of the local MACV headquarters building near where several ARVN and an American sergeant were standing. On the ground to their front lay a man on a stretcher. (MACV, U.S. Military Assistance Command, Vietnam.)

When the whirlwind of dust settled the sergeant approached and stood on the left front skid toe. "He's got gangrene—bad!" the man shouted to Justen over the drone of the helicopter. "They'll probably have to amputate! He's an officer! You'll be taking two of his men with you!"

Christian then watched as Conrad motioned for the soldiers to advance with the stretcher. As they came closer, he could see that the man's left leg was heavily bandaged, the bandage also badly soiled. "Why did it take so long for them to call?" Christian asked over the intercom. Justen relayed the question to the sergeant.

The sergeant shrugged. "Sir, please don't ask me why these people do what they do!" Christian could hear the man's reply shouted into Justen's keyed microphone.

Christian watched as Conrad and Finch helped the Vietnamese soldiers load the stretcher into the center of the cabin area. Then the stench of the infected leg drifting from the back hit him. He saw Conrad waving his hand in front of his face.

Conrad said, "Mr. Justen, sir, after liftoff, can we keep the doors open?"

"Whatever you guys want. It's up to you," Justen said.

The crewchief then directed the two ride-along soldiers to be seated and buckled in. Appearing oblivious to the smell, they jabbered excitedly with smiling, glowing faces, as if this was a long-awaited moment...the trip of a lifetime.

When everything was ready, the two doorgunners announced:

"We're set in the back."

Justen remained on the controls. "Coming up."

They took off and headed due west climbing quickly to three thousand feet. Christian thought the night air darker than before, having an even eerier blankness to it. After several minutes, Justen turned the aircraft north. Christian said:

"According to my map, we should take up a heading of about zero four zero to go to Can Tho. Aren't we over the—"

"U Minh," Justen said, finishing the statement for him.

Chills ran up and down Christian's spine. The U Minh: *Forest of Darkness.* He had heard of it, a region of ragged forests, thick mangrove swamps, barren mud flats, and interlacing rivers and canals, where he was told several Viet Cong Main Force units trained and from which they staged military operations. True or not, and because it was an area left virtually alone by ARVN and U.S. ground forces, it was not difficult to understand how it had become a legend, much like the Lost Dutchman's gold mine in the Superstition Mountains of Arizona. *U Minh...U Minh...U Minh...*its very name made him shudder. He knew that now they were well inside its eastern boundaries. In the inky blackness, Christian could not see the terrain below but sensed an evil place beneath them. He knew that if they went down here, their chances of survival would be very slim.

Justen broke the spell. He began to flash the landing light on and off...on and off.

Christian breathed deep. "What are you doing?"

Justen didn't speak. He continued every few seconds moving the switch on the right-pilot collective control lever up and down...up and down.

"Morse code?" Christian asked.

Two clicks over the intercom (meaning yes, affirmative).

Justen began the series of flashes again. J-A-K-E. "You're spelling your brother's name, aren't you?"

Justen jerked his head toward the lieutenant. "How did you know—?"

Immediately, Christian noted the terseness in Justen's voice. "Lieutenant Whitaker told me. You think he's being held in this area?"

"I have a strong hunch he is."

"Sir! Receiving fire! Nine o'clock—looks like a fifty!" Conrad announced from the rear.

Justen quickly glanced left. Christian looked over his left shoulder. He saw the green glow of an enemy tracer, having the apparent size of a baseball, arcing toward them. Others followed. Reactively, Justen pulled in power and began a climb; he leveled off at four thousand feet. Two more tracers flew toward them then the danger ceased. Justen ran the Morse code series one more time, then kept the landing light off. He turned the helicopter northeast. "You have the controls," he said to Christian. "Fly heading zero six zero now. Should take us straight to Can Tho."

Chapter 2

THE OVERHEAD SPEAKER OF THE Colorado Springs's Continental Trailways bus terminal blared the final call for a bus departing to the north and made its second call for one leaving to the west. Travelers going on the southbound bus, destination Dallas and various stops in between, still awaited their first boarding announcement. Several passengers responding to the call for the northbound bus said their final good-byes, turned and made their way toward a set of double doors. There were other gatherings of people, but one in particular, a rather large group, was focused on a youth of medium height adorned somewhat awkwardly in the shiny newness of his army dress green uniform. More than half of those around him were ex-high-school classmates, while in the background stood the young man's father, along with an eleven-year-old daughter.

Sandy Adamson reached up and tried to fit a finger between his neck and the collar of his shirt. As he did a pair of slender hands found their way around the knot of his tie and unbuttoned the top button. "There," said a young woman's soft voice. "No one from the Army is here to check up on you. Certainly, you should be allowed to relax as you travel."

Sandy looked down. A pair of emerald-green eyes, flecked with gold, gazed back. "Thanks, Katie," he said, taking her hand and holding it firmly by his side.

"Hey, Sandy, do you get to start flying right away?" Bobby Cordova asked. Bobby had been a teammate in track, the anchorman in the mile-relay event. Sandy had always run the third position, handing the baton to Bobby.

"No. There's a four-week 'preflight phase' I'm supposed to go through first," Sandy said.

"What's preflight?" asked Chuck Ryan, another teammate who had thrown "shot" and the discus.

Sandy shrugged. "I don't really know. I guess it's where they try to make you quit."

"You're not going to quit, are you, Sandy," stated Debbie, Chuck Ryan's girlfriend.

"Not on your life," he replied with a wide grin.

"They say hovering a helicopter is the hard part," mentioned someone off to his left.

"Yeah, that's what I've heard."

"Will you be going to Vietnam right after your training?"

"I think so," Sandy answered, hoping to avoid that particular subject.

"Yuk, that's the last place I want to be," Bobby remarked.

"I'll go where they send me," Sandy stated. He felt the pressure of Katie's hand.

Victor R. Beaver

There were other questions, for which he groped for answers. Finally, his father, noting the time, came to his side and quietly placed two twenty-dollar bills in his hand. "For whatever you need, Son."

"Thanks, Dad."

"Give us a call right away when you get in. Your mother will be wanting to hear from you."

"Yeah, sure. Are you going?"

His father nodded. "It's getting late. Time for Melissa's bed." Then he motioned his daughter forward. "Go ahead and give your brother a hug."

Melissa stood on her tiptoes and gave her brother a kiss and a hug. "I'm going to miss you, Sandy. I'll write you every day." And then she said, "I know you can fly; I have lots of faith in you."

A lump caught in Sandy's throat. "Thanks, little buddy. I'm going to miss you, too."

His father gripped his hand. "Good luck, Son."

Just then the overhead speaker announced the first boarding call for his bus. Sandy shook hands all around and endured several pats on the back. He picked up his small overnight bag and with his hand on Katie's shoulder led her to one side. "Well, here I go again."

"Promise you'll call me right away, too?" she said.

"I promise," he said.

"I'll be home from church around eleven. I don't plan on going anywhere afterwards."

Sandy gazed down. This was always the hardest, going off to the unknown, as he had done when he left for basic training nearly three months before. "I'm going to miss you, Katie."

"I'll miss you too, Sandy."

"Now don't forget, I'll be home at Christmas, when we get our break," he reminded her. "That's only ten weeks away."

She tried to give him a cheery smile.

"I love you, Katie."

"I love you, too," she answered.

Sandy took a quick glance around and then drew her to him. He kissed her tenderly on the lips. Katie responded with a quiver. When he withdrew, he saw her eyes brimming with tears. "Hey, where's my big girl?"

She forced a timid smile. "I-I just worry about you."

"Please, I'll be okay."

She nodded. The speaker announced the second boarding call. Sandy quickly gave her another kiss and then with his overnight bag, moved through the double doors. He stepped to the bus and gave his ticket to the driver. Moving along the aisle he found an empty window seat where he could see her. He waved and she blew him a kiss. Already his heart ached for her, on top of the feeling he had just felt when she pressed her small breasts against his chest.

Shortly, the bus backed out of its stanchion and pulled out into city traffic. After a few minutes of maneuvering, it turned and began moving up an on-ramp; the bus accelerated and before long driver and passengers were lumbering full speed southbound down the freeway.

Sandy sat back and sighed. For a moment he stared straight ahead. Everything was happening so quickly. It seemed like yesterday he had graduated from high school. Now he had endured two months of basic training and had already graduated from that! Would the next nine months go by as fast? Afterwards, though, he knew it meant one thing: Going to Vietnam. Would he be ready? He hoped so. He wanted to be worthy in this life—to be capable and brave.

Sandy reached up and tugged at his tie. When it was off he stood and slipped out of his dress coat and stowed it neatly on the overhead rack. Then he sat back down and closed his eyes. All he wanted to think about was Katie: how she looked, how she felt, how much he wanted her. He breathed deep. A relaxed calm came over him. Someday they would marry. How would it be, he wondered, to be in bed with her, to be making love to her? The notion was almost beyond his comprehension.

As the bus traveled south past the base of Cheyenne Mountain, Sandy saw the lights to the entrance of NORAD's underground complex, his father's last assignment before retiring from military service. After a few more miles he dug in his bag and found a transistor radio. He put the earplug in and turned it on. He heard his and Katie's favorite song, sung by Jerry Vale. It washed over him like a gentle breeze...

> *"In the misty moonlight,*
> *by the flickering firelight...*
> *Any place is all right,*
> *long as I'm with you..."*

They had formally met a month after the start of his senior year. From the moment he first saw her, he knew he wanted to know more about her, and through simple detective work learned her name, that she too was a senior, and also a transfer from another school in the city. Their lockers were practically side-by-side and it was during that first month that he gathered the courage to speak to her. One day, after the last class bell had sounded, he saw her putting her books away. He swallowed the lump in his throat.

"Hi."

She turned. "Hello."

He stood transfixed. "Would you...do me a favor?"

She said, "Sure, what is it?"

"Would you go to Homecoming with me?"

She gave him a sideways look. "Wow, that's some favor."

"Would you?" He felt his heart thumping in his chest.

"Gosh, I don't even know you," she stated, unsure how she should respond. She wasn't unfamiliar with him, though; on more than one occasion she had taken note of his shy yet serious manner.

He extended his hand. "My name is Edward Sanders Adamson. But I like to be called Sandy."

She extended her own and he felt its delicate softness. He waited for her answer.

"Well, Sandy," she said, contemplating his light blue eyes, "I'll have to let you know."

He was crestfallen. He thought she might be waiting for some other boy to ask her, but then gave him a pleasant smile, re-casting her spell on him. She said, "Don't you want to know my name?"

"Oh, I already know it. You're Katie Lee Williams. You transferred from Billy Mitchell High."

She grinned. "Well...you sure do your homework."

He blushed. That night he hardly slept. The next morning he was waiting for her at her locker. He spied her long before she saw him. When she caught sight of him, she smiled. His heart skipped a beat.

"Well?" he said, trying hard not to appear too eager.

"Yes, I can go."

"You *can* go? What do you mean? Did you have to get permission?"

"Yes, from my mother. She's kind of funny about that." She saw his puzzled look. "She comes from a rather strict family, who still live in the Boston area."

"Oh...I see."

"I'm supposed to tell you ahead of time that I have to be in early."

"Okay—no problem," he said.

"Good. Then I guess we're set."

From that day on he walked her to all her classes, no matter how far they were from his own. Half the time he had to dash like a madman to keep from being late. But he didn't mind: his enthusiasm for this lovely green-eyed girl had no bounds. He found, too, that five minutes walking down a crowded noisy hallway didn't allow for any meaningful conversation, so he asked for her phone number. Evenings, then, after he did his homework, he called and they talked about everything. He learned that her father, a veteran of World War II, was the manager of an auto parts store. Her mother, head nurse of obstetrics at a local hospital, had also been a veteran, an army nurse stationed in England during the war, which was where and when her parents met. She had an older brother who was in the navy, an electronics technician first class onboard a ship somewhere in the Pacific. She had plans to attend college and study music.

"And what is it you want to do with your life, Edward Sanders Adamson?"

"I want to be an architect," he said. Though he stated it in all seriousness, deep down he wasn't sure at all. Being an architect, though, had a certain noble ring and he did want to impress upon her that he had worthwhile ambitions, whatever they turned out to be.

Homecoming was in mid-October. It was their first real date and his first meeting with her parents. True to her New England-born heritage, Katie's mother was a stern looking woman who spoke with a high, tight-strained voice. Upon his arrival she offered him a cup of tea, which he declined. She asked him questions about his family and what his plans were after graduation. Sandy thought her mother overly protective of her daughter. When Katie finally entered the room, he stood, his eyes blinking in disbelief. She looked far lovelier than he ever imagined. She gave a quick little skip to her step, then did a twirl to show off her dress. He barely noticed the dress, so intent was he on the sparkle in her emerald-green eyes. He presented her with a corsage, which her mother pinned to her dress. Her father had them pose for several pictures. When it was time to leave, Sandy placed a wrap around Katie's shoulders and opened the door. "Be home by eleven o'clock," her mother said.

"Yes, ma'am," Katie replied.

They danced to every slow song played. With her head nestled in the crook of his neck, he sensed the soft fragrance of her hair, which made his head swirl. They moved very well together, he thought—in perfect concert. "You're very beautiful, Katie."

"Thank you. And you look quite handsome yourself," she said, lifting her head to gaze at his face.

The golden flecks in her eyes dazzled him, while the color of her hair, a deep auburn hue, enthralled him. He bent and touched his lips to her forehead. "I want to be something special someday," he told her.

"You will. You're going to be an architect."

"I don't know," he said. "I might change my mind."

"Well, whatever you decide," she said, as she danced cradled in his arms, "I'm sure you'll be good at it."

"Do you really think so?"

She looked up. "Of course...don't you?"

"Yes, I hope so."

They left the dance early and parked in front of her house. Sandy turned off the engine. Katie, after checking to see if anyone was peeking from behind a curtain, snuggled into his arms. She offered herself to be kissed. He said, "Listen, Katie, if you don't mind, I'd really rather sit and talk. I like kissing, but sometimes...well—"

Right away he saw her hurt and puzzled look and thought, *Now I've blown it.* This was not coming out at all as he intended. He wanted to explain how he had dated one girl whom he liked a lot, but since she had no curfew there were times when they would sit and kiss for hours. It was so frustrating.

"Sandy," she said, looking at him with an amused smile, "I think you're one in a million. And I agree, people do forget to be friends first."

"Then you understand?"

"Yes, I understand." She then drew him toward her. She looked into his eyes and said, "I really like you, Sandy. I want to be your girl. But you'd better kiss me once in awhile or I'll wonder if you're serious." And with that, she kissed him gently, yet firmly, on the lips.

The bus slowed then turned into a small parking lot in front of an all-night diner. It was after midnight and they had just crossed from New Mexico into Texas. The driver announced a thirty-minute rest stop and opened the door. As Sandy stepped from the bus he saw a young man in an army summer-tan uniform standing next to the entrance of the diner, a tightly packed duffel bag at his feet. "I'm going to get something to eat. Would you like to join me?" Sandy offered. He spoke more to the uniform than to the face, which he tried hard not to look at, for fear he might burst out laughing. It had been years since he recalled the puppet character Howdy Doody, famed for its reddish-orange hair, face full of freckles, and ears that stuck out like Dumbo the Elephant.

The face full of freckles lit up. "Sure."

"Where you headed?" Sandy asked, as he opened the door to the diner.

"Fort Wolters, Texas. Helicopter pilot training."

"Oh, yeah? So am I," Sandy said, in disbelief. "What's your class number?"

"67-15. How about you?"

"Why hell, that's mine too," Sandy said, extending his hand. "I'm Sandy Adamson."

"Seymore. Seymore P. Cutter. Glad to meet you. And don't ask me what the P stands for...I ain't telling."

Inside the diner they found two seats at the counter. After the waitress had taken their order, Sandy asked his newfound friend:

"Are you from around here?"

Seymore nodded. "Yep. Born and raised. I was in Dallas, though, living with my sister when I got my greeting from Uncle Sam. I had just started working at this rinky-dink fast-food joint."

"So you were drafted?"

"Nah...I went ahead and joined."

"Me too. I was supposed to go to college, but I couldn't see doing that."

After a few minutes, the waitress brought their order. Seymore sipped at his coffee. He asked, "You gotta girl?"

Sandy nodded. "We're almost engaged. How about you?"

Seymore raised an eyebrow and shook his head. "No way, Jose." Then with an infectious grin he put his cup down and flicked both ears with his fingertips. "Freckles, red hair, and these flaps...I'm definitely slated for bachelorhood."

Sandy laughed. Already he liked this guy, kind of kooky yet with a serious side to him. "You'll find someone."

"Ha! Not if I can help it."

After boarding, Sandy offered Seymore his window seat. Within minutes, Seymore had his head pressed against the window and was fast asleep. Sandy leaned back. He closed his eyes. Images of Katie flooded his mind...

It was a Friday night in late January. He had taken her to a basketball game and afterwards to their favorite place for something to eat. "You've been awfully quiet," he said, looking at her from across the table. "Anything the matter?" During the whole of the evening she had not been herself. Something clearly was troubling her. He was afraid there might be something wrong between them, but he couldn't guess what. He reached over and touched her hand. She looked at him with a long face.

"They're sending Brad to Vietnam," she said.

Sandy's eyes widened. "They are?...Where?"

She told him her brother's ship would be anchored off the coast of Vietnam, somewhere near the DMZ (demilitarized zone).

"When did you find this out?"

"He called this morning," she said. "His ship was in Hawaii, at Pearl Harbor."

Sandy sat back, slightly relieved, glad that her troubles had nothing to do with them. But he could see she was shaken and this unnerved him. He had finally met Brad during Christmas, when her brother came home on leave. Sandy remembered how impressive he looked in his navy uniform.

"Oh, Sandy, I'm so worried!"

He reached again for her hands and held them tight. "He's going to be fine, Katie. He'll be onboard his ship. He won't actually be *in* Vietnam."

Her shoulders slackened. "Yeah, I-I guess maybe you're right..."

In early March it was her turn to notice a certain preoccupation in him. She thought he might be worried about making the mile-relay team, but watching him during practice she knew he had that cinched. During his warm-up sessions, though, he kept doing something very curious. Every now and then he would look to the south, his hands over his eyes to shield the sun. He appeared to be searching for something, but she didn't know what. This went on for several days. Then one day as he was doing his stretching exercises he stood and faced south. She came down from the bleachers. "For heaven sakes, Sandy, what are you looking for?"

Victor R. Beaver

He had both hands up around his eyes, formed like a pair of binoculars. "Do you hear it?"

"Hear what?"

"There—I can see it!" She followed the point of his finger. After a few seconds of searching, she saw the tiny speck coming toward them. The noise it made became louder and louder, until it was a thundering clatter against her eardrums. It was a helicopter out of Fort Carson, and though they seldom flew over the city, this one passed not more than five hundred feet above them. She saw Sandy waving at it. He turned and shouted at her. "Wow!—isn't that neat? I'd love to fly one of them!" Her hands were pressed against her ears. She hadn't heard a word he said; she just smiled and nodded.

On a Saturday morning in April he came to her house. "Can we go for a drive?"

They drove north until they came to their favorite parking place, a hilltop overlooking the city. He parked the car. The huge Pike's Peak massif loomed before them. "Katie, I've got something to tell you."

"Yes?"

"After graduation, I'm joining the army."

She wasn't sure she heard him right. "You're joining the what?"

"The army. I've been to see the recruiter. I took a bunch of tests. I'm going to be a pilot—a helicopter pilot."

"Wh-when did you do all this?" she said, stunned.

"About a month ago. I had to take a physical examination. I got the results back today. I passed."

She peered at him. "But, Sandy, what about college? What about architect school? What made you change your mind?" She felt suddenly out of breath.

"College will have to wait," he answered. "This is something I really want to do." He paused and looked at her. And then he asked, "What do you think?"

She struggled to catch her bearings. "How long will you be in for?"

"Initially, three years. But I'll have a three-year commitment once I finish flight school."

"And after flight school...where will you go?" She was certain she knew the answer.

"Wherever they send me, I guess."

"Vietnam—?"

His heart skipped a beat. "Yes...probably, I'm not sure." He wanted to sound nonchalant, wishing her to believe that where he might go was secondary to what he wanted to do: fly helicopters. But he knew that wasn't true. The more he thought of it, the more he realized that where he belonged was in Vietnam, doing his duty. Going to college, he felt, when his country needed men to fight, seemed wrong. He had read several magazine articles saying that if the United States didn't stop the Communists in Southeast Asia, his country would end up fighting them on its own shores. This made perfect sense to his young, impressionable, then seventeen-year-old mind.

Sandy gripped the steering wheel, feeling the strain in the muscles of his arms. He turned to look at her. He saw the tears welling in her eyes. "Look, Katie, going to Vietnam is a long way off—almost a year. Anything can happen. The war could be over by then," though deep down he hoped it wouldn't.

She looked at him through a veil of tears. She felt her body trembling. Ever since Brad had left for Vietnam the war had taken on a whole new meaning. Until then she hadn't realized how far she, her parents, in fact, most of the people she knew, were removed from it. Now she paid close attention to the headlines, about furious battles for numbered hills, enemy body count, and worst of all, the tally of U.S. servicemen missing, wounded, and killed in action. At night she watched the evening news and noted that the live combat coverage was becoming more and more graphic. Vietnam was now being called the "living-room war." She said, almost pleading, "Aren't there other places you could go?...*Anywhere?*"

"But I want to go over there—" he sounded.

Katie felt as if she had been kicked in the stomach. She closed her eyes; a wave of nausea came over her. Quickly she opened them. What was happening to her? She was remembering her response to her brother's last letter, received a few weeks ago, stating they were very close to the shore and could see explosions. From that time on she began having terrible dreams, of coming home and finding her mother in tears and learning the horrible news that Brad had been killed. Just then she tried to imagine Sandy flying in a helicopter, the noise it made, how exposed and vulnerable he would be. If her dreams about her brother were unnerving, how would she fare with Sandy actually *in* Vietnam?

She didn't know what to say. She remained silent trying to collect her thoughts. What am I *supposed* to say? she wondered. *What kind of response does he want from me?* "Oh...Sandy," she said heavily, "I love you. I-I'm just so afraid. I want you to be okay. Promise me you'll be okay—*Promise?*"

Eagerly, he said, "I'll be all right, Katie, I promise. After all, I'll have you to come home to."

The first sign Sandy and Seymore had that they were nearing their destination was their view, off in the distance, of a large brick building they later learned was the Mineral Wells Hotel. With the early morning sun as a backdrop, the hotel dominated the landscape like a tall sailing ship on a calm sea, and the closer they got, the more apprehensive they became.

After several more minutes the bus slowed and entered the outskirts of the town. It lumbered along making several turns before coming to a stop in front of the depot, a squat, stucco-sided building overshadowed by the huge hotel one

Victor R. Beaver

block away. As they got off the bus, a sign on the outside of the depot immediately got their attention:

**OFFICER & WARRANT OFFICER CANDIDATE
REPORTEES:
Day or Night: For Transportation
To USAPHC, Fort Wolters, Texas
Call Post Transportation: #3447**

"What do you think?" Sandy asked.

"Let's take a cab. We can arrive in style," Seymore said. "Once they have us in their sights, they're going to be on us 'like stink on shit'—as the saying goes."

"Yeah, I agree."

Chapter 3

THE CAB DRIVER KNEW EXACTLY where to take them. He turned onto a side street that went past a row of two-story wooden barracks all painted white with green trim. Through the cab windows Sandy and Seymore saw several soldiers double-timing in starched fatigues. Seeing their shaved heads, it looked like basic training all over again.

After the last set of barracks, they rounded a curve and stopped near a small building that had a sign out in front that read:

WELCOME TO 5TH WOC COMPANY
"PREFLIGHT PHASE"
UNITED STATES ARMY PRIMARY HELICOPTER CENTER
FORT WOLTERS, TEXAS
New Candidates Report to Company Orderly Room

"Good luck, fellas," the driver said, after he helped them off-load their gear.
"Thanks."
The cabby drove off.
"Would you take a look at that," Sandy said. Several hundred feet away they saw a soldier doing push-ups. Hovering over him, with voices booming, were two men in army dress greens. "Boy, those guys sure have healthy lungs."
"What did I say?...'Like stink on shit,'" reminded Seymore.
They turned and saw three more soldiers running around a large PT (physical training) field that sat on a slight rise just beyond the orderly room. "Care for a little exercise before brunch?" Seymore quipped.
The newcomers picked up their baggage and began to lug them toward the orderly room. They spied another soldier coming from a set of barracks off to their left. He had on an OD (olive-drab colored) cap, starched fatigues, and covering his eyes was a pair of aviator sunglasses. On his left breast pocket they could just make out an orange felt tab with a black stripe down the middle. As he came closer they saw centered on his cap the letters W.O.C. made of brass pinned on a round yellow plastic disk. The soldier slowed and stopped. "Have you guys signed in yet?"
"No, sir," Seymore said.
"Well, git on in there. Leave your stuff outside."
"Yes, sir."
The two men moved quickly into the orderly room. Once inside, the company clerk took their records while they signed the company roster. Sandy asked, "Who's that guy wearing the orange tab with the black stripe?"

"Oh...you'll find out soon enough," the clerk said. "He's one of the holdover seniors."

"He seems real friendly," Seymore said.

The clerk smiled. "Yeah, *real* friendly..."

After about ten minutes of typing and paper shuffling, the clerk told them they would be in Flight Alpha One. Their barrack would be straight across from the orderly room on the other side of the supply building. "After you dump your gear, you can pick up your bedding and sheets," the clerk said. "Supply opens in half an hour. You'll be getting the rest of your issue tomorrow or the next day. There'll be other forms to fill out once you get settled in. That's all I've got."

"Okay." They turned and walked out the door.

"CANDIDATES! Don't you know you're supposed to salute a senior candidate when you see one?" It was the friendly soldier.

"...Wha-What?!..."

"Drop and give me ten! AND SOUND OFF!"

"Yessir!" Sandy and Seymore dove for the ground.

"Louder, candidates. I can't *hear you!*"

"...FOUR!...FIVE!...SIX!..."

Sandy did his ten push-ups and stood at attention. Seymore struggled to his eighth push-up and began to slow down. "Don't stop, candidate! I want ten. What is your name, candidate? I can't see your nametag."

"Cutter, sir. Seymore P."

"That's not how you say it. Keep pushing. *Do ten more!*"

The holdover senior turned and faced Sandy. He read the nametag. "Adamson. Where are you from, Candidate Adamson?"

"Colorado, sir."

"Negative. Negative. You say, 'Sir, Candidate Adamson, I'm from Colorado, sir.'"

"Sir, Candidate Adamson, I'm from Colorado, sir!"

Seymore finished his second set of push-ups and stood. The senior candidate surveyed the pair. He looked at Seymore. "Where are you from, Candidate Cutter?"

"Texas, sir! I mean, sir, Candidate Cutter, I'm from Texas, sir!"

"Gawd! I might have known."

"Are you from Texas, sir?" A moment ago, Seymore thought he detected a slight drawl. He diverted his eyes for an instant to read the man's nametag: *TYREE*...a good Texas name.

"I'm from Arkansas. I hate people from Texas. TEXAS SUCKS! Down, both of you, and give me another ten—!"

As they finished, one of the post shuttle buses pulled up and stopped where the cab driver had originally let the pair off. Tyree turned. "Aah...more bodies.

You two are dismissed. Get out of my sight!—ON THE DOUBLE!" Then he strode off to meet the new reportees.

The two newly signed-in warrant officer candidates stumbled toward their assigned barrack. By the time they reached their destination their arms and backs ached from the dead weight of their loads. They struggled up the short flight of stairs leading to the back door of the building. Cutter huffed as he opened the door. They both plunged forward and found themselves in a short narrow hallway marked: OFF LIMITS TO ALL WARRANT OFFICER CANDIDATES.

"Oh oh..." Seymore groaned.

"What's the—"

"CANDIDATES! Can't you read? Drop and knock out ten!" boomed the voice.

With the man square in their way, Sandy and Seymore slammed to the floor, one practically on top the other; they grunted through more torture. All Sandy could see as he pushed up and down were two spit-shined low-quarter shoes and the knife-like crease in a pair of green dress pants; they belonged to the tactical training officer of Flight Alpha One.

"I can't hear you, candidates. Let's begin *again*—UNTIL WE GET IT RIGHT!"

"One!...Two!...Three!..." they chorused.

"LOUDER! FASTER! Sound off like you got a pair! Start again, *damnit!*"

"ONE! TWO! THREE! FOUR!..."

By the seventh push-up, Sandy felt his arms turn to rubber. Midway up the next push-up he stopped, unable to budge one inch higher. He couldn't go back down, either; he didn't have the strength to do it slow enough in order not to collapse.

"What's the matter, candidate? I need to see ten push-ups..."

"I-I...c-can't," Sandy muttered.

"*Christ!* You guys are pathetic. *Stand up!* UP! UP! UP!"

Exhausted, they stood braced at attention more out of fear than protocol. Inside their skulls, though, their minds spun dizzily. Through eyes watering with perspiration, Sandy stared into the office from which the man had come. Two crossed sabers in their sheaths hung on the wall behind a desk. The letters *B TROOP 1st SQUADRON 9th CAVALRY* appeared on a red and white cavalry troop banner that also hung on the wall. Images of horsemen in blue and yellow in a long column with dust rising around them came to his mind.

Chief Warrant Officer Bryan Carlyle glared at his new charges. With menacing eyes, he stalked them. To him their status in life was barely above that of amoeba. He edged around their backsides, then stopped; he stared at a spot below Cutter's right ear. What he saw was a patch of previously unshaved whiskers. "Candidate Cutter, did you preflight your face this morning?"

"Sir, Candidate Cutter...I beg your pardon, sir?"

Carlyle roared, "DID YOU SHAVE TODAY, CANDIDATE CUTTER—?"

"Sir, Candidate Cutter, no sir! I haven't had ti—"

"Candidate Cutter. You need a haircut. You need a shave. You need to get into the proper 'winter' dress uniform...AND YOU NEED TO GET OUT OF MY BARRACK—*UNTIL YOUR SHIT IS SQUARED AWAY!"*

"Sir, Candidate Cutter! Yes, sir!" The red-haired candidate turned and bolted for the back door.

"Not that door, you idiot. THROUGH THE BAY AND OUT THE MAIN SIDE DOOR! And when you get outside, *give me one hundred push-ups!"*

Turning to Sandy, he said, "Candidate Adamson, get this baggage out of my sight."

"Sir! Candidate Adamson! Yes, sir!"

Sandy struggled to shove the two duffel bags and his overnight bag out of the narrow hallway and into the candidate bay area.

"Not that way, Candidate Adamson. Take that crap out the back door and double-time the gear around to the main side door."

"Sir! Candidate Adamson! Yes, sir!"

"MOVE IT! MOVE IT!" Carlyle drummed him outside practically toppling him over backwards. Carlyle then turned and charged into the candidate bay area. "EVERYONE, DOWN! GIVE ME TEN!" Fifteen candidates, most of whom had been watching the tirade out of the corner of their eyes, hit the floor pumping. "LOUDER! LOUDER! I want to *hear you!"*

Weighted down by over a hundred pounds of luggage, Sandy slugged his way around the right-hand side of the building. He saw Seymore by the stairway in the front leaning rest position, mostly flat on his stomach, barely moving. "I'll leave your stuff on the other side of the door," he told his beleaguered friend.

"Th-thanks."

How he managed to get up the stairs without dropping anything, Sandy Adamson never knew. A candidate coming out of the building kept the door open for him. He bounced off walls as he plowed his way through another narrow hallway and into the same first-floor bay area he had just vacated. A shaved-headed candidate in starched fatigues and spit-shined boots greeted him. A silver-looking disk was pinned to the man's right collar; pinned to his other collar was his WOC brass. The man said, "I see you made it."

Sandy braced. "Sir, Candidate Adamson! Yes, sir!"

"Forget that stuff. I'm a low-life like you...the temporary platoon leader, though, until we get this show on the road. My name is Bartlett, Frank Bartlett." He helped Sandy ease the load off his shoulders.

"Thanks. My name is Sandy—"

"Adamson. I know, we heard you say it about fifty times."

Sandy smiled. "Right..."

"At first, I wanted to assign bunks in alphabetical order, but that's impossible, since not everyone's arrived." Frank Bartlett pointed to a candidate seated on a bottom bunk with an artist's sketchbook on his lap. "Tom Adkins is our resident Michelangelo. His top bunk is empty." Frank helped Sandy to the cubicle. In other cubicles Sandy saw candidates either spit-shining their boots or setting up their wall- and footlocker displays for inspection. Frank asked if he liked to read.

"Yeah, sure, but do you think we're going to have time?"

"Doubtful, at least not in the beginning," Frank said. "I try to get through a couple of books a week. Maybe we can swap titles. It'll keep us from going crazy."

Adkins stood and introduced himself and helped Sandy stow his gear. Afterwards, he turned the sketchbook around for Sandy's inspection. It was an excellently detailed drawing of the bay area depicting several candidates performing various tasks. "That's pretty good," Sandy said.

"Thanks." Adkins then handed Sandy a thin orange booklet. "Here, you might want to look through this." It was the WOC Handbook: *The Candidate Bible.* Sandy took and scanned it. From A to Z, it covered every aspect of a candidate's existence while in flight school. It told how to "precisely" set up personal displays for inspection, how to "precisely" wear the uniform, even how to "precisely" stand in the chow line. It told when the married candidates could visit with their families who resided in the area, where they were allowed to meet, and how they were to conduct themselves.

Nothing was left to the imagination.

Since the helicopter was a precision machine, the candidate "student pilot" was to be a precision instrument in the cockpit.

Precision—

"Impressed?" Tom Adkins asked.

"I'll say. Wait till Seymore gets a load of this."

Seymore P. Cutter came panting into the bay area toward the cubicle. "I promised myself...I'd do ten extra push-ups a day...until I knocked out...the remaining seventy-five..."

Sandy nodded. "I'll help you get your gear upstairs."

"Upstairs!—God, I'll never make it..."

As Sandy Adamson began to unpack, he detected an acute orderliness and sense of purpose around him. Each man was there for one reason and one reason only: to learn to fly a helicopter. Each man had only one expectation: to use that skill to fight a war. And each man knew exactly where he was bound after flight school: Vietnam. Exhilaration passed through him. For the first time in his life, Sandy felt he was wholly among his own kind.

Sandy examined his head in the latrine mirror. He and Cutter needed a haircut—*fast.* Adkins clued him in with a quickly drawn list of "essentials" they would need from the PX: cotton balls to smooth Glo-Coat over the heels and toes of their boots: Kotex pads for the bottoms of their footlockers (to keep the bottom from scraping the floor): and a myriad other little goodies necessary to make it through preflight training, the officer-development phase of flight school.

"We've got to go to the PX."

"What for?"

"These."

They double-timed the two miles to the main post exchange. They turned in their uniforms to have patches sewn on. Since it was being remodeled the barbershop was closed, so they bought an electric razor and scissors and gave each other haircuts. They emerged from the PX restroom nicked, cut—hideously bald.

They double-timed back.

Formation for the noon meal.

"Flight Alpha One—FALL IN! RIGHT FACE! Forward...*MARCH!*"

Outside the messhall they waited in line at parade rest. To move forward, each man came first to attention, advanced a step, then returned to parade rest. Body stiff, eyes looking straight ahead, breathing slow and measured.

Inside, they sat stiff-backed. Bring the fork straight up, then cut a 90-degree angle directly to the mouth.

Senior Candidate Tyree roamed between the tables. He glared at them one at a time, searching for the slightest provocation to pounce. Then someone belched.

Seymore's eyes grew wide with horror. "Oh, shit...!" he whispered.

"CANDIDATE CUTTER! What did I hear?"

"Sir! Candidate Cutter, I couldn't help it—"

"Give me ten!"

"Here?"

"Affirmative!"

"Sir, Candidate Cutter, yes, sir."

They double-timed back to individual barracks, usually in pairs, scanning the company area for the "enemy," the tactical training officers.

"Jesus," Sandy whispered, "would you look at that?" They slowed to observe five new reportees standing at attention. One of them, a compactly built man, wore the green beret of the United States Army Special Forces. Over his left breast pocket were five rows of ribbons, and above them a pair of master jump wings and the CIB, the coveted combat infantryman badge. They perked their ears as they scuttled by.

Like two skulking vultures, Tac Officers Armstrong and Douglas stood next to these new men. "Well, what do you suppose we have here, Mr. Douglas?"

"Looks to me like a Sneaky Pete," replied Chief Warrant Officer Douglas.

The Special Forces veteran, wearing the rank of sergeant first class, said nothing. The other men around him stood like statues.

"Where did you serve in Vietnam, Candidate Cottrell?"

"Cai Cai, sir, in the Delta. That was my third tour."

"That's not how you reply. *Drop*—but let's make it twenty."

Cottrell hit the ground and was finished before anyone could blink an eye.

"Impressive. Very impressive."

"Have you ever eaten rattlesnake meat, Candidate Cottrell?"

"Yes, sir."

"Mr. Douglas, he still hasn't got it right," said Chief Warrant Officer Armstrong. "Perhaps a little instruction. But first, a little PT." Armstrong pointed toward the oval track. "Take these men and do five laps. We're going to have your thinking cap screwed on tight before these four weeks are up. DO YOU READ ME, CANDIDATE COTTRELL!?"

"YES, SIR!" And with the other new reportees quickly assembled in a line, he was gone.

Tac Officer Douglas swung around just in time to see Adamson and Cutter disappear behind the supply building. "CANDIDATES! *POST!*"

Armstrong pointed toward the PT field. "Laps! *Five!*"

After the third lap, Seymore began to vomit at the edge of the track. "That's okay, I don't remember eating it anyway."

By 1400 hours, all members of the new class had arrived and were signed in. "Okay, listen up," Frank Bartlett said. "I've got the word on the bunking arrangement."

"Don't tell us," spoke someone from the back. "We'll be staying at the Mineral Wells Hotel, in individual rooms, with room service and a wake-up call at nine A.M. Just be in by midnight."

"You wish," someone else commented.

Frank said, "The last alphabetical name will bunk with the first...then so on and so forth. Adamson, Cutter, you've got cubicle one."

"Christ, right next to his office," Seymore groaned.

"Adkins, Cottrell, number two."

"Yo."

"Alexander, Cottondale, number three. Candidates Allen and Cochran, number four..."

By the time all the shuffling had ceased, amid curses and shrieks as pinched fingers and sore backs packed footlockers and baggage up and down stairs, it was three thirty.

"FLIGHT ALPHA ONE! Formation at sixteen hundred! The uniform will be fatigues and fatigue cap. The company commander will be addressing us. All the tacs will be in the area—*so look sharp!*"

At exactly 1600, like rats deserting a sinking ship, three hundred and eighty-five warrant officer candidates of the newly formed Class 67-15 poured out of their respective barracks and formed in eight separate flight platoons in front of the commander's platform.

Victor R. Beaver

"Candidate Company Commander...*REPORT!*"

Ned Symington, a former infantry company first sergeant, saluted. "Sir! Candidate Symington! All present or accounted for, sir!"

Captain Richmond, the 5th WOC Company commander, returned the salute. "STAND AT—EASE!"

Eyeballs clicked toward the platform. Richmond was dressed sharply in greens. Like the other officers and warrant officers present, he wore the distinctive badge of U.S. Army Aviator above his left breast pocket. He surveyed the new class through a pair of aviator sunglasses, checking them over like a herd of cattle. And then he bellowed:

"Most of you have met the staff!" The staff moved among the ranks, eyeballing each candidate with the scrutiny paid a *Playboy* centerfold (however with not near as much relish). "These men," Richmond continued, "are your tactical training officers. It is their job to weed out those undesirables who can't cut the mustard." The captain paused to let the words sink in. Not a man stirred. "Uncle Sam doesn't want to get a person half way through the solo phase only to find out he can't take the pressure of flying. *It costs too much money!* Your tac officers will give guidance and counseling in matters relating to officer development. They are here to provide you with the incentive to stay—or quit! You may be inspected at any time during the day or night. Your personal area in the barracks and your uniform must always be at the highest standard of appearance and repair. Your personal integrity must equally be of the highest caliber. An officer's word is his bond. Your leadership capabilities will be severely tested. I cannot stress enough, gentlemen, how important self-discipline is, not only while you are here in preflight, but during the entire nine-month program. I guarantee, we aim to make you measure up—*or get out!*"

The company commander again paused for effect.

"NOW—!" he thundered. "I want to offer each of you the opportunity to resign. No questions asked. No black mark against your record." He surveyed their faces; not one eye blinked. "I guarantee it won't be a disappointment to me or my staff. We don't want you here...if you don't want to be here." He stood silent, moving his head from left to right. And then he gave the next command:

"COMPANEEE...!"

"FLIGHTS...!"

"Atten—HUT!" Captain Richmond looked over his herd. "Any man wishing to resign, may do so now. Take one step forward—and fall out!"

He waited ten seconds—an eternity—and no one stepped forward. The captain looked from side to side; not one soul stirred, not one head turned; there was not a movement anywhere, except the silent wavering of the 5th WOC Company guide-on in the breeze.

"Okay, men, stand at ease. I wish you the best of luck. When you complete this course, if you do, they'll make you a warrant officer and pin wings on you and make you fly. I hope someday you don't regret it.

"Now, one more item needs to be discussed: Grundy Day. I'm sure you've heard it through the grapevine, but I'd like to highlight the directive put out by the post commandant. There will be no Grundy Day the third Saturday of preflight, as was customary in the past. Colonel Eddington will no longer tolerate this kind of demonstration. To ignore this directive by any member of this class shall constitute grounds for immediate dismissal. DO I MAKE MYSELF PERFECTLY CLEAR!?"

The new class gave a thunderous reply: "SIR! YES, SIR!"

"Okay, tomorrow you will begin your first phase of training: Preflight. Don't lose sight of your real goal here. That's all I have. Dismissed!"

"COMPANEEE...!"

"FLIGHTS...!"

"Atten...HUT!" Again, Symington saluted the man on the platform; he did an about face. "Flight Platoon Leaders! *Take charge of your flights!*"

When they returned to the barrack after the evening mess, Sandy saw that the first week's chain-of-command roster had been posted. He groaned.

"What's the matter?"

"I've been picked to be platoon leader this week."

Seymore saw he had been picked squad leader for First Squad. "Look who's the platoon sergeant."

Just then, Willie Cottrell appeared in the hallway. Pinned on his right fatigue-shirt collar was the rank of sergeant first class. He flipped Sandy the silver-looking disk Frank Bartlett had been wearing earlier. "Look's like Carlyle's picked you and me to start this shindig off. I've got a squad leader's meeting set for nineteen hundred."

"Okay...thanks," Sandy said.

"No problem." Willie looked at him. "Hey, why the long face?"

"I hope I don't screw this up," Sandy said. "I just got out of basic training."

"Don't worry. We'll work it out together."

"Thanks...I appreciate that."

Both the upstairs' and downstairs' bay areas were a beehive of activity.

"Jesus!—all my uniforms are wrinkled!"

"Who's got some Brasso?"

"Here," someone yelled. "Don't use it all."

"Where are you from?"

"Fairbanks, Alaska."

"Oh, yeah? What are you, an Eskimo?"

"For crissake—no!"
"Did that prick Tyree go home?"
"What home? The guy's got his own room in Alpha Four's barrack."
"Someone ought to short-sheet his ass."
"Don't worry, he's gonna get his."
"I hear the tac for Bravo Four is worse than Carlyle. Walks around with white gloves when he inspects. I saw him. He's got a little black mustache. He looks just like Hitler."
"What's Grundy Day?"
"You got me."
"It's on a Saturday, the third weekend of preflight," Frank Bartlett explained. "We're all supposed to get dressed up in crazy uniforms, 'arrest' our tac officers and throw them in the Mineral Wells's jail. Then we're supposed to march to the flight-line barracks and serenade our departing Blue Hat brothers, the ones leaving next for Fort Rucker. It is—or at least it was—an accepted tradition."
"So how come it's been outlawed?"
"Because," Frank said, "the last class got a little too rowdy. They threw a couple of the tacs into one of the downtown motel swimming pools."
"Well, what was so bad about that?"
"Nothing—*except they stripped them naked first!*"

Willie Cottrell lit a cigarette. Gathered around him were Ron Bowden, Seymore Cutter, and two other squad leaders. Sandy Adamson stood quietly off to the side. "We gotta make sure," Cottrell said, "that whatever we do in this barrack, it's uniform."
"How come?"
"Because, if it's minor and it's wrong, chances are the tacs won't notice it, as long as everybody's done it the same."
Ron Bowden, blond-haired, age thirty, an ex-Huey crewchief with a Vietnam tour behind him, spoke up: "I've been getting some talk about Grundy Day. The word is out that we ought to say the hell with it and do it anyway."
"I don't like it," stated Darryl Chancey, squad leader for Fourth Squad. "Some of us waited too long to get into this program, to have it pulled out from under us for insubordination." Chancey had already been pegged a whiner and complainer; no one liked him; so far, Cutter was the only flight platoon member who could stomach his grumbling.
Willie looked toward Ron. "Hell, I'm game. We can probably get away with anything if the whole class is behind it. Besides, they can't dismiss everyone. *Christ!*—they need us all in Vietnam."

"LIGHTS OUT IN TEN MINUTES!" Cottrell's voice rang throughout the barrack. "Seymore! Get your squad back into the latrine! It looks like hell!"

"Yes, sir!"

A mad dash for a last minute piss call. Those shaving slashed through the last of their whiskers. Sandy remained seated at his bunk, putting the finishing shine on his boots. "Adamson," Willie said, "I'd advise you to take care of that later, after you see the men are doing their jobs."

"Okay...yeah, I understand."

At exactly 2227, the back door opened. A uniformed figure entered and stood in relative darkness, watching the last minute flurry of activity before the final call for lights out. At 2229, the figure stepped forward into the light and walked quietly toward the middle of the bay area. Suddenly, someone shrieked:

"ATTEN—SHUN!"

Everyone stiffened. The clamor upstairs continued unabated until someone in the stairway shuttled back up the stairs and passed the word. Meanwhile, Chief Warrant Officer Carlyle had continued to go slowly past the stiffened bodies on the first floor. The very air they breathed was charged by his presence. It was as if some frightening creature had stolen in and was browsing among gravestones. Each man tensed as the tac officer neared, relaxing slightly once he passed. They waited, barely twitching a muscle...

Carlyle stopped. He turned. With deliberate slowness, he moved his head from side to side. And then his eyes fell upon Sandy Adamson standing less than ten feet away. The young warrant officer candidate chilled to the tac officer's cold-hearted stare. After a long moment, Carlyle spoke:

"Candidate Platoon Leader, call everyone down from upstairs."

"Sir, Candidate Adamson, yessir."

They stood in four rows, two on each side of the bay. "At ease, smoke'em if you got'em."

Zippos flicked; the smoke swirled.

"We haven't been formally introduced. I'm Chief Warrant Officer Carlyle, your tactical training officer for the next four weeks. I've been here in this capacity for six months. I don't particularly like the job. The hours are shitty and I do very little flying. I'm not happy, but I go where the Army tells me.

"By definition, my purpose in life is to observe your initial officer development. I'm also a glorified baby-sitter. If you've got minor personal problems, I'm supposed to help you resolve them. But if you got big personal problems—your girlfriend is pregnant, your mother is about to kick the bucket, your wife wants a divorce—these I can't help you with, and won't. You shouldn't be here if that kind of crap is on your mind. You married guys with your families here, I have no sympathy for. You were strongly advised not to bring them. This is a highly concentrated program requiring all of your attention—and I'm real serious, gentlemen—*all* of your attention. Learning to fly a helicopter is not a piece of cake. How many of you have any stick-time?" Bowden, the ex-Huey crewchief, and two others raised their hands. "Did you try to hover? What was it like?"

"Hovering's like trying to rub your belly and head in two different directions at once," Bowden said.

"And beat your meat, too," one of the others added.

A ripple of laughter threaded through the ranks. Carlyle, stern-faced until that moment, cracked the slightest smile. "I probably couldn't have said it better myself."

Then he said, "Anyway, it takes a lot of concentration. You've got beaucoup things to think about. Mostly, you've got to keep from running into each other out there. Guys, this place is like tiptoeing through a minefield. And believe me, Rucker isn't any better. In fact, it's worse.

"To put all of this into perspective, my real purpose here is to make you as miserable as possible. Now maybe I shouldn't be telling you this, but by God, I don't want anyone leaving for the flight line unless he's damn sure he wants to be there. Besides, I'm going back to Vietnam in eight or nine months. I don't want any fools in the same airspace as me. *You got that?"*

A subdued "Yessir" filled the bay area.

"Come on, guys," Cottrell said. "Sound off!"

"SIR! YES, SIR!"

Carlyle said, "Do your job. Snap to when addressed. Be sharp. And you'll have no cause to worry. Any questions?"

There were none. Willie Cottrell called them to attention. Again, they became like statues—rigid, scarcely breathing. Carlyle scanned each of their faces. At last:

"EVERYBODY!—*drop and knock out ten!"* then he turned and was gone.

Finally, the lights were out. Sandy slid into his bunk. He laid back and stared at the bottom of Seymore's mattress above him, the events of the day spinning in his head. He had expected the harassment and the push-ups, but found it difficult to understand why any of it was necessary to learn how to fly. "Seymore, are you awake?"

"Yeah, how could I be asleep? I only ache from head to toe. And my ears are still ringing from all the shouting."

"What do you think about all this?"

"Think? Who thinks? I just react."

"The perfect automaton."

"I wished..."

As he stared into the darkness, Sandy's mind went to Katie. It shocked him to realize that he had not thought of her once since his brief phone call to her from the PX when he and Seymore had gone for their haircuts. It was as if she had dropped off the face of the earth. *Seymore's right. They don't want us to think...they just want us to react. This isn't any different than basic training. We learned to march and shoot by the numbers. Will we learn to control a helicopter*

the same way? It doesn't make any sense. As he drifted off to
thoughts were of tomorrow. He wondered what their first real day
ficer candidates would be like....

Chapter 4

THE LIGHTS BLASTED ON ACCOMPANIED by a racket of clanging and banging. "ALL RIGHT, LET GO OF YOUR COCKS AND GRAB YOUR SOCKS! PT FORMATION IN TWENTY MINUTES!" Willie Cottrell had taken the lid off one of the latrine trash cans and was beating on it with a broom handle. "UP! UP! UP! AND AT'EM!" he yelled.

"Jesus, who wound that sonofabitch up?"

"What time is it?"

"Four fifteen..."

"Christ, I thought wake-up wasn't until four thirty."

"CANDIDATE COTTRELL! WHO AUTHORIZED EARLY GET UP?" Tac Officer Carlyle stood outside the door of his office, at the edge of the bay. He was dressed in heavily starched fatigues and on his head he wore a black polished helmet liner.

The ex-Green Beret came to attention; he peered straight ahead. "Sir, Candidate Cottrell, no one, sir. No excuse, sir."

"Around here, Candidate Platoon Sergeant, we do things by the book."

"Sir, Candidate Cottrell, yes, sir."

"Wake-up is exactly o'four thirty—and not a minute before. DROP AND GIVE ME TEN!" Carlyle moved down the middle of the bay. "EVERYBODY—BACK INTO YOUR BUNKS!"

Carlyle turned. "Candidate Adamson, did you authorize early get up?"

"Sir, Candidate Adamson, no, sir."

"Then how come you've got a flight platoon sergeant running around doing as he damn well pleases?"

"Sir, Candidate Adamson...I...don't know—"

"You don't know! WHO'S IN CHARGE OF THIS FLIGHT? YOU OR CANDIDATE COTTRELL?"

"I am, sir..."

"Then act like it, damnit! Drop and give me ten!"

Class 67-15 charged out to the physical training field under hundreds of stars visible in the cool pre-dawn sky. Ned Symington began the exercises. The tac officers wove in and out of the ranks and watched as the men squatted and bent and hopped and swiveled and did the hated push-ups. After the "daily dozen," Symington led them onto the racetrack where they began running laps. Senior Candidate Tyree chased and nipped at the heels of the ass-draggers.

"Okay, everyone, listen up," Cottrell said. "This week our flight eats last in the messhall; then we rotate each week thereafter. In the meantime, we can get started on the details. Formation for class is at o'seven thirty."

The Sky Soldiers

Seymore asked, "Do we have to eat?"

"Yes, Candidate Cutter—*everybody eats!*"

In the line outside the messhall the new warrant officer candidates stood rigid as stones, while the tacs moved alongside with deliberate slowness, their eyes cocked, their foreheads furrowed. They were like vultures that fed on an unbuttoned pocket, a curl of loose thread, a patch of unshaven whiskers. When they found a discrepancy, the offender was dropped for an immediate ten push-ups.

"Candidate Adamson, get a cigarette lighter," Chief Warrant Officer Carlyle said. He had been eyeballing Seymore's uniform up and down for a full minute.

"Sir...?"

"I said get a lighter."

"Sir, Candidate Adamson, yes, sir."

Sandy went to Cottrell standing at the end of the line. "Willie, I need your cigarette lighter." Willie handed it to him. He went back and stood next to Carlyle.

"Now, Candidate Adamson. As Candidate Flight Platoon Leader it is your duty to inspect your men *before* they appear outside the barracks. I will show you how to properly preflight this uniform. See all these loose threads? We're going to burn each one." Carlyle singed seventeen strands of thread that had unraveled from the seams of Cutter's fatigue shirt and pants. "See how it's done?"

"Sir, Candidate Adamson, yes, sir."

"I CAN'T HEAR YOU!"

"SIR, CANDIDATE ADAMSON, YES, SIR!"

"Down, both of you! And give me seventeen push-ups—APIECE!"

After breakfast, they had twenty minutes to prepare the rest of the barrack for inspection before falling out for class.

"FOURTH SQUAD! OUTSIDE FOR POLICE CALL!"

"Seymore!" Cottrell yelled. "Get a man back on those shower stalls! They're a mess!"

Every man scurried about like ants on a disturbed anthill. The floors were buffed, window ledges cleaned, and glass made to sparkle. The latrine detail swept, scoured, disinfected, and polished. Old used toothbrushes were poked into every corner and crevice. Finally, with what seemed like only half the work done, Cottrell yelled, "OKAY, EVERYBODY, WRAP IT UP! WRAP IT UP! LET'S GO—OUTSIDE FOR FORMATION!"

One final touch given to individual displays, locker doors opened for inspection, bunk covers stretched so tight you could bounce a quarter off them. Everything was set.

Sandy gave the barrack one last look. He noticed a few items not quite "uniform," but they seemed minor. Carlyle was going to have a hard time finding too much wrong, he decided. He felt satisfied.

"FALL IN!"

Victor R. Beaver

Three hundred and eighty-five men slapped to attention.
"LEFT...FACE! FORWARD...MARCH!"

Classes were conducted in old wooden one-story buildings located next to the 5th WOC Company area. The instructors were chief warrant and commissioned officers who, in sharp contrast to the tac officers, presented their material helpfully and calmly. By eleven o'clock, the new candidates had been bored to death by subjects ranging from customs and courtesies of the military services...to how to balance a checkbook. They were given a smoke break once every fifty minutes. But when they got outside, the tac officers took the opportunity to inspect, harass, and mete out their favorite punishment. In the chow line their angry presence made the pressure build. Before the end of the day five candidates would resign.

Because each flight had gone to different classes, Flight Alpha One marched back to the barracks on its own. Sandy did as he had seen a couple of the other candidate flight platoon leaders do, he remained off to the side of the platoon while his platoon sergeant counted cadence and gave marching commands. As a young man just out of basic training, many of the formalities of soldiering and drilling were still foreign to him. The ex-Special Forces sergeant had taken quite a bit of the load off his shoulders. Even the early morning goof-up didn't dim his respect for the older, more experienced veteran. As far as Sandy was concerned, Cottrell had not been wrong waking the men fifteen minutes early. But he was beginning to realize the importance of sticking to the rules: ten push-ups per infraction could leave a man an exhausted lump in no time at all.

Cottrell halted the platoon in front of the barrack. Tac Officer Carlyle came and stood before them like a prima-donna statue, his uniform immaculate, his eyes hidden behind a pair of sunglasses. "Candidate Adamson, prepare the men for inspection."

"Sir, Candidate Adamson, yes, sir."

Cottrell's voice boomed. "FLIGHT...!"

"Negative negative negative, Candidate Cottrell. I want Candidate Adamson to give the commands."

The tac officer took several slow steps and stood next to Sandy. "I'm waiting, Candidate Adamson..."

"Yes, sir...I mean, sir, Candidate Adamson, yes, sir." He tried to think. He said, "Flight...Prepare for...Inspection!"

No one moved. The command (as worded) meant nothing to them. The men continued to stand ramrod straight.

Sandy took a deep breath. *What is the command? Willie was about to say it. I know I've heard it a thousand times...What is it—?*

"I'm still waiting, Candidate Adamson."

"Sir, Candidate Adamson, yes, sir."

An eternity passed. Beads of sweat formed on the young candidate's brow. His mouth became dry. And then it came to him. "Open ranks...March!" *That's it!* Like a precision machine, the flight moved. First Squad took two steps forward, Second Squad one, while Third Squad remained in place. Fourth Squad took one step back, and they all dress-right-dressed.

"Ready...FRONT!" Sandy felt a wave of relief. The ranks were open for inspection.

"Take notes, Candidate Adamson."

Carlyle passed in front of each candidate. He shook his head, dropping every other man for push-ups. Sandy nervously added up the demerits.

When Carlyle was finished, he went to the front, turned and faced them. "Disgusting—everyone of you—*disgusting!* If you turds preflight your aircraft the way you preflight your uniforms, there won't be one of you who gets out of this program alive. Candidate Adamson, take charge of this fouled-up flight!"

"Sir, Candidate Adamson, yes, sir!"

Inside the barrack, Sandy stood in shock. The first-floor bay area was in shambles. Flight Alpha One had failed its first barrack inspection miserably.

Seymore gawked at the disorder in their cubicle. Sandy's bunk had been overturned and lay at an odd angle on the floor. His own bed had been ripped apart, as if some wild boar had been rooting for food beneath the covers. His can of shaving cream sat propped upside down on the desk, stuck in a mound of foam. Red grease pencil had been used to draw an arrow toward the can from an encircled note: RUST ON BOTTOM RIM OF CAN—50 DEMERITS. More than a dozen red circles enshrined minute specks of dust, each speck costing them ten demerits. Both footlocker displays had been overturned, the contents a scrambled mess on the floor.

"This red shit ain't never gonna come off," Seymore P. Cutter moaned.

Darryl Chancey rushed up to Sandy. "Look at this!" he shrieked. In the palm of his hand Chancey held a hardened wad of gum. "I got a hundred demerits for this! It was stuck under my bunk on the frame! Probably placed there by the last joker who slept on it!"

Sandy blinked. "Damn...you're kidding."

"No, I'm not."

"Well, go back upstairs and help get your bay area cleaned up."

Chancey blurted, "You should see it. It's worse than this!"

"Well, get on up there then," stated Sandy. "We've got fifteen minutes till chow. We can't leave the barrack looking like this."

"What about these demerits?"

"Jesus, Chancey, we all got demerits. Get upstairs!"

After he was gone, Sandy said, "What the hell is with that guy?"

"He's a flake," Adkins said, his artist sketchbook in hand. "I went through Basic with him. He goes nuts over everything."

Victor R. Beaver

Willie Cottrell came and stood by Sandy's side. "Cheer up. Wait till you get to Vietnam. This mess ain't shit compared to a direct hit by a mortar...or the aftermath of a firefight."

Sandy relaxed slightly. "Yeah...you're probably right."

* * *

"OKAY—LISTEN UP!" CALLED WILLIE Cottrell. "We're going for our flight gear. The bus should be here anytime." It was 1030. They had just returned from class and were dealing, again, with the devastation left by Carlyle. The second day's inspection found fewer mistakes, but both bay areas still looked like a tornado had gone through them. The demerits were mounting fast.

"Damn, Seymore. What's he finding wrong with your bunk?"

"Beats me," Seymore groaned, as he lifted his mattress and sheets off the floor, "but I've got a sneaking suspicion my whole aviation career is riding on whether Carlyle can bounce a quarter off my bed."

When the bus arrived they moved on board excited as children on a field trip to the zoo. The driver took them to an area of post where railroad tracks ran past long rows of buildings. Inside one of these buildings they filed past a long, chest-high countertop, where enlisted men on the other side handed them, item by item, the tools of their new trade: two flight suits, leather gloves, flight helmet and helmet bag, flight jacket, E6-B computer, plotter, kneeboard, flashlight, and the requisite number of flight training manuals. Back outside they stood in loose formation, some of them trying on their new jackets, others checking out the fit of their helmets. All donned their brand new Army aviator sunglasses.

Tom Adkins thumbed through one of the training manuals. It was filled with vector diagrams and drawings of airfoils and formulas and complicated explanations of the theory of rotary-wing flight. He sighed. "Oh, Jesus, it looks like they also want us to know how to build a helicopter...not just fly them."

Seymore held a queer-looking device that had a flat, rectangular metal plate that slid inside a ring of metal. One side had a plastic window to view the plate. The other side displayed an apparent hodgepodge of embossed numbers around a stationary and moveable disk.

Pete Cochran, an ex-airline first officer, explained: "It's your E6-B flight computer. With it you can calculate true airspeed, wind correction angles, ground speed, fuel consumption, and much more. You can even multiply and divide with it."

"Now how the hell am I gonna fly and screw around with this?"

"That's easy," Cochran replied. "First chance you get, toss it out the window and use your INS."

"What the hell's an INS?"

"Inertial navigation system. To explain it would take the better part of several months."

Back at the barracks they dug into the WOC Handbook to learn how to display these new "toys." They wondered, too, if they would ever get to use them...So far, flying seemed the last thing they were destined to do.

* * *

"GENTLEMEN, PLEASE OBSERVE THE maps spread before you," said the platform instructor. Mid-week. It felt as if they had been in preflight forever. The days were so jam-packed that every waking moment seemed an eternity unto itself. So far, ten voluntary resignations had occurred. Most of these were old-timers, unwilling to endure the petty harassment. No one in Sandy's platoon, though, had quit. He was beginning to detect a strong cohesiveness among the members of the flight.

"We will begin," the instructor continued, "by orienting our map to grid north, always at the top. If you'll notice at the bottom there are symbols that denote declination, or the variation in degrees grid north is from magnetic north. You will also see another line, capped by a star, which tells the slight amount of deviation true north is from grid north. The layout of this map is called *Universal Transverse Mercator.* Naturally, this map represents a very small portion of our earth. And because we are so far south of grid north, these vertical grid lines appear parallel to one another, or straight up and down. In other words, this map does not display or represent the true curvature of the earth. But our magnetic compass, the tool in the aircraft we use to guide by, points to the magnetic north pole, which is slightly removed, like I said, from grid north. And true north, or north relative to Polaris, the North Star, is again slightly offset from that. Unfortunately...all of this...may seem...confusing to you. But we must realize...there are three kinds of north..."

He stopped. The candidates had just eaten lunch. The instructor glanced from face to face, noting, aside from the several drooping eyelids, that nearly all of them held a look of total bewilderment. "Er...uh, let's move on to terrain features, gentlemen. Right now, I think we may have better luck getting that across."

Dear Katie,

I'm writing this letter under my bed covers using a flashlight to see by. It's after lights out. I wish I could say how much I miss you, but they keep us so busy, I haven't even had time to think about you. I'm platoon leader this week and I hardly have a moment to myself. So far, though, I like it. The guys I'm with are great. We are a tight group. My bunkmate is a guy named Seymore P. Cutter. He's a real card. He looks like Howdy Doody. We hound him to tell us what his middle initial P stands for, but he isn't talking...

Victor R. Beaver

Chapter 5

COBRA HALL WAS A COLLECTION of offices, briefing rooms, and academic classrooms that lined an exposed second floor walkway running the full length of a large hangar. First Lieutenant Mike Nolan paused, glanced up, then bounded the long flight of stairs leading to the walkway. He was a short, compact man, age thirty, square-jawed, with hair cut skin-close, and a pair of darting eyes the color of gray stone. When he reached the top, he paused again and surveyed the more than two dozen men in flight suits assembled in groups of twos and threes on the landing. They were the newest class members of the AH-1G Transition and Gunnery Course (conducted at the Hunter-Stewart aviation training complex located near Savannah, Georgia) of which he was about to become a part. He strode toward a tall, dark-haired chief warrant officer standing alone next to the rail.

The warrant officer shifted his posture. "Good morning, sir."

"Good morning." Nolan took a deep breath. "This must be the place."

"Yessir...if you're here for the Cobra transition."

"That's exactly what I'm here for." He looked around. "Where's the coffee machine?"

The warrant officer pointed. "Over there. But I think all that's left is soup and hot chocolate."

"Better than nothing."

At the coffee machine, Nolan sipped his drink. He studied his surroundings, glancing from man to man. Old infantry habits die hard. "Know your men!" "Guard your perimeter!" "Utilize maximum firepower!" "Offense is the best defense!" Fort Benning "school for boys." Infantry OCS (Officer Candidate School), 1965. The tactical training officers were everywhere—day and night—in front of you, by your side, behind you, always yelling. The pressure was intense, but he had withstood it, because he knew from his first Vietnam tour in 1963, as a MACV NCO advisor, that the enemy could deliver decidedly worse. When he returned to Vietnam three years later he wore the gold bars of second lieutenant and given command of his own platoon. And six months to get it right. In six months he had lost only five men: three killed in action and two gruesomely wounded by booby traps.

Nolan strode back to the dark-haired warrant officer. He glanced at the man's nametag: *GRANGE*. He saw, too, that the man wore the large yellow and black combat patch of the 1st Cavalry Division. Nolan pulled out a pack of cigarettes and offered him one.

Grange took it. "Thanks."

"You staying in the Q?"

"Yessir...Room Two O Five." Grange bent to receive Nolan's lighted match.

The Sky Soldiers

"I'm in Two Ten, just down the hall." Nolan lit his own and blew the match out. "Maybe we can join forces and quiz each other on the limitations and emergency procedures."

Grange nodded. "Fine by me, sir."

Just then a door opened and a curly-haired warrant officer poked his head beyond the door frame. "Okay, you guys can come in now. The captain's about to start the briefing. By the way, who's the class leader?"

"I am." A commissioned officer in Class A dress greens stepped forward. "I'm Captain Nettles."

"You got a flight suit, sir?"

"Yeah...sure, but I didn't think—"

"Sir, we'll be doing some flying after the briefing."

"Sorry, I didn't know."

"Oh, yessir. That's what this course is all about, sir—flying."

They all filed in, the old and the new, a blend of combat-experienced pilots and those recently graduated from formal flight training. The class totaled thirty rated student aviators. Jardine, the one who had called them in, began to read from a list of names matching students with flight instructors. He pointed at the tables where they were to sit. "Garner and Thomas, you've got me. I'm Jardine. Sit over there. Grange and Nolan, your instructor will be 'Daddy Don' Pollard. Sit right there—and have fun. Nettles and—what the hell? Finken—"

"—binder, sir. Duard D. Finkenbinder."

"Okay, you guys got Mr. Monkton."

Shortly, everyone was seated.

Captain Smith, the flight commander, stood before them. "Good morning, gentlemen. Welcome to sunny southern Georgia. Bear with me, we've got a lot of ground to cover and very little time to do it.

"As you know, the AH-1G is virtually brand new in the Army inventory. It's been designed to replace the old Bravo- and Charlie-model Hueys, still out in the field, and, I might add, still doing a damn fine job."

"Here-here," sounded several old-timers raising clinched fists.

The captain grinned, then continued: "But it will take some time before we fully deploy this helicopter." He turned slightly and pointed toward a picture of one of the sleek-looking gunships in a sixty-degree nose dive. "The Cobra is quite literally the first helicopter developed to be used specifically as a weapons-firing platform. A very stable weapons-firing platform, I might add.

"Gentlemen, this aircraft is good for only one thing: to bring death and destruction upon the enemy—with just the simple press of a button. It has no other purpose. And neither do the pilots who fly it." The flight commander glanced around the room. "Gentlemen, with this helicopter we are going to teach you how to ruin, disfigure, mangle, smash, rip, break, split, batter, torpedo, tear to pieces, and demolish any god-damned thing Charlie decides to throw at you—" He took a deep breath. "Any questions?"

"Yessir, I got one. Does that thing have a piss tube?"

For a moment, there wasn't a sound to be heard. And then the whole room broke down. When the laughter subsided, the captain said:

"Negative...What the hell's your name again?"

"Finkenbinder, sir. Duard D."

"Where are you from?"

"Kansas, sir...Holcomb, Kansas."

"Incredible."

The captain continued: "Today, you'll be given your 'dollar ride'—a non-graded flight. You'll sit in the front seat, the co-pilot slash gunner's station, while your IP starts the aircraft, goes through the run-up checks, and hovers to the take-off pad to fly. During flight he will demonstrate some of the capabilities of the aircraft...a high-speed dive, for instance, with a two-G pullout...steep turns around a target...and he might even opt for a high-speed, low-level, pop-up auto-rotation. That, gentlemen," he stated, "is as good a roller-coaster ride as you'll ever find."

He went on. "Your IPs have all been factory-trained. They are very knowledgeable and very capable, plus they all have at least one Vietnam gunship tour behind them. Each has over a thousand hours of instructor-pilot time. Listen to them. Draw on their experiences."

He paused and again surveyed the room. "Good luck in the course. I think you'll find it damn rewarding." He looked toward Jardine. "Mr. Jardine here handles the daily briefing, so I'll give the controls over to him."

The chief warrant officer asked for an ID tag check, then requested one of them to read the weather. A moment later, he pointed: "You—how about a safety tip?"

"Me? Uh...during preflight watch out for...Watch out for the sync elevators! It does have sync elevators, doesn't it...?"

Jardine rolled his eyes. "Yes, it has a pair of sync elevators. Thank you, Mr. Finkenbinder, for that timeless—and forever necessary safety tip."

Then he said, "Okay, you're all released to your IPs. This is Friday. Next week we'll be on afternoon flight line. We'll start on the daily questions and I'll also be calling on a couple of you to stand and recite certain emergency procedures—from memory. I suggest, too, you get into those aircraft limitations. Have a safe flight. That's all I've got."

The room soon buzzed with a dozen separate conversations, each instructor laying out his own way of presenting the training program.

Nolan and Grange looked about for their flight instructor. Soon they saw a large broad-shouldered man ambling toward them, carrying a white porcelain coffee mug. As he came closer they noticed that he practically bulged out of his faded gray flight uniform. With sleeves rolled up, his forearms appeared as two hambone-like appendages. A tuft of gray chest hair protruded above the top of his white T-shirt. Both men were quick to see that he wore a set of master aviator wings. When Daddy Don Pollard got to their table, the two men were standing—taut with anticipation.

Pollard extended his hand and introduced himself. He then turned his chair around so that the back was toward them. He sat down, pulled out a thick cigar from one of his upper zipper-pockets, and unwrapped it. With his tongue and lips he moistened it, then poked it between his teeth. He rummaged in his pockets for a book of matches. When he found it, he struck a match and put flame to the cigar's end, drawing deeply several times until it was lit. Nolan and Grange watched as blue-gray smoke engulfed the man's balding head. Pollard took several more deep draws, his eyes intent on watching the smoke swirl from the cigar's lighted end. Then he began to lay out his brand of instructing: memorize systems, checklists, limitations, capabilities, nomenclatures, effective firing ranges, and emergency procedures. "In fact," he said with a grin, slowly fanning through a lop-eared heavily marked AH-1G operator's manual, "memorize this goddamn book and you and me will get along just fine." Pollard then stood. "I gotta go piss. This coffee goes through me faster than beer. When I get back we'll go out and run through a preflight."

All the aircraft were parked on square cement pads on a large asphalt ramp near the hangar. When they came to theirs, Nolan and Grange were impressed at how large the fuselage was broadside, though it presented a very narrow silhouette head-on. Right away Nolan saw that Daddy Don regarded the ship with a certain reverence. Similar to practically all two-pilot fighter aircraft, it had tandem-seating, one pilot behind the other. The ship looked sleek, fast—and deadly.

The full preflight took two hours. Pollard left no stone unturned. He examined every nut, bolt, and washer, checked every control tube, electrical connection, and safety wire. All mechanical linkages and hydraulic control lines were looked at, tugged at, and felt. The support tubes, transmission mounts, engine mounts, and coupling devices—every component was critically eyed and its function explained by the old IP, the man practically a walking AH-1G encyclopedia.

"This is the right-side turret-ammo compartment door." Pollard opened the small door that was then held parallel to the ground, secured by a chain. "Within this compartment we can carry four thousand rounds of 7.62 ammo or three hundred rounds of forty mike-mike." He explained that in an emergency, during a rescue, for example, a man could ride seated on the open compartment door.

Behind an access panel that had been unscrewed and swung down by maintenance personnel for preflight inspection, he pointed out a portion of the total hydraulic system (similar to the power steering system on a car). "Check these servos real good. You do have a back-up system, but should you lose both, you've got an accumulator that stores about four full strokes of collective lever action." Pollard eagle-eyed them. "Gentlemen, don't squander this precious little reserve. Once it's gone, that's it—you might as well try maneuvering a concrete bunker."

The burly IP crawled underneath the belly of the ship that sat a little over a foot above the ground. Nolan and Grange stooped to watch. Pollard then took a fuel sample from each of the sump drain ports. Next, he pointed to an opening beneath the main mast and transmission area. "Just like in the Huey, this is called the 'hellhole.'" It was an access opening on the belly to view the guts of the ship around the transmission casing. Nolan had decided during his first introduction to the Huey two months before, at Fort Rucker, that it was like looking at the innards of a living creature, an indecent exposure of things not meant to be seen.

Daddy Don directed their attention to the top of the ship. He pointed to the mast retaining nut. "Jesus nut. Same-same as on the UH-1. You lose it and you'll wish to Jesus that you'd have checked it better. And make sure it's safetied properly." He tugged and grunted at the control linkages. He insured that the control rods that led to the main rotorblade pitch-change and collective-lever assemblies were secure. "Memorize the nomenclatures of these components. You won't be carrying a crewchief, so you'll have to know their tolerances."

Air ejector area, electronics compartment, a glimpse down the length of the inside of the tailboom. A critical check of the "forever necessary" tailboom attaching bolt nuts—no slippage marks allowed. Synchronized elevator, gearboxes, vertical fin, tailrotor, each component of the Cobra—or any helicopter for that matter—was as essential as were the individual parts of the human body. Each part had a function. "Guys, we haven't got the luxury of ejector seats and parachutes to save our asses. Anything goes wrong with this ship and we may well have our hands full."

By the time the man completed the preflight they knew they had been given more information than either of them could digest in any four-week course of instruction. "Now, I don't expect you to remember everything I said today," Pollard mused, "but this crap has got to be jammed up and jelly tight between now and when you take your first checkride, in two and a half weeks. No shooting until this helicopter is known inside and out. Is that understood?"

They both nodded.

"Okay, Lieutenant, hop in. We'll take this snake up for a spin." Pollard looked at Grange. "We'll meet you back here one hour after takeoff."

"Roger that."

Nolan had never felt so exposed. At one thousand feet above the ground, they swept forward at a neat one hundred and fifty knots, nearly twice as fast as he had flown in the Huey. During the first high-speed dive, Nolan had the sensation of being in the front seat of a roller coaster. He found himself leaning back with his arms and legs braced; he had to force himself to relax.

Before liftoff, during the cockpit and engine run-up procedures, Pollard had asked him to read the checklist, to get him familiar with how each check was done. Finally, after what seemed like an eternity, the chief warrant officer brought the aircraft up and hovered to the take-off pad. Nolan was impressed with how smooth and steady the ship was in the hands of this capable individual.

He peered into the tiny adjustable mirror attached up and to the right on the metal canopy support brace that sectioned off the Plexiglas windshield. He looked at Pollard's face outlined by his helmet. The mirror was set so eye contact could be maintained between the two pilots. "Monday, when I'm seated there in the front and you're here in the back," Pollard had said during the run-up, "I'll be able to read in your face and your eyes how you perceive what's happening."

Pollard guided the ship on a southwesterly heading, to a large marshy area several miles from the Fort Stewart main post complex. He demonstrated a cyclic climb after a high speed dive, negative-G flight and the recovery technique, pitch-cone coupling, transient torque, and the proper roll-in technique for a rocket run. Finally, after three simulated rocket attacks, Daddy Don asked Nolan if he wanted to fly.

"Sure."

"You have the controls. Remember the ratio of four to one. It doesn't take much movement with that dinky cyclic control stick to make this aircraft do what you want."

Nolan placed his feet on the pedals. He rested his arms on the padding next to the flight controls. The collective pitch-control lever was a short handle that moved with just the ease of his left wrist. And the cyclic was very different than he was used to. In the Huey, the cyclic control stick (for directional control) sat between his legs; in the front-pilot seat of the Cobra, it was off to his right, not in his direct line of sight with the travel of the aircraft. His control inputs felt awkward.

He tried a few turns. "Lead with right pedal when you're going right and left pedal going left. The reason is transient torque," Pollard told him. He explained a little more of the theory behind this wandering movement. Nolan felt the words barge in one ear and fly out the other. Ten minutes later, they were on their way back to the airfield. Pollard was on the controls; he had the airspeed indicator registering VNE (velocity never to exceed). "You and Grange get into those emergency procedures and aircraft limitations this weekend. Come Monday afternoon I want to hear them roll off your tongues."

"All right," Nolan said.

After they landed and were shut down, a POL truck came and topped off the fuel tank. Pollard had left to make a phone call. Nolan helped Grange strap in. "What are you smiling at, sir?"

Victor R. Beaver

"Us. You and me," Nolan said. "We probably got the best instructor in the course. But it's not going to be easy. Cinch up tight, my friend. In the next four weeks, we're going to get the ride of our lives."

"That's fine by me, sir," Grange replied.

"Call me Mike."

"Okay, Mike. I go by Dave."

Chapter 6

THE MEMBERS OF FLIGHT ALPHA ONE stood in the chow line rigid as blocks, moving forward only when the next candidate entered the messhall door at the top of the stairs. Chief Warrant Officer Armstrong and Senior Candidate Tyree roamed the line like crazed bulls. With each man they found a discrepancy in either appearance or stance. Sandy Adamson watched as Pete Cochran, the ex-airline pilot, was ordered to the ground. Armstrong bellowed, "I can't hear you, candidate. LOUDER!"

"...FOUR!...FIVE!...SIX!..."

Armstrong went to the next man. Frank Bartlett had one of his back pockets unbuttoned. "Candidate Bartlett, did you preflight your uniform before leaving the barrack?"

"Sir, Candidate Bartlett, yessir."

"Did your flight platoon leader?"

"Sir, Candidate Bartlett...no, sir."

Armstrong took out his pocketknife and opened it. He reached around and sliced off the offending, unused button. He ordered Bartlett to the ground. The chief warrant officer turned. He stood face to face with Sandy Adamson. Tyree advanced on Sandy's flank. Armstrong said, "Candidate, you have the sorriest flight I have ever seen—"

"Sir, Candidate Adamson, yes, sir."

"You admit it?"

"Sir...I—"

"DROP AND GIVE ME TEN!"

Sandy plummeted to the ground. The two men hovered directly overhead. "Are you motivated, candidate? You don't act motivated or your flight would be *squared away!*"

"Sir, Candidate Adamson, yes, sir."

"'Yes, sir' what, candidate?" Tyree yelled.

"Yes, sir, I am motivated, sir—" Sandy huffed the words out as strong as he could.

"Do you really want to be a helicopter pilot, Candidate Adamson?" Armstrong said.

"Sir! Candidate Adamson! Yes, sir!" He was up to push-up number seven.

"I don't believe you, Candidate Adamson. You're a sorry damn excuse for a warrant officer candidate."

Sandy strained through push-up number eight. He was certain he had done at least two hundred push-ups that day for every conceivable reason. At number nine, he was drained; every one of his muscles ached; his head pounded and his breathing was labored; he felt dizzy. This is all going so wrong, he thought. Suddenly he hated the two men standing over him. How could they know how motivated or unmotivated he was? After the tenth push-up, Sandy stood.

"Drop, candidate, and give me another ten," Armstrong said.

Sandy went down again, slowly this time. Out of the corner of his eye he saw Ron Bowden go to the ground and start doing push-ups, too. Armstrong turned. "What are you doing, candidate?"

"Sir, Candidate Bowden, push-ups, sir!"

"Oh?...and were you ordered to?"

"Sir, Candidate Bowden, no, sir!"

Suddenly, Sandy saw Cottrell drop, and then like dominos the rest of the flight plunged to the ground. At first, Armstrong and Tyree just gaped at each other. Then Tyree began to rush from man to man, ordering them to stand. No one did. Armstrong's anger became equally vehement.

While his classmates sounded the count, Sandy began to regain his strength. He thrived on their enthusiasm and they in turn fed one another. Without anyone knowing the full import of their actions, Flight Alpha One was showing the kind of unity the cadre (inadvertently) was intending all along.

As one man they sprang to attention. Armstrong's face was flush. He rushed to Cottrell and ordered him to the ground. As the ex-Green Beret went down, so did the rest of the flight. Their count became a thunderous roar. Out of breath, his voice weak, his throat raw, Armstrong threw up his hands, turned and walked away. Tyree did the same.

* * *

THURSDAY. THEY HAD JUST RETURNED from their morning classes. Upon their arrival Carlyle informed them that an Awards and Decorations ceremony would take place on Saturday at the large parade ground near the flightline barracks. Curiously, he did not mention yesterday's demonstration, which made Sandy nervous. As they went inside the barrack, they found it again in shambles.

"Damn!" Sandy blurted, as he surveyed the mess for the fourth day in a row. On top the cubicle study table he saw a note.

Candidate Adamson—See me after last class at 1645.
CW2 Carlyle

Sandy showed the note to Willie. "What do you think?"

"You got me," Willie replied. "Listen, if this shit was easy, anybody could do it."

Sandy shook his head. "Willie, you always have a way of making everything so simple."

The Sky Soldiers

"Hey, fifteen years in this man's army has taught me at least one thing: Don't sweat the small stuff. One way or the other they're going to ship your butt to Vietnam. I was over there, all totaled, for twenty-nine months—on the ground. Believe me, I think flying choppers is the better way to go."

Sandy canted his head. "So what's your point?"

"Carlyle doesn't think you want this program bad enough," Willie answered, "and he's going to try to make you quit." He peered into Sandy's eyes. "You've got to admit, you've been leaning on me pretty heavy."

Sandy rifled Willie an angry look. He knew it was true. "You're right...but I'll never quit."

"Hey, don't tell me—tell Carlyle."

It was 1645. Sandy checked his uniform and stepped to the door. He knocked.

"Come in."

Sandy entered and closed the door. He saluted. "Sir, Candidate Adamson, reporting as ordered, sir."

Carlyle returned the salute. "At ease."

Sandy relaxed his stance, feeling weary and depressed. He couldn't believe so much was riding on his performance as Candidate Flight Platoon Leader. Somehow the end result of the flight training program had become elusive. He wanted to fly, if given the chance—wasn't that what they were all there for?

Carlyle leaned back in his chair, twirling a pencil between his fingers; he stared at an open folder on his desk, the candidate evaluation folder.

"Candidate Adamson, the condition of this barrack is despicable."

"Yes, sir...No excuse, sir."

"What are your intentions, Candidate Adamson?"

"Sir, Candidate Adamson, my intentions are to try harder, to do the job expected of me to the best of—"

"Candidate Adamson, why are you here?"

"Sir...?"

"Why do you want to be a helicopter pilot?"

For a long moment Sandy was silent. As he had learned early in the army, a question asked by a superior always warranted a "correct" answer. He took a deep breath. "I...want to fly."

Carlyle laid the pencil down. "Have you always wanted to fly?"

"No, sir...I can't say that I've always wanted to."

"You do know," Carlyle stated, "that in all likelihood you'll be going to Vietnam—*if* you graduate."

Sandy perked his ears. The tac officer had said "if" tentatively. "Yessir...I know that."

"You also know that America is fighting an undeclared war in Vietnam. How do you feel about that?"

Again, he wondered what the right answer might be. And wondered, too, where these questions were leading. "I...I don't know how I feel about that, sir."

"Have you ever seen a dead person, Candidate Adamson?"

Sandy frowned. "Yessir."

He remembered the day so plainly. He was seven. His family was living in Germany, in a small town near the base where his father was stationed. He was walking past a cemetery accessed through a large iron gate. The gate was open and he decided to go in. He walked along a worn, red-brick path to a gray-stoned building. Inside the building the lighting was dim. And then he saw him. There encased under glass, for final viewing, was an old man dressed in a dark, threadbare suit, his hands folded across his chest. For the longest time he stared at the wrinkled, pasty-colored face and tried to plumb the depth of its stillness... *wondering where the soul had gone.* The mystery of it perplexed him still.

"Do you think I'm being too hard on you?" the tac officer asked.

"Sir...I—No, sir, I don't think so."

"Candidate Adamson, there are forty-eight men in this flight and each one of them is a potential aircraft commander. If you think for one minute that all you're going to have to do when you get to Vietnam is manipulate the controls of a helicopter—*Mister, you'd better think again.* Over there you're going to be responsible for a quarter-million dollar aircraft and the lives of your co-pilot and crew, and any troops or passengers you may have to carry. And they're going to expect you to be in command—"

"Yes, sir, I understand—"

"Don't interrupt me, candidate. I had you pegged as pretty levelheaded. But you seem to think that this flight runs on its own good merit, that you can sit by and let each man do his own thing, go his own way, that you're not that necessary in the grand scheme of things. Well, that's a big fat negative. Every man must do his job—*and that includes you!* Do I make myself perfectly clear?"

"Sir, Candidate Adamson, yes, sir!"

"Good. This is your week to be a platoon leader. I expect you to act like one!"

"Yes, sir!"

"Saturday morning, these bays had better be standing tall."

"Sir, Candidate Adamson, yessir! They will be, s*ir!*"

"You're dismissed—"

"PLATOON SERGEANT COTTRELL!"

"Sir...?"

"Get the squad leaders together," Sandy said firmly.

"Yessir!"

* * *

SATURDAY MORNING. 0700. SANDY Adamson had just checked his watch: inspection in half an hour. He felt tense, excited. No matter what happened, Carlyle would never be able to say he didn't give his all. He had never been a quitter; he wasn't about to start now.

"Seymore—get a man on this commode."

"All right already...Jesus...Christ..."

Upstairs, Sandy ran his hand on the backside of a wall-locker. "Dusty! Damnit, Chancey, tell your guys to clean behind them, too. If Carlyle sees this he'll rip you and me both a new asshole—"

Sandy scouted every cubicle, checked every corner, slid his hand over every possible surface. He carried the WOC guide in one hand and a ruler in the other. If nothing else, he could honestly say he had inspected every man's wall- and footlocker display by the book.

"I've got a man to rake the leaves, like you told me," Willie Cottrell said. Sandy was looking out from a second-story window.

"Good. I'll be down in a minute to inspect."

Five minutes later, Sandy stood before each man, giving every uniform a thorough once over.

It was now 0725. Carlyle appeared in front of the orderly room and was now coming toward the barrack.

"Keep working," Sandy ordered. "At exactly seven thirty, I'm going to call for a formation outside. And remember, if one goes down for push-ups, we all go down."

Carlyle entered through the back door.

"ATTEN—HUT!"

"Carry on," Carlyle said. He looked at Sandy. "Candidate Adamson, come into my office."

Sandy stood at attention, back stiff, arms taut, heart thumping.

"Is the barrack ready for inspection, Candidate Adamson?"

"Sir, Candidate Adamson, yes, *sir!*"

"I hope so. If this flight fails inspection, you're going to wish like hell you never met me."

Sandy's heart skipped a beat. "We won't fail—Sir!"

"We shall see."

They were outside. "OPEN RANKS...MARCH!"

Carlyle went from man to man. Sandy walked beside him, notepad in hand. The first discrepancy came with the tenth man. A faint patch of unshaven whiskers under the left jaw. Twenty demerits. In the next row a candidate had a scuff

Victor R. Beaver

mark on the toe of his boot. Ten demerits. In the back row another flight platoon member had one of his WOC brass slightly off center. Fifteen demerits.

Inside, Sandy followed again. The tac officer went from cubicle to cubicle. He bent and tiptoed and wiped his hand over every surface. His discerning eyes peered into every corner. Unlike the previous days, Carlyle was finding it difficult to note any gross errors; he assessed demerits for flecks of dust that had fallen in the interim.

Finally, Carlyle came to Seymore's bunk. He took out a quarter. Sandy saw that his Howdy Doody friend had his fingers crossed. "What do you think, Candidate Cutter? Will I get a flip?"

"Sir, Candidate Cutter, yes, sir."

"I hope so, Candidate Cutter."

The tac officer dropped the quarter from four feet. It hit and did one flip. "Very good, Candidate Cutter. You're learning."

Carlyle called them outside for another formation. He stood before them with Sandy at his side. "Today's inspection was a far cry better than I've seen. It looks like you all put some real time and effort into your work. I believe that one of your members was sufficiently motivated." Carlyle turned and looked at Sandy. "I would like to think that these inspections serve a useful purpose: to help you develop an eye for detail unlike you've ever done. If you don't find out what's wrong with your aircraft before you fly, you're going to wish like hell you had after you get off the ground. They say a helicopter is nothing more than a mass of rivets and bolts flying in loose formation...just looking for the opportunity to scatter everywhere. After this past week—the way this barrack looked after I inspected—you'd better by God believe it. Keep up the good work."

* * *

NEARLY THREE THOUSAND MEN WERE assembled on the parade ground. There were forty flight platoons of warrant officer candidates, four student-officer companies plus members of the school's permanent staff. Seated on bleachers off to one side were several dozen onlookers. A brisk wind made flags and guide-ons wave and flap with a smart snapping sound. In the background were the flight-line barracks, eight three-story buildings built of pale stucco, aglow in the warmth of the mid-morning sun.

Earlier, Class 67-15 had marched from the 5th WOC Company area two and a half miles on a winding and hilly back road until they crested the last hill and these sacred halls came into view. Shortly afterwards, as they began to pass down the company streets, they saw veteran candidates, in preparation for the ceremony, quickly form into platoons and companies, while angry tac officers shouted at stragglers and meted out the ubiquitous push-up.

The Sky Soldiers

The 5th WOC Company cadre began to bark frustrated commands. "Quit rubber-necking, you people. EYES FRONT! Your left...your left, your left right left..."

"Sheee-it, they don't look any different than we do, with their damned skinned heads," someone commented.

"Hey, aren't those guys our Blue Hat brothers?"

"Yeah, those are the guys leaving next for Rucker."

"Betcha they can't wait to get the hell outta here."

"Okay, you people. CAN THE CHATTER!"

The PA system sounded across the parade field. The post adjutant, a lieutenant colonel, began speaking: "Good morning, ladies and gentlemen. We are here today to honor seven men who distinguished themselves in combat in the Republic of Vietnam. I regret to say, however, that one of these men is not with us. He is being honored posthumously. On behalf of the post commandant, I extend my deepest sympathies to the family and friends of this individual.

"All of them are pilots, except for a member of the candidate corps, an ex-Huey crewchief going through the flight training program."

The ceremony lasted half an hour. Sandy stood in the front of his platoon and saw clearly the men whose valor had warranted these accolades. They were indeed men of flesh and blood, however they had given that extra measure which set them apart from others. Their awards were two Silver Stars and four Distinguished Flying Crosses. Ron Bowden, of Flight Alpha One, received one of the Silver Stars, for saving the lives of his fellow crewmembers after his aircraft was shot down in heavily forested terrain. The seventh, given posthumously, was the Distinguished Service Cross, the nation's second highest award.

* * *

THE PHONE RANG SEVERAL TIMES. "Hello...?"

"Hi, Katie, it's me, Sandy."

"Oh, Sandy—How are you?"

"Great. Just great."

"I got your letter yesterday," she said. "You sounded down. Is everything okay?"

"Yeah, everything's fine now. This morning we had an inspection. We passed. Then we went to this ceremony, you know, where they give out medals. There was a guy who got the Distinguished Service Cross. That's the nation's second highest award. But he wasn't there."

"How come?"

"He got it posthumous. They presented it to his wife."

"Oh, Sandy...how awful that must have been."

There was silence. Suddenly he wished he hadn't told her that. "Listen, sweetheart, I'm with a really great bunch of guys. I can't wait for you to meet them."

"I can't wait, either..."

"You'll really like them," he added.

"I'm sure I will."

"Katie, could we talk...about something?"

"Sure, what is it?"

He took a deep breath. "I graduate from flight training in July. Let's get married then."

"Married?...What?...Sandy, I—are you sure? Gosh, that's such a big step. Shouldn't we talk about it?—give it a lot of thought?"

"I've already thought about it," he said. "We could do it at one of the post chapels. It would be a military wedding, you know, with crossed swords overhead—the whole bit. What do you say?" At that moment, he regretted that he was not on one knee presenting her with a ring, the way he had always envisioned.

"Oh, Sandy...I just don't know. What about Vietnam?"

"What about Vietnam?"

"Well, you'll be over there. I'll be here...all alone."

"I know. It'll be tough. But we could do it, don't you think?"

"Sandy...I-I don't know—I'd be so worried."

"Katie, aren't you going to be worried anyway...even if we aren't married? I don't understand."

"Yes, of course, but it-it wouldn't be the same."

"Well, how would it be different?" He felt a terrible constriction across his chest.

"Please, Sandy, don't ask me to explain—"

"You do love me, don't you?"

"Of course I do, Sandy, please don't ever doubt that." She wished she knew what to say. She wished she understood her fears better—her true feelings for him this past week. "This is really such a bad time, Sandy. We're all worried about Brad. We don't know how he is from day to day. It's just terrible—this not knowing."

"Oh, yeah, how *is* Brad doing?" He had completely forgotten about her brother.

"So far he's okay," she said, her voice wavering. "We got a letter from him just yesterday. He says they're always firing their guns."

Sandy breathed deep and sighed. "He'll be all right, Katie. Honest. Gosh, what kind of danger could he be in...a couple miles off shore?"

"I-I don't know, Sandy. I'm really scared. I don't know why."

"How do your folks feel?"

The Sky Soldiers

"I'm not sure...they don't ever really say."

He decided to change the subject. "Okay, listen, we'll talk about getting married later. Over Christmas break. What do you say?"

"Yes, Sandy, that would be...better."

"You do miss me, don't you, Katie?"

"You know I do, Sandy."

"I miss you, Katie—really, really bad."

After he hung up, he went to the dayroom and found a place to be alone. He sat down and put his hands over his face. He was so confused. He tried to sort things out, but his attempt to do so made everything worse. *What would it be like for her with me over there, if we were married? Would she be even more beside herself with worry? How can being married make such a difference?—It doesn't make sense.* He slammed his fist against his leg. *Damn! How can I be so callous?...I don't want to put her through that!...But if we don't get married, would she worry less?...What's the right thing to do?* The knot in his stomach tightened. Maybe he should break from her completely. But he found that thought so unbearable, he dismissed it immediately. And then it hit him, a revelation so potent it went off in his head like a bomb. With utter certainty he knew that if anything bad were to happen to Brad, he would lose her for good.

Sick at heart, Sandy went in search of Seymore. He found his friend in their cubicle fretting over the shine on his boots. "Seymore, will you be the best man at my wedding?"

"Wedding? What wedding?—Right now?"

"No, you dufus—in July, when we graduate."

Gathering his wits, Seymore reached up and felt Sandy's forehead. "Are you feeling okay? You must have a fever."

"I feel fine. Will you?"

Seymore nodded. "That's a big ten-four, good buddy. I'd be proud to do the honors."

"Thanks, Seymore. You're a real pal."

Victor R. Beaver

Chapter 7

"MR. SLATER, I'VE GOT YOU on the mission planning board for tomorrow," Captain Slote said. "Your AC will be Mr. Dreyfuss. You'll be resupplying Vinh Long Province, flying out of Sa Dec. Briefing will be at o'six hundred."

"Yes, sir."

It had been two days since Kip had taken his stan ride with Lieutenant Whitaker; and for two days he had come into operations practically every hour on the hour to check the scheduling board, hoping to see his first in-country mission posted. Each time Henry would shake his head and he would go back to his room or to the club or go visit the little PX down the street from the company area. The second day after his arrival he and Mac had gone downtown to shop for a pistol belt for his .38 and a plastic mapcase for his operational map of the Mekong Delta. He spent his evenings in the Tiger's Den with Leo, Mac, Henry, and Oakerson, getting completely sloshed, usually stumbling into bed at one or two in the morning, vowing each time he woke to curb his alcohol intake (however, with little success).

Looking at the slight growth on Kip's upper lip, Captain Slote said, "And by the way, Major Drummond doesn't allow officers or warrant officers to grow mustaches."

"Really, how come?"

"It's just his policy, *Mister* Slater."

"Well, maybe I can grow one when the new CO arrives."

"Hopefully not," Slote replied.

Early morning. Slater ran his hand along the underside of the tailboom, continuing back until he came to the left-side synchronized elevator and the vertical fin that supported the tailrotor assembly. He had learned that it was customary in the unit for the peter-pilot to perform the preflight inspection while the aircraft commander checked out an SOI, received a mission briefing, which included whom to contact and where, a weather outlook, and any additional instructions.

Slater had met Dreyfuss, recently promoted to CW2, in the officers' dining room at 0530. The aircraft commander had said very little, giving Kip the impression that his presence in the cockpit would be more a nuisance than a need. Dreyfuss also walked with a slight limp. Off convalescent leave now for three weeks, his left foot had taken a small hunk of shrapnel during a combat operation near Mo Cay. Mo Cay, Kip learned, was one of several notorious locations in the Delta where the VC roamed with near virtual impunity.

"Mr. Slater."

Kip turned. "Yes?"

"You've got a choice. Ham and lima beans or meatballs in sauce." Rusty White, the ship's assigned crewchief, held out two individual C-ration meals for Kip's inspection. Slater had met White when he came out to preflight, along with Ron Larkin, the gunner.

"I'll take the meatballs. What does Mr. Dreyfuss like?"

"Ham and eggs, the lousiest combination there is."

"You guys get along with him all right?"

"Yessir. Ron and I, we can't complain. Mr. Dreyfuss is quiet, usually, and a damn good pilot. He doesn't screw around like some we've flown with." Rusty lifted a Gott-cooler full of ice water onto the cabin deck. He shoved it back against the transmission bulkhead, between a set of nylon passenger seats.

"Screw around? What do you mean?"

"Well, some ACs like to do low-level flying where they don't think there are any Charlie. Trouble is, the sneaky little shits can be anywhere—especially where you least expect them."

When Dreyfuss finally appeared, Kip and Rusty were on top the aircraft cabin checking the main rotor system. "Everything okay up there, Chief?" Dreyfuss asked.

"Yessir," Rusty replied. "Mr. Slater wanted me to show him how I inspect the head when I do my 'daily.'" He turned to Kip. "Anything else, sir?"

"No, that's okay. We might as well get down."

After they climbed down, Dreyfuss opened the right cockpit door and placed his flight helmet and chest protector (chickenplate) on the seat. He carried a loaded carbine and two bandoleers of ammunition. He placed the carbine against the side of the ship and draped the bandoleers on the inside handle of the open door.

Dreyfuss handed Slater a small booklet that had been in his left breast pocket, attached to a nylon cord looped around his neck. "Here's the SOI. Do *not* lose it. It's a court-martial offense if you misplace it. Afterwards, they hang you and cut off your balls." Kip grinned, stifling the urge to laugh. Dreyfuss said, "I'll have you work with it and make the radio calls. I'm getting short. If I get a wild hair, I might let you fly. Otherwise, you'll be better off the first day in the left seat just watching what's going on. How does that sound?"

Kip shrugged. "Sounds fine."

"Okay, let's untie and swing the blades."

As the two pilots got into their respective seats, Ron Larkin went to the rear of the tailboom, unwrapped the nylon strap from around the tail stinger, and then rotated the main rotorblades until they were ninety degrees to the fuselage. He released the tie-down hook from the tip of the blade and stowed it in the back cabin area. Meantime, Dreyfuss had quickly strapped in and was going through the pre-start checks, flipping switches and setting dials almost faster than the new peter-pilot could follow. Shortly, he called out, "Coming hot!"

"Clear!"

Dreyfuss started the clock and with the "trigger" switch pulled energized the igniters, which began to "fire" with a familiar tick-tick-tick sound. Behind them the turbine engine began to whine and the main rotorblades overhead began to turn. In a little over a minute, Dreyfuss was bringing the throttle to full rpm. With the main generator and inverter on, he told Kip to turn on the radios. "You get the rest of the cockpit checks; I'll call for hover-taxi instructions." The two pilots then put their helmets on.

In another moment they were airborne. Dreyfuss climbed the aircraft to two thousand feet then turned due north. Before increasing their speed, Dreyfuss signaled for Rusty and Ron to close the cabin doors. Then he spoke to Kip over the ICS (intercom system). "Okay, we flight follow with Paddy Control on three four four point four UHF. Give them a call and tell them were off Delta Seven en route to November Three. Those are the flight-following coded identifiers for Soc Trang and Sa Dec. Tell them we're at two thousand feet. Estimated time enroute about thirty-five minutes. We'll call tally-ho when we arrive at Sa Dec. Request flight following and artillery. It's important to copy *all* the artillery information."

"Yeah, okay." Pencil in hand, Kip made his radio call. The voice coming back sounded young yet experienced. "Roger. We have arty coming out of Juliet Two, azimuth zero five zero, range nine thousand four hundred meters." The controller then gave a shell trajectory height in feet above ground and suggested a southerly route around Can Tho before proceeding north.

Having scribbled most of it down, Kip looked quickly to Dreyfuss who nodded agreement. Again, Kip tried to sound professional speaking over the radio. "This is Tiger Zero Nine Eight, roger."

"Okay," said Dreyfuss. "We'll just aim for Can Tho first before going on to Sa Dec."

The aircraft commander now took up a new heading to the northwest. Slater consulted his map. To their right flowed one of the major tributaries of the Mekong River, the Basaac, less than four kilometers away. He saw dozens and dozens of sampans gliding over its smooth-flowing, muddy surface. He also saw a line of PBRs (river patrol boats) scouting along the shore. It made him wonder just exactly where the VC were, how well hidden or obvious they would be when it came time for him to confront their presence.

To keep oriented, Kip matched terrain features, mostly canal and river intersections, with symbols on his new operational map. He peered straight ahead. "That should be Can Tho...twelve o'clock. Sa Dec is about thirty-eight klicks due north of there." He tried not to feel foolish, but he wanted Dreyfuss to at least know he could read a map.

The day was crystal clear. Everywhere there were varying hues of browns and greens, all vivid in the early morning light. Dreyfuss pointed to something in

The Sky Soldiers

the distance. "See those outcroppings, those dark nodules? That's the very southern portion of the Seven Mountains region, one of several VC strongholds. They've got caves all around there where they can hide and stash shit in. Those three particular nodules are just this side of the Cambodia border. The other four mountain outcroppings, strung out in Cambodia, probably got gooks hidden in them too." Kip checked his map. From their location, he estimated the mountains on this side of the border to be at least a hundred kilometers away. The map also showed their average elevations to be slightly over two thousand feet. Dreyfuss said, "Except around Ha Tien and the Cement Plant, they're the only raised relief in the entire Mekong Delta. Everywhere else is flat. Perfect—as you can plainly see—for growing rice."

After several minutes, flying over a patchwork of rice paddies, an intricate lacing of narrow winding rivers, and numerous isolated clusters of trees and vegetation, Slater asked, to break the silence: "Where are you from, sir?"

Dreyfuss glanced at him. "Don't call me 'sir.' Over here we don't even call lieutenants 'sir.'"

"Oh...okay, sure."

"I'm from Fort Wayne, Indiana. I grew up on a pig farm."

"Oh yeah?" Slater replied. "My father works at a feed store, in Hutchinson, Kansas."

Dreyfuss nodded.

Kip said, "I understand you got wounded."

"Yeah."

"What happened?"

Dreyfuss shrugged. "Just got hit. What can I say?"

"How did it feel?"

"It felt like I got slammed by a rock. I didn't see any blood at first—just a rip in my boot. Then it started to hurt, real bad."

"So you got a Purple Heart."

Dreyfuss nodded. "Yeah, big deal, I got a Purple Heart."

They slipped past Can Tho on the left, continuing northwest until they were beyond Binh Thuy's airport traffic area. Dreyfuss then turned the helicopter due north. "Binh Tuy and Can Tho have the longest runways in the Delta. Besides U.S. Air Force fast movers and VNAF Skyraiders, a gang of Navy SEALs also operates out of Binh Tuy. Try not to work with those guys, they're loco."

Sa Dec loomed ahead. "Call Paddy Control and tell them we've got a tally-ho on Sa Dec. Tell 'em we'll report liftoff later." As Slater transmitted on the radio, Dreyfuss slowed the aircraft and told Rusty and Ron to open the doors. He began a descent to fifteen hundred feet. "Okay, look up Sa Dec's FM frequency in the SOI. Give them a call and tell them we'll be there in five to six minutes."

Victor R. Beaver

Slater fumbled through the little booklet for over a minute before finding the right frequency. He dialed it in and began transmitting: "Gold Digger Two Five, this is Tiger Zero Nine Eight."

A gravelly voice came back. "Go ahead, Tiger Zero Nine Eight. What's your ETE?"

"This is Tiger Zero Nine Eight. We'll be there in about zero five minutes."

"Roger that."

Dreyfuss skirted the west side of Sa Dec. When they neared the Mekong River, he began a wide turn to the east. "We land in the middle of a soccer field. We approach from over the water, the only decent approach path in. Trees surround the field on the other three sides."

Kip spied a large cluster of old French colonial buildings in the center of the city, side-by-side with numerous large Banyan trees. The French architecture gave the city the appearance of a medieval fortress, as if built to guard the river. Kip felt the aircraft slow again. Dreyfuss banked right, rolling out on a southerly heading. They were now over the river. The AC started a descent. Kip strained to see an opening in the midst of the city's layout, but saw no such thing. Below them brown-faced children stood in sampans and waved. He waved back. They reacted with excited laughter. He looked to see if any of them held a weapon, wondering if any of the stories he had heard were true.

Slater glanced again to his front. They were heading directly toward the heart of the city. He resumed his search for the soccer field. *Where the hell is it?* And then he saw an opening on the other side of a high, brick wall. The helicopter began to shudder as Dreyfuss steepened the approach to the landing zone. At the far end of the LZ Kip could see an American soldier standing with his arms raised, acting as a ground guide. As they continued the descent, Kip performed a textbook low recon of the landing zone. And then his eyes locked onto the razor-sharp concertina wire strung along the top of the wall. As Dreyfuss had described, Banyan trees with limbs as big around as the trunks of smaller trees crowded the soccer-field walls as well as the buildings nearby.

Rusty announced: "You're clear of the wall."

"Clear right," piped Larkin.

Dreyfuss brought the Huey to a hover in front of the American soldier, a staff sergeant who recognized him and grinned. The sergeant was holding fast to his hat. "Coming down," Dreyfuss said.

"Clear down."

The sergeant, a burly man with a massive handlebar mustache, came to the helicopter's right side. He cracked a large smile and poked his head through Dreyfuss's window. "Well, I'll be go to hell!" he boomed over the noise of the engine. "How ya doing, sir? Long time no see! I got word you had your goddamn foot blown off!" He looked at Dreyfuss's feet resting on the anti-torque pedals. "Musta been a scratch, huh, sir?" The man's eyes gleamed as he spoke.

The Sky Soldiers

"Oh, yeah, right, just a scratch..." Then Dreyfuss spoke to Slater over the intercom. "Sergeant O'Brien. I thought he'd DEROS'd. He's a kick in the ass. He'll treat us right."

"Sir, I got one terrific schedule for you today!" O'Brien shouted. "Might as well shut down! Got hot coffee and fresh cinnamon rolls in the mess!"

"Okay, Sarge, but you gotta remember—I'm short!"

"Oh yeah? How many days, sir?"

"Twenty-one and a wake-up. After this week I get to skate. No more flying. I just may get out of this idiotic war alive!"

O'Brien grinned. "Shit, sir—I extended!"

"God, what did you do that for?" Dreyfuss said.

"Gotta mama-san downtown! She's got three of the cutest kids I ever saw. I'm just like their daddy!" O'Brien's faced beamed as he spoke.

MACV province headquarters was housed within one of the French colonial buildings adjacent to the soccer field. Once inside, Kip found the messhall to be a large, high-ceilinged room furnished with six long tables, each table covered by a bright red-and-white-checkered tablecloth. Upon sitting, a frail-looking Vietnamese woman served them coffee, then brought out a pan of piping-hot cinnamon rolls, the biggest rolls Kip had ever seen. Their sweet, just-baked smell filled the whole room. He closed his eyes...*I'm in heaven!*

"Okay, here's the scoop, sir," O'Brien said, bringing out his notepad. "We got four re-supply runs to make: one to Lap Vo, one to Ap Tan Phong, and two to Hac Long. Hac Long has more stuff than I think you can take in one lift. Then break for lunch. After lunch, you'll be taking a Captain Harvey to Saigon."

"Saigon—*all right,*" Rusty said. "That means we can go to the Tan Son Nhut PX and I can get that telephoto lens I've been meaning to buy."

"Now hold onto your shorts," O'Brien said. "I've got to have you back ASAP—if not sooner. You've got to go back to Ap Tan Phong, to take a USAID guy for a pow-wow with the district chief at fourteen hundred hours. The meeting should last about an hour. You'll shut down and wait for him. I might get you released by fifteen thirty. How's that sound?"

"Better," Ron Larkin said. "I'd rather get home early."

After they ate, they went back to the helicopter. Fifteen minutes later, O'Brien appeared in a jeep pulling a small trailer loaded with cardboard boxes, wooden crates, and several cans of ammunition. Two ARVN who jumped out of the jeep to help with the loading accompanied him. Rusty and Ron roused themselves to supervise the loading process. To make more room they folded the passenger seats up and secured them against the transmission bulkhead.

"All of this is for Lap Vo," O'Brien said. "I'll have the load for Ap Tan Phong right here ready when you get back."

Dreyfuss nodded. Again the two pilots proceeded through the start procedures and soon had the ship up to operating rpm. "All set in the back?" the aircraft commander asked.

"Clear left."

"Clear up right."

"Okay...let's see how this goes." Dreyfuss began to apply power. Like a beast of burden, the engine groaned; the rpm drooped then recovered. "Gutless wonders these L-11 engines," Dreyfuss said over the intercom. He applied more power. "Well, we're light on the skids. Just a little more torque and we should be hovering...I hope."

Dreyfuss applied two more pounds of torque pressure and the ship lifted to a one-foot hover. "Well...Alfie seems to be holding steady at about thirty-two pounds. We probably won't get much more out of him without bleeding off rpm." "Alfie" was the name Rusty and Ron had given their ship. Several months before, Ron Larkin had had the face of Alfred E. Newman, Mad Magazine's toothy main character, painted on the nosecone (the radio compartment cover). Below the face were the words *The New Yorker.* Dreyfuss maneuvered the aircraft until they were at the southernmost end of the soccer-field LZ. "Hold onto your hats—and pray for a sudden rising gust of wind at the right moment," he said.

Dreyfuss guided *Alfie* forward. The winds, slight as they were, were still coming out of the northwest, but would be of little use for providing additional lift until after they cleared the wall. The helicopter moved slowly at first, picking up speed gradually. The far wall loomed larger and larger. Slater was certain they wouldn't become airborne in time to clear it. And then, as if drawn skyward by some unseen hand, *Alfie* lumbered into the air, clearing the wall and the concertina wire by a scant three feet. Once on the other side, Dreyfuss, to increase airspeed, allowed the helicopter to settle toward the river's surface. He guided *Alfie* past several sampans, narrowly missing the first one in front of them. Then he added power and eased back on the cyclic to gain altitude. Slater felt his heart beating in his throat. That the aircraft got off the ground and cleared the wall seemed predestined by the good grace of God. But Slater knew it was Dreyfuss's intimate knowledge of the aircraft and deft handling of the controls that had actually done the job. *Lordy Lordy, do I have a lot to learn!*

They climbed to fifteen hundred feet, still over the wide Mekong River, before Dreyfuss turned the helicopter west. Kip made his required radio call to Paddy Control, then began to thumb through the SOI for Lap Vo's frequency and callsign. "Have you been to Lap Vo before?" he asked Dreyfuss.

Dreyfuss nodded. "Maybe seven or eight times, at least. It's a small district town, very quiet, housing a MACV military advisory team. The landing pad is a square mound of dirt, built up about a foot above waterline. A dirt path leads from it to the road. They might land us on the road, since we won't be shutting down. That way we can unload directly onto their jeep."

Within a few minutes, Lap Vo came into view. As they got closer Slater could see that it didn't look any different that any other village or town they had flown over that morning, a collection of thatched huts surrounding a more permanent downtown structure of mostly stucco-sided buildings with red-tiled roofs. Large clusters of banana trees, nipa palms, and other tropical growth hid most of the dwellings, making the town appear like an island of plant life in a sea of rice paddies. In time, he would come to know that provinces in Vietnam were like individual states in America, and that district towns were like county seats within the provinces. Though hundreds of roads crisscrossed the Delta, most of them built of hard-packed dirt, and easily traveled during the dry monsoons, it was the dozens and dozens of canals (many of them constructed during the French colonial period) and the hundreds of winding riverways that were the people's main thoroughfares. The sampan, a long canoe-like boat, some large enough to house and raise a family, plied these waterways, bringing meats and produce from the countryside into the cities.

Slater keyed the radio to report their inbound time. A reply came quickly back. "This is Whiskey Charlie Two Five, roger. We'll be standing by with smoke."

Dreyfuss brought the helicopter around the north side of Lap Vo and began a slow left-hand turn to allow Kip to see the landing pad. "I've got purple smoke," Kip said. "And it looks like a couple of Americans next to a jeep."

"Whiskey Charlie Two Five, Tiger Zero Nine Eight, we got your purple smoke," Dreyfuss radioed.

"This is Whiskey Charlie Two Five. I confirm purple smoke. Could you land on the road? Over."

"Affirmative," Dreyfuss returned.

"Doesn't look like there's much wind," Slater said, seeing the drift of the smoke. "It's still coming out of the northwest, though."

"We'll descend over that open area downwind of the pad and road, then make our approach over the road," Dreyfuss said. "We can set down perpendicular to the road after we come in." The AC then looked to the back and ordered the cabin doors opened. When this was done, Rusty and Ron brought their M-60s up to level, loaded the belted ammunition, chambered a round, and sat back with their fingers on the trigger.

Slater tensed. He had felt no danger going into Sa Dec, a large city, but he felt fear now. "Don't we need gunship cover?"

"What for?" Dreyfuss replied.

"I don't know. Aren't we in a war?"

"In the Mekong Delta? Get real. Besides, during the day Charlie sleeps. At night, that's when he comes out to play."

Slater swallowed. "So, where's the war?"

"It ain't at Lap Vo, I can tell you that," Dreyfuss said. "Try your luck in the Seven Mountains region, or around Vinh Quoi, or Mo Cay, or how about Nam Can. But do it after I'm gone. I've had about all I can stand of this place."

With more airspace to maneuver in, their approach to Lap Vo was shallower and faster than their arrival into Sa Dec. Dreyfuss brought the ship to within a few feet of the dying smoke canister. The downwash from the rotorblades made the last of the smoke disperse and the surrounding trees bend away. Kip noticed several clusters of small children in front of them, arching forward into the powerful wind. "The kids make a game of standing there," Dreyfuss said. The children's faces were stretched taut, their eyes squinting; a few were hiding behind the others. "Okay...tail coming left."

"Clear left," Rusty said.

"Clear on the right," stated Ron.

Once the ship was on the ground, the children straightened and watched the two American advisors move forward from the parked jeep. Rusty got out and started unloading, while Larkin remained in his seat, languorously aiming his machine gun at a treeline a hundred meters away. One of the advisors, a short, wiry black staff sergeant, stood on the toe of the left skid. He had a wide, happy grin on his face. "How ya doing, sir? We got some mail for you to take out. Did we get any?" The man handed Kip a small bundle of letters tied together with string. Kip took the letters and placed them in the narrow space between the center console and the left cockpit seat.

"Did we have mail to deliver?" Kip asked Dreyfuss.

"O'Brien didn't give me any."

Kip shook his head. The sergeant's face changed from happy to sad. Kip felt bad. "Maybe later today something will come in," he told the sergeant. "We can make another run. How's that sound?"

The sergeant's expression changed back into a wide grin.

"What are you telling him?" Dreyfuss asked over the intercom.

"Uh...later some mail might come in? We could bring it out then?"

"Oh, shit, I can see you're gonna get along real well over here. Make all the grunts happy but piss off your crew. Do you realize how boring it is for them sitting back there behind their guns?"

"Well, we're here to take care of these guys, aren't we?"

"Yeah...I suppose."

When they returned to Sa Dec, O'Brien was waiting with the supplies for Ap Tan Phong, a small hamlet located eighteen kilometers southwest of Sa Dec. Rusty and Ron began loading. When they were done they got into their seats and plugged their helmets back into the ship's intercom. This time the burly sergeant handed Kip two small packages and a dozen letters tied together. "Here's some mail and a couple of care packages. I also got word that you might have a passenger coming back with you!" he shouted into Kip's keyed microphone.

"Ask him who," Dreyfuss said.

Kip relayed the question. O'Brien said, "A Vietnamese woman...an older woman!" The MACV sergeant gave them a hapless look. "Sorry, that's all I know!"

Kip said to Dreyfuss, "Wow, she must be someone important."

"Yeah, sure, Mrs. General What's-Her-Face, Chief of National Security," the AC answered.

Kip checked his map. Again, a canal led directly to their destination. After they were airborne, Kip thumbed through the SOI for the Ap Tan Phong callsign and frequency. "Rusty Harbor Two Five, this is Tiger Zero Nine Eight, inbound your location. Estimating arrival in zero five minutes."

"This is Rusty Harbor Two Five, roger. We'll be standing by with smoke. We've also got a passenger for you, one-each female-type. She's a medevac. Over."

"Roger that," Kip replied.

"She probably got her back strained from too much stooping and bending in the rice paddies," Rusty commented from the back.

"Bull," Ron said. "She's probably VC. She was in a firefight last night, got shot up, and we're the ones who have to haul her ass in for treatment."

Kip turned in his seat and faced toward the back. Frowning, he said, "You guys are full of it."

"It's happened before—believe me," Dreyfuss interjected.

They made their approach to yellow smoke, touching down several feet short of the canister. The same scene played again. The children were there in bunches, giggling, pointing, all of them barefooted. They seemed clean and healthy—and happy. Though he had only been in-country a week, Kip was beginning to realize that the war was not quite as constant everywhere as the nightly news in the United States portrayed, nor were the Vietnamese people as impoverished, particularly the children.

An American captain dressed in camouflage Tiger fatigues approached. He held onto his hat as he stooped low under the rotorblades. Behind him followed a sergeant. A jeep was parked at the edge of the village about thirty meters away. Around it was a crowd of villagers, mostly older people. In the front seat sat a slightly younger woman, her face a study in pain. Next to her, standing outside the jeep, was another American, giving comfort.

The captain spoke loudly through Kip's open window. "We got a pregnant woman here! She isn't any spring chicken! My medic says she's about seven months along and getting ready to deliver! He thinks the baby's all cockeyed! She might need a C-section! We need for you to take her back to Sa Dec! Is that okay?"

Victor R. Beaver

Kip looked over to Dreyfuss. The aircraft commander had heard most of what was said over the din of the engine.

Dreyfuss breathed deep. "I don't like this. She could pop en route."

"It wouldn't happen that quick—would it?" Kip said.

"Shit, you never know," Dreyfuss replied. "It happens in the back seat of taxicabs in the States—seems like all the time—doesn't it? And what are we?—nothing more than glorified cab drivers."

"Is she having contractions?" Ron asked over the intercom.

Kip relayed the question to the captain. "They're irregular! I'll send my medic with you, and those two women!" he said, turning and glancing back toward the jeep. "They're her relatives! How does that sound?"

Dreyfuss thought for a moment, then shrugged. "What the hell," he said. "If she delivers en route, it'll be a first for me. Tell him okay."

With the supplies off-loaded, Rusty and Ron put the seats back down and secured the leg-posts to the floor. The captain and sergeant returned to the jeep and waited for the command to bring the passengers forward. "Here's where I wish we had a damn stretcher," Rusty said. "I swear, we might as well have one. Our slicks haul more medevacs in a week than Dustoff does in two months."

When the ship was ready, Ron signaled for them to approach. The medic gingerly guided the pregnant woman under the helicopter's turning rotorblades. The captain and sergeant, assisting the woman's two relatives, a pair of ancient-looking crones barely able to walk, followed them. Suddenly, Kip remembered his camera. He had yet to take a picture that morning. He reached for it, opened the case, and set the shutter speed. By the time he was ready, he saw the agony the woman was in and lost heart. To use the camera now, he thought, would be insensitive and unkind.

Dreyfuss brought the aircraft carefully to a hover. To eliminate any uncomfortable airflow through the cabin, the two crewmen closed the cabin doors before liftoff. The two machine guns, without their human element of control, now pointed harmlessly downward outside the helicopter.

During the climbout, Dreyfuss told Slater to call ahead and ask that an ambulance be standing by. O'Brien's gravelly voice answered that it would be done.

"Good, she'll have that much more lead time," Dreyfuss said.

Kip looked back at the pregnant woman. Her face was gaunt, both from worry and pain, her dark eyes wide and fearful. In a moment her lips parted and she began a quick session of breathing. Slater saw that she had a mouthful of discolored and disfigured teeth. The medic, a small, fair-haired staff sergeant named Collins, checked his watch. He raised three fingers: contraction three minutes apart.

Suddenly the woman let out a loud guttural cry heard even above the din of the helicopter. Frantically, the two older women tried to calm her. Collins spoke quickly to Larkin. The gunner relayed:

"Sir, the medic says he's never delivered a baby. We gotta hurry!"

Dreyfuss said, "Crap—tell him I'm pedaling as fast as I can!"

The aircraft commander applied more power. The air outside the ship whistled past with the increase in speed. The helicopter began to rattle and shake, as if at any moment it might tear itself apart. The airspeed indicator registered 115 knots.

To save time, they raced straight toward the center of the city. Dreyfuss overflew the soccer field, then made a steep descending turn to the right, slowing *Alfie* as he did. When they returned to a level attitude, Kip saw the landing zone directly to their front, less than three hundred meters away. Even on a steep approach angle, Dreyfuss wasted no time losing altitude.

Kip looked back. The pregnant woman was now on the floor with her head on Collins's lap. Breathing hard, she had her hands over her belly while her dark eyes darted back and forth between her two relatives. It was then that Slater thought of the father. *Where was he?...Who was he?...Did he know what was going on?...Was he a Viet Cong?...Was she a Viet Cong?*

Kip turned and faced toward the front. He braced himself. They were coming in fast—way too fast. Everything—the buildings, the trees, the wall surrounding the soccer field, the concertina wire on top the wall—all seemed to be rushing at them at breakneck speed, as though he were riding in a derailed lead engine careening out of control. Kip closed his eyes. For a split second his mind projected an image of the on-rushing landing zone. He opened them as Dreyfuss began to apply power to stop the dreadful sinking sensation. The next thing he knew, the helicopter was shuddering; then it smoothed out and it felt like *Alfie* was gliding on a pillow of air. He looked down through the Plexiglas chin bubble; he saw the top of the wall and curl of deadly concertina wire pass beneath them.

"The tailboom's clear of the wall," Rusty White reported.

"Clear on the right," sounded Ron Larkin.

Slater sighed, then relaxed; he leaned forward. At the far end of the soccer field he saw the ambulance, a leftover relic from some bygone war. Near the vehicle, two Vietnamese medics stood over a stretcher placed on the ground. Sergeant O'Brien towered over the little men.

Dreyfuss slid *Alfie* onto the ground from a fast-running hover. The helicopter came to a halt twenty-five meters from the ambulance. Rusty and Ron opened the cabin doors. Ron got out and stood and signaled for O'Brien and the two medics to approach the helicopter. Sergeant O'Brien hustled them forward, toting the stretcher by himself as he did. Collins, concerned over the woman's contractions, directed everyone's actions. She shrieked as she was lifted. The two older women watched petrified. The woman was placed on the stretcher and rushed to the ambulance.

Both Dreyfuss and Slater remained seated in the cockpit. They watched as the woman was loaded into the back of the ambulance. Then one of the Vietnamese medics piled in behind her. They saw the two older women try to climb aboard. The second medic shoved them aside and closed the doors. O'Brien gestured for him to re-open the doors. The medic refused. Jabbering excitedly, the little man turned, gesticulated wildly, then went quickly to the driver's side, got in and drove away. By then, O'Brien was furious. His face had turned beet red. They saw the burly sergeant tear his hat from his head and throw it to the ground.

"What the hell is that all about?" Slater asked, dumbfounded.

Dreyfuss pounded his hand against the doorframe. "Fucking gooks—fucking gooks! That's how they treat their own people. God *damn—!"*

A few seconds later, O'Brien directed Rusty and Ron to help the two women into his jeep, after which they and Sergeant Collins returned to the ship. O'Brien spoke over the radio. "Tiger Zero Nine Eight, take Sergeant Collins back to Ap Tan Phong. Return to this location ASAP. Over."

When they returned from Ap Tan Phong, O'Brien met them with the first load of supplies for Hac Long. When they asked about the woman, he told them she arrived at the hospital okay, was carried in, and that he would let them know the outcome as soon as he could. The four crewmen nodded.

By 1145, *Alfie's* crew had completed both re-supply lifts into Hac Long. They refueled and went to the messhall for lunch. Afterwards, they waited at the aircraft for Captain Harvey and the trip to Saigon. They barely remembered the excellent meal they had been served, so riveted were their thoughts on the fate of the pregnant woman and her relatives.

The flight to Saigon took forty minutes. They dropped Captain Harvey off at Hotel Three, the main Tan Son Nhut heliport, refueled and shut down. Dreyfuss told Rusty he had exactly fifteen minutes to go to the PX and be back with his new camera lens.

They left the heliport by way of the same routing and checkpoints they followed coming in. By the time they were back in open country, Slater's head was swirling. "It takes a couple of trips into that madhouse to get the hang of getting in and out. You'll learn," Dreyfuss assured him. During their departure, Slater thought downtown Saigon looked like any large American city, with its tall modern buildings and traffic-packed streets. He did note two major differences: many of the buildings had red-tiled roofs and the wide boulevards were green-filled with Banyan trees. Off in the distance Slater could see the Saigon River, a brown ribbon of water that snaked its way past the city's east side. Before reaching the outskirts of the city they overflew thousands and thousands of refugee shanties, so close together one domicile was indistinguishable from the next. Saigon, *Paris of the East,* was a seething cauldron, and testimony to one of war's unrelenting facets: The forced relocation of vast numbers of people.

"Gold Digger Two Five, this is Tiger Zero Nine Eight. We're inbound. Estimating your location at two five past the hour," Slater reported over the FM radio.

"This is Gold Digger Two Five, that's a rog," O'Brien came back. "I've got a release for you. Meeting set for this afternoon has been canceled. You may proceed to home station. Thanks for your help today, guys. Over."

"Roger that," Dreyfuss answered. "Good copy. Good Copy."

O'Brien came quickly back. "Oh, I almost forgot...she had a boy. Five pounds eight ounces. The woman was a little further along than seven months. Mother and son doing just fine—!"

"All right!" Rusty exclaimed over the intercom. Kip felt tingles up and down his spine. Dreyfuss reached over and slapped him on the shoulder, the first sign of camaraderie the aircraft commander had shown him all day. Slater felt embarrassed; he smiled and looked back at Ron Larkin, who gave him a thumbs-up. The gunner's face displayed a wide grin.

"Well," Dreyfuss said, smugly, quickly regaining his composure, "we've got plenty of fuel to make it home." He gestured with a sweep of his hand that Slater was to take the controls. "You may fly if you like. Turn left heading two zero five. I'll call Paddy Control."

Elated, Slater reached for the cyclic control stick. "I've got the controls."

Victor R. Beaver

Chapter 8

THE MEETING WAS SET FOR SUNDAY at midnight. A representative from each flight would be present. The idea had been growing since day one and now everyone felt it: the undercurrent of tension and excitement. If it worked, Class 67-15 would go down in warrant officer candidate history....

"I still don't like it," Darryl Chancey grumbled. "We could all be expelled—"

"Oh for crissake, Chancey, they're not going to do any such thing," Seymore replied.

The two men were in the first-floor latrine. Seymore held a bottle of toilet bowl cleaner in one hand and a hard-bristle brush in the other. He stooped and began to swish milky water around in one of the bowls, while Darryl watched from several feet away, his hand over his mouth and nose to ward off the strong disinfectant smell. In a moment, the redheaded candidate stood and turned the flush handle. A loud roar of rushing water bounced off the walls. Seymore moved to the next bowl.

"'No Grundy Day on the third Saturday of preflight.' Those were Captain Richmond's exact words," Chancey stated. "Plus it's insubordination if we go against the commandant's orders."

Seymore poured the liquid in and began to scrub. "Look," he said, "even guys like Cottrell and Bowden and that ex-first sergeant Symington want to do it. Wouldn't they shit-can the whole idea if they thought anything could go wrong?"

"What the hell do they know?" Chancey said. "Besides, I'm not going to jeopardize myself by following some stupid tradition outlawed by the post commandant."

Again Seymore flushed the toilet; he watched the cloudy water disappear. "Damnit, Darryl, don't you see, the whole class has to participate—or we won't get away with it!"

Chancey shrugged. "Count me out. I'm not interested in what the whole class wants to do."

Seymore gave Chancey a disgusted look. He handed him the bowl cleaner and brush. "Why don't you help me instead of being such a pissant quibbler—!"

"A what?"

"Never mind...never mind."

* * *

SANDY ADAMSON WALKED BRISKLY along the sidewalk that led to the main post exchange. For the first time since he arrived at Fort Wolters, he felt good, really good. The day was warm, the sky was clear, and there was that first hint of autumn in the air.

Earlier he had given up "command" of the platoon to Frank Bartlett. Tom Adkins, the artist, became the platoon sergeant, while Willie Cottrell took over the duties of candidate company commander from Ned Symington. From now on, at least while they were at Fort Wolters, command responsibilities would be rotated once a week, so that each candidate could be evaluated on his leadership abilities.

The PX was not yet open when Sandy arrived, so he went to the cafeteria and ordered a cup of hot chocolate and sweet roll.

As he sat down, he noticed several candidates from his class gathered in the corner near the pinball machines. He had seen it before, the large square plastic case around which they were grouped. Inside the case was a model helicopter with spinning rotorblades, a sort of coin-operated training arena. Outside the case were two control handles. The helicopter was attached to a flexible horizontal rod that extended from a fixed point on the far side of the board. Electrical wires connected the helicopter to the control handles. The person manipulating the controls could make the little aircraft go up and down, forward and backward. The object was to guide it across a horizontally arced obstacle course of trip levers and unevenly elevated landing pads. Score was kept electronically with each successful maneuver. All of a sudden, there was a roar of laughter and then curses. Sandy went over to watch.

"Damn!—You missed again. Can't you fly that thing? That's the third time."

"Hey, I'm not doing so bad," Mark Allen said, his hands on the two handles.

"Well, hurry up. Let someone else have a turn."

Sandy looked on, fascinated. Mark Allen, a member of Flight Alpha One, was a tall, well-built, good-looking candidate from Wilmington, Delaware, a real ladies' man Sandy had decided when they first met. Observing Mark on the controls, Sandy could see that a high degree of skill and coordination was required to make the helicopter "fly" right.

On the fourth trip across the board, Allen tripped one of the levers, recording a score. In the same instant the machine stopped; he put another quarter in the slot.

"Hey!—come on. Give us a turn—!"

"Can it, you guys. I've got four more quarters and I'm going to master this thing. One of the candidates in the class ahead said that if you can fly this, you could fly the Mattel Messerschmitt."

"You mean the TH-55?"

"That's the one."

"What about the OH-23?"

"Na," Mark Allen said, shaking his head; he continued to concentrate on the task at hand. "Another guy told me that flying the 'twenty-three' is like flying an old washing machine. He said that when you put a control movement in it, it takes a day and a half for anything to happen."

"You're kidding—"

"That's what he said."

Sandy checked his pocket for change and found three quarters. The line was short; the PX wasn't due to open for twenty minutes. In spite of what Katie had said the day before, he wanted to see the PX's selection of engagement rings to keep the gloom of her concerns from overwhelming him. A half-hour later he was at the controls of the tiny helicopter. His efforts made him wonder if he had chosen the right profession: the helicopter "crashed" four times before he logged a score. And the line behind him had grown to ten more anxious enthusiasts, each eager to get a head start on his flight training.

* * *

MIDNIGHT. RON BOWDEN AND WILLIE Cottrell were there representing Flight Alpha One. Ned Symington, the ex-first sergeant, and a host of others were present. Ned and Willie, the two old-timers in the class, were appointed co-leaders. "What's the story, you guys?" spoke Ned. "Did we get a consensus?"

"Yeah, as best as we can figure," said Harmon, the representative from Flight Alpha Three. "Pretty much the whole class is behind it."

"It'll blow their minds if we pull it off a week early. That was a cool idea you had, Willie," said Mayberry. A former church choir director, Mayberry had been selected to lead the class in serenading their senior "Blue Hat" brothers at the flight-line barracks.

"Who should we pick to be General Grundy?"

"We're working on it," Symington replied.

Zeigler, another ex-Green Beret, looked toward Willie. "I hear that one of the guys in your flight is against this whole thing."

"Who?—Chancey? Don't worry about him. He's mostly bluff, a goddamn crybaby. We can handle him."

"Oh, yeah—How? We agreed there'd be no rough stuff," Zeigler reminded. "We can't let this thing get out of hand."

"Come on, Zeig...you know me," cooed Willie. "Would I do anything rash?"

"Yeah, I know you all right. You didn't get that Silver Star at Cai Cai for sitting on your ass."

Cottrell laughed. "You've got to know that when a Special Forces camp gets overrun, everyone gets a medal, just for being there—"

"Okay—enough," Symington said, looking at the faces around him. "Let's get this damn thing organized. Bravo Two, your bunch will be directing traffic on post."

"Check."

"Lindl, Alpha Four, you guys will gather up the tacs when they show up—and the CO and XO, if they come in."

"What about the First Sergeant and his clerks?"

"Let'em be. They never give us any shit."

"Alpha One will be the Mineral Wells's jail detail. You'll need four or five guys for that."

Ron Bowden nodded. "That's a rog."

Cottrell looked at a piece of paper with the other assignments. "Bravo Three, you'll need to detail about five guys as scouts to reconnoiter that back road leading to the flight-line barracks. We'll be marching at o'six hundred."

"What about the MPs?"

"Yeah, we'll need a man to act as a liaison," remembered Willie, "someone who can explain what we're doing. They won't be expecting anything like this on the second weekend."

"I'll volunteer," said Olivette, the representative from Flight Bravo One. "I used to be an MP."

"Good. Make sure you tell them we're going to 'police' ourselves."

Symington looked toward Lindl, responsible for the round-up team. "Remember, there'll be no—I repeat—no rough stuff. When you 'arrest' the tacs, they have to come of their own accord. Be gentle, but persuasive."

"How persuasive?" asked Lindl.

"Inform them that we're going to resign—the whole damn class."

"What?"

"They'll never believe that shit," Zeigler said.

"They'll have to," Symington replied.

"Resign?...The entire class?"

"That's what I said. Me and Willie decided." Suddenly everyone was talking at once. "Now hear us out. Quiet, goddamnit! Tell'em, Willie."

Cottrell lit a cigarette. He inhaled then blew the smoke out with force. "We're almost going against the commandant's orders on this. I say 'almost' because Captain Richmond said, 'No more Grundy Day on the *third* Saturday of preflight training.' By doing it on the second Saturday, we don't violate the letter of law, though we sure stomp on the spirit. And if they decide to do something, what they could try to do, to save face, is force the leaders of this shindig to resign. That's everyone here in this room. But, if the whole class decides to resign—and signs their intent to do so—we got them by the balls. They can't do jackshit to anyone."

"Okay...okay," Zeigler said. "But how do we get everyone to agree to that? A lot of guys, including myself, waited long and hard to be here."

Ned and Willie eyed each other. Neither man was certain he had the kind of persuasive power needed to convince this group of professional soldiers how important it was to carry Grundy Day off the way they decided. But they had to try.

Victor R. Beaver

If General Grundy and his day were to go down a hero's death, they could think of no better way to "bury" him than to offer themselves, that is the whole class, as a sacrifice. General Grundy had always been regarded a symbol of honor and unity. In war, every man depended on every other man. One man's failure to perform could mean the destruction of an entire unit. But a helicopter pilot flying over the jungles of Vietnam had an added responsibility: the life and death struggle of the man on the ground, the grunt, the lowly foot soldier, depended almost entirely on his support. Each pilot had to be daring enough to go into "hot" landing zones to carry in ammunition and supplies, and to perform urgent medevacs when necessary, often at great risk to himself, his ship, and his crew. It was understood that a helicopter pilot had the decision-making latitude to perform a task or not, every time his services were requested. It was for this reason that General Grundy's spirit had to be remembered. "And so," finished Willie, "that's the long and the short of it. We'll give the guys an option. The entire class must agree to resign...or there'll be no Grundy Day."

"No Grundy Day—?"

"That's right. No Grundy Day," Symington repeated.

The two co-leaders looked upon solemn faces.

"Those are the only options?" Zeigler said.

Ned and Willie nodded.

"We're all supposed to *volunteer* to resign?" Pete Cochran said, aghast.

"How else do we pull it off?" Mark Allen stated, his eyes alive with excitement. It was Monday, right after evening chow. Seymore and Sandy along with Pete and Mark were in the dayroom. An hour before, Frank Bartlett, Ron Bowden, and Willie Cottrell presented the committee's ultimatum to the flight.

"He's right," Sandy agreed. "It all makes perfect sense."

"Oh, yeah? Well, what if they accept our resignations?" Cochran said. "What the hell will we do *then?*"

"No way," said Mark. "This post would be in deep kimchee if that happened."

"Come on, Pete, what do you say?" Seymore urged.

Sandy said, "It's one for all and all for one—just like The Three Musketeers."

Cochran's shoulders sagged. "I don't know, guys. I just don't know. This whole thing is fraught with peril—"

"Well, you've got to decide soon," Mark said. "The list is already going around."

"Let me think on it, man. Just let me think—!"

* * *

THE SECOND WEEK OF PREFLIGHT WAS a repeat of the first, as would the third and fourth weeks. Eight hours a day were spent in classes; their subjects were Leadership, Map Reading, Dismounted Drill (marching and standing at attention), Physical Training, the UCMJ (Uniform Code of Military Justice), Customs and Courtesies of the Services, and Administration. Examinations were given based on instruction presented during class or in study assignments. At 1700, the candidates moved to the messhall for evening chow. Following mess, each candidate was allowed to take care of personal matters. Fathers went to the dayroom to visit their families, while most of the single guys went there to read, listen to music, play ping-pong, or shoot pool. Between 1900 and 2030 hours they observed mandatory study hall. After study hall each candidate prepared his uniform and personal displays for the following day's inspection. The lights went out at 2230. No candidate was allowed to be in his bunk one minute before or out of his bunk one minute after lights out.

Academic grades along with a practical demonstration of leadership were the two main areas of concern. The barracks were inspected daily. Personal appearance was always subject to severe scrutiny by the company staff. Compliance with school standards was mandatory. Individual responsibility with respect to performance, discipline, and conduct was considered to be of the utmost importance. Academic failure, lack of leadership potential, and serious breaches of discipline were grounds for elimination. *Elimination.* It was each man's greatest fear. Just the idea of being there, with their vision set on being at the controls of a helicopter, made each man covet this rare privilege.

So, after the committee's ultimatum, a vociferous dialogue took place among the members of the class. To be eliminated from the flight program was one thing; to volunteer to resign was quite another. They wanted to hold Grundy Day, though, and this was their dilemma. They wanted to show the establishment—and their fellow upperclassmen—they had the courage, the spirit, the unity—*and the balls*—to abide by the tradition one more time. They had made a promise to General Grundy and to themselves; they wanted both to be remembered; thus they were committed.

By Wednesday, they were all in agreement, except Darryl Chancey, whom they now watched like a hawk, especially Seymore. He now tolerated Chancey's grumpiness as an offspring might tolerate the same in an aging, petulant parent.

"I'm still not going to do it," he told Cutter.

"That's okay, Darryl. No one's going to force you to sign anything. Don't worry about it."

"That's good. I think you're all being stupid."

"Maybe so. But just promise me one thing. Keep quiet. Don't ruin it for the rest of us."

Victor R. Beaver

Class 67-15 prepared for Grundy Day like creatures hidden underground. The tac officers saw nothing, heard nothing, suspected nothing. There ran through the ranks a slender thread of communication—a passing word, a wink of the eye. "The Inspection," code name for the event, was being plotted like a covert war against a hideous enemy: The System.

Yet still throughout the week their numbers declined as those less committed to the program tendered their *actual* resignations. Every flight was affected except Flight Alpha One, which had yet to lose its first man. Those who departed did so like patriots abandoning a lost cause; most were disheartened that so much emphasis was placed on the nonsensical, the mundane, the picayune. A moot point always became blown way out of proportion by the tac officers. And as they left they abandoned that which might have been.

But all who stayed gained a kind of momentum. They drew strength from each other and formed friendships that would last a lifetime. Their goals were clear: to be above the earth: to be commanders of their ship—a helicopter: to be masters of their fate, in almost the literal sense of the word. In the Republic of Vietnam lay their destinies; most of them believed they would be fighting to maintain the freedom of a beleaguered people. Little did they know that all they would really be fighting for...would be their lives.

Chapter 9

IT WAS EARLY MONDAY AFTERNOON. Dave Grange sat in the back seat of the Cobra, strapped in, sweat pouring from his forehead. Pollard stood beside him outside the cockpit, one foot placed on a small step protruding from the right side of the massive fuselage, the other supported by the open turret-ammo compartment door. As the late October Georgia sun beat down, Pollard explained the aircraft's pre-start procedures to Dave, while Mike Nolan, standing on the cement's hot surface, listened and observed from below.

"As you can see," Pollard said, "most of the interior check simply insures that you have the necessary circuit breakers in and that all the electrical equipment is off before you crank. And you sure as hell don't want any ARM switches on, do you?"

"You got that right," said Dave. Having served his previous Vietnam tour as a Huey gunship pilot, he had seen the result of such an oversight. A 2.75-inch rocket (from another gunship) accidentally discharged from its tube during refueling, went clean through a board fence, through the windshield of a parked jeep, then exploded killing two unsuspecting American cavalrymen asleep in their tent.

As Dave continued to read each checklist item, Pollard pointed to their location in the cockpit, explained how to check it—and why. Then he had Dave sound off with the proper response. They came to 'Rain removal and heat switch (ECU)—OFF.' Dave frowned. "What the hell is an ECU?"

Daddy Don grunted. "ECU stands for 'environmental control unit.' Among other things, it's your air-conditioner."

"Air-conditioner?" Pollard might have had it on last Friday, but he couldn't remember. "Can we turn the damn thing on now?"

Ignoring Grange's misery, Daddy Don said, "The ECU also provides heat, removes moisture from the air supplied to the crew compartments, defrosts, defogs, and de-ices the canopy; it even removes rain from the canopy."

"I like this aircraft already," Mike said, looking up at Pollard's sweat-drenched back.

"And sometimes the cooling system works a little too good," Pollard said. "Little balls of ice spit out at you—with some velocity."

"No shit—?"

Pollard took out a handkerchief and wiped his brow. With a wry smile, he asked, "How're you doing? Hot enough for you?"

"Great—couldn't be better, just like Viet 'fricking' Nam." Even with the canopy open, Dave felt as if he were seated inside a pressure cooker. Finally: "Item fifty-three 'Cockpit light—OFF—check condition and security.'" Dave found the light, checked it, and then said, dolefully, "Off and secure." He shook his head. "Item fifty-three…God, you'd think we were trying to get a damn B-52 off the ground…"

Pollard glared at Grange, then glanced down at Mike Nolan. "By checkride day you guys will know these checks—and the rest of the cockpit procedures—by heart." Dave's eyes glazed over; Mike stared disconsolately into space. Pollard scoffed at them. "Surely, you don't expect Charlie to wait around after an attack while you take your sweet time using a checklist to get this snake started and airborne, do you?"

Pollard now had Dave begin the engine-start sequence. He continued to instruct from outside the cockpit; eventually, he would move to his front-seat position, after the engine was started and the rotorblades were turning. Unlike the Huey, where student and instructor sat side-by-side (separated by approximately two feet of open space), the tandem-seating arrangement of the Cobra made it nearly impossible for the IP to know if the student was checking the right switches or circuit breakers. Seated up front, Pollard would be extremely vulnerable. Because of this, his instruction had to be more than adequate the first time—it had to be perfect. He explained that a wrong switch thrown at the wrong time, or an instrument not interpreted correctly—and therefore reacted to improperly—could cause a serious accident and possibly two fatalities. "Or if either of you guys freeze on those back-seat controls, there's no way I can override you. Remember, you've got four-to-one leverage on me." Pollard practically snarled at them. "When it comes right to it, you guy's pretty much got me by the balls. And if you fuck-up—and I mean bigtime—and you're still alive, I'm gonna kill ya." Mike and Dave looked at one another, each cocking an eyebrow. Then Daddy Don grinned. "Well, I might just beat the shit out of you." And with that said, Pollard again wiped his brow and continued, step by tedious step, about his merry methodical way.

By the time Pollard was seated and strapped in, most of the other IPs in the ships around them had completed their engine run-up checks and were hovering to the take-off pads. Pollard adjusted the little mirror and looked into Grange's eyes. The lanky pilot bent his head slightly to see Daddy Don's face. Both men had waited until the last minute to put on their flight helmets. Sweat now gushed from their brows. Mike continued to stand outside on the cement parking pad below. He had his helmet on and was plugged into the ship's intercom system by a long cord extending from a small access opening on the fuselage. Pollard asked, "Okay, how do you hear me?"

"Loud and clear," said Dave.

"Good. Let's try to keep eye contact as we go through these run-up checks."

The engine run-up procedures was a forty-four-item list and took another half-hour to complete. With each check, Pollard again explained what, how, and why. It was SCAS that fascinated Mike.

"SCAS. Stability and control augmentation system," Pollard said. "You were wondering how I could pick this baby up the other day, with that little bit of wind we had, without even a quiver? SCAS, a Cobra pilot's best friend, especially when it comes to firing the weapons." He spoke now nearly verbatim out of the book. "SCAS is a three-axis, limited authority, rate reference augmentation system. SCAS cancels undesired motion of the helicopter during flight. This is accomplished by inducing an electrical input into the flight control system to augment the pilot's mechanical input.

"When the aircraft is being acted upon by outside forces, forces such as winds or a gust of wind that might affect the stability of the aircraft, SCAS evaluates those forces and acts to balance the aircraft against them. It does this by electrically feeding, through three separate axis channels, the automatic response to these forces. It's almost like an auto-pilot. As you know, an auto-pilot can maintain a set course, airspeed, or altitude. SCAS, however, only keeps the aircraft stable. This stability is necessary to fire your rockets and other armament systems accurately."

"What about pilot input," Nolan asked, "such as overcontrol? Or not enough control input, especially at a hover?" To him, SCAS "input" sounded like an IP assisting a student on the cyclic control stick, countermanding a new student's inclination to jockey the stick back and forth, which causes the helicopter to dance the rock n' roll.

"No-no, SCAS is limited authority, not total authority," Pollard rumbled. "It can't overpower you, although you could have a SCAS hardover. If you don't react properly to that, SCAS could fly you into the ground. Just remember that when you come to a hover, try to be as still as possible on the controls. Let SCAS take care of the little bumps and knocks of the wind."

Some fourteen separate checks later they were ready to depart. Pollard told Dave to close his canopy door. Mike unplugged, re-stowed the cord, secured the little access door, and moved to the edge of the ramp. He then watched as Dave brought the AH-1G light on the skids and then to a wobbly three-foot hover. Their transition into the Cobra had officially begun.

* * *

THE NEXT SEVERAL DAYS WERE MUCH the same. During each flight period Pollard explained something new about the engine-start and run-up checks and expected them on the following day to recall what they had learned. At night, in the BOQ, the two neophyte "Cobra jocks" drilled each other over and over on the aircraft systems, limitations, and emergency procedures. Understandably, their sleep was no longer restful. They worked almost as hard in their dreams, with their subconscious mulling over their expanding knowledge, as they did awake. Pollard was very specific about what they had to know. "You guys aren't going to have a goddamn crewchief around to baby-sit your asses," he told them. "If you're stuck at some LZ with a maintenance problem, you're going to have to tell the mechanics—before they come out to fix it—exactly what's wrong. Plus," he said, again eyeing them sternly, "you've got to know what constitutes a 'red X,' a grounding condition. You practically have to be your own TI—maintenance tech inspector."

It was late afternoon Wednesday. Student and instructor were high over the little town of Ellabell, north of the Fort Stewart main post complex. Nolan had been performing a series of turning maneuvers.

Daddy Don spoke to him over the intercom. "You're doing pretty good, Lieutenant. You're doing pretty good. But you're still forgetting the transient torque effect. When you go into a turn, you've got to keep this puppy in trim. Lead with left pedal when going left and right pedal when going right. Just speed up your crosscheck, Lieutenant."

"Okay-okay," Nolan said, mulling over the phenomena called transient torque. Banking left, the engine senses a loss of lift, it automatically supplies power to compensate, the increase in torque pressure causes the nose of the aircraft to yaw right. Going to the right, the engine senses an increase in lift, it automatically reduces power to compensate, torque pressure decreases, the nose yaws left. Normal student reaction: play with the collective pitch-control lever, jockey the cyclic, fiddle with the anti-torque pedals. Result: overcontrol. Solution: when turning, "step on the ball," *keep the aircraft in trim!*

Chapter 10

BY THURSDAY CLASS 67-15 HAD BUILT its excitement to a crescendo. The tac officers were bewildered. No man could be singled out for disciplinary action without causing whole flights—and sometimes the entire class—to bare itself for equal punishment.

The committee met twice more to iron out last-minute details. As organizers, though, they came together under a cloud of foreboding. Outright military insubordination was not to be taken lightly. In the past, Grundy Day had been an accepted tradition, an event the whole post looked forward to. Now little joy went into the preparation: only a certain countenance of purpose.

Ned Symington said, "The uniform will be whatever hodgepodge the guys want. And remember, tell them not to wear any identifying tags." He looked at Mayberry. "Did you get the songs run off?"

The ex-choir director nodded. "I've got a couple of the wives doing it right now."

Harmon said, "I can't believe the tacs don't suspect anything. We've got to be as obvious as a train wreck."

"Apparently we're not," Ned stated, "or they'd let Willie and me know."

A couple of other items were discussed. Lindl asked, "Who's gonna be General Grundy? Has anyone decided?"

"Don't worry," Willie said. "We've got just the man for the job."

Zeigler said, "So what's the big goddamn secret?"

"The secret is," replied Symington, "the candidate we've picked doesn't know he's it—yet."

* * *

FRIDAY AFTERNOON A SPECTACULAR thing happened. A lone TH-55A helicopter approached and circled above them. It let down and came to a hover at the far end of the PT field. After several pedal turns, it settled gently onto the ground.

The skies were filled with these little reddish-orange specks. Morning, noon, and night they heard the faint flutter of their small rotating wings and the throaty sound of their lawnmower-like engines. But they could never quite catch a good glimpse of one. None of the flight corridors passed over the 5th WOC Company area. Their skin prickled as they edged toward the one that had landed before them.

The pilot sat alone in the cockpit, keeping his gaze straight ahead. With his helmet on and sunvisor down, he looked like some alien creature that had just arrived from outer space. After a minute, he cut the fuel and the engine died. The blades slowed, until they came to a full stop.

The pilot began unstrapping as they advanced closer. A moment later they saw him take his helmet off and place it on the vacant seat to his left. He put a blue baseball cap on and got out. He smiled at the throng around him. He had a salty, jaunty air about him; he probably had all of a hundred and two hours of student-pilot flight time.

"What's the story?" someone asked.

The senior candidate spoke. "Since they've outlawed Grundy Day, to mollify you, you get to check this thing over. Who knows, maybe it'll turn out to be a tradition."

"Oh...yeah?"

They surrounded the little training helicopter and looked it over good. The cockpit was enclosed by one large Plexiglas bubble appearing much like the eye of a giant preying mantis. Behind the cockpit sat the engine; to the left and above the level of the engine sat the fuel tank. Three small rotorblades drooped to eye level. The tailboom, a small-diameter hollow tube attached to several hardpoints around the engine, extended rearward. It supported the tailrotor and tailboom airfoil assembly. Overall, it looked so fragile. *How could it fly?*

"Christ! All that's holding this thing together is a few nuts and bolts and chicken wire," one candidate said.

Another candidate put his hand on the windshield; it seemed to give at his slightest touch. "Shit—it's made of plastic."

Then someone pointed to a lever on the left side of either seat. "What's that?"

"The collective pitch-control lever," answered the pilot. "Up lever makes the helicopter go up, down lever—down."

"Hell, that seems simple enough."

Someone placed his finger on a short metal tube protruding the front. "What's this, an extra-short machine-gun barrel?"

The pilot laughed. "Not hardly. It's a pitot tube. Air molecules ram into it to give an indication of how fast you're traveling through the air." He pointed to a dial inside the cockpit. "That's the airspeed indicator."

"What's the top speed of this thing?"

"Ninety knots is VNE."

"What's a knot?"

"What's a VNE?"

"Is the goddamn thing hard to hover?" a candidate finally asked.

"Well...I'll tell you," said the senior candidate, about to give the standard spiel, "it's like trying to rub your tummy, pat your head, and jerkoff. If you can do two at once, you're pretty good. If you can do all three—you're a helicopter pilot!"

The Sky Soldiers

Saturday morning. The lights glared on at 0515. The voices of Frank Bartlett and Willie Cottrell stormed into their dreams. "UP UP UP AND AT'EM, BOYS! PT in five minutes! Afterwards, we prepare for 'The Inspection!'"

Everyone scrambled into their jogging shorts, tennis shoes, and sweatsuits. "I thought we were going to get all duded up for this?" someone commented.

"Not yet, you dumbshit—after PT."

Class 67-15 formed up on the PT field. The skies to the east had not yet begun to lighten. Senior Candidate Tyree roamed their ranks as they performed their exercises. He saw a laggard and charged over to him. "You. Candidate!—PUT MORE INTO THOSE JUMPING JACKS!"

"Sir! Candidate James. Yes, sir!"

Halfway through the daily dozen, Mayberry went and stood alongside Ned Symington. Symington nodded.

Mayberry shouted out, "Let's sing 'My Country Tis of Thee.'"

A strange thunder of voices sounded (mostly off key) as Mayberry guided their efforts. Furious, Tyree stormed up to the ex-choir director. "Who said you could sing, candidate? This is a PT formation. NOT A GLEE CLUB! Down and give me ten!"

"Yes, sir!" Mayberry shouted, as he and the rest of his classmates plunged to the ground.

After the last push-up, they all bounced up. Mayberry said, "Okay, let's sing 'Onward Christian Soldiers.'"

This time their singing was more subdued. Tyree tried to stop them, but their unity was complete. Even Chancey, sandwiched between Adamson and Cutter, raised his voice an octave to spite the senior candidate's ranting and raving.

When they were done, Ned called for the run around the track. Tyree caught up with those candidates trailing behind. But his harangues fell on deaf ears. Frustrated, he moved to the center of the field and stood, hands on his hips.

After the second lap, Mayberry began singing *God Bless America*. Breathlessly, the class joined in.

"Isn't that it? The signal—?"

"Not yet. Wait till we get around the curve. Don't you keep up with the changes?"

On the back straight-a-way, Mayberry let out a loud war holler.

"Now that's the signal. LET'S GO!"

The throng became a wild, stampeding mass, aiming straight for Tyree. Three hundred and fifty-seven strong, they surrounded him, closing in tight until he could barely budge.

"What is this?" he demanded, squirming amid the crowd.

"This, Senior Candidate Tyree—*Sir!*—is the official beginning of Grundy Day."

"Grundy Day? It's been canceled. Who authorized it—?"

Victor R. Beaver

"What do you mean 'Who authorized it?' We authorized it," they shouted. "And in the name of General Grundy, YOU'RE UNDER ARREST!"

"Candidate Chancey."

"Yes...?"

"Would you come here, please?" Willie and Seymore stood at the foot of Chancey's bed. Slowly, the bewildered candidate approached.

"What have we here?" Willie Cottrell said, holding a metal object in the palm of his hand.

"What is it?" Chancey asked, eyeing curiously the pearl-handed knife Willie held out for his inspection.

"My my, a switchblade knife," said Seymore. "You surprise me, Darryl. Whatever possessed you to own one of these...?"

Darryl Chancey's eyes grew wide. "Hey, where'd you get that—?"

"We found it—in your footlocker."

"That's bull, it was in my car—in my glove compartment."

"Then you admit it's yours?"

"Yes-no, I mean...sort of."

"I'd certainly say it was yours," Willie said, turning the knife over.

Chancey looked closer. "What the—?"

"It's got your name engraved on it...tsk tsk tsk," scolded Seymore.

"Engraved!—I never did that."

"Someone did."

"One of you guys did it," Chancey asserted.

Willie and Seymore frowned. "Now why would we go and do a thing like that?" said Willie.

"I-I don't know." Sweat beads had broken out on Chancey's forehead. "Hey, what's this all about?"

Seymore said, "We, me and Willie, that is, were wondering what might happen...if this...somehow...got into the wrong hands."

"You wouldn't dare."

"Could get you eliminated," the ex-Green Beret said.

"Why are you guys doing this?"

"Don't you know?"

Chancey sneered. "You jerks can't get away with this."

"Oh, it seems the evidence is quite clear."

Chancey slumped. They had him. "Okay-okay, I'll sign your damn resignation form. Is that it?"

"Why, Darryl, you humble us. But we've got a much higher, nobler purpose for you," Willie said, the drama in his voice rising slightly.

"Would you like to hear it?" Seymore offered.

"Yeah...what is it?"

The Sky Soldiers

"Have you ever been on a horse?" the redheaded candidate asked.
"A horse?—*Never!*"
"Well, you'll probably do just fine."

Everyone dressed in their most outlandish outfits. Cutter had the crazy notion to wear his skivvy shorts around his neck, plus a sock hanging down from each ear, secured by a rubber band. Sandy had his dress green blouse on inside out. Adkins, the artist, wore a combination of fatigues, dress greens, and PT uniform. Cottrell brought out an old Eisenhower jacket. Not one of them donned any flight training gear: these were sacred.

Before assembling outside, they made sure their barracks were ready for inspection. The chaos they created looked worse than any previous inspection tour brought about by the tac officers.

Class 67-15 looked like a large group of freaks going to a sideshow, as they wove their way along the two-mile-long back road that led to the flight-line barracks. A lone military police car came alongside just as the sun broke over the horizon. Having been briefed earlier by Olivette, they moved to the rear to protect the column, knowing also to leave well enough alone.

Recalling last weekend's march to the Awards and Decorations ceremony, the back road went over a series of hills. When they crested the last hill they saw them again—the flight-line barracks—those sacred halls—their home to be in two weeks. Their excitement grew as Symington ordered them to pick up the pace.

Finally, they were assembled on the street that ran past the 3rd WOC Company billeting area. Mayberry took his position to their front. A long, three-story building loomed behind him. He raised his arms and everyone took a deep breath:

*"God rest ye merry gentlemen,
let nothing you dismay...
Remember Christ our Savior
was born on
Christmas Day..."*

Within moments windows were opened and heads poked from the upper stories.
"What the hell's going on down there?"
"Sir, Candidate Mayberry, it's Grundy Day, sir!"
"Grundy Day?...Christ on a crutch..."
The ex-choir director prompted his throng to raise the sound level. A boot hurled from a third-story window. It landed with a thud at Mayberry's feet.
"Let's now sing 'Winged Soldiers Are We,'" he shouted.

Victor R. Beaver

"Saber wings will lift us
when we get the call
Through the dawn like eagles
we will soar...
Roll the pitch and throttle,
cyclic to the wall
Listen to the Army's eagles roar...

"We're winged soldiers, we
fly above the best,
Defenders of the land
and the free...
From the sky we do or die
and let the angels rest,
Winged soldiers are we...

"Charging through the jungle,
hear our rotors roar
Down from in the valley
to the hill...
Fighting aviators out
to win the war
We're the Army's escadrille...

"We're winged soldiers, we
fly above the best,
Defenders of the land
and the free...
From the sky we do or die
and let the angels rest,
Winged soldiers are we...

"Rotorblades are churning,
diving for the fire...
Screaming in like eagles for the kill
After our inferno, troopers
must admire...the eagles
of the Army's escadrille...

"We're winged soldiers, we
fly above the best,

*Defenders of the land
and the free...
From the sky we do or die
and let the angels rest,
Winged soldiers are we..."*

Somehow their harmony was perfect. Each man had poured his heart and soul into the song. Even Mayberry was touched, as he wiped away a lone tear.

"That was good...that was good," someone said from a second-story window.

"Here-here," came an appreciative chorus of voices.

"Hey, we thought Grundy Day was canceled."

"The hell," Mark Allen shouted. "You can't keep a good class down!"

"Aren't you guys early? S'posed to be the third Saturday...not the second."

"Neat trick, huh?"

"Hey, you guys got balls," shouted someone from the far end of the building.

"Roger that. Didn't want to disappoint our brothers in Blue."

"Say, where are you from, you look familiar...?"

"Milwaukee."

"Is your name Harrison?"

"Yeah, how did you know?"

"I dated your sister!"

"If you did, *she* was my brother—*I don't have a sister!*"

"What are your requests?" asked Mayberry, of the more than five-dozen faces looking down from practically every window.

"Singing requests...?"

"Yeah."

"You gotta lullaby for a hangover? Jesus—my head's splitting wide open."

"Let's sing 'When Those Caissons Go Rolling Along,'" Mayberry sounded, "the revised version—"

*"Over hill over dale we won't
hit the dusty trail...
As those caissons go
flying along...*

*"Up and down, flit about,
rotors turning 'round about...
As those caissons go
flying along...*

"It's a sky high ho and

Victor R. Beaver

> *off to Nam we go...*
> *Shout out your number*
> *loud and strong—*
> *SKY HO!*
>
> *"And where 'ere we go the*
> *grunts will always know*
> *that those caissons are*
> *flying along..."*

"BRAVO! BRAVO!" they shouted.
"What the hell's a caisson?" blurted one of the senior candidates.
"It's an ammunition wagon—you dummy."
They sang several more songs. Then, after the sun was well established in the sky, they bid their senior Blue Hat brothers adieu and began the long march back to their barracks. What awaited them, none of them knew....

When Tac Officers Douglas, Armstrong, Carlyle, and several others arrived, they were "arrested" and escorted to the Mineral Wells's jail. A newsman and photographer from the local newspaper were on hand to record the event. The escort crew then brought the cadre back to the company area and "ordered" them to remain in the orderly room until further notice. With scowling faces and murmurs of future disciplinary action, they complied; not a one tried to resist.

When Captain Richmond, the company commander, appeared, he was promptly "overcome" and "ordered" to wait in his office. He was told that formal proceedings were due to take place in less than an hour. A pair of "guards" was posted over him. Earlier that morning, an anonymous phone call to his residence had alerted him that the outlawed tradition was in progress.

Richmond sat arrow-straight at his desk. "You realize," he said to the two stone-faced candidates "Lording" over him, "that I'm only going along with this because I don't know how far you will go to keep me detained. But I can assure you that none of this will be tolerated—not even in the least." He looked right at them. Neither candidate blinked an eye nor said a word.

At strategic corners around post small bands of "renegade" candidates greeted the arriving traffic. Their outlandish unmilitary appearances were met with cautious grins and stares.

"Mrs. Eddington, ma'am...Is Colonel Eddington there, please?" a man's voice said over the telephone.
"Yes...just a moment. Who may I say is calling?"
"Captain Thomlin, ma'am. The duty officer."
"I'll get him."

The colonel came on the line. "Yes, what is it? Speak up."
"They've done it, sir."
"Done what?"
"Grundy Day, sir. They've pulled it off."
"What—?"
"Yes, sir. They're right now all over post. What do you want me to do?"
"Nothing...nothing. I'll be right in."
"Yessir."

Symington gathered his organizers. "Is everyone back?"
"Yeah."
"Okay. In five minutes, I'm going to call formation. We'll have the cadre in the middle. We'll box them in, just like we discussed."
Zeigler spoke. "Where's General Grundy? None of us have seen him."
"Hidden. Don't worry—he's about to make his grand appearance."

"COMPANEEE..."
"FLIGHTS..."
"Atten...HUT!"
In spite of their ridiculous appearance, Class 67-15 snapped smartly to attention. Captain Richmond, Lieutenant Lee, the company XO (executive officer), and all but one of the tac officers were present. With arms folded they looked at the group around them, some feeling awkward, others glaring at their insubordinate charges with icy stares. The ceremony began.
Willie Cottrell, the ex-Green Beret, came solemnly to the forefront. He said:
"As everyone knows, Grundy Day has been a tradition for more than several years. Upon our arrival, however, the post commandant declared this tradition outlawed. Unfortunately, General Grundy was never given a formal demise."
"What does he mean ...'demise?'" someone whispered.
"Dying, a burial, you idiot."
Willie continued: "It is our intent—if General Grundy is to be no more—to have him formally surrender. This was the reason we planned and executed this final 'Grundy Day.' Our company commander, Captain Richmond"—Cottrell looked at the CO—"clearly said there would be no 'Grundy Day' on the third Saturday of preflight. Nothing was said about the *second* Saturday."
Lieutenant Lee raised an eyebrow...then let go an amused smile.
"We, the warrant officer candidates of Class 67-15, do hereby declare the formal surrender of General Grundy..."
In the next instant, the steady roll of a snare drum filled the air. And then, as if the trio had materialized out of nowhere, a rider on a black horse led on foot by Seymore P. Cutter came slowly forward. The clippity-clop of hooves echoed off barrack walls. The ranks parted and the horse and rider, both masked by black

Victor R. Beaver

hoods with slit-openings for the eyes, came into their midst. The rider was wearing the uniform of a general; however, on each epaulet he wore ten stars and above his left breast pocket there dangled more than forty medals. A saber was strapped to his side, in a finely etched sheath. Chief Warrant Officer Carlyle gasped when he saw that it was one of his sabers "the General" was wearing.

Cutter stopped the horse. He nodded for the General to dismount. The General did, awkwardly, for he had never in his life been on a horse.

The General felt for the ground, stood for a moment to steady himself, then went ponderously toward Captain Richmond. The drum rolled on.

The General withdrew the sword and held it across his forearm. He bowed as he had been instructed to do.

Sensing the seriousness of the affair, Captain Richmond took the offered saber and bowed in return.

"With the surrender of this sword," read Warrant Officer Candidate William Everett Cottrell, *"I do hereby vanish into antiquity. But my spirit shall live on. Wherever there are men who must go forth into battle, I, General Grundy, chief of all U.S. Army helicopter pilots, do hereby direct, in my eternal absence, that each pilot give every available measure in support of the soldier on the ground. For he shall always fly above the best..."*

At that moment a bugle began to play in the background. It was the lonesome, woesome sound of *Taps*. For what seemed like an eternity the notes rose and the notes fell. Gradually, the notes were carried higher...higher...higher into the sky. Then, as if it had been planned—but in fact it had not—a white Huey, one of the post's medevac helicopters with a red cross painted on the sides, flew overhead. Everyone turned their eyes skyward. Their attention was so acutely fixed to its passage that none of them saw nor heard the horse and rider disappear quietly, and forever, from view....

Colonel Eddington, commandant of the United States Army Primary Helicopter Center, was fuming. He arrived in a huff, storming through the doors of the post's large white headquarters building with Captain Thomlin, the duty officer, close behind.

"I want the candidates responsible for organizing this breach of discipline—Immediately," he growled.

"Sir...there are two men outside right now. You passed right by them."

"Those two NCOs—?"

"Yessir."

"Send them in!"

At his desk, the Commandant tried to formulate his thoughts: "This is unconscionable," he stated aloud to the four high-ceilinged walls. *How dare they go against my orders—? What's happening with this army, anyway? And it's getting worse. A commander can't tell a man what to do anymore without wiping his ass and explaining every little detail. And now, for crissake, even E-7s and E-8s are a party to this...this...this rebellious outrage!* "Well, there will be hell to pay," he mumbled, as he looked at the door the two men were about to enter. "After I eliminate these perpetrators, the entire class will be on restriction. No one will be allowed to leave the company area—Not even the married candidates!"

Captain Thomlin escorted Cottrell and Symington into Eddington's office. Willie and Ned came forward, snapped to attention, and saluted. The colonel saluted quickly back. He asked Captain Thomlin to leave the room.

The colonel scrutinized the two NCOs. They were in their Class A dress green uniforms. Their chests were decorated with a variety of medals ranging from the Good Conduct ribbon to the Silver Star. They exuded the very essence of straightforward military bearing and discipline. The two men combined represented thirty-three years of military service, of which six had been spent in a combat zone. The colonel saw that Symington held a brown envelope. He shook his head, unable to fathom how these two fine men could be the violators of a direct order.

"Stand at ease."

They shifted.

"What is the meaning of this?"

"Sir," Symington began, "we represent Class 67-15. We did in fact willfully violate the Commandant's direct order not to conduct Grundy Day. As the duly authorized representatives of our classmates, we—"

"You two organized this...this Grundy Day?" the colonel interrupted.

"Yes, sir, we were co-leaders."

"How many others were involved?"

"Quite a few, sir." Cottrell took the envelope from Symington and handed it to him. "In here we have the signatures of three hundred and fifty-seven candidates, ours included."

"Three hundred...and...fifty-seven..." the colonel repeated slowly.

"That's correct, sir. Class 67-15 would like to resign."

"What?—Resign?"

"Yes, sir. Resign."

"The entire class—?"

"That's correct, sir."

"I will accept only your resignations." *I can't have an entire class quit!*

"It's all or nothing, sir."

"First Sergeant Symington, are you in accord with this?"

"Yes, sir."

"I don't believe it."

"Check the envelope, sir."

"Damnit—you can't *all resign!*"

"Sorry, sir..."

Eddington looked at Cottrell, then at Ned Symington. "I don't know what you two are trying to gain from this, but it won't work. This act of insubordination will definitely go on your records."

"Yes, sir," replied Willie.

Captain Thomlin called over the office intercom.

"What is it?" grumbled the colonel.

"Sir, I think you'd better come outside and see. I'm not sure what to think of it."

"Of what, man? Quit speaking in riddles!"

"Well, sir, the whole class is here, standing at parade rest."

"What? Oh, for crissake..."

Eddington ordered Symington and Cottrell to follow. The colonel, along with his weekend staff, stood on the porch of the headquarters building and surveyed the scene. On Zeigler's cue, Class 67-15 snapped to attention. Instead of the hodgepodge mixture of "uniforms" they were wearing earlier, everyone was dressed smartly in their greens.

Zeigler saluted. "Sir! Candidate Zeigler! The class of 67-15 presents itself for disciplinary action! Sir!" When he dropped his arm, the entire class took one step forward and came to parade rest. The colonel's jaw dropped; his staff stood wide-eyed in shock.

Everywhere there was stillness—and a profound silence—except for the American flag waving in the breeze, the metal snaps clinking against the flagpole. For a long moment the colonel's eyes went from face to face as he tried to understand what clearly was the most inspiring sight he had ever seen. Incredible! All of these men were willing to take full responsibility for their actions! Gradually he relaxed. He felt the tenseness of the last half-hour leave him. If he had had a dozen sons, he would want every one of them to be just like these men.

And then he spoke: "Men, I...I'm not really sure what to—" He cut himself off. He thought of a time long ago, of a far-off place, of a bygone war, of the Bataan death march. He had been one of the survivors. Each step of the march was still etched clearly in his memory. He drew a deep breath. "You men are placed on restriction for two weeks. And I do not accept your offers to resign. Yes, you did violate my order, but I'm beginning to understand you had good reason to do so. When you get to Vietnam," he said, as he began to choke on his words, "it will be your unity, your sense of brotherhood, that will carry you through." They knew about the death march. Their emotions swelled, their throats constricted in empathy for him.

The colonel saluted then quickly turned. He walked alone back to his office. As he sat down at his desk, he noticed the envelope. He took it and opened it. He read its contents:

We, the Warrant Officer Candidate Class of 67-15, do hereby submit this letter of resignation from the Warrant Officer Flight Training program, for the planning of and participation in Grundy Day. Said participation we did in direct violation of the order prohibiting Grundy Day, as issued by the Commanding Officer, United States Army Primary Helicopter Center, Fort Wolters, Texas.

Let it be known, however, that Class 67-15 did violate said order in the spirit of unity among men of honor and that there was no intent to violate the lawful will of the United States Army to produce capable men soon bound for Vietnam, hopefully as United States Army helicopter pilots.

Three pages of signature followed. The colonel read the list, and as he did so he was certain he was reading the names of some of those who would make the ultimate sacrifice in South Vietnam…

*…Adamson, Adkins, Alexander, Allen, Babyak, Bartlett, Bowden, Boyter, Chancey, Chaney, Cochran, Cottondale, Cottrell, Creal, Cutter…*the list went on and on…

Victor R. Beaver

Chapter 11

A LIGHT RAPPING SOUND ON HIS door brought Slater out of a deep sleep. "Mr. Slater, sir...?"

"Huh?"

"It's o'five hundred, sir. Time to get up...single-ship 'swing' with Mr. Randall. You're going to Ben Tre."

"Okay, I'm up...thanks."

* * *

JOURNAL ENTRY, 2 NOVEMBER 1967, Soc Trang AAF

Have flown 31 hours in 4 days. Max flight time in a 30-day period per company policy is 140 hours. But we're in a combat environment, so guys are pushing past that figure all the time. Everyone really looks beat. Of course, drinking and staying up late doesn't help at all.

After I flew with Dreyfuss, I paired with WO1 Wainwright on a VIP flight out of Bac Lieu. We picked up the 21st ARVN Division commander and took him to Saigon. The jeep ride from the Bac Lieu airstrip to the local MACV compound (in Bac Lieu) paralleled a one-mile section of canal. The Vietnamese who lived along the canal used it for everything: laundry, swimming, bathing, drinking, dish washing, defecating, fishing, washing their water buffalo, urinating, even brushing their teeth! We shut down at Hotel Three, the Tan Son Nhut heliport. The PX there is huge! Filled to the gills with stereo and camera equipment. I finally bought a fan. What a relief. Wainwright very casual, easy-going. Let me fly more than half the time. I need it. I'm still not used to the left seat. Very awkward. It's hard to see to the right over the instrument-panel glare shield.

I flew re-supply the next two days, out of Can Tho and then Chi Lang, a Special Forces camp near the Cambodian border, in the Seven Mountains region. Still no shots fired. Where's the damn war?

The new CO will be here next week. Found out he's a graduate of VMI, Virginia Military Institute, an outfit that pumps out bigger assholes for career officers than West Point, someone told me. Major Drummond, the current CO, is in the club every night, drinking like a fish right along with the rest of us...

Just then Leo burst into his room. "Kip, we've got our first combat assault. It's tomorrow—by God!"

Kip looked up. "Where?"

"Vinh Binh Province, staging out of Tra Vinh. I'm flying with Wainwright, in White Three position. You'll be with Justen, Tiger Trail." Leo pulled out a pack of cigarettes, took one and lit up. He blew out smoke in hurried puffs. "It looks like a biggy. The Outlaws and the Knights are also lifting."

Kip breathed deep. "Our first CA."

"Come on, this calls for a celebration. Meet me over at the Tiger's Den. I'm buying."

"Okay...sure, let me finish this journal entry."

The Tiger's Den next door to their hootch was packed, as usual. Members of their sister company, Warrior slick and T-Bird gunship pilots, were there, too, indulging, like the rest, their second favorite pastime: alcohol consumption. Women and flying ran a close first, but since the airfield lacked an abundance of women, flying always won by default. It was way past midnight before anyone hit the sack.

He heard footsteps in the hallway, and the sound of voices, and cursing, and then a tap on his door. "Mr. Slater, are you up? It's four A.M., sir."

"Yeah...I'm up."

"Briefing's at five, sir."

"Okay. Thanks."

He stood under the showerhead, his eyes closed, the water going full force on his face. There were voices; water ran from open faucets; a toilet flushed; a screen door slammed.

"SHORT! Thirty-seven days and a wake-up, you turkeys!"

"Fuck you, Baumburger—!"

A towel snapped. Ouch! You sonofabitch."

Someone whistled. "Hey, Henry, you got any razorblades?"

"Here—from now on buy your own."

"What's for breakfast?"

"The usual shit, Oakerson. Powdered fuckin' eggs."

Kip turned the water off. His head felt light, his stomach queasy. *This damn drinking's got to stop. How the hell do these guys do it? What time did we get to bed? Oh...God...it was about one, maybe a little after. Mac wanted to listen to the Peter, Paul and Mary tape again. Henry cried. What was he crying about? Something about his beloved frickin' Vikings.*

Naked bodies. Men. Few were well endowed. Some were hairy-chested, some had no hair. Some were short, some tall. Some were large-boned and heavy-set, others chunky with flabby stomachs, and some were thin and wiry. Some were good-looking; most, though, had ordinary features. Naked and dripping wet, there wasn't a one that looked like a helicopter pilot. *What does a helicopter pilot look like, anyway? This is insane...why am I looking at them at all? Because, you're a writer; a writer is curious about everything.*

Victor R. Beaver

Jonesy said, "I didn't get a letter yesterday, either—damnit."

"What do you think's the matter?"

"Hell if I know. One thing for sure, she hates for me to be over here."

"Crap, Jonesy," bellowed Baumburger; "your wife's probably *glad* you're over here!"

"GODDAMN! This water's hot," cried Randall. "Hasn't anyone told that little papa-san to turn the heat *down*!?"

"Bitch...bitch...bitch."

Outside. On the sidewalk. Half dark. The towel was wrapped around his waist. The air suffocating. Dank air mixed with stinkbugs...thousands of them dead on the sidewalk under the street lamps. *What an acrid odor. Jesus...acrid. Not too bad. My vocabulary is improving. Aplomb. Now there's a neat word. Aplomb...aplomb...*

Kip was in his room. *I've got to sit down. My boots...my boots...! Where are my boots? Oh, yeah, I remember. I took them off last night in Leo's room.*

"Hey, Leo...you in there?"

"Yeah, come on in."

"I need my boots. They're in your room."

"I thought I smelled something dead."

Dressed now. *Where's my map? Where's my gun!? Man o' man...I feel so shitty...*Kip laid down on his bunk, closed his eyes, then shot back up. *I can't lay down! Ooooh...God, give me five more hours of sleep—*

In the dining room. The smell of bacon, coffee. The room felt steamy, humid. He could hear the cooks; a pot clanged; bacon sizzled. There were a few pilots seated. Oakerson sat hunched over a plate of powdered eggs. Henry and Mac each had their hands wrapped around a mug of coffee.

Kip pulled out a chair. "Mac, where are you in the formation?"

"I told you last night."

"Tell me again."

"I'm Red Lead. My AC is Randall," he said.

"And I've got Jonesy," Henry reminded him. "We're Purple Two, right in front of you and Justen."

"What's he like?"

"Who?"

"Jonesy. What's he like as an aircraft commander?"

"Flaky...like Oakerson—"

"Hey—be nice," cried Fred.

"But mostly he's an ass," said Henry. "He's always got his crewchief and gunner polishing the aircraft. He never lets them sit still. I'll bet his wife Dear John's him."

Leo walked in rubbing his hands together, his eyes filled with anticipation. "What the hell's with you?" asked Kip.

"We're going to get into some heavy shit today—I can feel it."

Henry smirked. "No way. Here's what's going to happen," he said. "We're going to take those fuckin' ARVN gooks out into the boonies so they can do their required two-mile hike. We'll start lifting at ten thirty. Then we're going to pick those little shits up at two and deposit them back at Tra Vinh. I'll betcha fifty bucks not one shot is fired. The whole day. Our doorgunners won't even get to suppress."

Leo extended his hand. "Shake, Robin Henry. It's a bet."

"What for?"

"One shot fired."

"By Charlie? No way—"

"Yep."

"You're on," Henry said, "—but let's make it a hundred. I need the cash."

At the aircraft Kip met Justen's crewchief and gunner. "You bring your flashlight, sir?" Conrad asked.

"No....I didn't."

"You can borrow mine."

"Thanks."

"Plus, I got a case of C's. I already got Mr. Justen's picked out. There's plenty of good stuff left."

"Oh, yeah...I bet."

Preflight. Kip started at the front and worked his way down the left side, then along the right side back toward the front. He opened the engine cooling fan compartment door. *Tailboom attaching points—bolts secure. Good. The oil-cooling fan turns freely. Good. The support brace installed. Good.* He tipped open the right-side engine cowling access door. *Oil level...a little low, but not to the bottom line.* He unlocked and removed the fuel cap. *Aaaah...yes, plenty of fuel.*

He climbed on top of the cabin. *Check the main rotor system over real good. Wither it goest...so goest thou. If it's attached, that is. I need to sit.* He sat on the engine air intake screen. *Let me see. I've checked the Jesus nut, the hydraulic fluid, the cowling is secure, the short shaft, the main generator, the filler caps secure, the damper action, the blade grip reservoirs, the pillow block reservoirs...the...the....*"Damn—I could go to sleep right now."

Out of the semi-darkness a face looked up at him, a dark, olive-tanned face. "You okay?"

So, the illustrious, tight-lipped Mister Justen, my aircraft commander. "Yeah...I'm fine."

"We crank in ten minutes," Justen said. He turned to Conrad. "Where's Finch?"

"He went to get another can of ammo."

From on top the aircraft cabin, Slater spied dark shadows moving about the other helicopters. He heard voices, cursing, someone vomiting. There was the sound of metal against metal, machine guns being mounted, ammo belts being placed in rectangular feed cans. He saw the source of other sounds. One of the perimeter guards stirred, stood, stretched his arms out wide...and yawned. The man turned and gazed at the crews readying their ships. After a moment the guard sat down and faced the open fields and the road that ran past the east perimeter fence. From the road came the tinkling of bicycle bells, workers going into the city. Later, after the helicopters were gone, the children would come by, chattering and jabbering, on their way to school.

The eastern skies began to lighten. Kip saw the guard take out a cigarette and light it. He observed the man contemplate the breaking dawn. A moment later Kip climbed down from the cabin top; he slinked his alcohol-ravaged body into the left seat and strapped himself in.

At 0545, they cranked. Within two minutes there were more than a dozen spinning main rotorblades at flight idle rpm going to full throttle. Within three minutes, the radios began to chatter:

"This is Tiger Lead...radio check on Fox."

"White Two is up."

"Yellow Three's up."

There were several other responses, not necessarily in order. "Red Three has you weak but readable."

"Tiger Trail is up," Justen said.

"Has anyone heard from Oakerson?"

"This is Yellow Lead...Fred's finally cranking," Baumburger said.

They made radio checks on VHF and UHF. Lieutenant Whitaker called the tower for permission to form up on the runway. Permission was granted.

Each ship slid forward from its protective revetment and began to hover toward the runway. The positioning reminded Kip of a square dance, with one aircraft giving way to another— *"Your turn to curtsy, my turn to bow"*—until all the helicopters were lined up on the hard-surface airstrip in straight-trail formation. "Lead, this is Trail, looks like everyone is ready," Justen reported.

"Roger," Trent replied. "Tiger Flight...Lead will be pulling pitch in one zero seconds."

From their trail position, in the half-light of dawn, Kip could make out about half of the fourteen rotating beacons, a red anti-collision light flashing on top each ship's engine cowling. He saw an equal number of (what appeared to be) overlapping, spinning main rotorblades. Anticipating liftoff, Justen applied torque pressure (power) to bring the helicopter light on the landing gear. Then Kip saw Lead, far in the front, in a climb. Then White Two lifted, then Wainwright and Leo's ship White Three...Four...Five, until he observed a mass of helicopters bloom upward, like pigeons startled into flight. And then they too were off the ground and climbing. "Lead, this is Trail, your flight is up."

"Roger that. I'll hold sixty knots until we're formed. Tiger Flight, come up Vs of Five."

For as long as he would live, Kip Slater would never forget the scene that played before him. Once each helicopter had gained altitude and had achieved some airspeed, the group seemed to split apart. Then, in near breathless anticipation of a mid-air collision, he watched each helicopter race toward the ones ahead, slow down at the last possible second, and then slide gracefully into its assigned position. When their ship, the last one to play catch-up, came within a hundred meters of the others, Justen reported: "Lead, this is Trail, your flight is formed."

"Roger. Lead will be picking up speed." That there had been no collision between helicopters was a testimony to the expertise of the pilots involved. Many of the ACs had seven to eight hundred hours of combat flight time, nearly half of it spent in formation. In the months to come, Kip would watch the same scene play again and again. Now, it was exciting—a challenge—something he never dreamed he'd be doing. In the coming year, though, flying would become so exhausting, so mind numbing, he would pray to do anything else.

Journal Entry, 3 November 1967, Tra Vinh airstrip

It's 9:30 A.M. We're parked along the southeast side of the Tra Vinh airstrip, just inside the city limits. A fuel truck has topped off all the tanks. So far no lifts. The ACs got their briefing from Whitaker. Nine other slicks are here. Five from the 114th (the Knights) and four from the 175th (the Outlaws), both assault companies based at Vinh Long. The Vikings have a heavy fire-team here (3 aircraft). The Mavericks, the guns for the 175th, have 2 light fire-teams. Our Vikings are on station now. No word yet when we're going to lift. Parked on the far side of the runway are a maintenance chopper and Dustoff.

The ARVN are "camped" alongside the helicopters, eight to nine soldiers per ship. Staying a respectful distance away, they laze about, watching us strung out in our hammocks or hanging around the ship. Some are curious and come closer. Conrad tells them to di di mau, meaning scat. They turn away, jabbering. None appear to be hurt or angry by this. They look no older than 14 or 15. They point and giggle; they seem curious about everything. They smell horrible. Their body odor is hard to describe: a swampy, putrid, musty smell. Their weapons are WW II vintage: carbines, BARs, and the M1 Garand. The officers pack .45-caliber pistols. The large size of their weapons seem way out of proportion to their small stature.

Victor R. Beaver

>*Jonesy and Henry are parked ahead of us. Jonesy has his crewchief and gunner polishing the tailboom. What an ass. I've got a book to read while we wait. Guess I'd better get stocked up. I met 2Lt Paul Christian today. Found out he's the "awards and decorations" officer. He likes to read. He offered to exchange paperbacks with me. He seems likeable, real easy-going. Well, here comes Leo. I wonder what's on his mind...*

"What's that book you're reading?" said Leo.

Slater turned the book over. "It's 'Battle Cry.' I'm studying Uris's writing style."

Leo checked his watch. "Shit—it's ten o'clock. I'm bored."

Finch came over to them. He had just finished heating a can of Cs. The can of fuel, situated on the ground several feet from the helicopter, was still aflame. "Sir, you want to use the fire? I'm done."

Kip put his journal down. "Yeah, thanks." His box of C-rations was next to his seat. "Leo, go get yours. We'll eat."

With his P-38, Slater opened the can of meatballs in tomato sauce. He stirred the contents then squatted down, perching the can over the flame. The squad of ARVN soldiers watched him. Kip looked up and smiled; they smiled back. After a few minutes the sauce began to bubble; he stirred. In another minute he tasted it. It was ready.

Kip was still eating when Leo returned. "The fire's out, Leo. You'll have to get some more fuel."

"Okay." Leo took the can and turned. The ARVN squad, the nine brown-faced men, now had their eyes on him. "What the fuck you looking at?"

"Leo...be nice."

"Yeah, right." Tannah held the can up and pointed. "Can," he said. They nodded. "For cooking yum-yum." He rubbed his belly. They nodded again, each of them grinning. Leo held the can upside down. "Empty. Must have cooking fuel." He nodded his head and pointed toward the helicopter. "Yes-yes," one of them said. Leo laid down next to the landing gear and moved underneath the belly of the ship. He positioned the can directly under a fuel-sump drain valve. He pressed his finger against the valve and let the liquid spill into the can. When the can was three-quarters full, he released the pressure on the valve and moved out from under the aircraft. He took a match and struck it. "Match...makes fire." They nodded and began an exchange of unintelligible chatter. Leo shook his head and lit the fuel. A purple-blue flame appeared, fluttering above the top of the can. *Ooohs* and *aaahs* came from the little group.

Next, Leo took a can of Cs from the small rectangular box; his audience looked on. "Processed horse meat," he stated; "it's for dogs but our army thinks it's good enough for us." They nodded again. He opened it, then balanced the can on top of the flame. He stared at it for a moment. He took a spoon and, again,

The Sky Soldiers

looked at his audience. "Spoon," he said, holding it up, revering it as if it were an icon. He poked the spoon in the can. "Stirring now and then keeps the yum-yum from sticking."

Kip stood. The Vietnamese soldiers looked away. "Oh-oh, Leo. It looks like you dinked around a little too long."

"Huh...?"

Kip's gaze was far down the line. He saw rotorblades becoming untied and turned ninety degrees to their fuselages. He saw Whitaker give the signal to crank.

"What's happening?"

"I think this is it, Leo...We're cranking."

At the word 'cranking,' Derek Justen opened his eyes and swung out of his hammock. Conrad went to untie the blades. Finch began putting on his chest protector. Justen quickly stowed his hammock in one of the ship's cubbyhole compartments. He got into the front seat, strapped in, and began setting switches and the throttle. Leo kicked over the can of fuel; he spent a moment putting out the flame spread across the ground. "Leo—you'd better get going," Slater said.

"Yeah...yeah, I'm going." He turned to Kip, who was buckling on his pistol belt. "What the hell do I do with this?" Leo held the open can of C-rations.

"Toss it," Justen told him.

Leo pitched the can at the feet of the squad of soldiers now assembling their packs and weapons. One of them kicked the can back. "You bastard," Leo Tannah hissed.

Kip was just beginning to strap in when Justen called out, "Comin' hot."

"Clear."

"Good luck, Leo."

"You too, Kip."

Justen brought the engine to full rpm. Conrad beckoned for the ARVN to board. Kip watched as they climbed in on both sides. For the first time he noticed how lightly equipped they were. They certainly weren't overly stocked with ammunition. A few had concerned looks on their faces; none, though, seemed frightened or panicky.

"Lead, this is Trail, your flight is ready."

"Roger, Trail." Several minutes passed. Then Lead said, "Flight, looks like we have a hold."

"Roger..."

Kip looked ahead. Out of each ship he could see legs dangling and rifle barrels pointed toward the ground. He glanced behind him. None of the soldiers acted at all like he expected men to act going into combat. They're either incredibly brave or incredibly stupid, he thought. *Maybe Henry is right. Maybe all we're doing is taking them out for a little stroll in the rice paddies.* At that moment he took it all as a sign to relax. He could see that Justen was irritated. In the back Finch and Conrad seemed both tense and bored.

With all three radios on, Kip began to hear smatterings of different conversations. Major Drummond in the C&C (Command and Control) ship, high over the LZ more than thirty kilometers away, was speaking to Tiger Lead: "Tiger Lead, Tiger Six, expect at least a five minute delay."

"This is Tiger Lead. Roger that," came Whitaker's reply.

"Flight, this is Lead, reduce to flight idle rpm." In response, Justen rolled the throttle back; the sound of the engine decreased. Kip sat with his left elbow out the window. The air inside the cockpit was hot and the longer they sat the hotter it became. He felt listless, drowsy...He sweltered with his flight helmet on. The ARVN sat placid; their brains appeared to be baking under their steel helmets.

After fifteen minutes, Whitaker ordered his flight to shut down.

With the blades tied down, and the soldiers assembled outside the ship, Justen withdrew his hammock and tied it again between two posts inside the cabin. He refitted himself within the plastic weave and closed his eyes.

Slater looked at his watch. It was almost eleven o'clock. Up at four, he had got less than three hours of sleep since yesterday morning. Feeling sluggish, he sat down on the cabin floor and laid back, resting his head on his flight helmet bag. He opened his book and began to read. His eyes became heavy. He closed the book and placed it on his chest.

The next thing he knew Conrad was nudging his boot. "Wake up, sir. We're cranking."

Kip sat up. He looked at his watch; it was now eleven thirty. He couldn't believe he'd been asleep. He moved into his seat. Again, Justen had the battery switch on and was setting the throttle control.

Within minutes all aircraft were cranked. The ARVN moved back onboard. Once they were situated they held the same posture as before. Kip felt lethargic, from both the high humidity and heat, and the short-lived nap.

Kip watched as Lead picked up to a hover. "Tiger Flight, this is Lead. We'll be pulling pitch in one zero."

And then they were off. Kip noted the time: it was 11:34 A.M.

"Lead, this is Trail, your flight of twenty-three is off."

Lieutenant Whitaker spoke to Major Drummond. "Tiger Six, Tiger Lead, flight of twenty-three off Tango Victor en route to RP Two."

"Roger, report zero five from RP Two. I'll have more for you then—break, Viking Two Two, this is Tiger Six."

"Go ahead, Six."

"Tiger Lead flight of twenty-three are inbound to RP Two."

"This is Viking Two Two. Roger that."

"How's that east side now? Are you taking anymore fire?" Drummond asked. The 121st AHC commander was at two thousand feet directly over the

LZ. In the cabin behind him sat an ARVN battalion commander and three staff officers, each wearing headsets, maps open, all staring at the land below out the right side of the ship. They saw the Viking heavy fire-team down low, still reconnoitering the proposed LZ. For those in the C&C bird, the whole process was tedious and time-consuming. How to bring in twenty-three helicopters loaded with human cargo to engage a tenacious and wily enemy?

"Negative fire, Six. Negative fire."

Whitaker guided his flight on a southeasterly heading, paralleling the Song Co Chien, one of the major tributaries of the Mekong River, flowing into the South China Sea. They were at two thousand feet. RP Two was about twenty-six kilometers from Tra Vinh, over a small cluster of hootches seven klicks east of Cau Ngang, a hamlet near the mouth of the river. Flying time would be about ten minutes. Kip looked at his map. Justen reached over and pointed on the chart where he thought the LZ might be. "It's desolate there. Real swampy. The ARVN are going to be knee deep in mud. There won't be any place dry for us to land."

Slater listened and nodded.

Justen dialed in the Viking VHF working frequency. They heard conversation:

"Two Two, Two One."

"Go."

"Your ten o'clock. See that cluster of trees, right near that pool of water?"

"Roger that."

"I see movement."

"I got it—I got it."

"I'm breaking right in three seconds."

Kip said, "Sounds like they might be into something big."

"Sounds like it."

With the additional nine aircraft from the other assault companies, the close-knit formation weaved and bobbed in front of them for over a quarter-mile. All the while Kip remained tense as he watched the helicopters maintain the barest separation between spinning main rotorblades.

"Tiger Six, Tiger Lead, we're now zero five minutes from RP Two."

"Roger, Lead. I'm going to have you orbit the RP. Do right-hand turns."

"This is Lead, roger...right-hand turns."

"Now what's happening?" asked Kip.

"They're not ready for us," Justen replied. "We orbit the RP. Could be one turn, two turns—or twenty."

Four minutes later, Lead began a shallow right-hand turn. Each ship followed suit, with the aircraft on the outside of the turn playing catch-up with those on the inside. Soon the flight was heading to the northwest. After about two minutes,

Lead began another turn to the right. Three orbits later, Justen said, "You fly. This crap wears me out."

After his second full orbit, Slater was exhausted. Never had he poured so much energy into a task. Formation flying required his utmost concentration. The task's inherent danger, complexity, and his inexperience, all took its toll. Meantime, the conversation between Tiger Six and the gunships continued:

"Six, this is Two Two, we're now receiving automatic weapons fire from that southeast treeline."

"Roger. What do you estimate the strength?"

"Company size, maybe larger."

"Can you see anything?"

"Negative. They're bunkered in good."

"What's it look like now for bringing the slicks in? What about that area just to the southwest...near that short section of river?"

"Looks good. It's far enough away, easily three hundred meters."

Drummond said, "It's pretty flat...little cover, though, do you agree?"

"There's some small brush, a few tree stumps."

"Okay. I'm going to split the flight up. We'll bring ten ships in on the first insertion. See how it goes. Can they suppress on the left?"

"Roger that, Six."

"Okay...that's real fine." Drummond spoke on his UHF radio. "Tiger Lead, this is Tiger Six."

"Go, Six."

"Depart the RP on a heading of one six five. Come up staggered trail right. Bring in ten ships. The thirteen ships left behind will do one more orbit, then I'll have them do the same. I'll let you know when to turn to your final landing heading of two three zero. You'll be landing to smoke about three hundred meters from the objective, a one-hundred-meter-long treeline. There are several such treelines. Look carefully for the smoke. The troops should bear to the left rear, about eight o'clock, when they off-load. You can have your doorgunners use suppressive fire on the left side only."

"This is Tiger Lead, roger."

Trent Whitaker gave his instructions to the flight. A minute later the first ten helicopters departed from the RP. Red Lead became the command ship of the remaining aircraft. WO1 Randall was now in charge of thirteen combat assault helicopters with McNamara as his second-in-command. The second flight began another shallow right-hand turn. Within another minute the two separate flights got their instructions:

"Tiger Lead, Tiger Six. Start your turn heading two three zero. Break. Red Lead and flight, depart the RP heading one six five."

"This is Red Lead, roger that," Randall replied.

"Red Flight, this is Red Lead. Come up staggered trail right." Thirteen aircraft acknowledged.

"Execute...Now."

The formation shifted. Slater thought, *This is it...this is it!* Just then an image of his mother flashed across his mind. He wondered what his family was doing right now. Were they in bed, or possibly just going to bed? Did they have any idea what he was doing? How could they? He was already certain that what was taking place in or near the LZ was more than anyone expected. *Oh God...Oh God...are these to be my last moments on Earth—?*

"I have red smoke," Whitaker stated over the UHF radio.

Drummond said, "Roger that. Break. Viking Two Two, Tiger Six."

"Go, Six."

"Is the smoke out yet?"

"Roger that...we're dropping it now. Smoke's out."

Justen, hearing the discrepancy in what was being said, told Slater:

"Oh boy, I think Charlie's got our number."

"Why? What's happening?"

"The smoke. Trent's got red smoke...but the guns just now threw smoke out."

"What's the color?" they heard Drummond ask.

"This is Two Two. Red smoke is out."

"This is Tiger Lead, roger...I have red smoke."

"Six, this is Two Two."

"Go."

"Are the Mavericks inbound yet?"

"Standby—Break, Maverick Two Six, Two Six, this is Tiger Six. Are you inbound?"

"Affirmative Six, this is Two Six, we're inbound—estimating on station in zero five minutes."

"Roger, Two Six."

Randall's flight of thirteen helicopters was three kilometers behind Whitaker's flight of ten. Kip remained at the controls. Flying from the left seat still felt awkward, especially in formation. He wondered about the descent into the LZ: that would be the true test of his skills. How would he react under fire?...Would he panic?...Would he be able to maintain his position in the formation?...Would their ship take hits?

The radios continued their incessant chatter. Tiger Lead was fifty meters from touchdown. "Tiger Lead, Tiger Six. Do you have that treeline to your left front?"

"Six, this is Lead, affirmative."

"Look farther to your front—do you see another red smoke?"

"Negative—I say again, negative."

"Tiger Six, this is Two Two. That last smoke was a dud."

"Roger that. Break. Tiger Lead, this is Six, you're landing to the wrong smoke!—I say again, you're landing to the wrong smoke. Pick up and go three hundred meters farther to your front!"

"It's too late, Six—we're down. They're already jumping out."

"Lead, White Three taking fire!" Kip recognized Leo's voice.

"Yellow Lead is taking fire—from nine o'clock!"

"Lead, this is Six, you've got to get those troops back on board!"

"No dice, Six. It's too late. Besides, they wouldn't have a clue. Break. Flight, this is Lead, we'll be pulling pitch in zero five."

"Viking Two Two, this is Maverick Two Six. What's the story?"

"The slicks are receiving fire from a treeline to their nine o'clock position. Do you have us in sight?"

"Roger that."

"Red Lead, Tiger Six."

"This is Red Lead, go, Six," Randall replied.

"Do you have Tiger Lead in sight?"

"Affirmative...It looks like he's lifting."

"Roger that," Drummond said, his voice a little calmer now that Trent's flight was off the ground. "Look three hundred meters forward from point of lift-off—"

"Six...this is Two Two, I've got another smoke out."

"Roger—break, Red Lead, did you get that?"

"Roger, I now identify purple smoke."

"Two Two confirms purple smoke."

"Land there," stated Six. "Land there. Do not suppress. You'll hit friendlies. I say again—do not suppress on the left side."

"Roger that."

Kip looked across the instrument-panel glare shield at Purple Two, Jonesy and Henry's aircraft. From his vantage, to maintain the correct angle on them, the rear crosstube attachment point on the left landing gear had to be in direct line of sight with the front crosstube attachment point on the right landing gear. He was hardly maintaining that line of sight. His flying had become erratic. The inevitable had become a reality. Without taking his eyes off Purple Two, he sensed they were on descent now into the LZ. Continually, Kip pulled up close to Purple Two, then dropped back. "Bring it in," Justen told him. "Now bring it down. Keep your angle, *damnit.* You're going to lose complete sight of him!"

Slater felt the urge to urinate. He gritted his teeth and placed a near death-grip on the collective and cyclic. At that moment he wished Justen would take over control of the ship to put him out of his misery—and out of bodily danger of his own ineptness. He felt shame to even dare claim he was a pilot. To top that, he was scared witless that at any moment a bullet would come ripping through his body.

As they descended, the humidity began to envelop them as though entering a large sauna. The odor of dead and dying vegetation assailed them. There also came the acrid, eye-watering smell of spent cordite.

With every fiber of his being, Kip Slater fought to maintain control—of himself and the aircraft. When he saw Jonesy's helicopter touch down, he felt their ship close to the ground. He diverted his attention ahead and saw the marking smoke in front of Randall's aircraft whip about by the rotor downwash. They touched down with a jolt. He was about to place the collective pitch-control lever full down when he felt Justen's pressure against his movement. "Don't. We're in mud. We'll get stuck and never get out."

The ARVN quickly evacuated the ship. As they sat there, with the landing gear barely touching the ground, Slater became more fully aware of the terrain to which they had descended. They were in a no-man's land, near the edge of the coast, a swamp, uninhabitable, yet thriving with mankind's fiercest activity: *War*. To his left he felt the concussions caused by the impact of 2.75-inch rockets fired from the gunships. There was an occasional rattle from several ARVN rifles; the little brown men were laying prone in the mud not more than fifty feet away. He saw a Maverick gunship pass by on the left, then break left. The radios continued to belch a cacophony of chatter. Viking Two Two reported receiving fire. A split second later, Kip heard:

"Tiger Six, Two Two, my co-pilot's been hit. Bronski's been hit—"

Slater's eyes widened. *The polar bear's been hit!*

"Roger, Two Two. How bad?"

"Looks like he got it in the arm. It looks bad."

Justen said, "Red Lead, your flight is ready."

"Red Lead is coming up."

Again, Kip found himself concentrating with all his might on Purple Two. As Two began to lift, so did he. As Two began to move forward, Kip began to move forward in lock step. As Purple Two began to pick up speed, Kip added power to accelerate. And as Jonesy and Henry's aircraft began to climb, Kip practically willed Justen's aircraft Tiger 986 into the air…to get away from the first real hell he had ever experienced in his life.

"Red Lead, Tiger Trail, your flight is up."

Chapter 12

THURSDAY NIGHT. MIKE AND DAVE were in the BOQ. "I ordered a pizza," said Dave.

"Did you get some beer?" Mike asked.

Dave sighed. "If I had even one beer right now, I'd fall asleep—sure as hell."

"Yeah, me too. Okay, let's run through these emergency procedures again. Our illustrious Mr. Pollard really got the ass when we screwed up the generator-failure procedure."

"God, no shit. That aircraft is an electrical nightmare."

For the next two hours, they ran through the checklist, reciting what they would do if this happened or that problem developed. The proper procedure had to be stated verbatim out of the book. A misplaced word or phrase was enough to bring down the wrath of Daddy Don.

At the stagefield, it was practice practice practice. Normal approaches, steep approaches, normal takeoffs, max performance takeoffs. They performed high-speed, low-level autorotations, anti-torque malfunction maneuvers, "simulated" hydraulics off, standard autorotations, one-eighty autos. Emergency governor-control hover work. Hovering autos. It was one maneuver after another. Talk on the radio. Call for takeoff, when turning base, on final approach. Check systems before landing...before takeoff...on downwind...on base. Simulated forced landings en route to and from the stagefield. Collective pitch down, establish glide, check rotor rpm within limits, check N1, airspeed...and trim trim trim.

In the aircraft. "What would you do if your AC inverter failed?" Pollard asked. "Don't hesitate—rattle it off, rattle it off."

"Main inverter circuit breaker, check in. Standby inverter circuit breaker check in. Inverter switch, move to standby position. SCAS, re-engage. Main inverter circuit breaker, pull out."

"How many inverters do you have?"

"One."

"Wrong. Two, dummy. You just said 'Inverter switch, move to standby position.'"

"I did?"

At the table. "Lieutenant Nolan, explain pitch cone coupling."

Nolan blinked, thought for a moment, then drew a deep breath. "Pitch cone coupling. Pitch cone coupling is a characteristic of the flexible yoke of the 540 rotor head installed on the AH-1G, to automatically reduce pitch under loading to keep the rpm within limits. Any maneuver, however, which produces severe loading on the rotor may overspeed the system, unless the pilot applies collective pitch. The effect," Mike recited, "is greater as airspeed increases. Loading the rotor, caused during flight by G-loads from a maneuver, forces the blades to cone upward."

"Mr. Grange, when does rotor loading normally occur?"

"During power-on or power-off flight, such as during a pullout from a high-speed dive or a flare in an autorotation."

"Okay, good. You guys are learning. You've got to remember, the Cobra's high maneuverability makes it imperative the pilot check the rotor rpm and use correct coordination to keep the rpm with limits. You guys got that?"

The two men nodded their heads.

The first weekend came and went. Neither man left the BOQ, except to eat. They were together morning, noon, and night. They studied, memorized, and were mesmerized by questions. They quizzed each other over and over. By Monday morning both aviators were drawn tight as a drum. Checkrides were scheduled after the following weekend, on Tuesday. There was so much material to cover and so little time. In their academic classes, platform instructors covered the AH-1G aircraft systems: electrical, hydraulics, the flight control system; the power train, fuel system, and lubrication system. They followed a drop of oil from the oil case through the oil pump and filter, to the engine casing, down through the scavenger pump, the oil cooler, and back to the oil case.

And Daddy Don continued to pressure them:

"Mr. Grange, when does the engine oil pressure caution light come on?"

"Below twenty-five psi."

"Lieutenant Nolan, when will the engine oil bypass caution light illuminate?"

"When oil becomes three point eight quarts below spillover. Bypass will occur if the engine oil bypass switch is in automatic."

The day before in academics they began to study the aircraft's armaments systems. They were now learning to be killers: High-tech killers.

* * *

WEDNESDAY MORNING OF WEEK TWO. A dense fog had settled over most of the East Coast. It was a no-fly day.

"Okay, listen up." Mr. Jardine, the briefing officer, was speaking. "This warm front is going to be around through tomorrow. If we don't fly tomorrow, we'll be coming in this weekend to make up time. We're gonna meet your checkride schedule. And that's a promise."

The students moaned. The IPs, however, sat down at their respective tables and rubbed their hands together like kings at a feast. The potential confiscation of a weekend didn't phase them; it was part of the job. But each day rushing out to do the preflight and to get precious flight time took them away from equally precious table-talk time. Hands-on flying, honing the student's piloting skills, was, of course, essential. Now, however, each IP could get into the meat of his subject. And it was a time for in-depth drilling, to see how well their students were learning.

Six hours of uninterrupted table talk. Daddy Don was in his element.

"Okay, we're going to talk about low-G and negative-G flight." Pollard's icy stare prompted Mike and Dave to perk their ears. "First, what is it? It's that flight condition in a helicopter when the weight of the helicopter becomes negligible—to non-existent—to its turning mast and rotor system." They frowned. They had heard this before, but still didn't quite understand it. "Imagine, if you will, a rotating system, and beneath that system, hanging, an airframe and engine. First, let's place these entities at a three-foot hover. As the engine is supplying torque pressure which causes the rotor to turn and to provide lift when collective pitch is applied, the clockwise motion of the rotor, as viewed from the cockpit, causes the fuselage to want to turn in the opposite direction...or counter-clockwise underneath it. This, as you both know, is compensated for by tailrotor thrust, the amount of which is controlled by the pilot with his anti-torque pedals, which also helps maintain his heading at a hover. As long as the fuselage represents weight to the rotor system, things are kosher.

"Now, let's put ourselves in flight. Visualize a rotor system turning free above a fuselage, not lifting, if you will, a quantity of weight. But that mass, that weight, is still attached physically to that rotor system. And that mass has the thrusting action of the tailrotor still being applied to the tailboom. Which way will the fuselage roll if the rotor is providing lift—but not the opposing twisting action?"

They thought for a moment. "It'll roll to the right," said Dave.

"Exactly, due to tailrotor thrust. Now, what would your normal 'gut' reaction be with the flight controls to counter this? A right roll causes you to think—"

"Apply left cyclic...to stop the roll," Mike said quickly.

"That's right—very good. But a left cyclic-control input to a turning rotor that is not supplying lift to a quantity of weight—what do you suppose will happen?—especially if you apply left cyclic abruptly."

This time they each gave Daddy Don a puzzled look. "That left cyclic movement will cause the 'stops' on the turning rotor to hit the mast, probably sever it, and...well, I don't have to spell it out for you." They grimaced. No turning rotor system. Nothing to glide with. All they could envision was a Cobra out of control. *Impact. Explosion.*

"So what do we do?" asked Mike.

"First of all...you try like hell to avoid that condition. Unfortunately, you'll find yourself more near that condition in a Cobra than in most other helicopters. With this ship we can do a quick cyclic climb, reach our safe altitude for a dive, to then roll over the top of that climb for a rocket run. As you nose the aircraft over, that's when the Cobra approaches weightlessness. What should we do? I'll tell you. Add just a little collective pitch...that'll help. The added pitch in the blades will start to lift that mass—pull it along with the rotor system, as the rotor wants, theoretically, to fly off into space. But, if you ever find yourself in a right roll...apply aft cyclic."

"Aft cyclic?"

"Aft...bring the cyclic slowly back to return the rotor to positive thrust." Daddy Don emphasized this with his right hand, pretending it was on a cyclic control stick, bringing it back gently. "Not left. But slooow...ly back."

Thursday. More fog. More table talk. Flying on Saturday was now a certainty. Even the old pilots there for the transition were keyed up and on edge. And the instructors were drained. They had browbeaten and quizzed and explained until they were blue in the face. If they couldn't fly on Friday, it meant flying on Sunday, too.

Friday, no fly.

"Listen up," Jardine said. "Be here bright and early tomorrow morning. 0500 hours. Saturday's forecast calls for clearing skies. Sunday, same-same." A round of expected moans chorused through the room. "Zin loi, brother, as they say in Vietnam."

"That's it," Pollard said. "I've done talked myself silly. If you haven't got anymore questions, I haven't got anymore answers."

As they were leaving, Dave Grange looked at Pollard. "How about a beer? We're buying."

Daddy Don looked up. "Huh? Na...you guys don't want anymore of me. Besides, I got a date."

"Your wife?" Mike queried. It had never occurred to him to wonder if the man was married, single, or divorced.

"No-no...I'm divorced. Was married. For seventeen years. Had three daughters. This gal I got now, I've been dating about six months. Her name's Elaine. She works on post, in finance. She's from Australia."

Nolan and Grange smiled at each other. Pollard scowled. "Now don't be thinking what I think you're thinking," he said.

"We're not thinking anything," Dave retorted.

"Look, she's a smart lady. She isn't any shack job. She's also one helluva a cook. And I can't figure for the life of me what she sees in me. But I'm not gonna complain."

"Okay, okay." Both men suppressed the urge to laugh.

Nolan and Grange eyed this gruff individual who in a short time had earned their solemn respect. Pollard was a hard IP. He demanded from them their very best. Though there were times when they thought his expectations unreasonable, he never asked them to know or do something without explaining why. *"Just because the Army wants it done that way..."* wasn't good enough for Daddy Don. More than most of the other instructors, he was acutely aware of the ship's limitations and capabilities. Yet there were aspects of the AH-1G still not known nor written in any book, which told him this aircraft was to be treated with respect. The Cobra was fast, modern, and highly complex. It was an aircraft that demanded the kind of pilot who could divide his attention many times over in the span of a few seconds. Pollard's job was more than to teach two people to manipulate the controls of an aircraft. Split-second value judgment, proper analysis of a problem, thinking and reacting quickly, and being right one hundred percent of the time was what he was after—and nothing less. In Vietnam, their lives would continually be on the line to destroy an unseen enemy who could strike them quickly and sometimes easily from the sky. It was this aspect of the war that drove Pollard to push these two men to their limits. He intended that not one of his charges should die because they lacked something he could have given them in the short time they were together. To survive the AH-1G Cobra gunship each student had to know and understand it explicitly. This Pollard had control over. To survive the war, though, would be up to them, on their quickness and cunning—and their luck. "Well," Dave declared, "when this shit's over, we're treating you and your lady-friend to a steak dinner."

"When this shit's over, I'm gonna deserve it...after you guys," Pollard grumbled.

"Ah...come on now..."

"Just kidding. Listen, you guys, and I mean this...you've been a couple of my best." He paused. "You're both good pilots, good learners, and you're both eager to do it right. But mostly," he said, "you both got common sense. What more could an IP ask for?"

The Fort Stewart officers' club informal lounge reminded Grange of a northwest logjam. They did, though, manage to find two seats at the far end of the bar. It was the Friday afternoon "Happy Hour" and pilots were everywhere. Many of them were students, commissioned officers still in flight training. An equal number were veteran pilots, mostly chief warrant officers assigned as flight instructors to the newly opened Hunter-Stewart flight training complex designed to siphon off the overflow of students coming out of Fort Wolters. Nolan could see their faces etched with the lines of many hours of combat flight time. They wore on their upper right sleeves the patch of their last unit of assignment in Vietnam, and there was a colorful assortment: the 1st Aviation Brigade, the "Screaming Eagles" of the 101st, the "sky troopers" of the 173rd Airborne Brigade, the American Division, the Big Red One of the 1st Infantry Division, the 4th Infantry, 9th Infantry, the 25th Infantry, Special Forces, MACV, USARV, and the granddaddy of them all, the 1st Cavalry Division (Airmobile). Theirs was a large patch, a wide black diagonal and horsehead on a distinctive yellow background.

Grange's 1st Cav patch stood out along with the rest. Even Nolan felt a special kinship toward that first group of pilots who in late 1965 carried forth the very essence of the airmobile concept, a concept whereby a whole battalion of infantrymen at once could be brought into the sacred and hitherto untouched realms of the North Vietnamese Army. There was, though, among all Army pilots, young and old alike, regardless of unit, a camaraderie that seemed evenly matched by few other branches of the service. Only the Marine Corps as a whole could boast a prouder *espirit de corps*. But Nolan was beginning to see a spirit different in kind than anything the Marines ever had. The technical expertise required to fly a helicopter banded together a different breed of person: an intelligent, daring individualist, someone who perhaps was more exposed to death by being in the machine he flew—loud, low, and slow above the ground—than the infantryman on the ground. Nolan had spent his time on the ground and was more than aware of the plight of the grunt, the groundpounder, the lowly foot soldier. Theirs was a separate and dirty hell and on his second Vietnam tour, when hidden among the clods of broken earth and splintered and shattered bombed-out trees, he had never been so glad to hear the loud wopping sound of a helicopter inbound to re-supply him and his men or extract the dead and wounded—and wondered the special courage of the men so willing to lay down their lives as a matter of honor and brotherhood. It was in that moment that he shuddered and was grateful for the enormity of their sacrifice....

Chapter 13

AFTER GRUNDY DAY THE CANDIDATES settled back into the routine. Everyone was emotionally drained, including the company staff. Captain Richmond tried to mount a campaign of harassment, but his cadre couldn't quite muster their original vigor: Class 67-15 had stolen their thunder.

* * *

CANDIDATES ADAMSON, ALLEN, AND Cutter were in charge of contacting Texas Women's University in Denton to invite the girls to the preflight "phase" party. Inviting them was tradition...and in the past, the college administration had always been happy to oblige.

The occasion, a semi-formal affair, was to be held on the last Friday of preflight. On the following day, Class 67-15 would move to the flight-line barracks. Officially, the party was an opportunity for the cadre to observe the future warrant officers in a social setting. Normally, congeniality and proper adult behavior would be assumed. However, three days before the evening in question they were told: "You will conduct yourselves as gentlemen—and not like caged heathens! IS THAT UNDERSTOOD!?" shouted Captain Richmond from his raised platform.

"SIR! YES, SIR!"

"Us?...Caged heathens?"

During the week before the party their emotions were subdued. Each was wondering what lay ahead during their first few days of flying. They had heard so many horror stories about screaming IPs...engine failures...unfair checkrides...pink (colored) gradeslips..."prog" rides for unsatisfactory progress...flight deficiency setbacks and eliminations. It began to dawn on them that the real stumbling blocks to their silver wings were yet to be challenged. And woe is the candidate who was the last to go solo in each respective flight: his solo wings would have to be sewn on his baseball cap *upside down.*

On Friday, though, they woke to a whole different tune. "I feel...gooood," sounded Seymore P. Cutter. "Tonight we party—" And all the rest of the day they were as high-spirited as colts in spring. How many girls were coming? A couple of hundred? Enough for all the unmarried guys?...Yes?...No?...Maybe?

Hardly.

"Yes, ma'am...Yes, ma'am...I'm sorry to hear that, ma'am. Perhaps they will in the future, ma'am. Thank you, ma'am." Sandy hung up the phone. He had made one last call to Denton to find out how many buses they would need to bring the ladies to Fort Wolters.

"Well, damnit, how many?" Mark Allen asked.
"One bus," Sandy said.
"Just one?" Seymore groaned.
"Yep, just one." Sandy held up a single digit for emphasis.
"Well, that's about forty, maybe fifty girls," Mark decided quickly. "Jesus, I thought there'd be a lot more than that."
"How many girls?" asked Seymore.
"Twelve—maybe."
"Twelve—?"
"Only the more responsible ones—so says Mrs. Tucker—are being allowed to come."
"But damn there are over two hundred of us."
"Why so few? What did she say?" Mark asked, his voice sounding exasperated. "The last class got almost sixty."
"She said, and I quote, 'You're lucky, young man, that I am allowing these few to attend your function. The last time our ladies went, more than a dozen came back thoroughly intoxicated—and one of them was pregnant.' Unquote."

When the girls finally did arrive there were in fact forty-one that came through the Fort Wolters NCO Club door (many late-comers had shown up at the bus departure-point in front of Administration on the sly). Of the forty-one, only four were considered attractive; a dozen were passable; the rest were marginal at best. But then, neither were all the men handsome and dashing...even by a long shot.

Because Cutter and Allen had volunteered to escort the ladies from Denton on the bus, the two managed to cull their pair of fillies early. Allen corralled Marie Robbins, the prettiest of them all, while a plump, cheery girl from Austin, named Callie Henderson, lassoed Seymore.

Mark Allen, Seymore, and Pete Cochran, along with their dates, were seated at one of the large round tables. Pete's wife, Cheryl, a very forward and inquiring type with short, ash-blonde hair and a soft-cheeked face, had come by bus from Oklahoma City where she worked as a fashion coordinator at one of the city's large department stores. Sandy sat by himself at the table with them; he watched their faces illuminated by the flickering candlelight.

By ten o'clock everyone was having a great time. All the girls from TWU, as well as most of the wives, had become quite relaxed. Requests for slow songs had become more frequent. By eleven o'clock, couples were dancing so close together they appeared a shade less than outright lewd. But the staff didn't seem to mind: *"Eat, drink, and be merry, for tomorrow ye may be dead,"* was the motto they, too, lived by.

"You're awfully quiet. What are you thinking?" Cheryl Cochran asked Sandy. Pete had gone for another drink, and Mark and Seymore were on the dance floor with Marie and Callie.

Sandy was still nursing his one and only drink so far that evening, feeling slightly the dizzying effects of the alcohol. He glanced over at her. "I don't know. I'm just watching everyone dance."

The band started to play another slow song. Cheryl canted her head. "Well...would you like to dance?"

Sandy hesitated. "Are you sure Pete won't mind?"

"Not at all."

She guided him to the dance floor. They came together and she began to move easily with his lead. "Where are you from, Sandy?"

"Colorado."

"Oh, do you ski?"

"Not really. I've tried it. I'd rather climb. I've been up several Fourteeners."

"What's a 'Fourteener'?"

"A mountain peak between fourteen thousand and fifteen thousand feet in elevation. There are over fifty of them in the state."

"That many?"

"I don't do any technical stuff, though. I just trudge up the side. Usually, it takes all day to go up and back. Once I get started, I don't quit."

She said, "You don't seem the type that quits. Do you have a girl, Sandy?"

He nodded. "Yes. Her name is Katie."

"Are you guys serious?"

"Oh, yeah, we're...well, I haven't given her a ring yet, but I'm hoping we can be married this coming July, when the class graduates. I've already asked Seymore to be my best man."

Cheryl grinned. "Your friend, he's funny—and he's cute."

"Cute—?"

She nodded. "He has a kind of lovable charm. Girls really go for that."

"They do?" Sandy looked toward Seymore, dwarfed by Callie Henderson's buxom form. Lord help him, he thought, if she's the one to sink her hooks into him.

Sandy paused, then said, "Do you mind if I ask a personal question?"

"No, go ahead."

"What do you think about all this?"

"What, the party?"

"No, I mean the flying...plus, well, you know...us probably all going to Vietnam?"

"Oh..."

"I mean, you're a wife. How do you feel about Pete going over?"

The Sky Soldiers

She pondered for a moment. "Right now, I don't give it much thought. I'll probably give it a lot of thought the closer he gets to graduation."

"Are you afraid?" he asked.

"You mean like...what if he dies?" She tilted her head and gave him a serious look. "Sometimes it really frightens me," she said.

Sandy sighed. "I can't imagine that it wouldn't."

The music ended and the band announced one more song before taking a break. "Let's sit this one out," Cheryl said.

"Okay."

She guided him back to the table. Sandy saw that Pete was still at the bar, talking to several classmates.

"I know what you're thinking," she said, "but Pete and I don't talk about him going to Vietnam like that. That would be too morbid. We're pretty philosophical. What will be will be. We'll pray for the best...what else can we do?" Cheryl saw the strained look on Sandy's face. "How old are you, Sandy?"

"I'm eighteen. So is Katie. She's a freshman in college."

"Do you and her talk about Vietnam?"

He shook his head. "No. It's a real sore subject with her right now. She's got a brother over there. He's in the Navy onboard a ship. He's probably safer there than driving here on the streets. But she's worried anyway."

"That's too bad. Maybe later you can discuss it." Then she said, "I'm glad Pete's going over as a pilot. I'd hate to think of him being in the infantry. Those guys have it the worst, I think. With him being a pilot, it should be a little safer, at least that's what I'm hoping." She took a sip of her drink. "Pete loves flying. He's wanted to be a pilot ever since he was a little boy. I have lots of confidence in him."

The last song before the break ended. The club jukebox now supplied the music. Mark and Seymore guided their dates to the table and sat down. Pete approached, holding a pair of fresh drinks. "You've had enough," Cheryl scolded. Sandy could tell hers was a loving scold. Pete's face held a lost puppy-dog look. At that moment, Sandy envied the ex-airline pilot whose wife had taken the time to talk to him.

"Listen to her," Pete stated; "ain't she just like a wife? I love her dearly." Still holding both glasses, he raised them high. "Toast...to my beautiful wife. She's my living proof that flying is the best thing you can do with your pants *on.*" He took a sip from each drink, bent and gave her a kiss. Bleary-eyed, he straightened, but not before she gave him a quick, gentle cuff to the head.

Mark Allen stood and raised his glass. He misquoted slightly an old Irish toast. "When the first one of us dies...may he be in heaven a half hour before the devil knows he's dead."

Suddenly, Sandy shivered. He thought of Carlyle's question of him: *"Have you ever seen a dead person, Candidate Adamson?"* And then he wondered which one of them would not be coming back? Just then a familiar tune began to play on the jukebox. It was his favorite Christy Minstrels's ballad. Listening now to the words and hearing the melody, his mood changed to melancholy, making him reflect on the people around him—why they were there—where they were eventually going. And he thought, too, of Katie—how much he loved and missed her.

> *"Today while the blossoms still*
> *cling to the vine,*
> *I'll taste your strawberries,*
> *I'll drink your sweet wine.*
> *A million tomorrows shall all*
> *pass away, ere I forget all*
> *the joy that is mine,*
> *—Today."*

The following morning they were plagued by the most god-awful hangovers. Cottrell awakened them the same way he had done the first day of preflight—he banged on a garbage can lid with a broom handle. "Gentleman, as long as your hair hurts, you know you haven't left the world of the living—at least not yet."

CW2 Carlyle ordered them out for one last in-ranks inspection. He eyeballed them from stem to stern. "Stand still. Quit weaving. Jesus H. Christ—you people smell horrible!"

When he got to Seymore, he moaned. "Your brass is on upside down, Candidate Cutter. Do you intend to fly that way? Drop and give me ten."

"Sir, Candidate Cutter, yes, sir…I mean, no, sir."

And as they had done since the first week, they all went down together.

"All right, you turkeys. Get up. GET UP! Starting Monday, you'll meet your flight instructors. Guys, let me say one thing if I don't say another: Listen to what they're telling you. They've got a lot to teach and damn little time to do it. And keep your heads on a swivel. Watch out for the other guy! There, I've thrown in a couple extra. And good luck. I'll probably be seeing some of you in Vietnam after you graduate in July. That's when my time Stateside will be up. I guarantee they'll wring more than one tour out of you—that's if you survive the first."

"That's all I've got. *Go!*—You're dismissed!"

As they were leaving in civilian convoy for the flight-line barracks, to enjoy their elevated status as brand new student pilots, members of the next new class were arriving at the 5th WOC Company area to begin their month of "preflight" training. "Was it as tough as they say?" an incoming candidate asked.

"Na…you guys can handle it," said Seymore. "We softened them up for you."

"Oh…sure."

"CANDIDATES! POST!" they heard Carlyle shout. "DOUBLE TIME!...DOUBLE TIME!"

"Well, there's the shit. And you guys are the fan," Seymore yelled as they drove away in Mark Allen's Impala.

"Christ,"—they heard a timid voice cry—"what the hell have we set ourselves up for...?"

At the flight-line barracks, a group of Yellow Hat seniors were standing on the periphery, anxious to exercise their new status. They were to be afforded by all junior classmen the same courtesies and respect as actual military officers. They were to be saluted, referred to as "sir," and given first preference wherever they went, whatever they did. With the old Blue Hat class gone, they were now the "top dogs."

"YOU—CANDIDATE!...POST!" A solitary finger was pointing at Mark Allen.

"Sir, Candidate Allen, yes, sir!" He dropped his duffel bag and hurried forward. He saluted.

"Where are you from, Candidate Allen?"

"Delaware, sir..."

"WHAT WAS THAT?"

"Sir, Candidate Allen, Delaware, sir!"

"Drop and give me ten."

"Sir, Candidate Allen, yes, sir!"

At first, the rest of them were stunned, loaded as they were with bags and gear. Then they remembered and plunged to the ground alongside Allen and counted push-up cadence.

"SO—!" roared half a dozen fresh-charging seniors, "we have 'unity' and 'brotherhood' and all that neat shit."

Seymore, alongside Allen, said, "Sir, Candidate Cutter, yes, sir!"

"Well, Candidate Cutter," said a medium-built senior now stooping low to look Seymore square in the face. "When you fly in the 'fifty-five' or the 'twenty-three' and your engine quits, I'll bet you a million dollars not one of your classmates pulls the fuel on his aircraft and goes down with you—"

Everyone stopped. There was a long pause. Finally Cutter said, "Sir, I think there is a strong element of truth in that. Yessir, a strong element of truth..."

Flight Alpha One had the rooms on the top floor, north end, of a modern three-story barrack. They were now members of 3rd Warrant Officer Candidate Company, the "new" Blue Hats. A holdover senior, wearing an orange tab behind the WOC brass on his cap, directed them to choose whom they wished to room with...even which room to bunk in.

"We really get a choice?" Sandy asked, incredulously.

Victor R. Beaver

"That's affirmative," the senior candidate said. Thin and wiry, Senior Candidate Walker sported an inch-growth of light blonde hair and had a soft-spoken, easy-going manner about him, just the opposite of Senior Candidate Tyree.

"Hey, this place just might be all right."

"What's our tac like?" Tom Adkins, the artist, asked.

"Mr. Drakeman? He'll be too good for you guys, that's for sure."

Seymore, Sandy, and Mark decided to room together. Theirs was on the west side of the building. The concrete floors were shiny, polished almost like glass. There were three desks and three bunks and three sets of built-in wall lockers, and three separate overhead storage areas. The room had an airy, expansive feel to it, unlike the tiny cubicles in the open bay barracks they had just left. They plopped their gear down and flipped a coin to see who would get the lone bed: the losers would have to share the bunk-bed arrangement. Mark won the toss.

"I get the bottom bunk this time," Cutter said, "since you had it last."

"Okay, okay, you don't have to be a crybaby about it."

Ron Bowden had been chosen to be the interim platoon leader during the move, Pete Cochran, the platoon sergeant. Willie Cottrell and Ned Symington were the candidate company XO and CO, respectively. By two o'clock most of the class was settled in. Symington had called one formation directly after the noon meal, which most felt still too hungover to partake. He explained that they had a different responsibility now: to "really" conduct themselves according to the WOC Handbook, to salute and treat with respect the senior candidates as they hoped someday to be treated. "And tone it down with the pushups," he exclaimed. "We've got to save our strength for flying!"

"Flight Alpha One. Formation at fourteen forty-five hours," Ron Bowden called down the hall.

Heads poked out from doorways.

"What for this time, damnit? I'm not done setting up my displays."

"Our tac, Mr. Drakeman, wants to give us a briefing."

"Oh...good enough for me."

They were seated on the grass in the shade of a large sycamore. CW2 Drakeman and Senior Candidate Walker were in front of them. Like Walker, Drakeman, they quickly found, also had a casual, easy-going manner about him. They wondered when the boom would fall.

"Smoke if you got'em," their new tactical training officer said.

Zippos flicked; the smoke swirled.

"Gentlemen, welcome to the flight-line barracks. I'm not going to bore you with any kind of pep talk. This is my first class as a tac officer. Frankly, I'm not cut out for this job. Why am I admitting this? Because I'm not a hard-ass—not by a long shot. You're about to start flying and I remember how tough it was. The last thing you need from me is a heavy ration of shit everyday. I'm not going to scream at you or harass you. I'm sure you got a bellyful of that in preflight.

The Sky Soldiers

You're here to learn to fly, not march or dig a foxhole. Therefore I mean to make it as easy as I can for you. My rules are simple: keep your rooms clean and orderly, do your lessons on time, hold fast to the SOP as outlined in the WOC Handbook, and I'll leave you alone. I'll inspect rooms daily. I'll conduct in-ranks inspections. I'll point out discrepancies. I expect them to be corrected. I will mete out demerits, but I want you to know that I'm as concerned as you that you get time away from here. You need to bug out on the weekends...so you can come back relaxed for a new week of flying.

"You married guys, I know it's tough. It was recommended that you leave your families behind. For some that was impossible. Yet I can't play favorites just because they're here. That's why I don't want to be too hard on all of you. This way everyone gets a break." He paused and surveyed their faces; mouths stood agape.

"I'll entertain any questions you have...about flying...about Vietnam...about what I expect of you."

There were none. No one wanted to shatter any bubbles. They couldn't believe their good fortune: a tac officer who acted like a real human being and a senior candidate willing to clue them in on the weeks to come.

Cutter raised his hand. "Sir, I...uh...think I speak for all of us. We appreciate your attitude. You won't be disappointed. We do have one request."

"What is it?"

"With your permission, sir, Candidate Adkins"—Seymore pointed to their resident Michelangelo—"would like to do some artwork in the latrine, on the walls and shitter doors. Paintings of helicopters and such."

Drakeman frowned.

"It would really help morale, sir," Cutter added.

The mild-mannered warrant officer thought for a moment. Nothing in writing said it couldn't be done. *Why not? It would be just like in Vietnam. We painted helicopter nosecovers with all kinds of artwork.* "Sure. Go ahead. But I want to see sample drawings before you paint."

"Yessir. Thank you, sir."

Finally, Ron Bowden, who had his wife living in the area, spoke up: "Sir, when can we release the married guys to be with their wives and families? It's been a long four weeks, sir...if you know what I mean."

Drakeman cracked the slightest smile. "Okay, here's the deal. As soon as your displays are set up and your bunks are made, I'll inspect. If everything looks fairly regulation...release time will be at eighteen hundred. That'll be for everyone. I'll expect you all back tomorrow, Sunday, at fourteen hundred hours."

Victor R. Beaver

Chapter 14

COBRA HALL. CHECKRIDE DAY, A DAY each student would be allowed to demonstrate his mastery of the flight procedures associated with the AH-1G aircraft. Captain Smith, the flight commander, began to match students and checkpilots. "Mr. Grange and Mr. Finken—"

"—binder, sir. Duard D. Finkenbinder."

"You'll be with Mr. Cuthbert."

"Captain Nettles and Lieutenant Nolan, you'll be with Mr. Jardine."

"I'll be taking Mr. Thomas and Lieutenant Doyle."

"Mr. Pollard, you'll have Mr. Anderson and Mr. Quincey."

When the captain finished, everyone moved to the proper tables; introductions were exchanged and the evaluations begun.

"Captain Nettles," started Jardine, "recite the emergency procedure for a 'Hydraulic System 1 Failure.'"

The class leader squirmed. "Yessir..."

Jardine smiled. "Sir," he whispered, "I'm a warrant officer. You don't have to call *me* 'sir.'"

The captain's face flushed. "Sorry..." Nettles thought for a moment. "The procedure is 'Emergency collective hydraulic switch—OFF. SCAS—disengage yaw channel. AC weapons sight circuit breaker—OUT. Perform running landing, fifty knots minimum airspeed. On final approach, emergency collective hydraulic switch—ON.'"

Jardine nodded. "Very good, sir. Lieutenant Nolan, what are the indications of an 'inlet guide vane actuator failure,' in the closed position?"

"If the guide vanes fail in the closed position, a maximum of twenty to twenty-five psi of torque will be available. N2, N1, rotor, and EGT readings will be normal until we apply collective pitch. An attempt to apply power above twenty to twenty-five psi of torque will result in deterioration of N2 and rotor rpm and an increase in N1 and EGT readings." (Turbine engine performance indicators: N2, an equivalent term for engine speed or rpm; torque, in psi, pounds per square inch, the amount of twisting pressure imposed on the engine output shaft to the transmission; N1, or gas producer turbine speed, in percent; and EGT, exhaust gas temperature, indications in degrees Celsius.)

"How do we react to this?"

"Well...we shouldn't place the governor switch in the emergency position. This won't—"

"Please, Lieutenant," Jardine interrupted, "just answer the question."

Nolan nodded. Rule Number One when taking an Army flight checkride: Don't answer a question that wasn't asked. "Okay. 'Collective—maintain N2

The Sky Soldiers

rpm. Wing stores—jettison as appropriate to maintain altitude. Land, planning for a minimum power approach.'"

"Very good." Jardine looked toward Captain Nettles. "Sir, how do we, with the collective pitch control lever, maintain N2 rpm?"

"We...this means that...we—I can't remember. I'm sorry..."

Jardine glanced at Nolan. "I think what he's trying to say," Mike offered, "is that we don't use anymore power than we have to, within the limits of what torque pressure is available, to maintain flight and the N2 in the proper rpm range."

Jardine looked toward Captain Nettles. "Do you agree with that, sir?"

The class leader nodded. "Yes, that's...that's what I was going to say."

Jardine said, "Sir, I'm not trying to embarrass you. For us, it's just as important to know what you don't know...as what you do. Please, don't feel bad if you can't remember something. If you need more time in the course to get it right, that's what we're here for."

"Okay, yeah...sure."

Jardine decided to try the first "one eighty" autorotation. He asked Nolan to sit back and watch. At the stagefield, this maneuver required that they turn one hundred and eighty degrees from their original groundtrack (simulating an engine failure with a turning maneuver to land the aircraft aligned into the wind), to land on the outermost hard-surface lane. (There were usually four to six hard-surface lanes, appropriately spaced, several hundred yards long, at a training stagefield.) They had already gone through all of the other required maneuvers. Mike Nolan felt good. He glanced at the ship's clock. Two and a half hours had passed since Jardine asked the first question at the table. The preflight and run-up procedures took half an hour. Jardine asked for the identification of parts of the aircraft and how these parts functioned. Nettles wanted to fly second, so Nolan went through the SCAS checks, explaining how SCAS worked and what steps to take if it malfunctioned.

They were now on the close-in downwind. Jardine requested permission to land. The stagefield tower operator radioed for them to stand by. Jardine said, "It looks like the winds are coming out of the southeast...at about eight knots. This means we'll have to keep our pattern out...enter the maneuver just before we get to the end of the lane. Do you agree, Lieutenant?"

"Sounds good to me."

Jardine called the tower again. "Tower, are we cleared to land on Lane Six?"

"Roger, Falcon Two Three, clear to land Lane Six, winds are one six zero at eleven knots."

Jardine's first entry had them slightly wide and just short of the lane. He made a power recovery, with Nolan calling off the EGT and N1 readings as power (torque pressure) was re-applied to the rotor system. On his second try,

Jardine adjusted the downwind groundtrack a little farther out from the lane and entered the autorotation sooner, to compensate for the added wind velocity. This time he was right on the mark. They were lined up nicely on the extended centerline of the lane. Both pilots could see that with the aircraft's apparent rate of closure they would easily make the short, hard-surface runway. Jardine began the deceleration, trading off airspeed for additional lift. At fifteen feet he applied a small amount of cushioning pitch (to slow the helicopter's rate of descent slightly), then used the rest of the pitch in the blades as they floated down to affect a smooth touchdown; there was practically no ground run.

"Okay, Lieutenant, it's your turn."

"I have the controls," Nolan said.

Nolan followed Jardine's exact flight path after liftoff. He entered the maneuver at about the same spot, putting the collective pitch control lever to the full down position. He spoke aloud the subsequent steps that made up the rest of the maneuver, more for his own benefit than Jardine's. "Okay, throttle to engine idle, add right pedal—trim is good. Now turn left." Nolan diverted his attention outside the cockpit for a split second then back inside at the instrument panel and began to call out: "N1 stabilized and rotor rpm...in the green." His attention focused inside, however, made him inadvertently apply just the slightest amount of right cyclic movement, which slowed their rate of turn. Nolan felt left pressure on the cyclic control stick. When he looked up and out, he could see why. He wasn't banking the aircraft steep enough to get the ship around to line up on the lane. Jardine's left cyclic input was adding the necessary control input to complete the maneuver.

With Jardine's help, Nolan avoided a power recovery and was, thereby, able to land the aircraft. The touchdown was fast and the result was a longer than normal ground run, with the skids (landing gear) sending sparks flying off in all directions along the smooth paved surface. "If your engine fails over a water-filled rice paddy, Lieutenant, I don't think you can afford *any* kind of touchdown speed. You'll ball it up for sure. Let's try it again."

"Okay."

On the close-in downwind, Nolan again made the initial call to the tower requesting permission to land.

"Falcon Two Three, clear to land Lane Six."

"He didn't give the winds," Nolan said.

"I think they're the same," Jardine replied. "Okay, you're coming up on your entry point. Let's enter...Now."

Nolan did as he was told. But this time, as he was bringing the nose of the helicopter around to line up on the lane, he could see right away they were going to land short. "Power recovery," Nolan announced.

"Good call, Lieutenant, good call," the warrant officer remarked. Jardine noted the windsock; the winds had changed considerably since their last attempt, causing them to be well short.

Nolan began to roll the throttle clockwise to rejoin the rotor and N2 needles. Meanwhile, the descent continued. As he brought the engine to full rpm, Nolan looked outside toward the lane then returned his gaze inside to check the instruments. At four hundred feet altitude, he began to apply torque pressure to stop the descent. It was then that he noticed the first signs of trouble. At first he was unable to detect that the torquemeter needle was unable to register above twenty-two psi; and then he saw the N1 and EGT gauge readings indicate higher values than he was accustomed to seeing. "EGT...now seven-twenty. N1 is climbing—!"

Suddenly, Nolan knew exactly what was happening. He quickly reduced collective. "I think we've got an inlet guide—"

"—vane failure," Jardine called; he had recognized the problem, too. "I've got the controls," he announced.

"You've got the controls."

"How coincidental," Jardine remarked. "I'm glad now we talked about this problem at the table." The instructor applied forward cyclic to pick up speed. He saw that indeed they were limited to twenty-two psi of torque—and no more; the slightest increase of collective caused the rpm to drop. What he wanted now was to fly the aircraft at minimum power, at an airspeed fast enough to be safe, yet try to gain a little more altitude for their trip around the traffic pattern. Jardine continued their present course over the lane with the airspeed indicator reading eighty knots. "Tower, this is Falcon Two Three, we're doing a go-around Lane Six. We're declaring an emergency."

"Roger, Two Three. State your problem and intentions. Also state your fuel, please."

"Fuel is seven-fifty pounds. We've got an inlet guide vane actuator failure—closed position. We're going to leave the pattern. I want to swing out on a wide left downwind. I can't pull anymore than twenty-two pounds of torque without an N1 or EGT rise. We'll make a wide base and then set up on final. We'll do a running landing."

"Roger, Two Three. Crash-rescue will be standing by. Clear to land Lane Six." The tower then directed all other traffic in the pattern to remain in position if they were on the ground, or give way to Jardine's aircraft if in the air.

They were now half a mile out on the downwind leg. Jardine felt more comfortable. He had managed to creep the aircraft up another hundred feet by sacrificing a little airspeed in the process. They were now indicating seventy-eight knots. The aircraft was well under control. "Lieutenant Nolan, go ahead and take the controls. No better time than now to practice a real emergency," Jardine said.

"It's just a simple running landing. How many of them have you done with Daddy Don? Dozens...Right? You can handle it."

Nolan felt more than confident. Each day with Pollard, each hour in the cockpit, had all come down to this. They could not easily climb: their power was limited by the failure of the inlet guide vanes to open. Turning sharply was out of the question. Turning required power to maintain altitude. They dared not descend, at least not yet, not until they were lined up on the lane prepared to land. Everything had to be just right. An attempt to increase collective pitch would cause the N2 and rotor rpm to bleed off; a decrease in collective pitch and they would lose precious altitude, that they might not be able to recover before it was time to descend. Suddenly, Nolan saw that he was never steadier on the controls.

Nolan brought the AH-1G around. On Jardine's suggestion, he flew a longer downwind before turning base. On final, they were about a half-mile out, still holding their altitude. Nolan made all his turns very shallow, to maintain altitude and airspeed—especially altitude.

"We've got it made, Lieutenant. Keep up the good work. Plan on touching down at the start of the middle one-third of the lane. If we end up being too shallow on our approach angle, we can compensate by landing short of that point—with at least the first one-third to touch down on."

"Okay," Nolan said.

With very little help from Jardine, Nolan brought the ship over the approach end of the lane doing about sixty knots. Nolan touched down on the centerline, right at the beginning of the middle third. The landing was smooth, a grease-on; Nolan kept his heading with the anti-torque pedals. The aircraft slid about seven helicopter lengths before finally coming to a stop. "Nice, Lieutenant...very nice!"

Back at the briefing room, Daddy Don was beaming. "Lieutenant, you did good. You did good."

Dave was also smiling. He shook Nolan's hand.

"It wasn't anything. Just a dumb run-on landing," Nolan said, embarrassed by all the praise and attention.

"Well, hell, that ain't even what I'm talking about. Of course it was nothing more than a simple run-on landing." Pollard dropped the amenities of rank and protocol and placed his arm around Nolan's shoulders. "What's really important is how quickly you analyzed the problem. Jardine was impressed with that. You could have screwed up a perfectly good Cobra had you called it wrong. I'm proud of you. Congratulations."

"Well...you were a good teacher. I'd like to buy you a beer," Nolan said.

"To hell with that noise. I'm buying you one—both of you. Next is gunnery!"

Chapter 15

"INCOMING! INCOMING!"

Slater turned his head. He tried to open his eyes, but his eyelids felt like they were glued shut.

"INCOMING!...MORTARS!...MORTARS!"

The airfield emergency siren began as a low wail, and then increased in pitch. Kip lifted his head and groaned.

CRRUUMP!...CRRUUMP!

The next split second lasted an eternity. In that time, nothing—absolutely nothing—made sense. He had no idea where he was or who was yelling at him. It took a monumental effort to shift his body and sit.

CRRUUMP!...WHUUUMP!

"Kip! C'mon—!" shouted Leo from his doorway.

Slater stood and lunged forward. Out in the hall he met a rush of men clothed in nothing but their undershorts.

CRRUUMP!

Once outside, Leo turned; Kip followed. Arms and legs and torsos jostled him as everyone crowded into the bunker opening. A second later he found himself in pitch darkness. The strong musty smell of the bunker hit him at once. He felt Leo's arm push him down and then he found himself seated on a wooden bench. A Zippo flicked, illuminating Mac's face as he lit a cigarette. Within moments the bunker bore the sounds of irritated men, their collected groans subdued somewhat by the wail of the siren and the muffled bursts of the mortars.

WHUUMP!......CRUUMMP!

Kip leaned back and drew a breath. He became aware of the din of two Huey gunships right outside the bunker. Then he heard them come to a hover and move forward for takeoff.

"Time—?" someone called.

"Fifty-one seconds," said Randall.

"Not bad...not bad," Kip heard Baumburger reply. Within another few minutes the sound of both gunships diminished, so that all they heard were the wail of the siren and the sound of exploding mortars...sometimes near...sometimes far away...

"Fifty-one seconds...?" Kip stated in disbelief.

CRRUUMP!.....CRUUUMP!

"So far their best lift-off time is forty-eight seconds," stated Robin Henry. His voice sounded almost reverent.

It was then that the queasiness Kip felt in his stomach caught up with him. He felt the urge to vomit, dreaded it, and managed to hold it back. Then he said, "I gotta get outside."

Victor R. Beaver

Leo held him back. "Oh no you don't."

"Oh yeah, who's gonna stop me—?"

WHUUUMP!....CRRUUMP!

"So, okay...I'll stay. God, I feel so miserable...*Jesus...!"*

CRRUUMP!....CRRUUMP!....WHUUUMP!

"I don't know what Charlie's been up to," said Baumburger, "but he's been a helluva lot more regular than this."

"Yeah, seems like we've had about a three-week lull." Slater recognized Wainwright's voice.

"I thought maybe they were saving up for the Christmas truce—give us a triple whammy," Oakerson said.

"Well, it ain't Christmas yet," exclaimed Robin Henry.

A few minutes later the explosions ceased. Everyone began to venture out from the bunker. Kip stepped outside, took a deep breath, then stumbled to the base of a cluster of banana trees; he began to vomit. After another moment the siren sounded the "all clear" signal. Henry and Mac began to follow Leo back into the hootch. "Kip, come on, we're going to the club for a drink," said Leo.

"Screw you..." he groaned.

"Yeah, come on, Slater," Henry urged. "You gotta celebrate your first mortar attack—"

"Celebrate...celebrate," Kip muttered, now beginning the dry heaves. Somehow his fuzzy brain recalled the ironic statement: *"Vietnam...It ain't much, baby, but it's the only war we got."*

It was morning. "Kip, come with me," Tannah said.

"Where to?"

"Over to the Warriors. Last night one of their hootches took a direct hit."

Slater followed Leo to the 336th company area. They found a clean-up crew working with shovels and a black, zippered body bag. The mortar round, one of them related, had entered through the roof. When it exploded, shrapnel shredded everything: wood framing, bedding, stereo equipment, clothing, footlockers, wall-lockers, you name it—it got wasted.

Then they went over to where one man was scooping up what looked like a soft, mushy coagulation of red material mixed with dirt. Another man held the body bag open. "What's that?" Leo asked. The man with the bag looked their way, his face grim. He turned back to the man with the shovel, saying nothing. The man with the shovel held it still. Leo examined the shovel's contents. His eyes grew wide. "What is it?"

"Can't you tell, sir?"

"It...looks like..."

"It's a hand."

Leo then looked inside the bag. He peered for a long moment before he turned away. He went several steps before his knees buckled and he began to heave.

* * *

REVOLT WAS IN THE AIR. EVERYONE was exhausted. At least a dozen pilots were pushing 150 hours flight-time in a given 30-day period. A typical day began at four or five in the morning and ended in the evening around six or seven. Even when they lagered (stood by waiting for the next lift) at the staging sites, who could rest or sleep? The heat and humidity, the constant noise of the gunships coming and going (rearming and refueling), the boredom—and sometimes the panic—all took their toll. Formation flying day after day numbed them. Once back at the airfield they drank. In bed by one or two in the morning, they were awakened a few hours later by CQ runners to start a new day—and the same routine all over again.

Several pilots were in front of the dispensary door. Lieutenant Oremsby, the Blue Tiger platoon leader, stood behind one of his aircraft commanders, a WO1 named Capola next to go in. Behind Oremsby stood Henry, Randall, Slater, and Tannah, all waiting to see the flight surgeon. The ploy was to get medically grounded for a couple of days of rest. "How many hours you got?" Oremsby asked Capola.

"One fifty-eight on the dot," the AC said.

Oremsby sighed. "My ass is fuckin' beat. This shit sucks. Crew rest has been out the window for so damn long."

"What do you think the new CO's going to be like?" Capola asked.

"Who the hell knows? Not me—"

"Well, you're the fuckin' lieutenant."

"So—?"

Henry said, "Captain Slote thinks that because he's a VMI graduate, he'll be a stickler for the regs."

"Good. Maybe he'll bring some fuckin' sanity to this shit."

"Are you shitting me? A guy like that? Give me a break."

* * *

JOURNAL ENTRY, 13 NOVEMBER 1967, Rach Gia

What a peaceful place. A small coastal village on the Gulf of Thailand. Lt. Whitaker and I are here to buy a load of shrimp and crab for the Hail and Farewell party tonight. FNGs (Fucking New Guys) in, short-timers out.

Victor R. Beaver

> *Capt. Ketchum and Fred Oakerson went to Saigon for the steaks. Ketchum, one of our new officers, is a big burly dude with a huge walrus mustache.*
>
> *Major Drummond left a week ago. Major Maes, the XO, has been in charge. Major Neely, the new CO, showed up the day before yesterday.*
>
> *Dreyfuss will DEROS in two days. Baumburger will then be the resident short-timer. Yesterday he and Leo flew together. Baumburger let Leo "bomb" a couple of hootches with grenades in a "free-fire" zone near Vinh Quoi.*

"Step right up, folks. Don't be shy," Captain Ketchum bellowed. "How do you like your steaks? Speak up—I ain't got all goddamn night." The burly captain stood behind a glowing barbeque pit, tongs in hand. He wore a tall white hat borrowed from one of the messhall cooks. They were on the lawn outside the operations hootch. Music played from Leo's stereo set up on the porch. A large selection of other food was on a long table. Since it was a company function, all were invited: cooks and clerks, hangar mechanics, gunners and crewchiefs. Major Neely took the informal gathering as an opportunity to wander among the men and introduce himself. With Captain Slote and Major Maes at his side, the new CO greeted everyone with a forced smile and an extra firm handshake. He was dressed in starched jungle fatigues, spit-shined boots, and his hair was cut skin-close. Everyone smelled a rat.

"Got a medium rare one." "Here's a burnt one—tough as a frickin' boot." "You want me to do what with your steak? Only thirty seconds on each side?! Oakerson, you're a goddamn cannibal!"

"What do you think?" Slater said, popping open another beer. They had finished eating an hour ago and were sitting in wooden lawn chairs on the grass gazing upon a bright silvery moon.

"About what?"

"About the new CO," Kip said. "Do you think he'll let us keep our mustaches?"

"Who knows..." Leo said. After Drummond left, several men decided to test the waters. Their growths were mostly stubble, a "dirty" upper lip. Unable to grow mustaches during flight training, Leo and Kip vowed they would sport ones with long curly-cue ends once they got to Vietnam. Their arrival into the 121st ended that notion. Drummond, at the beginning of his command, had declared them "un-military," thus prohibiting them among his officers.

Leo took a deep draw of his beer, swallowed, then belched. The two men looked toward the southern horizon. They saw the red blinking anti-collision lights of the two T-Bird gunships performing the nightly airfield security duties while the Tigers held their company party. Their appearance had a calming effect on Slater. For the first time since his arrival he felt at ease. The balmy night air, the banana trees swaying in the breeze, the music, the company of men he was with, their camaraderie, all lent to his euphoria. Then Leo's reel-to-reel began playing one of his favorite Frank Sinatra songs:

> *"When I was seventeen,*
> *it was a very good year...*
> *It was a very good year for*
> *small town girls*
> *and soft summer nights.*
> *We'd hide from the lights...*
> *on the village green,*
> *when I was seventeen..."*

By eleven o'clock, most of the pilots and crews had dispersed. Tannah, Slater, Mac, and Henry found themselves at a booth in the Tiger's Den, a round of mixed drinks before them. In one corner of the club, seated at a round table covered with green felt, were the serious card players, a mixture of military and civilian (technician) personnel. Slater watched them. Cards flew across the table and bets were made. Several nights before, he saw one gambler rake in several thousand dollars in MPC as his winnings, which almost prompted him to try his luck.

The sound of the first two booms deafened them. Everyone froze. "Isn't that outgoing...?" someone asked. "Sounds like it..." someone else said. At the northeast end of the airfield, outside the perimeter fence, was an ARVN artillery battery. In the evening, usually before midnight, the ARVN would lob a half dozen shells out to the rice paddies, H&I (harassment & interdiction) fire. *Wake up, Charlie, you bastards! You don't let us sleep, we ain't gonna let you sleep, either!* was the rationale.

BOOM!....CRUUMP!....BOOM!....BOOM!.....CRRUUMP!

"Which is it?" "Fuck, I can't tell—"

"It's both—incoming and outgoing," someone yelled.

CRRUUMP!.....CRRUUUMP!

All of a sudden the mad dash was on. Arms and legs and bodies jostled and intertwined going through the two narrow side doors of the club. Shouts and curses added to the din of the stampede as men tried to keep from spilling their drinks. Kip and Leo followed Henry and Mac as they leaped over the back of the booth they were sitting in and into the mainstream of the evacuation.

CRRUUMMP!...CRRUMP!....WHUUUMP!

"Jesus—that shit's close!"

Finally the siren sounded its shrill wail.

"There's the signal. It's incoming..."

"Thank God. I never would have guessed—"

Victor R. Beaver

Outside, men were running—scrambling toward the bunker, down the narrow corridor that separated the club from the set of officers' quarters next door.

CRRUUUMMP!...CRRUMP!

Kip plowed behind Leo, who pushed Henry in his wake. And then they met the "logjam." A couple of drunk Viking gunpilots, chief warrant officers, old-timers each well into his second Vietnam tour, had stumbled over one another trying to be the first to one of the gunships set for a quick-start. What followed was a time-worn discussion between them:

"God almight damn, Buck. Watch where the hell you're going!" Ben Logan cried.

"What—?" Buck Crenshaw replied. "You tripped me, you lop-eared, sorry-ass excuse for a mule-headed idiot. Git off my back. I gotta get to the helicopter!"

"Bullcrap. You ain't in no condition to fly!"

"The hell—! You're the one that's sloshed."

"Me? I'm a helluva lot more less drunk than you and a damn sight more or less sober—!"

"Now that made a lot of fuckin' goddamn sense!"

CRRUUMMP!...WHUUMP!.....CRRUUMP!

The two men were helping each other up as Kip and Leo skidded to the bunker opening. Kip turned to see how the old-timers were doing. Both had stumbled again over each other's feet. He looked toward the two Viking gunships. They were scooting forward for liftoff even before reaching normal operating rpm (or so it seemed). Their rotor downwash blew back dust and other debris. Logan and Crenshaw stumbled to a tottering halt at the edge of the revetments as the two Huey gunships lumbered away.

"Buck, if you hadn't been in my way—!"

"Me? In your way? Ben, it was your feet I tripped over!"

The explosions ceased within a minute after the two gunships were airborne. Two minutes later the men ventured out from the bunker. Shortly after that the two gunships returned to parking.

"Look—!"

"What...?"

Lieutenant Richards, one of the newer gunpilots, bare-chested and seated in the left seat, opened the cockpit door. Not only had he taken off without a shirt, he was minus his pants, boots, socks—*even his skivvy shorts!*

Amid hoots and catcalls, the bare-assed lieutenant jumped from the ship and made a mad shivering dash for his hootch. Robin Henry, in his drunken state, sighed contentedly. "Them's my Vikings..."

* * *

THE ENTIRE COMPANY OF OFFICERS was seated in the back briefing room of the operations hootch now called Slote's Piece-of-Shit Turquoise Shack. (The walls on the inside of operations had become such an abominable eyesore and a glaring reminder of how little they respected their company operations officer, that they could think of no worse name to give it.) Most of them sat slouched, cigarettes dangling from between their lips. Several had smuggled their drinks over from the Tiger's Den and tried (in vain) to keep them out of sight. They were expectant, curious, and irritated. The meeting was now cutting into their viewing of X-rated flicks to be shown that evening in the movie room in the Den. They glanced at their watches, hoping the briefing wouldn't be too long.

Major Maes, the company executive officer, stood before them next to the podium. "Gentlemen," he said, "there will be no smoking during the briefing." A dull rumble of complaints. "And there will be no drinking." Another rumble of complaints.

In the next instant, Neely appeared in the doorway. Maes stiffened. "Gentlemen, the company commander..." Everyone rose and stood loosely at attention.

Neely advanced to the podium carrying a folder. He opened it and pondered its contents; then he looked up. "Be seated, gentlemen." They sat. And then he spoke: "Let me begin by saying how fortunate I am to be here as your new commanding officer. I have been looking forward to this assignment for quite some time—and with tremendous pleasure. The Soc Trang Tigers have a commendable reputation, a proud history, one that is the envy of all assault helicopter companies in Vietnam." The men stiffened, nodded, then frowned. "This past week I've had a chance to look around, check things over. I must say you have all made quite an impression." The new CO paused. To the man, they envisioned the only kind of impression they could have made: they liked to drink, they liked to fly (but not to the extreme of utter exhaustion), and they all counted down their days to DEROS.

"There are several items, then, I want to discuss with you tonight, changes if you will to our combat program." That did it: their ears perked; their antennae turned.

"Item number one: Flight hours. Your previous commander's policy was that no pilot should fly more than one hundred and forty hours within thirty consecutive days without approval of the flight surgeon. I understand the last part of this policy was very loosely applied."

Neely paused. Half the men nodded their heads while several "no shits" sounded.

Henry elbowed Leo and whispered, "I think here comes the giant shlong."

"Gentlemen, since we operate in a combat environment, and defeating the enemy is our primary goal, by whatever means we see fit, I'm instituting this policy: Each man will judge how much rest he needs, to include the amount of flight time he can handle in any given thirty-day period. If a man can handle more than a hundred and forty hours, I certainly won't stop him from going well about that value; and he won't need the flight surgeon's approval."

Most of them squinted their eyes then rolled them. "Now there is a clever sonofabitch," someone in the back whispered.

"Item number two: Alcohol consumption. Gentlemen, your rate and quantity of alcohol intake is *abominable!*" The tone of Neely's voice raised their eyebrows. "From this moment forward the Tiger's Den will open no earlier than fifteen hundred and close no later than o'one hundred hours. Each of you is an accident waiting to happen. You need to be alert when you fly. I intend to raise the combat efficiency of this unit by one hundred percent. Therefore, this nearly constant drinking has got to *cease—!"*

"We don't drink *all* the time, do we?" someone muttered in the back.

"Item number three: Military bearing and courtesy. This includes saluting, uniforms, haircuts—and mustaches." Neely looked at Captain Ketchum whose mammoth brush covered his entire mouth. Kip and Leo slid down in their seats and covered what little growth they had managed the past week. "We are completely lacking in this area. First and second lieutenants outrank warrant officers. Captains outrank lieutenants. I want to see you people saluting each other. Your uniforms," Neely stated, "are sloppy, almost a disgrace."

"What," whispered Leo, "is all this bullshit?"

"This," answered Randall, "is a man who intends to be a general someday."

"Mustaches, gentlemen," continued Neely, "are out. Period."

"Crap."

"Finally, the enlisted personnel." Neely peered around the room. "They are undisciplined and unruly. I will not tolerate enlisted men who look and act like pirates. As officers, you will exercise your prerogative to correct them. Is that understood?"

A few nodded their heads.

"In the next several days I want to see improvement in all areas. Gentlemen, we're going to make the Flying Tigers of Soc Trang a name synonymous with honor and glory. I also intend to raise the number of combat awards and decorations. From here on your actions in combat will be duly noted.

"Are there any questions or comments?" Neely surveyed the room. Seeing no arms raised, he said:

"That's all, gentlemen. You're dismissed."

Chapter 16

THE MEMBERS OF FLIGHT ALPHA ONE filed into the large flight-briefing room with their brand new flight helmets in hand. "Find yourselves a seat, gentlemen, three to a table," spoke Mr. Goddens, the flight commander, standing behind a large brown podium. He was a short, stout man dressed in a white shirt and gray slacks. He was a member of Southern Airways, Inc., the civilian-contracting firm charged by the Department of the Army to conduct the first phase of flight training. "I'll give you a couple of minutes to get acquainted with your IPs before we start the briefing."

Frank Bartlett, Tom Adkins, and Sandy Adamson introduced themselves to their flight instructor, a man in his early thirties, who extended his hand and said, "Fellas, how're you doing? The name's Gressing. Bud Gressing. Go on, take a seat."

"Thank you, sir."

As Sandy pulled out his chair, he happened to glance at the next table over, where Seymore, Ron Bowden, and Darryl Chancey were getting seated. Their IP was a large, broad-shouldered man whose massive head sported a shock of red hair that flared out from around his ears in great curls. His voice boomed as he spoke. Seymore gave Sandy a look of total consternation; Sandy returned one of total sympathy.

With an eager, infectious smile, Gressing put his three fledgling aviators at ease. He was a tall, large-nosed, bald-headed man with light blue eyes that seemed to laugh when he spoke. He told them to kick back and relax. "Ya'll can't learn nothin' if you're all tensed up." They learned that he was a CW2 pilot in the Texas Army National Guard, that he lived in the Fort Worth area and commuted daily to Downing Army Heliport, and that he enjoyed the challenge of instructing, he'd been doing it for eight years. He also mentioned that he owned a helicopter crop-dusting service. Sandy looked him over as they listened to him explain what they would be doing the first couple of days of flight training. His flight suit was well faded with the edges frayed, due to many, many washings. He wore it jauntily with most of the zippers open, an unforgivable sin for any warrant officer candidate. For an instant, Sandy tried to imagine how many flight hours the man had: thousands, he was certain. "...And we'll be having you boys soloing in no time at all. How's that sound?" Sandy heard Gressing saying.

"About how long will that take, sir?" Frank asked.

"Give or take an hour or so...oooh, I'll have you up there all by your lonesome in fifteen...maybe sixteen hours of dual instruction."

"When will that be?" said Adkins.

"Less than three weeks from now," Gressing replied.

Victor R. Beaver

A few minutes later Mr. Goddens got their attention. He outlined the course of instruction and talked sternly about safety. He spoke of the need to keep heads on a swivel, eyes darting around, always watching out for other aircraft at the stagefield and when leaving or coming into the heliport. "Gentlemen, I guarantee you won't live through a mid-air collision with another TH-55. And if you do live, I guarantee you'll wish you hadn't. So keep those eyeballs clicking. Is that understood?"

"Sir! Yes, sir!"

"One other thing. Listen to your flight instructor. Do what he says. You and he together are what's going to get you through your training. Any questions?" There were none. "You're released to your IPs. Down time is eleven o'clock. Aircraft tail numbers are posted."

After several more minutes of table-talk and getting individual flight records prepared for daily use, Gressing said, "Who'd like to go first?" Then he added, as he reached down by the table to pick up his flight helmet: "The other two will ride the bus to the stagefield."

Sandy raised his hand. "I'd like to go first...if it's all right." Frank and Tom both nodded their approval.

"That's the spirit," Gressing said, hitting the tabletop lightly with his fist. "Well, then, let's git. We're a'wastin' daylight."

Gressing picked up the logbook to their assigned aircraft and the two strolled out onto the ramp. The skies to the east were getting lighter. The ramp and all the helicopters parked on it were bathed in a soft pink glow. As Gressing and Sandy walked toward their aircraft, others of his class followed in the quick-paced footsteps of their instructors. Puppies, thought Sandy, smiling, we're like little puppies following our masters.

At the aircraft, Gressing released each of the three main rotorblades from their tie-downs and secured the tie-downs, neatly bundled, in the front of the instrument panel. Next he connected the battery and checked the battery voltage and afterwards the anti-collision and navigation lights. The walk-around inspection took twenty minutes with Gressing explaining what was critical to check and what kind of discrepancy might cause a "grounding condition." He said, "When in doubt, always call a tech inspector. And if you're still in doubt—don't fly it."

Next, Gressing instructed Sandy how to buckle in, put on his helmet, adjust the chin strap, and plug into the ICS—the intercom and radio system. He helped him set the anti-torque pedals for the length of his legs. Once both men were seated, he showed Sandy how to check the flight controls for any kind of binding, or excessive play, called "slop." From memory, Gressing began to set knobs and switches and check instruments. Sandy followed his every movement. He was certain he wouldn't remember a thing the next time he flew with this man. And this thought made him nervous.

"Relax," Gressing said, sensing the lad's concerns. "In a couple of days, you'll be strapping into this thing like you were born to it."

"Yeah, sure..."

With his flight helmet on, and his body cinched in tight by his seatbelt and shoulder harness (his ass already feeling numb from the tight, webbed seating), and his eyes darting about, and his mind contemplating all the unfamiliar wizardry associated with the little trainer, Gressing looked at him and said:

"You ready?"

"Yes, sir."

"Well then, let's start'er up." And with a loud "CLEAR!" voiced heartily from his left-seat position, Gressing engaged the starter and fiddled with the fuel mixture. Sandy listened as the engine coughed once, twice, a third time—and then "took off," making a deep throaty sound, like that of a rough-running outboard engine, the sound, however, muffled by the insulation of his tight-fitting flight helmet.

Next, Gressing began to engage the clutch. Soon the three rotorblades were whirling overhead, a fast-spinning blur, sounding much like the fluttering of a thousand tiny bird wings. Over the intercom Gressing explained what instruments to check and how to check them. Within minutes Sandy's head was swirling with a dozen all seemingly unrelated details.

Gressing keyed the microphone switch and called the tower for hover-taxi instructions. A jumble of numbers, all foreign and confusing, came rapid-fire back over the radio, which Gressing acknowledged. Within another few seconds, Gressing, with a twist of the throttle, began to drive the engine and rotor rpm to higher indications. When the engine tachometer needle read a fast 2,900 revolutions per minute, Gressing began to move the lever to his left upward until the helicopter began to feel light, airy. Suddenly they were two feet above the ground, with Gressing holding the aircraft steady over the now vacated parking spot.

The TH-55A "training helicopter" rocked and weaved ever so slightly as Gressing hovered the ship toward the taxi-way centerline. It felt to Sandy like they were on a pillow of air. The rotor system, in fact, was creating it's own "relative wind," that airflow across a wing (with the wing at just the right angle and speed) that causes it to become airborne, thus allowing the little trainer to "fly" at a slow-moving pace just above the ground.

Sandy looked around. He saw a ship coming out from its pad guided expertly by the instructor. To their left, Sandy saw another helicopter come up to a hover occupied by only one pilot. "You got a solo student there," remarked Gressing. "One of your upperclassmen. Soon you'll be doing that, going out all by yourself."

Sandy's eyes widened. *Solo...*

Victor R. Beaver

They slowed. The ship ahead of them was over one of the large takeoff pads. The pad, painted white, had a black Maltese cross in the middle of it. There were three such take-off pads marked A, B, and C.

"He'll be lifting here in a second, then it's our turn," Gressing said.

Sandy felt the gooseflesh rise all over his body. In the next few minutes all that he had been waiting for all these past months would come true: a cherished dream realized. How often had he thought of this very moment? Hundreds and hundreds of times. He felt like the luckiest person alive. How many young men would trade places with him? This had to be the ultimate adventure—*learning to fly a helicopter!*

The helicopter to their front received its clearance to take off. Sandy watched as it began to lift upward, its tiny tail jockeying slightly, its rotorblades overhead a nearly invisible blur. Soon it appeared as small as a dime.

It was now their turn.

Gressing called the tower and was given permission to take their position over the Maltese Cross. He brought the little ship forward. And then they were cleared to take off. "Okay...hang onto your hat...'cause here we go."

Fascinated by Gressing's obvious expert handling of the controls, Sandy watched him bring the lever to his left up slightly more. His right hand clutched at the control stick in front of him and he moved that ever so slightly forward. His feet pressed at the two anti-torque pedals, the left quite a bit more forward than the right. The rpm gauge remained steady at 2900 by the twist of the throttle in his left hand. *And he was making it look so easy!* Every part of the ship and its control was an extension of the man himself—every movement performed because it had to be performed. The helicopter and the man were one. And then they were climbing. He watched the ground recede from them; to their front the horizon seemed to blossom out before them; and then he glanced at his watch: they were airborne at exactly thirteen past seven.

They flew east over US Hwy 180. To their left was the Fort Wolter's main post complex. To their front he observed the pall of yellow haze that hung over Fort Worth, some forty miles away. Below them, Sandy noticed cars moving nearly as fast as they were. This seemed odd until he remembered that the top speed of the little helicopter wasn't much greater than most vehicles moving over the ground. Though they were a mere five hundred feet above the earth, the young warrant officer candidate felt like he could see all of Texas. And what a grand feeling it was!

"Well, young fella," Bud Gressing said, "how about you taking this cyclic control stick and seein' if you can't keep this little critter aimed straight ahead. We want to keep our altitude, too, so don't start a nose dive on me. I'll handle the throttle, the pedals, and the collective."

"All right," Sandy said. He moved his hand forward and gripped the handle of the cyclic control stick.

"Look out toward the horizon," Gressing instructed. "See the tip-path plane, the tips of the rotorblades spinning above the horizon?"

"Yessir."

"Good. What we want to do is keep the same apparent distance between it and the horizon." He felt Gressing's hand move the stick forward and back; the tip of the spinning blades moved down and up (with respect to the horizon) in sync, causing the helicopter to speed up and slow down equally in sync. (The helicopter also began to lose and then gain altitude as well.) "See how I did that?"

"Yessir."

"So, fore and aft movement makes us go faster and slower, and if we don't do something with the power lever here," Gressing said, indicating the control lever both to his and Sandy's left, "we'll descend or climb. Left and right movement of the cyclic makes us go left and right." And then Gressing said, "See that silver-looking water tower to our front about seven miles away?"

"Yessir."

"Let's aim for that...Sounds simple enough, huh?"

"Yessir."

After about three minutes, Sandy was exhausted—and completely flustered. He tried to keep the tips of the helicopter's spinning blades at just the right position above the horizon, but to no avail. At times he would have the ship careening for the ground; other times aiming for the heavens. He'd fixate on the spinning tips and not realize he was in a turn to the left or the right. Then he'd concentrate so hard trying to point the ship toward the water tower, that he'd forget the tip-path plane and be in another climb or dive. It was maddening.

"It takes what's called a 'crosscheck,'" Gressing said, momentarily relieving the lad of the cyclic control stick, "or better still a division of your attention between the two concerns. Glance at the tip-path plane and then look at the water tower for a second...and then peek at the tip-path plane...and then at the tower. Keep your eyeballs moving. If you stare at one thing too long, everything else goes haywire. You got that?"

"Yessir."

"Well, let's try it again."

Miracle of miracles, it worked! He'd look at the tips of the blades and their relation to the horizon and then glance at the tower, still some distance away. And then back to the tip-path plane...then back to the tower. He found he could keep altitude and their direction toward the tower much better, which pleased him immensely.

"You're getting the hang of it."

For the next fifteen minutes Gressing had him manipulate the other flight controls, also one at a time. The anti-torque pedals and the collective pitch-control (power) lever were easier to handle by themselves than the cyclic, but

Victor R. Beaver

when it came time to maintain rpm with the throttle (which was much like that of a motorcycle's), he had fits again. He would make the rpm wind up and Gressing would have to check it with a quick twist in the opposite direction; he'd start to reduce it too far, and again the instructor had to react with opposite movement. In no time at all, Sandy felt he was a spastic misfit, a fraud, undeserving of Gressing's patient attention.

"Fella, I think you've got the makin's of a pretty good pilot—" the instructor suddenly exclaimed.

"You're kidding...I do?"

"Why, hell yeah—" And then Bud Gressing gave the young student pilot a hearty, joyous laugh. "Man o' man, can you believe they pay us to do what we're doing. Ssssshh...don't breath a word of it to anyone."

Finally they came to the Tuy Hoa stagefield traffic pattern, from the southeast (the stagefields were given names of actual places in Vietnam), entering on a right downwind. Other helicopters were already in the pattern, so Gressing told Sandy to keep his eyes peeled for their movements. Gressing turned the aircraft on base and then final and then brought the TH-55A to a hover over Lane One. He moved the ship toward the base of the tower. Next to the tower sat a small white wooden building called the stagefield house, a place where students could study or seek refreshments from the coin-operated machines. Around the house Sandy saw his classmates, those who rode to the stagefield on the bus. They all appeared eager to have their first turn at the controls with their flight instructors. Gressing put the ship on the ground. "Get ole Frank Bartlett over here. We'll see what his mettle is made of." As Sandy was unbuckling, Gressing said, "You did good. I'll have you soloing in no time."

Sandy went to Tom and Frank, saying to Frank that he was next. He then turned and gave Gressing a thumbs-up. He felt great. "How was it?" Frank asked, taking his flight helmet out of the bag.

"No sweat," Sandy replied. "Piece of cake...piece of cake."

Chapter 17

"**D**AMNIT, LOOK AT ME," DADDY DON Pollard growled, as he adjusted the little mirror from his front-seat position to get a better look at Dave Grange's face in the back.

"I am," Grange answered, peering hard at Daddy Don. For the past two days the old IP had been riding them unmercifully. Mike and Dave both sensed something wrong...something eating at the man.

They had just spent, for the second morning in a row, a nearly intolerable one and a half hours preflighting both the aircraft and the AH-1G's armament systems. Afterwards, thirty minutes more were spent in the cockpit performing the run-up checks. With the Cobra now gun-configured, their training had elevated to a more critical—and dangerous—plane.

The day before had been all demonstration. Pollard went over the cockpit "switchology" essential for the safe operation of the weapons systems. He reiterated time and again how important verbal confirmation was over the weapons' switch positions between the front- and back-seat pilots. "Remember, I can't see what you've done. I have to trust you. Don't pull a *gabroni* on me—!"

When they got to the firing range they spent the first fifteen minutes discussing the radio terminologies essential for safe range operation. "Range Control has to know, just like I do, exactly what you're doing—whether you're 'hot' or 'cold', armed or safe. Is that understood, Lieutenant?"

"Of course, *Mister* Pollard."

During the first firing demonstration, Nolan sat in the front seat while Pollard, during several passes over the range, fired off multiple pairs of 2.75-inch rockets and let go short and long bursts from the two pod-mounted 7.62mm high-rate automatic guns. When the rockets left their tubes they made a high-pitched *swiffing!* sound and emitted a trail of intense light and smoke. The rocket pairs crossed paths about fifteen hundred meters in front of them, then detonated a split second later. Each set of explosions enveloped the target, an APC (armored personnel carrier) or an old World War II tank, with gray smoke. Then they heard a *WHUUMP!...WHUUMP!* about a second later. When Pollard fired the minigun system, they heard the sound of the guns immediately, but the rounds stitched the ground silent as death down range.

The front seat of the Cobra was the co-pilot "slash" gunner's station. (Before any pilot who flew in the Cobra later in Vietnam could advance to the back seat, the aircraft commander's station, he had to do his time in the front seat.) Pollard showed them how to prepare the TSU (telescopic sighting unit) for firing, how to set the range and adjust the retical. Wherever the gunner looked, sighting through the unit with the "action-bar" depressed, so pointed the turret on the front of the ship. Housed within the turret were the barrels of the minigun and the tube of the

40mm grenade launcher. A separate trigger fired each weapon. "Fire three-second bursts minimum when shooting the miniguns," Pollard had told them at the table.

"Helps keep the guns from jamming," Dave offered, already familiar with the miniguns by his previous gunship experience.

"Roger that, you got the picture, Mr. Grange."

The turret was activated by electrical impulses sent from and by the movement of the TSU. The minigun barrels (and the 40mm tube) within the turret could swivel left and right, up and down. The turret could also go to the stowed (fixed) position, allowing the back-seat pilot to fire the turret weapons, aiming them by pointing the nose of the ship at the target. (This action was likely to be taken should the front-seat pilot become incapacitated or killed.)

In the beginning Nolan's lack of experience with the TSU caused the miniguns to jam several times. They had to set down on one of the range pads, pointed down range, while the armament people worked to fix the problem. "Okay," said Pollard, as they waited for the jam to be cleared, "let me run through this shit again. The turret always goes to the stowed position when you release the action-bar. With the action-bar depressed, you begin, by telescopic movement, to move the turret. If you move the telescopic sight without first depressing the action-bar, the turret will not move—until you depress the action-bar. And then, goddamnit, the turret will fucking jerk, instead of move smoothly, to where the TSU is pointed. You got that?"

"Yes, I do."

"Good. Same-same now when you release the action-bar after shooting. The low rate of fire is two thousand rounds per minute; the high rate is four thousand. *Jesus*, even the low rate is fast. So don't release the action-bar with the trigger still depressed. What's going to happen? The turret will jerk to the stowed position, even while it's firing. Plus, when you release the action-bar and the trigger at the same time, there is an automatic clearing of the weapon of unexpended rounds; at the same time the barrel continues to rotate as the turret is slewing. The turret's quick stowing movement with this going on can also cause a jam. Release the trigger first, then point the TSU forward before you release the action-bar. Keeps the turret from slewing too quickly. And saves wear and tear. How's that sound, Lieutenant?"

"Gotcha."

"You'll learn, Lieutenant...you'll learn," said Pollard; his voice sounded anxious, testy.

Firing the chunker, nickname for the M129 grenade launcher, was like spitting exploding fist-size rocks at a target. It was an anti-personnel weapon capable of firing at a rate of 400 rounds per minute fragmentation-type projectiles in ten-second bursts. The effective-kill bursting radius of a 40mm projectile was 15 me-

The Sky Soldiers

ters. As the old saying went, *"Close only counts in horseshoes and grenades...and nuclear bombs."*

"Control, Falcon Two One, going hot across the line," Dave Grange reported. It was their third day on the range. Dave was in the back seat. He had fired the turret in the stowed position. He was now coming around for his first rocket-run, in high-speed configuration. (Nolan was in the stagefield house, awaiting his turn to fly.)

"Roger, Two One," came the reply from Range Control.

From three thousand feet, Dave rolled in on the target using a 45-degree dive angle. At twenty-five hundred feet he pressed the button on top the cyclic control stick and fired off three pairs of rockets. (Had he been watching his diving run from a distance, he would have detected a momentary stoppage of their movement in flight due to the rockets' sudden burst from the tubes.) A moment later the six rockets exploded, sending out a shock wave that could be felt on the ground as far as ten miles away. The target, an APC, ripped and shredded after many such hits, disappeared in gray smoke. Dave continued the dive to release another pair of rockets. He adjusted the aircraft's pitch and roll attitude to have the cross hairs on the M73 reflex sight exactly centered. He was passing through seventeen hundred feet when he noticed the aircraft not precisely in trim. He spent another split second adjusting the pedals to center the trim ball. By thirteen hundred feet he was ready to fire. Pollard came over the intercom: "When the hell are you going to shoot—?"

Dave glanced at his altimeter. He saw the needle passing through one thousand feet and realized his mistake. He felt Pollard come on the controls and begin to pull the Cobra out of the dive. "You're an experienced gunpilot," he heard Pollard saying. "Can't you recognize the symptoms of target fixation—?"

"God, what was I doing?" Dave said, "I can't believe it—"

"Range Control, Falcon Two One, breaking left—systems are cold," reported Pollard.

Dave "safed" the systems.

"Roger, Falcon Two One."

"Is the master-arm switch off?" Pollard asked Dave.

"Yes."

"Then announce it to me!"

"I'm announcing it now! Christ! What's with you?"

"Never mind...never mind."

Pollard was on the controls in the front seat. He and Nolan had just made a low pass over the range, with a right break to leave the range for the return flight to the airfield. The armaments systems had been checked and any unexpended ammunition unloaded before departure. Don Pollard brought the ship around tight in the turn; the positive G-forces pressed Nolan into the seat; his head and stomach felt strange; these sensations he hoped to get used to over time. When Pollard and Dave returned after their flight period together, Nolan detected strong tension between the two men. Dave climbed out of the cockpit and gave Mike a look of discouragement—and bewilderment.

"Lieutenant Nolan," came Pollard over the intercom.

"Yes, go ahead."

"How many pounds of thrust is the AH-1G rotor system capable of delivering?"

"About twenty-one thousand pounds."

"At or above what airspeed does the rotor system deliver this amount of thrust?"

"At or above one hundred fifty knots indicated," Nolan recited.

"At what altitude do we begin a high-speed dive?"

"At three thousand feet."

Pollard then asked, "At what minimum altitude should we begin our pullout?"

"At one thousand feet...or one hundred seventy knots."

"Wrong answer, Lieutenant. But why?"

Mike peered at Pollard in the little mirror. *Wrong answer...but why?*

"I'll explain, Lieutenant. If we begin our pullout at one thousand feet, we won't be indicating a positive climb until six hundred feet—or less. Remember it may take as much as five hundred feet of altitude *loss* to fully recover from a high-speed dive. At five hundred above the ground, Lieutenant, Charlie could blow your shit away with a simple pop gun. You don't want that, do you, Lieutenant?"

"No, of course not...I understand that."

"Do you really, Lieutenant?"

In the little mirror the two sets of eyes locked on to each other. "Yes—I do, *Mister* Pollard."

* * *

THE TWO MEN WERE LEAVING COBRA Hall. It was late Friday afternoon. "What say we go have a drink—I'm buying?" Dave offered.

"Sounds good to me," Nolan replied. "But let's go someplace quiet. The officers' club is beginning to drive me nuts."

All afternoon Pollard had badgered them over trivial matters, small mistakes they made that even they knew were of no real consequence. On Thursday, Daddy Don had talked them through the switch positions and firing sequences. Today he required them to do it on their own. All three men were drained.

The Sky Soldiers

The night before the two "stick buddies" immersed themselves in the components of the M134 and M129 armament systems. Pollard also required them to be familiar with the operation of the 7.62 miniguns and the 2.75-inch rocket launch apparatus. Pollard had earlier discussed emergency situations that could occur with the weapons: "runaway" guns or a rocket misfire. They had to recite what they would do to handle the emergency. "Above all—keep the helicopter pointed down range," he exclaimed.

After changing into civilian clothes, Mike and Dave drove to the outskirts of Savannah and stopped at a quiet-appearing lounge. They found an empty booth in one corner and ordered their drinks.

"What do you think is the matter with our main man?" Nolan asked.

"Beats me. He sure has turned the tables on us."

"Maybe something's gone haywire between him and his woman."

"Could be."

"I wonder if that's the reason I never got married," Nolan stated. "Women. You can't please them." And then he said, "Besides, I'd rather be fishing than fussing with a house, a bunch of kids, and a white picket fence. My old man's got a fishing charter business in Marathon, on the Florida Keys. We're going in together after I retire."

"So, Mike, you're a 'lifer,' eh?"

"Like hell, goddamnit. I'm a career combat soldier," Mike responded. "There's a big difference. A lifer is a ticket-punching sonofabitch whose only interest is to get the most for doing the least. Usually, he does it by kissing ass, not sticking his neck out, nodding yes to every goddamn little thing his commander says. Whatever job he does, he's only in it for what he can get out of it, usually nothing more than a good OER, than how much he can put into it. He's in it for the rank and the retirement. Me, I just want to do the job, any job, the best I can. The reward, or in this case, the rank and retirement, will come of its own accord. Sure, I'm looking forward to retirement. Deep down I'm a civilian at heart. Who isn't? I'd also like to make major before I go. That's realistic. I won't go any higher. Beyond major, they start taking away parts of your brain, to turn you into a spineless sonofabitch. They'll have a hard time doing that to me. I haven't got a whole lot of gray matter to give up. Besides, I'm too cantankerous. In my own realm I'm as bad as Pollard. God, he's been a real shit." Mike changed the subject. "What about you? What are you in this man's army for? It's gotta be something."

"Oh, the experience, I suppose. My country hasn't got a war to fight, so—"

"You're country? Where the hell you from?"

"Canada."

"Canada? Well, I'll be damned. Where at in Canada?"

"Prince George, British Columbia."

"No shit. So you came to the United States to get into a war. That's ironic. Our guys split and go to Canada to avoid the war. That's pretty weird."

"Yeah, I guess."

"Doesn't it seem weird to you?"

"Not really. We Canadians are a pretty tolerant people. And I have to admit, we like a good fight. But your people who have come up to Canada to avoid the draft, they have to do what's right for them."

"They're a bunch of chickenshits, if you ask me."

"You think so?"

"I know so."

"Perhaps. Interestingly, though, I grew up in a strict religious family. Seventh Day Adventist. My father was a minister. He's dead now. He was a pacifist, but I also knew him to be a man of high principle. He preached that a man faced with a moral dilemma would be better off stating for all to hear 'I can't,' rather than 'I won't,' if asked to do something his conscience doesn't allow. He said this would indicate that he was willing to suffer the consequences of his actions. 'I won't,' my father told me, implies a kind of childish rebellion." Dave Grange paused and signaled for the waitress to replenish their drinks.

Nolan thought for a moment. "Seems to me, then, a lot of our guys, by going to Canada, are saying they *won't* be drafted."

"I tend to agree, but then their only alternative is jail. I don't believe they belong in jail, either. Maybe, too, that's why so many of your countrymen allow themselves to be drafted, since because to them the only alternative *is* jail. Those who fled to Canada are suffering the consequences of their actions, you can bet on it, by being isolated from their homes and families."

"Bullshit. They could join instead of being drafted. Then they could pick their MOS. Hell, maybe they could avoid going to Vietnam altogether—"

Dave raised an eyebrow. "Mike, have you ever wondered about true pacifism?"

"No, why should I?"

"Take the Amish, for example. They live in an orderly society because someone is willing to do the fighting for them, if not directly then indirectly. But what if there was no one around to defend them? Would they just stand before an enemy to be slaughtered? Their homes and possessions ravaged? Aren't their lives, the fruits of their labors, worth anything? Maybe I didn't have to go to Vietnam, but someone has to."

"And you, a Canadian citizen, have volunteered where some of our guys won't. That really rubs me the wrong way."

"Funny, but Vietnam was just happening when I joined your Marines," Grange said.

"You were in the Marines?"

"For four years. Then I left and joined the Army to get into the flight training program."

"How old are you, anyway?"

"Almost twenty-six."

"Shit, I had you pegged a lot younger."

Dave said, "You were over there as an advisor. You know what the Viet Cong are like. They're ruthless. Their propaganda has everyone believing that the Americans are the aggressors. Well, I admit your country has fumbled and stumbled and your news people are damn hard on you. That doesn't alter what purpose you Americans have over there."

"And that is...?"

"Wolfhounds. To keep the wolves at bay."

Saturday was spent deep in the books and the procedures. The two men, as they had done on the previous two weekends, drilled each other again and again on the armament systems, on the switch positions, on the gunnery emergency procedures, and range control radio calls and range operating procedures. They wanted to be sharp Monday morning to keep Pollard's wolfish anger at bay. Deep down, though, they knew they weren't driving each other to be the best just to satisfy Daddy Don: they were doing it to insure their own survival; they wanted "to make the enemy die for his country, his ideals."

On Sunday, Dave asked Mike if he would accompany him on a quick trip to Parris Island, the East Coast Marine Corps recruit training depot. "I want to see an old friend," Grange said, "a gunnery sergeant I used to know. We were at Da Nang together in '65. The last I heard he was a DI pushing boots. When he knew I was interested in flying, he tried to get me a flight training slot at Pensacola, but the red tape was horrendous. I thought I'd see how he was doing."

The drive took less than an hour. As they passed through the Parris Island gate, a husky yet trim-looking corporal, wearing a white service hat, blue trousers with red piping, and tan shirt and tie, saluted them smartly.

"Damn, that's impressive," Nolan commented.

Dave grinned. "A marine pays a high price to wear that uniform."

They found the address they were looking for. It was a single two-story barrack set off on a side street near a row of Quonset huts. Dave had gone through boot camp at Camp Pendleton, on the West Coast. What he saw was a mirror image of the training he had received six years earlier. Shaved-headed recruits, about fifty of them, were in the hot sun, on a grassy strip of ground, in the push-up position, arms straight, heads up, teeth gritting at the strain. Dave had no idea how long they had been in that position, but they looked like they were well into their torture. Two drill instructors, their hands behind their backs, were walking up and down the row of men. Dave parked the car along the side of the road to watch.

Victor R. Beaver

"Fucking maggots. DOWN! Let's go down—AND HOLD IT!" they heard one of the DIs say. His voice boomed across the grounds.

Each recruit lowered his upper torso, inch by measure inch, until his nose just touched the ground. Arms quivered, bodies shook, faces were gripped in pain; sweat poured from every forehead.

"LET'S HOLD IT…HOLD IT…HOLD IT…" For what seemed an eternity the men held the nearly impossible position they were in, until one of them collapsed. The two drill instructors raced over to the prone-positioned lad.

"GET UP! GET UP! GODDAMNIT!" they shouted no more than two inches from the young man's ears. "WHAT'S THE MATTER, MAGGOT? This isn't shit compared to what Victor Charlie will do to you! You just killed your whole squad by quitting, you dip-shit little cunt! GET YOUR ASS UP! GET UP! GET UP!" Somehow, either out of desperation, self-preservation, fear, or just plain pride, the recruit began to raise his torso. One of the DIs had his hand on the lad's head, forcing it down. The recruit strained to keep his head from being shoved into the ground. Mike and Dave, even from this distance, could see the agony he was in.

"I know exactly what he's thinking," Dave said. "This very instant he's wondering how on this green earth he's going to last one more second like that. He could give a shit less about the next minute or the next hour or the next day. All he wants to do is survive the next second. And if he can do that, then he prays to survive the next. And then the one after that."

They watched for another minute. The recruit, over whom the DIs hovered, had not given up. "He'll make it," Nolan said. "Somehow."

"Yeah, just like we'll make it past Daddy Don—somehow."

"Yes, sir, I know who you're talking about," said the gunnery sergeant seated at the desk. "Sergeant Stephen Travois went back to Vietnam about two months ago. We got word a couple of weeks ago he was a KIA. Got it on a patrol near Quang Tri."

Grange's face turned white. "KIA…?"

"Yes, sir. I'm sorry."

"Yeah…Thanks."

Chapter 18

"**P**ERCIVAL. CHRIST ON A CRUTCH! Are you trying to kill me—?" blasted Red Fleming, Seymore's flight instructor, over the intercom. The helicopter had halted after bouncing and jostling nearly halfway down the lane. At the moment they sat cockeyed in front of the stagefield control tower. Seymore could see Mr. Goddens, the flight commander, in the tower, behind the tower window, tearing out the last of his hair.

"No-no, sir," screeched Seymore P. ("P" for Percival) Cutter.

"That was the worst autorotation I have ever seen," cried Fleming. "When God was giving out brains, hand-eye coordination, and just plain good old country common sense, what did you tell him? 'Oh...no, none of that for me...thanks anyway—'"

"Sir," pleaded Seymore, "if you'll just give me one more chance. I-I promise I'll do better—Please!"

Seymore cringed in his seat. This verbal onslaught from Fleming had become a daily ritual. No matter how earnest his intentions, he could not bring himself to put the cyclic control stick forward to level the aircraft during the last portion of the landing. It went against his grain—his survival instincts. Instead, he would bring the cyclic stick back—as far back as he could, like drawing in the reins of a horse. This was fine, until it came time to touch down, then the technique was to sort of let the reins go, which Seymore couldn't bring himself to do. On this last descent to the lane without power, Fleming had almost kept his promise. "I'm not going to say a word, Percival," he had told him on the downwind. "I'm not going to touch the controls. If you screw up this time, you're getting a prog-ride. And if this ship is a pile of rubble—I'm going to kill you. Even if you're dead!" But Fleming couldn't help himself. He added the necessary forward cyclic at the last possible moment, muscling the control stick away from Cutter and salvaging what would have been a disaster had he not.

"One more time, Percival," Red Fleming said, the sound of his voice as sweet as honey, "if you don't level the skids, you're going to strike the ground with the aft skids and damage the struts, the rotorblades could flex down, chop off the tailboom, and with it the tailrotor. Without a tailrotor, Percival, this helicopter will spin like a top and crash. Do you want that to happen, Percival?"

"No, sir. Absolutely not, sir."

"Then put the damn cyclic forward after you pull initial cushioning pitch, for crissake—"

"Yessir-yessir."

Fleming twisted the throttle to increase the rpm. He shook his head. "What I'd like to know is how I can get the best two students I've ever had with Bowden and that wimp, Darryl Chancey, and with you, Percival, I have scraped the bottom of the barrel. If I can't let you go solo, I'm not going to let you live, either. Do you read me?"

"Read you? Yessir, loud and clear."

"Good. You have the controls."

"I have the controls, " Cutter said.

Seymore managed somehow to limp the trainer into the air with just the slightest goading from Fleming. Normally, Red Fleming screamed at him throughout the takeoff and all along the crosswind and downwind legs. Then on base he would remain silent, building up a head of steam for his tirade turning from base to final. But this time, even on the downwind, Fleming kept quiet. ("He's trying to figure a way to make my death look like a suicide," thought Seymore, as he looked ahead for the landmark to turn from downwind to base. "So far, all my gradeslips have been written as if to reflect I have no respect for life—neither his nor mine. It would be easy enough. He could send me solo anyway in the next seven days or so and then when I crash and die, he could wash his hands of me. Oh, Lord, that's what he's planning—I just know it!")

At the turning point from downwind to base, which was over a small farm pond, Seymore cleared himself right, called the tower and requested permission to land on Lane One, and then banked the helicopter to the right. He started a descent. "What are you doing now, Percival? I thought we were supposed to maintain our downwind altitude when we do an autorotation." Fleming was being obnoxiously calm.

"Ooooops...Sorreee..." Seymore brought power back in. As he stared at the "joined" rotor and engine tachometer needles, trying to keep them at the proper indications with the throttle, he began a climb above the required altitude.

"Percival, watch your altitude. Watch—Oh, God..."

"Altitude?...What?" trembled Seymore.

"Never mind, Percival...never mind. Turn final now. You're going to overshoot the lane—TURN NOW!" screamed Fleming. Seymore felt the cyclic stick jam to his right. The aircraft went into a sharp bank. Fleming next moved the cyclic left and leveled the ship. They were now lined up on Lane One. "You have the controls."

"I-I've got'em..." Seymore bleated over the intercom.

"You've got'em?...You've got'em what—?"

"Sir, Candidate Cutter, I've got the controls, sir...?"

"Oh Jesus..."

As the training helicopter puttered forward, Seymore kept jerking the cyclic around, trying to line the ship on the extended centerline of the lane, at least how he perceived that imaginary line to be. The aircraft wallowed like a fish out of water. In the left seat, Fleming fumed.

Seymore eyeballed where he should begin the maneuver. "I'm going to enter now," he said. Red Fleming kept silent. "Now...sir?" Cutter looked quickly to his left for guidance.

"Don't stare at me. There's the lane—just do it. What are you waiting for—Christmas?"

"Yessir—I mean, no, sir. Oh, shit...here goes."

Seymore put the collective pitch-control lever full down, rolled the throttle clockwise—the rpm revved up!—which brought Fleming asshole over elbow for the controls. Seymore caught his mistake as Fleming's hand grasped the handle. "Sorrreee..." he said, rotating the throttle now counter-clockwise. They were now in the descent.

"Let's get the damned thing in trim, Percival. Add some right pedal—PLEASE!"

"Yessir, right pedal coming up." Seymore jammed the right anti-torque pedal practically to the stops. The ship swerved madly.

"Percival, you're not driving a goddamn bulldozer—"

"That's correct, sir."

"Remember, Percival, this one has to be good."

"It will-it will."

As the descent continued, Seymore took a deep breath. His mind began to go through the steps: at thirty-five feet, start the deceleration; hold the attitude which allows the helicopter to slow down and at the same time to build or maintain rotor rpm; at five feet, pop in a little cushioning pitch; then as the aircraft settles, put the cyclic forward and pull in the remaining pitch to soften the landing. *I've got it. I can do it. I can—*

"You're starting your decel too high, Percival—we're still a hundred feet up." Seymore then felt Fleming's hand on the cyclic, holding it forward to keep the ship from decelerating too soon. As they descended farther, Fleming said, "Okay, now we're at thirty-five feet." Fleming took his hand from the cyclic. Seymore felt the cyclic stick ram backwards. Not realizing how much of his own counter-pressure he had been applying, Seymore felt the helicopter lurch nose up. Fleming grabbed again for the cyclic. At this point, Seymore didn't know who was flying—him or Fleming. "We're at five feet, Percival, you can apply your initial cushion."

"CUSHION?—Now?" cried Seymore. The beleaguered lad, now OBE (overbecome by events), made an abrupt upward movement with the collective lever, which Fleming also had to check.

"I have the controls—let go of them, Percival. There's no sense in fiddling around anymore today." And with that, Fleming moved the cyclic forward and leveled the skids, using the last of what little rotor rpm was left in the system to soften the landing. The aircraft touched down as gently as a leaf landing on a pond.

Seymore let out a low whistle. "That was a perfect landing, Mr. Fleming. How do you do that?"

"Percival..." Red Fleming said, as he reduced the collective lever to the full-down position and began to bring the rpm back up to the normal operating range, "...I am a transmitter of information and piloting skills. You are supposed to be a workable receiver. The Army has bench-tested you and declared you fit to receive my instruction. Now let's get this straight: my transmitter is always on, up to power, and tuned to the proper channel. I have told you how to do it. I have shown you how to do it. I have helped you do it. But you have persisted, Percival, in always being off frequency and at minimum reception sensitivity. *Plus, you are the most uncoordinated human being I have ever known! Do you read that—?"*

"Yessir," Seymore P. Cutter replied.

"Tomorrow," Red Fleming said, "we'll try it again."

"Tomorrow, sir? I believe tomorrow is Saturday."

Fleming sighed, gratefully. "God sure works miracles in strange ways...doesn't He?"

"Sir...?"

* * *

ACADEMIC CLASSES TOOK UP THE OTHER half of each day. Morning flight line, afternoon classes. Afternoon flight line, morning classes. They were near the end of their first week. They each had about six to eight hours of "dual" flight instruction under their belts. Their blue caps were beginning to fade and lose their stiff shape. Though none of them had soloed, it came as no surprise that Ron Bowden, the ex-Huey crewchief, might be the first. But it came as a complete shock that Darryl Chancey might be the second. Red Fleming, their IP, had nothing but praise for these two. "Aah, what can I say," he said to Bud Gressing one day, "...two out of three's not bad. How are your guys doing?"

"They're doing fine...just fine. The Adamson boy, that lanky, blonde-haired kid, he's my best. Real solid. Good head on his shoulders. Frank Bartlett, my bookworm, is just a little on the slow side. He tries to analyze everything. But he'll come around...no problem."

Red Fleming sighed. "I'll trade my slow one for yours."

"Thanks...but no thanks."

It was after lunch. The doors were open and the warm sunlight poured in. A soft autumn breeze stirred the pages of their notebooks. Their aerodynamics theory instructor stood before them on a raised platform. He held a three-foot-long pointer. A mock-up of a TH-55A rotor head sat on rollers next to him. They tried to show interest, but they kept dozing. The instructor droned on:

"When we move the collective power lever up," Mr. Spencer said in his neat, compact voice, his every word spent like a miser, "we affect a change through these control tubes, which then moves this stationary trunnion, which then moves this rotating swashplate, which then changes the pitch angle in each of the three blades. This causes the aircraft to ascend." Herbert Spencer, also a civilian, was a prim, middle-aged man in his late forties, and never having been in the military, found it much easier on his ulcers to be oblivious to most of his surroundings. Why disturb someone's ecology? His paycheck came to him whether his students were awake and absorbing the material consciously, or asleep and absorbing the same material "unconsciously." As of yet, sleep-learning hadn't been proved ineffective. As a matter of fact, he could swear he learned Spanish that way, listening to a tape-recorder while asleep during the night. Besides, on the day of the test he always reviewed what "possible" questions might be on the multiple-guess quiz, and hinted at the "possible" answers. His students never failed one of his exams. Thus, whenever he paused and looked about the room and saw the majority of the class preflighting the inside of their eyelids, he did not stir them...lest they be dreaming of flying.

* * *

A CHILL WAS IN THE AIR. STREAKS OF sunlight broke through the branches of several cottonwoods in a field nearby. The windsock in the northeast corner of the Tuy Hoa stagefield hung limp; the winds were dead calm: ideal conditions for a fledgling helicopter pilot. Three ships were in the traffic pattern; the others had not yet arrived. Soon, furtive breezes would kick up as the sun rose higher; the little trainers would buck and twist, giving the students a run for their money. It was up for grabs whether a rodeo bronc rider had it any easier to stay on top of the game.

Sandy Adamson was beginning to feel confident. He was reacting without the hesitation of surprise he had done the first several days to Gressing's simulated forced-landing announcements. He found himself automatically putting the collective lever full down and turning quickly into the wind and picking a suitable place to land (though they never actually fully autorotated to the ground except at the stagefields). Gressing was still helping with the power recoveries, but this didn't bother him; it was so easy to overcontrol the throttle and cause the overspeed governor to kick in, creating all manner of wild gyrations.

Square traffic patterns no longer posed a problem. On the climb out he maintained the proper ground track so as not to drift over into someone else's lane—which could be a prelude to a mid-air collision. Just the thought of two helicopters colliding sent shivers up and down his spine. Also, he had his landmarks picked out and was reaching his altitudes at about the right spots before turning from upwind to crosswind and from crosswind to downwind. He had already selected the best available forced landing areas outside the traffic pattern, should Gressing suddenly blurt "Simulated forced landing—!" the three most anticipated (and sometimes most dreaded) words in a student's rapidly expanding aviation vocabulary. They were beginning to believe the helicopter couldn't fly if at least one engine "failure" didn't occur during each training flight with an instructor.

Sandy was about to complete a normal approach to the close end of Lane Two. They were seven feet above the ground when, as had become routine, he felt Gressing come lightly on the controls. It was always at this point that Sandy became uncertain who was supposed to be flying, him or Gressing. A second later Gressing announced: "I have the controls."

"You have the controls," Sandy said, again feeling the heat rise in his chest. Gressing began to hover the helicopter toward the far end of the lane for another practice takeoff. "Sir...I'd like to hover."

"You would, huh?"

"Yes, sir," Sandy said. Immediately he regretted his boldness. But it was always at this point when he felt the most frustrated: *Why isn't he letting me do it? I should be soloing in another seven to eight hours and I haven't even begun to hover. What is he waiting for?* How often had he listened to or seen off in the fields nearby, the wild antics of his classmates, as they described or fought desperately the crazy gyrations of a machine gone mad? *At least they have tried and failed. I haven't even done that!*

"A couple more flights. Trust me, I know the signs," Gressing told him.

The signs? What signs? What is this, some kind of "witchcraft" method Gressing used? He sat back in his seat dejected. He knew that he couldn't really fly a helicopter until he could claim that he had hovered it, had picked it up and set it back onto the ground without assistance (which at this point few of his classmates could claim either). Just like flying an airplane, he overheard Pete Cochran saying one day: "Until you can land the silly thing, you can't claim you can fly it."

* * *

IT WAS FRIDAY AFTERNOON HAPPY HOUR. The Pizza Pub was packed. Located next to the messhall, the pub served as a convenient watering hole and an outlet for pent-up frustrations from the rigors of student flying. Lone Star beer in large pitchers adorned the tabletops, as did circles of sausage and pepperoni and mushrooms on crusted bread, cheese and sauce. The students sipped the sallow liquid out of large paper cups, gulped down the wedges, and belched loudly. Cigarette smoke swirled, the jukebox blared "wailing" country tunes (described by none too few as "cowshit" music), and the whimpering, spontaneous voices of sixty fledgling aviators could be heard amongst the collective din.

"Piss on it...just piss on it," one lad lamented.

"What the hell's the matter now?" said his friend.

"I'll never be able to hover that little sonofabitch...never."

"Look, don't feel bad. My IP assigned me all of Parker County to do my hoverwork in. I was crossing the Parker County line, going into Fort Worth, when he finally took the controls. He accused me of jerking off the helicopter."

"Where were you going?"

"Going—? I didn't want to go anywhere—I was trying to set the damn thing down so I could get out and take a piss!"

"Hey, slick, I heard your IP cut the throttle on you over a wide open field."

"Yeah, that's right—"

"And you turned toward the only cluster of cottonwoods within ten miles."

"Bullshit—that was Greiner, my stick buddy, who did that."

"That's not what I heard, turkey."

"Well...I was trying to get it into the wind."

"My IP wanted to give me an enema yesterday."

"What?"

"Yeah...he wanted to stuff the cyclic stick up my ass. Said I had no respect for God's gift to aviation."

"Who did he say was 'God's gift to aviation?'"

"Him—of course!"

"What stagefield you working out of?"

"Vinh Long."

"Really? Did you know they had a mid-air collision there a couple of classes ago?"

"No shit—?"

"Yeah, really."

"What happened?"

"They said the IP was showing his student how to chase down a coyote."

"And then what happened?"

"The coyote pulled pitch and flew into a buzzard. There were nuts, guts, and feather everywhere—!"

Victor R. Beaver

Chapter 19

SATURDAY MORNING INSPECTION. Seymore P. Cutter, Mark Allen, and Sandy Adamson, snappy looking in their Class A dress greens, stood about in their room fidgeting like little school children. Down the hall they heard the company cadre going from room to room and now theirs was next.

"Oh, God...I just remembered," Seymore whispered, pointing at his upper locker. "I forgot to get rid of the Playboy magazines—"

"Are you kidding?" Sandy hissed.

"I was going to take'em out last night. Jesus, if they find them, I won't be going to Denton tomorrow—"

"You're a degenerate," Mark Allen stated. "Serves you right."

"Hey—I'm only human..."

Sandy said, "Callie's going to think you're deserting her already."

Both Mark and Seymore had planned a picnic with the girls at a state park near Denton. And then Mark became concerned. "Crap. I might get grounded right along with you, you idiot—just for being in the same room."

Seymore gave Mark a quick "sorry about that" smile. But then he reversed course. "We can't let them look up there. I'll go nuts if I don't get out of here this weekend. Fleming's got me so rattled, I-I can't shit...I'm backed up, man!"

"All right—all right, hold onto your shirt, I'll think of something," Mark said quickly.

Footsteps approached. In the next instant, Major Bond, the company commander, appeared in the doorway. Behind him were Captain Manley, the executive officer, and Mr. Drakeman, their tac officer. "ATTEN—HUT!"

"Stand at ease, men," Major Bond said, as he entered the room. The trio relaxed, but only slightly. "How are you candidates doing today?"

"Sir, Candidate Allen, just fine, sir—just fine. Gotta heavy date this weekend. A real pretty little thing from Denton. Met her at the preflight party."

"You and her serious?" Major Bond asked as his eyes swept the room, his gaze falling upon their study desks. "Lamp off center...ten demerits." Drakeman made the note.

"Yessir, I'm real serious about that little gal...if you know what I mean, sir."

"Marriage?" The CO poked his head into Sandy's wall-locker. "Uniforms not spaced correctly...ten demerits."

"Yessir," Allen said. "That's if she'll have me, sir."

"Have you bought a ring?" the executive officer asked, now speaking to show an interest.

"Not yet, sir. I was going to buy one this weekend, in the PX. I was planning to slip it on her finger tomorrow, during church service, sir."

Sandy rolled his eyes. Major Bond said, "Floor dusty in this corner...fifteen demerits."

Next, the CO looked toward Seymore's upper locker. Mark's eyes grew wide. "Sir!—Pardon me, sir. Are-are you married?"

Bond turned. Manley frowned. Drakeman coughed. Sandy and Seymore both held their breaths. "Yes. Four years. Happily, I might add."

"That's very nice, sir. She must be a very lovely woman."

The major nodded his head. He went now toward the bunkbeds. Sandy and Seymore stiffened. He stood in front of Seymore. "Why are you sweating, Candidate Cutter? Are you feeling all right?"

"Sir, Candidate Cutter...couldn't be better...sir," Seymore squeaked.

Bond frowned. "You'd think it was the middle of the summer here, without the air-conditioning running."

"Sir...sometimes it gets pretty hot," continued Cutter, his voice barely above a whisper. "We spend a lot of time...waxing and polishing the floor...we take great pride in our room and equipment. We haven't a thing to hide—"

Mark cringed; he stiffened the moment Major Bond looked his way. "Yes...I'm sure. Well, take care of these discrepancies, Candidate Allen," the major said, now going toward the doorway, "and maybe that young gal will say 'yes' tomorrow."

"Sir, Candidate Allen—yes, sir. We will, sir. Thank you, sir. I'd like for you to meet her, sir—!"

"I'm sure I will. Carry on."

* * *

"LOOK—!" MARK ALLEN WAS POINTING AT one of the helicopters near Lane One. Sandy turned and stared. They were standing together outside the stagefield house. The air all about them was noisy with the throaty sound of more than a dozen TH-55s. An instructor was getting out of the left seat of the helicopter they had their sights on. He re-buckled his abandoned seatbelt and shoulder harness. The man then took his helmet off, exposing a shock of red hair. "Bowden's going solo!"

Fleming turned and gave Ron a thumb's up. By now the stagefield house had emptied. Everyone stood gawking, anxious to see one of their own go on his first solo flight. They could not contain their eagerness—or their envy. Bowden had about eleven hours. The average flight time to solo was fourteen to sixteen hours.

They now watched as the ex-Huey crewchief picked the helicopter up to a hover. He was steady. Then they watched as he moved forward toward the departure end of the lane. Bowden was hovering like he'd been born to it. He stopped. They saw him do a clearing turn to the right. Back now to the departure heading. Steady...steady...Then they saw him begin the climb-out. Shivers coursed through each of them. Eyes were wide. It was hard to fathom that Bowden was in the aircraft by himself—*but he was!* After what seemed like an eternity, they watched him turn the ship right. He was on the crosswind. Their heads turned.

Bowden continued to climb. Again, time stood still. He banked the aircraft again to the right. He was on the downwind, the longest stretch of the traffic pattern. By now Bowden's ship seemed but a large speck in the sky. There were other specks ahead of and behind him, but their eyes were riveted only to his.

Each man had now turned his whole body to keep track of Bowden's progress. Their eyes followed. The little trainer moved slowly. Then their view of the solo aircraft was blocked by the control tower. Everyone shifted to try and catch an early glimpse of it. "There he is," exclaimed Mark.

"He should be ready to turn base," Willie Cottrell said.

"Yeah, right over that cottonwood," Adkins commented.

Bowden now banked right. They saw him start a descent. Everyone's heart skipped a beat. In another minute Ron Bowden would be on final, to make his first of three approaches to the lane. The tension mounted. Some of them breathed heavily, and, oddly, were beginning to tire. In fact, as Bowden flew, so did they—with a fair amount of body language—performing every portion of Bowden's flight as if it were their own. By the time his solo period was over, they would all be limp with exhaustion.

"He should be turning final...right about...now," Sandy stated.

The helicopter was now on final descent. The closer it approached the louder it became. And then the TH-55A went past them. Bowden ignored his audience. He guided the ship down to the far end for another takeoff.

Seymore watched Bowden's second liftoff from inside the stagefield house. He was alone. He saw the helicopter climb out until it once again became a small, reddish-orange speck. He followed Bowden's progress on the downwind. Gradually, his eyes held a blank stare. The lad wondered about his future if he couldn't go solo. And then he envisioned himself in Vietnam humping through the jungle...*sweaty...sticky...bugs and serpents...and mud and sharp elephant grass...and the sound of ammo belts and hardware, rifles and machine guns, metal scraping metal...hot...hot!...HOT!* He slammed his fist into the wall. "You sonofabitch, Red Fleming...*You sonofabitch!*"

"ONE...TWO...THREE...HEAVE!" Arms and legs went out at odd angles as Ron's body sailed through the air— *SPLASH!*

"AGAIN! ONE...TWO...THREE...HEAVE! This time it was Chancey who went topsy-turvy into the Buckhorn Motel swimming pool—*SPLASH!* Drenched and shivering, yet smiling and happy, they both crawled out of the water and ran barefooted and hatless to the bus; the rest of Flight Alpha One followed.

After Bowden had completed his final trip around the pattern and had landed and was outside the helicopter, they rushed over and smothered him with backslaps and handshakes. An hour later they watched Darryl Chancey take his turn. After Bowden, though, the wide-eyed curiosity had become worn but not the thrill. To commemorate the event: a nearby motel swimming pool dunking by one's own classmates. Their first set of aviator wings had just been earned—*their solo wings*.

Willie Cottrell tossed Bowden's boots to him as the bus was pulling away. "Okay, you jack-asses," he called out to the rest of the flight. "If Ron and Darryl can do it, so can we!"

* * *

"YOU'RE GOING TO SIT THERE, SEYMORE, until I say you can go. No beer drinking…no pizza…no nothing," Sandy Adamson stated. "You have to learn this or Red Fleming will drop you like a hot potato. Think about it," he pleaded, "they'll ship you to Vietnam as an infantryman. You don't want that, do you?"

"Oh God, no—" Seymore bleated. They were in their room. It was Wednesday evening. Seymore was seated in one of the room chairs with both his feet propped against Sandy's feet. Sandy was sitting on Seymore's bunk. In Seymore's left hand was a broom handle; he moved it up and down like a lever, simulating the collective pitch-control lever of a helicopter. Clutched in his right hand was a mop-bucket squeezing handle; the bucket sat between his legs; the handle was the "cyclic." Seymore's feet against Sandy's represented the anti-torque pedals. He would press the left "pedal" when increasing collective power and/or throttle, and press against the right "pedal" when reducing power and/or throttle.

"Okay," Sandy said, "you are now in the descent, making a normal approach. The pad is coming closer—" As Sandy spoke, Seymore had his eyes closed trying hard to visualize it. "Now think about it, Seymore…" continued Sandy "…you're having to bring the collective lever up, and move the cyclic slightly forward…so let me see your movements." Sandy expected Seymore to press against his left foot, as he moved the broom handle up, and twist the "throttle" on the handle clockwise (to regulate the rpm), to simulate coming to a hover over the landing pad. Instead, his friend twisted the broom handle counter-clockwise and pressed against his right foot. And for some reason, Seymore brought the bucket handle back into his belly. "No, Seymore, you're doing it all ass-backwards. Jesus—forget about riding a horse!"

"Horse?—what horse?"

"Never mind—never mind, let's try it again."

Victor R. Beaver

* * *

"I HAVE THE CONTROLS," BUD GRESSING said.

"You have the controls," Sandy replied. They had just completed a normal approach to the lane. Again, as was Gressing's technique, he took over control of the aircraft as the student was about to terminate to a hover. Sandy drew a quick breath and exhaled.

"Whaddya, say? You think it's about time?" spoke Gressing, as he moved the helicopter off the lane. A moment before he had called the tower and told them he would be repositioning to the pasture south of the stagefield.

"Sir...?"

"To hover. Are you ready?"

"Hov?—yes, sir."

"Okay—hang on." Gressing scooted the helicopter across the pasture until they were about a quarter-mile from the stagefield. He brought the ship around until they were facing a small formation of rocks jutting from the ground fifty feet to their front. There were no other obstacles in the open pasture, except a small herd of Herefords about two hundred meters to their right front; they had lifted their heads and were now watching. (Having no capacity to remember the past, or project the future, these creatures were looking on as if seeing for the very first time what was about to happen. This hovering, then, would be a "brand new" experience for their dull-witted stares, as it would be for the student pilot in the right seat.) "Okay, you have the controls," Gressing said. "Let's keep this little puppy aimed straight toward those rocks there. Keep us at about a two-foot hover. You shouldn't have any problem. The air is dead calm."

"Yessir, I have the controls."

It was a tussle. When Gressing gave him the controls, the ship was as steady as a cow's brain. After five seconds, with Sandy not moving a muscle to change anything—or so he thought—the helicopter started (somehow on its own) to buck and weave and dance and do a little rock n' roll. (A helicopter at hovering-rest tends to become un-rested if left attended to by a nonmoving-moving force.)

LESSON #1—HOVERING

Instructor Pilot: "Are you checking to see if the flight controls work?"
Student Pilot: "Yes, sir."
Instructor: "Do they work okay?"
Student: "Yes, sir, I-I believe they do..."
IP: "You let me know if you need any help."
SP: "Yes, sir, I-I certainly will, sir..."

If he wasn't chasing the engine and rotor tachometer (rpm) needles with erratic throttle-twisting and a wild-eyed stare, he was eyeball-locked onto the rocks and climbing away from them with an armful of collective pitch (lever), mesmerized by and amazed at their (the rocks') stationary-ness. Then he developed a severe case of leg-lock: his right leg wasn't strong enough to overcome his left, to keep the ship pointed toward the rocks. And then the little trainer began to swerve left...pitch nose up...back up...and go up. If that wasn't enough, Sandy decided to reverse course: collective down, add right pedal, cyclic right, reduce throttle. The rpm drooped, the ship became sluggish, and then began to wallow like a fish dying out of water. "Life—it needs rpm...Life!" Gressing lamented, adding just a touch of clockwise throttle to keep the rotorblades from coning upward. The engine whined. The ship was breathing again. "Sir," Sandy moaned, "I don't feel so good."

"Come to think of it...neither do I," Gressing replied. "I have the controls."

"You have the controls."

Gressing climbed the aircraft up three hundred feet and flew eastward, traveling about a mile from their original spot. Again he came to a hover, this time aiming the little training helicopter toward a large cottonwood three hundred feet to their front. Gressing held the ship steady over the ground. He said, "Be real easy on the controls; keep your crosscheck going—just like you do in the traffic pattern. Crosscheck. It's your bread and butter. Look out about fifty feet, toward the tree, and then glance back inside the aircraft, and then back toward the tree. Don't stare. I know you can coordinate all the controls at once—you've done it many, many times in the traffic pattern. Now don't let me down. You have the controls."

Sandy put his feet on the pedals, his left hand grasped the collective lever and throttle, he placed his right hand on the cyclic control stick, and he started his crosscheck. "I have the controls..."

"It was a miracle!" Sandy blurted to Seymore, who was now listening with just the slightest interest. "Before Gressing repositioned us, I was such a spastic misfit." They were in their room. Seymore had just returned from his shower and Sandy was reiterating for the third time his feat. "One minute all my body parts acted like they had a mind of their own. Then Gressing took the controls, we flew away, he gave the controls back to me, and then it happened—I was hovering!"

"Yeah...that's great...Congratulations."

* * *

"PHEW...YOU GUYS SMELL LIKE A COUPLE of French whores," Sandy said. It was Saturday afternoon, end of the second week of flight training. His two roommates had dates with Marie and Callie again. "For a couple of confirmed bachelors, those girls sure have you two on a leash."

"Nay," Mark retaliated, "we are merely suitors. Our task is to share our wit and charm. To behold the fair sex. To appreciate. Besides, our armor is ironclad. You sure you don't want to come along? That school is packed with fine-looking women. Bet we could scare something up for you."

"No thanks," Sandy said.

"Well...ta ta," spoke Seymore. "Don't wait up, we'll probably be late."

"Don't be late. We have formation tomorrow afternoon at four o'clock."

In Frank Bartlett's room, Sandy plunked himself down in an empty chair. Frank's cigarettes were on the study table. "You mind if I try one of these?"

"No...go ahead."

Sandy fished one out and lit up. He took a puff and blew the smoke out. "These aren't half bad. Maybe I should take up smoking."

"What's the matter?" Frank asked. "You look like you're hungover or lovesick, I can't decide which." Frank had his head on a pillow propped against the iron railing of his bunk, his nose stuck between the pages of Dostoyevsky's *Crime and Punishment.*

"I keep thinking about my girl Katie. I'd like to get married before shipping over, but I don't think she'll go for it."

"Probably a smart thing." Bartlett placed the book by his side on the bed.

"Why?"

"It's rough on a marriage, being separated like that."

"How do you know?"

"It's how my marriage ended."

"You were married? I didn't know that. What happened?" Sandy took another puff, then started coughing; he put the cigarette out.

"I was stationed at Long Binh," Frank began. "I helped to put bodies in caskets that were being shipped home. I made the mistake of writing to my wife and telling her what I did and what I saw, how it felt to see day after day all those dead. I was never in any danger, but she didn't know that. Vietnam was Vietnam. And in Vietnam a war was going on. Then one day I got a letter. She wanted out—a divorce. I suppose I depended on her too much. She couldn't handle it." Frank fell silent. His eyes took on a distant look. "All those bodies...going home to loved ones. I could almost feel their pain, their anguish. It was too much for me. I thought my wife would understand."

"How long ago were you divorced?"

"It'll be one year this December."

"I'm sorry."

"It's okay." Frank lifted the book from his side and replaced the bookmark. "Do you want some advice?"

"Yeah...sure."

The Sky Soldiers

"It's got to be tougher on the homefront. Dead is dead. Only the living will ever feel the true pain of death. Does that make any sense?"

Sandy nodded. "Yeah, that makes sense."

"Let your girl decide on her own. Remember, she'll be the one left behind if you don't return."

Sandy's eyes took on a faraway gaze. "I'll be coming back..." he whispered.

Frank looked at Sandy sympathetically. "Yeah...I hope you do."

Victor R. Beaver

Chapter 20

"BE AT EASE, MR. SLATER." MAJOR NEELY, seated behind his desk, had returned Slater's salute smartly. He picked up a pencil. Before him was Slater's field 201-file. "I see you have two years of college, Mr. Slater. It says here your major was journalism."

"Yessir."

"Do you like to write?"

"Well, sir...I do make a stab at it. I keep a journal."

"I see." Neely sat back in his chair. "I noticed, too, you don't have an extra duty. It must be an oversight on Lieutenant Whitaker's part."

"I suppose so, sir."

"You would like an extra duty, wouldn't you, Mr. Slater?" Neely was twirling the pencil now between two fingers.

"Yessir, if you say so, sir." *Isn't putting in twelve to fourteen hours a day out in the AO, most of it spent flying, extra duty enough?*

"It's hard to evaluate a man based solely on the fact that he's a pilot," Neely resumed. "You're all good pilots; some are better than others, of course, but...well, you know...for me to approve your officer evaluation report, I must see you perform in other ways. Don't you agree, Mr. Slater?" Neely was now tapping his desktop with the pencil's eraser end.

"Yessir...I suppose I do," Kip answered.

Neely grinned. "That's good...that's good. I like your enthusiasm, Mr. Slater. Very commendable."

Let's see now, thought Slater, perform in other ways. *I could sharpen thirty pencils every Monday morning...Or inspect the latrines...Or hold the enlisted men at gunpoint to buy U.S. Savings Bonds...Or check them for VD...Or ride herd on the little papa-sans who do the yard work in the company area—anything to show my true worth as an officer and gentleman in the United States Army of America.*

"Well, considering your background in journalism," Neely stated, "I thought you might like to be the assistant Awards and Decorations officer. You'll be working with Lieutenant Christian. It requires a lot of writing. A good narrative is a must to be able to award the men Bronze Stars, Silver Stars, DFCs...and the like. Who knows, one of our men might even merit the Distinguished Service Cross. Or the Medal of Honor. Why...it could even be you, Mr. Slater."

Oh sure, the Medal of Honor. Let's see. Most recipients of the nation's highest award usually get it by throwing themselves on a grenade or flying through a hail of bullets. Posthumous recipient, I believe, is the correct terminology posted on the citation. "The Medal of Honor, sir?...No thank you, sir."

The Sky Soldiers

Neely frowned. "Aaah...yes—Well, suit yourself," he said, then leaned forward. "I guess that's all, Mr. Slater."

Kip turned to go. "Mr. Slater...aren't you forgetting something?"

"What would that be, sir?" said Kip, turning back.

"You forgot to salute."

"Oh...sorry, sir."

Kip saluted. As he was about to turn the second time, Major Neely said, "I've assigned your friend, Mr. Tannah, the duty of U.S. Savings Bonds officer for the enlisted men. Give him a hand if you would...you know, encourage the men to put their money into something secure and worthwhile. No telling what they're wasting their hard earned combat pay on."

Probably booze, beer, and the whores downtown—just like the officers, thought Kip Slater.

"You will help him, won't you, Mr. Slater?"

"Yes, sir. I certainly will, sir."

They were so drunk none of them could steer a straight course or maneuver upright without leaning against the other—or a nearby pole or tree—or the wall of a building.

"I gotta go pissh..." Robin Henry said.

"I gotta go pissh, too," Leo Tannah repeated. He was leaning against Mac, who was leaning against Henry, who was jammed against Kip Slater, who was wedged between the trunks of a cluster of banana trees. How they managed to get outside the club, and into their present contortions, none of them knew.

"And me..." Mac said, "...I gotta piss bad."

Slater said, "I gotta piss bad worse."

Before leaving the club, which closed at 0100 sharp per Neely's directive, they had watched a pair of Viking gunpilots raise the tips of several banana fronds into the two overhead fans. They were pretending to track the main rotorblades of a Huey helicopter. Their pretensions were, in fact, a serious helicopter maintenance procedure. A severely "out of track" blade could cause the helicopter, in flight, to shimmy and wiggle like a tone-deaf belly dancer. This was not good for loaded bladders—or severe hangovers. Their make-believe blade-tracking efforts on the turning fans caused a rip-roaring hoopula among the many bystanders. However, after much effort, the previously "perfectly tracked" overhead fan blades had now become "perfectly out of track."

"Do you know the philoshophee of a dog?" Henry belched.

"No, what?"

Henry aimed his gaze skyward, in deep thought. "Something about...piss on it."

"Piss on it? Piss on it 'what?'"

"Just piss on it...I don't know, I can't sheem to remember the rest..."

Several moments of silence passed. Mac started to laugh. "Yeah, I get it—I get it. Enlightening...very enlightening."

Slater, struggling to get himself free, said, "You wouldn't know 'enlightening' if you were struck by it."

"Well then, let's do it," Henry said.

"Let's do 'it' what?" Leo said.

"Less piss on it..."

"On 'it' what?" Leo blurted.

"Less go piss on Neely's door..."

"What—?"

Henry repeated, "Less go piss on Neely's hootch-door."

"Funny," Mac declared, "I could have swore you said let's go storm the Bastille."

Major Danforth R. Neely's quarters was three hootches down from the club, in a secluded, darkened area surrounded by several large clusters of banana trees. Luckily for the quartet, the door itself was wreathed in almost total darkness, the light from the street lamp one building over unable to filter through the miniature "jungle." The four had stumbled "quietly" near the front steps, had stopped, and were now looking the situation over. With their hearts thumping in their throats, they hesitated for a long moment. "Would this be a 'firing-squad' offense?" asked Mac.

"Hell if I know," Robin Henry replied.

Just then Leo dropped his fatigue pants. "Let's fuckin' do it."

"Yeah...shit—let's do it," the others chorused, then dropped their fatigue pants likewise.

Belligerent and teeter tottering, they approached the door managing somehow to stop at the first step. "Let's let'er rip," Kip snarled, as if directing a firing squad.

And they did. A loud splattering noise that sounded like a "thundering" waterfall.

For the longest time their nearly clear liquid streams poured and poured. It seemed as if they would never stop—as if they were destined to meet their "Maker" (should Neely appear with a gun and blow them all away, one shot apiece) here on the front steps of the hootch of the commanding officer of the "World-famed" Soc Trang Tigers. But the longer they peed, the less they cared; it was too late. If they were caught, Neely would have them dead-to-rights. It would be very difficult to explain this particular piece of action now being perpetrated by four (level headed, mature, and highly responsible) Army warrant officer helicopter pilots. Finally, Kip said, "Hey, Henry, what if Neely opens the door?"

"Huh?"

"I say again, 'What if Neely opens the door?'"

"That's what I thought you said." And then Henry started to laugh, as the solution, so perfect, so clear, came to him. His laughter was hysterical, an infectious, nonstop, knee-bending, tear-jerking laugh, which none of them could contain once they, too, began laughing. "If," Henry said, "that sombitch opens the door...we'll just have to—*piss all over his legs!*" And with that, Henry keeled over backwards, wracked by his own convulsion. The others followed suit. Had the MPs appeared it would have been a simple matter of scooping them up (like a puddle with a paddle) and depositing them in the nearest "dipsty-dumpster."

After they were buttoned, and were turning to leave, Kip stopped. Somehow, in his semi-comatose state, he remembered something important. He did an about-face, raised his right arm and saluted the door. "Screw you, sir, and the horse you rode in on—Sir." As he turned to go, he said:

"Medal of Honor my ass..."

* * *

LEO TURNED HIS GAZE SKYWARD TOWARD the sound of the approaching helicopter. "That must be Fred and Lieutenant Christian."

Justen nodded. He continued to pull on his cigarette as he watched the speck become larger and larger.

It was ten o'clock in the morning. They were shut down at the Ca Mau airstrip. Earlier, they had re-supplied the outposts to the north and northeast of Ca Mau. But to re-supply the ones to the south, called "two-ship" area, required a second lift helicopter to provide support and cover. To go farther south, to re-supply Nam Can, required full gunship escort.

After Oakerson and Christian landed and had shut down, Christian got out and with the rotorblades still slow-turning behind him, approached Justen, who was leaning against the side of his helicopter. He noted that Justen's gaze seemed fixed in space, his mind apparently deep in thought. "You hear anything out of these MACV folks?" he asked the chief warrant officer.

For a second or two, Justen didn't speak. And then he turned his head toward Christian. "About what, sir?"

"You know...about your brother?"

"No, not lately, sir."

"They do have a pretty good intelligence network here, don't they?"

Justen shrugged. "As good as any, I guess."

Christian twisted his mouth slightly, then frowned. Whenever he was around Justen, he didn't know quite what to say, or even how to act. For the short time he had known him, though, he had come to admire Justen's resolve, his stoic determined manner. "What's it been now, two years and still no word?...Do you really think he's alive?"

Justen pondered the question for a moment. And then he said, "Sir, with all due respect, I don't know if Jake is dead or alive. Right now he's listed as MIA. Here's my position. I don't care what I have to do, how many times I have to extend, I'm not leaving this country until I find him. Or at least what's left of him. I don't think about anything else, and I don't worry about anything else. He's my brother. Plus, he has a wife and two children. I also have to think of them. I have to somehow try and keep their hopes alive."

It was one thirty by the time the two crews had finished their re-supply trips to the southern outposts, Dam Doi and Bay Hap. One last run remained, to Thoi Binh, eighteen kilometers north by northwest of Ca Mau. In spite of its proximity to the U Minh Forest, the military advisory team there had reported no noticeable enemy activity in the past several weeks, so Justen told Oakerson and Christian they could head back to Soc Trang if they wanted. Fred, his nerves shot after returning from Bay Hap, was only too happy to comply.

Staff Sergeant McAfee, the team NCOIC, greeted Justen and Tannah at the Thoi Binh outpost LZ when they arrived. He was a tall, narrow-shouldered man, wearing a set of sweat-drenched camouflage Tiger fatigues. Three RF/PF soldiers accompanied him to help with the off-loading. "What a cheap bunch of sonsabitches!" McAfee shouted to Justen over the din of the helicopter engine when he saw their meager ration of beer. His eyes lit up, though, when he saw the toilet paper. "Well, at least they didn't skimp on the shit-paper! I got two of my guys with the runs! I'm liable to come down with it myself! You might as well shut down!" Then he told Justen, "The captain's got a request!"

"What is it?"

"He wants to do some sight-seeing! We might have something for you!"

Suddenly, the shackles rose over Justen's entire body. "What did you see? How long ago?"

"Better let the captain explain! He's got the map! Besides, it'll give these men a chance to off-load these stores!"

Once the engine was off and the blades had slowed, Justen got out. He told Tannah to remain behind and help with the off-loading. He then followed McAfee through the maze of concertina wire that surrounded the outpost. The outpost was like most of the others around Ca Mau, a circular buildup of dirt surrounded by a moat, land mines, barbed wire, with the defensive positions located strategically around the perimeter. The American team that lived inside the compound had their own housing made of building material which had been requisitioned, borrowed, or "confiscated." Their living quarters, nearly as primitive as the Vietnamese defense-force soldiers they advised and supported, were heavily sandbagged and were covered with ample canvas material to keep out the rain. Justen stooped low behind McAfee and entered through a make-shift door into a small command room. Captain Tafoya, the team leader, stood in his T-shirt and skivvy shorts. He had been napping on his cot when Justen landed. He was now in the process of heating water for coffee.

"Derek, good to see you. How about some coffee?" said Tafoya.

"Sure. How's it going out here?"

Tafoya wagged his right hand. "You know, so-so. What do you hear from Valerie?"

"Got a letter from her just the other day. How about you?"

"It's been about three weeks now. I'm concerned how she's holding up." Herman Tafoya had been a classmate of Jake's at West Point, and had also attended Jake and Valerie's wedding. He became assigned to the Thoi Binh outpost seven months ago and was as interested in Jake's whereabouts as Derek. Whenever he could communicate with Justen, he did, and gave his usual report, which usually amounted to nothing. Occasionally, the farmers who worked the fields surrounding Thoi Binh would glimpse unusual sampan traffic, often late at night, but were never cognizant of their occupants or contents. If Jake, or any American, was being transported into or out of the Forest, it was information they were unaware of as a rule.

"Yeah, me too. Damn, I wish I could tell her more than I do. I never know what to say." And then Derek said, "McAfee said you might have something."

Tafoya lifted a map. He pointed to a sharp hook along the Song Trem Trem, a river that wound like a snake through the upper reaches of the U Minh. The location in question was about twenty kilometers north-northwest of Thoi Binh. "Two days ago an Air Force FAC spotted two sampans parked side-by-side just as the river turns south. He didn't see any activity around them. Could be something...you never know. We'll take a look." Tafoya poured out two cups. He took a sip from his cup. "He's a prisoner, Derek. I don't doubt it one bit."

"Yeah, but the goddamn Army won't confirm it. And that's the shits."

Tafoya reached out and touched Derek's arm. "It may be the shits all right, especially for Val, but at least he isn't a confirmed KIA. Missing in action is small compensation, don't you think?"

"Yeah...I suppose."

Tafoya said, "Let me get dressed and we'll go."

Back at the aircraft, Leo Tannah, on a whim, suggested that Conrad get some stick-time in the left seat. Justen agreed. When they lifted Leo was seated in the left door-gunner's well, behind Conrad's M-60.

They climbed to two thousand feet, heading north by northwest. The cabin doors were open. Unlike Finch on the right side, who had let go of his M-60, allowing it to point straight down against the swivel stop, Leo continued to hold the left-side M-60, aiming it left and right at clusters of nipa palm or any kind of growth that looked suspicious.

After several minutes of flying time they came to the northern portion of the U Minh. Below them was swamp and low vegetation. Justen could see the form of the river ahead by the trees bordering it on both sides.

Justen looked back; he eyed Leo still grasping the M-60. "Tannah, no shooting unless you clear it with me first. You got that?"

"I got it."

They flew west of the hook. Justen then directed Conrad to circle to the right. Tafoya was seated on the rightmost cabin seat, looking down. He held tight to his carbine. A pair of banana clips taped together protruded the magazine chamber. He began to point at something. "A house—in that cluster of palms."

"Yeah," Justen said. He saw the roof of what looked like a small plantation building, overgrown by vegetation.

Tafoya said, "Innocent-looking, huh?"

They made three orbits, looking for any kind of movement or activity. Suddenly, Justen took over the controls and turned the ship sharply left; they were now flying on a southwesterly heading. After two minutes, Justen felt something strange, a vague, gnawing feeling that went up and down his spine. *This...this place,* he thought, and then shivered. He began to run the series of flashes with the landing light, spelling Jake's name using Morse code, even though he knew it wouldn't be seen, in the bright of day, as he intended.

"What's happening?" Tafoya asked.

"Nothing...I thought I saw something," Justen replied, suddenly irritated with himself. He felt foolish. *Goddamn reckless showmanship. You're getting to be a dippy bastard, Justen. You've been over here too long. Are you going to start paying attention to ghostly superficial impressions now? What kind of bullshit is this? If you're not careful they'll ship your ass back to the States and you'll never return—*

Justen looked back. Leo Tannah, his knuckles bared white, continued to have a firm grip on the handles of Conrad's machine gun. And then Derek saw him lean forward, slightly raised off his seat, peering almost straight down. The gun was also pointing nearly straight down. "Tannah, what do you see?"

"A sampan—" he said over the intercom. "It was moving near the edge of the canal and now it's gone beneath some palm trees."

"How many people did you see in it?" Tafoya asked.

"I couldn't tell. We're too high. Come left and I'll try to spot it again."

Derek banked the ship hard left. Leo found himself looking straight down. At two thousand feet they had way too much altitude to make out any detail. In the first place, the sampan had barely caught his eye; now it was gone. His grip on the M-60, though, hadn't relaxed, and he found himself with his finger on the trigger, ready to shoot—wanting to shoot—at something—*anything.*

Justen now had the helicopter level. Tafoya had moved to the other side of the cabin and was looking downward too, his carbine off "safe." Leo strained to identify the exact spot where he saw the boat disappear, but all along the canal it looked the same. And then he heard a sharp crack. Tafoya heard it too and was shifting his rifle up, his finger on the trigger. Leo interpreted Tafoya's readiness as all the signal he needed to start shooting. As he began blasting, he shouted over the intercom: "Receiving fire! Receiving fire! Nine o'clock!"

Justen had looked back at the first rattle of gunfire. He saw Leo hunched over the machine gun, his upper torso jiggering with each pull of the trigger. He could see Leo's teeth bared, his eyes straining to see where his tracers were going. A second later he saw Tannah swivel the gun back and forth, spewing hot lead everywhere. Tafoya strained to see the exact spot where Leo was trying to hit, but it seemed that the whole area was now a target. If there were a dozen sampans hidden in the trees, each was likely to take a hit.

"Tannah. Cease fire! *Cease fire*!" Justen screamed.

Leo kept firing. It was almost as if Justen's cries spurred him on. Justen watched incredulously. "CEASE...FIRE!" he cried one last time. The gun stopped. It had jammed.

"Tannah—what the hell are you shooting at?"

Leo didn't answer. He was pulling the bolt back, working feverishly to clear the jam.

"Tannah—!"

After a few more seconds of fussing with the gun, and realizing he couldn't clear it, he slammed Conrad's M-60 down to its stops. Leo said, "I told you, I was receiving fire. And I returned the fire—"

"What did you see? Tracers? Someone in a sampan? What?"

"Negative. I heard shots being fired—the captain heard them too."

Tafoya nodded, confirming Leo's declaration. "I heard a shot," he said. "I think there was only one, though."

Everything happened so fast that when Justen turned back around in his seat he saw that the aircraft had gained several hundred feet of altitude. He adjusted the controls to level the ship. He felt his heart racing. Why did it matter that Tannah stop firing? he asked himself. They probably were fired upon, though he hadn't heard any shots. *What's with you, Justen? What are you so goddamn worried about? You could be flying right smack over the top of Jake and never know it—how could you? Or he could be a thousand miles away. Shit, he could be dead, for all you know. How many times have you implicated that he was alive, as though it were a fact. You don't know. YOU DON'T KNOW AT ALL!*

What were the odds that Leo could accidentally hit Jake, he thought? A million to one—they had to be. And trying to locate him in this large track of forest and swamp—if indeed he was down there—had to be the ultimate assumption, a fantasy, totally out of the realm of common sense.

They spent several minutes trying to re-locate the sampan, then gave up. It was futile. If Victor Charlie was anything at all, he was a master at camouflage.

They turned and headed toward Thoi Binh. They dropped Tafoya off and then, after refueling at Ca Mau, lifted for Soc Trang.

Leo was back in his left cockpit-seat position, at the controls. "I heard shots," he told Justen. "So did that captain."

"Forget it."

"I'm serious…I did."

"Damnit!—I said forget it."

The Sky Soldiers

Chapter 21

"**M**R. GRANGE, EXPLAIN THE purpose of the 'override pilot' switch."
It was early Wednesday morning. The three men sat hovering over hot cups of coffee. The likelihood of doing any firing that morning was slim. For the second time during their training a dense fog had settled over much of the East Coast; again, it was time for table-talk.

Dave Grange cleared his throat. For the past several days Travois's death had been on his mind. He was thinking of him now as Daddy Don was speaking.

"Come on," Pollard urged. "I haven't got all day."

"It's an emergency switch," Dave began, taking a deep breath. "It permits the gunner to take command of the armament subsystem when...when the pilot in the back is...incapacitated."

Pollard nodded. "Okay." He looked at Mike Nolan. "Explain a little more about how this switch works."

Nolan said, "Placing the 'override pilot' switch in the ON position energizes the pilot override relay, transferring control of the armament subsystem and pods to the gunner."

"What happens to the turret with this switch in the ON position, Mr. Grange?"

"I...beg your pardon...?"

"Come on, damnit. I want you to snap out those answers!"

Suddenly, a heat rose in Dave's chest. "Go to hell!"

Pollard's eyes widened. "What's the matter with you?"

"With me?—What's the matter with you?" he said. "You've been acting like a total ass lately. You tell me what's the matter—*Mister Pollard.*" Shocked by his own outburst, Dave quickly recovered. He found himself glaring into the older man's eyes. The tension between instructor and student lasted several more moments and was felt all over the room.

Pollard looked around, embarrassed. "Come on, let's go to the snack bar and get some breakfast. I'll buy."

Pollard poked at his eggs with a fork. He said, "I've got a younger brother...by ten years. He's in Vietnam. I got word right after your aircraft qualification checkrides that he was MIA. He was flying with the Twenty-fifth Infantry, out of Cu Chi. He's a gunpilot..." Pollard lifted the fork and picked at his grits. He tried to eat, but the food was tasteless. "I never talked to him about flight school; he went on his own. The report said he got shot down south of Dau Tieng, in Three Corps. That's all it said." Daddy Don took a deep breath. For a long while he was silent. Then his voice became small and broken. "He's not MIA...He's dead."

"Dead? You don't know that," Nolan stated.

"The hell I don't..." Pollard said. "Listing pilots as MIA is the polite way of telling the folks back home they haven't recovered the body. Or if they have...they haven't been able to identify his...the charred remains."

Nolan and Grange frowned. Pollard's gaze became distant. They could see the welling in his eyes, the red puffiness. "I've got to go," he said in a barely audible whisper; then he stood and walked away.

* * *

"YOU'RE GOING TO BE A WHAT?" NOLAN blurted.

Pollard nodded. "You heard me...I didn't stutter. I'm going to be a dad—again." It was early Thursday afternoon. They had just returned to the briefing room after a grueling four hours of flying. The fog had dissipated by 0900 and they had rushed out to the aircraft to make up lost time. The students had flown in the front seat to practice firing the wing-store armament systems using the "override pilot" switch, simulating their action if the rear-seat pilot became incapacitated.

"A dad...?" Grange repeated. "I'll be damned. I didn't know you still had it in you."

Daddy Don scrunched up his face. "The hell you say. I got more piss and vinegar in me than both of you put together," he defended. "My 'can do' still keeps up with my 'want to.'"

"What about all those diapers?...The midnight feedings?...What if it's a girl?" said Nolan, deciding to lay it on thick.

"Damnit, it's going to be a boy—"

Then Pollard's shoulders sagged. His face took on a look of remembrance. He raised his eyebrows. "Crap...you're right," he groaned; "what the hell did I get myself into?"

Pollard then announced that he and Elaine were going to be married on Saturday and that Mike and Dave, of course, were invited. Jardine was to be the best man, while Elaine had asked Pollard's youngest daughter, Cynthia, age twenty, to be her maid of honor.

On Friday, the members of the Cobra transition course flew their final training flight. It was an informal checkride with another instructor, a chance to experience different flying and firing techniques. Nolan and Grange each paired with a black chief warrant officer named Tillerman. They walked away with yet more information about the AH-1G to take with them to Vietnam.

The wedding was conducted in one of the post chapels. Elaine, an attractive woman in her early thirties, was dressed in an elegant white linen suit and held a bouquet of lavender orchids. She exchanged vows with a nervous yet proud groom who looked deceivingly in control, in his military dress blue uniform.

Several of the instructors in Pollard's flight, meeting Elaine for the first time, were eager in their approval. They wondered, though, how she had managed to overlook Daddy Don's gruff exterior to find the sensitive person he was on the inside. Nolan and Grange had more than a professional interest in Pollard's happiness. He had become a kind of father figure they could look up to and respect. In Elaine, the two students believed their instructor had found a soul mate. As a native of Australia, her accent and warm personality gave her an air of distinction they found very reassuring. Clearly, she was a woman who would stand by her man, especially should Pollard's worst fears about his younger brother proved true.

An hour before the wedding, Pollard had asked them to come to his apartment, to lend him moral support, he claimed. When Mike and Dave arrived he made them each a drink, pouring an extra dollop of rum for himself to steady his nerves. They teased him about his impending post-nuptial doom: the advent of a little one in the nursery.

Daddy Don took a long pull on his drink. They could see that something else was on his mind. He said, "I have something to show you," then disappeared into the bedroom. Returning with an envelope, he handed it to Mike to read first. "This is my brother's last letter to me. It was sent about a week before I got word that he was missing." Nolan took the letter out of the envelope and read:

Dear Donald,

Glad to hear you're doing okay. I'm now at the mid-point of my tour and suddenly time seems to have stood still. I have a short-timer's calendar that I've been marking off daily. Unfortunately, doing that makes the time go slower, so now I mark the days off whenever I get the notion. If it's a week later, I can wipe out seven days at once.

I got my aircraft commander orders posted last week. I still fly cover for my lead bird. We have yet to lose any gunpilots (thank God). The Scouts are taking it in the shorts, though. Their average longevity is less than three months.

Last night five 122mm rockets hit our base. The shit was really flying. I was never so goddamn scared in my life. Unlike mortars, these things can penetrate just about anything we build. And noisy! Christ, I dread the sound almost as bad as the flying shrapnel. One rocket hit the mess tent. Guess what we'll be eating for the next week?—C-rations. The worst news is that four men were killed. Arms, legs, chunks of flesh, brains, you name it, were scattered everywhere. This morning I saw this funny-looking glob of brown

Victor R. Beaver

"hair" stuck to my tent. Hair! That's what it was! A part of some guy's scalp. I nearly freaked.

Donald, I never thought this until a couple of weeks ago, but this war is a bunch of political bullcrap. It scares the shit out of me to think I could get killed over here—for what? Nothing.

Sorry this letter sounds so morbid. I didn't mean for it to. But at least I got said what I needed to say. Now I'll be okay, good for another six months, that's if I get through it.

Give my love to all,
Doug

Mike gave the letter to Dave. He read it and then gave it back to Daddy Don, who, folding it, said, "I distinctly remember a strange feeling come over me after I read it, like I was never going to see him again." He shrugged; his face held a deadpan expression. "I hope to God I'm wrong."

The wedding reception took place late that afternoon, at the Fort Stewart officers' club. At nine o'clock that evening, Dave and Mike approached Pollard.

"We've got to be going," Mike said.

"What? Already?" Don Pollard retorted. "I'm just getting in the mood to party."

"We both have to get up early," Dave said. "I'm heading home for a couple of weeks to see my mom and the rest of my family."

Mike said, "And I'm going to the Keys. My old man and I are going to fish and drink beer until we wobble. But we've got something for you." Mike then took a flat, rectangular object wrapped in gift paper from behind his back.

"What's this...?" Daddy Don said, his eyes glazed over from the drinking and the happiness he felt.

"A little memento..." Mike said, handing the gift to the instructor, who opened it. It was a wooden plaque. Engraved on a brass plate were the words:

"It's hard to soar like an Eagle,
when you're surrounded by Turkeys..."

On the back there was another brass plate and more engraving:

TO "DADDY DON" POLLARD
OUR MENTOR & FRIEND
Given by
CW2 DAVID GRANGE & 1LT MICHAEL NOLAN

"You bastards. What's this crap…'turkeys?' You guys ain't friggin' turkeys." His face was beaming with pride and embarrassment, though. He looked at the plaque, rereading the front and back. Pollard turned away. He removed a handkerchief from his pocket, blew his nose with a loud honk, dabbed at his eyes, then turned back to face them. "You didn't have to do this," he said.

"We know," Nolan admonished. "We shouldn't have. For a whole week and a half you were a real shit."

"Yeah-yeah…I'm sorry."

"We got something else for you," Grange said, "but we couldn't bring it." He had been holding a large white envelope. Dave fidgeted with the envelope as he spoke. "We didn't know you liked to barbecue until you mentioned one day you were going home to have a 'rib out.' We vaguely recall you once inviting us…but we we're so immersed in our studies—thanks to you—that we had to decline the offer. Jardine told us you 'live' to barbecue. So, Mike and I, we went together on this. It's your wedding present." Dave handed the envelope to Pollard who opened it and withdrew a glossy blow-up of a large black barbecue grill, the kind of outdoor grill a true connoisseur would be proud to own. "When you go to your apartment, it's all set up on your patio in place of the old one."

Wondrously, Pollard looked at the photo. "I…I can't believe this. Goddamn you guys, what the hell did I do—?"

"Oh…not much. You just gave your best and expected nothing less from us. That's all."

"I-I don't know what to say…"

"You don't have to say anything. Just keep doing what you're doing." Mike Nolan offered his hand. "Mr. Pollard, you're the finest instructor I've ever met. Thanks for everything."

"That goes ditto for me," Dave Grange said.

The following day, Chief Warrant Officer (W3) Donald M. Pollard received word that his brother was officially listed as "killed in action," vicinity Dau Tieng, Republic of Vietnam. Remains to be shipped home as soon as possible.

Chapter 22

SANDY ADAMSON HAD JUST TURNED the aircraft from crosswind to downwind. It was their second circuit in the traffic pattern and twice on the last downwind Gressing had given him a simulated engine failure. He was approaching the fifteen-hour level. So far, aside from Bowden and Chancey, only two others had soloed, Dwight Alexander and Pete Cochran. In the beginning, Cochran's instructor pilot had the usual doubts about having an ex-airplane pilot for a student. Old fixed-wing habits were hard to break, but Cochran proved the exception to the rule.

"Simulated forced landing—!"

Sandy hesitated momentarily, then pushed the collective lever down. "About caught you napping, didn't I?" Gressing said over the intercom.

Sandy guided the helicopter toward a large area of open pasture. Gressing announced power recovery. After Sandy brought the throttle back to full rpm, and had started the climb back to pattern altitude, he said, "Yeah, I was thinking more about how I misjudged the winds on that last normal approach to the lane right as you whipped the throttle off on me."

Gressing wagged his finger. "It don't work that way. In the flying game five minutes ago is ancient history. You've always got to be thinking ahead of the aircraft. It comes with experience."

"Yessir."

Once they were back in the traffic pattern, Gressing told him to request permission to do an autorotation to Lane One. "I want a good one—I don't want to have to assist on the controls at all. Can you do it?"

"Yessir, I'll sure give it a try."

When they were lined up on final, Sandy judged the entry point and bottomed the collective. He then rolled the throttle counter-clockwise to the stop. He checked his trim, adjusted the pitch attitude, and then used the cyclic to stay centered on the lane. He decelerated at thirty-five feet and then applied the cushioning to land. He put the cyclic forward to level the landing gear just before touchdown. "Excellent," Gressing exclaimed. "You did that all by yourself—I didn't have to touch the controls at all. *Good job.* Now bring the rpm up and let's hover to the sod area in front of the tower. Set it down there."

"Yes, sir." This is it, Sandy thought. He recognized the signs. The gooseflesh rose all over his body as he brought the engine back to normal operating rpm and hovered the helicopter as he was told. Once on the ground, Gressing began to unbuckle. The instructor opened the left door and swung his leg over the cyclic and got out. He turned and secured his now vacant seatbelt and shoulder harness. Still plugged into the intercom system, Gressing reached over and pressed the switch on the cyclic to talk:

"All right. I need to see three turns in the pattern: three normal takeoffs and three normal approaches. Come to a hover at the close end of the lane, and then hover down the lane to the take-off end. Make sure you do your clearing turns. Call the tower for takeoff, and when turning from downwind to base. The aircraft is all yours. Good luck."

"Yes, sir. Thank you, sir."

Gressing unplugged from the intercom system, closed the door, and moved away from the helicopter. Once in front of the tower, he stopped and turned; he took his flight helmet off and put it under his arm. He gave Sandy a thumbs-up.

Sandy turned his gaze toward the far end of the stagefield lanes. "Tuy Hoa Tower, Three Five Five X-ray in front of the tower, ready to hover for takeoff Lane One. First supervised solo."

Permission was granted. The winds were from the east, almost right down the lane. Sandy brought the rpm to twenty-nine hundred. He looked to his right and then to his left. He brought the helicopter to a hover. Then he began to move forward. I'm alone, he thought... *really alone.*

Without Gressing in the left seat he felt confident, yet awkward. And then he realized: *I am being given the rarest of privileges...my first solo in a helicopter.*

At the end of Lane One, he did his clearing turn and called the tower. "Tuy Hoa Tower, Three Five Five X-ray, ready for takeoff Lane One."

"Three Five Five X-ray, roger, cleared for takeoff...winds zero eight zero at five knots."

"This is Three Five Five X-ray, roger."

Well...this is it. If anything goes wrong, you're the only one who can do anything about it. No one can save you—but you.

He checked his instruments: all gauges were showing in the green range. He looked to his front and found the distant object he normally used, a lone cottonwood tree, to guide on (in order to maintain a straight course and not drift into someone else's take-off path). He took a deep breath, exhaled, steadied himself, then applied power and proceeded into a climb.

Close to the ground he felt relatively safe. But once he passed through one hundred feet, he realized how vulnerable he was. He glanced to his left. *Gressing's seat really is empty!* He looked back to his front. He was now approaching the point where he would turn onto the crosswind leg. It came, he checked right, and then moved the cyclic right; the aircraft continued to climb. His mind was darting about, racing off in a hundred directions at once. Ahead of him was another helicopter turning downwind. He had to keep his proper spacing on that aircraft. Check the altimeter, the rpm, the pressure gauges. He moved his scan outside again. Keep it moving: up and out, from left to right. Look for other aircraft, birds, traffic pattern turning points. Then back inside the cockpit to see the gauges. All still in the normal operating range. Check tip-path plane...airspeed

Victor R. Beaver

...altitude...trim...rpm. Division of attention: it was the most critical student-pilot performance indicator on the daily gradeslip.

He was too busy flying to worry about probabilities. He had been too well trained to be anxious about the dangers inherent in what he was doing. All of Gressing's patient instruction had come to this: the man had had enough confidence in him to let him be on his own, the mother sparrow shoving its young out of the nest.

Now he was abeam the tower. Soon he would be turning onto base and setting up a descent. As he approached the turning point, he called the tower: "Tuy Hoa Tower, Three Five Five X-ray, approaching base. Request to land on Lane One."

"Three Five Five X-ray, this is Tuy Hoa, roger. Clear to land Lane One. Winds are calm."

"Three Five Five X-ray, roger."

Check the gauges again: all in the green arc; now look outside: look right, clear right, turn right. Sandy began the descent and banked the helicopter right. The aircraft ahead of him was going to Lane Two. No factor. An aircraft in the left-hand traffic pattern was approaching head on. *He'll be turning for Lane Three, I hope. Yeah, he's doing it. Good.*

For a moment Sandy's gaze locked onto the aircraft going to Lane Two. He heard the rpm start to build. Quickly, he checked inside; he had forgotten to reduce throttle as he reduced power. Crosscheck crosscheck crosscheck. *Keep those eyeballs moving,* as though hearing Gressing's voice echo back at him.

"Don't stare—damnit," he said aloud over the intercom. The sound of his voice startled him; he grinned. "Yeah, don't stare..."

He was now lined up on final. Pad One was the nearest of the four painted on the lane, which were spaced evenly apart. He would be making his first normal approach to it. He waited until he saw the approach angle he was to use...about five to eight degrees. Wait...wait...there it is, now start the descent. Reduce power, check rpm. Looking good. To his right he saw out of the corner of his eye people standing around the base of the tower and outside the stagefield house. He saw Gressing off by himself, arms crossed, critically watching. His classmates were still coming out to observe, especially those on the verge of soloing. He was on display; he had an audience. And then he remembered: out of forty-eight student pilots in Flight Alpha One, he was the fifth to go solo.

Steady. Steady. Keep the descent going, keep the angle, watch the rate of closure, slow the aircraft as necessary to keep it going at an apparent brisk walk. The TH-55A began to jiggle as it came closer to the ground. It wanted to wander, but Sandy held tight to the reins. "Oh no you don't...I'm the guy in charge, not you..." he said aloud, as if speaking to a puppy during its first time on the leash.

As he brought the helicopter over the pad, he saw that his control touch at a hover had never been better. He held it steady for a moment then began moving forward down the lane, conscious of his classmates' envious stares. Again, he saw Gressing giving him the thumbs-up. His heart skipped a beat. Moving down the lane for another takeoff, he began to relax—but not too much.

He took off and made another approach to Lane One. During his third circuit in the traffic pattern he began to feel like this was "old hat." He had never felt so confident...so powerful...so in command of his own destiny. He shivered at the enormity of it all. He was a king—*a Viking god!* The world lay at his feet—literally.

As he came to a hover over Pad One for the third and final time, he looked toward Gressing who motioned for him to set the aircraft down on the parking ramp. He nodded and moved off the lane and scooted past the grassy spot where Gressing had got out and let him take control. He brought the ship over one of the numbered spots on the ramp and with just the slightest wavering placed the helicopter on one of the cement parking pads. He reduced the engine to idle rpm. Gressing walked toward him, his face beaming. The instructor opened the left door, extended his hand and gave Sandy a firm handshake. It was then that Sandy noticed the front of his flight suit: even in the cool of December it was drenched in sweat. In the past, he had worked on his uncle's farm in Iowa, haying, weeding the beans and the corn, milking the cows, shoveling manure, feeding the pigs, until he thought he would drop from exhaustion. When he ran the mile-relay race, he did so until he was breathless, his legs turned to rubber. But in all his life he couldn't remember ever working harder to do anything so right...as his first flight alone in a helicopter.

It was because his life had depended on it....

He dialed. The phone rang twice. "Hello..."
"Hi, Dad."
"Hey, Sandy. How's it going?"
"Great. I've got some good news. I soloed today."
"You did. Wow, that's terrific! How was it?"
"All right. It really felt good."
"In how many hours?"
"A little over fifteen dual hours. I'm the fifth to solo."
"The others will be coming right along, huh?"
"Yeah. Right after me, Willie Cottrell soloed. Remember, he's the ex-Special Forces guy I told you about?"
"Well, that's great, Sandy. We've all been waiting to hear about it...Oh, by the way, are you still coming home for Christmas?"
"As far as I know."
His father said, "Reason I asked...Katie called a couple of days ago."
"Oh yeah?"

"She said she hadn't heard from you lately...so naturally we were concerned."

"I've been pretty busy," he said. "I really haven't had time to call or write her." He knew the reason for not telephoning; he couldn't bear to listen to her concerns for her brother, mainly because he knew no way to assuage her fears. Somehow, very subtly, Brad's presence off the coast of Vietnam had driven a wedge between them.

"You can call her and charge it to us if you want."

"Okay, Dad, thanks."

"Here's your mother. She's chomping at the bit to talk to you."

"Okay, I'll talk to you later."

"Again, congratulations, Sandy. Keep her low and slow."

"Sure, Dad."

His father got off the phone and then he heard his mother's voice.

"Hello, Sandy..."

"Hi, Mom...I guess you heard I soloed?"

"Yes, that's wonderful. We're so proud of you. Was it hard to do?"

"Not really. I had a good instructor. He's been real patient. At first I was a little scared...but I did all right."

"We missed you for Thanksgiving. Melissa cried when she looked at your empty chair. Did they fix a nice meal for you guys?"

"Yeah, Mom...they sure did."

"We were wondering why you didn't phone. We were expecting a call."

"I know, Mom." He remembered why he didn't want to call. He felt so homesick that he knew if he telephoned it would only make it worse. Instead, he and Frank Bartlett went to the Mineral Wells Hotel after dinner and sat and talked in the lounge. It took his mind away from home and family...And away from Katie.

His mother sighed. As she spoke, the strain in her voice came definably over the phone. "The news...it's getting more frightening every day. This Vietnam situation is taking its toll on everyone. The number of soldiers reported killed each week is giving me nightmares—"

"I'm really sorry, Mom. We don't hear much news," he lied. "I guess we're too busy learning to fly."

"Sandy, your father mentioned something about you being sent to Fort Carson, since it has helicopters. Do you think you could get stationed there?"

"I...I don't know, Mom."

"If you asked, perhaps they would consider it...don't you think?"

"Maybe..." he said, wishing she hadn't brought the matter up.

"Could you try?"

"I'll try, Mom." But he knew he wouldn't, and that it would be hopeless, anyway, even if he did. "We get to fill out a 'dream sheet' where we'd like to be sent. I'll put down Fort Carson as my first choice...How does that sound?"

"That would be great, Sandy. You never know." He detected relief in her voice.

"Well, I've got to go, Mom."
"Sandy...about Katie."
"Yes?"
"She called us the other day. We talked."
"I know. Dad told me."
"She'd appreciate a letter, a short note...doesn't have to be long."
"I know, Mom. Like I said, I've been real busy."
"I'm sure you have. Well, anyway, you take care, Sandy. Call us anytime."
"Okay, Mom...thanks. I'll do that."
"We love you, Sandy," she said. "Be careful."
"I will, Mom...I love you too."

* * *

THE FLIGHT SOLO PARTY WAS SET FOR next Saturday afternoon, a picnic planned by the wives to be held at one of the lakes on post. Much to everyone's dismay, Drakeman had selected Darryl Chancey to be platoon leader during the week prior. Naturally, the power went right to his head. One day he collared Willie Cottrell for not seeing him in time to receive the salute due him by a lesser-ranked candidate. Willie took him aside. "Back off, Chancey. Remember, I've still got your switchblade." It was also do-or-die week for anyone who hadn't soloed (in each respective flight). They faced either a setback or complete elimination, depending on the individual's prog-evaluation. Thus far the flight had experienced one failed prog-ride given a week ago to a student named Auten, who, as rumor had it, was a spastic misfit when it came to hovering, even after eighteen hours of dual instruction. Red Fleming was certain that Seymore P. ("P" for Percival) Cutter was a shade worse, but was sticking to his guns *"...to make a silk purse out of a sow's ear."* (To Seymore, he promised nothing short of death if he couldn't let him go solo.)

Tom Adkins, the flight's artist, had practically taken up residency in the latrine along with his murals of helicopters interwoven into a variety of Fort Wolters' training scenes. And he had plenty of help. Tom assigned members of the flight to do the large scale background painting, while he took care of the detail work. So far, Drakeman had not turned down one original drawing offered for his approval.

Victor R. Beaver

On Thursday afternoon, Sandy asked Mark: "Are you and Marie getting serious?"

"Huh?...Serious? Not on your life. What the hell kind of question is that?"

"I was just wondering." He was having difficulty understanding how Mark could date someone as nice and as attractive as Marie Robbins without falling head over heels for her—like he probably would have done. He said, "Mark, have you ever been engaged?"

"Never. Being engaged is like putting a noose around your neck. Getting married is like being hanged. Hey, man, life is too short to get all tangled up like that. Keep it simple. Besides, the last thing I want is a wife while I'm in Vietnam. She'd be plumb worried about me. And I'd be plumb worried about her being worried. I don't need that kind of crap."

Seymore came into the room.

"I'm going on sick call," he said.

"What?" said Sandy.

"You heard me. The thought of flying with Fleming one more time makes me sick to my stomach. I'd rather be sittin' on top a Brahma bull than next to him in the cockpit," Seymore moaned. "And if I don't solo, they're going to ship my ass over to Vietnam with a pack and a rifle and I'll never be seen again—"

"All right, if that's the case, we've got just enough time to go through the motions. Get your mop bucket and broom handle. I've got your pedals."

"Oh Jesus, I'm all pretended out, amigo."

"Sit down, damnit. Or shall we pretend you're crawling through the jungle?"

"So...I'm sittin' already—*I'm sittin'...*"

The Sky Soldiers

Chapter 23

INDIVIDUAL FLIGHT TIME AMONG THE pilots assigned to the 121st Assault Helicopter Company soared. By the time Slater had reached day twenty-six, his flight hours in-country stood at one hundred and fifty-eight. Though his average was a low 6.1 hours per day, he logged on some days as many as nine and ten hours. Lately, most of their combat assaults had been with the ARVN 9th Infantry Division, based at Vi Thanh, one of the division's main staging areas. For Slater, Mac, and Tannah, and the other peter-pilots, the assaults had become sickeningly routine. During the morning hours they would lift two and three battalions of infantrymen into selected landing zones, wait an hour or two, then spend seemingly endless blocks of time picking them up and moving them to an adjacent rice field not more than three or four kilometers away. Flying became so monotonous that Slater found himself fast asleep, when not at the controls, to be awakened by his AC during descent into the LZs. Oftentimes, Neely would have the troop-carrying slicks orbit an RP (airborne reporting point) for twenty minutes and more until the ARVN commanders could decide where they wanted their troops put next. Orbiting in formation for any length of time was their greatest challenge—and had become their greatest bane. Like the helicopter, the pilots and crew, too, had become as machines in a factory that stamped out the same product day after day. Flying had truly become mind-numbing work. In fact, a truly "hot LZ" would have been an almost pleasant diversion, something to help them pretend they were contributing to the war effort.

During that period they refueled many times, taking on and expending enormous quantities of JP-4 (jet fuel). They were unable to fathom the cost in American dollars it took to seek—yet rarely find—the Viet Cong. It was generally believed that Charlie knew of every assault mission two days before the pilots were even aware of their assigned positions in the formation. And if the VC's intelligence-gathering network broke down, it would have to be the deaf, dumb, and blind who were not aware of an operation in any particular area. The combined efforts of the American and Vietnamese forces were as obvious as a herd of stampeding buffalo. Once the ARVN were deposited into the field their activities, too, became sickeningly routine. They burned deserted hootches, absconded meager supplies of rice found during their searches, scattered chickens and ducks left behind by their owners (at least the ones they couldn't catch), and cut wide swathes through hard-worked rice paddies. Occasionally, they would detain one or two or a group of local farmers, question them and let them go. Few Americans doubted that the individual Vietnamese soldier wanted anything more than a pleasant afternoon stroll in the rice paddies. And why not? When his so-called combat duties were done for the day, and the American helicopters and crews had deposited him back at the staging area, awaiting him were wife, children, extended family, a hot meal of rice and vegetables and cooked meat, and his own bed—all the comforts of a *real* home.

* * *

UP AT 0400, BRIEFING AT 0500, AIRBORNE by 0600. Destination the Vi Thanh airstrip. Heavy overcast skies made the morning seem dark and foreboding. Patches of ground fog lay below as they joined in formation.

"Damn," cried Fred Oakerson, as he cringed in his right-seat position. "What the hell is that shit-head doing—?" Captain Slote, flying lead, with Robin Henry as his peter-pilot, had just flown through another patch of cloud.

"Crap if I know—" Kip Slater replied. His head swirled as their ship became enveloped for several seconds at a time by gray mist. The rotating beacon and the navigation lights reflecting inside the cloud caused an eerie sensation to roll through his body. He fought the desire to fly by the "seat of his pants." Vertigo (spatial disorientation) was a pilot's worst fear when flying in clouds. He had to trust his flight attitude instruments implicitly. Flying off Lead in the White Two position, though, meant Kip had to trust Slote more than his own instruments. Most of the pilots in the unit thought their operations officer an ignoramus, with justification. Kip, however, had an even lower opinion: Slote was right now proving to be a blithering idiot. "No wonder Henry wants out of operations and into the gun platoon. It may be his only way out from under Slote's thumb."

Oakerson glanced back and forth between Lead and White Three, urging Kip to hold back. "Let me take the controls," he said, grabbing for the cyclic.

"I can handle it—" Kip replied. Oakerson's disquietude, unnerving most of the time, gave Kip the smug feeling that he was more on par with the man even though Fred had much more Vietnam flight time.

The twenty-minute flight to the Vi Thanh airstrip found them landing in a bleak, drizzling rain. After lighting JP-4 fires, the crews broke out the Cs and sat hunched over their food, stirring, mumbling, cursing in abject frustration…

Journal Entry, 8 December 1967, Vi Thanh airstrip

> *Paul Christian (now a first lieutenant) has come to an interesting conclusion. We might not be the guys wearing the white hats over here. We airlift the ARVN into LZs and all they do is pillage and plunder their own people. And we're their goddamn taxi service!*
>
> *Paul and I have been working together in the orderly room. Awards and Decorations. A joke. Neely has cooked up a scheme for most of the Viking gunpilots to receive the Bronze Star with V-device (for valor), which no*

doubt they deserve. But come on. The medals have got to count for something. At that rate we'll all be getting a Bronze Star, just for flying!

Neely has our first "mandatory" social affair planned for next Saturday night. He's invited a bunch of bigshots from Can Tho to attend. He's also lined up half a dozen American women who work in Saigon to be there, too.

Well, here comes Fred. I guess it's time to start our air-taxi service...

"So what's the story, Fred?" Kip noticed that Fred's face had lost all its color.

"You're not going to believe this, but the guns have stirred up a real hornets' nest. They think they stumbled onto a battalion of VC—"

"You're shittin' me."

"I shit you not...!"

They found the radio chatter nerve shattering during their first descent into the LZ. The rattle of machine-gun fire from the gunships had also been nearly constant. Rockets pounded a heavily wooded canal near the landing zone, which lay less than ten kilometers from the Vi Thanh airstrip. Smoke poured from several burning hootches and the moment the ARVN made their attack they were cut down by an avalanche of machine-gun fire. During the first lift the doorgunners were allowed to suppress, but no time thereafter for fear of hitting friendlies. Major Neely directed traffic at the base of a two-thousand-foot overcast. To give his men a taste of what it was like to run an air-assault operation, Neely picked a different co-pilot each time he flew C&C. Today, Leo Tannah was it.

The second and third lifts went in quickly to support the initial deposit of troops and they too came under intense fire. In no time at all the ARVN casualties had multiplied. After the second lift, two of Slote's radio transmitters became garbled and unreadable. Wainwright and a new peter-pilot named Munson moved forward to take up lead duties.

By noon, three ARVN infantry battalions had been airlifted into the foray, with a fourth, the reserve battalion, gearing up to join in. As fresh troops were committed, the more seriously wounded were evacuated by several of the rear helicopters in the formation. For Slater the battle seemed to grow fiercer by the minute. By two o'clock the skies overhead had cleared. He watched as two sets of F-4 Phantom jets came screaming in to deposit their loads of the ferocious, air-sucking napalm.

They hot-refueled six times in less than nine hours. By the time Slater had to relieve the pressure on his bladder, he noted that he had not been out of his left-seat position *in eight solid hours.*

"You gotta go?" he asked Oakerson, as he began to re-buckle his seatbelt and shoulder harness.

"Go...?"

"Leak. You gotta take a leak?"

"No..."

Kip took the controls, twisted the throttle to full rpm, then moved out of the way for the next ship to refuel. After ten minutes the flight was formed again in straight trail on the Vi Thanh dirt and gravel airstrip. As more troops began to assemble for loading, Reinhart, Oakerson's crewchief, motioned for the soldiers to step back. He had seen up and down the line other troops being held in place for some reason.

With his head back, his mouth open and lips fluttering with each breath, Oakerson for the moment was out of the war while blissful sleep overtook him. As the soldiers continued to stand and wait for the signal to board, Kip heard a radio conversation between Neely and one of the Viking gunship pilots. The words "shut down" came across and reactively he rolled the throttle off and moved the fuel switch back. Oakerson woke to the sudden reduction in engine noise. "Wha-what...are you doing?"

"I heard Neely say 'shut down,'" Kip told Fred.

"Oh..."

More chatter came over the radios. But at the moment both men had tuned it out. And then they heard Wainwright, Tiger Lead, say over the VHF radio: "Tiger Flight, go ahead and load these troops. Trail, let me know when we're ready."

"This is Trail, roger."

"The hell we're shutting down," said Oakerson, who began to reset the throttle and flipped the fuel switch back on. The rotorblades, still turning overhead, had just begun to slow down.

"Lead, it looks like Fred doesn't want anymore of this shit. He just shut down." Randall was speaking from the aircraft directly behind.

"What?"

Oakerson got on the radio and explained.

"That's okay," Wainwright replied. "When you crank back up, Major Neely wants two aircraft to depart the formation to pick up ARVN KIAs."

Kip Slater stared out the left window. Stretched out in three neat rows, most of them wrapped in their own rain ponchos, were the dead. He watched as four men to a wrapped body sloshed through the wet paddy toward them. As the ARVN came closer he turned to see Reinhart indicate how he wished for the bodies to be placed in the cabin area of the ship. The soldiers responded stoically. No matter how hard he tried, Kip Slater could never quite fathom the true state of mind of the ARVN combat soldier. Even now they showed little emotion over the deaths of their comrades.

Slater felt strangely out of place. Behind him were six soul-departed men, with two more yet to be loaded. He had never in his life been this close to a dead person and the moribund drama held him spellbound. It was the loading of the last body, though, that made him grasp the true horror of war. Four soldiers carried an unwrapped body face up and placed him on top of the others. The sight and smell of the dead man, his eyes open and staring vacantly into space, the mouth open in a contorted expression, his head wound a mass of congealed blood, brains and bone, were more than Kip could stand. The rise from the pit of his stomach came so fast that he had no time to open the left cockpit door. Kip Slater vomited out through the open window.

At Vi Thanh, a team awaited them to off-load the dead. Before their gruesome task was done, Oakerson's crew would make seven such trips while the main body of helicopters continued to shuttle fresh troops into the fray. As the day wore on, so did the struggle. For one brief period near the end of the day there seemed a slight tapering of the actual fighting, but as dusk fell the enemy came back at their tormentors even more furiously than before.

Slater was on the controls; the engine was at flight idle rpm. The unloading team had just finished removing their fifth load of bodies and had lain them in a grassy area on the north side of the airstrip. Ahead of them several returning helicopters from the main flight had deposited more of the walking wounded. Awaiting each flight, too, were the women. The men, bandaged and in shock, came down one side of the airstrip like living zombies, unseeing and uncaring. Kip looked on. A young Vietnamese woman with terror-stricken eyes approached one of the returning men who seemed not to notice her. She moved into his path backing up as he went forward. Kip watched as she gestured in a beseeching manner a question she had posed the soldier. At the man's response, the woman collapsed at his feet and began to weep. Expressionless, the man moved on. Slater could only assume that the woman had just learned her husband was dead.

"Tiger Six wants you to go to Can Tho," Wainwright said to Oakerson over the radio. "You're supposed to pick up some staff folks and a couple of newspaper people at the pad in front of the tower and return to Vi Thanh." A moment ago, Wainwright had ordered his flight to shut down for the first time since early that morning.

"Roger that," Oakerson answered. It was dusk. They were approaching Vi Thanh with the last of the dead. Fred looked toward Kip who rolled his eyes. Kip tapped at the fuel gauge. "We'll need to get gas first."

Once they were on the ground, Walls, the gunner, refueled the ship while Kip opened a can of ham and lima beans and began gulping the contents down cold. The food dropped to the pit of his stomach like chunks of lead. He wished he had even a cold cup of coffee to wash it down.

The trip to Can Tho took seventeen minutes. As they flew, Kip began to feel the full impact of his exhaustion. He stared blankly ahead; their four o'clock wake-up seemed ages ago.

At Can Tho they met five men in camouflaged uniforms. Two of them were without nametags or rank. One carried a camera. Kip assumed them to be from the press. Everyone clambered aboard.

"You want to fly?" Oakerson asked. "I'm too pooped."

"Okay...sure," Kip said, placing his hands and feet on the controls. For the first time since becoming a pilot, he dreaded being on the controls. His eyes were heavy and his body yearned for sleep. "Okay, tell me again where we're taking them?"

"To Vi Thanh," Fred answered drowsily.

"Oh, yeah..."

As they approached Vi Thanh, Kip saw the slicks cranked and in the center of the airstrip, getting ready for another lift. He made his initial contact with Wainwright who radioed back that they were to drop their passengers off, proceed to Soc Trang, and return with aircraft parts. After he acknowledged, Kip gave an exuberant sigh of relief. He was not up for any formation flying, especially at night. Flying back from Can Tho, Kip was so drowsy all he could think about was being in bed asleep back at Soc Trang.

Before leaving Can Tho, Oakerson had fallen asleep and had remained so during the landing at Vi Thanh, while the passengers debarked, and throughout the liftoff for Soc Trang. The ship approached Soc Trang from the northwest. Oakerson awakened as Kip slowed to have the doors opened and pinned back. Fred looked back into the cabin area. "Where are the passengers?"

"Vi Thanh."

Oakerson nodded. He looked to their front. "What's that ahead?"

"Soc Trang?"

The AC nodded again. He watched as Kip tuned to the tower frequency. "What are you doing?"

"I'm going to call the tower."

Oakerson paused. "What for? This place doesn't have a tower."

"Soc Trang?—sure it does, Fred."

"Huh? What are you talking about?"

"We're at Soc Trang, Fred. Don't you recognize it?"

"Soc Trang? What the hell are we doing here?"

"Aircraft parts, Fred. We're here to pick up parts and take them back to Vi Thanh. Go back to sleep."

"Sleep? I haven't been asleep."

"You coulda fooled me."

After landing, Kip gave the controls over to Oakerson and went into operations for coffee. Slote was standing behind the counter, his fatigues fresh and his face cleanly shaved. Because their radios couldn't be repaired at Vi Thanh, he and Henry had returned to Soc Trang, remaining there to perform operations duties. "Mr. Slater, I have you scheduled again with Mr. Oakerson tomorrow. You'll have the same position in the formation. Lieutenant Oremsby will be Tiger Lead."

"Yessir."

On the return trip, Oakerson and Slater traded off flying; as the one at the controls began to nod he would give the task of flying over to the other. In the back, both Reinhart and Walls slept. With the transmission bulkhead to their backs, warm and vibrating, it was never difficult for even the most well-intentioned crewman to doze, especially during single-ship flight. During formation flying, on the other hand, their full attention was required to watch the position and movement of other aircraft in the formation, a state of mind they oftentimes fought to maintain. All other times were moments of intense activity. In the landing zones, they made sure the pilots didn't run the tailrotor into trees, shrubs, buildings, and soldiers that were boarding or exiting the ship. They opened and closed the cargo doors on request, and during landings and liftoffs readied their M-60s for the action that never seemed to come. At the staging areas they refueled the aircraft, supervised the loading of troops or cargo, and waited, along with the pilots, for the next mission. Once at the home station, after the pilots had left to turn in the SOI (to then go to their rooms, take a quick shower, dress and proceed to the officers' club for dinner and another evening of drinking), gunner and crewchief would spend two to three hours more cleaning weapons, inspecting and servicing the aircraft. Afterwards, they would eat, shower, do their own share of drinking, then sleep, to be awakened the next morning to start the same process again. (In spite of their own lot, most pilots thought a crewman's life of flying an even more thankless drudgery. While some of the crewmen might agree, most saw their time in-country proceeding more quickly to DEROS working the flight line than if they spent their days performing as clerks, cooks, hangar mechanics, or motor pool personnel. Plus, they were exempt from perimeter guard duty, a chore sometimes so tedious during the night that no amount of caffeine or threat of court-martial could help keep a person awake.)

The Vi Thanh airstrip was pitch black when they returned. Before shutting down for the night Oakerson ordered the aircraft refueled. As Walls pumped the gas, both pilots dozed. When the refueling was complete the two warrant officers were awakened. Fred turned the landing light on, came to a hover, then began to move the ship toward a spot behind the last aircraft on the left side of the dirt strip. The helicopter hovered slowly, sometimes stopping, sometimes drifting sideways, then moving again, until they were within fifty feet of the last aircraft. Beneath them, moved by the rotor downwash, Kip saw the tall grasses on the side of the airstrip waver and undulate, casting its hypnotic spell. Within seconds he began to feel one with the ship...*floating...floating weightless...drifting...willingly...wantonly toward sleep...*

He blinked. "*FRED!*"

The sudden outburst caused Oakerson to rear back on the cyclic control stick. Slater had his hand behind the stick to check Fred's sudden movement.

"Wha-what!?" cried Oakerson.

Both pilots now struggled against each other on the controls. The helicopter heaved and danced for several seconds before either pilot calmed down enough to decide who would take full control of the ship. "Take the aircraft," Fred declared.

"Okay...I've the controls." Fully alert, Kip steadied the ship. His heart, though, felt like it wanted to throb right out of his chest. When he had looked up from his drowsed state, Fred had moved their ship to within ten feet of the helicopter ahead with no sign of stopping. What caused his mind to finally see what his eyes were only able to detect, Slater never knew.

Reinhart guided him toward a level spot.

"That's good, sir...Clear down left."

Kip placed the helicopter gingerly on the ground.

"What happened?" Oakerson asked.

"You must have been...somewhere...I don't know—*asleep?*"

"Oh, God, no shit...?"

"We about hit that guy's tailrotor. Do you remember hovering from the refueling port?"

"No...I-I don't remember a thing. All I remember is landing and then putting it down for refueling; and then I vaguely recall picking the aircraft up. After that..." His voice trailed off. "I can't believe I was asleep..."

The Vi Thanh airstrip was once again dashed in darkness. Moments before, Reinhart, using a flashlight, finished performing perfunctory maintenance, checking the oil levels, the engine deck, the rotorhead and tailrotor sections. Walls half an hour before had wiped the guns down, oiled them, then covered them for the night; he was now fast asleep in his hammock. Oakerson had stretched himself on the hard cabin floor and was snoring loudly. Kip sat in his seat in the cockpit and peered into the blackness. He had taken his fatigue jacket off, folded it, and was using it as a pillow. He heard Reinhart's footsteps approaching, coming from the ship ahead. "Did you get some hydraulic fluid?" Kip asked.

"Yessir."

"That's good."

"I haven't checked the logbook," Reinhart said. "How much time did we get today?"

"I added it three times. We got fifteen point seven hours." Kip sighed. "It sure beats the twelve point two I got the other day with Randall."

The crewchief let out a low whistle. "Sir, if we keep flying like this, we'll be pulling 'intermediates' every two to three days and hangaring them for PEs every eight days."

"No shit."

"Sir," Reinhart said, "you did a good job back there. Mr. Oakerson would have hit that other aircraft for sure if you hadn't looked up when you did."

Reinhart's praise met only silence. He then listened quietly. He heard a slight fluttering and then the sound of steady breathing. "Have a good night, sir. I'll be joining you in a minute. After I bring the logbook up to date."

* * *

IT WAS WELL AFTER THE EVENING MESS. Kip had spent the afternoon in the orderly room with Paul Christian. The two Awards and Decorations officers were swamped with work and had skipped the evening meal. Kip plunked himself down in Leo's wicker chair. Leo grabbed a beer from his refrigerator and handed it to him. Kip popped it open and took a good long swig. "You're not going to believe the latest shit," he said to Leo.

"Try me. Nothing surprises me anymore."

"Slote has recommended Neely for the Silver Star."

Leo's eyes widened. "What for?"

"For the action the other day at Vi Thanh."

"For the action at Vi Thanh. What the hell did *he* do?"

"He was Cn'C," Kip replied. He shrugged. "I guess Slote figured he did something."

"He didn't do shit. Remember, I flew with him the whole fuckin' day. All we did was orbit the gunships. First, at two thousand feet, then at three thousand. We were never in any kind of danger. What?—he gets a medal for doing circles at three thousand feet?"

"Hey, it ain't me," Kip said. "That's not all. Neely has recommended Slote for the Distinguished Flying Cross with V-device."

"For doin' fuckin' what?" This time Leo leaned forward, his brow furrowed.

"For being Tiger Lead."

Leo blinked and shook his head, as if trying to clear the cobwebs. "But he was only lead for about thirty minutes; his transmitters were crap—barely readable. Wainwright and Munson had to take over. A couple of warrant officers. What are they getting?"

"Bronze Stars with V-device."

"You're *kidding—?*"

"No, sir, I kid you not."

"Well, I'll be go to hell," Leo said. "Neely and Slote are sure scratching each other's ass."

"That's a damn ten-four," Kip replied.

"And as usual the warrant officers are getting the proverbial screwing. Jesus—does that ever piss me off."

"You and me both." Kip slugged down the rest of his beer. He said, "Suddenly, the idea of getting a medal over here has lost all its pizzazz."

For a moment Leo was silent. And then he said, his eyes looking past Slater: "Screw the pizzazz. Just point me to the free-fire zones. As far as I'm concerned they can stick their medals up their asses."

Journal Entry, 12 December 1967, Soc Trang AAF

I got a big surprise today. On the mission planning board, where all our flight time is posted, mine stood at 182.2 hours in a 30-day period. Several others were over 190. Capola broke 200 by 0.3 hours. Fred and I logged 29.4 hours during the three days we spent at Vi Thanh. Yesterday, I flew courier with Derek Justen to Saigon. I wallowed in the casualness of the flight. It was glorious.

The Sky Soldiers

Chapter 24

MOST OF FLIGHT ALPHA ONE HAD soloed by their eighteenth flight hour. By Tuesday of the fourth week Seymore P. Cutter was the only student who hadn't. Seymore had twenty-one dual flight hours. If he wasn't permitted to solo by hour twenty-three, he faced elimination or leaving the flight to the class behind. It was no secret that Red Fleming, Seymore's instructor, was one of the hardest IPs around. To any student who did well, he was as sweet as if he was dealing with his own grandmother. To the student who did poorly, but showed some inkling of coordination, Red Fleming was harsh but fair. To the student who had no apparent coordination, he was unmerciful. Red Fleming had another foible: He felt it his duty to weed out the Army's undesirable flight students, rather than let the checkpilots do it (for fear, mainly, that they would let them slip through the cracks). If one of his students wasn't good enough to go solo or pass a checkride (at least in his mind), he wasn't good enough to continue in the flight program. Therefore, Fleming would mount a campaign short of the "intimation of murder" to force that student to quit. Seymore was one of these students.

* * *

SEYMORE HAD JUST TURNED THE HELICOPTER downwind. It was late afternoon. Red Fleming was sitting in the left seat, smoking a cigarette, appearing somewhat relaxed. (Covertly, Fleming, as was any good instructor, was spring-loaded in the ready position to counter any wild-ass move his student might decide to make.) Oddly, Fleming was becoming more and more resigned to certain little facts about life (particularly about Seymore). There was no doubt that the lad had tested his skills as an instructor in every possible way. (If asked, Seymore would have to admit that his one and only flight instructor had called him every conceivable name in the book.) He has taken a ton of verbal abuse lately and seems quite calm in spite of it, even showing signs of hope, thought Fleming. He was no longer twisting the throttle in the wrong direction, or wiping out the cockpit with the cyclic, or jockeying the collective up and down to maintain altitude. His flight path in the traffic pattern still resembled, to some degree, that of a sidewinder snake, but at least he wasn't racing away from the traffic pattern, heading for God knows where, like some politician hell-bent for re-election. The lad still flew out of trim, but with the doors on, now that they were going into colder weather, it didn't matter, since the relative wind couldn't sweep through the cockpit to snuff out his cigarette.

"You know, Percival," Red Fleming began, "I've been told that all it takes for a person to learn to fly a helicopter is that he have ten fingers, ten toes, a temperature of ninety-eight point six, and that he not be blind, deaf or dumb. They

Victor R. Beaver

even say that I should be able to teach a chimpanzee to fly, given enough time of course. They say all I have to do is provide the right motivation, you know like…dangling a banana or carrot. Do you agree?"

"Er…yessir. If you say so, sir." (Up periscope. Down handles. Scan 360 degrees.)

"Well, I've been thinking," Fleming said.

"Yessir, you've been thinking." (Target: one flight instructor. Bearing: two seven zero. Range: one foot. Mark.)

"It's dawning on me—you know, a kind of vague insight. I've been a flight instructor for about ten years now. Looking back, I've begun to realize something." (Ready Tube One. Ready Tube Two.) "I've never got a dime more pay when one of my students made it, nor a dime less when he didn't." (Turn to heading three two zero. Standby to fire Tubes One and Two.) "This means I've been taking this instructing stuff way too seriously. I take it as a personal insult when an uncoordinated student does poorly, when in reality that's just the way God put him on this earth." (All ahead one third.) "Now you take yourself for instance…"

"Yessir." (Target changing course. Turning starboard. Right full rudder.)

"I think maybe I've been handling you all wrong."

"You have?—Sir?" (Up handles. Down periscope—down periscope. All ahead full.)

"Percival, my boy, how bad do you want to solo?"

"Sir—?"

"You want to pretty bad…don't you, Percival?"

"Very, very bad, sir. I want to solo in the *worst* way, sir. (Up periscope—up periscope. Down handles. Scan.)

"Well, Percival, I think maybe I might be able to let you go—*IF!*…you can do me one good autorotation. How does that sound?"

(White flag. White flag. It looks like a surrender, boys. Secure Tube One. Secure Tube Two. Prepare to surface. Prepare to surface.) "It sounds great, sir. One good autorotation coming up, sir—"

Seymore turned from downwind to base. "You will level the skids, won't you, Percival, when you pull in the last of the cushioning pitch…?"

"Oh, yessir—you can bet your life on that—*Sir!*"

"*NO!*—No-no. I'm not a gambling man, Percival. Besides, God only knows how many more of your kind I may have to train. But if you do screw up this time, I'll still be able to rest in peace."

"Rest in peace, sir?"

"Yes, because when you're in the infantry, you'll still make excellent cannon fodder."

"OUCH—*damn*…that hurts."

"Come on, Seymore," Sandy said. "You can do it. Just one more stitch—" Seymore sucked at the tip of his bleeding finger. More than two dozen members of Flight Alpha One were gathered around him in the room breathing down his back as he put the final touches to his blue cap.

He tied off the thread and managed to stick himself one more time. But he felt only joy as he put his cap on and stood. Everyone began to clap. Seymore glanced from face to face, the pride he felt obvious in his wide grin. Sandy reached up and tweaked the cap once for final straightening. Seymore's solo wings, however, looked very odd sewn upside down, the penalty for being the last in the flight to go up alone.

"You look good, Seymore," Ron Bowden declared. "We're proud as hell of you. *You finally did it!"*

"Speech—speech!"

"Gosh, guys...I-I don't know what to say."

"SAY!?" rang out Willie Cottrell. "Just say you'll buy the first round of beer! How about it, guys—*to the Lone Star pissing hole we go—?!"*

* * *

"GENTLEMEN, WE WILL NOW DISCUSS the concepts Controlled and Uncontrolled Airspace. Later in the period, I will explain the difference between instrument and visual flight rules, or IFR and VFR," spoke Mr. Giovanni, another of the civilian platform instructors assigned to Southern Airways, Inc. It was Friday morning and they were attending their last class of the day. Ever since their first flying day, the pace in academics had been brisk. Their subjects—meteorology, navigation, aeronautical chart interpretation, rotary-wing aerodynamics, FAA regulations and air safety procedures—had all come at them in big chunks, called "blocks of instruction." Most of it was thrown at them like shit at the ceiling in the hope that some of it would stick.

Mr. Giovanni was a towering figure, tall and stoutly built. Perched on his nose was a pair of dark, horn-rimmed glasses. He peered at them over the top of the lenses, giving them that "Ben Franklin" look. He was a man who loved to read Aristotle. "A thing is what it is—the Law of Identity: A is A," he liked to quote. "A is not Non-A—the Law of Non-Contradiction."

"Let us begin with the idea of Either-Or," he began. "We are either flying in Controlled Airspace—or we are not." Their eyes were held open wide by the power of the man's singular, unequivocal voice. Their attention was riveted to his every utterance.

"First, we must define our terms. What is the strict definition of air traffic control? Simply put, it means the controller tells you when to fly, what route to fly, how high to fly, to create a buffer of airspace around you and other aircraft. All for what reason?"

Not a man stirred.

"Why...to avoid creating a collision hazard. Simple."

He went on. "Therefore, for air traffic control to have the legal jurisdiction to do this the concept 'controlled airspace' was instituted. Controlled airspace is defined in the book as that airspace designated at Control Area, Transition Area, Control Zone and Continental Control Area. Period." He paused. "Uncontrolled airspace is that airspace which has not been designated as Control Area, Transition Area, Control Zone, or Continental Control Area. Period. Therefore...no name of any other airspace..." he stated slowly, methodically, "...is considered controlled airspace...unless it has the title of...one of these four names. Period."

Seymore raised his hand. "Isn't an airport traffic area 'controlled airspace?' The tower operator at Downing sure gets pissed when we don't do what he says."

Giovanni straightened. The pursuit of logic. It was his forté. "Mr. Cutter, is the title 'airport traffic area' listed among the four I mentioned?" He hated to call the students by the title of candidate.

"No, sir."

"Then an airport traffic area—by title—is not controlled airspace. Period."

"Yessir..."

* * *

FLIGHT ALPHA ONE NOW NUMBERED forty-nine candidates (they had lost Auten as a flight deficiency setback and had gained two flight deficiency setbacks from the class ahead.) Of that number, seventeen were married. Willie Cottrell, Dwight Alexander, and Pete Cochran were the only married candidates whose wives had not accompanied them to Fort Wolters. Several of the unmarried candidates had steady girlfriends back home, and one or two of them would come for special occasions. But most of the single guys came to the flight functions without dates, the competition around most military bases notoriously keen for the few women available.

Ron Bowden's wife Rose, an older, very likeable woman without children of her own, had early on elected herself flight den mother. Without being too much of a busybody she took under her wing the other wives in the flight, especially those with young children, to whom she had become like a nanny. Her spirit and energy, too, were present whenever the flight planned a social gathering (which happened quite often). She was also a terrific cook, Italian food being her specialty. Anyone who came to visit her and Ron in their apartment was usually greeted with some mouth-watering delight she was preparing.

Flight Alpha One conducted its solo party on a mild December afternoon on the last Saturday before the Christmas break. A slight breeze came off the lake where they had reserved their picnic spot. Willie and Seymore stood at two barbecue grills, while Frank and Ron manned the taps on the kegs. Mark and Marie flitted a Frisbee back and forth as several children ran around them playing tag. Sandy, Cottondale, Chancey, and several others tried their hand at fishing. Callie Henderson, Seymore's date, eyeing the feast with relish, helped adorn the picnic tables with napkins, plates, and silverware, while several wives relaxed and held babies and small children in their arms or laps. Rose Bowden shooed away idle hands trying to snatch the delectable treats. Tom Adkins had his sketchpad out and was furiously trying to capture every scene. Soon Willie and Seymore reported that the chicken and pork chops were done. Rose clinked a fork against a glass and began to speak:

"Come on, everyone, gather around," she said, waving her arms in a sweeping movement. "Time to eat. But first let's say grace."

Ron led them in a short prayer. Rose then began to ladle out one of her specialties: stuffed ravioli topped with a rich red sauce, all her own recipe. Within moments everyone had plates heaped high.

A few moments later, Rose raised a glass of wine. She called again for everyone's attention. "I would like to propose a toast. To all you men. You have reached another milestone. This flying a helicopter, I know is not an easy thing. You have all soloed and that is something to be proud of." She looked toward her husband Ron. "You all studied hard and so I know there is a lot of bookwork most people don't know about that goes along with learning to fly. May we all continue together. I would like to see each of your faces at the end when you graduate and get your wings." She held her glass higher. "Toast...to each of you and to your loved ones...they too share in this accomplishment." Glasses clinked and they each took a swig of their drink.

Ron Bowden then hugged his wife. "She is quite a motivator," he declared. "She wouldn't let me get to 'sleep,' if you know what I mean, until I got my studying done." Everyone chuckled. Rose blushed and looked away, embarrassed.

"So he always studied," she said.

* * *

IT WAS JUST BEFORE THE EVENING MEAL. Mr. Drakeman stood in front of the formation holding a piece of paper. "Candidate Adamson, you've got a message to call this number. I believe it's urgent." Sandy came forward and took the paper. His heart skipped a beat when he saw it was Katie's home phone number.

The telephone rang several times. "Hello...?"

Sandy recognized Katie's mother's voice. "Hello, Mrs. Williams. This is Sandy Adamson, how are you?"

"Oh...hello, Sandy." Her voice trembled, sounding uneven.

Victor R. Beaver

His knees went weak. "Is...Is Katie there?"

"No...no she's not. Sandy—"

"Is-is she okay?"

"Sandy, I have some very sad news for you. Our son Brad was killed."

For a moment he was too stunned to speak; a lump formed quickly in his throat. He said, "When?"

"It happened yesterday," Katie's mother said. "We got the news this morning."

What do I say?—What do I say? "I'm-I'm so sorry, Mrs. Williams."

"I know you are, Sandy." She explained that Brad's body was being shipped home tomorrow. There would be a memorial service Friday night. The funeral would be on Saturday morning. "Will you be able to attend?" she asked.

"Yes...yes, ma'am. My leave starts Wednesday evening. I should be getting in sometime Thursday afternoon."

"We'll be looking forward to seeing you." And then she added: "Sandy, Mr. Williams and I would like for you be one of Brad's pallbearers."

He had to clear his throat. "Okay...I'd be hap—I mean, yes, ma'am."

She said, "I'm afraid Katie is taking this pretty hard. Right now she's over at Susan's. Would you like the number?"

"Yes, ma'am."

He dialed right away. As he dialed, his heart was in his throat. What was he going to say? For a split second he wished, before dialing, he had collected his thoughts, but it was too late. *Killed...Oh my God. It's happened—!*

"Hello?" It was the voice of an older man.

"Is Katie there?"

"Who may I say is calling?"

"A friend of Katie's. I'm Sandy Adamson."

"Just a minute, I'll get her."

The few seconds that passed seemed an eternity. "Hello, Sandy."

The sound of her voice, so fragile, made every muscle in his body go limp; he barely had the energy to speak. "Katie, I-I just talked to your mom. I'm sorry...I'm so very sorry. Are you okay?"

For a moment there was silence. When she spoke, it was just a murmur, as if there was hardly any life left in her. Her voice sounded soft, unhurried, even-paced. Katie related how she found out the news. She was getting ready to leave for school when the doorbell rang, and when she went to answer she was greeted politely by two men in uniform, plus the pastor of their church. She had no idea what they wanted, but their faces were very somber. They asked to see either her mother or father. Her father had already gone to work. When her mother appeared, she saw her face turn white. It was then that she understood the purpose of the visit. The two men in uniform asked them to sit down and said they had some very bad news about Brad. "They explained," she said, her voice almost

The Sky Soldiers

inaudible, "that there had been an accident onboard ship, an explosion, and that he had been badly burned..." Katie's voice trailed off and she began to cry. In a moment Sandy heard someone else come on the line.

"Hi, Sandy. This is Susan."

"Susan—I feel so terrible...I wish I could be there."

"I'm sure you do. Look, Katie needs a little time. She's still pretty much in shock. Maybe you could call her tomorrow, at her home. I think she'll be doing a little better then."

"Okay, yeah...that's probably a good idea."

"Sandy, she's real concerned about you. Are you doing all right in training?"

"I'm doing fine."

"She mentions that you'll probably be going to Vietnam right afterwards. With what's happened to Brad, she's really frightened for you."

"Yeah, I can imagine," he said. Suddenly, he had a vision of the same thing happening again: the doorbell rings: there are two men in uniform and a minister standing before her: they ask to come in and they explain that...that...he shook his head to clear the image. "I don't know what to say, Susan. Just tell her that I love her and that I'll be home soon, on Thursday."

"Okay, Sandy...I'll tell her. Meanwhile, you be very careful."

"I will."

After he hung up, he remained in the booth and gazed out across the large open space that lay between the two 3rd WOC Company barracks. He watched as several pairs of candidates made their way toward the beer and pizza parlor next to the messhall. It would just now be getting crowded. He had gone in there once, before Seymore's solo-flight celebration, but walked right out; it just seemed so loud and boisterous. As was typical, everyone was drunk and he had heard that occasionally tempers would flare and a fight would break out. Sandy opened the door of the telephone booth and began to walk toward the parlor. He fell in behind a pair of warrant officer candidates who looked remarkably alike. "Mind if I tag along. I need a drink bad."

"Hell no...you come right along," one of them said. "The more, the merrier."

By the time Mark and Seymore found him, Sandy had a beer in one hand and a cigarette in the other, and both arms draped over his new-found buddies. They were in a larger group singing along to lyrics coming from the jukebox. "Hey," he yelled, "I want you guys to meet the Parip...Paripovich twins, Andy and Randy." He slurred his words badly and his eyes were way out of focus. "And of course you know who I am, I'm Sandy Pari...povich. They adopted me. I'm a third twin brother—"

At midnight Mark and Seymore hauled him up to their third floor room and tried to put him to bed. But he fought and struggled and cursed like a madman. After they got him calmed down, Sandy told them about Katie's brother; then he began to wail. "I can't never put her through that again...never...never...got to break up with her. Got to do it…got to…do it…" at which time he slumped down, passed out on the floor.

Mark shook his head. "What do you think, pal?" he said to Seymore, who was seated on his bunk, a lighted cigarette in his hand.

"About what?"

"It ain't worth it, is it?"

"What ain't worth it?"

"Getting all tangled up with someone when you know you're going to a place like that."

Seymore, half-tipsy himself, thought for a moment, then nodded. "Yeah…it ain't worth it. Especially it ain't worth it to them. We get killed and they get left behind. It just ain't worth it. I'm sure glad I ain't tangled up with nobody. I'm with you, man. Gotta keep it simple…"

Chapter 25

MAIL CALL. EVERY DAY FROM FOUR to six in the evening, come rain or shine, the small post office window was open. Always a much awaited daily ritual, it was their only real link to the outside world...a world supposedly much safer and saner.

Holding several letters, Kip Slater turned and walked back toward his hootch. One was from his mother, which he dreaded opening; another was from his brother, with whom he was playing chess by mail; and there were two others, from a couple of girls he had known in college; their letters had a nice, fresh scent to them. He opened his mother's letter first—to get it over with.

Dear Son,
I hope this letter finds you alive and well. I'm so frightened of the news. Things over there are so horrendous. Are you okay? I pray every day that you are not in any trouble. Please, you must write more often and let us know if you're in good health. I am fraught with worry for you. I just know something bad is going to happen...

These letters from her were so exasperating. Every one he received made him feel like she was writing to a corpse. She practically had him dead and buried! It was driving him nuts. He wrote back:

Dear Mom,
I'm okay. I'm eating good. I'm healthy. I've not had any trouble. Please, you're letters are not the least bit uplifting. Tell me some good news from home once in awhile, anything. I'm not in that much danger, believe me...

Dear Son,
How dare you treat my feelings so casually. I'm your mother; I have a right to know how you're doing—

"Yes, Mother..."

P.S. Those idiots! You got another draft notice yesterday. Your father had to physically go down and show them a copy of your orders sending you to Vietnam.

* * *

"TURN IN THE SOI," RANDALL TOLD HIM. "I'm bushed. My ass is dragging."

Slater grinned. "Now-now, you've got to be up for the party. Remember, it's mandatory."

"Oh shit...the party, I almost forgot."

"Hey, they're gonna have a bunch of round-eyed women there," Kip reminded.

"Oh sure, guess who's going to get'em. I was at the last function. Every woman was scooped up by the brass—the horny bastards. You won't be able to get within ten feet of one of them broads."

Slater watched for a moment as Randall went toward the hootches. He then turned and went into operations. They had flown re-supply out of My Tho that day. Kip learned that Randall was from Burbank, that he had attended UCLA for two years, and that when he quit to go full time as a lifeguard at Santa Monica State Beach, he received his draft notice. "I went down to the recruiting office," he told Slater, "with the intent of joining the Air Force. I got sidetracked by this frickin' Army poster with a guy and his helmet and a helicopter pictured behind him."

In operations, Henry was busy behind the counter posting tomorrow's missions. He turned as Kip came through the door. "Here's the SOI," Kip said. "Have you seen Leo?"

"The last I heard he went downtown with a couple of Blue Tiger gunners, Mangrum and Pickett. Do you know them?"

"No, I don't think I've ever flown with them."

It was after six when he got his shower and shave out of the way. In his room Kip put on his Tiger sport-shirt and splashed on an extra measure of aftershave. He had a small mirror over his table. He gazed at his reflection. His face had grown thin since he'd been in-country. His eyes looked worn from gazing into harsh sunlight all day. As he went out his door and down the hall, he wondered what the American women looked like. He imagined them young and pretty; he suspected strongly that they would be otherwise.

The small room sectioned off in the officers' mess for the wet bar was crowded when he entered. All the men were dressed in civilian clothes, casual shirts and pants. How strange it seemed to see no one in jungle-fatigue uniform. He counted seven American women. Indeed, two of them were slender and very attractive. Three were overweight, with faces that made them look middle-aged. The other two, in his estimation, were beyond "repair"; however, they did not lack for attention. He knew none of the battalion headquarters' staff by sight but figured them to be the ones standing around Major Neely, who was smiling at them, yet who was also glancing about the room reassuring himself that everything was in order. Major Maes, the company XO, stood by Neely's side, looking nervous. Before Neely came into the unit, Maes was known to have several quick drinks in the evening before retiring; now he rationed himself accordingly. Kip went to the bar and ordered a Seagram's and Seven. He stood off to the side and watched the women. Randall was right; all of them were accounted for; and not a one stood with any of the lieutenants or warrant officers. Captain Slote leered over the shoulder of one of the girls, who was talking to an older, gray-haired man. Kip figured him to be the battalion commander.

"Pssst..."

Kip turned. He had just finished his first drink and was working on his second.

"Leo—"

"Sssssh...Come here," Leo said, motioning from the doorway.

"What's up?" Kip said, moving toward his friend.

"Up? Yeah...yeah—Up. I'm up."

"Up?" Kip repeated. "What are you talking about?"

Leo moved into the room. The two men stood alone against the wall near the door. Kip frowned, deciding quickly that Leo was acting very strange. He said, "So, how'd it go today? Were you pretty busy?" Leo had not flown that day. Lieutenant Oremsby had assigned him the duty of helping to arrange the mess for the dinner party. Leo had been more than delighted to do it. He had had enough flying lately to last into the coming year. Leo stood next to him, glancing drowsily about the room; then he started to giggle.

"Hey...pretty busy...fun busy..."

Kip gave Leo a quizzical look. "What do you mean?"

"I'm feeling pretty good," Leo said.

"Well, I can see that. How much have you drunk?" Kip then noticed that Leo's eyes were bloodshot.

Leo shook his head, waving his finger across his face. "Ain't had hardly a drop to drink, Kip, old boy."

"Like hell..."

"No, I'm not shittin' you. Hardly a drop. Got into something better."

Kip looked around the room. Everyone was engaged in conversation with someone. Not a soul was looking their way. "Leo, what's the matter with you, anyway? What the hell *have* you been doing?"

Leo grinned. "Nothin'...'cept gettin' high."

"High? What do you mean 'high'?"

Leo came closer. He patted his shirt-pocket, which bulged with his pack of cigarettes. "It's in here."

"What's in there, Leo? You're not making a lick of sense."

"It's 'shit.' The very best 'shit' I have ever smoked."

"Smoked—?"

Leo reached up and put his finger to Kip's lips. "Gawd—not so loud." And then he whispered, "Have you ever smoked grass before?"

"You mean...*marijuana?*" Kip replied. And then he drew back. "Are you kidding? Not on your life. That stuff will get you hooked on heroin—"

"Oh crap," Leo blurted, rolling his eyes. "Where'd you hear that shit from?"

"I don't know...somewhere."

"Don't believe that junk. You want to try some?"

Kip furled his eyebrows. "Here?"

"Sure," Leo answered. "Ain't nobody here gonna care. Look at'em; everyone's already half drunk."

Kip shrugged. He had never in his life ever taken any drugs, not even in college. None of his friends smoked. To him marijuana was the same as the hard stuff: one led inevitably to the other, at least that's what he had read, therefore that's what he believed. He couldn't fathom that normal people did that. He looked at Leo and frowned.

Leo took out his pack of cigarettes. He tilted the pack. Out slid a "rolled" cigarette. Leo took the "cigarette" and licked it thoroughly. He lit one end. Next he put the cigarette between his lips and took a long, deep drag. The smoke swirled. Kip looked around. No one seemed the least bit interested—or alarmed—at what Leo was doing. Leo held the smoke in his lungs, then handed him the cigarette, now smoldering nicely. Leo expelled the smoke in one great burst. "See how it's done?"

"Yeah." Kip took and put the cigarette to his lips. He pulled deeply. Leo stood watching, grinning, his eyes sleepy and now more bloodshot than before. Kip blew the smoke out and took another drag. He blew the smoke out again. "I don't feel a thing," he told Leo.

"Well, no wonder, you're honking on it like a regular cigarette. But don't worry, you will. Take another hit."

Kip pulled deeply again, wondering what everyone must be thinking and also wondering why he wasn't feeling the effects of the smoke.

It was his fifth deep drag that did him in. He felt a tremendous surge from the pit of his stomach. His head felt like it was being flooded by a hot rushing liquid. "*LEO!*—Oh God, I'm going to be sick. Let me out of here!" He bolted for the door. Once outside he went to the side of the building and dropped to his knees. The contents of his stomach came up so fast that he had no time to dread the moment. He retched until he was depleted. "Hey-hey," Leo said, dropping by his side. "You okay? Jesus, I didn't think you'd get sick. Pretty good 'shit,' huh?"

"Fuck...Leo..." He could barely speak. "What the hell happened?—Man...I have never in my life been that sick that quickly."

"You'll be all right. Pretty soon you'll be floating. Everything will be just fine. Trust me."

Slater remained there on his knees, weak, weaker than he had ever been. No morning-after hangover had ever left him so ragged, so thoroughly spent. Sweat now broke out on his forehead. And then a warm feeling began to filter throughout his body. He thought he might vomit again, but the feeling, instead, turned into a kind of vibrating tingle. When he sat back on his haunches, he felt heavy. He looked toward the light that lit the entranceway to the officers' latrine shining a little more than fifty steps away. The narrow pathway between the Tiger's Den and the first set of officers' quarters seemed like a long tunnel. Everything, as he looked around, seemed far...far...away...

As he sat there tilting his body first one way, then the other, sensing like he was in a tailspin, his mind became bombarded by a dozen vivid impressions. Then, after what seemed like an eternity, he glanced at his watch and saw that from the time he bolted from the club only a couple of minutes had passed.

"Leo—I feel like I've been sitting here forever. What's happening?"

"You're stoned. Ain't it great?" And then Leo started to laugh. "I forgot to tell you. That's 'one-hit shit' you just smoked."

"What the hell is 'one-hit shit?'"

"Dummy, you only need one good drag—'hit'—to get high!"

Journal Entry, 16 December 1967, Soc Trang AAF

> *What I'm about to relate seems totally incredible. That I actually did what I did last night, especially where I did it—literally in front of colonels, majors and captains—is hard to believe. And then this morning, I got the scare of my life. Major Maes remarked to me that I sure got my head "smoked up" last night. I nearly blew out a mouthful of coffee all over him. Then his later remarks to me made me realize he was using the term "smoked" in another way: that I had apparently got quite drunk. Holy Mother of Jesus.*

* * *

WORLD NEWS, AND NEWS ABOUT VIETNAM, usually came to them over the Armed Forces radio network, AFVN. In the aircraft, when the communication radios weren't going a mile a minute, there was usually the opportunity to listen to the latest poop over the ADF (automatic direction finder) navigation receiver, which could also be tuned to any normal radio broadcast station. Kip twisted the dial and found the station. He and Wainwright and crew were en route to Chou Doc. The DJ's voice was clear, sounding much like any stateside announcer, cheery and exuberant:

"*...And on the military front, General Earle Wheeler, Chairman of the Joint Chiefs of Staff, suggested that the single most important factor prolonging the* war is Hanoi's calculation that there is a reasonable possibility of a change in U.S. policy before the collapse of the Viet Cong...

"Other news this hour...retired General David Shoup, former U.S. Marine Corps Commandant, at a luncheon was quoted as saying, '...it is pure unadulterated poppycock to believe U.S. presence is necessary in South Vietnam to prevent a Communist invasion of the United States. The administration is trying to keep the people worried about the Communists crawling up the banks of Pearl Harbor or crawling up the Palisades or crawling up the beaches of Los Angeles,' unquote."

Kip frowned. He looked toward Wainwright, who smirked. "Someone's probably gonna get their ass in a ringer for putting that kind of shit out on the radio," the AC said. "Jesus, why don't they just play music. The news over here always depresses me."

* * *

LEO AND KIP WERE ON ONE SIDE, PICKETT and Mangrum on the other. "Hit it. Hit it," Leo cried.

"I'm trying—Jesus, Leo...Oh shit, there it goes—"

Both Pickett and Mangrum cheered. "We win—the foosball championship of the *universe—!*" The two gunners shook hands and congratulated each other. Leo spun the two handles he had been operating, his face flush. They were on the outskirts of downtown Soc Trang, formally call Khanh Hung, at one of the city's public tennis courts, a typically shoddy and rundown affair. (Since the big battle southwest of Vi Thanh, the action in the Delta had slowed, enough to allow everyone a day off every three to four days.) The foosball table was off to one side of the tennis court, near a small, stucco-walled building. Large Banyan trees provided most of the shade around the tennis court. Since the party, the four men, two pilots and two gunners, had become good friends. Both Mangrum and Pickett always had an ample supply of the "dinky dou" weed, which they willingly shared with Kip and Leo. Slater was getting to like the feeling it gave him—a feeling of total peace and tranquility. Plus, all of his senses became so incredibly heightened.

"Would you gentlemen care to join Evan and me?" Jeff Mangrum said.

"Doing what?" Leo asked.

"Well, we have this little place we go to occasionally..."

"The girls are...how you say...very clean," said Evan Pickett, smiling.

Kip's ears perked. He liked the flavor of this conversation. "You mean...you're going to a whorehouse?"

"Yeah...yeah," Mangrum said. "Can you dig it?"

"Count me out," Leo stated.

"Come on, Leo," Kip said, "where's your spirit of lust and adventure?"

"I'll meet you back at the airfield," he said.
"Okay, whatever you say."

The trio meandered down several back streets until they came to a small side street where a row of plaster hootches sat on a cul de sac. Evan opened the gate to one of the houses and the three walked up the dirt path to the door. Jeff knocked. In a moment, a young-looking, very pretty Vietnamese woman opened the door. Hesitant, she looked out at them half hidden in the shadows until she recognized who they were and the purpose of their visit. Smiling, she motioned for them to enter.

It was dark inside, and very cool, as if they had stepped out of a sauna and into an air-conditioned room. Kip took a moment to get used to the dim lighting. When his eyes adjusted he saw two children huddled behind the young woman, and beyond them a good-looking slightly older woman, very dignified, standing in an inner doorway. He heard a strange rooting sound coming from behind her. In a moment the snout of a small pig appeared next to the older woman's legs, followed by the rest of its head, and then its whole body. Kip thought, *What the hell am I doing here?* as the younger woman guided them down a short hallway with the two children close behind. They then turned into another hallway about twice as long. Kip saw three closed doors on one side of the hall. All the while cooking smells and earthy noises permeated the house with the flavor of a barnyard.

Kip said to Evan: "I haven't got a rubber."
"That's okay, they're clean. Which one do you want?"
"Which one?"
"Yeah," Jeff said. "You get your pick. Evan and I have had them all."

To Kip's amusement the two gunners were indicating either the young woman or the older one, and a third woman, the loveliest Vietnamese female he had ever seen, now appearing at one of the doorways. His eyes lit up. "Can I have her?"

"Sure," Jeff Mangrum said. "She's new. Isn't she beautiful? And so young. An excellent choice, Mr. Slater. A very excellent choice."

Kip smiled. It sounded as if Mangrum was commending him for his good taste choosing an expensive wine or some delicacy from an expensive restaurant menu.

Evan nodded for the lovely young Vietnamese woman to come forward. She came and gingerly took Kip by the hand. She led him into the room and closed the door.

Kip looked about. The room was practically void of furniture. A mattress lay on the floor in one corner covered by a dingy yellow sheet. In the left adjacent corner stood a small wooden table upon which sat a wash basin filled with water, the table placed near a drain hole in the cement floor. A single bulb hung down from the ceiling; it's dim light spread feebly about the room making the affair he was about to engage in seem even more seedy and unclean. The girl began to remove her pants and shirt. Kip followed her every movement, his desire for this delicate creature now becoming greater by the second.

He was still feeling the effects of the last marijuana cigarette he and the rest had smoked. His manhood strained inside his pants.

The girl laid down on the mattress. So far she hadn't said two words to him. He noticed that her breasts were small but well proportioned for her size. She removed her panties. Smiling, she said, "Numba one teetee."

"What?" Kip said.

"Teetee numba one. No need plotection. Doctor always lookee."

"Oh..." he said, now unbuttoning his shirt. He looked for a place to hang it. She sat up and indicated he could place it on the mattress. Next he peeled off his pants. Her observation of him, he noticed, seemed nonplused. He wondered if she had the dreaded "brand X" venereal disease, whatever the hell *that* was. Rumor had it that if you were to catch it, you could never return to the States. Not ever. But she did look very clean and for some reason he trusted her.

With his pants off and laid on the mattress alongside his shirt, he kneeled on the edge of the mattress. She pointed at his feet. "Shoes?"

"Oh...sorry, I forgot."

He turned and sat down and pulled his low-quarters off. She laid back again and Kip moved next to her. He looked into her eyes. She seemed like such a child, but he knew that so many of the Vietnamese people he had seen either looked much younger than they actually were, or much, much older.

His whole body now seemed on fire. She reached for him and guided him to her. He held back. He put two fingers to his lips, indicating that he wanted to kiss her. Her mouth was small yet lucious. She shook her head. "No kissee...no kissee."

Well, he had heard that about prostitutes. To do their job, with someone different as often as they did, they could not get emotionally involved. Kissing would give the impression that she liked him. He shrugged...and then...and then...

It was over so quickly. The young woman moved from beneath him. She got up and went over to the drain hole. She doused herself with water from the basin on the table. In another moment she was dressed; she motioned for him to do the same.

When he got his shoes on he stood and she held out her hand. "Five hundred P. That numba one good time, huh?"

"Yeah...I guess so," he said, giving her a five hundred piastre note (equivalent to about five American dollars).

"You come 'gain soon?"

He nodded. "Yeah, sure."

In the hall Kip met Jeff and Evan. They were smiling. "So, how was it?"

"I think I'd rather ask a gal out to dinner, pay twenty bucks for a meal, then hope like hell I get laid." He scrunched up his face. "It was too clinical for my blood."

"Yeah, we sorta agree."

But Slater found himself wondering when he and Mangrum or Pickett would be back. The next time he wanted to be really stoned....

Victor R. Beaver

Chapter 26

"STUFF AS MUCH FOOD, AMMO, and first-aid supplies as you can into your pockets," Whitaker told them. The White Tiger platoon leader's eyes were deep-set and serious. He held his operational map with a slight quiver.

"How many troops are we lifting in for the security force?" Randall asked. He was leaning against the side of Trent's ship, behind Lieutenant Oremsby.

Oremsby turned. "About two hundred," the Blue Tiger platoon leader said.

"Damn, that's hardly more than a company," Oakerson blurted.

Trent nodded his head. "There won't be enough time to put more into the LZ, Freddy my boy."

They were at the Ca Mau airstrip, parked on the north side of the runway, near the elongated body of water that ran parallel to it, eighteen lift helicopters and six pairs of gunships. Each of the Delta's four assault helicopter companies was contributing to the operation. Phase I of the evacuation of Nam Can, in the middle of the Ca Mau Peninsula, was about to begin. "We've got to get in and out as fast as we can," Whitaker continued, "before Charlie has a chance to assemble and react."

Kip Slater looked toward Derek Justen, whose gaze remained fixed on the water's edge. The two had been paired together. The other Tiger pairings were Tannah and Baumburger, who had two weeks to go before DEROS, Oakerson and Munson, Paul Christian and Trent Whitaker, Oremsby and McNamara. Robin Henry was now an aircraft commander; his peter-pilot was a gum-smacking nineteen-year-old from Arkansas named Westy Harper. The first two landings into the LZ would bring in the security force, to guard the LZ during the evacuation proceedings. Only the dependents, women and children, were to be airlifted out today. Phase II, the complete abandonment of the Nam Can outpost, would come later, after the first of the year. Nam Can was impossible to resupply without making a major airlift operation out of every run into there, thus the reason for the abandonment.

Justen sat silent, his fingertips holding steady the cigarette he was smoking, the smoke drifting straight up in the dank morning air. He peered at the mist rising off the surface of the water, thinking of Jake. If he was alive, and if they hadn't moved him too far from Bay Hap, where he had originally gone down, a location a mere six miles north of Nam Can (where Derek neither thought nor felt Jake was being detained for reasons he couldn't explain), he would most certainly hear and perhaps even see all the helicopter traffic sometime during the day. What would he think? That rescue was close at hand? And when it didn't happen, what then? Would he lose all remaining hope and fall deeper into despair? Would it push him beyond the edge and drive him mad?

Justen had no answer. Just like he had no idea how long he would remain in Vietnam, nor how long Jake's lovely wife, Valerie, could endure the pain and frustration of not knowing, from day to day, the fate of her husband. As was the case with practically all MIAs, the lives of those concerned were put on hold—with no apparent end in sight—rarely ever any good news to break the deadlock. Weeks and months of nothing. Months piled on months piled on years. No word of life...nor of death. Contrary to what Tafoya had told him, at least in death there was finality, a resolution, a dismal resolution, but a resolution nonetheless. Afterwards, life goes on. Yes, Justen knew nothing definitive about Jake, nothing he could pin his hat on, but of one thing he was certain: If Jake was not dead, then he would have to be a POW; he could not be anything else, or he would have appeared sometime soon after the crash. Thus, in spite of the frustration of not knowing, Jake's MIA status at least allowed a sliver of hope...and a very faint sliver at that.

Kip began to fill his fatigue pockets with foods from the C-ration cartons and first-aid materials from the packets that normally went with the ship. His holster had every slot filled with a .38 round. He wished he had had the foresight to bring an extra box of shells. He hadn't yet found an extra personal weapon like Leo's Thompson sub-machinegun, or Henry's pump-shotgun, or Randall's BAR (Browning automatic rifle). The two M-14 rifles strapped over the armor plating of each pilot's seat as part of the ship's normal complement of armament, added some comfort. Next to the rifles several bandoleers filled with M-14 ammo clips also hung over the armor plating. Neither doorgunner had a personal weapon. In the past he had thought it silly that Conrad always carried brass knuckles and a switchblade. But every form of defense they had onboard could be needed, even brass knuckles.

Kip looked up. Coming from the village, in single file, were the troops, with the ARVN platoon leaders assigning eight men to a ship. They looked heavily armed and loaded with extra gear. He hoped they were stocked to the gills with ammunition. As they came nearer, Slater saw that their faces were somber. He noticed, too, there was very little of the usual banter between the Vietnamese soldiers and the American crews; still shouldering their equipment, they simply sat down on the ground to await eventual liftoff.

Kip glanced at his watch. Only two minutes had passed since he last checked it. They would be lifting in forty minutes. He watched Finch, Derek's gunner, unload the belted M-60 ammunition from Conrad's feed tray and reload it, taking great pains to do it exactly right. On top the aircraft Conrad was making last minute checks of the rotorhead. "How's everything look up there, Chief?"

"Okay, sir," he said. "I was just...checking the play in these pitch-change links...again." Conrad's voice sounded strained.

Finch went to the right side of the ship and did the same to his ammunition. Kip went around to watch. After a moment, he asked Finch how the M-60 worked. Finch explained in detail the gun's firing functions. "You gotta watch your firing rate, though; don't want to overheat the barrels. That's why I always carry a coupla extra. See these heavy leather gloves? It's in case I have to change a hot barrel."

"I see," Kip said. After a moment, he asked Finch where he was from.

"LA...same as Conrad. We're cousins. Our mothers are sisters."

"Hell, I didn't know that. You guys hardly ever speak to each other."

Finch shrugged. "We grew up together. We've said it all."

Kip moved away from the helicopter; he sat down near the edge of the landing strip. Everyone was tense. It was the mission. Everyone had to be thinking the same thoughts. From the very beginning, Kip believed the evacuation to be suicidal—or very nearly so. The area surrounding Nam Can had been enemy-controlled for so long that it seemed ludicrous to call it government territory. The outpost had outlived its function ages ago: that of listening for and monitoring enemy re-supply movements into the southern tip of the Mekong Delta from the Gulf of Thailand and the South China Sea. Practically all traffic was VC. And then it dawned on him: *this was a suicide mission!* The realization of it settled like a knot in the pit of his stomach. None of us is assured of a reasonable chance of getting through this day alive, he thought. They didn't even ask for volunteers. They didn't say diddlysquat to us. We get here and they tell us that if we go down, we're on our own to get back as best we can, that no aircraft can be spared to rescue a downed crew, that no gunships will be permitted to provide air cover which might jeopardize the mission. *What the hell kind of shit is that—?*

He shuddered and took a quick breath. For the first time since he arrived in Vietnam, he thought of death—of his own dying. He had given it so little serious thought—until now; and here he was—face to face with it. He closed his eyes; he tried to imagine that he was dreaming, but when he opened them, the reality of the moment was even more vivid. He began to shake. His nerves were becoming raw, more so by the second. He closed his eyes again. He wanted his mind to conjure a different place...a different time...he wanted to go back into his past...where it was safe. But the fear of his own dying crept in, stealing across his thoughts, permeating his body. His bowels tensed. He breathed again, deeply, but expelled his lungs in a burst. He looked at his hands. He was wringing them, as if trying to squeeze from them his feelings of dread and uncertainty. He closed his eyes and tried to think. What day is it? It was December—but what day? *I have to know.* He fumbled through his mind searching for a date. He reached for his journal. He wanted to write something down on paper...to say one last thing to someone. And then he remembered: it was his mother's birthday.

Journal Entry, 21 December 1967, Ca Mau

I don't know what to think. If this writing is too maudlin, time will tell. As I write these words, I feel strangely at peace. My name is Keith Perry Slater and this is my Last Will and Testament. To my mother and father, Martha and Vernon Slater, I hereby bequeath all of my earthly belongings, except the following: to my brother Dale, I bequeath my sterling-silver chess set. To my sister Janice, I bequeath my set of Encyclopedia Britannica. May God have mercy on my soul...

He left his journal with the medic on the Dustoff helicopter.

"Looks like it's time to crank," Finch said, who could see the crewchief in the first ship untying the rotorblades. Kip, already in his seat, buckled his straps. He closed his eyes; never had he dreaded a moment more in his life.

Within minutes all the blades were turning. The ships moved onto the dirt strip in straight trail. "Lead, this is Trail, your flight is ready."

"This is Lead...I'll be pulling pitch in one zero. After liftoff come up staggered trail left."

They climbed to fifteen hundred feet, two separate flights, nine helicopters apiece. Below them was a land mostly covered by water, the water made invisible by mangrove. To their left, just above the horizon, the sun shimmered. Kip looked toward the lead ship. He and Justen were in the first flight of nine aircraft. The six ships ahead of them weaved ever so slightly.

The flight flew past Dam Doi and continued on a southerly heading. The RP was a set of coordinates ten kilometers northeast of Nam Can. They would approach the outpost low-level from the east with the sun to their backs.

"You want to fly?" Justen asked.

"No."

Lead began a slow descent. In the distance, two pairs of gunships, approaching from the right and left, closed in to protect them. Kip looked at the doorgunner of the gunship situated to their immediate left. The gunner sat on the right side of the helicopter, his helmet sunvisor pulled down, his chest protector securely fastened. He gripped his M-60, pointing it earthward ready to fire. He looked to Kip like some kind of futuristic warrior. Could this also be how American crewmen in their high tech machines appeared (as some kind of alien beings from a far-off galaxy) to the Viet Cong, those little, brown, primitive men who lived and fought on the land below?

Within moments they were skimming the treetops. Their speed, this close to the ground, made Slater feel like they were on some kind of raceway. They never low-leveled to the landing zone. The feeling he got was both terrifying and exhilarating. At any moment he expected tracers to come streaking across at them.

Never had he felt so vulnerable. So far, even the guns were quiet. Usually, they fired at anything and everything that moved. Kip pressed himself as far back in his seat as he could, wishing the armored plates attached to his seat could encircle him. How fragile was this aircraft, he thought. *Its occupants...they were even more so.*

Lead now angled to the right. Their heading was to the west. They were now above the Song Qua Lon, the river that ran past Nam Can.

And then he saw them: Viet Cong flags. One here and one there and then another over there. It seemed they were everywhere, each waving in the breeze with impunity, blue above red with a centered yellow star. But still no shots had been fired. Not one crackle. It was eerie. Kip shivered. Charlie had to be everywhere below them, yet he saw no movement; he expected them to be scurrying about like ants. And then he thought of a different analogy: he felt like they were being suspended over a pit of dozing rattlesnakes, dangling by a thread. Should someone cut the thread, they would fall into the pit and rouse the snakes. How many dreams had he had like that? Again, he shuddered.

The closer they got to Nam Can, without a shot fired, the better he felt. But why was Charlie holding back? What were the VC waiting for?

And then he thought—*the LZ!* They had it zeroed in; it was surrounded by machine-gun positions; the moment they came within inches of the ground the Viet Cong would jump out of spider holes; the second their skids touched the ground land mines would detonate.

That's it. They're going to wait until we've landed then mortar the hell out us.

And then he saw it...the Nam Can outpost. The flight had slowed to a crawl, their airspeed just above ETL (effective translational lift); any slower and they would begin to sink with their loads toward the earth...into the trees...the water. *Into the pit.* He sensed the vipers hissing now. The shackles rose all over his body, yet still there was no gunfire.

Lead banked to the right. The flight followed. Out his left window Kip saw the Nam Can compound in greater detail. It was an oval-shaped island of dirt, about two hundred-fifty feet long by one hundred-fifty feet across, with walls built of mud, encircled by a narrow moat. Barbed wire sat along the ridge of the walls; concertina wired coiled down slope to the moat. Numerous thatched and tin-roofed huts sat in the center of the compound. More readily in view were several mortar pits: two four-deuces and several eighty-one millimeters, their tubes pointing nearly straight up for close-in fire support. Radio antennas stuck out at odd angles. Kip had never been to Nam Can; he could see now why it was so dreaded an outpost to re-supply. He had never in his life felt so surrounded by the aspect of death. How anyone could live here day in and day out, was unimaginable. The combination of fear and boredom (mostly fear) would certainly drive a person mad, he thought.

Several men inside the fortress were smiling and waving at them as they flew past. On impulse, Slater waved back. And then he saw the women and children in clusters inside the compound near one of the entrances, their meager belongings in hand.

The flight slowed more. Up ahead, Slater could see that the LZ was just large enough for nine ships—if they kept a tight formation. It sat north of the compound, on the right side of a north-south running canal. Tall trees bordered the LZ on the north and east sides. Trees also bordered the narrow canal heavily on the left. Luckily this time they were unloading troops. Were they to be lifting troops out, with the amount of fuel they still had on board, it would be doubtful they could rise to treetop level. Kip looked to their right front. They were now within twenty feet of the ground. Any second now and they would all be sitting ducks. He shifted his holster with pistol over his crotch, like so many other pilots did, a small amount of armor to protect the family jewels

Justen brought the aircraft to within inches of the ground. Even before touchdown, the troops were separating themselves from the ship, to put as much distance between them and the huge target it presented. Slater watched as they moved hurriedly to the edge of the trees, their weapons pointed into the dark growth of mangrove. The ARVN weren't shooting; they weren't providing themselves with suppressive fire. *Why not—?*

"Lead," said Trail, "your flight is ready." The voice came across sparingly, as if even a radio crackle would disrupt the slithering vermin that surrounded them. In the voice, Slater detected an exact duplication of his own fears. He grew more pensive by the second. They had to be off the ground now. The second flight of nine aircraft was a quarter-mile behind them. He saw Lead rise, clear the trees and scoot. The other five aircraft in front of them did the same. Justen brought the helicopter off the ground; he began to accelerate the ship forward, gaining a slight amount of altitude as he did. The wall of trees was directly to their front. With a fair amount of body language, Slater willed the helicopter to clear the tops. They did. With nothing but clear sky ahead, they climbed to higher, safer altitudes. He took a quick glance to his right. Justen was wreathed in sweat. It was then that Slater took his first deep breath since descending from fifteen hundred feet.

They orbited the RP for seventeen minutes. The reports coming back were negative; the LZ was quiet. Kip felt relief, but thought they were being led into a false sense of security. But then if this was a suicide mission, it would have to be Victor Charlie who wanted death. No American or ARVN soldier would arbitrarily stir this placid, yet seething nest.

"Lead, this is Six, the LZ is ready for first civilian extraction. Depart the RP with the first nine ships heading two one zero. I'll let the second nine know when they should depart."

"This is Lead, roger…"

Victor R. Beaver

Slater flew the second trip in. The women and children were grouped in small clusters in the landing zone, now called the PZ (pickup zone), spaced appropriate distances apart. When Kip saw them, he thought a more frightened, anxious and bedraggled group would be hard to find.

He watched as they were helped aboard. After the women and children, Finch helped two ancient and feeble papa-sans to crawl on the cabin floor. When they were all loaded, Conrad reported nineteen human bodies packed into the fold. Luckily, they were mostly babies and small children, each weighing no more than ten to perhaps thirty or forty pounds. To the men remaining inside the Nam Can compound, the cargo they saw climb into the bowels of the ships were their most precious possessions, their wives and children. Included unexpectedly were a few old mama-sans and papa-sans, people to whom they gave their most revered respect. Neither group knew when next they would see each other—if ever.

Kip brought the ship to a hover. The old D-model groaned. He tried to move the helicopter forward, but the aircraft began to settle to the ground. The moment it did Justen took over the controls.

The rpm, as Justen slid the ship forward, was down to 6200. The low rpm "warning signal," a nerve-splitting audible tone sounded like a mournful, disconcerting bleat over the intercom system. To quiet it, Derek reached up and pulled the circuit breaker that controlled the flow of electricity to the audio-signal generator. Ahead of them, Kip saw the other ships straining under their loads. The aircraft weren't easily maneuverable, and in their holds were non-combatants, useless cannon fodder, in military parley, should a ship be forced down. It was during this time that Kip became the most terrified: the Viet Cong would let loose now—they'd just have to. Their targets were such easy pickings—!

But still there was no sound of gunfire. The anticipation grew more maddening by the minute. He would be satisfied with one shot fired, at least—*by anybody!*—just to relieve the tension.

Ahead still were the trees. They seemed taller now, huge impediments. A living barricade. For a heavily loaded helicopter, they were as much the "enemy" as Victor Charlie. Deftly, Justen manipulated the controls…coaxing…urging…cajoling the aircraft to ascend through the dank, fetid air. They seemed to move forward an inch at a time. Kip was certain they weren't going to make it: there wasn't enough distance to both accelerate and climb.

Derek continued to "milk" the collective, to raise the rpm a notch, to recover the slightest bit of power. Kip watched as the other ships in front of them were somehow drawn upward; they seemed to clear the trees at the last possible second. And then, after an interminable amount of time, they too rose through ETL…as if pulled by strings from above. They labored into flight as their skids (landing gear) and the nose of the aircraft scraped the treetops. Derek then moved the cyclic ever so slightly forward and added right pedal, to increase airspeed and power. When the rpm crept past 6400, he added the slightest bit of collective power and they began to climb. The vipers had almost had their first meal.

The flight to Ca Mau took a little over twenty minutes. The lift helicopters deposited their loads of human cargo on the airstrip. Kip noticed there were only a few concerned people to greet them. After they debarked, the women, the children, the old people, all seemed to wander off aimlessly, unknowing their fate, or from where their next meal would come. It seemed so unfair. It was then that Slater formed a strange conclusion: for this "suicide" mission there would not have been a lack of volunteers. Not one pilot or crewmember would have refused. Even Oakerson would have stepped forward. "Nervous-nellie" Fred would not have been able to stand the chiding had he declined.

It was time now to extract the security forces. Kip felt like he was aging by the second. On the way back in, each moment they didn't take fire, made him feel rickety. The first loads of troops to be pulled out would be assembled in the PZ. The second load of troops to be pulled out would be at the edge of the PZ, barely able to provide the minimum of cover and security until the second flight of aircraft made their approach, at which time they would scurry onboard and be gone along with the first lift.

As the first flight slowed, Kip began to think. The second nine aircraft were only a few minutes behind them. The troops would have to move fast. Timing was very critical. With the security forces disassembling, this would have to be when Charlie unleashed his fury. Thank God they were lighter. Each ship was down to three hundred and fifty pounds of fuel. They would have less trouble clearing the trees. But that amount of fuel equated to a little over thirty minutes of flying time until fuel exhaustion. (An unwritten policy few pilots violated was to never allow the fuel gauge to read less than five hundred pounds. From the moment the engine was started, the procedure was to seek someplace to refuel 1.5 hours later. Today, that policy had been massively disregarded to perform the mission.)

After they touched down, Justen gave control of the aircraft over to Slater. With sweat now pouring out from under his flight helmet, Slater placed his feet on the pedals, his hands on the cyclic and collective. He watched as the troops hoisted themselves onboard. There were no laggards. In fact he had never seen the ARVN propel themselves so quickly. This time when he brought in power and came to a hover and began to move forward along with the others, each helicopter practically leaped through ETL—as if drawn back to Ca Mau like a magnet. With his thoughts riveted to their now 320-pound quantity of fuel, Slater took no time to appreciate that no mortars fell as they departed the Nam Can LZ for the third and final time.

Kip Slater rejoined their ship with the rest. To conserve fuel, Lead told them they could fly a loose trail formation. This would prevent jockeying the collective power lever up and down to maintain a tight formation, an act that in itself consumed the precious liquid at an alarming rate. The gauge was now at two hundred and ninety pounds.

Kip's gaze was now almost exclusively fixed to the fuel quantity meter. He knew Justen could easily handle an autorotation, should their engine quit for lack of gas, but that wasn't what bothered him. He was convinced that Victor Charlie was everywhere below. Were the Viet Cong aware of their dilemma? Kip couldn't believe they were otherwise. In fact, he could swear he felt the points of their fangs sinking right now into his skin.

The fuel-gauge needle seemed to drop at a gallop. It now read two hundred forty pounds. Every minute that passed was almost ten pounds of fuel gone. Justen beeped the rpm down to 6200. This would help a little to conserve gas.

Ca Mau came into view. The fuel gauge registered one hundred sixty pounds. In the next instant the master caution light illuminated. Both Justen and Slater glanced at the caution panel segment lights: the 20-minute low-fuel warning light was on. Justen reset the master caution light. Technically, Ca Mau was within easy reach...less than twelve kilometers away. But the "low-fuel" warning light was not always accurate. Twenty minutes or two minutes of gas remaining—many pilots thought it could be either. The gauge now read one hundred and twenty pounds. Kip Slater felt his "pucker factor" increasing by the second.

Ca Mau was now ten klicks to their front. One hundred and five pounds. The gauge now seemed to drop ten pounds every time he glanced at it. *So quit looking, goddamnit. If the engine quits, so be it—!*

They were on a very long, extended right base for landing to the east. Kip snuck a peek: ninety-five pounds.

A few minutes later he watched as the first ship turned onto final. Thus far no one had dropped like a brick due to fuel exhaustion. *We're going to make it—we're going to make it. I can feel it in my bones. No sweat—no sweat. Piece of cake.*

Eighty pounds. He banked the aircraft to the right—gently. He didn't want the fuel in the tanks to slosh even momentarily to empty.

Seventy-five pounds of fuel, hardly more than the weight of an ARVN soldier dripping wet. They were now on final. Half a kilometer to go. Derek told him to keep the airspeed up, and to plan to land on the grassy area to the side of the dirt strip. They were now in a descent. One hundred meters before touchdown. Seventy pounds. "You want me to beep up the rpm?" Kip asked.

"I'll do it." Justen pressed the little rocker switch on the main control area of the collective lever until the N2 tachometer registered 6400 rpm.

One hundred feet...seventy-five feet...fifty feet. "Slow up just a little," Justen told him. "That's good...that's good."

Twenty-five feet. Sixty-five pounds. Kip began to bring in the power. It was his intent to come to a hover. "Keep your speed up," Justen told him, "do a running landing—for practice.

The Sky Soldiers

"Sure...why not."

Kip kept the ship moving forward, allowing the skids to touch the ground at a slight run. Sixty pounds were indicated on the fuel gauge when they came to a stop. He put the collective lever full down. And then the engine died. Lights all over the caution segment panel started to come on one by one. And then there was a kind of deafening silence, the first bit of quiet in their helmets since they cranked over two hours ago. (Surprisingly, during the entire mission there was very little radio chatter; what they had heard was mostly the sound of the turbine engine behind them and the droning of the rotorblades overhead.)

Justen moved to turn the fuel switch off, but too late, the fuel-control unit had cavitated. He twisted the throttle counter-clockwise and turned off the inverter switch. After the rotorblades had stopped turning, Justen flicked the battery switch to OFF. Kip had been staring at the fuel gauge. Before all electricity was turned off it read a measly fifty-eight pounds, a little more than a presumed six minutes of fuel remaining. "Well, so much for twenty minutes of fuel left when the twenty-minute low-fuel warning light comes on," Kip remarked.

Kip remained motionless in his seat. He had removed his helmet and was staring straight ahead. Justen unbuckled his seatbelt and shoulder harness; he removed his flight helmet. Kip said, "You know...I was just thinking. Not one shot was fired...all day...by anyone. The ARVN didn't shoot. The guns didn't shoot. And neither did Charlie. What the fuck, over?"

"You got me," Justen said.

"Apparently, we didn't want to start anything, and neither did they. We won't shoot if you don't." Kip paused. "Now why the hell can't we operate like that everyday?" Justen got out of his seat. Once outside the aircraft, he gazed at Slater, his eyes narrowed, listening. Slater continued: "Whose idea was it to give this war, anyway?"

Justen peered at his peter-pilot. He said, "Slater...you need to get laid."

Kip's head jolted. Something inside him stirred, tingled. He thought back to the lovely little Vietnamese prostitute. Oh what he wouldn't give to be in bed with her right now, high on the dreaded weed. What a fitting conclusion to the day. Anything to take the razor-sharp edge off his emotions. His nerves couldn't be anymore frayed had he been placed in the electric chair, with everything set to jolt him into eternity, and then told at the last second his execution had been stayed.

He said to Justen: "You know...I heartily agree."

Chapter 27

THE BUS PULLED INTO THE COLORADO Springs's Trailways bus terminal early Thursday afternoon. Sandy sat and stared out the window at the gray wall of the loading area as passengers around him gathered their belongings and moved down the aisle.

When the last passenger had debarked, he moved from his seat and into the aisle and put on his dress coat and saucer cap. He reached for his overnight bag and took the book he had tried to read during the long twelve-hour trip, and with them in hand, began to move toward the front of the bus. His legs trembled as he stepped onto the pavement. In that instant he wished he could have turned around, got back on, and just kept right on going.

The terminal waiting room was crowded with holiday travelers. He saw his father coming toward him, weaving his way around small groups of people.

"Hi, Dad."

"Hello, Son,"

They shook hands. "How was the trip?" his father asked.

"Long. Very long."

"I'm sure it was…all things considered." They went to the baggage claim area. Sandy fumbled for his claim check. His father cleared his throat. "Again, your mother and I are very sorry about Katie's brother."

Sandy nodded. The day after he found out about Brad, Sandy had telephoned his parents and told them the tragic news. After he hung up, he gathered his courage to call Katie. Her composure, at least, was a little better than the day before. They spoke for a couple of minutes. She explained that Brad's body would arrive the next day accompanied by someone in the Navy, appointed as his official body escort. Because he had been so badly burned, his remains would be nonviewable. He cringed when she told him that. He wished at that moment that he could reach out and take her in his arms and hold her, comfort her. "I'll call you when I get in," he said.

"Okay, Sandy…" For a long moment there was silence. Then she said, "Come home to me, Sandy. Please—please…I need you."

"I'll be there, Katie. I-I need you, too—"

He recalled the earnestness in her voice, how her words made him tingle all over, a sensuous stirring in his groin. Right now, though, he dreaded the thought of later going to see her.

He and his father spoke little during the drive home. Just before turning onto the street where they lived, his father said:

"Listen, Son, your mother is pretty upset."

"I know, Dad."

"If you could, try not to talk too much about your training. If she asks, that's fine."

He nodded. "I understand."

His mother met him at the front door as he came up the steps. She hugged him, then led him into the house and to the kitchen. Melissa, his sister, greeted him with her usual childlike enthusiasm, lifting his spirits slightly. His father placed his suitcase in the hallway and asked if he wanted something to drink. "How about a beer?"

"Yeah, a beer...that sounds good. Thanks, Dad."

The two men sat at the kitchen table. Sandy saw that his father looked tired. The homefront must be wearing him down, he thought. "How's work, Dad?"

"Okay. I still get those damned midnight calls. Two days ago we had a derailment south of Fountain. Just a couple of cars. It didn't mess up the signals too bad. We got that cleaned up this morning. I told Hanks you were coming home and that I wanted some comp time. He didn't argue."

Sandy's mother sat down at the table. She reached over and cupped his hands in hers. She tried to smile, but he saw that it was a strain. "I'm going to make a casserole," she said. "You can take it over to Katie's when you go."

"Okay...sure. Thanks, Mom."

She let go of his hands and reached up and pulled his head toward her and kissed him lightly on the forehead. She said, "I love you."

He blushed. His voice cracked. "I love you too, Mom."

His mother got up and went to the refrigerator and began drawing out the food she needed to prepare the dish. Father and son glanced at each other. Sandy remained silent as he sipped at his beer. Finally, he said, "I'm going to go lay down."

"Aren't you going to call Katie?" his mother asked.

"I will. But first, I need to close my eyes. I didn't get any sleep on the bus. And this beer's already making me drowsy."

He went to his bedroom on the lower level of their triplex home. When he closed the door, he felt suddenly at ease.

He sat on the edge of his bed and removed his shoes. He stretched out and laid his head on the pillow. For a moment he stared upward, his eyes focused on the hundreds of tiny, irregularly placed holes in the ceiling that were a part of the design. He then searched for the many familiar patterns he had conjured during the countless hours he spent in the room. He saw the dog's head, the parachute, the pipe with the curved neck, the image of a bird's wing, and he saw his favorite, the one he had always been a little ashamed of, the shapely bosom of a woman. He thought of Katie. What would it be like, he wondered, to see her naked? To watch her take off her blouse, and then slowly undo her bra? And then to gaze upon her breasts, small and shapely like he imagined them to be? And then to see her undo her skirt and let it slip to the floor? And then, above all, to watch her take off her panties? And then to come to him—*to actually come to him.* He closed his eyes. He felt the strain in his groin and shook his head. *You're pitiful—pitiful!* He couldn't believe himself. *Katie's brother is dead. He's at the funeral home. What does someone look like who is burned...burned beyond recognition?* He shuddered at the enormity of it all.

The room was dark. Sandy heard a soft rapping sound at the door to his bedroom. He looked at the luminous clock on the nightstand next to his bed: it wasn't quite five o'clock. He had been asleep for nearly two hours. "Come in," he said.

The door opened; he felt his father's hand touching his feet. "You awake?"

"Yeah..."

"Katie just called. She wanted to know if you got in. I told her you were pretty pooped. She understood."

Sandy was up on his elbow. "I wish I didn't have to go over there."

His father sat down on the side of the bed. "It's never easy to face something like that," he said. "For a couple of months during the war, I did duty with a military color guard. Mostly funerals. It was not fun. I tried to imagine how the loved ones felt. Of course, I found out firsthand years later when my dad had his stroke. He gave us no warning."

Sandy nodded. "Funny, but I thought Grandpa would live forever. To this day I still find it hard to believe he's dead."

"Yeah, me too. They had him tied to a bunch of tubes. He wasn't breathing on his own. We had to let him go."

"I'm sorry," Sandy said. He reached over and touched his father's arm.

His father shook his head. "They say that in peace sons bury their fathers. In war fathers bury their sons." He paused. "Well, at least my father didn't have to..."

Sandy saw the barren look in his father's eyes. "Didn't have to what, Dad?"

"Oh nothing..."

Holding the casserole his mother had prepared, Sandy raised his hand, hesitated, and then rang the doorbell. The sound came loudly to him outside on the steps. He wondered how often it had rung during the past several days: many times he was certain. As he was driving up he noted the different cars parked in front of Katie's house, all the out-of-state license plates. He glanced at his watch: it was almost six. He was dressed in Levi's and a flannel shirt and was wearing his high school letter jacket. Before leaving the house, he asked his father to take his military uniform to the cleaners, so that he could wear it during the funeral.

Katie's father appeared at the door. "Yes?"

"Good evening, Mr. Williams."

"Oh hello, Sandy. Good to see you. Come on in."

He entered and stood in the hallway. In the living room he could see people standing and sitting, talking quietly, visiting, their faces harboring varying levels of grief and concern. He nodded to each of them as Katie's father made the introductions. Then Sandy excused himself and went into the kitchen, where he was met by other members of the family, some of them children, most of them women who were setting out food to be served for dinner. He gave the casserole to a heavy-set older woman who thanked him and placed it on the table, next to other similar dishes. Except Katie's father, he had encountered no one he knew. Not seeing Katie right away and noting the relative calm of everyone, relaxed him slightly. "Katie's upstairs," he heard Mr. Williams saying from behind. "I told her you were here."

Sandy turned. "Mr. Williams, my folks...well, they're real sorry. So am I. I wish I knew more what to say."

Charles Williams nodded. "That's okay. I know it's difficult. We're glad you're here. Brad would have appreciated it."

Sandy was unprepared for the change he saw in Katie. Her face was ashen and all the sparkle had gone out of her eyes. He could see she had been crying. She came to him and buried her face on his shoulder. Holding her, with his lips brushing her hair, he whispered how sorry he was. She pulled back, looked up at him, and managed a weak smile. She introduced him to the people in the kitchen and then took him out onto their enclosed back porch, where they could be alone. She put her arms around him, inside his jacket. She nestled her head under his chin and this time held him tightly. Her body was pressed into his and he felt his excitement rise strong and firm. His lips were in her hair and he heard himself saying over and over how much he loved her, how much he wanted her and needed her. He could feel her body heaving; again she was crying. "Sandy, I'm so scared. I don't know if I can go through with this. I miss him so much. Why did this have to happen? Why now? Why at Christmas, of all times—?"

He remained silent. After a moment she pulled away and peered at him. "I would die if anything happened to you, Sandy. I wouldn't be able to handle it. Promise me you'll be all right. Promise me." In her face he saw, instead of sorrowful concern, a purposeful, yet desperate determination.

Sandy reached out and took hold of Katie's shoulders. He tried to speak, but the speech he had prepared at Wolters, and recited during the trip, caught in his throat. Everything was a jumble. When he was with the guys in the flight, all there for one reason, everything was clear, everything made sense. Here, in front of Katie, her brother lying in a cold dark coffin, nothing made sense. "Katie, I'm going to be all right. I wish I could promise you that, but you know I can't. No one can. You'll have to trust me. What happened to Brad must have been a freak thing—"

Abruptly she stamped her feet; she clinched her fists. "Yes—it was a freak thing. And that's just the point. He wasn't supposed to be in any danger. *But you will be!"*

Her sudden outburst caught him off guard. Her eyes flashed dangerous sparks. He drew back.

"Why did you join, Sandy? Why did you think it was so important to go before you were called? Tell me," she cried.

"God, Katie. It's my duty—it's everyone's duty."

His equally sudden comeback softened here. "Your duty? Oh, Sandy, let someone else do that duty. Why do you have to do it? Why do you think you have to save the *whole* world?"

He shook his head. "But that's just it. There is this world and I am a part of it and I want to help make it better. Is that so preposterous?" As he spoke, he recalled an event in the latter part of his junior year, a meeting he had with the minister of his church. He had been feeling these strange fears, fears of dying accidentally, senselessly. He told the reverend he wanted to die for a reason, full of meaning and purpose. He remembered the man looking at him strangely, curiously, as if he were some kind of aberration, a deviant. Then, instead of sympathizing with him, the reverend became curt, angry. Sandy remembered leaving the office hurt and bewildered, fearful that the man might inform his mother and father what he had just disclosed.

Katie sighed. "Okay...okay, it isn't so preposterous, but that won't make me feel any better if anything happens to you—"

He tried to smile. "Look, this has to be the worst time to talk about this. The guys I'm with are a great bunch. Many of them have already been over there, and in much greater danger than Brad was ever in. They came back. Now they're going through flight training and are willing to go back again. I trust them. I know war isn't supposed to be fun or glamorous. Believe me, that's not how I think of it. But you've got to remember the kind of person I am; I won't run from what I believe in doing. Sure, there are a lot of people who oppose what we're doing over there. Congress hasn't officially declared war. Maybe they should...I don't know." He shrugged. "I guess what I'm trying to say is, all the years spent fighting in Vietnam, right or wrong, is just so much water under the bridge." He paused; he looked at her, into her imploring eyes. "Katie, wouldn't quitting now be the worst thing to do? Wouldn't that make Brad's death be for nothing?" He watched as her eyes once more clouded over. Then she was in his arms, with her head buried deep in his chest. "Katie...Katie, please don't turn me inside out. Lately, I admit, things have become kind of confusing. I love you so much, you are so precious to me. I wish we were married. Will you marry me?"

She lifted her head and looked at him. She saw a stranger peering down at her. He was taller, more confident, his shyness was gone. He was fast becoming a man: *He had learned to pilot a helicopter!* A thrill passed through her. He was already a hero, just the way he imagined himself to be. And then, in her mind's eye, she saw all the guys on campus, most of whom had long hair and wore peace beads and walked around slouched, hunkered down in their down-filled coats. They passed out anti-war literature that she would take and read and save in a folder she kept under her bed. Her more outspoken professors talked about the war and the bombing of innocent civilians and the alleged American atrocities being committed. She found herself caught square in the middle, between her concern for Sandy and her world on campus.

"Married?"

"Yes. This coming July...when I graduate."

She shook her head. "Sandy, my parents would never permit me—"

"Your parents? Permit you? What have they got to do with it?"

"Sandy, they're my parents—"

"Okay-okay. You're right. I'm sorry." He wanted to hold her again, but he dared not. "Look, I've got to go. I'm exhausted. I didn't get any sleep at all on the bus."

She nodded, then reached up and touched his face. "Will you be here in the morning? Let's go for a drive. I need to get away from these people. Tomorrow night is the memorial service. And then Saturday's Brad's funeral. Sometimes I feel like I'm coming completely to pieces."

"I know what you mean. I'll be here at nine thirty. Is that early enough?"

She nodded. "That's fine..."

He left the porch through the outside door. She stood and watched him go, and when he was gone the feeling that came over her was the same feeling she felt last April when he told her he was joining the service. Looking back, she realized that it was during that moment that their worlds had split apart, as if the planet had exploded and they were on different chunks going out into space. Would they ever again be together like before? She doubted it, more so now than ever. Dejectedly, she knew she was being left behind while he sped toward his own uncertain future. "I hate what they do to us," she stated aloud. She thought of the many anti-war discussions on campus, on the one hand, and on the other, the political claptrap that came through the President's official channels on the conduct of the war. The government treated the war as if it were an errant child, misguided yet salvageable. How do you salvage men's lives? How do you reattach their souls? *How can I ever have my brother back?* screamed her heart in the cold clear night.

* * *

IT WAS SATURDAY MORNING. THE MOURNERS attended Brad Williams's funeral under a pale blue sky with the Pike's Peak massif looming large in the background. A cold, strong wind swept down its eastern side and slammed at them in a tireless fashion. Sandy Adamson, along with the other pallbearers, had his shoulders bent into the wind. Twice he glanced up to see Katie next to her parents under the awning as they stood over Brad's final resting-place.

They halted Brad's flag-draped casket under the awning near the ground opening, then repositioned themselves off to the side. Sandy went and stood next to Katie, who seemed not to notice him.

He put his arm around her shoulder and looked out. Thirty yards away was the color guard, men in uniform with rifles, at parade rest, waiting to render the country's final salute. He glanced about and tried to read the faces of those within his immediate view. He gazed down at Brad's coffin and then looked out toward the mountain. Snow-clad in the pristine beauty of this late December morning, he recalled the one and only time he had ever climbed it. It was in late May, right before high school graduation, he was with Katie, and it was her first climb. He brought his gaze inward and looked toward the pastor of Katie's church, a small baldheaded man who shifted his weight from foot to foot against the cold, gauging the crowd for the right moment to begin. As the seconds ticked by, Sandy thought of yesterday. The morning—in fact the entire day—had ended in confusion.

He had met Katie at the promised time. Her eyes were red and puffy, wet with tears. She had on jeans, a blue goose-down jacket, partially unzipped, and underneath a pale blue mohair sweater. He had on Levis, a brown cotton shirt, and his letter jacket. They drove to their favorite parking spot atop one of the bluffs that overlooked the city. Sandy turned the engine off. He turned the collar of his jacket up. Katie, looking down at her lap, fingered a rumpled ball of tissue. They sat still, neither saying a word. Sandy looked out toward the city, and then at the base of the mountain. He lifted his gaze higher, until he was peering at the top of Pike's Peak. He saw plumes of snow whipping off the summit by the wind. Behind them the morning sun beat through the rear window. Katie began crying again. Sandy reached over and took her in his arms. She turned and burrowed into him, pressing her head into his chest. She repeated over and over that she was so afraid. She had no idea how she could go through the funeral. Why Brad? Why not someone else? Why now? Soon she was saying that she didn't want him to leave her, that she couldn't bear the thought of him going to Vietnam. At a loss for words, he held her tight and stroked her head; her body heaved in his arms. She struggled to get closer to him. Teary-eyed she looked up and began to smother him with kisses. He felt her tears smear over his face. With one of her elbows pressed lightly into his groin, he soon became aroused. Within moments the frustrations of the past several weeks spilled from both of them. Lips crushed against lips. In spite of her weeping, her body felt warm and pliant. He put his right hand underneath the back of her coat. He felt the clasp of her bra through the soft material of her sweater. Her right hand roamed over his chest. By now her breathing had become labored. He sensed the wellhead of her desire matching his own. "Katie," he said; "Oh God, Katie...I want you...I want you so badly." "Sandy," she replied, "if you want me, you can have me—" Her spoken consent, words he thought he would never hear, sent a spasm throughout his body. He felt strong, the tension within him increasing by the second. His right hand roamed over her back, down under her arm, he felt the soft mound of a breast. In a moment he had his hands underneath the back of her sweater, struggling to unclasp her bra. The clasp released. He reached around and touched her nipples. Hungrily, she urged him on, her left hand now over his still clothed groin. He felt the small of her back, palm on flesh, the cloud of mohair over the back of his right hand. Any moment he felt he would explode. His hands now groped the zipper of her pants. Meantime, she had the top buttons of his shirt undone, then her soft auburn hair flat against his chest. He caught a whiff of her hair, a soft scent that sent him reeling. His whole body vibrated like a violin. Her eyes were closed. He felt the elastic band of her panties; he struggled, she assisted, allowing him to go on. She bit his neck, feverish nips that sent chills up and down his spine. And then he heard sounds emit from her lips that had no definition—except that he knew he was giving her profound pleasure—pleasure that lifted her from the world and beyond. She crushed herself against him; fury matched fury. And then the very fabric of his being exploded. She arched against him and she too was overcome.

They drove back to her house in silence. He seemed at a loss what to say, afraid to break whatever spell had been created between them. She was back where she was when he came for her, in some dimension that didn't seem to include him, no dimension which he was familiar. He had driven her back to the reality of Brad's death, to the upcoming memorial service, which they attended that night, back to the reality of the scores of relatives and friends who had come to pay their last respects. During the remainder of the day and into the night, not one word was spoken about their brief encounter. When he said goodnight and tried to kiss her, she offered herself calmly, the feel of her lips hardly in motion. When he got home, he telephoned and her mother said she had gone to bed. That night he lay in his bed and tried to recapture the excitement of that morning; he stroked himself but something kept him from building any kind of momentum. He lay awake for the longest time, finally drifting into sleep sometime before dawn...and the morning of Brad's funeral.

The pastor cleared his throat. He spoke: *"The Lord is my light and my salvation; whom shall I fear? The Lord is my life's refuge; of whom should I be afraid? When evildoers come at me to devour my flesh, my foes and my enemies themselves stumble and fall. Though an army encamp against me, my heart will not fear; though war be waged upon me, even then will I trust."*

Victor R. Beaver

Sandy listened; the words echoed in his mind: *"...though war be waged upon me, even then will I trust...even then will I trust...even then will I trust..."* He strained against the blowing wind to hear the rest of the sermon. And then after several more quotes from the Bible and a short eulogy, the pastor closed the funeral liturgy with the Lord's Prayer. There had been two soldiers standing nearby. They lifted the flag from the casket, took their time to fold it in the prescribed manner, and then one of them carried it to the Navy ensign assigned as Brad's official body escort. The two men exchanged salutes. The ensign turned and went to Katie's mother. He gave a short, prepared speech, something about a grateful and caring nation, and then handed the folded flag to her. In the background, Sandy heard the NCO in charge of the rifle-bearers give a command. Seven men raised their rifles and fired. Twice more the command was given and twice more the men fired. Twenty-one shots. And then from another part of the cemetery, standing alone, the bugler sounded *Taps*. Sandy remembered during preflight that it was such a lonesome, mournful sound. He wondered if Brad's spirit was lingering nearby, watching the ceremonies of his family's final farewell...

When the bugler was finished, the pastor nodded to everyone that it was done. Several more minutes were spent exchanging condolences. Sandy escorted Katie to the funeral car reserved for the immediate family. He kissed her on the cheek and said he would meet her back at the church. Her face grimaced with tears.

* * *

"I WISH I COULD HELP YOU, SANDY," HIS mother said. "She's in mourning. It could take weeks, maybe even months, for her to be herself again. You'll have to give her time."

Sandy nodded and stared at the cup of coffee on the kitchen table in front of him. He thought back over the last several days. After the graveside services, there was the gathering at the church, where food was served and last farewells were said before everyone returned to their homes and their regular lives. He remembered that whenever he tried to be at Katie's side, she treated him with indifference, which made his heart sink even lower. By the end of the day, she was so cool toward him, he wanted to go anywhere he could to be alone.

Later that evening he called her house several times but either her mother or father would tell him she was in her room and didn't feel well, that she wasn't up to speaking to anyone. The next two days he went to her home three times and each time was told she couldn't see him. Both Mr. and Mrs. Williams were sympathetic. But they could do nothing for him. On the evening of the third day, Christmas Eve, he brought his gift over and when she met him at the door, he saw that her eyes were red and swollen. She thanked him for the gift, asked him in (she said that it could only be for a moment) and told him that she and her parents were preparing for church, that they probably wouldn't be back till late. She gave him a feeble hug, brushed him lightly on his cheek with her lips, and then led him back out the front door. With the door closed behind him he remained standing on the front porch, the lump in his throat so hard he found it difficult to swallow. He went to his car, started it, and then drove away, feeling a longing for her so profound he wanted to cry. Once on the highway, he drove to their favorite parking spot where a week before they had had their first awkward moment of sex, so close to the real thing that he could almost sense the very essence of it still. Sitting there, looking at the twinkling lights of the city, a blanket of white everywhere to reflect the stars of the black-blue night sky, he tried to envision his life without her. It was so bleak and barren—so vastly empty—that he wondered if life was worth living.

    He went through Christmas Day in a daze. Even the wonderful meal his mother had prepared could not lift his spirits. He excused himself and went to his room. There he spent the rest of the day staring at the ceiling, wondering if he should call or go see her. And then he thought what was the use; she hadn't called him even to wish him Merry Christmas, which caused him to accept the belief that she no longer wanted him in her life. And when he felt certain it was true, he cried until he no longer held any tears.

    He blinked his eyes and came out of his thoughts. He took a quick sip of his coffee and then stood. "I think I'll go pack," he told his mother. "I'm heading back to Wolters."

    "But I thought you didn't have to leave until after New Year's," his mother said.

    "I don't...but I can't stay around here any longer. At least back there she won't be so close and at the same time so far away."

    His father drove him to the bus depot. This time it was just the two of them in the terminal waiting room. "I'm sorry, Son. If you don't mind, I think you and Katie are now in two different worlds. You split apart when you decided to join the Army and not go to college."

    "I know, Dad. I made my bed. Now I have to sleep in it."

    "Call us when you get in."

    Sandy nodded. "I will...and thanks."

    "For what?"

    "For holding down the fort."

    His father smiled. "You be careful. Keep her low and slow."

    Sandy smiled. "Sure, Dad."

    They shook hands. And Sandy was gone.

Victor R. Beaver

The Sky Soldiers
A Saga of Men in War

Part Two
Mike Nolan

War Is The Province of Physical Exertion And Suffering

IN ORDER not to be completely overcome by them, a certain strength of body and mind is required, which, either natural or acquired, produces indifference to them. With these qualifications, under the guidance of simply a sound understanding, a man is at once a proper instrument of War; and these are the qualifications so generally to be met with against wild and half civilized tribes. If we go further into the demands which War makes on its votaries, then we find the powers of understanding predominating.

From Ernest Hemingway's anthology *Men At War.*

The Sky Soldiers

Chapter 28

"**HEY, KIP,**" YELLED LEO. "Happy Friggin' New Year, ya sorry-ass shit."

Slater, standing in the doorway that led from the dining room to the Tiger's Den, waved a two-finger salute.

"Get on over here—where the hell you been?" Leo called.

Kip wormed his way through the drunken New Year's Eve crowd. He was wearing a helmet liner, his pistol belt, and a black armband. "You jerk, don't you remember? I'm the OG—Officer of the Guard tonight."

"Me?...Remember? I don't remember shit."

Slater looked toward Oakerson. "Did your mama-san get the word, Fred?"

Oakerson groaned. "Yeah...she laid it all out." Fred's mama-san was his guardian angel if ever there was one. Somehow she almost always knew when the airfield was going to be mortared, and before she left for the day she would lay out his steel pot and flakjacket for him to wear that evening.

Leo said, "If she knows so goddamn much, she's gotta be VC."

"Listen, you turkey, if she was VC would she be warning me—?"

Henry said, "The man's gotta point."

"How's it going on the 'duty?'" asked Mac.

"So far, so good. At the stroke of midnight, though, every guard on the perimeter decided to let go a clip of ammo. Did you hear it?"

"Christ, yeah, we heard it," Leo said. "And them fuckin' ARVN shot their damn One O Fives, too."

Slater shook his head. "For sure we'll get mortared tonight."

"Tit for tat," Mac stated.

"That's a big ten-four," said Slater, remembering that on Christmas Eve, right after midnight, in spite of the Christmas truce, Charlie had lobbed in one lonely mortar round. It impacted at the far end of the runway near VC Village. With few exceptions, only the airfield control tower operator and the perimeter guards at that end of the field knew that the round had landed. Mac had OG duty. He and his Sergeant of the Guard investigated and found a large, four-inch-deep dent in the runway's surface.

The following day Slater went and examined the point of impact. "Peace on Earth, goodwill toward men," he muttered; then added, "You bastards." Afterwards, a sense of gloom came over him and he kicked at a chunk of rubble lying nearby sending it skidding to the edge of the runway. At noon he went to the enlisted mess, where the kitchen crew had put on the traditional Christmas feast: turkey, ham, dressing, cranberry sauce, mashed potatoes (the dried variety), gravy and rolls. He picked at his food for a few minutes, then got up and went to the hootch.

Victor R. Beaver

As he went past Leo's door, he glanced inside. Spread out everywhere were open boxes of cookies and candies and other goodies received from home by most of the men of the Blue Tiger platoon. All day pilots and crews partook of the treats. Though everyone maintained an air of joviality about them, it was merely a thin guise under which they hid their true feelings. It was hard to forget where they were—and why. Slater declined Leo's offer to come in and select something to eat. Instead, he complained of a stomachache, went to his room and crawled into bed. Feeling homesick and depressed, he stared at the exposed rafters overhead until past mid-afternoon. At three thirty, Leo talked him into going downtown, along with Robin Henry, Jeff Mangrum, and Evan Pickett. Robin Henry, on orders from Major Neely, had signed for a three-quarter-ton truck from the motorpool to distribute candies to the children of Khang Hung (Soc Trang). As they drove through the streets, each toss of candy brought squeals of delight and fierce competition as the children scrambled for the treats. "Bribery will get us everywhere," Kip remembered saying. He also saw the icy stares of the mothers who crowed angrily at the older children who overwhelmed the younger ones as they grabbed the candy; and the defiant looks from the young teenage boys who stood and watched with their arms locked across their chests; and the blank expressions on the faces of the old mama-sans and papa-sans who gazed from darkened doorways at this outlandish Western behavior. Eventually, he allowed the glee of the children to overshadow the resentment he saw around him and for a short time came out of his doldrums feeling reasonably good about being in this far-off country eight thousand miles from home. When they returned to the airfield he joined Mangrum and Pickett and the other enlisted crewmen and celebrated the remainder of Christmas Day with them instead of with his fellow pilots in the Tiger's Den.

It was 0300. Slater and his Sergeant of the Guard, a hefty staff sergeant named Hargrave, were driving along the east perimeter fence. Slater sat in the right seat, smoking a cigarette. As they went past the guard stations, Hargrave nodded at the men on duty to insure they were awake. Curled under their rain ponchos to keep out the nighttime chill, the men stared back passively, their M-14 rifles laid across their laps. The machine gunners sat next to their M-60s, the belted ammo for their guns laid out neatly, ready to be fired. To Slater's right were the helicopters, parked in their protective revetments.

One helicopter in particular loomed ahead. They continued along slowly until Slater asked Hargrave to stop. Three days ago he, Leo, McNamara, and Paul Christian all took their aircraft commander checkrides. The following day each was assigned his own ship. The jeep halted next to Tiger 098, *Alfie.* Slater shined his flashlight on the forward radio-compartment access door. He saw the toothy grin of Alfred E. Neuman staring back at him. After he had received his AC orders, Rusty and Ron had come to him and asked that he be their new aircraft

The Sky Soldiers

commander. Ever since Dreyfuss had left they had been without an assigned AC, waiting, they said, especially for him. It flattered him so much that he went to Trent Whitaker and quickly made the arrangements.

"That your ship, sir?"

Slater nodded. "Yeah."

"Looks like it could stand a new paint job," Hargrave said, noting the peeling paint that described Alfred's face. "There's a papa-san downtown who does it for about ten bucks." He saw the wording inscribed beneath the face. "What does it mean 'The New Yorker?'"

"My gunner, Ron Larkin, is from New York. He's the one who had the face painted on it in the first place."

"Kinda strange how the CO lets you guys keep all these different paint jobs," Hargrave mused.

Slater nodded. Major Neely was a stickler for standardization, yet he allowed a favored "Tiger" tradition to continue: each aircraft had something different painted on its front. Leo had been assigned Tiger 078, *The Roadrunner,* which had the words "Beep ...Beep" painted underneath the speeding cartoon-bird. Robin Henry, before the Nam Can evacuation, didn't like the display on his ship, so he had the little papa-san downtown copy a *Playboy* centerfold. Painted on the nosecover was a voluptuous, naked woman, her long blonde hair spilling down over a pair of well-developed breasts. The Viking gun platoon helicopters were all painted the same: On each nosecover was a caricature of a Viking warrior, with horned helmet, blonde beard, under each arm a slew of rockets, and in both hands machine guns blazing away.

Slater glanced toward the sergeant. "Yeah, it is kinda strange that our illustrious CO lets us do that."

Hargrave put the jeep in gear and resumed the drive along the perimeter line. In the quiet of the early morning, Slater had time to reflect on his first day as an aircraft commander. The opportunity came two days after his checkride with Derek Justen. Typically, new aircraft commanders are paired with the more experienced peter-pilots. Slater drew Castillo, a pilot who had come into the unit three weeks after him, a twenty-year-old from the Boston area. The day began quietly enough. They flew to Cao Lanh, base of a Special Forces headquarters unit. They arrived at 0800 and were given the usual VIP treatment: a hot breakfast, a tour of the premises, and a few souvenirs, which included four VC flags. The NCOIC (noncommissioned officer in charge) laid out a varied schedule and promised an early release. This put everyone in an expansive mood. The first hour they flew "chase" behind another aircraft carrying a Vietnamese three-star general. Afterwards, they re-supplied three Special Forces A-team outposts on the Cambodian border that lay west of the Parrot's Beak. While working with one of the A-teams, they performed a short recon flight along the border, medevaced a wounded mercenary soldier at Cai Cai and flew him to Moc Hoa, and then went to Saigon on a courier flight, returning to Cao Lanh at 1330. At 1420, they were directed to go to one of the Navy Mobile Riverine Force barracks ships, the *Benewah,* anchored on the Mekong River near My Tho, land on it, pick up two individuals who would be wearing civilian clothes and return to Cao Lanh. On the return trip, Castillo looked back at the two men dressed in white cotton shirts and blue slacks. They were each carrying leather briefcases. He said to Slater over the ICS: "Obviously CIA."

Slater nodded. "Obviously."

Later in the day, at 1537, Slater and his crew were seated on the floor of *Alfie* playing cards, enjoying a smoke, waiting for what they thought would be their early release. When the sergeant who had been coordinating their activities appeared, he informed them they were indeed released from his jurisdiction, but added: "You guys are supposed to go to Vinh Long and report to Outlaw operations."

"What for?" Slater asked.

The sergeant shrugged. "You got me, sir. I'm just passing the word. Thanks for all your help today." Then he walked away.

Rusty White groaned and went to untie the blades. As Ron Larkin was donning his chest protector, he said, "Something's fishy, sir."

"What do you mean 'fishy'?"

"I don't think Outlaw ops is inviting us to any picnic."

Within minutes they were airborne. Castillo turned the ship to the southeast. Rusty said, "Sir, do you hear that noise?"

Kip perked his ears. "What noise?"

"I hear a tapping sound," the crewchief said.

Slater strained to listen. Yes, he did hear something, a faint tapping sound back in the transmission area. "What is it?"

"I don't know, sir. Could be one of the servos, or worse, something wrong with the transmission fluid filter. Do you think maybe we should abort and go on to Soc Trang?"

Slater, hearing the tapping sound again, turned and caught Rusty hitting the floor with a wrench (hard enough to be heard over the din of the engine). "Neat trick, Chief, but it won't work."

"Thought I'd give it a try, sir."

From the moment Slater first spotted the LZ, he knew this was going to be no picnic. From one thousand feet and descending, he could see the three downed helicopters they had been briefed about, one of them still smoldering. The LZ was boxed in on all sides by heavy foliage. It was about the size of an extra large football field. Their ship was in the number six position in a formation of seven in staggered trail left. After they had refueled at Vinh Long, they were told to head northeast and contact Outlaw Six, the 175th AHC company commander.

The situation was bad. Three aircraft had taken dozens of hits; two doorgunners had been killed, one pilot was severely wounded, another pilot had suffered minor wounds. All three aircraft had to be abandoned. The wounded had been picked up by Dustoff but drew a casualty during the rescue, a medic who later died from a gunshot wound to the head. The rest of the crews were still on the ground, within the ranks of the ARVN forces. Other ships had taken hits but had managed to limp out of the landing zone and fly back to Vinh Long. Preliminary reports indicated that the ARVN had bumped into two companies of Viet Cong, well entrenched and armed to the teeth, at a location north of Cai Be, near the Mekong River. Later, after they joined the formation as a replacement ship, they learned that Charlie was also sporting two .50-caliber (anti-aircraft) machine guns with which to do battle.

"Mama mia..." Castillo said over the intercom.

"Mr. Slater." It was Rusty's voice.

"What—?"

"Don't you wish now we'd have checked out them servos?"

"Yeah, Alfie don't like where we're going," harped Larkin.

"Can it, you guys. I'm trying to concentrate. Jesus—the two of you could aggravate a dead person." Slater's heart raced a hundred-fold faster than the speed at which *Alfie* carried them forward. He saw two Maverick gunships cruise by, sending forth a volley of rockets to prep the LZ. Gray smoke enveloped several locations near the left treeline where they hit. Again, it seemed they were involved in madness that held no possible hope of return. As the pilot in command, though, Slater maintained his composure. At the controls, he guided expertly off the helicopter in the White Five position. As the flight descended below the surrounding trees, he kept his attention riveted to the task at hand, abating his desire to investigate the downed Hueys. He heeded little the sound of rockets fired by the gunships impacting on either side. When the troops belched from the ship, his poise remained steadfast, his whole being prepared for liftoff. After they cleared the trees and had gained several hundred feet of altitude, it was then that he realized how little he had paid attention to the thought of being killed, wounded, or severely maimed. All his attention had been riveted to flying: checking the gauges, maintaining formation, landing, and then departing.

After two more lifts into the LZ they were released. The following day he learned that those American crewmembers that stayed the night in the LZ with the ARVN forces were credited with three VC kills. However, one of the Americans, a pilot and former flight-school classmate, was hit and had to have his right leg amputated.

"Sir, how about a cup of coffee?" Hargrave asked. He had just pulled the jeep in front of the airfield operations hootch, a small three-room building that housed the airfield commander's office, the office of a secretary, and the ready-room from which the two men conducted their evening guard duties.

"Sure." Kip got out of the jeep and followed the sergeant inside, who then proceeded to make a fresh pot. "Looks like Charlie is proving Oakerson's mama-san wrong this time," Slater commented.

"Sir?"

Kip told the sergeant about nervous-nellie Fred's mama-san. Hargrave nodded. "You wait, sir. Pretty soon the shit's going to hit the fan around here."

"Oh?...How do you know?"

"I don't. Just a hunch. Maybe because we're long overdue. Besides, I don't think Charlie can stand the status quo anymore. This stupid war is probably going a little too slow...even for him."

* * *

EARLY EVENING, TWO DAYS LATER. "Henry, what the hell are you doing?" Leo Tannah asked, who happened upon Robin carrying a box filled with folders and papers and the SOIs. His two operations clerks followed close behind with the radio equipment.

"Moving to the command bunker."

"How come?"

"Neely's bright idea. You can turn your SOI in at the bunker."

"What?—is he expecting some shit tonight?"

"Nope, but the command bunker is closer to his hootch. From now on when we get mortared, at least at night, everything will be handy for him. We'll move back to 'The Shack' in the morning."

Leo said, "It'll be your luck they bomb that turquoise piece of shit tonight."

Henry scowled. "If that happens, I'll kiss Neely's ass—"

On the following day, those who came approached the devastation in awe. The back room where Neely had held his first company briefing was in shambles. Finger-size splinters of shrapnel were everywhere. Streams of sunlight poured through two large gaping holes in the roof. The mission planning board sported several ragged gashes. The bunk where Henry would have been sleeping, had he stayed the night, was demolished.

Early that morning, at 0215, thirty mortar rounds had hit the airfield. Besides the damage done to operations, one Tiger aircraft took a direct hit and was a congealed mass of magnesium and aluminum; the only part of it recognizable as a helicopter was the last five feet of the tailboom. Four other Tiger aircraft and a Warrior ship received minor shrapnel damage.

Wide-eyed, Tannah and Slater examined Slote's Piece of Shit Turquoise Shack. They watched as Henry sifted through the debris as he tried to locate the few personal effects he kept there. "Henry," Tannah said, "you are the luckiest sonofabitch I have ever known."

Henry's face was ashen. All the while he searched, he said nothing.

"Looks like Neely inadvertently saved your ass." Leo grinned. "Paybacks are hell, aren't they?"

"Get screwed, Tannah—"

Victor R. Beaver

Chapter 29

THE LITTLE MAMA-SAN PADDED softly down the narrow hallway, clutching a pair of boots. When she came to the room where they belonged, she paused then opened the door.

Her eyes widened. Instead of sleeping like she had seen him doing ten minutes before, the man in front of her sat on the edge of the mattress, his hands gripping the steel frame of the bed. She saw his upper torso glistening with sweat and his chest heaving as he gasped for breath. Then their eyes met.

How many times had she seen that harrowing look, as if while he slept he had fought some desperate battle and lost? "You hap 'nother bad dream?" she asked. Justen nodded. She bent her head and reached toward him. "Soon, you be okay. I watch."

After a moment, when his breathing subsided, Justen let go of the bed frame and vigorously rubbed his face. She saw him grab for his cigarettes and light one. He inhaled and exhaled slowly several times. Only when she saw him do this did she allow herself to relax.

Satisfied that all was well, at least for the time being, she bent down and placed his boots under his cot. She rose and went to the closet and scooped up his dirty laundry. She retraced her steps out the door, backing up as she went.

In bright sunlight, she went to one of several faucet-heads attached to two-foot-high pipes sticking out of the ground. She turned the faucet on and let the water fill a medium-size metal washtub. She took his fatigue shirts and began soaking them in the water. Momentarily, she began to voice the melody to her favorite song.

She liked being his mama-san. He had been in her country a long time. It was like a piece of him was Vietnam: her country was his country. There were other soldiers she worked for, washing and ironing their clothes, shining their boots, cleaning their rooms, but none like him. His room was practically bare. He didn't have the usual collection of stereo equipment, or a refrigerator filled with beer and soda, nor did he decorate his walls with a fancy calendar that would tell him when his time to return home had come. No, his room was not like the others at all. He kept no books, or camera equipment; there hung no captured VC flag on the wall. His only other furniture, besides his bed, was a table that served as a desk, and a metal folding-chair. And even the tabletop was bare, except that it held two framed pictures, family members she assumed, and the letters he received from them all stacked in a neat pile at one corner. It saddened her, though, that he hardly ever spoke to her. And he never smiled. She believed it was because of the terrible dreams. She wanted to help him, but she didn't know how.

The shirts had been soaking in the tub for several minutes when she lifted them and laid them on the cement. She next took a bar of soap and began to

The Sky Soldiers

scrub. She puzzled over him. Would he ever leave her country? Why had he stayed so long? Did he not want to see his family? And then she thought of her husband, serving in a ranger battalion near the DMZ. She hadn't seen him since last year. She was very anxious now to see him. He was due home in two and half weeks to celebrate Tet, the Vietnamese lunar new year.

Derek Justen smashed his cigarette in an ashtray on the nightstand near his bed. He grabbed a towel and his shaving kit and headed for the latrine.

Inside the latrine, he stood under the showerhead, the strong stream of water pummeling his face. He closed his eyes. Immediately there came the image of a bamboo cage, the same image that appeared in his dreams. And he saw the bars. Bathed in the dimmest light, he saw the pair of soiled hands made into fists gripping the bars. He saw the face, grimed with dirt. In the face he saw the eyes, glowing like hot coals. Even now, as he stood under the showerhead, with his eyes still closed, Derek looked deeper into the "hot coals," like he always did when he dreamed this dream. They were eyes that, at first, appeared to bear no sense of vision, or reveal any feeling, or need, or desire. Always, when he awakened, he wondered why these particular images appeared? where they came from? how they became implanted obviously deep in his subconscious? What basis in reality did they have? Had he seen a picture somewhere, in a magazine, for example, of a man inside a bamboo cage, broken and in despair, beyond feeling, compulsion, desire? The dream was repetitive, always the same, never varying. Why? Why did it always have to be the same? Why couldn't it be different by even the slightest degree? Was it a netherworld communication? Did it somehow explain why he always felt such a strong pull toward the northern reaches of the U Minh? The dream was eerie, diabolical, it smacked of the insane. It was driving him crazy. Because of the dream he dreaded sleep, struggled against it, kept awake as long as he could, but then sleep always overtook him, captured him, brought him into that other reality, the very reality he could only presume Jake was living, a prisoner in a cage, a pair of imploring eyes, pleading...pleading...*Don't leave me here...Get me out... Get me out!* Shuddering, Derek wrenched the showerhead off.

He toweled himself, shaved then went to his room. He lit another cigarette, sat down on his cot, and looked at the photos on the table top. One of them was a picture of Jake and Valerie on their wedding day, the same day Jake graduated from West Point. In her wedding dress, Valerie appeared radiant and happy, lovelier than he had ever seen her. The other picture was one of her and the children: Robbie, five and Jill, three, a picture taken several months after she received the news of Jake's crash landing; in it she looked tired and worn. Still there was that hint of her former loveliness, right below the surface, straining, hoping to be let out. He gazed at the pile of letters he got from her, all neatly stacked. By this stage in his tour, Valerie was writing about once a week. When he first got in-country her letters to him, arriving almost daily, spoke only of Jake's MIA status. Now she penned barely two sentences concerning her fears and frustrations. She concentrated on the children, how they were doing in school, how fast they were growing. At the beginning of his tour, he wrote back not quite once a week. Now his letters were spaced about a month apart, and were uniformly short and also, sadly, to the point. He wished he could comfort her better. Though he was in touch with the senior province advisor at Ca Mau also about once a week (who as of yet not ever given him any kind of news that even remotely smacked of the kind he wanted to hear), he found it difficult to send the same message to her as often as he might, that of nothing significant to report.

Justen's mama-san entered the room. She looked at him. And then her gaze went to the framed pictures.

In all the months she had known him, she never asked who the people were in the photos. There was little resemblance between the man seated before her and the one in the wedding picture. And now more than ever this puzzled her.

"Maybe you family?"

He peered at her. "No...not my family."

"No you wife?" she said. "No you wife?"

"No."

"No you...?" she said, to reassure herself that who she was pointing at in the picture was indeed not the figure of Derek but of some other man.

"No, not me...my brother."

She nodded. "He fly?"

"Yes—*No.*"

She noted the hardness in his voice and stepped back.

He reached toward her. "I'm...sorry."

Her eyes softened. "You brotha hap pretty wife."

"Yes, she is very beautiful. My brother is a very lucky man."

"Where him?"

"That...I don't know."

"Long time no see?" she said.

Justen nodded. "Yeah, long time no see."

"Someday, you see, then maybe you go home?"

"Yes, I hope so."

Pleased that everything seemed all right, she bowed and left the room. As she padded down the hall, it dawned on her that when he spoke of his brother he was looking more at the other photo, the one of the woman and the children, than at the photo the brother was in.

* * *

JUSTEN HAD JUST RETURNED FROM mail call. He took Valerie's latest letter and began to read:

My dear, dear Derek,
  I hope this letter finds you in good health and that the holidays were bearable and that perhaps you have learned something about Jake, which will end this horrible nightmare. It is now over two years since Jake was listed as missing in action. Derek, I cannot understand for the life of me why we don't know something by now. How can the Viet Cong keep a man prisoner without informing the authorities? Aren't they bound by the Geneva Convention like we are? I know, I've asked all these questions before and the answer is always the same. But I don't know how much longer I can go on. I can't even visualize what my own husband looks like anymore! I don't know what to say to the children. If he comes home, will he be different? Oh God, Derek, how much so? Will he still love me? Will I still love him?...

Derek stared at the letter. It was the first time in months he had received one from her written in such a despairing tone. After he finished reading the rest of it, which tapered off talking about the children, he wrote back:

Dear Val,
  You have to hang in there. Jake must never believe for one second that he doesn't have you to come home to. If he is alive, and I'm certain he is, knowing you're waiting for him is keeping him alive. For him to have the slightest doubt would kill him. You must understand this...

Valerie put the letter down. She stood at the living room window watching the snow drift down in large, wet flakes. Before opening Derek's letter she had put the tea kettle on and now heard its urgent whistling.

At the kitchen counter, she poured the water and put the tea bag in and sat down to contemplate Derek's response to what she had written. What *had* she said in her last letter that had given him the impression that she might not wait for Jake? *Oh Lord, what he must think of me—!*

Lately, though, she had been feeling more and more out of control with bouts of insomnia. There were times when she would lay awake until long past midnight, her mind filled with images of Jake being tortured by his captors—if he was a POW, something she always had to remind herself. When she did sleep, she dreamt that he was dead, his body hidden, rotting, where no one would ever find it. She would then awaken wreathed in sweat, unable to regain sleep.

She returned to the living room and sat down in Jake's easy chair. She stared out the window mesmerized by the falling snow, lying over the ground like a white blanket, piling up and up. She tried to think of her husband, what kind of life he lived—if he was alive...*if...if...if!* How could two years go by without a word?—*How?* How could a country like America, the greatest country on earth, fail so miserably to learn the simple whereabouts of one of its soldiers?

    She took a sip of tea. She laid her head back against the soft cushion. She and the children had continued to live in post housing at Fort Sill, in the same quarters they occupied before Jake's assignment overseas. The arrangement with the Department of the Army was that he would return to Fort Sill after his one-year tour of duty and take over an artillery battery as a captain. She had been comfortable with that. She was relatively comfortable, too, with the way the war was being conducted. Jake had assured her that duty in the Mekong Delta would be far safer than if he were stationed farther north. She remembered being relieved by that. She recalled one news headline in particular the day he left, in late June 1965, whereby President Johnson had ordered an increase in U.S. military forces if the situation demanded it. Well, at least he'll have plenty of company, she recalled thinking, which she soon learned translated into having plenty of company at Fort Sill, as she found herself among many other wives whose husbands had also deployed to Vietnam. She became active in several support groups, attended all social gatherings whenever she could, and felt a measure of contentedness in spite of Jake's absence as a mate and a father to the children. She wrote him long letters about the children, her on-post activities, how much she loved and missed him. He responded with letters that told how idyllic his life was, how he flew once, sometimes twice a day, rarely spotting enough actual enemy activity (or at least recognizable as such) to get excited about, or do anything about, considering the strict rules of engagement. He mentioned how he was back on the ground in the tiny officers' club at province headquarters, usually around five o'clock in the evening. He lived comfortably in a high-ceilinged room with a large fan turning overhead. The thick cement walls of his room offered a kind of natural air-conditioning as well as protection against mortars. He ate a good breakfast in the morning and a fulfilling dinner at night, watched a movie whenever they got a new one in, and occasionally played poker, keeping his bets down to a dull roar. All of this gave her the impression that the worst that could happen to him was that he might fall off a barstool and crack open his head. For nearly six months she was at peace, her need to be concerned a far cry less than many of the other wives whose husbands were in more dangerous locations.

    Then the news came that Jake had been forced down by engine failure and that he had crash-landed not far from where he was stationed. The Army, upon inspection of the crash site, listed him as missing in action, and because there was sufficient evidence that he had been taken from the wreckage of his plane under his own power, they also presumed him to be captured. Over two years later, though, his POW status had not yet been officially corroborated.

She took another sip of tea and noted that the snow had stopped falling. She returned to the kitchen and refreshed her cup with water and then went back to Jake's easy chair. She thought of Derek. She recalled the day he left for Vietnam. He had spent his last three days of leave with her and the children before he was to report to Oakland Army Depot, the main debarkation point for soldiers reporting to Vietnam. Before that he had been in Washington, D.C., at the Department of the Army, in the hip pocket of the officer in charge of keeping track of MIAs and POWs. She remembered him looking gaunt in his uniform, his ocean-blue eyes deeply troubled.

It was six in the morning on the day he was to catch his flight to Oklahoma City and then another to San Francisco. He had loaded his duffel bag and suitcase in the taxi and had returned to the front door. "I'll write as soon as I get my assignment," he said.

She nodded. She was dressed in a robe, her arms folded in front of her.

"Are you going to be okay?" he asked her.

"Yes..."

"Give Robbie and Jill a hug for me."

"I will...you be careful." As she spoke, she reached out and touched his arm, giving it a gentle squeeze. She said, "Thanks for coming. You've been a lot of help. I know Jake would appreciate it." And then tears came to her eyes and she increased the pressure on his arm. "Please...please, Derek, you must be careful. I would die if anything bad were to happen to you too—"

"Don't worry—don't worry, I'll be all right." And then he added: "I'm going to find him, Val—somehow I'm going to find him."

She nodded, feebly. She knew it was what he was supposed to say. After he was gone, she returned to her bed and laid awake thinking of him, how strong he was, how much he reminded her of Jake. She thought of the previous three days. Derek caused a feeling inside her that she couldn't quite define. There was nothing in particular he did. Perhaps, she thought, trying to pinpoint it, to get it clearer in her mind before it became something she couldn't manage, it was the way he knew that everything would be all right, that someday Jake would come home to her. When Derek left, Jake had been missing less than six months.

The sun shone through the window. Everywhere outside was a brilliant white. But she seemed not to notice. Instead, she closed her eyes and thought of how many days were in twenty-four months: Over seven hundred. And then she tried to imagine how far, if converted to distance, seven hundred days would extend in a straight line. In her mind's eye—and because the length of many of her days alone with the children seemed endless—the line seemed to stretch forever, to finally fade into a kind of gray gloom, exactly like each and every day had now become. Tears came to her eyes. *Oh, my darling, darling Jake, can you last another day?...Another week?...Another year? Can you last forever, like it seems I must until we are together again? Please, God, help me...help me to last....*

Chapter 30

AFTER CHRISTMAS, CLASS 67-15 returned reluctantly to Fort Wolters and again to the task of soldiering. Usually, it took a day or two for mild to severe cases of homesickness to pass; but once they strapped themselves into the cockpit, the excitement they felt for flying revitalized them. Sandy Adamson would have spent the last days of the old year alone had Frank Bartlett not appeared in the barrack on New Year's Eve day equally in the doldrums. "How did it go at home?" Frank asked. The two men were in Sandy's room seated at the study tables.

"God, Frank, it was awful. If I never attend another funeral, it will be too soon."

"How did it go with your girlfriend?"

Sandy shook his head. "We broke up—I think. She did, I didn't." He went on to explain the events leading to the funeral, relating shyly the fumbling sexual encounter. Frank listened, pulling slowly at his cigarette, pondering the younger man's dilemma. "I don't know why she acted so strangely toward me, especially after...after—well, you know what I mean. What the hell did I do?"

"You didn't do anything...at least not directly," Frank answered.

"What do you mean?"

"You've got one frightened woman on your hands," he said. "Right now you can bet she's frightened of the world—of a world she doesn't understand. And she certainly doesn't understand her brother's death. I'm afraid it's going to take a long time for her to recover."

"So, what do I do?" said Sandy.

Frank shook his head. "There isn't much you can do. It doesn't help, either, that you're so far away. And it doesn't help a damn bit that you'll be going to Vietnam after you graduate. Her retreat from you is a form of self-preservation."

Sandy nodded, the look on his face despondent.

"Right now she's trying to put as much emotional distance between you and her as she can. That way if something does happen to you, it won't hurt so bad."

"Well, that sure sucks."

Frank reached over and placed his hand on Sandy's shoulder. "Believe me—I know."

Sandy nodded, remembering their conversation before the Christmas break. He stood, trembling. He felt as if he were in a kind of netherworld, between two realities: the loss of Katie and that he might actually die in Vietnam. Boy, had he got himself into a pickle when he decided to join the army and be a helicopter pilot. As he was filling out the paperwork at the recruiting office, all he could think about was how neat it would be to fly a machine that could go practically anywhere—and he would be the one controlling it. Now he understood what Carlyle meant that day he called him into his office: *"...you're going to be responsible for a quarter-million dollar aircraft and the lives of your co-pilot and crew. They're going to expect you to be in command."* Suddenly he was no longer trembling. Yes, he had made his bed and now he had to sleep in it. Brad's death merely speeded up a process that was inevitable. Katie had begun to move away from him the day he told her he wasn't going to stay at home and go to college, that he was going into the military, just like his dad had said.

"More appropriately," Frank continued, "I would call it psychological self-preservation. I think it's a phenomenon of this war more so than any other. I attribute it to television. Let me tell you, the major networks aren't holding anything back. You couple that kind of war coverage with the fact that we don't seem to know what the hell we're doing over there and you have yourself a potent mixture of public fear, frustration, and outrage. There is a lot of anti-war sympathy being generated in this country, at practically all levels. I think most of it is valid."

"You do?"

"Never forget, Sandy, that the men who fight on either side are pawns to those who supposedly have grander schemes in mind."

"That's bullshit—" Sandy blurted. "I-I know why I'm going."

"You do?"

"Sure, to fight communism. If we don't—"

"—stop them in Vietnam, we'll be fighting them on our own shores." Frank smiled.

"You don't believe that?" said Sandy.

"Hardly."

"So, Frank, why are *you* going back again?"

"That's a good question. When I find the answer, I'll let you know."

* * *

THEIR FIRST CHECKRIDE WAS DUE in two weeks, to be administered by military checkpilots charged with overseeing the quality of flight instruction given by the civilian instructor-pilot force. Each training flight now took on extra meaning. Plus for every hour they flew with their instructor they logged 1.2 hours (and more) by themselves to build their pilot-in-command time. Without an IP onboard to tell them every move to make, they led themselves into difficult, and sometimes dangerous, flying situations and were expected to get themselves out.

Sound flying judgment was not something learned overnight. Nor was it found between the pages of a book. Nor could an instructor plant it entotal in a student's mind. It began with a seed that was already present somewhere in the psyche of the person, to germinate, be born and then nurtured. The environment had to be just right. A good instructor was someone who created the proper atmosphere for learning, one where the student didn't fear making a mistake (as long as it wasn't one that could do him bodily harm or kill him). A relaxed, congenial atmosphere...

"Now where are you going, Percival?" Red Fleming asked.

"Where? Why...north...t-toward the stagefield, sir..."

"The stagefield is behind us, Percival. And behind us is the direction of north. *We're going south—!"*

In academics they were inculcated daily with information, some of it interesting and relevant, most of it, though, explained dryly, without much fanfare. Meteorology, dead-reckoning navigation, aviation regulations and procedures, and aerodynamics continued to be the hot topics.

"Gentlemen," the instructor said, "when a cold front moves rapidly, its leading edge steepens." He moved his pointer to the large diagram covering the blackboard. A few raised their heads. It was afternoon, right after lunch, the worst time to be given "vital" information. "This lifts the warm air ahead of the front abruptly and accelerates the cooling and condensation process. As the water vapor condenses in the form of clouds, large amounts of energy are released in a relatively narrow band along the leading edge of the front. This concentration of energy causes the turbulence and violent weather associated with the rapidly moving cold front." They nodded half-heartily.

"Now, frequently, with a rapidly moving cold front, lines of thunderstorms may develop ahead of the cold front." It was the word "thunderstorms" that perked their ears. "These are known as prefrontal squall lines, and they generally form parallel to the cold front. These prefrontal squall-line thunderstorms are usually more violent than cold-front thunderstorms, and they can form ahead of the cold front by as much as seventy-five to three hundred miles. Should you see, coming from the direction of the cold front, a huge black wall of clouds hugging the ground, steam-rolling toward you"—the instructor slammed the pointer flat against the blackboard making a loud snapping sound—"that is an onrushing squall line. You'd best be looking for a place to land—Quick. Is that understood?" Wide-eyed now, they nodded, because in flying, self-preservation was the name of the game.

It was their aerodynamics class that remained their most boring subject. All they really wanted to know was which flight control made the helicopter go up, which made it go down, which made it turn left, and which to the right. They couldn't imagine at any time during flight, especially during an emergency, having to deal mathematically with the equation for the lift force:

$$L = C(L)qS$$

where L is lift in pounds, C(L) is the coefficient of lift, q is dynamic pressure (psf = ½ rhoV^2), and S is the airfoil surface area in square feet.

The three sat hunched over their VFR Sectional maps, trying to understand the magenta and bluish shading that identified the vertical divisions between controlled and uncontrolled airspace. They had a regulations test coming up and so far neither Mark nor Seymore could make heads or tails out of the Basic VFR altitude structure. Sandy tried to explain one more time the way Bud Gressing had presented it to him, but he shook his head exasperated: "For crissake, it's not that hard, guys!"

They all, however, had a tussle with the magnetic compass. With its lead-lag error factor, rolling out before or after the heading they were actually turning to, compensating for the turn rate, dealing with the acceleration-deceleration problem, the little "whiskey" compass, as it was popularly termed, really did act like a drunken fool in the kerosene liquid within which it rotated. It seemed to weave and swerve and "dance" all the time, making it nearly impossible to read (with any kind of accuracy), much less understand.

When it came to dealing with the winds aloft forecast, most of them cringed. "How did that damn saying go—True Virgins Make Dull Companions?" Seymore moaned.

"Yes-yes. For godsake, Seymore, must I spoon feed you everything—?" Sandy proclaimed. "The winds aloft are given reference true north. You must change their direction into magnetic, so you can decide how to counteract them with a wind drift correction angle referencing your magnetic compass. Unfortunately, the aircraft's compass usually has a deviation problem, due to electrical fields generated inside the cockpit. First you add or subtract the variation to or from the 'true' direction given. This becomes the magnetic direction. Next you figure your wind drift correction bases on your magnetic course. Then you correct for deviation…to get your actual…compass…heading. Seymore, why are your eyes crossed? Damnit, are you listening to me—?"

Victor R. Beaver

Chapter 31

"OKAY, LISTEN UP." A HEAVY-SET Air Force sergeant stood before them. "Sorry for the delay. When you deplane, you will see two shacks. One is for the officers and the other is for enlisted personnel. Move quickly to them once you get on the ramp. Your baggage will be unloaded shortly. Are there any O-6s on board?" There were none. The sergeant smiled. "Well, then, welcome to the war in South Vietnam. Uncle Sam appreciates your attendance—"

It took an hour for duffel bags and suitcases to be off-loaded, stacked in piles next to the shacks, and for the men to identify and claim them. Mike Nolan, now a captain (his promotion had come while he was on leave), found his luggage and dragged it off to one side. He lit a cigarette and pondered the activity around him. Being here now felt old hat to him. "Vietnam...the revolving-door war," he mused.

During the flight over, he noted that nearly a quarter of the passengers had served previous tours. Already he was beginning to feel like he had never left, that he was merely moving to another part of the country. What had changed? Nothing, really. The humidity stifled him, sapping him worse than in Georgia or Alabama...Open cooking fires and the omnipresent odor of rotting vegetation wafted through the air, so powerful he thought he could cleave it with a knife...Expended jet fuel made his eyes water. And there were the sounds. Bien Hoa Air Force Base, as he remembered from a year ago, after his tour with the 173rd Airborne Brigade, still hummed like a well-oiled machine. Fighter, transport, and other support aircraft wheeled about everywhere. Dozens of men wearing fatigue pants, T-shirts, and sporting a variety of headgear criss-crossed the ramp in jeeps, bicycles, and tugs in support of these high-tech machines. He turned at the sound of two F-4 Phantom jets thundering down the runway, remembering what a Marine Corps major, a Phantom pilot, once told him:

"The F-4 is proof that if you put enough engine behind a chunk of metal you can make anything fly—*even a concrete shithouse.*"

So what *had* changed?

Only the day and the year. It was January 14, 1968.

Again, the heavy-set Air Force sergeant stood before them. "The buses will be here momentarily," he bellowed. "You've got a half-hour ride to Camp Alpha, Ninetieth Replacement Battalion, Long Binh, where you will process in, be given your in-country assignments, and issued your jungle fatigue uniforms. You should be out of there by tomorrow or the next day."

They spent twenty minutes more sweltering in the hot sun, waiting for the buses to arrive. Once they did, it took another twenty minutes for everyone to load their gear as each man vied for space to stack his belongings and also have a place to sit. By the time the drivers pulled away, everyone's Stateside uniforms were drenched in sweat.

"What are these screens over the windows for?" one man asked.

"So Charlie can't lob a grenade through'em," another answered.

Those who had never been to Vietnam were hit by culture shock. The bus ride took them along narrow streets lined with clapboard shanties, sewage standing in open puddles, and toddlers, naked and dirty, playing gleefully amid the filth and the squalor. On either side of the road they saw Vietnamese men squatting on their haunches, smoking rolled cigarettes, smiling and nodding their heads at the passing newcomers. In the background they spied women stooped over open cooking fires, or hunched down grappling with dirty laundry, the lassitude in their faces making them look old long before their time.

They pulled into Camp Alpha trailing a cloud of dust. Again, the enlisted men were separated from the officers, assembled and marched down an incline to their billets situated not quite a quarter-mile away. The officers remained in place, their billets located in a grove of tall trees. Nolan dragged his duffel bag and one suitcase and propped them against the wall of one of the screened-in wooden buildings that served as sleeping quarters.

"Listen up, gentlemen," sounded the voice of one of the camp NCOs, dressed smartly in pressed jungle fatigues. "Your first order of business is to exchange your American greenbacks for MPC, military payment certificates, funny money. After that you will receive several lectures concerning your health in a tropical climate and a war zone. Here you have to worry about malaria, the plague, dysentery, hepatitis, venereal disease—you name it, Vietnam's got it. And we want you to know what you can expect from the enemy: Charles, Chuck, the VC, the Viet Cong, Victor Charlie, or them goddamn little rice-propelled sonsabitches." A ripple of laughter threaded through the group. "In short, drink only potable water labeled as such, don't mess with the whores downtown without protection, and refrain from picking up foreign objects you may find lying about on the ground. They could go boom."

By 1700, Nolan had completed most of his in-processing. He, along with several others, had also received his initial issue of clothing that included jungle fatigues, OD underwear, combat boots, and a few other odds and ends that added up to more weight than he wanted, for the moment, to lug around. He found an empty bench, sat down, and lit a cigarette.

The camp loudspeaker sounded: "Captain Nolan, please report to the orderly room."

When he walked in, he met a tall, sandy-haired, first lieutenant dressed in faded jungle fatigues. Sewn above his left breast pocket were a set of aviator wings. "I'm Jeremy Hardin," the lieutenant said, extending his hand. "I've been sent by Major Elroy, the Two Thirty-fifth CO. He asked me to check on any of our newly-arrived officers. Battalion has a funny way of rearranging assignments

Victor R. Beaver

once a man gets to Can Tho. He needs a replacement ops officer, if you're interested."

"Sure, I'm game," Nolan responded.

"I've got a Huey parked a half-mile from here. I've also got a jeep outside. I was on a parts run to our maintenance depot. On the way back it's just you, me, and the crewchief. If you want you can fly leftseat."

"Sounds like a plan. Let's go get my gear."

As they drove along, Nolan learned that Hardin was one of the 235th Aerial Weapons Company platoon leaders. An ROTC graduate out of the University of Texas, El Paso, Hardin was married, had a five-year-old son, and was planning to go into dentistry when he finished his military commitment in two years. "My old man has a ranch east of El Paso, but I'll be damned if I'm going to baby-sit a bunch of stupid cows. And I'm not going to stay in the army, either. It's bad enough I've got to ride herd on nine warrant officers who don't give a shit about their OERs, or their damn personal appearance, or even how stupid they get when they're drunk, but some of my officers aren't a whole helluva lot better."

It was after eight o'clock when they landed at Can Tho. Hardin hovered the Huey toward an empty revetment near a large open hangar, parked and shut the aircraft down. Meanwhile, Nolan had caught sight of several barebacked men inside the hangar working under bright lights on two Cobra gunships; both AH-1Gs had their main rotors removed. He wondered how good a target the lights made for adjusting impacting mortars.

"You can do your in-processing tomorrow," Hardin said, as the main rotor came to a full stop. One of the maintenance jeeps had arrived a moment before and was now off-loading boxes of helicopter parts. "Tonight, you can bunk with us."

Hardin commandeered another jeep and helped Nolan with his baggage. The drive to quarters took less than three minutes. Stepping inside Hardin's hootch, Nolan expressed surprise. The BOQ turned out to be one of several fairly new, solidly built, air-conditioned wood structures set on concrete slabs. The interior, however, had been redesigned to house five pilots instead of six and with the extra space the present occupants had fashioned themselves a bar, generously stocked. An elaborate stereo system completed the proverbial den of iniquity. (Nolan learned later the local R&D engineers had been bamboozled into building two more pilot hootches to compensate for the commandeered space.) "They're putting in an evacuation hospital here," Hardin told him. "We're expecting a dozen American nurses to be on staff. The other officer hootches are pretty much like this one."

"And the hootch with the best arrangement will reap the greatest rewards," quipped Nolan.

On the following morning, Nolan spent in-processing into the battalion, with orders cut officially assigning him to the 235th.

That same afternoon he met Major Elroy, the 235th commanding officer. Less than an inch taller than Nolan, Elroy had deep-set gray eyes, a medium build, and a short, brush-like haircut. "My S-3, Captain Dane," he said, "who you'll meet tonight, is DEROSing in forty-five days. I need to have you well entrenched before he's gone. You're not going to get much flying once you take over. How does that make you feel?"

Nolan shrugged. "Sir, it's fine by me. I'm pretty flexible."

"Good. You'll get a fair amount of front-seat time, though, before that happens, so that you can have a decent understanding of our AO. But I doubt you'll ever make AC on this tour. Those who do have put in a lot of orbit time. They've earned it."

That afternoon Nolan took up quarters with the rest of the company staff, in a hootch next to operations and the orderly room. The following day he received his in-country standardization ride from CW3 Grant Widlow, an old-timer like Daddy Don Pollard. Once that was done Hardin took him on an orientation flight beginning at the western edge of the Parrots Beak, that chunk of the Cambodian border that juts zigzag-like into the northern reaches of the Mekong Delta. From there they flew westward along the border over the Plain of Reeds, past the Seven Mountains region, to the Gulf of Thailand.

The day after he met more of the men of the company and found the younger members eager to do battle with Charlie. These men were not yet weary of the war; they probably wouldn't become so during their first combat tour. Among them was a real anticipation of doing a number on the Viet Cong in the Mekong Delta. The second-tour pilots knew this would never happen. Besides, the mood back in the States was for winding down, letting the South Vietnamese shoulder more of the actual fighting. All these older pilots wanted to do was get through their second tour unscathed—by beating the odds that they wouldn't.

* * *

WORLD WAR II HAD JUST ENDED WHEN Nolan's mother died. His father, a merchant marine seaman, upon hearing the news, quit his ship at the next port and came home. He sold the house they lived in, bought a fishing boat, and went into the charter fishing business. Allowed to bring aboard any belonging that could be stowed in one of the boats many compartments, Michael chose his *Superman, Batman,* and *Combat* series comic books. He also brought aboard a horde of plastic toy soldiers, which he would arrange and rearrange as two opposing forces on his bunk, on the deck, wherever he could find space and not be in the way.

Victor R. Beaver

He continued his public-school education at Marathon, a town more than half way down on the Florida Keys. After school, as he awaited his father's return from a day of fishing, Michael would walk and comb the beaches. He wore an army web belt with attached canteen, ammo pouch containing an empty M-1 ammo clip, and .45-caliber pistol holster housing a cap gun. He carried his toy soldiers along with him in a cloth bag (as well as an ample supply of fire crackers, cherry bombs, and M-80s). He built sand forts and created scenes filled with pitched battles, mock casualties, and heroic deeds.

When Michael was thirteen the Korean War broke out. He puffed himself up and went to the Army recruiting office to join. The sergeant, quick to sense the boy's true age, rejected Michael's efforts but held him spellbound with his own exploits, real or imagined. This sent the lad ever deeper into a lifelong dream of soldiering. Before the war ended, Michael tried once more to enlist, but they still weren't taking underage consignees, so he had to make one more retreat, vowing that next year, come hell or high water, he would have his name signed on the dotted line. At the end of his junior year, Michael told his father he was quitting school. Because he was not yet eighteen he asked his father to sign the waiver allowing him to enlist. His father agreed. During the years they had spent together the two had become as stolid as two ships crossing paths in the night.

On the morning of the big day, his father drove him to the induction station in Miami, gave him a five-dollar bill, and told him that when he returned he wanted him to be his partner in the charter business. Before that time the older man had never once said he expected his son to join him. "I'm going to make the army a career," Michael told his father. The older man nodded. "After you put your time in, the offer will still stand."

It had been several days since he had unpacked. Nolan sat on his bunk, his back against the wall. He glanced around his hootch-room, made comfortable by a fan, a small refrigerator, and a simple stereo system. He looked down to his left. On the bed next to him was a small overnight kit. He unzipped the top and took out the last of his belongings, to be placed where he could examine them from time to time.

He took the framed photo that had been covered in cloth and held it in front of him. It was a picture of him and his father at the dock at Ben's Marina in Marathon. Between them, hanging head down, was a 295-pound blue marlin. In the background was his father's boat, the *Laura Lee,* named after his mother. The struggle to bring the fish in had taken Nolan six hours; and in that time his father never once offered to help. When the battle was done, his hands were bloody; his arms as hard as two lengths of taut rope; and the muscles in his back and shoulders felt as though they had been stretched by a medieval torture rack. After the prized catch was finally hauled in, his father said:

"You never called for help, so I figured you didn't need any."

Michael peered into his father's face. It was sunburned and whiskered, with the skin leather-like tough. He wanted to tear into him, rip him apart, and scatter his shredded body and taciturn mannerisms to the sharks. He thought of his mother and wanted to let out a torrent of pent-up sorrow and grief. In a moment, though, all had passed. He looked at the fish, at his hands, and said:

"Okay, I can accept that. It's better this way."

He placed the picture on the stand next to his bunk. Then he took out a white plastic box. He opened the box and there fit snugly inside was a blue velvet case. He removed the case and opened it. Inside were two gold oak-leaf clusters. They were the gold clusters of the rank of major in the United States Army. He bought them the day he graduated from OCS, along with his gold second lieutenant bars. He brushed them lightly with his fingertips. He took one of the insignias, held it up for a moment, examined it, and then replaced it in the case. He closed the case.

He placed the case next to the picture. He took a cigarette and lit it. He sat back and relaxed full against the wall next to his cot. He pulled lightly on his cigarette. In his mind's eye he saw himself standing in his Class A dress green uniform, the hands of someone, another man, perhaps a commanding officer, pinning one of the gold clusters to the epaulets of his dress coat. It was a ceremony he played again and again in his mind whenever he opened the case to look at them.

He smiled. Everything was on track—his career, his life—everything. Barring the unforeseen, he would retire in eight years as a major. And return to the Florida Keys—to his father and home....

Victor R. Beaver

Chapter 32

EVERY DAY AT THE STAGEFIELD it was practice, practice and more practice. Normal takeoffs and landings. Steep approaches. Maximum performance takeoffs. Autorotations. Simulated engine failures.

Checkride day drew nearer and nearer. Bud Gressing had his three students primed. He and Frank Bartlett had left Downing Heliport on a dual flight. Sandy Adamson was in the bus on the highway going to the stagefield, to take Frank's place when his dual flight was completed. Tom Adkins, the resident Michaelangelo, had one of the training helicopters all to himself.

Adkins peered ahead, his gaze just below the horizon. *Where is it?* He checked his watch. *It should be there—I'm right on time.* He felt his heart sink. His breathing became shallow, his grip on the cyclic control stick slackened. And then, suddenly, there it was, the lead engine of the train. He checked above the horizon both left and right for "enemy" airplanes. There were none. Incredible. *An unprotected supply train! How can this be—?*

Adkins felt his body stiffen. He tightened his seatbelt, then the nylon strap of his helmet. His right hand now held a death grip on the cyclic control stick. He checked the rpm. Everything was set. He toggled one of the ICS switches. *There, the guns and rockets are armed.* He drew in more power. The wind whistled past. The helicopter shuddered as if it might shake itself apart. The two opposing forces were now approaching each other head-on. "Prepare to meet your maker," the artist hissed. He checked his watch. With every second that passed the train loomed larger and larger, the lead engine appearing now like one great, black, thundering dinosauric form. Adkins hunched his back; the hairs on the back of his neck bristled. The angle had to be perfect. Absolutely perfect. Nothing less would do—

In the next instant, he knew he was committed. There was no turning back. The fate of the free world hung in the balance. He was the vanguard for the forces of good against evil. It would be a fight to the finish. Was he prepared to die? Yes! He was the cream of the best, the chosen...*the Divine Wind...*

The angle for attack came closer...closer...*There!* He began his dive. From fifteen hundred feet the speed of the ship began to build. Could the little training helicopter handle it? Could it? Yes—*it would have to hold!*

He had the front engine now in his sights. His trigger finger twitched. *Steady. Steady. Take your time. When you fire, don't jerk it...squeeze it, like you were fondling the breasts of a woman. Caress the trigger. There...yes...you've got it. Fondle the trigger.*

He checked his speed and then the trim. The earth rushed to meet him. From the earth he came, to the earth he would return. It made sense. He was one with the Universe, though at the moment he was above the earth, a soldier from the sky. Yes! He was also a soldier from the sky. *A Sky Soldier!*

At five hundred feet he squeezed off the first pair. The "rockets" crossed paths much too early. They "exploded" on either side of the lead engine. Again he trimmed (to make the aircraft more streamlined as it flew through the air). He squeezed off a second pair. They streaked forward. The two rockets this time met head-on with the train. A large, fiery explosion. *Yahoo!* He fired off the final pair. They too found their mark. The train careened off the track, plunging down an embankment. He watched as the cars behind the engines sandwiched into a pile of rubble.

The artist, turned fighter pilot, began his pullout. He had stopped his descent not more than a hundred feet from the devastation he had just created. He flew through a thick column of smoke. As he began to ascend, he looked back. Two flatbed cars coupled together, still on track, their decks covered before with canvas, suddenly came alive with men firing machine guns. The bullets "zipped" through the air around him. Upward he climbed, until he was out of range. He glanced back one more time. He laughed. ***Mission complete.*** He headed for the stagefield.

"Adkins, what the heck are you doing?" said Willie Cottrell, standing back to get a better view. "Did Drakeman approve this?"

The young Michaelangelo looked up. The main latrine wall was nearly all outlined with the largest mural he had yet to undertake. "Sure. What do you think? Do you like it?"

Willie gazed at the outline. He frowned. "You've got rockets…mounted on a TH-55…attacking a train—?"

"Yep. Anything wrong with that?"

The ex-Special Forces sergeant shook his head. "I guess not. Boy, you sure got some kind of wild imagination."

"Shee-it," Adkins grinned. "It didn't hardly take any imagination at all."

* * *

SANDY ADAMSON FELT A WAVE OF nausea pass through him. He wiped his forehead. "Seymore…I-I feel sick…"

"Boy, I'll say. You look white as a sheet. What's the matter?"

"I-I don't know…I feel hot…weak…"

It was Friday at noon. They had been outside in formation and had just heard a pep talk given by Major Bond about their upcoming checkrides. The air temperature was a mild 65 degrees, but Sandy felt like he was on fire. Mark and Seymore helped him up the stairs to the room. They unclothed him and put him to bed. Willie Cottrell stood over him. "He's got some kind of bug. He needs to go on sick call."

Sandy tried to sit up. "I'm not...going on sick call...got checkride..."

Willie eased him back down. "Okay, take it easy. Try to get some sleep. Maybe you'll feel better later."

By late afternoon, though, he was worse. He had tossed and turned and twice in three hours had gone to the latrine to vomit. By the time Willie returned, he saw the horrid condition Sandy was in. Willie felt his forehead. "Mama mia, you're hotter than hell." Again, Sandy tried to rise, but Willie nudged him back down. "You're going on sickcall, pal. Whatever you got, can't be good. I'm calling an ambulance."

In the emergency room, the diagnosis was immediate: pneumonia coupled with the flu.

He spent his first night in the hospital delirious, his dreams crazy, mixed up, nonsensical. In and out of sleep, he drifted continuously between the real and the imaginary. More than a dozen times he cried out, "Katie...Katie, I want you—*I need you!*" and would toss and turn until he became hopelessly entangled in his bedsheets. Twice he fell out of bed and had to be helped back in by a nurse's aide. In his dreams, Katie always appeared as if standing on an expansive blinding white surface. She remained constantly out of reach, retreating farther from him as he went toward her.

By morning, his condition had changed little. Afternoon trailed into early evening, with his subconscious remaining a labyrinth of buried emotions. Seymore came and comforted him.

By Sunday morning his stomach had settled enough for him to take in fluids. Again, Seymore was there, this time to feed him.

On Monday, Sandy woke feeling lonely and depressed. Even his immediate world seemed to exist in some distant past, even, at times, in some other dimension. On Tuesday, he tried to get out of bed, but was so weak he collapsed. He stood again, determined to find his clothes. He knew that if he missed one more day of training he would be setback to the class behind. A nurse ordered him back into bed. Late that afternoon he began to feel better. A doctor came and listened to his chest. He shook his head. "You need another night here."

Wednesday morning. A doctor unfamiliar to him examined him. "How are you feeling?"

"I feel great...good enough to fly," Sandy said, his voice still sounding weak.

"Sure you do."

"I'm serious, sir. Please, you've got to let me go. If I miss one more day, they'll—"

"Set you back." The doctor frowned. He'd seen too many candidates under similar conditions adamant about sticking with their original class. "Well, do you think you can get back to the barracks?"

"Yessir."

"Okay, I'll release you for flying this afternoon."

At the flight line, Gressing looked at the ashen-faced lad. "You look like death warmed over."

"I feel fine, sir."

"Okay, here's the story. The last day for checkrides is this coming Monday. I convinced the flight commander that in spite of the days you've missed, I could have you ready. What do you think?"

"Let's go for it, sir."

"Okay, but we've really got our work cut out for us."

Gressing spent the first part of the flight period reviewing all the maneuvers. When Sandy took the controls, it was all he could do to hold the helicopter straight and level.

Gressing shook his head. "You've got to put more into it, son."

"Yessir."

"You sure you want to do this?"

"I have to, sir...I know I can do it."

By the end of the period, Sandy's flight suit was drenched in sweat. He had made only moderate progress. Thursday morning saw most of his color return, and he was also able to eat a good noon meal. That afternoon, both Frank Bartlett and Tom Adkins took their checkrides and came back with scores in the high eighties. During Sandy's dual flight period, Gressing saw some improvement. But in the back of his mind doubted the lad could pass a checkride—not yet, anyway. By Friday, Sandy had got most of his strength back. Gressing said:

"I wish like hell you didn't have the weekend to go through before your checkride. It would be nice to have a dual period on Monday, for review."

Sandy said, "Don't worry, sir, I'll manage. I know I can do it."

"Well...I sure hope you can. You've got the heart."

During the rest of Friday's training period Gressing sat back and let Sandy work on the maneuvers he wanted most to practice. Finally, when their time together had come to an end, and Sandy was shutting down the engine, Gressing said over the intercom:

"Okay, this weekend get plenty of rest. Review your emergency procedures. On Monday, eat a good breakfast and come in with a positive attitude. Remember, just do like you've been taught."

Sandy took his helmet off. As Gressing was about to get out of the helicopter, Sandy said, "Thank you, sir...for your faith in me. I won't let you down."

Gressing smiled. "No, no you won't. But more importantly, you won't let yourself down."

The following Monday he was up and ready. It was do or die. At the flight line he met his checkpilot, a grizzled-looking chief warrant officer with a no-nonsense expression etched across his face. Still, Sandy felt confident. But once

Victor R. Beaver

the checkride started his confidence fell flat. Each maneuver he performed left him with the impression that he was failing miserably. Nothing he did had the polish he had acquired with Gressing before his sickness. After the flight, the checkpilot led him back to the briefing room. Sandy was certain of the outcome.

As the two sat down at the table, the checkpilot gave Gressing, who was standing off to one side, a stern look. "How do you think you did, son?" the warrant officer said.

"Not so good, sir," Sandy replied.

"Well, perhaps not your best, but I'll tell you what, you showed very good judgment in every one of your maneuvers. And you always had the aircraft under control, even though your control touch was a little rough. Wish I could give you a grade better than eighty-one."

Sandy frowned. "You mean...I passed?"

"Sure, what did you think?"

"I don't know. I guess I thought everything had to be perfect, or it wasn't right."

"Nah...I don't do any of those maneuvers perfect and I'm a checkpilot. And if you were perfect, your instructor and I would be out of a job. What counts most is that you always strove for perfection." The man extended his hand. "Congratulations. I don't know what score your IP expected you to come back with, but if you'd have had a little more time, I'd say you'd have been in the nineties." Sandy's eyes lit up. And then the checkpilot said:

"Here's a word of advice. They don't engrave the scores you make on the back of your wings when you graduate. You just learn to fly the best you can. Let the scores take care of themselves."

"Yes, sir. Thank you, sir."

* * *

FLIGHT ALPHA ONE MET THEIR MILITARY flight instructors in a small flight briefing room (building) next to the messhall. As they walked into the briefing room they saw hung on the walls a variety of plaques and souvenirs. The plaques were mementos of appreciation given by previous classes. The souvenirs were mostly trophies brought home from Vietnam: an AK-47 assault rifle, several VC flags, two captured Viet Cong single-shot rifles, a North Vietnamese pith helmet, a canteen sporting a bullet hole, and a whole display of MPC, military payment certificates, "overseas" money the men used to make purchases in Vietnam. Most of the instructors were young, barely older than the students they trained. They wore an assortment of colorful patches on their upper right sleeve, a testimony to the combat units they served with in Vietnam. Sandy, Mark, and Seymore managed to get the same instructor, a soft-spoken rotund captain named Oliver Crandall, who had just returned from his first Vietnam tour. Seymore, not used to a flight instructor who didn't bellow when he spoke, gave Sandy a meek, worried look, as if at any moment the boom would crash down on his head.

The captain chose Mark Allen to fly with first, while Sandy and Seymore rode the bus to the stagefield. During flight with each respective student, Crandall watched them perform normal stagefield work—approaches, takeoffs, a couple of autorotations—to give him an idea the level of their flying skills. Before his first flight with them, though, he defined at the table what their training goals would be: confined area approaches, pinnacle approaches, slope landings, that is, landing on ground that had a slight incline, and later, cross-country navigation, and then a brief period of formation flying. He explained high and low recon techniques, and told them that from now on they could expect a simulated engine failure anywhere, anytime.

"What did you fly in Vietnam?" Seymore asked.

"Chinooks. If there wasn't an LZ hacked out for us to land, we blew the area down with our rotorwash." He smiled, expecting them to laugh. They had no idea the downward velocity of the winds created by a CH-47's tandem rotorblades.

Before Captain Crandall completed his first dual period with Seymore, Seymore had lathered himself into a tizzy. "Candidate Cutter."

"Sir!—did I do something wrong? I'm sorry—"

"No-no. I was just going to say, your approach to the lane was pretty good."

"It was...?"

"Yeah, you sort of had me fooled."

"I did? How did I do that—sir?"

Crandall gave a roly-poly laugh. "My first impression of you was that you were a spastic misfit. I guess it just goes to show you can't judge a book by its cover, can you?"

Seymore relaxed. "Yeah...I guess not."

The days that followed were intense. In academics they were introduced to the E6-B flight computer, a hand-held, metal and plastic, circular and rectangular device which they used to calculate true airspeed, a wind correction angle, ground speed, their fuel flow, all the planning data necessary, using this tool, for effective cross-country flying. They became immersed in the navigation charts. They plotted courses, checkpoints, en route times, and the fuel required to complete a long trip. Crandall introduced them to the confined areas (usually a small open space surrounded by trees or other barriers) in their training area. Different colored tires (old, used, painted tires), placed in the middle of the landing zone, signified which ones they were able to work under certain conditions. A red tire meant that, due to the confined area's high degree of difficulty, they weren't allowed to perform an approach and landing into it without an instructor on board. A yellow-tire confined area was one that the student could go into alone (solo), however only after a previously accompanied "practice" approach with an instructor. The white-tire areas were the least difficult and all solo students were permitted to go into them without prior dual practice. Some confined areas were more favored than others, due to their proximity to the stagefields, and these were competed for fiercely. It was not unusual to see three and four training helicopters (with solo students on board) orbiting one white-tire confined area while another was making its approach and landing into it.

Once in the landing zone (with the ship firmly on the ground), a student was required to bring the helicopter to flight-idle rpm, friction down the controls, get out of the helicopter, and step off his departure path out of the confined area—to insure he had enough room to lift off safely. That it was a time consuming process was an understatement to say the least. But they took to learning these advanced skills with enthusiasm, knowing that these steps were essential to bring them to their ultimate goal as Army helicopter pilots.

Chapter 33

ROBIN HENRY APPEARED AT KIP'S hootch-room door. "Henry—I'll be go to hell—look at you," Kip exclaimed.

"I made it," Henry said, puffing out his chest. He had on the trademark of the Viking gun platoon—a black T-shirt tucked in his jungle fatigue pants.

Leo nudged into Slater's room. He vigorously shook Henry's hand. "Let's go to the club. This calls for a celebration."

"Drinks are on me, guys," Henry said.

Seated at one of the booths, Leo pulled at Henry's arm. "What do you think my chances are? Did Captain James give any indication when the next opening might be?"

"Gosh, Leo...I didn't ask. You gotta keep bugging him, like I did. You'll make it."

"Okay, yeah...sure."

Later, when he was alone with Slater, Henry said, "The Vikings don't want him; he's too reckless; he flies too close to the edge. They want someone who isn't so eager."

"Yeah, I understand."

* * *

ONE DAY CAPTAIN SLOTE SCHEDULED Slater and Tannah to fly together, single-ship "swing" (re-supply) for the Chau Doc Province. Slater was designated as pilot-in-command.

They lifted from Chau Phu, the provincial capital, at ten o'clock. Tannah was on the controls. On board was an American Special Forces captain and the Chau Doc province chief, an ARVN lieutenant colonel, accompanied by two of his aides. The Vietnam-Cambodian border was to their right, marked by a canal that bent and turned toward the southwest past the Vietnam portion of the Seven Mountains region until it spilled into the Gulf of Thailand. The massive granite outcroppings reminded Slater of medieval castles overseeing the landscape below.

The captain and the province chief scanned a topo map. After a moment, one of the aides began to point to the left, toward the base of one of the mammoth outcroppings.

Leo glanced left. "I've got purple marking smoke."

To their front, Kip saw more smoke. "I've got yellow marking smoke...coming from the border outpost—which is where I thought we were going."

All heads looked left, then to the front. "What do you make of it?" Slater asked the Special Forces officer over the intercom.

The captain shrugged. "I don't know. We haven't been able to make radio contact. Our map-destination is that outpost you see ahead, along the canal." The captain then peered left. "We shouldn't be going to any location near the base of the mountain there. We do have a patrol, though, in that area. I wonder if they're in trouble?"

Leo looked back. "Which one are we going to, captain?" Leo's sharp-edged tone drew a raised eyebrow.

The captain gave Leo a stern look back. "Continue straight ahead."

Slater flipped his ICS switch to "private." Leo did the same. The two pilots were able to converse only between themselves; no one else could listen. "I don't like this," Kip said.

"Two marking smokes." Leo peered ahead. "I sure hope these bastards know where they want to go—and where they're supposed to be going."

Kip glanced back. The captain and the province chief were checking both the map and the land below, while the two aides jabbered excitedly among themselves. "I don't think anyone back there knows what's going on, Leo."

"Well, the original destination was supposed to be that outpost ahead."

Kip glanced again to the back. "Why would they be confused by this?" His voice had grown tense.

"Hell if I know—"

Kip felt a tap on his shoulder. The two pilots flipped back to normal intercom.

The Special Forces captain said, "Land at the yellow smoke, along the border. We're disregarding the smoke near the mountain. It's probably our patrol—signaling for God knows what. But we're not in radio contact with them. Best to forge ahead."

"Are you in radio contact with the border outpost?" Leo asked.

The captain shook his head. He pointed again to their front. "Proceed there."

Kip nodded. "Roger that." *And three bags full.* This whole situation now smacked of foreboding. He sighed heavily. *Goddamn...why can't anything over here ever be simple?*

"Doorgunners—lock and load." Leo spoke to Slater's crew as if they were his own. "Fire at anything suspicious—anything that moves."

"Leo—" blurted Slater. "Rusty, Ron—*cancel that!*"

"Hey—"

"Hey nothing—they're my crew, Leo. You're going to get me thrown in jail."

"I'm just trying to protect my ass."

"You let me worry about your ass. I'll tell my crew what to do—not you."

The Sky Soldiers

Leo circled the outpost once, then set up for an approach to the north, to keep from overflying Cambodia. Kip scanned ahead. For a border outpost, it was scantily fortressed. As they descended lower, he could see several Vietnamese soldiers standing off to one side, holding casually to their weapons. They were hatless, barefooted men, appearing barely in possession of anything more than the happy wide grins they held on their faces. He looked back at the captain:

"Shall we continue?"

The Special Forces advisor gestured the go-ahead. "Trust me, this is the right place."

Later that evening.

"Kip."

"What." They were in the bar. Leo approached him from the far side. Martha Reye, who had visited the Tiger's Den earlier, was gone. Her outspoken charm, her loud voice, her wide, eager smile, and especially the way she filled out a set of jungle fatigues had fascinated Slater. A full-figured woman, she seemed like the type that could gobble a man up, rattle his bones, then spit him out like so much confetti. She was the first celebrity he had ever seen in person and he adored her.

"Got something to tell you."

"What, Leo?" Kip took another sip from his drink.

"You know that other smoke we saw today, near the base of the mountain?"

"Yeah...what about it?"

"I just talked to that Special Forces captain by telephone. They were set up for us."

"Who, Leo?...Who was set up for us?"

"The VC. They had two machine guns set up in a cross-fire."

"What—?"

"Remember the ARVN patrol that was supposed to be out there?"

"Yeah...?"

"Remember the gunfire we heard when we were lifting from the outpost? The patrol had stumbled onto them. The VC were trying to lure us in. If we'd have gone in there, Kip—we would have got ourselves *killed.*"

Journal Entry, 19 January 1968, Long Xuyen

Two days ago a gruesome thing happened. An ARVN soldier wasn't watching where he was going and walked into Randall's tailrotor. He fell to the ground in a heap—his head sliced cleanly down the middle.

Randall and Leo are crazy. Yesterday, we lifted the ARVN into a cold LZ. As they started to walk along the paddy dikes, Randall hovered next to them, knocking them off into the mud and water one by one. Leo decided it looked fun to do and joined in.

And now I feel like a jerk. This morning, as we were landing to re-supply a small hamlet southeast of Long Xuyen, I happened to overfly (by about 30 feet) a large gathering of people attending a graveside funeral. I saw my rotor downwash lift the yellow and red South Vietnamese flag draped over the coffin and send it flying.

* * *

THE BULLETS SKIPPED TOWARD THEM like rocks hitting the flat surface of a pond. Rusty White spied the muzzle flashes and sent a volley of return gunfire. Meantime, Slater, at the controls, kept the descent going. As loaded as they were it wasn't in the game plan to do a go-around (to abort the landing) though the urge to do so nearly overwhelmed him.

They had left Ca Mau ten minutes before, stacked to the gills with 4-duece mortar ammunition for the outpost at Dam Doi. Though technically a "two-ship" re-supply outpost, and because a cover bird wasn't available, Slater talked his crew into doing the mission anyway, due to the fact that the folks on the ground were down to their last two mortar rounds. From ten kilometers out, they were in radio contact with one of the Dam Doi MACV advisors who briefed them on the two known enemy sniper locations in the vicinity of the outpost. One was less than a hundred meters west of Dam Doi, in a cluster of nipa palm. The other was due northeast, near a 90-degree bend in the river that ran past the west side of Dam Doi. The nipa-palm location had opened up first.

The landing pad, a twenty by twenty square (feet) of raised, hard-packed ground, was connected to the compound by a narrow footpath. Like Nam Can (before the evacuation), the Dam Doi outpost housed a company of RF/PF soldiers and members of their immediate family. Unlike Nam Can, five American advisors kept residence at Dam Doi.

Slater brought Alfie to within inches of the landing pad, to a canister of dying yellow smoke, and plunked down. Crouching low, several Vietnamese soldiers rushed forward and with Ron's help, began to off-load the ammunition. In the background were crouched more than two dozen hopeful passengers, old men and women, mothers and small children, all eager and willing to risk life and limb to get on board once the unloading was done.

Kip looked toward his gunner. "Ron! We can't take anyone out!" he shouted.
"Yes, sir!"
"You've got to keep them back!"
"I'll try, sir!"

When the last box of ammunition was on the ground, the throng stampeded forward, squirming and struggling and elbowing one another past Larkin in spite

The Sky Soldiers

of his best efforts to keep them out of the ship. Slater heard Rusty's M-60 fire at the sniper location again, a sharp cracking sound that rattled his senses. Kip looked toward Larkin, urging him to do something—*anything!*

"What am I supposed to do, sir?" he exclaimed. At his feet was an old papa-san on his knees, pleading to be helped on board. Slater caught Ron's hapless, frustrated look. Meanwhile, Rusty continued to blast away at the sniping gunfire. Finally, Slater motioned for Larkin to help the man aboard and to get aboard himself.

Ron plugged back into the intercom system. "I'm ready, sir—let's di-di the mau outta here—!"

It was Harper's turn to fly. The gum-chewing peter-pilot from Arkansas started to move the helicopter forward. Feeling close to panic, Slater glanced back. He saw a woman inside the cabin with outstretched hands trying to grab onto a small girl who scurried alongside the lifting ship. At first their fingertips were mere inches apart, then the gap widened as the overloaded Huey became airborne.

As they lumbered out, gaining precious altitude seemingly by the thimbleful, Rusty continued firing until he lost sight of the cluster of nipa palm. In the same instant, Ron's gun began firing. "Receiving fire from three o'clock—" the gunner called over the intercom. Slater could see the bend in the river where the second VC location was known to be. He told Harper to break right. Doing so, he felt, would put the aircraft almost directly overhead and harder for the VC to take aim and shoot. Ron was standing as he fired, and then his target, too, became lost from view.

When they reached two thousand feet altitude, Slater began to breathe easier. He looked at the sea of faces behind him. The woman whose child was left behind was crying. He tried to count heads but lost track after fifteen.

"We've got twenty-one, sir," Larkin told him.

Back at the airfield. Slater was in his room. A knock sounded on his door. "Come in." His crewchief stood before him. "What do you need, Rusty?"

The crewchief held out his hand. "Gotta present for you, sir."

Kip examined the twisted chunk of lead. "Where was this?"

"It was lodged in the soundproofing next to your seat, right above your head. I think it entered through the right cabin side. It must have come from that second sniper location."

"I'll be damned..."

"You've taken your first hit, sir. I guess you're no longer a cherry."

"Thanks. That's real comforting."

"Anytime, sir. But let's keep this kind of thing down to a dull roar. Alfie does not like going into bad places."

"Believe me...I'll keep that in mind."

Victor R. Beaver

* * *

KIP SLATER AND JEFF MANGRUM FOLLOWED Kim Thi An up the flight of wrought-iron stairs to her apartment. She unlocked the door and invited them in. They found themselves in the kitchen, a small bright room that contained a table, a sink, an ancient-looking gas-burning stove, and a tiny PX-bought refrigerator. Large windows on two adjacent walls looked down at the courtyard below. So far Kip liked the location of her apartment, right behind the Soc Trang MACV compound. The sight of the American compound gave him a secure feeling. He wondered if he would ever be able to spend the night here. It would be nice if he could.

"Did Eddie buy the refrigerator for you?" Mangrum asked.

She nodded. "Yes."

"Do you have any beer?" said Kip.

Again she nodded. She opened the refrigerator and brought out two cans of Falstaff beer. She opened them and they each took one. Slater took a sip. It wasn't as cold as he liked, but it still tasted good. "So, what do you think?" Mangrum asked. Eddie Barrow, one of the civilian tower operators, and a good friend of Mangrum's, had returned Stateside, his contract period up. He had spent two years at the airfield and had kept the woman in room and spending money, with the agreement that he be her one and only bed companion. Now that Barrow was gone she was in the market for another man. Slater had picked up on the idea several days before. Mangrum agreed to introduce them.

"I like it," Kip said. "And she's very pretty."

"She's half French," the gunner said.

"Yeah, I can tell." Kip saw that her face was long, her eyes slightly rounded. Mangrum went to the door. Slater asked, "Are you leaving?"

"Yeah. You don't need me around to work out the details, do you?"

Slater grinned. "No, of course not."

"I'll see you back at the airfield."

"Thanks."

"Don't mention it."

Alone with this lovely French-Vietnamese woman, Kip said, "I understand you work at the MACV compound."

She nodded. "Yes...I am a secretary."

She spoke with just a slight accent. Her eyes, he noted, had a sorrowful look. *What must she think of me?* he wondered. *We're performing nothing more than a business transaction, yet with such underlying implications.* A moment of silence passed between them. She indicated that he should see the rest of the apartment. Next to the stove was a doorway that led from the kitchen to another room. The door itself was nothing more than a series of colored beads suspended from the top of the doorframe to just above the floor. Kip entered. It was her bedroom, very narrow, very small, and very dark. To his immediate left was a slab of cement and in the middle of it, a drain-hole, and beside the drain-hole a pail of water: The bathroom. Against the right wall was a small table that held a lamp; above the level of the table was a heavily curtained window. To his front, against the left wall, was a bed. Kip sat down on the bed. Kim Thi An turned on the lamp and sat next to him. "How much?" he asked.

"Five thousand P," she said.

Slater nodded. "That's about fifty dollars a month."

"Yes."

"Okay. Do you want the money now?"

"Yes, if you have."

Kip got out his billfold. He gave her fifty dollars in MPC. She took the money and put it in a small case she retrieved from under the bed. "Okay...now what do we do?" Slater said.

She indicated that they should go to bed.

"Okay, but...do you have anything to smoke? You know, dinky-dou weed?"

"Yes, I'll get." She stood and went to the table. She opened the drawer and pulled out a small plastic cigarette-rolling machine. Jeff had told him that she always kept an ample supply. In a couple of minutes, she had a cigarette lit and smoldering. Slater drew on it slowly, deeply. He held the smoke in. After a moment he exhaled...slowly. He took one more deep drag and exhaled. And then his body sagged as the warm liquid rush filled every pore. He was stoned. His mind collapsed and he began to see things in slow motion.

Meanwhile, Kim had got up and was undressing. He sat back on her bed and watched. The first thing he noticed were her perfect-pyramid breasts, the nipples pert and upturned. Then he saw that her skin was smooth and dusky. Her long dark hair, previously pinned up, hung down past her waist and had just the slightest wave to it. She stood before him and he could smell the musty aroma of her body. She helped him undress. As she did, every molecule in his body felt vibrant and alive. Next, she laid down beside him. He indicated that he wanted to kiss her. They had known each other less than an hour. He found her lips soft, warm—and yielding. His organ felt strong...extremely sensitive. Like he had hoped, the intake of the marijuana had done its job.

She moved her lips down along his neck, then lightly over his chest, tantalizing him. With her hand she massaged his manhood. After a few minutes, Slater knew he could take no more."Kim—wait..." He held her hand and she stopped. His body felt aflame as she slipped alongside him. Gently, he coaxed her onto her back and then positioned himself above her. She reached for him and guided him toward her. Slowly...slowly...slowly he went into her, into her silken softness. After he was deep within her, all he wanted to do was hold still, to feel every licentious part of her. In his smoke-filled state of mind, with the dusky color of the

Victor R. Beaver

room around him, he saw that she was indeed incredibly beautiful. *I am lost in you and I am safe. Right now the rest of the world does not exist. There is no war...no pain...no suffering...no killing...no dying...no weeping—no anything: there is only the here and now. I am at peace.*

An hour later he was dressed. He spoke to her about when he might return. "I want to come here often," he said. "I want to spend all the nights I can with you." At the moment he couldn't imagine anything that would ever stop him from doing just that.

She smiled and opened the door for him. Gingerly, he descended the stairs. At the bottom, he looked up; she waved and he waved back. There was plenty of daylight left, and he wanted to stay, but he knew he must get back to the airfield.

He walked out of the courtyard. Once past the MACV compound, he hailed a cyclo driver. As the driver sped the little motorcycle-driven buggy toward the airfield, he thought that life was good. He had a small piece of the world that seemed completely apart from the war.

Chapter 34

MIKE NOLAN SAT PERCHED IN THE front seat of the lead ship of a pair of high-orbiting Cobras, looking down. He watched a company of Cambodian mercenaries as they moved slowly through the reeds, led by two Special Forces advisors. So far the troops had turned up nothing: no caches of food, medical supplies, weapons, or ammunition. "Sun Devil Two Six, this is Sierra Red," came the American voice on the ground.

"This is Two Six, go," Hardin answered.

"We'll be taking our lunch break now."

"This is Sun Devil Two Six, roger that."

Nolan glanced in the tiny rear-view mirror. Hardin's eyes were hidden behind his helmet sunvisor. Mike shifted in his seat and looked up. The sun shone so bright, the sky so hazy, it appeared the two were as one. He closed his eyes. Sleep, if I could just go to sleep, he thought. For the past hour and a half they had been orbiting over the eastern edge of the Plain of Reeds, a wide expanse of land covered by waist-high grasses and occasional clusters of low-lying trees. Narrow waterways meandered through the Plains, providing the Viet Cong their primary avenues for transporting supplies and ammunition across the Parrot's Beak. To relieve the monotony of the mission, and the landscape, the VHF radio crackled with idle chatter between the two ships: a word or two, an observation, a comment, a joke. "Sun Devil Two Six, this is Two One."

"This is Two Six, go," Hardin replied.

"I'm down to about five hundred pounds on gas."

"Roger. I'm close to five-fifty." There was a short pause. Hardin came back over the VHF radio: "Two One, this is Two Six, let's give it another ten minutes. Call back to Mike Hotel for me. Have the other team launch. I'll inform Sierra Red."

"This is Two One, roger."

Nolan opened his eyes. He shifted uncomfortably in his seat. He felt the heft of the .45-caliber pistol under his left armpit, digging into his ribs. The fiberglass chickenplate, secured by his shoulder straps to the front of his chest, cut into his upper thighs. On several occasions Nolan felt his legs going to sleep and he would have to shift the shield to regain his circulation.

"Sir, you doing okay?" Hardin asked.

"My ass has just about had it," Nolan replied. "And my eyes are about to slam shut."

Hardin let out a chuckle over the intercom. "I hear you. This shit's boring. You want to fly?"

"Yeah." Nolan placed his feet and hands on the controls. He began his cross-check of the instruments. Earlier, during their first orbiting session, Nolan became so drowsy he couldn't keep his head from falling sideways into sleep. Hardin responded by offering to trade control of the ship every ten minutes or so. "Better get used to it," he had said. "Most of the time this is about all we do—one big circle-jerk."

They orbited twice more. Nolan looked east. He caught sight of two black dots against the hazy sky coming toward them. "Sun Devil Two Six, this is Two Four. I've got you at my twelve o'clock."

"Roger that," Hardin said. "Sierra Red is right below us. They're eating lunch."

Hardin took the controls. He turned the aircraft east. The wingbird followed. The two relieving Cobras loomed larger. Nolan saw the fanged white teeth and blood red mouth painted beneath the cockpit area of both ships. In another moment, the two AH-1Gs glided overhead. A formidable sight, they looked to Nolan like two dark missiles—sleek and deadly. After several minutes of flying, Hardin announced: "Moc Hoa, dead ahead."

Nolan peered at the horizon. Kien Tuong's provincial capital appeared as flat as the landscape around it, a collection of brown, single-story thatched huts surrounding a slightly more modern inner city. On the western edge of the city was a dirt airstrip. As they approached, he could just make out the one lone revetment that housed an O-1 Bird Dog aircraft, one of the many little spotter planes based across the Delta (tasked with locating Charlie and calling in and directing air and artillery strikes on sightings found).

Hardin entered left base to land to the north. In a moment, Hardin banked left and lined the ship up on the runway. Nolan looked to his right, where the armorers had set up their cache of rockets and 7.62mm ammo. He saw the driver of the fuel truck get into the front seat, to start the truck and drive over to refuel them. "So, what do you think, sir? This orbiting stuff is for the birds, huh?" commented Hardin.

Nolan said, "It's okay for now. But I'll tell you what, watching those guys on the ground, I think I prefer to be down there with them. I guess once a grunt, always a grunt."

Hardin slowed the Cobra and came to a hover over the dirt strip. He kicked in right pedal and hovered toward the fuel truck. Over a grassy area he kicked in left pedal and settled the aircraft onto the ground. Hardin started the clock for the two-minute cool down. He wiped his brow. "I try not to use the air conditioning too much. With it on we suck fuel like crazy. Let me know, though, the next time we go up when you need it on." When the clock registered two minutes, Hardin rolled the throttle off and pulled back the main fuel switch. The rotorblades took their time coasting to a stop. The driver of the fuel truck, a little Vietnamese papa-san, ancient as dirt, pulled up along the right side of the fuselage. He dragged the hose out while Hardin's crewchief came over to do the actual refueling. Hardin finished filling out the logbook and got out. "Lunch time," he said to

Nolan, retrieving his box of C-rations from inside his flight helmet bag stowed behind his seat. "Good ole ham and lima beans. My favorite. I'll drain a little JP-4 and get us a fire going."

With Hardin out of the aircraft, Nolan sat for a moment and stared straight ahead. He felt a slight breeze waft through his hair, a minute respite from the sweltering heat. He glanced left. Across the runway he saw several Vietnamese children gathered near the barbed-wire fence that enclosed the O-1. The mechanic had the engine cowling off and had torn into the engine. The children watched; the mechanic ignored their stares.

It was so different this time. He remembered that a little more than a year ago, after his six-month stint in the field, he was in the hip pocket of the brigade commander, chasing after him with a notepad and pencil, yet feeling like he was being drug around on a leash. He had endured it because he looked forward to flight school, wondering what it was going to be like. He envisioned, after graduation, airlifting men into combat, bringing in supplies, picking up the wounded. But this, this going around in circles, watching combat soldiers move along the ground, this was so tiresome, so irksome, so damned debilitating that already he felt like turning in his wings to be back alongside "the troops."

He looked at the gauges in front of him. His feet rested on the pedals. Thank God Elroy needed a replacement operations officer, he thought, something to sink my teeth into. He had met Captain Dane several days before, a tall, good-looking, dark-haired West Pointer who was the least pretentious man he had ever known, especially for a Point graduate. He had the S-3 job down to a fine art and was more than willing to pass on his favorite organizational tidbits. Nolan liked the man immediately, and was almost sorry Dane was going home.

But right now he was wondering if he had taken the right path with his career by going to flight school. As each day passed, the harder it was to accept that he might never again lead men on the ground as he had done on his first tour as a MACV NCO advisor, and then later as a second lieutenant with the 173rd. Lately, the thought had begun to gnaw at him. There were moments, in fact, when he worked himself into a pure fit.

Hardin's voice startled him. "Sir, I'm going into the MACV compound for a Coke. You want me to bring you back one?"

"Absolutely. And I think I'll take advantage of that shade over where the armorers are, maybe take a short nap. The last thing I want you to do is fire me as your co-pilot for dereliction of duty: sleeping on the damn job." Disgustedly, Nolan shook his head.

Hardin laughed. "Don't be so hard on yourself, sir. Christ, you never know what Charlie might pull next. With a wife and kid back home, I'm damn glad the Delta isn't anymore active than a slow-turning windmill."

***

Victor R. Beaver

LEO TANNAH BEGAN, "BLESS ME, FATHER, I have sinned. It's been four months since my last confession. I've not been to Mass since Christmas. I've also taken the Lord's name in vain many times. Oh, and I've done other things that I shouldn't have done." He paused, curious what the chaplain must be thinking. It was his first confession in Vietnam. "I'm embarrassed to say this, but I've smoked marijuana three times. Actually, Father, it was pretty good stuff." He cringed at his last statement. "I promise, though, not to do that again." He breathed deep and clasped his hands together. He stretched his arms and shoulders taut. "This next thing I confess...I don't know how you'll take...but Father, I'm always anxious to find the Viet Cong. I'm anxious for my doorgunners to fire their M-60s. Is that good or bad? I don't know. This is war. Aren't the VC trying to kill us, too? What's fair for them goes the same for us, doesn't it, Father?" Leo froze. *Does he hear this kind of confession all the time? Or is this something brand new? Am I being too honest? I shouldn't have come...but it's a sin not to confess.* "Father, I left college to join the Army. I wanted to come to Vietnam. I think it's every American's duty to fight whenever he can. But there are times, Father, when I don't know who the enemy is. Lately, I've been asking the advisors we support if I can scout their free-fire zones. They tell me I can shoot at anybody I see. Is that okay, Father?" Leo shook his head. "I'll do anything to help win the war. It's gone on long enough. Certainly God is listening, but do you think He understands?" Leo waited a moment, then added: "Oh yes, I had the opportunity to be with one of the women downtown, but I passed it up. Well, thank you, Father. I guess I'll be going."

    Tannah walked briskly to the orphanage, located on the west side of the city in a quiet peaceful neighborhood surrounded by Banyan trees. He had visited there several times in the past. The first time came right after he arrived at the airfield, when he accompanied Captain Kearney, one of the airfield flight surgeons, on his weekly visit. There he met several of the nuns, including Mother Caruso, a patient and tenacious woman who was in charge of the orphanage. Equally dedicated, "Doc" Kearney tirelessly administered to the children and encouraged his medical staff to do the same. One day, just before Christmas, Leo was present when a "care" shipment arrived from the United States, arranged for by Kearney. It contained case upon case of soap, canned luncheon meat, clothing, diapers, bed linens, and baby bottles, along with large quantities of penicillin, vitamins, protein supplements, and antibiotic ointments. Leo had helped to sort and store this generous donation and instantly became one of Mother Caruso's favorites. She asked that he visit often.

    Mother Caruso's soft brown eyes gave off a saint-like glow when she saw Leo. In her late fifties, she was a slightly built woman of Portuguese descent, who had a tendency to speak in several languages at once whenever she became excited. She wore a clean white habit and a wooden cross that hung on a long chain around her neck. "Leo...Leo, what brings you on this fine day? Come, sit down. You look troubled—what is it?"

Leo bowed slightly. "Thank you for seeing me. I know you're busy...but I was wondering if there was anything I could do, any errands to run? I have a day off. I went to confession a little while ago—"

"And for penance, the priest sent you here?"

"No-no, of course not...How did you know?"

She waved a hand. "It is not important. I know you come when you can, but I think, too, you find other diversions...like drinking? Isn't that the way of all pilots?"

Leo blushed. "Yeah...pretty much that's true. Me and the guys, we spend quite a bit of time in the Tiger's Den. But you know, I'd really like to come here more often. I-I think it would be good."

Mother Caruso nodded. "I agree. We have much for you to do...I could keep you busy forever. I should know, I've been here almost thirty years."

Leo spent the remainder of the day in the garden. One of the little orphan girls, someone he had never seen before, took a sudden liking to him. Her name was Mei Le. Without saying a word, she took his hand and guided him down the long rows of squash and cucumbers and stalks of broccoli. She helped him pick at weeds and occasionally tossed pebbles at dogs that had free rein of the orphanage grounds.

Before he left, Mother Caruso said, "We are having a small celebration tomorrow morning, in preparation for Tet. You're welcome to come. Captain Kearney and some of his men will be here."

Leo smiled. "If I'm not flying, I'd like to come. It depends on the schedule."

"Try if you can, Leo, and bring a friend. It was such a delight to see you with Mei Le. She is one of our new ones. She lost her father during that big battle early last month near Vi Thanh. Her mother committed suicide shortly after, we think out of grief."

The following day he flew re-supply out of Can Tho and thus was unable to take Mother Caruso up on her invitation. For the first time, though, flying had been pleasant. And then after two relaxed courier runs to Saigon early in the afternoon, he and his crew were released to go home. Back at the hootch Leo took his rosary beads from the silver box he kept them in and began to finger them one by one. How long has it been since I've looked at them, he thought?... *This place can really tear at a guy, but still I like it here in Vietnam. I like the idea of being in combat. Why? I shouldn't...yet I do. And I'm never afraid. I especially like it when we find Charlie...*He sat on his cot and held the beads and began to speak softly the prayers he had learned in Catholic school. He thought of Mei Le, the little orphan girl, who yesterday held his hand in the garden. I am just like her, he thought. I, too, have been in an orphanage. Unlike Mei Le, though, he had been adopted before his first birthday. Several years back, he had the notion to locate his biological parents, but then thought, What would be the point? He loved the two people who had taken him as their own and raised him and it was them he owed his allegiance. The day he joined the army his adopted father was so proud. To have a son go off to war was, to him, the height of patriotism. He had come to the United States from Poland in the early thirties, a man already middle-aged, with a wife and sister. When America entered the war in 1941, his age, his flat feet, and a recently discovered heart condition made him exempt from military service. Presently, he worked in the Pittsburgh area, in the same defense factory he had worked for years, helping to build bombsights.

Leo finished saying the prayers associated with the rosary beads and placed the beads in the box. He heard music coming from the club. He rose and fixed his fatigue cap on top his head. He checked himself in the mirror that sat on top his stereo equipment. He exited his room and strolled across the narrow pathway that separated the hootch from the club. He walked in. He plunked his money down on the bar, ordered a Black Velvet and Seven, and picked up the cup containing the liar's dice. When he asked Jonesy, the OIC of the Tiger's Den, standing behind the bar, what movie was playing that night, the grumpy warrant officer told him to get screwed. McNamara sat down next to him; quietly, he said:

"Jonesy's wife is suing for divorce. And the movie tonight is 'Doctor Zhivago.' It's supposed to be over three hours long."

Chapter 35

"MR. SLATER, I NEED TO TEST-FIRE my gun. I replaced the operating rod and rod yoke last night," Larkin said from the back. Throughout the morning they had been flying re-supply out of Bac Lieu. It was now after lunch, almost one o'clock. They were en route to Lac Hoa, a tiny village on the coast near the mouth of the Basaac River. They carried a load of ammunition, food, and other supplies.

"Okay," Kip said over the intercom. "We'll swing south. You can shoot toward the ocean. How's that sound?"

"That'll be good, sir," the gunner replied.

Slater motioned for Westy Harper, his peter-pilot for the day, to veer right, toward the open waters of the South China Sea. Out of character, Rusty asked if they could low-level. Kip frowned and thought for a moment. The surrounding area was flat, with little vegetation. "Yeah...what the hell..." He looked back toward Rusty, who gave him a wide toothy grin—an *Alfie* grin.

Kip told Harper to start a slow, straight-ahead descent. Their flight path now was perpendicular to the coast. The water ahead was a light brown color and didn't begin to turn blue until after some distance from shore. For as far as they could see, the South China Sea was smooth as glass. "Let's not get too far out," he told Harper. "We'll parallel the shore and let Ron blast away. Shouldn't be anything out there to hit, 'cept water..."

"Okay," Harper said. The Arkansasan began a slow turn to the left. When they were about a hundred feet above the water's surface, Kip told Harper to maintain that altitude. Looking inland, Kip saw scattered hootches sitting on stilts and a few Vietnamese fishermen watching the helicopter as it flew by. It was hard to tell how deep the water was...a few inches or a few feet—or even more.

"Can I shoot now?" Ron asked.

"Yeah, go ahead." A split second later Kip heard the rattle of machine-gun fire on his right side. Over the water the sound was like a hammer hitting against wood. Every fifth round was a tracer. Kip saw streaks of orange flying outward, toward the right front and down as Ron swiveled his gun left and right, down and out. Then he saw what looked like dark stationary posts in the water, perhaps the leftover supports of a pier after a bad storm. The posts, however, were some distance from shore. Their speed this close to the surface, their angle from the objects, and his concentration on Ron's firing, made it difficult to determine what the objects were...until it suddenly dawned on him—*they were people!* Barebacked, brown-skinned men, in knee-deep water, looked at them from where they stood, petrified by the sound of the gun.

"Cease fire," Kip yelled. "*CEASE FIRE!*" Immediately, Kip grabbed the controls and started a climb.

Ron stopped firing. "What—? How come?" Ron's voice had the quality of a man who had just seen a ghost.

"People!—didn't you see them?"

"You're kidding. Is that what they were? I-I didn't know—"

As they gained altitude they looked back to see the "objects" moving toward the shore. Kip felt the panic rise in him. Had they hit anyone? God, if they did, what would the implications be? Even if they hadn't hit anyone, they still fired at them! What was the provocation? *God Almighty damn...why me?* How would he explain *this* to Neely? To the staff folks at Can Tho? To the American senior advisor at Bac Lieu? As they flew along, now at fifteen hundred feet, all he could think about was his court-martial. Neither Rusty nor Ron nor Harper said a word. Maybe they were thinking the same thing. Kip gave the controls over to Harper to make the approach into Lac Hoa. "I've got to think..." *God do I have to think—!*

Back at Soc Trang, Slater sat alone in his room. There was a knock at the door. The color drained from his face. "Who is it?"

"Open up, fucker, it's the MPs."

Fuck... "Come in."

The door opened. "Surprise!—it's only me."

"Leo!—*goddamn you!*"

"Hey, Kip, ole buddy what the fugg you doing? You wanna go eat—or shall we just drink our dinner tonight?"

"You're smashed—"

"Yeah, I got started early. Hey—guess what? They gotta cool movie playing tonight. 'Doctor Chivvy-go'...sumpthin' like that."

"I don't care—leave me alone."

Leo sat down next to Kip on his bunk. He reeked of booze. Leo said, "Whattsa matter...ya sick?"

Kip took a deep breath. "I screwed up, Leo—bigtime."

"You did?...How?"

Slater explained everything. He described how after completing the remainder of his re-supply missions, he departed Bac Lieu and made his descent to the airfield fully expecting to see the MPs waiting for him in front of operations; and when they weren't there, expecting Captain Slote to have him report to the orderly room when he turned in the SOI.

"Well, didja report?"

Kip shook his head. "No. I'm betting the news hasn't gotten here yet. *But it will.*"

Leo let out a low whistle. "I can't believe you did that. How come you shot at'em?"

"We didn't do it on purpose," Kip fumed. "They're going to send me to jail, Leo—I just know it."

Leo stood. Kip looked up. Leo's alcohol-soaked body was draped before him. And then Leo said, "Nah, don't worry 'bout it. Hey, man, we're in Vietnam. Who the fuck cares who you kill."

* * *

"TIGER NINE EIGHT SIX, THIS IS TANGO Six, Tango Six. Over."

"This is Tiger Nine Eight Six, go ahead," Justen said, speaking evenly into the microphone.

"What is your ETE? Over."

"Eight to nine minutes. What do you have for us?"

"One of my patrols southwest of my location reported hearing the motors of a couple of sampans. They think one of them is rather large. We had a similar situation a couple of days ago and it turned out positive. We'd like for you to check it out. What we think the VC are doing is re-supplying one of their mortar positions. Did you get the coordinates? Over."

"Roger that. We got them copied." Justen shined his flashlight on the grease-pencil markings on the plastic overlay of his operational map. Their flareship duties (flying airfield security) had been interrupted to perform their current mission. The gunships had remained behind to orbit the airfield. In the back was his regular crew (Conrad and Finch), plus Bradowski, the flare handler, and Lewis, the .50-caliber gunner. Also seated in the back was a MACV first lieutenant named Towers and his Vietnamese counterpart, a pockmark-faced lieutenant who sat still as a mummy, content to let the Americans run the show.

"This is Tango Six, roger—good. Give another call when you get closer in."

"Roger that, will do."

With the lights of the airfield well behind them, what lay ahead was an exaggerated darkness. Vague definitions appeared on the ground and then Justen saw a curve in the treeline that looked like a loop. "We've just gone past the Tiger's Tail. Vinh Quoi is about seventeen klicks ahead. Fly heading two seven zero."

Jim Ellis, a warrant officer and recent transfer from a cav troop based at Tay Ninh, in III Corps, banked the helicopter left.

"Frontseat." The voice was that of Lieutenant Towers, callsign X-ray Six.

"Go ahead."

"Did you get those coordinates?"

"I did, sir," Ellis responded. "Copied them on the windshield."

"I've got Whiskey Romero 650145," Towers said. "Is that what you copied?"

Justen said, "I copied two sets. The set you copied sounds like the second set, but you got the last three digits backwards." For a moment there was silence. "I think they want us to check out the first set which is in the area east of a northwest-southeast canal, the one that runs to Thanh Tri. Call Tango Six and tell them we're about five minutes out."

"Okay, that's fine. I'll give'm a call, " Towers said. He keyed his mic: "Tango Six, this is X-ray Six."

"This is Tango Six," came the voice again from the ground.

"We're now five out. Confirm that we can fire anywhere around the target."

"This is Tango Six, roger. The only restriction I have right now is that my patrol is still coming in. Should be here in about five minutes. After that, you have permission to fire anywhere in that area. I'll keep you informed. Over."

"This is X-ray Six, roger."

"Frontseat, I've got the second set of coordinates plotted near Victor Quebec on the northwest-southeast canal line. Do you confirm?" Towers asked.

"Negative," said Justen. "I've got the second set of coordinates plotted on the thin canal that runs mostly north and south, about a klick south of there."

Towers re-plotted the numbers. "Yeah…yeah, you're right," he said. "I don't know what's the matter with me. I can't seem to get these damn figures right tonight. By the way, why were we given two sets to check out? Tango Six seems concerned only about the one where his patrol sighted the large sampan."

"Hell if I know," Justen said. "They're not that far apart. Let's check out the first set. Looks like a small hamlet northeast of Vinh Quoi." And then he said to Ellis: "Aim more to the right. Vinh Quoi should be at our ten o'clock position, about four klicks away." After a couple of minutes they could make out the definition of a large cluster of trees and hootches. A canal ran past the hamlet, one that stretched in a straight line to Ca Mau, forty-five kilometers away. Like Nam Can and a few other locations, the Viet Cong ranged around Vinh Quoi with near utter impunity.

Justen spoke to his flarehandler: "Bradowski, get a flare ready."

"Got one ready now, sir."

"Lewis, get the fifty ready."

Lewis lifted the heavy belted ammo and chambered one of the big rounds. The gun was mounted on the left side of the aircraft. Special mounting supports had to be installed on the floor of the helicopter to keep its recoil from causing undue stress elsewhere on the ship. A slow rate of fire was also recommended. Lewis patted the long barrel when the gun was ready. He swallowed a half-mouthful of Skoal and said, "I got the big guy ready, sir."

"Tango Six, this is X-ray Six. We're about to drop the first flare. Do you have anyone nearby to observe? Over."

"Negative, not at this time. From where I sit I might be able to give you a little guidance. Are you concerned about your location? Over."

"That's affirmative. Is your patrol in?"

"Roger that. They're coming in now."

Justen said to Bradowski: "Go ahead with the first flare."

Bradowski heaved the silver-looking canister out the right side of the ship. "Flare's out, sir."

Ellis put the helicopter in a slow right turn. In a moment, the initial burst of light came—the small explosion that discharges the parachute from the canister. This was followed a few seconds later by the second burst of light, the ignition of the flare's million-candlepower burn. The ignited canister, suspended beneath the parachute, shined an intense white light. The light illuminated a near perfect quarter-mile circle of the earth below. Shadows danced about like ghosts. Ellis looked toward the right front. And then he declared, "Holy shit. Would you look at all the sampans—!"

Justen leaned forward, chill bumps all over him. He heard Ellis counting aloud over the intercom:"I see one...two...three...four—God, there's got to be at least a dozen sampans, all bunched together. What a haul. Christ, they're all lined up in the middle of the canal—*like sitting ducks!*"

"X-ray Six, this is Tango Six," came the American voice from the ground. "You're over the wrong area. You're dropping too far east. Your target is about eight hundred meters to your seven o'clock."

"Shit, tell him about all these sampans—" said Ellis.

"Tango Six, this is Tiger Nine Eight Six, we've sighted about a dozen sampans here. Several of them are very large."

"Disregard—disregard. Those are probably friendly. Go south...I say again, go south. Over."

"Roger that."

"Friendly—? How the hell can that many sampans all in one location be friendly?" Ellis erupted. "This really sucks. Jesus, it looks like a damn invasion force down there."

Another radio transmission crackled from the ground: "From the canal junction at Victor Quebec, go about eighteen hundred meters farther south. Over."

"He must be talking about the second set of coordinates," Justen stated, wondering himself why so many sampans were all congregated in one location. He told Ellis to turn left. The flare came to within a hundred feet of the ground and fizzled out. Once again, everywhere below was dashed in total darkness.

"This is Tango Six, you appear to be circling too far east. Go now to your nine o'clock position."

"Tango Six, this is X-ray Six," came Towers's voice over the radio; "understand our target is on the large northwest-southeast canal? Over."

"That's a negative. Go about one klick south on that canal. There's the intersection of a smaller canal. From there, go eight hundred meters south. The target is in that vicinity. Over."

Aggravated, the MACV lieutenant shook his head. "Christ, by the time we get this mess cleared up, the bastards will have cleared out—"

After a minute, they found the intersection they wanted. "Sir," spoke Conrad. "Me and Lewis have been watching this light. It's been going on and off. Real irregular. Right now it's to our nine o'clock. Want us to bust it?"

"Negative," Justen said. Then: "Bradowski, get another flare ready."

"Roger that."

"X-ray Six, this is Tango Six. You appear to be right over the area."

"This is X-ray Six, roger that. We're going to drop another flare."

Justen said, "Heave the flare."

"Flare's out."

They waited. After about a minute, Ellis said, "It's a dud."

Justen asked Bradowski: "How many flares are left?"

"Three, sir."

"Let's try another."

Bradowski readied the next flare. Conrad squirmed in his seat. He said, "I see the light again, sir. Just a couple of flickers. Can't really tell what it is." Ellis then put the ship in a hard turn to the left. Justen looked left.

"I don't see anything," he said.

Lewis aimed the big fifty downward, ready for the command to fire. His mouth worked steadily on his Skoal. He said, "It's gone out again, sir."

At three thousand feet they were at the optimum altitude for a flare to ignite and give maximum duration of light before burning out, just before hitting the ground. But they had no gunship below to engage the enemy should they be spotted. They were much too high for either of the two M-60s to do any good, and almost out of effective range for the .50-caliber machine gun to hit a point target with any kind of accuracy, especially while flying. "Descend to two thousand feet," Justen told Ellis.

"Roger that."

When they reached two thousand feet, Justen ordered Bradowski to heave the next flare.

Again they waited. Nothing but darkness. Justen turned. "Damnit, Bradowski, are you sure you're setting those flares right—?"

"Yessir—"

"Get another one ready."

"Yessir. After this one, sir, we'll only have one left."

They watched this time as the parachute deployed and the canister ignited, but made a quick descent to earth. "A goddamn streamer," Ellis stated. "I'll bet some contractor back in the States is making a killing off this shit they're selling the Defense Department."

Conrad fingered the trigger of his weapon. "Sir, I'll bet this light that flickers every now and then is our target. Let me give it a quick burst."

Derek Justen breathed deep. Something inside him demanded that he be sure of the target. Goddamn this war and its rules of engagement. How do they expect men to fight when the enemy was everywhere and nowhere, a good guy during the day, minding his little patch of rice paddy, a sonofabitch at night, sneaking around outside the perimeter of every goddamn RF/PF defense compound around? And then the image of the man in the bamboo cage flashed in his mind. Hands gripping the bars, eyes two cavernous holes. He tried to shake the image, so vivid he could practically count the hairs on the back of the man's hands. The pictures persisted a moment longer, then subsided, like they always did after he awakened. "Okay, bank right." He looked back. Bradowski was poised with the last flare. Justen looked up. A high, thin overcast had formed and hid the stars from view. He looked down; the definitions of treelines were gone. Everywhere below was pitch black. Glancing toward the airfield, he could just make out the blinking red anti-collision lights of the two Viking gunships circling low near the airfield. He checked the ship's clock. Not quite eleven. If this last flare didn't work they would proceed back to the airfield defeated. The thought stung him. *I've been here twenty-two months. Twenty-two months. When will it end? Or will it ever end? I'm so exhausted...so tired...Anywhere but here...anywhere ...So futile, everything...the whole goddamn war...futile. What does it matter if we find and bust one lousy sampan?...There are thousands of them all over the Delta...hundreds of them belonging to Charlie.*

"Drop the flare."

"Flare's out."

They waited. Justen barely breathed. And then it came, the initial explosion; the parachute billowed out, followed by the trail of white phosphorus smoke.

"X-ray Six, this is Tango Six. You appear to be a little too far north."

Suddenly, Conrad cried out, "I've got a sampan—right at the canal junction. It's a little bit removed from where Lewis and I had the light."

"I see it," Ellis said.

Towers said, "The light might have been a diversion—maybe."

"God, it's huge—!" Ellis exclaimed.

"There's a smaller one next to it," Lewis stated.

"Tango Six, this is X-ray Six, we've got'em—we've got'em! We'll bust'em for you—"

"Good show—good show. Give'em hell, guys. Give'em hell!"

"Okay, Lewis, go at him," Justen ordered.

Lewis pulled the trigger and began a steady, slow rate of fire. Justen felt the recoil from the big .50-caliber machine gun reverberate throughout the ship. He watched as one tracer after another fled into and around the target. So far there was no return fire. Ellis continued a tight left-hand turn around the sampan as Lewis kept the hammer down. "Get lower," Justen said.

Ellis turned toward Justen. "Roger that."

The first sound of gunfire aimed at them came from their right. Finch saw muzzle flashes and then tracers. "Receiving fire—three o'clock!"

"Return fire," said Justen.

Finch's M-60 sounded like the rattle of tin cans behind a car going down the road compared to the heavy thunder of the fifty. In the next instant, the fifty was silent. A link had caused a jam during recoil. "Damn!"

"A jam?" said Justen.

"Yessir."

"Can you clear it?"

"I'm trying."

Meanwhile, the flare continued its slow wavering descent. Ellis leveled off at one thousand feet. The flare began to veer toward the two sampans. The two canoe-like boats were now lodged against the bank. And then Justen saw movement, several escaping black-clad figures clawing their way along the ground toward a lone hootch not far from the water's edge.

The burning canister was within two hundred feet of the ground. It drifted toward the target. Finally it landed. The grasses on the bank near the sampans ignited. Quickly the flames spread. And then the hootch and the sampans were on fire. In another moment, the escaping figures were also engulfed in flames.

The first explosion sent out a shock wave so powerful that it seemed to slam everyone in the aircraft against their seats. Immediately, Ellis began a climb. The second and third explosions came thirty seconds later. From two thousand feet and climbing, they shuddered at the sight of the towering inferno. After two orbits, the conflagration died down. Justen slipped his hands on the cyclic and collective, his feet on the pedals. "I've got the controls. Whatever those bastards were up to, I guess we interrupted the hell out of it."

"Yeah, but I'll bet there's something to that dozen sampans we saw," Ellis stated.

"Let's hope there isn't," Justen said, somewhat satisfied, his eyes set on the airfield ahead.

The Sky Soldiers

Chapter 36

THE BEGINNING SCENES SHOW LARA, played by the lovely Julie Christie, cloaked in a heavy black winter coat as she comes upon her friend, Pasha, a Marxist, on the street handing out subversive literature critical of the Czar. Pasha asks if she's going to attend the rally later that evening. Lara tells him she can't, that she has important school studies to attend to. Several scenes later show the Czar's cavalry form a line across one of Moscow's wide streets. It's nighttime. With drawn sabers, they wait to confront the Marxist demonstrators. When the mob appears around the corner, the order is given to charge. Everyone scatters. The horsemen cut down the demonstrators as they run. Yuri Zhivago has seen the slaughter from a balcony doorway. The next scenes show him giving aid to the wounded and dying. One of the cavalrymen rides up and tells Yuri to go inside, back into his home.

The lights glared on.

"Hey, what the fuck, over—?"

"Turn that goddamn thing off," Whitaker ordered, stepping into the beam of light coming from the movie projector. The projectionist, an enlisted man, did as he was told. The White Tiger platoon leader had on his steel pot, flakjacket, .38 pistol in a holster slung under his arm, and web belt hung with canteen and first aid pouch. "Okay, listen up. As of right now we're on Red Alert."

"What the hell for?" someone called out.

"Because I said so," Whitaker replied.

"For how long?"

"Until further notice. White Tigers, you can remain right here. The rest of you guys, dump those drinks and report to your section leader."

Within moments, the movie viewing room behind the Tiger's Den buzzed with aggravated men bristling with curiosity. Leo nudged Kip on the shoulder. "What's going on?"

"Now how the hell would I know?"

Robin Henry drained the last of his drink and made for the Viking readyhootch.

"Maybe the Russkies decided to drop 'the bomb,'" Mac said.

"McNamara, Tannah," said Whitaker; "Oremsby wants all Blue Tigers to report to the orderly room—on the double."

"Okay-okay, we're going."

Whitaker checked his watch; he surveyed his pilots. "The word is out. Sometime to night, Charlie's going to hit all major installations, all over the Delta—all over Vietnam, in fact."

"I thought we had a truce?—for this Tet thing?" said Westy Harper, the little gum-chewing Arkansasan.

295

"I guess we don't," Whitaker stated.

Slater said, "What do you want us to do?"

"For one thing, get your gear and be ready to defend the perimeter. I've ordered all crewchiefs and gunners to report to the bunkers near the revetments."

"Are you shitting us?" said Munson.

"No, I'm not shitting you." Whitaker lit a cigarette. "Chances are we're going to get mortared pretty heavy tonight...probably more than once. An hour ago the flare ship shot up a couple of sampans. Justen said they got a couple of good secondaries. That's all I know. Good luck."

In his room, Slater strapped on his pistol belt, located his steel pot packed away in his closet, and donned his flakjacket, which he had never even tried on much less worn. He zipped the front and felt its tightness across his chest. Within the past month he had managed to get an M1 carbine and several bandoleers of ammunition. He picked up the rifle and sat down on his cot and held the weapon across his lap. He removed the magazine, opened the chamber, checked it was clear, and pulled the trigger. *Click.* He cocked the rifle and this time took aim at a tack pinned on the wall. *Click.* He remembered the day he got it. Right away he liked its small size, its lightweight heft. When he carried it, with the sun to his back, he admired the way his shadow appeared on the ground as he held it; it gave him a strange feeling of power.

He had never, until he joined the army, shot a rifle. He had never gone hunting, had never even owned a BB gun. But this...this weapon was for killing another human being and he wondered: Would he, could he, take another man's life? He decided that, Yes, he *would:* if one of his crewmembers was threatened: if the enemy came at him hell-bent on murder: if there was no alternative. But *could* he? It was a decision he hoped he would not have to make.

Slater often wondered if he could have been an infantryman, moving through the bush, never knowing when and where all hell would break loose. The thought fascinated him, but he always cast it aside when he realized how fragile the human body was; how death could come so easily (and unaware) with one shot fired from a sniper's gun...or from a sudden burst of automatic-weapons fire...or a tripped booby trap...or a barrage of mortar rounds...or God knows what. The grunt, the groundpounder, the infantryman always fought war the muddy, noisy, hell-fire and damnation way—the bloody, mangled-body way, with their skin close to the ground and only a tree or a bush or some large jungle leaf for cover. Which was what he liked about flying. Flying was as close to the action as a person could get without getting dirty, grimy, filthy and sweaty. But which was really better?—Or worse? As he had already decided—and experienced—flying required nearly total concentration, regardless the bullets whizzing past. A pilot's preoccupation with his machine, his manipulation of the flight controls, the gauges in front of him, the other aircraft in formation during an assault, all was like a panacea. The infantryman, on the other hand, and in most instances, was forced to deal with his tormentors head-on, bullet for bullet, perhaps even face to face—two grapplers locked arm and arm in mortal combat.

Slater shuddered. Once more he wrenched the bolt back. He lifted the stock to his shoulder. He swung the barrel until it was pointed at his short-timer's calendar tacked to the wall above the table that served as a desk. It was the standard calendar, a large pin-up drawing of a woman sectioned three hundred sixty-five times to represent the days in a year. The countdown moved across her body until the final days of a soldier's tour happened upon her licentious parts. He took aim at the cleavage of her breasts, then moved the point of the barrel slightly right, until he believed it was pointed at her heart. *Click.* Could he kill a woman bent on killing him? A young boy or girl? *If we are attacked tonight, if the entire countryside rises against us, will we have to beat them back with sticks after the last bullet is fired?*

He heard movement in the hall. There came a loud knock and his door opened. Kip stood and jammed the clip back into his gun. He was facing Leo and Mac. "What's up?"

"Oremsby's got us going out to the perimeter. How about you?"

"Same-same."

The first bunker they came to found Oakerson hunkered down next to Walls, his gunner, positioned behind an M-60, along with several other men. As the trio went along trying to find a location that could accommodate extra bodies, they happened upon a crew of men behind a revetment working to fill a half pallet of sandbags that had been delivered to them along with a truckload of sand. One man stood nearby with a flashlight while the others struggled to fill the bags. After a few more steps, they came to Mangrum and Pickett, alone, perched behind a hastily drawn barricade, their M-60s aimed outward toward the darkness. After a few moments, Leo, Kip, and Mac were situated on the ground beside them, behind a waist-high berm of sandbags, their own weapons covering the blacked-out rice paddies beyond the perimeter fence.

The next hour passed quickly. Two Viking light fire-teams patrolled the perimeter while the flareship kept pace above them at three thousand feet dropping an occasional flare. As each flare descended, eerie shadows danced before them and they nervously panned their weapons left and right seeking evidence of the impending attack. They saw nothing, except what their imaginations determined they should see.

From somewhere down the line, a dancing shadow brought a burst of machine-gun fire. Tracers raced outward like streaks of rocket-propelled fireflies. And then other machine guns opened up, the airfield perimeter sounding like a free-for-all shooting gallery. After a time, Slater realized that Charlie would have to be bent on suicide to attack this part of the perimeter across the open field where they aimed the barrels of their weapons: There was no cover anywhere.

Victor R. Beaver

Kip checked his watch: 0212. It had been nearly two hours since Whitaker announced Red Alert. In the next instant, as he was about to rest his head against his arm, which lay across his rifle, he heard in the distance one of the gunships fire a pair of rockets. Heads turned, hands gripped weapons, heart rates became elevated. "Do you see where they're shooting?" he asked.

"It looks like right into the city," Leo said.

"God," Mac blurted; "that's exactly what they're doing—"

Next they heard muffled explosions and the distant rattle of gunfire. They watched as the second gunship fired off three pairs of rockets. The attack was finally happening, as predicted, but at no point around the airfield. "They're after the MACV compound," Mangrum said. "And province headquarters, too...I'll just bet." After another minute, there was no doubt where the VC had focused their attack, as the sound of rifle- and machine-gun fire from within the city became more distinct.

For the next ten minutes they had nearly a front-row seat. The flareship kept dropping flares while the gunships fired into the heart of the city. Slater couldn't believe his eyes. And then it struck him. *Kim Thi An!* Her apartment was right behind the MACV compound. Was she okay? Had her apartment been hit? "Damn—"

"What's the matter?" Leo asked.

"Oh nothing...nothing." He hadn't told Tannah his arrangement with the woman. It was a part of him he didn't want anyone to know. He had gone back only once since the afternoon of the negotiation, and now, from the looks of it, it would be a long time before he would go again. Already he was wondering if the lovely French-Vietnamese woman was dead or alive—and regretted that she might already be dead.

They watched the light show for another few minutes. And then it happened. The explosion was so loud that Kip wondered for a moment what had happened to his hearing. It seemed that he was enveloped in a kind of silence; then came the ringing sound. And then, gradually, he began to hear voices. It took some time before the voices returned to a relatively normal tone. He realized, next, that he was laying stomach down, his right cheek flat against the ground. "Incoming! Incoming!" he heard Mac's voice cry out.

"No shit, Sherlock—"

"Yeah, my mommy didn't raise no dummy."

KABOOOM!

"That shit's close."

The siren sounded.

KABOOOM!"

"Hey—*my helmet!"*

"Shit, the sonofabitch hit me right in the arm!"

"Hand it back—!"

KABOOOM!....KABOOOM!

Slater used his hands to cover the back of his neck. So far every mortar attack he had been in had caught him inside, either in his room or in the club. Soon after he would find himself in the bunker, the sound of the explosions usually muffled. Outside now, under an actual rain of steel, the explosions deafened him.

KABOOOM!

Slater kept still, his hands now covering his ears. He could not recall drawing himself into the fetal position, but saw that Mac and Leo were similarly poised. The ground shook with each detonation and then they were pelted by chunks of runway.

After a few seconds, Slater heard screams somewhere down the line. Someone had been hit! The cry sounded primordial. There were more explosions, but this time a little farther away. After what seemed like an eternity, there came a kind of metallic silence. Until now, he had never thought that silence could be so loud. The ringing sound was gone. It had been the ringing in his ears that muffled the sound of the explosions.

Slater opened his eyes. A fly alighting several times around his mouth had waked him. The hot sun beat down. He eased up on one elbow and looked around. To his front he saw Tannah seated behind Pickett's machine gun. Leo yawned, pulled out a pack of cigarettes, and lit one. To Leo's left, Kip saw Mangrum spooning the contents from a can of C-rations.

Slater then focused on two prostrate figures lying several feet away covered by rain ponchos. For a moment he thought whoever was underneath was dead; then one of the figures moved. Mac flipped back his rain cover and through squinting eyes began to assimilate his surroundings. A moment later, Pickett stirred under the other rain poncho.

Slater watched as Leo repositioned himself behind Pickett's M-60, placing his hands back around the firing mechanism. Then his gaze fell upon several flare parachutes that lay in white clumps out beyond the perimeter fence. As he looked beyond, at the first visible treeline, Slater pondered his friend. He knew Tannah had not been more than arm's length from the weapon all night. After the initial mortar attack, there had been two others. During both subsequent attacks, Leo remained upright at the gun, sweeping it back and forth, firing short bursts, the noise it made masked by the exploding incoming mortar rounds. There had been no apparent targets. When quizzed, Leo explained that it was just in case Charlie was out there. Slater agreed with the rationale, but deep down knew Leo just wanted to fire the gun.

"Leo..."
"What?"
"Are you hungry?"
"Yeah."

"I'll go see if they've got anything hot to eat."
"Okay."

Slater glanced around as he went across the runway. He saw evidence everywhere of last night's attacks: pockmarks in the runway, chunks of asphalt scattered about, several small-size craters in the lawn near Slote's Piece of Shit Turquoise Shack, a shredded cluster of banana trees. He noted that dozens of sandbagged-positions had been built around revetments, against buildings, in ditches. He went to his room first to see if it was intact. It was. He gathered his journal, some letter-writing materials, and a few books. Everyone was wearing a steel pot, an odd sight, he thought, for an airfield. He met an enlisted man going past the company orderly room, who commented that he should go check out the airfield communications center, saying that it had taken a direct hit. It was only a short block away, so Kip went to investigate.

What he saw had to be a technician's worst nightmare. The damage appeared deviously intricate. Several racks of complex electronic equipment were in twisted shambles. Various bundles of wiring lay in disarray like so much colored spaghetti. Kip estimated it would take several weeks to rejoin the wires and route them to their proper connecting points.

At the officers' mess, Kip was told he had to sign for rations from the enlisted mess. He returned to the perimeter carrying two cases of C-rations.

He opened one of the cases. Everyone grabbed a favorite meal. Mac and Pickett lit two JP-4 fires. An hour later, as they sat smoking, they saw two dark specks coming out of the sky from the north. A moment later the two specks became larger; they made a wide descending turn to the right, then banked left.

"They look like F-100s," Mangrum said.
"I wonder where their target is?" Slater said.

The two Supersabres now came straight toward them. "Shit, I'll betcha they're going to bomb downtown—" All morning they had heard sporadic gunfire from that quarter.

The two jets screamed past. The men plugged their ears. A second later they saw bombs explode in the center of the city. Dark gray smoke billowed upward. The two jets streaked skyward, then swept left to prepare for another pass. After two more bomb-runs, they shot skyward a final time and were gone.

Slater could only imagine the condition of the city now. He was certain, after the ordnance expended last night and this morning, that a good portion of it was nothing but rubble. He wondered, too, about Kim Thi An. The thought that she might be dead suddenly tugged at his heartstrings. With his notebook open he sat to one side and penned a hasty letter home on a blank sheet of stationary.

Dear Mom and Dad,

I'm all right. Things aren't as bad in the Mekong Delta as they must be elsewhere. Don't worry if you don't hear from me for a while. Last night we were placed on permanent Red Alert...

He put the letter in an envelope, sealed and addressed it. Where ordinarily he would have placed a stamp, he wrote "free." Small recompense, he thought, for risking one's neck in a war zone: A soldier's mail is sent home at government expense.

* * *

AS HISTORY WOULD TELL IT, THE COMMUNIST command, "whether by accident or design," launched an initial wave of attacks one day in advance of the others, concentrating mostly on major cities in II Corps. In the early morning hours of January 30, seven cities, each accommodating major U.S. military installations, were hit: Nha Trang, Ban Me Thuot, Kontum, Hoi An, Da Nang, Qui Nhon, and Pleiku. (That this first wave occurred gave some impetuous to be on alert for the others.) The second, and much larger, wave of attacks came in the early hours of January 31. Every major city from Quang Tri near the DMZ to Ca Mau deep in the Mekong Delta, to include hundreds of smaller district towns, were subjected to mortar and rocket barrages, most of these barrages followed by ground assaults and spearheaded by VC sapper attacks. To the Marines at Khe Sanh, a major combat base in I Corps, this sort of activity was nothing new. The base's 6,000 troops had sat hunched in bunkers and trenches and had lived in a tense state of siege since January 20. Surrounded by NVA (North Vietnamese Army) artillery, the rain of steel on Khe Sanh was practically a round-the-clock affair. For the population of Saigon, on the other hand, long immune to anything except occasional terrorist bombing attacks, thirty-five Communist battalions, hurling from all directions, came to them as a complete surprise. And no location within the city was sacred. The elite Viet Cong C-10 Sapper Battalion, two hundred fifty members strong and backed by nearly five thousand local force troops, most of whom had infiltrated the city in the days before Tet, was tasked to take and hold the presidential palace, the United States embassy, the National Radio Station, and other principal targets. Outside Saigon, principal U.S. military bases such as Long Binh, Bien Hoa, Lai Khe, and Chu Chi were also encircled and attacked.

During Tet, several battles raged for days, and the destruction was appalling. The fight for Hue, the longest and bloodiest battle of the Communist offensive, lasted from January 31 to February 24. U.S. Marines and ARVN soldiers had to fight the North Vietnamese Army from house to house, and in the process the two opposing forces gruesomely disfigured Vietnam's most exotic city. Fifty percent of the provincial capital of Pleiku was destroyed. Within the confines of

Victor R. Beaver

Saigon, American F-100 jets and VNAF A-1E Skyraiders pounded some of the more heavily populated sections of the city. Cholan, Saigon's Chinese district, was methodically destroyed by fighting raging day after day, until the U.S. Army 199th Light Infantry Brigade, on February 10, finally came in and secured the Pho Tho racetrack, where the Communists had set up a command post and field hospital.

And finally, at long last, war came on a grand scale to the Mekong Delta. Ben Tre, one of its principal cities, "had to be destroyed [by allied forces] to be saved." Other principal cities: My Tho, Vinh Long, Sa Dec, Can Tho, Khang Hung (Soc Trang), Chau Phu, and Ca Mau, all were savagely attacked. The allied airfield at Can Tho suffered more than a dozen helicopters destroyed. Vinh Long, home of two U.S. assault helicopter companies, was practically overrun. In fact pockets of Viet Cong resistance remained within the Vinh Long perimeter for several days. In many places, resistance to the attacks was disorganized. For example, occurring in the vicinity of Vinh Long, to add insult to injury, in the confusion of battle an element of an ARVN armored cavalry detachment held a vicious firefight with their own river assault group boats stationed in the Mekong River.

Aside from these more impressive attacks enemy mortars and vicious ground assaults also battered many of the Delta's district towns. Dependent primarily on the larger province cities for food, supplies, and ammunition, and the use of helicopters to deliver them, many MACV outposts, after the initial wave of Viet Cong attacks, became dangerously low on ammunition and other critical assets. Several towns were almost overrun. To make matters worse, practically every American gunship and every troop-carrying helicopter in the Delta, to defend its own, had become largely unavailable for fire and logistic support elsewhere. And since most of the ARVN command (and its soldiers) was stationed in the large province cities, and was tasked principally to defend these cities, they would not have been able to provide a sizable reaction force even if helicopter support was available.

* * *

SOC TRANG ARMY AIRFIELD REMAINED under siege for eleven days. Every available pilot, gunner, crewchief, mechanic, cook, service technician, and administrative clerk manned the perimeter day and night. After several days, however, re-supply ships, one and two at a time, began to venture out, go to the major installations, provide whatever service requested, then scoot back home. During these missions, shots were exchanged while landing and departing such unlikely places as Vinh Long, Can Tho, Sa Dec, Chau Phu, Ca Mau, Vinh Loi (Bac Lieu), and Phu Vinh (Tra Vinh). Two and three times a night the Soc Trang airfield was mortared, flares illuminated the surrounding paddies, and the men braced themselves for the always-anticipated ground attack (which, incidentally, never came), and wondered when normalcy would return. Most of the men neither bathed nor shaved for days. One night, based on an intelligence report that the Viet Cong were really going to plaster the airfield with mortars, Neely decided to evacuate his helicopters to Vung Tau. The flight to this nearby coastal city over a portion of the South China Sea was so dark, and without a visible horizon, that the pilots flew by their attitude instruments practically the whole way.

The casualties mounted fast, most combat related, a few not. The Viking gun platoon, always in the air, suffered a doorgunner killed, a gunshot between the eyes. Two other Viking crewmen were badly wounded in separate skirmishes. At the airfield, shrapnel from mortars wounded more than a dozen men. A Warrior instructor pilot, conducting a stan ride with one of the unit's new pilots, crashed the ship outside the perimeter during a low-level engine-out procedure. The aircraft caught fire and burned. The instructor escaped with massive burn injuries, but was unable to save the new pilot who died in the flames. Few men had seen him or even knew the new pilot's name.

From across the runway on the fourth day of the offensive they watched as one of the Viking gunships planted itself next to the airfield hospital. There was a flurry of activity and a moment later the left-seat pilot was extracted from the ship. Slater looked upon the proceedings through a pair of binoculars.

"Who do you think it is?" Leo asked.

"I don't know. I can't tell."

Tannah took the glasses. Giving them back, he said, "I'll go see."

When he returned his face was white.

Slater felt his heart rate quicken. "Well...who was it?"

"It's Henry. He's dead."

"What?...Robin?"

"Shot through the left side of his back."

Kip stopped breathing. "How—?"

Leo's voice cracked. "One goddamn bullet. Somehow it came right through that little bit of space between the left side of the seat and the sliding armor plate. Purely, a lucky shot."

Kip sat down. "No, I don't believe it...you're joking."

"I swear to God," said Leo.

# Chapter 37

AT FORT WOLTERS THE NEWS OF THE massive Tet offensive electrified the entire candidate corps. There was talk everywhere that flight training might be shortened. But the rumor had little fizzle. Besides, regardless how much flight school was cut short, by the time Class 67-15 arrived in Vietnam, the heavy fighting surely would be done.

Before the attacks, the count of Americans killed or wounded in action averaged five hundred per week. Afterwards, within the first twenty-four hours, the reported U.S. casualty count was well over two thousand. The Army also reported the number of enemy killed or wounded in the first dawn of attacks to be a staggering ten thousand. If these figures were even remotely correct, many in the class felt that once they did graduate, the war would already be ended and won.

* * *

THEY STIRRED RESTLESSLY AT THEIR tables. Unfolded before them were sets of VFR navigation charts covering the areas of Mineral Wells, Fort Worth, and Brownwood, Texas. Their platform instructor, a blonde-haired twenty-year-old chief warrant officer, no taller than the shortest man in the flight, had them reviewing VOR (visual omni range) station symbols. He aimed his pointer at a circular object on a map hung on the wall. "This is a compass rose," he said, his voice soft and even. "The center of a compass rose depicts where a VOR station is located. You can see tic marks around the edge of the circle. Every tic mark is five degrees. Counting clockwise around the circle, we see that every thirty degrees there's a number. The first number," he said, his tone also very monotonous, "is three, representing zero three zero degrees. The second number is six, representing zero six zero degrees, then nine for zero nine zero degrees, all the way back to zero, which of course represents three hundred sixty degrees, or due north."

SNAP!

"Ah...shit," the little instructor blurted; he had slammed the pointer flat against the map. "Let's talk about what's happening in Vietnam. Christ, I was with D Troop, First of the Tenth, Fourth Infantry Division. I'll bet those guys right now are kicking ass and taking names—*Sonofabitch!*"

On the flight line, their flight instructors were equally preoccupied. Many were concerned about buddies left behind. More than a few stated they wouldn't mind being back in the action, while a couple openly declared Vietnam to be a waste of lives and equipment. But either way the atmosphere was charged and their training became even more fraught with meaning. Each instructor drilled his

The Sky Soldiers

students with renewed vigor. And each student felt that every bit of knowledge gained here and now might someday save his life—over there.

For many candidates it seemed that time stood still. After less than a week, the U.S. command in Vietnam declared a complete victory. General Westmoreland said in a statement that allied forces had killed more enemy troops in the past seven days than the United States had lost in the entire war. Lesser commanders felt that the backbone of the enemy had truly been broken and any further aggression would be futile. Sandy Adamson believed the war might not last much longer. He thought of Katie and decided now would be a good time to write. He took her picture from his wallet and began to compose...

Dear Katie,

I'm sure you've been following the news. The drift here is that the war may be over soon. I suppose I should be happy about that, and in a way I guess I am. If that's what you sense, then I'm sure you are too. I do want you to know, though, that I still feel the same about going, if I have to. I'm training very hard and I'm learning all I can to be a good pilot. I don't intend for this letter to sound strange or frightening, but the more I think about being over there the more I realize I'm not afraid to die. I believe that to die fighting for freedom is its own reward. I want you to know that I think of you a lot and I miss you something fierce. I wish it could be the same between us. I'm still not sure what happened over the Christmas break...

Sandy put the pen down. He tore the letter in two. He took another piece of paper and tried composing again. But he found that he couldn't begin...*It's better this way. If we had stayed together and I went over there, I'd just worry about her worrying about me. That wouldn't do me any good. Besides, once I get over there it'll take every ounce of energy I have to concentrate...*As he mulled over these thoughts, he felt no real consolation. He gazed at her picture and the way her emerald-green eyes sparkled and remembered something else about her that had always endeared her to him: the little skip she put in her step especially for him when she saw him at the beginning of each school day. *I love you, Katie...I will always love you. Someday I'll come home to you....*

* * *

SANDY ADAMSON HAD FINALLY BEGUN to fit the little training helicopter around him like a well broke in glove. He knew the preflight steps by heart, though he was sure to use the checklist just in case he might miss something important. Starting it up, he decided, was not that difficult, like turning over a car with a manual choke on a cold day, however with just a few more steps to follow. Getting it to move seemed about as easy as driving his father's Jeep, once he learned how: first you put in the clutch, shift into first gear, and then let the clutch out…slow and easy…while giving it gas. As he recalled, it was a horrible machine to learn how to drive, but his father, like Gressing, had been more than patient. In time, he and the vehicle had become one.

It was late morning. Sandy was flying solo, heading east toward the Downing heliport. Up ahead on the horizon he could easily make out the multi-story Mineral Wells Hotel. It would take a blind man to get lost around here, he thought, though Cutter had managed to do it twice with Captain Crandall seated beside him. Back at the briefing room, Crandall had said:

"Candidate Cutter, did you *really* pass your eye exam?" to which Seymore replied: "Oh, yessir. Both eyes are twenty fifteen." Crandall sighed and shook his head. "Incredible."

His senses sharpened, Sandy's eyes swept across the gauges. All in the green. With his gaze outside, he scanned from left to right for other aircraft in his immediate vicinity. There were none. He yawned, almost as if he were bored, happily that is. He then permitted himself a moment to enjoy the scenery. The dry Texas landscape stretched for miles in all directions. Juniper, piñon pine, and sage dotted the earth below, along with cattle foraging lazily in small clusters. Moving overhead at a brisk pace were puffy cotton clouds, his only competitors in an otherwise empty sky.

And then he felt it, a sudden high frequency vibration. The blood drained from his head. The machine felt like he was enclosed in a huge vibrator. Immediately, he looked for a place to land. He aimed the little craft into the wind and made a radio call. "Mayday! Mayday! Mayday! This is Two Three One X-ray. I have a severe vibration in my aircraft. I have the aircraft under control. I'm landing to an open field approximately five miles due north of Palo Pinto. Mayday! Mayday! Mayday!"

As he descended, the vibration increased. He wondered if the little ship would make it to the ground before coming completely apart.

When he came within twenty feet of the ground, Sandy found a level spot near a large cluster of dried sagebrush and put the helicopter down. He shut the engine down. After the rotorblades had stopped, he got out and went around the helicopter to inspect. Right away he saw what had caused the sagebrush to clump: an abandoned corner post with the guy wires still attached had caught the wind-blown weed one by one. In his haste to be earthbound, he had narrowly missed hitting one of the guy wires with the tailrotor. (Hitting a guy wire with the tailrotor would have, in most instances, severely damaged the tailrotor and probably caused the helicopter to spin out of control, due to the loss of the anti-torque feature provided by the tailrotor.) He cringed, realizing how close he had just come to having an accident. To calm himself, he went and sat inside the cockpit, giving little thought to what might have caused the vibration that had prompted him to be so quickly on the ground in the first place.

Fifteen minutes later, a small dot approached from the east. Sandy turned the radio on and keyed the mic to make contact. When the helicopter finally landed, he saw that it was a civilian maintenance test pilot that had come out to "save" him.

The man extracted a large juicy wad of tobacco from his mouth and tossed it to the ground. He went back toward the tailrotor. He shook his head. "You about screwed up a damn good aircraft, as close as you come to that fence post."

"I know," Sandy said glumly.

The test pilot looked at the leading edge of one of the tailrotor blades. A piece of thick adhesive tape, designed to protect a portion of the blade from premature wind and sand erosion, was beginning to separate from the blade. He ripped off the old tape, took a fresh roll from one of his flight-suit pockets, cut a strip and fixed it to the blade. "There. She's as good as new. You want to fly it back...or do you want me to?"

"Sir?"

"Shit, boy. All that was the matter was that the blade was a little out of kilter. I can't say she's perfect, but certainly better than before. Was she that hard to control?"

"I-I thought so," Sandy answered, now feeling about two feet tall.

"Well, you decide." And then the man said, "I'll give you a word of advice. Don't make no goddamn mountain out of a molehill. Usually, if you can steer a helicopter and all the controls go this way and thatta way"—the test pilot made pantomime control-input gestures with his hands and arms—"you can handle it."

Sandy nodded. He shivered again at the thought of what might have been. "I'll fly it back...if you're sure it's okay."

"Of course I'm sure." The pilot got out a package of Red Man and put a sheaf of dark brown leaves in his mouth. He studied the young man's face. He had seen the look before. He said:

"You ever drive a motorcycle?"

"No, sir."

"Me, I got a Harley, and it's about when you think you're God Himself master of the damn thing that it'll reach out and bite you. Same with a helicopter. Every moment I fly, I'm waiting for something to happen. I never relax—Never. You can't joyride a helicopter like you can an airplane. Okay, I've given my two-cent lecture. See you back at Downing."

"Thank you, sir," Sandy said, speaking a little more cheerfully.

The man grinned. "Think nothing of it. Remember, today you were lucky you didn't get a tailrotor strike. It was a freebie. One to think about."

"Yessir."

* * *

Victor R. Beaver

THE MAN STANDING BEFORE HIM WAS of medium height, slightly overweight, had dark brown hair, and wore a pair of jungle fatigues without rank or insignia. They had gone to Nolan's room and closed the door. Mike invited him to sit down. "Would you like something to drink...a beer? soda? iced tea?"

"Iced tea would be great," the man answered. He wiped his brow with a handkerchief.

Mike Nolan brought out a small pitcher of tea and a tray of ice. As he prepared the drink, he continued to mull over what he had been asked to do, thinking how he let Major Elroy talk him into it. In a moment, he handed the man his drink.

"I hope you don't mind relating what happened," the man said. "My magazine tries to get each story, particularly of this type, firsthand. From what I've heard, your deeds certainly warrant some kind of medal. Again, what are they putting you in for?"

Nolan sat down across from him. He took a sip from a can of Canada Dry. "The Silver Star," he said.

The man raised an eyebrow. From his briefcase he retrieved a yellow notepad. "I'll be jotting notes, if you don't mind."

Nolan shrugged. The whole affair had caught him off guard. Major Elroy had committed him before he had a chance to refuse. Normally, he hated to draw attention to himself. Elroy, however, was under pressure from higher command to highlight any acts of valor that occurred during the Tet offensive. "It's your show, you can run it any way you like," Nolan told the man before him.

"Okay...shall we begin at the beginning? Explain how you got to be where you were? Why weren't you flying?"

Nolan took a long pull from his drink. "When we were first placed on alert, Major Elroy asked that I remain on the ground rather than be assigned to fly."

"Why was that?"

"He told me, frankly, that it was because of my previous Vietnam ground combat experience."

The man made a quick note. "You were over here before? When and under what circumstances...if you don't mind?"

"My first tour was in 'Sixty-three. I was a MACV advisor. An NCO weapons man. I served in that capacity for eighteen months. My second tour was spent with the One Seventy-third Airborne Brigade, from December 'Sixty-five to the same month in 'Sixty-six. I was an officer then. I had a platoon."

"How did that tour go?"

"It was okay."

"Did you lose any men?"

Nolan nodded. "Yeah...three killed in action..."—his voice trailed off—"...and then a couple of others...taken out by booby traps."

"How bad?"

"Pretty damn bad."

"Elaborate."

"Both suffered multiple traumatic amputations." Nolan had used the medical phraseology written on the official report. He watched the reporter jot down another quick note. He added:

"To the best of my knowledge, they're both still alive."

"Are you saying, then, that that is the extent of the casualties of the men under your command? That seems like a pretty low figure."

"Yeah...well...I sure as hell wouldn't want to say it was more so I could gloat about it, for crissake—"

The man raised an eyebrow. He peered at Nolan for a moment. "That's quite a feat, wouldn't you say, though—only five men hurt or killed? How did you do it—that is, keep your men so well protected? Surely, you had your share of patrols. And battles."

Nolan felt the heat rise in his chest. "Dozens of patrols. Tedious, monotonous shit—nothing to write home about. A couple of battles, in fact a big one near the Laotian border. By the way, where are these questions leading? Aren't we getting off the subject?"

The man nodded. "Sorry. So you were selected not to fly on the evening in question. How did that make you feel?"

"It wasn't a problem. I graduated from flight training this last October and went straight into Cobra transition. Frankly, I haven't got enough time or experience in that thing to be worth more than a plug nickel—if that."

"So you were glad to be on the ground?"

"Let's just say I wasn't disappointed. Besides, not all aircraft were committed to fly airfield security, which meant at least one platoon of pilots would be somewhere on the ground, most likely on the perimeter."

"Had there been any attacks yet?"

Nolan shook his head. "None. That didn't occur until two hours later."

"So you and the other pilots were just out guarding the perimeter...?"

Nolan nodded. "Yes, that's right. I made sure they were spread out evenly, not all grouped in one or two bunkers. Buddies bunched together."

At that statement the reporter chuckled. "That's an odd thing to say. What do you mean?"

Nolan frowned. He hadn't meant for his comment to come out quite like that. "I just mean that as a rule warrant officer pilots, and even lieutenants without any kind of infantry experience, aren't going to deploy in the most effective way—not that we were doing anything extravagant."

"Okay, so you made sure, by your experience, that they were at least where they should be."

"Yes."

Victor R. Beaver

"Let's go back to the perimeter itself. Why weren't the VC stopped? Didn't anyone see them? How did they get in?"

Nolan breathed deep. At the beginning of Tet he had wondered that too, until he found out later that the VC had tunneled under the fence from the river that ran east and west on the south side of the airfield. "I'm sorry, I can't answer that."

"But you can tell me that it must have been easy for them, can't you?"

Nolan looked the man in the eyes. "Let's get something straight. You want to know exactly what I did to be recommended for the Silver Star. Anything beyond that is off limits, as far as I'm concerned."

"Okay-okay, I apologize."

Nolan began to relate the events as he remembered them. "I had just checked each bunker, to make sure everyone was awake. It was about a quarter after one. I was on my way back to our operations, going past the last revetment, when there came this explosion. Immediately I dropped to the ground. Several more explosions followed—about three in quick succession. Right away I knew what was happening. The VC were satchel-charging our helicopters. A mortar-round impact has a much different sound."

"So then what did you do?"

"I got up and started back the way I came. This time I saw aircraft burning a good five or six revetments down. I remember I had my forty-five out of the holster. The next explosion flattened me. For a few seconds I was stunned. I sat up and propped myself against the revetment wall I was next to. Red and green tracers were flying overhead in all directions. Suddenly, there were a couple of warrant officers by my side. I knew one by name and the other by sight only, someone who had just come into the unit. I told them to spread out. They scuttled several feet away from me and were now hunched like scared rabbits. 'What's happening, sir?' Higgins asked. 'The VC are inside the perimeter!' I told them. I remember they cursed. By that time, Charlie had blown up two more helicopters. The VC were having a heyday. I sensed that they were well organized, that every move had been planned. In rapid succession, they were setting off one and two satchel charges at a time. Plus, it had to be a suicide team. They were going strong with nothing to lose. I glanced around the revetment wall and didn't see anything. But I did hear noises, running footsteps. I looked toward Higgins. The other guy, I found out later, was Brady. 'Stay here,' I said. 'Where are you going?' Higgins asked. 'The bastards are a couple of revetments down,' I told them. 'I'm going to try and get behind them. I don't want either of you guys with me, especially with those cocked pistols. The guy named Brady said, 'Suits me.' Higgins asked, 'Don't you want us to cover you?' I said, 'If they kill me, cover me. It won't matter then.' I flicked my pistol off safe and scooted around the end of the revetment. I ran like hell to the next one. I was breathing hard. I remember cursing my three-pack-a-day cigarette habit. I kneeled. I heard movement, very hurried and loud. I remember feeling the blood throbbing in my temples. I had no idea what to expect if I were to charge around the corner. But I was running out of time. The aircraft that were burning were giving off plenty of light to see by, but it was the confusion that kept the little bastards moving around seemingly unnoticed. I kept low and began to edge around the revetment wall. Then I heard voices, speaking in Vietnamese. I knew enough of the language to tell that they were cursing, probably having difficulty setting the charge. I figured it was now or never."

"So what happened?" the reporter asked, nearly at the edge of his seat.

"Well, as I turned the corner, I found myself face to face with one of them. My forty-five was level with his mid-section and I remember the gun going off, almost as if it had a mind of its own. That forty-five slug sent him clean against his buddy, still trying to set the charge. In the next instant the buddy was all over me. His arms and legs were going in all directions, like a buzz saw. He clawed at me like a wildcat. We were the same height, but I had the weight advantage. But still, I was on my back and he was on top and I never in my life saw a pair of eyes so fierce. There was nothing I could do with the pistol, except hold onto it so he wouldn't get it. I even tried to keep my finger away from the trigger. We were in such a skirmish that I was afraid that if the gun went off—I'd accidentally shoot myself. We must have struggled for better than a minute like that. Finally, I managed to get a grip on his windpipe. He squirmed harder than ever; and I was fast running out of steam. And then he did something odd. He arched up and I got sight of something better to hang onto: his crotch. That was when I let go of the pistol and grabbed for his scrotum. I knew I had him then. He let out a scream that made me shiver up one side and down the other. He stopped thrashing long enough for me turn him over. Now I was on top, one hand clutching his throat, the other his balls. I gripped his windpipe so hard I heard it crunch. It took him less than a minute to relax—and then I knew he was dead. About three seconds later, I heard voices—American voices. I was so exhausted, I could hardly move. Then I heard shots. I hunted for my pistol, but I couldn't find it, so I said to hell with it and braced myself against the revetment wall. I was almost delirious. A couple more shots were fired. Not knowing what was what, I got up and started around the other side. As I did, I heard another shot, and then something slammed into me. It was a Viet Cong. His forward momentum laid me out flat. I remember smelling the VC I had just killed, but this one smelled worse. He lay limp on top of me so I figured he was dead. And then, like I was possessed, I heaved him off me. I remember seeing him slam against the revetment wall and slide down in a clump. As I was about to get up, I heard: 'Freeze!' It was Higgins. 'Stop!' I yelled. Higgins and Brady had seen this particular sapper somewhere and had given chase. After they finally got him, they saw me try to rise and figured I was still another Charlie."

By this time the reporter's eyes were practically bulging out of his head. "Obviously, they didn't kill you," he said.

"Yeah. But what's really funny, had those two warrant officers not seen and chased the one that slammed into me, I might have had to deal with him too…and I wouldn't have had the strength. Later, I remembered laughing. 'What's so funny?' Brady asked. That's when I told them thanks. 'What for?' Higgins said. 'For covering me,' I said."

Chapter 38

KIP SLATER GLANCED AT HIS WATCH. The luminous dials, barely visible in the inky black of night, read eleven thirty. "What do you think, Leo?"

Leo drew on his cigarette. For a second, the hot end glowed bright. He flicked the cigarette to the ground. "Piss on it."

"Yeah, 'Ours is not to wonder why, ours is but to do and die.' Isn't that how it goes?"

"Something like that," Westy Harper interjected.

Jim Ellis stood. "Where're you going?" Leo asked. Ellis had been paired with him for the upcoming mission.

"Back to the ship. Maybe I can catch some shut-eye. Beats worrying about it."

The briefing they had just received had been short, sweet, and to the point. During the early hours of Tet, two companies of Viet Cong had breached the Vinh Long airfield perimeter. The enemy, still on the airfield, dug in on the west side in platoon-size pockets, was heavily armed and well stocked with other supplies. During the initial invasion, Lieutenant Colonel Schaffer, the airfield commander, had been killed, along with thirteen other Americans. To re-enforce the airfield, a hastily assembled group of assault troops from Can Tho was to be airlifted directly onto the Vinh Long runway, at the extreme east end. Doorgunners on the lift ships would not be allowed to suppress with their M-60s. Only the gunships covering the assault had complete liberty to shoot.

Harper opened the left cockpit door and climbed into his seat. Slater looked toward the assault troops lounging on the ground several feet away, waiting to board. "Those poor bastards haven't got a clue what they're in for, do they?"

Leo took out another cigarette and lit it. "Now I know the definition of cannon fodder—and those guys are it," he said.

Slater nodded. The assault troops were made up of cooks and clerks, motor pool mechanics and aircraft maintenance specialists, and a few MPs. Most appeared awkward in their flakjackets, steel pots, and web gear. Though some were volunteers, most had been *volunteered.* Several were outright fearful and anxious, dreading what lay ahead. A few ran their hands over the cold steel of their weapons, their heads filled with visions of heroic deeds under fire. Others, feigning calm, lay on the ground and tried to sleep.

Randall and Christian appeared out of the gloom. "We crank in ten minutes," Christian told them.

"What's taking so long?"

Randall shrugged. "Tannah, how the hell would we know?"

"And remember," Christian said, "keep your rotating beacons off. Use just your position lights—on dim."

Victor R. Beaver

"Roger that."
Randall and Christian retreated into the gloom.
They waited. Ten...twenty...thirty...forty minutes. Then word came down the line. "Let's go, it's time to crank."
"Good luck, Leo."
"Yeah, you too."
Rusty White went to the rear of the ship to untie the blades. Weary, wary, the troops stood. Ron Larkin directed them to climb aboard. They bunched themselves on the cabin floor, as close to center as they could. None wanted their feet dangling outside the ship while in the air. They sat with the barrels of their rifles poked in the most unlikely places: under someone's nose, rammed deep into someone's gut, gouging the back of someone's neck.
Slater began the engine-start sequence. Westy Harper struggled into his seatbelt and shoulder harness. "What I'd like to know," he said, "is how this damn belt is going to save my ass if we fall out of the sky from fifteen hundred feet."
"Quit your belly-aching."
"What—I ain't got privileges to gripe."
"Stuff it. *We're coming hot—!*"
Slater pulled the ignition trigger. The igniters began to fire. The N1 tach generator began to rise, along with the EGT (engine gas temperature needle). The blades began to move and the N2 and rotor tachometer needles began to bounce (exactly like they were supposed to). When he saw, as the engine whined behind him, that everything was in order— *"the stars in their course"*—he began to relax. Maybe it was the sound of the engine behind him and the sweep of the main rotorblades overhead that calmed him. Or the glow of the cockpit lights. Or the feel of the seat around him. Or his shoulder harness and seatbelt fastened and tightened across his belly and down over his chest. Or maybe it was a combination of all of these things, all snugged in, surrounded by machinery, by gauges and switches and dials all bathed in a soft red light. Or maybe it was the night, the pitch-black night, a night without visible definition, as if he were wrapped in a darkened cocoon, safe and warm. Maybe it was about being a pilot, in control, the commander of his fate, of his immediate universe. Or then again maybe it was nothing at all.
After the inverters had been turned on, and the radios began to chatter, and the throttle was brought to full rpm, Slater glanced back. How many of these men, he wondered, would not live through this night? These men, who up to now never dreamed they'd be doing what they were doing, were now faced with the very real possibility of dying. And then he thought of Henry. Robin had wanted so badly to be in the Viking gun platoon that he unknowingly set in motion the exact chain of events that, perhaps, led to a more immediate end to his life...*Yet how can any of us avoid it? Is there some secret message that comes to us to tell us beforehand the moment of our demise? Could we sidestep it for a moment,*

maybe even indefinitely? Will I know the day I'm going to die...on the day that I actually do?

"Flight, this is Lead. We'll be pulling pitch in one zero," Christian called.

Harper, on the controls, added power and the helicopter became light on the landing gear. "It's blacker than a well-diggers ass," he said to Slater.

"Wait a little before lifting. Keep some space between you and the guy ahead. And watch your attitude indicator. You'll practically be doing an instrument takeoff."

"Ten-four," Harper responded. The sound of his gum chewing snapped over the intercom.

Lead lifted. After about fifty seconds, Randall, in the trail helicopter, announced: "Lead, this is Trail, your flight of ten is up."

"This is Lead, roger. Flight, come up straight trail—and keep it tight."

Slater looked out, his gaze intent on seeing the horizon. There was none. He glanced to his right, lowering his eyes toward the ground. He saw nothing but pitch black.

Again, he looked ahead. In the number six slot of ten aircraft, they were having to play catch-up with the helicopters that had taken off first. *I count one...two...three sets of position lights. Where are the other two? Oh...there they are. I think. God, they're a long way away...I guess. I can't really tell.*

"How's it going?" he asked Harper.

"I'm totally on the gauges."

"Yeah, okay, stay there. Keep the heading you're flying. I'll watch our rate of closure on the ships ahead."

"Check."

"Increase your speed...just a little."

"Gotcha covered, slick."

Another moment. *Why is it taking so long to catch up? Airspeed is ninety-five knots. Should be fast enough. This has got to be the biggest bunch of shit—blacker than black out and no fuckin' lights. Plus our LZ is smack in the middle of the Vinh Long airfield. I can't believe it. We're going to come in slow right over Charlie on the way in. These guys sitting behind me are going to get their asses kicked. Fuck, what am I saying? My ass could get kicked too—!*

Slater shifted in his seat; he bent forward. "I've only got three sets of lights ahead us. Jesus, where are the other two...?"

Harper said: "How's our closure?"

"It's okay..." *I think.* "Increase your speed just a bit more. I can't believe we're this far behind."

Jesus, my depth perception is shot to hell. Now I count four sets of lights. One set missing. Where is it? Ah, there's the fifth one. Shit—gone again.

He looked toward Harper. "You doing okay?"

"Me? Sure...Why?"

"No reason." Slater watched Harper's jaws working furiously on a wad of gum. "You got any extra sticks?"

"Sure." Harper reached in his pocket and handed him the pack.

"Thanks." Slater took a stick and handed the pack back. Harper reached over and put it in his pocket. Kip slid the wrapper off and undid the foil. He put the gum in his mouth. He began to chew. Peering through the windshield, he tried to relax. The ships ahead now appeared, by the look of their position lights (on dim), to be in a tight cluster, swaying slightly, bobbing up and down. He watched the lights. *They could mesmerize me, like the lava lamp Leo bought and let me borrow the other night. If I tilt my head just so, I can imagine that I'm flying through a dark tunnel...Hey, this is cool...cool. Jesus, why am I yawning? Crap, we're still not catching up. How come?*

Slater tapped at the glass covering his airspeed indicator: one hundred knots. *God, we never close this fast—never. Something isn't right...But what is it?* He leaned to his left and reached over and tapped the glass covering Harper's airspeed indicator.

"What's the matter?"

"Just checking. I can't understand why we haven't caught up yet."

Slater turned and glanced out his cockpit window, at the ground below. Black, blacker than aces down there, still. *No way to judge our speed. None. Zippo.*

He squirmed. He reached up and tapped his airspeed indicator again. *It appears to be working okay. But a hundred knots—?* And then he glanced up. A chill shot through him; his eyes grew wide. He grabbed the cyclic and pulled back.

"*Hey!*—what gives?" Westy Harper blurted over the intercom.

"I've got the controls!" Slater cried.

The nose of the ship rose like the head of a horse suddenly—violently—reined in. In an instant Slater slammed the collective down and banked hard to the right. They dropped like a rock.

"What are you doing—?" screamed Harper.

Kip quickly added power. "We fucking almost hit those guys!"

Harper glanced up. To his left he saw the white belly light of the number five ship not more than hundred feet above them. The little gum-chewing co-pilot looked toward Slater. Suddenly, his chest felt like it was being crushed by a vice. And then he felt the gooseflesh raise all over him as the full import of what had almost occurred—*a mid-air collision!*—sank in.

A few seconds later, Slater had the aircraft under control and had achieved a level attitude. He checked his power and locked his eyes onto the artificial horizon. He felt his heart beating madly in his chest. In another minute, he had the ship level with the other helicopters. Thirty seconds after that he had the helicopter in position, the sixth ship in straight trail formation.

"Jesus!—I thought you were watching those guys!" Harper cried.

"I was! I was!" Finally, Slater took a breath. "On a night like this, as black as it is, there's nothing to judge the rate of closure by. I'm sorry!"

"Fuck you!—you almost killed me!"

"I know—I'm sorry—*I'm sorry!*"

Leo Tannah and Jim Ellis, in the second to last ship in the formation, listened intently to a conversation between Neely and one of the Viking gunships. "Looks like the SOBs are near the outer edge."

"Is that the location nearest the perimeter?" Neely asked.

"Roger that, Six. It's about fifty meters from that perimeter bunker we discussed earlier—where we took fire."

"Roger," Neely said. "Do you think we should break the flight up? Bring them in two groups of five?"

"Negative. I think it's all or none."

"Roger."

As the chatter between C&C and the gunships continued, they heard firing in the background through keyed microphones. Several flares descended, casting an eerie halo of light over the airfield, like something out of a surreal movie. Beyond the light was infinite blackness. Gazing at the airfield, they saw flashes go off, like so many Roman candles, while tracers sped off in all directions. The red rotating beacons of the gunships could be seen down low, floating directly above the runway.

"Tiger Lead, this is Tiger Six."

"This is Lead, go," Christian replied.

"Bring your flight in now. Straight trail. Land as far forward on the runway as you can. No suppressive fire. I repeat, no suppressive fire."

"This is Lead, roger."

Christian began a shallow right turn. When he rolled out, the Vinh Long airstrip was three miles ahead. Leo saw several explosions, impacts from rockets on the left side of the runway, west end. Again tracers streaked everywhere. After two minutes, Lead reduced airspeed. Several seconds after that Lead passed over the runway's west end.

Leo was on the controls. A pair of rockets fired from one of the gunships countered a blast of enemy tracers. Tannah watched the explosions and shuddered. They descended lower. Three hundred feet above the runway. The gunshots going off sounded like firecrackers, a regular Fourth of July celebration.

"Parker. Receiving fire!—*ten o'clock!*" called Leo.

"I see it, sir!" replied his crewchief.

"Return fire!"

"I thought we couldn't suppress," blurted Ellis.

"To hell with that noise—!" answered Leo. The report from Parker's M-60 pumped Tannah's adrenaline faster and faster. They were now two hundred feet above the runway. Leo watched as several tracers from Parker's gun hit PSP and skipped off at odd angles. Just then the radios crackled, asking which one of the lift ships was firing. Leo was about to respond when three rounds stitched the floor between his legs. One bullet grazed the cyclic control stick and then passed through the greenhouse (skylight window) above his head. He felt the knock and gripped the cyclic tighter. Another burst of enemy gunfire. Leo felt the cyclic stiffen; the master caution light came on. The segment panel light on the center console told the story: *Hydraulics failure.*

Leo reached over and reset the master caution light. "Check the circuit breaker—" he said to Ellis. Leo tried to move the anti-torque pedals but they were stiff as boards. The collective lever felt locked in place. The cyclic control stick jiggered in his right hand. The helicopter felt controllable, but it was like driving a deuce-and-a-half truck without power steering.

Leo decided to break formation. "Yellow Four declaring an emergency. Hydraulics failure. I'm making a right break."

"Roger that, Four. We've got your right break," Viking Two Three replied.

Meantime, the front three aircraft had landed and had discharged their troops. Kip, in the middle of the pack, reported receiving fire. The gunships countered with mini-gun fire. Kip brought the ship to the ground. The troops jumped out and began running. The remaining aircraft, minus Leo's ship, landed and discharged their troops. A burst of machine-gun fire ripped into several men before they were able to take their second step. Empty of their human cargo, the lift ships took off and fled the carnage.

Leo, guiding his helicopter away from the airfield, watched the rest of the formation climb steadily to altitude. He turned south. "Jim, did you check the circuit breaker?"

No reply.

"Hey, Ellis—?"

Still nothing. Leo glanced left. In the semi-darkness of the cockpit he could see Ellis's head listing slightly to the right. He reached over and jabbed him in the arm. "What's this—sleeping on the job? Wake up."

Ellis's head now drooped forward. "Jim...? Hey, are you okay?"

Parker, listening, climbed out of his seat and struggled past the troops still bunched on the floor in the cabin of the ship. They looked at him curious and confused. When Parker got behind Ellis's seat he turned the man's head sideways. The eyes were open but stared at him blankly. Parker reached around and placed the tips of his fingers against Ellis's neck. He tried for thirty seconds to feel a pulse. "I think he's dead, sir," Parker reported to Leo.

"He's what?—Dead?"

"Yes, sir...I think so."

* * *

KIP SLATER SLID INTO THE THIRD PEW on the left side, along with Leo Tannah, Mac, and Fred Oakerson. He turned and watched the rest of the company file in, their expressions somber. After a few minutes, the chapel was full.

Captain Hendricks, a Methodist chaplain, got their attention. He stood before them in a set of ill-fitting jungle fatigues. "Gentlemen, simple words cannot convey the deep sorrow you all must be feeling at the losses of Warrant Officers Robin Henry and James Ellis. Rest assured that they did not die in vain. Your purpose here, though oftentimes vague, does have meaning. God willing, when this war is won, and the forces of good have overcome evil, you will look back and know that each American soldier who died here, like the leaves that fall from a tree in autumn, had to happen." The chaplain paused. He surveyed the men, imploring their wondering stares. He had always found it difficult to fill them full of patriotic symbolism, as it was his duty to do under circumstances like these. In fact, as a student of history, he often speculated the future historical perspective of America's involvement in Southeast Asia. Regardless the outcome, would it be said that America had to be here? Or just the opposite?

As the chaplain continued to speak, reciting the usual litany, his eyes locked onto those of one of the pilots to his right, seated in the third pew back. In them he saw neither resentment nor distress, neither fear nor hopelessness. In fact the eyes engendered bemusement, almost a mysterious lack of expression. The chaplain shuddered. He turned, viewing the man askance. Then he brought his attention full to the front. He said, folding his hands on top the podium, "...Let us pray. *The Lord is my shepherd; I shall not want. He maketh me to lie down in green pastures; He leadeth me beside the still waters. He restoreth my soul...*"

Leo mouthed the Twenty-third Psalm along with the chaplain and the others. "*Yea, though I walk through the valley of the shadow death, I shall fear no evil—for I am the meanest sonofabitch in the valley...*"

Mac and Slater, after the service, stood outside the chapel; each held a lit cigarette. Mac said, "Captain James has asked me to come over to the Vikings."

Slater frowned. "Oh, yeah? When did you find out?"

"This morning. He said that what happened to Henry was a fluke. What do you think?"

Kip shrugged. "It was Robin's time to go." He tried to sound nonchalant. "Just like Ellis...It can happen in the slicks, too."

"Roger that."

Slater tossed his cigarette to the ground. "Wait'll Tannah finds out."

Mac shook his head. "He's going to be pissed."

They stood silent for a moment. Mac said, "I don't want to be the one to tell him."

"Neither do I."

Victor R. Beaver

* * *

BRAVO LIMA ONE FIVE, BRAVO LIMA One Five, this is Tiger Zero Seven Eight. Have sighted two individuals in black pajamas, approximately nine kilometers west of Phu Loc. Coordinates are as follows. Are you ready to copy?"

"Roger that, Tiger Zero Seven Eight. Go ahead."

"They are Whiskey Romeo 652430. They are well within the free-fire zone Alpha November. Request immediate permission to engage."

"Roger-roger, good copy. Standby. Over."

"Roger that. Standing by." Smiling, Leo looked back at his crew. Parker, his crewchief, and Vitale, his gunner, had their M-60s ready to fire. "Looks like we got us a turkey shoot, guys."

"Yeah, well we'd better hurry, sir," Vitale said. "They're about to get away."

Leo diverted his attention out the window. The two figures were now moving briskly toward a treeline less than two hundred meters to their front. It was a piece of luck that they had been spotted at all. After he and his crew had completed their last re-supply run, Leo spoke with one of the assistant MACV advisors about scouting one of the area's free-fire zones. The advisor, a hard-nosed, barrel-chested captain, gave him the Alpha November sector to check out. It was a location, he told them, which lately had been free of any enemy activity, but likely to change at any moment. It was for this reason permission needed to be granted first before engagement.

Leo radioed: "Bravo Lima One Five. Need immediate permission to fire. They're getting away—"

"Roger-roger. You have permission to fire. Good luck and good shooting. Over."

"Okay, Vitale. Let's see what you can do."

Vitale's M-60 opened up. Leo directed Munson to do a wide circling descent to one thousand feet. Munson gazed at Tannah and then nodded. Meanwhile, the two pajama-clad figures, now under fire, had stopped and were looking up. Then they began to run, zigzagging toward the treeline. Leo watched as Vitale's tracers skipped around them. "Come on, Vitalie. Jesus, you've gotta hit'em—"

"Yessir, I'm trying!"

Leo took the controls. He reduced power. The ship began to sink like a rock. Leveling off at two hundred feet, Leo turned the aircraft until it was aimed directly at the fleeing figures. Vitale continued to fire but his shots were either long or short. Leo gave Munson the controls. He took out his Thompson submachine gun and pointed it out the window. He fired. The front figure went down in tall grasses. The other stopped, turned, and began running in the opposite direction. Munson immediately turned the ship left. "Parker. Get ready. You'll be seeing him out your side. To the right—in a second."

"Roger that."

When they rolled out, the lone figure had changed directions again. He now scurried back toward his fallen comrade. Munson banked the ship hard right. Leo aimed and fired. He missed. The man lay prone. Somewhere hidden in his clothing was a weapon, a rifle, which he lifted and aimed. They heard a distinct crack. Leo saw the man pull the bolt back, aim and fire again. He heard a *snap-clunk!* as the round hit somewhere on the ship. The VC hurried to get one more shot off. Parker fired and the VC ducked his head. The Viet Cong tossed his weapon aside, got up and began a sprint for the treeline. "We got him now, Parker, fire, *fire!"*

"Wait a second—I've got to reload."

Munson flew toward the VC with the landing gear at shoulder level. Leo pointed the Thompson again and fired. Bullets kicked the ground around him. "Missed—" Leo tried again but his Thompson was out of ammo.

The VC stopped and flung himself to the ground. As they flew past they saw that the little man had his legs drawn in tight, his arms and hands wrapped around his head. Leo grabbed the controls and drew the ship into a hard right turn. The man continued to lay doubled up on his side. Leo slowed the ship and then went forward at a brisk hover. "He's not moving. How come?" Munson asked.

"Beats me." Leo then gave the controls back to Munson. "Keep it steady right here." Leo looked down. The main rotor downwash flattened the grasses surrounding the VC; he lay there as if in the eye of a great storm. Leo unholstered his .45, chambered a round, and poked his arm out the window. He fired and missed. He steadied his hand, aimed and fired again. A dark wet spot formed on the man's lower right abdomen. Leo fired again. Five times. When the gun was empty, he told Munson to back away. The grasses around the inert figure remained flattened by the rotor downwash.

"Do you think he's dead?" asked Munson.

"Yeah...I think so."

At altitude, Leo keyed the radio: "Bravo Lima One Five, this is Tiger Zero Seven Eight. We have two confirmed Victor Charlie KIA. Within Alpha November free-fire zone. How copy?"

"Roger. Understand they were within the fire-fire zone?"

"That's affirmative," Leo replied.

"Good shooting, guys. Good shooting."

Victor R. Beaver

Chapter 39

DEREK JUSTEN LOOKED ON AS three Vietnamese soldiers unloaded boxes from a three-quarter-ton truck. Next to him stood a thin-faced MACV sergeant, one of the Vinh Binh Province advisors, who had arrived several moments before. Together they watched as Slater and Conrad lifted the crates into the helicopter. Inside, Finch arranged the C-ration cartons, ammunition boxes, packets of medical supplies, and six five-gallon cans of water on the cabin floor. "I don't know what's taking the colonel so long," the MACV sergeant said. "You'll play hell going in there without gunship support."

Justen pulled deeply on his cigarette. He took his map and unfolded it. The sergeant pointed. "See that canal just south of town?"

Justen nodded.

"It's heavily foliated," the sergeant said. "Captain Huddleston believes Charlie has a command post there—well guarded. On the way in, if you're going to get hit, that's where it'll come from. He reports that everywhere else the bastards are situated in groups of squad-size and better."

Slater came forward; he looked at Justen's map. "When did they run out of ammo?"

"They're not completely out," the sergeant said, "but dangerously low. They're out of food and medical supplies, though." The MACV sergeant paused. "Huddleston says he's down to a dozen One O Five shells. We're thinking that if you can get in with this load and out…maybe you could take them some shells."

Justen raised an eyebrow. "That might be pressing our luck," he said.

The sergeant nodded, then glanced up. A jeep came toward them. "Here comes Colonel Johnson. Maybe he's got some good news." The jeep halted and the men saluted. A tall gray-haired lieutenant colonel, the senior province advisor, returned the salutes.

The man eased out of the jeep. "How's it going, Sergeant Snyder?"

"Fine, sir. Any luck?"

The colonel approached, shaking his head. "Negative." He looked toward Justen. "I've been on the horn for the past hour. I couldn't raise one gunship. It's your call, son. If you want to reconsider, I'll understand." The older man had a pained look on his face.

Justen glanced at his watch: it was late afternoon, almost four o'clock. When they arrived at the Tra Vinh airstrip they were briefed that the Viet Cong, since the beginning of Tet, had surrounded Tieu Can, a small district town eighteen kilometers to the southwest. They were told further that an all-out VC attack on the town was imminent later that night. The supplies being loaded were desperately needed, but without gunship escort Justen thought the re-supply mission smacked of failure. He stood silent for a moment gazing at the ground. He had flown into Tieu Can more than a dozen times in the past. If they could come in low-level, paralleling the treeline that stretched west from the town, they might have a chance to get in unnoticed—at least until it was too late for Charlie to react. He looked toward Slater, then at Conrad and Finch. His chief and gunner peered back. Conrad, short and stocky, was as tough as a badger. Finch, a little taller, with muscles stretched taut over a wiry frame, and the quieter of the two, was like a coiled spring. Derek knew that whatever he decided, they would go along. Slater, his aircraft undergoing a 100-hour PE inspection, had been paired with him because no peter-pilots were available. Justen nodded toward the colonel and motioned his crew out of earshot. He said:

"Okay, I'm not going to pull any punches. It's plain as hell that without these supplies the advisory team at Tieu Can may not last the night. I'll let you guys decide. We can wait and maybe have gunship cover later tonight. Or give it a try right now, while it's still light. Frankly, I'd rather go in during daylight. If we fly in at dark and the VC do attack, the gunships are going to have their hands full." He eyed his chief and gunner. Conrad said, "Count me in, sir." Finch nodded agreement. Justen looked toward Slater. "How about you?"

Kip Slater breathed deep. His nerves were so raw-edged that he found it difficult to think. The deaths of both Henry and Ellis had affected him more than he realized. And he was still trying to piece together what Leo had told him. Tannah had killed the second of the two Viet Cong in the free-fire zone in cold blood, barely blinking an eye in the telling. "Why, Leo?...Why did you do it?" he had asked. Two days later, Tannah's reply still haunted him. "I wanted to know what it felt like to kill someone." Afterwards, he studied Leo's face long and hard. *What is this war doing to us? Have we become as bad as the Nazis. How did we get this way?*

Slater looked at Conrad, then Finch, and then Justen. He thought, Five Americans are in trouble. They may perish if they don't get these supplies. He gazed at the ship. The rear cabin area was filled to capacity, with no view out the other side. They had to be right at max gross weight. *Once again we'll be a slow-moving—perfect-sitting—fucking-duck target. Christ, when will this kind of shit end? I'll never see the end of my tour...Never.* He glanced at Conrad's M-60, on it's mount, pointed at the ground. He looked at the UH-1's silhouette, at the slightly upturned nose area, at the large fuselage and the long tapering tailboom. The rotorblades were untied, turned ninety degrees to the airframe; they teeter-tottered at the slightest wind. Could this one day be my coffin? he thought. It didn't look like one, but how many men had already perished in their ships? And to what end? When he joined the army to fly, one of the ways he justified doing so, because he knew he would also have to do penance in Vietnam, was that he might use the skill to fly somewhere in the civilian world, perhaps overseas, like Australia or maybe somewhere in South America. Plus, he had always wanted to write, and to do that meant, at least to him, accumulating as many life experiences as he could. He had always admired Ernest Gann, author of *Fate is the Hunter*. A flyer and adventurer, Gann had also turned himself into an accomplished writer. There were other pilots turned writers whom he admired: Nevil Shute, Richard Bach, Anne Morrow Lindberg, Antoine de Saint-Exupéry. A pilot, he felt, is someone who *really* has something to write about. It was then that he thought of his classmates during flight training. They couldn't wait to get to Vietnam, as if they had been asked to play-act in a John Wayne movie. Flying in Vietnam would be the ultimate adventure. But had he thought about it any differently? He couldn't recall. Yet day after day during flight school he took notes and then felt, upon his arrival in Vietnam, that now he was delving into the heart of life, on the cutting edge between it and death. But still to what end? To one day write the Great American War novel? And be on par with Hemingway and Leon Uris and James Jones and Norman Mailer? To do that he had to live—*to survive the war!* He shook his head. "Crap—let's do it." Justen nodded and said:

"There's really only one way in and out, regardless the winds or the weight of our load. We've got to make our final approach from the south, right along this canal"—Justen stabbed his finger at his map—"right where these guys think the VC have set up a command post. Finch, you'll be on that side. You've got permission right now to return any fire." He looked at Slater. "I'll take the right seat. How does that sound?" Slater gave a reluctant sigh. "It sounds fine."

They were at two thousand feet. Slater gazed forward. From seven kilometers out he saw the growth of trees that bordered Tieu Can on the east side. He saw the well-defined north-south canal that cut north out of town through rice paddies. A secondary canal curved south where the suspected command post was located, within two hundred meters of the town. To the west, he saw a long straight road; parallel to it on the north side he saw another treeline. The plan was to overfly the town on the north side and perform a cursory high recon, hoping to appear to the Viet Cong as if they were just passing by. They would then continue a southwest beeline for five minutes before descending. Once they were in low-level flight, they would snug the road and the treeline that lay west of town back toward the compound and the landing zone.

After a couple more minutes, they were directly over Tieu Can. Slater looked straight down. A single thoroughfare sliced through the town's middle, until it ended and opened into a large courtyard. The courtyard was the landing zone. Next to the courtyard he saw the MACV compound, enclosed by high brick walls. He saw the headquarters building, where the Americans lived and slept, the separate barracks for the RF/PF soldiers, and the old French stone fortress with observation tower. He saw clusters of town buildings abutting the compound walls on the north and west sides. Several Banyan trees overshadowed the southwest side of the wall. South of the Banyan trees was open rice paddy. And then he saw the two 105-howitzer cannons, their barrels aimed southward, elevated for a flat trajectory.

It was then that Slater understood the enemy's fevered interest in Tieu Can: *It was the two cannons!* With those in their hot possession, they could wreak havoc practically anywhere. When he mentioned this to Justen, he asked:

"But how would they get the shells?"

"I'm sure they'd find a way."

The town was now behind them. Justen continued flight until they came to the end of the west treeline. He then began a rapid descent to less than a hundred feet above the ground. The aircraft commander then brought the ship closer to the road and the row of trees that led to the town. He increased their speed to 110 knots.

They were now in low-level flight less than ten feet above the ground.

The Banyan trees bordering the southwest edge of the compound loomed larger with every second they sped forward. "Thirty seconds to go before we turn," Justen declared. Conrad and Finch tightened their grips on the handles of their M-60s.

Kip looked straight ahead. The south canal and treeline, where Huddleston said the enemy command post was located, was now less than three hundred meters to their front. Their present heading was east by northeast. They would turn due north just before reaching the treeline. The courtyard walls, and the LZ on the opposite side, would then be two hundred meters away.

Justen told Kip to place his hands and feet lightly on his set of controls—just in case. Feeling his heart rate quicken, Slater did as he was told.

Justen began to decelerate the ship. The turning point was now less than the length of a football field away. Slater glanced left. The Banyan trees to their left cast their huge branches outward, as if they would reach out and grab them.

Fifty meters...twenty-five meters...fifteen...ten...Justen brought the nose of the ship up slightly and banked left. He then corrected to a level attitude. Directly before them, and slightly left, stood the old French fortress and tower. To the right of it were the rooftops of the downtown dwellings of Tieu Can.

Justen continued slowing the aircraft. They now had one hundred and fifty meters to go before crossing the courtyard wall. Kip took a deep breath and felt his chest tighten against the armored breastplate held in place by his shoulder straps. Seeing the dense foliage near the canal on their right, Slater thought a battalion of men could be hiding there and no one would ever know.

At one hundred meters, Justen had the speed of the helicopter going at what seemed like a crawl.

At seventy-five meters they heard the first shots fired, the eruption of machine-gun fire from the suspected command post hidden along the south-canal treeline. Slater heard the rounds hit the right side of the aircraft. He heard Finch's M-60 open up. He heard more shots. Next he saw the Plexiglas windshield directly to Justen's front split as a round cut a flat trajectory across it. Later, Slater would recall how the ship suddenly lurched to the left, how the cyclic control stick felt immovable due to Justen's weight pushing against it, and how he had to jerk the cyclic stick back with one mighty rearward pull to keep the ship from slamming into the ground. He would recall, too, the horror he felt when he saw Justen's body slumped forward, practically smothering the flight controls.

In the next instant, Slater had the helicopter powered up with just enough forward momentum and height to clear the courtyard wall.

On the other side he saw several Vietnamese soldiers crouched against the base of the far courtyard wall. Next to them he saw two Americans, both kneeling, one holding a rifle, the other a PRC-25 (radio) handset pressed firmly to his right ear. In a swirl of dust, Slater lowered the helicopter to the ground.

For several seconds Kip Slater sat stunned. To his front he saw the American with the rifle pointing frantically at the underbelly of the ship. Confused, he frowned at his odd picture and then remembered Justen. Kip looked quickly right. Justen's whole left upper shoulder was covered in blood. The top of his flight helmet looked like a gopher had burrowed through it. The base of the helmet on the left side appeared as though an M-80 firecracker had exploded. What remained was an exposure of splintered fiberglass mixed with shards of black hair and blood.

Oh my God, the man is dead...!

Just then the right cockpit door opened. An American, wearing a floppy jungle hat, reached across to feel Justen's pulse. "Is he alive?" Slater shouted.

"I can't tell!" the man cried, then passed his hand across his throat indicating that Kip should shut the aircraft down. "You're leaking fuel everywhere!" Reactively, Slater complied.

Chapter 40

AFTER THE ENGINE WAS SHUT DOWN, Slater undid his seatbelt, opened the left cockpit door, and with his helmet still on, egressed quickly from the ship. He stooped low to check underneath the fuselage and saw the reason for all the frantic pointing. Fuel nearly poured from more than a dozen holes. He bumped into Conrad who was dashing around to the right side to see how Justen was doing. Together, they helped the American wearing the floppy hat lift him out of the ship. Meantime, Finch struggled out of his seatbelt and stepped to the ground, his right hand and arm badly bloodied.

After they hustled Justen away from the helicopter and had him stretched out on the ground near the far courtyard wall and out of harm's way, an explosion sounded. "Get down! RPG!" yelled the American captain who had been holding the handset. Slater ducked, then looked back at the helicopter. The rocket-propelled grenade had exploded near the wall they had just overflown, fifty feet from the tailboom. It was then that he saw for the first time half a dozen townspeople, each holding some kind of container, an open pail or pan, crouching low to the ground. The explosion had caused them to pause for a moment before moving forward again toward the downed ship. As he watched, the American with the rifle said, "They want to catch the dripping fuel." Slater raised an eyebrow and shrugged.

Slater turned and saw the American with the floppy jungle hat working feverishly to stop Justen's bleeding. The captain came and stood next to him. "Barry can fix him, if anybody can."

"Is he your medic?"

"Yes." The captain then extended a hand. "Glad you made it in. I'm Captain Huddleston. That's Sparky." The captain pointed at the man with the rifle, still kneeling. "He's our radio operator." The captain raised an eye at Slater's flight helmet. "You might as well take that thing off and stay awhile." Sheepishly, Slater reached up and lifted his helmet from his head.

"What unit are you with?" Huddleston asked.

"We're out of Soc Trang. The Tigers."

"As soon as everything settles down, I'll have Sparky get on the horn and let your command know what's happened."

"Okay...thanks."

Off to the side another American, a staff sergeant with gray wavy hair, attended to Finch's bloodied hand and arm. Kip stood for a moment and watched as Barry directed a pair of RF/PF soldiers to lay a stretcher out to lift Justen onto. Kip then glanced toward the ship. The rotorblades still hadn't come to a complete stop. Surrounding the helicopter, several Vietnamese men and women were watching their containers fill with the escaping fuel. Sparky came and stood by his side. "They'll use the fuel for cooking and anything else they can think of."

"We should have waited for gunship cover," Slater muttered.

"Sorry we couldn't have arranged a better reception for you," the radioman said.

Slater went to the aircraft. Amid the confusion of people, he examined the devastation made on the right side. Blood was everywhere. The right cockpit door had three holes right at thigh level. He spied two holes on the center console. And then he understood why Justen's leg and upper thigh were so bloody. He had been hit there too. He glanced at where Finch had been sitting in his right doorgunner position. The bolt on his machine gun had been shattered. He saw blood smeared over the soundproofing that covered the right side transmission bulkhead. On closer inspection, he saw where a round had penetrated from the bottom of the ship and had etched a grove on the surface of the soundproofing straight up through the cabin ceiling. Had it been an inch farther out, it would have driven right up Finch's spine. The last of the five-member American team approached, a tall stoop-shouldered black master sergeant who introduced himself as Abraham Morgan. "I'm the team NCOIC," he said, extending his hand. "If you like, I'll take you over to quarters and see what we can do to set you guys up. It looks like you all will be sticking around awhile."

In the team house, Justen was laid out on the main room floor. Barry had prepared an IV drip and in a moment had a line run into the underside of Derek's left forearm. "How's he doing?" Slater asked.

Barry, his eyes peering upward through a pair of wire-frame glasses, said, "Right now he's got a weak radial pulse. He's lost quite a bit of blood. I...don't know how he's going to do." As the medic spoke he had his kit out and was kneeling, trying to examine the wound on Derek's left shoulder. Slater felt compelled to wipe the medic's sweat-drenched brow.

Barry said, "I'm trying to figure where the damn bullet went." He breathed deep. "Wherever it went, it can't be good."

Slater turned and went outside. He drew a cigarette and lit it. His hands were shaking. "Jesus...Jesus, what have we done...?" he whispered to himself. He stared at the stone tower of the old French fort less than seventy feet away. He inhaled and then stared at the ground. He walked to the compound gate; looked at the aircraft. All the fuel had drained out and now only a few townspeople were standing around, mostly barefooted RF/PF soldiers with carbines slung over their shoulders, smoking and gawking at the downed ship. In his mind's eye, Slater saw a beached whale. *I could have been in the right seat. I should have been there. And then it would be me lying on the floor.* A shudder passed through him. He remembered Ernest Gann's book *Fate is the Hunter* and thought: *the slightest deviation sets a whole new world in motion. A zig versus a zag. What does it all mean? Why did Justen decide to change seats? Had I been in the right seat, how different would everything be? God...oh God, how close I've come again...*

The screen door to the team house opened. He heard footsteps behind him. The black NCOIC faced him. Morgan said:

"Barry says to tell you that Mr. Justen has a very slight skull fracture. The bullet that hit his helmet grazed his head and wound around until it exited the base of the helmet and entered his upper left shoulder. He's still unconscious. He thinks the bullet is lodged just above his heart. He needs a medevac." The master sergeant rubbed his chin. He shook his head. "Tough break."

"Where would another helicopter land?" said Slater, looking at the courtyard.

"Same place. There's room. We'd snug your ship up closer to that far wall and turn it sideways."

"How would we move it?"

"We'd figure a way."

During the next hour the crew settled in with their hosts. They were shown where they could shower, shave, and rest if they wished. They were taken to the kitchen and introduced to the cook, a wire-thin Vietnamese papa-san who was eager to prepare whatever they wanted, now that his stock had been replenished. Drinking water would be at a premium, but there were soft drinks and beer, enough to last several days. Slater was impressed with the team's living quarters. They had made what space they had comfortable and homey. Huddleston and his men were eager to show it off and equally eager to accommodate their guests. They were also relieved that the ammunition had arrived; plus the downed ship's one good M-60 and other weapons were a nice addition to their arsenal.

Justen's condition weighed heavily on everyone's mind, especially Barry's, who took to his patient like a mother in care of a sick child. Huddleston briefed them on the enemy situation. With a downed helicopter in their midst, the Viet Cong were sure to attack. For them to destroy it completely would make excellent propaganda. Abe Morgan gave them a tour of the defenses and assigned Slater and Conrad a location to go to if Charlie did attack. They were asked to man the flat space atop the fortress with Conrad's machine gun. It was an excellent defensive position with a near round-the-clock field of fire. During the tour, Slater carried his M1 carbine handily. Again, he had admired the shadow he and the rifle made on the ground. He was given extra ammo and another clip to use. They were introduced to the RF/PF company commander, Huddleston's counterpart, a short, slightly built man, very likeable, who smiled and couldn't thank them enough for bringing in the ammunition. He indicated that it would have been nice to get more cannon shells: they were down to their last dozen.

An hour later, Conrad had the damage to the helicopter assessed. The count was thirty-three bullet holes, with more than half that number doing critical damage to the ship, not to mention the ones that had wounded Justen and Finch.

Victor R. Beaver

Fourteen rounds had penetrated the fuel cells alone. Tiger 986 would have to be sling-loaded out—whenever the hell that would be.

In the beginning, Finch's wounds looked far worse than they actually were. Barry sewed five stitches between the thumb and forefinger. Finch's upper right arm had been grazed by a piece of shrapnel after his machine gun had been hit. Giving his wounds a good washing and dousing in alcohol, and covering them with bandages, made him look good as new. For pain, Barry administered morphine. Thus far, no medevac helicopter was slated to come in.

They had just finished supper. The papa-san cook had prepared fried rice and pork and vegetables. Every man was rationed a can of beer. Staff Sergeant Lunsford, the wavy-haired NCO who had initially administered to Finch's wounds, brought out a guitar and began to pluck at the strings. After a moment, he set the guitar aside, grabbed his rifle and went outside. "He's a short-timer," Sparky said. "Twenty days and a wake-up."

Barry had taken his meal in the sleeping quarters. Justen had developed a fever; his temperature was 103 degrees. Slater found the medic sponging the aircraft commander's head with alcohol.

"How's he doing?" Slater asked.

"Not good. Something's going on inside I can't figure out. I've given him another shot of penicillin."

Slater watched as Barry withdrew the thermometer from under Justen's tongue; he read the glass. "It's stable. We'll try to keep it that way."

"Take a break. I'll sit with him a while," Slater said.

"Thanks."

A light over Justen's unconscious form cast a yellowish glow. Bandages covered the back of his head. Camouflage cloth swathed his upper left shoulder, his right leg and right upper thigh. His skin had turned a slate gray. Slater watched Justen's labored breathing. As he sat there, Kip began to reflect on Justen's person. He was clearly the quietest, most remote, most non-communicative man he had ever known. Justen rarely went into the Tiger's Den; when he did, he had only one or two drinks before leaving for his room. There never seemed a break in his routine. Slater knew through conversation with Paul Christian about Derek's half-brother, presumed to be a POW in the U Minh Forest. He thought Justen's stoic manner admirable, but wondered how long the man could hold out waiting for information. Always alone in his thoughts, Justen must have long ago cut himself off from the camaraderie everyone else in the company thrived on and enjoyed...if ever it had developed at all.

* * *

The Sky Soldiers

THE FIRST SERIES OF EXPLOSIONS TERRIFIED the town into instant awareness. Everywhere men and women grabbed a child and scrambled for cover. As they cringed in corners and doorways, the Viet Cong began a methodical pattern of destruction that would by morning leave the town almost in ruins.

Upon hearing the first mortars hit, Slater grabbed his carbine and raced across the space between the team living quarters and the fortress. He plowed through the door and ran up the dusty stairs until he came to his newly assigned combat station at the base of the observation tower. Conrad had arrived a moment before and was laying the belted M-60 ammunition across the chamber of his machine gun. With Slater ready to feed the belted rounds, the two men crouched behind the M-60 and the parapet, the low stonewall that surrounded a good portion of the tower. They scanned southward toward open rice paddies. A full moon shown overhead. For several minutes their eyes searched the silvery darkness but there was no sign of any ground attack, no crouching figures advancing forward, no telltale muzzle flashes.

The explosions made a deafening roar. Fires broke out and began to spread from building to building, until it seemed the entire town was one gigantic inferno. Yellow-black smoke poured skyward. The flames, the smoke, the explosions, the staccato burst of gunfire reminded Slater of the first evening of Tet, an event that now seemed ages ago, yet had happened a little more than a week before. As round after round slammed into the town, Slater no longer believed the Viet Cong only after the downed ship: They seemed bent on the town's complete destruction.

They heard gunfire coming from the north. Slater shifted his position and peeked over the north parapet. Holding tightly to his carbine, he peered into the semi-darkness, through smoke and flame, until he could distinguish between incoming and return gunfire. A fierce firefight was raging between the VC and Popular Force troops stationed at the town's northern defenses. Conrad dismissed the probability of an attack from the south and scooted next to Slater with his M-60. The two men peeked over the wall. "Could it be a diversion?"

"It could be anything, sir," Conrad said. "One thing for sure, this shit's spooky."

Slater nodded. He shifted his gaze to the fires raging not more than seventy meters away. Some of the flames, though, had begun to die down; however the volume of rounds coming in had not abated. He sat back against the wall and felt for the first time since the attack began his heart thumping madly inside his chest. Suddenly, the thought that this might be his last night on Earth struck him cold. As the flames flicked skyward and the sound of gunfire enveloped his brain, he thought how sad it would be for his family to learn of his death. He saw them answering the doorbell and men in uniform introducing themselves—and his mother inviting them in—and then being told the purpose of the visit. He thought of his high school classmates who would hear that he had been killed in battle and he harbored the fanciful notion that they would declare him some kind of hero. He thought of his brother and sister and instantly felt a special protective warmth toward them, as if his demise here in this far-off country necessary to their immediate well-being back home. He decided right then and there that if the Viet Cong did mount an all-out attack, he would fight till his last breath. He squared his shoulders against the wall, looked compassionately at Conrad, Justen's spunky crewchief, and cuffed the side of the man's head.

"You okay, sir?" the chief asked, puzzled.

"I'm fine. Just fine. We're going to give'm hell...aren't we—?"

"You got that straight, sir," Conrad replied, gripping his M-60.

Slater grinned. A wave of calm came over him and for the first time in his tour he felt prepared to die. If it came tonight, so be it. He was ready....

From the very beginning, the explosions had made a faint impression on Derek Justen's mind. He became aware of someone near him, of a caring hand on his forehead that had the soft touch of a woman. Though he felt no pain, he did feel a dull ache somewhere on the backside of his upper chest, a throbbing ache like the beat of a wooden mallet against his back. There were sounds other than the ferocious din of battle, sounds he recognized as voices, frantic in tone and quality. He became dimly aware of being lifted and then carried for what seemed like an inexorably long time. Perhaps he had dozed. The next thing he sensed was darkness and a heavy mustiness. Both sensations conjured the image of heavy, long-flowing curtains, slate gray with a velvet lining. The curtains surrounded an elevated rectangular-shaped box enclosed within a small room. Surrounding him was a stillness like none he had ever known, a stillness so profound that had he imagined his heart without a beat, this would not be still enough. He was six years old.

"Justy...you may go to him," a voice behind him said.

He was just tall enough to see above the box's rim. He stepped closer and could see his father's face; it was the color of dry paste. It was small, too, smaller than he remembered. His father had always been a large man. But with the life force gone, so too was his great stature. The eyes were closed and the lips tightly pursed. The boy turned and looked at his mother. "I thought you said he was in heaven."

"Yes, Justy, he is in heaven, his spirit is in heaven. He is with God...God has called your father to Him."

"To be with God?"

His mother sighed. "Yes, his time had come."

"Where is heaven? Can I go there?"

"Someday, Justy...someday you will go there, you'll be with your father again." His mother put her arm around his shoulder. She regarded the older boy standing next to him. "Jake, you must say good-bye, too," she said. "He was good to you, just like your real father. Now they're both gone."

The two boys went closer. Derek stepped forward and touched his father's forehead. His mouth formed the words "Good-bye, Daddy," then he turned and buried his head in his older half-brother's chest.

The following morning was the funeral. Throughout the service, Derek remained still as stone. He stared at the casket, all the while wondering what his father was dreaming.

As the two boys walked back toward the funeral limousine, Jake said:

"Later, do you want to play with my new airplane, Justy?"

Derek's eyes began to swell with tears. He strained his chest to hold them back. His mother had said he must be a big boy. Big boys don't cry. He wiped at his eyes with his sleeve. "Okay, yeah, I want to play with your new airplane," he managed to say.

After they got home, Jake said, "Someday you'll go to heaven, too, Justy. We both will. Then we'll be with our dads."

Derek was sitting on his bed. He nodded. Then he blurted, "I'm not going to cry." He drew his chest out. "My daddy wouldn't want me to cry. I'm big now. I won't ever cry. And I don't think there's a heaven, *either!*"

"Justy, there is too!"

"No, there isn't."

"You still want to play with my plane?"

Derek frowned. He looked into Jake's eyes. "Yeah, let's play."

The shots that whizzed past put the two men on instant alert. It was a single volley and then all was quiet. Upon hearing the shots, Slater stiffened, turned and prepared to feed ammunition for Conrad. Again, braced for an attack, Conrad quickly trained his gun left, then right. They looked south toward open rice paddy, in the same direction the two cannons were aimed.

"Do you see anything?" Slater asked.

"Negative. Nothing."

Another volley came and the two crewmen ducked their heads below the parapet. Chips of stone breaking from the observation tower pummeled them.

"Now that's close!" said Conrad.

"No shit!"

They heard more gunfire, but the shots were directed elsewhere. They heard a thundering boom, then an explosion, followed closely by another boom. They flattened themselves against the wall.

"What the fuck—?"

"The cannons!" Slater cried. "They're firing the goddamn cannons!"

"Christ!—they could give a guy a little warning!"

Another loud boom, then instant explosion. And another.

Slater sat up and peeked over the top of the wall. He saw the two gun crews, in the small courtyard below, open the breeches and let the second set of spent shell casings eject to the ground. Four shell casings lay smoldering. "Well, they've got eight rounds left. I hope that's all we need between now and when we get the hell out of here—*if we ever do."*

"What were they shooting at?" Conrad asked.

Slater shook his head. "Beats me…empty rice paddy, far as I could tell."

Slater and Conrad stayed primed for action for another ten minutes. But no more shots were fired. Everywhere was quiet.

Two hours passed. At the first hint of dawn, Slater stretched and rubbed his eyes. Conrad shifted and turned. Both men stared at what was left of Tieu Can's downtown section. Most of the buildings, though badly disfigured, were still standing. The fires that had raged during a good part of the night were out. They saw several townspeople rummaging about the smoldering ruins. The two men glanced at the helicopter; miraculously it had survived the night without any further damage.

They heard footsteps. Sergeant Lunsford, the short-timer, appeared before them. "How're you guys doing?"

"Fine," Slater said.

"Papa-san's got coffee brewing."

"Does this mean the fireworks are over?" Conrad asked.

"For a while."

"How long have you been living like this? Has it been this way since Tet?"

"Pretty much, but last night was the worst."

They went below. In the command post, in the largest room in the fortress, they saw Finch curled up asleep in a corner near where Justen lay on the stretcher. Barry, too, was asleep, right next to Justen. "He fought Mr. Justen's fever through the most of the night," Sparky said. Several Vietnamese soldiers were also present, some already awake and moving, others just beginning to come alive. Their commander, Major Tu, haggard-looking, smiled at the two crewmen, turned and began to rouse the rest of his troops.

After several minutes, Captain Huddleston came into the room, followed by Abe Morgan. Each held a cup of coffee.

Huddleston spoke to Slater. "We need to move the chopper over against the far wall."

"Oh?"

"To make room for a medevac."

Slater turned at the sound of Barry stirring awake. The blond-haired medic sat up and checked Justen's pulse. Slater said, "How? Empty, that aircraft weighs close to fifty-four hundred pounds."

By now Barry was standing. "We've got to move it," he stated. "With that bullet in him, I don't think Justen will last through tonight."

The Sky Soldiers

Chapter 41

IT WAS 1000 HOURS. THEY HAD JUST moved the helicopter when Sparky appeared and told Slater he was wanted on the radio. In the team house Slater recognized Leo's voice.

"Where are you?" Kip asked.

"About ten klicks west. Coming your way. What happened?"

"We got the shit shot out of us—bigtime."

"That's what we heard. How's Justen?"

"Not doing good."

"What do you need for me to do?"

"Nothing. Are you assigned to Victor Tango today?"

"Negative. I'm on my way to My Tho. Thought I'd check with you. Are you sure you're doing okay? Want me to shoot the area up for you?"

"Standby and let me check."

Outside, Captain Huddleston was talking to Conrad, who was admiring his handiwork. Justen's crewchief had come up with the idea of using several rounded logs to put underneath the landing gear. They then rolled the helicopter forward, moving the back log to the front when the back of the skids came off the most rearward log. The job took the better part of an hour, but got done with plenty of muscle-power and determination.

"Sir, there's a chopper coming this way. One of my buddies," Slater said. "He wants to know if he can do some firing. Wherever you tell him."

"Is he in a gunship?"

"No, just a slick. Two M-60s, plus a box of grenades."

"Grenades?"

"Yessir."

The captain shrugged. "Okay. Why not. The medevac chopper isn't due for another hour."

Kip relayed to Leo where he could shoot. It would be at the treeline bordering the major canal leading north out of town. It was there they believed the main concentration of Viet Cong was located. "He's sure to stir up a hornet's nest," the gangly Abe Morgan said.

When Leo appeared overhead, Barry and Conrad were beginning preparations for Justen's evacuation. Slater was putting clean dressings on Finch's wounds, while Lundsford and a scantily clad Vietnamese RF/PF soldier, whom the Americans called Kung Fu, were helping the gun crew ready the two cannons. It was in Huddleston's mind to "throw" two 105-rounds into the south treeline a few seconds before Dustoff's arrival.

Leo's M-60s went to work almost immediately. From the ground they could see the smoke from his guns and hear the slight clatter they made, small potatoes against a force of perhaps one hundred men. Then Leo reported receiving fire. He climbed higher and ordered Parker and Vitale, his crewchief and gunner, to shoot until they had thirty percent of their ammunition remaining. Leo announced on the radio each time he dropped a grenade out the window. Slater peered at Morgan's frowning face, knowing that the team sergeant must be wondering Leo's state of mind.

"Well," Leo said over the radio, after he lobbed his last grenade, "we might have stung them a little."

"Thanks, buddy," Kip said.

"We'll stop back by later in the day."

"Roger that."

* * *

MIKE NOLAN HAD HIS MAP UNFOLDED on his lap; he peered ahead. He and Hardin, along with their wing ship, were tracking a one five zero course, paralleling the Basaac River, toward a rendezvous point over a district town called Cau Ke, thirteen kilometers northwest of Tieu Can. "Better give a call, sir," Jeremy Hardin said. "We're about zero five minutes out."

Nolan selected the rendezvous frequency and keyed his mic: "Dustoff Eight One...Dustoff Eight One, Sun Devil Two Six."

"This is Eight One, go."

"Roger, this is Two Six, we are five minutes from Charlie Kilo. What is your ETE?"

"This is Eight One. We're about the same. We are at two thousand five hundred."

"Roger roger...good copy. We're at three thousand. Let us know when you have us in sight."

"That's a rog."

The immediate plan was to pound the position south of Tieu Can, see what kind of return fire they got (they hoped none), then, if all appeared acceptable, they would allow the medevac ship to proceed inbound, low-level along the same treeline Justen followed the day before. Phase I of the plan, that of getting Dustoff Eight One in, seemed plausible. Charlie's head would be down, burrowed in. Phase II, getting Eight One out, was the iffy part. The Viet Cong by then would certainly have improvised. Fifteen minutes before, the extraction team had been in radio contact with Captain Huddleston, who briefed them on the enemy situation, where they could and couldn't shoot, and how long he expected the evacuation to take: less than ten minutes from start to finish. Nolan wrote everything down; then he and Hardin cooked up the plan and briefed their wing ship.

The Sky Soldiers

Nolan took down the TSU and readied the sighting unit for firing. It was his first front-seat flight since before the eve of Tet. During the start sequence, he reviewed the arming switches for firing. Major Elroy, true to his word, had him practically in Captain Dane's hip pocket before the latter's departure for the States. There was so much more to the S-3 (operations) job than met the common eye and Nolan was grateful for the chance to spend as much time as he could with Dane.

"Sun Devil Two Six, this is Dustoff Eight One. I've got a visual on you."

"Roger. Same-same with you."

"Understand our approach will be from the west?"

"Affirmative," Hardin answered. "We've been in contact with Perking Ambush Six. They're ready for the extraction."

"Roger that."

As the two Cobras thrummed by overhead, the medevac ship banked hard right to follow. The left-seat pilot turned his head and said:

"You guys ready in the back?"

Vaughn, Dustoff Eight One's medic, a recent transfer from a ground unit up north, keyed his intercom: "Ready, sir, except..."

"Except what?"

"Do you think we'll be back before one o'clock? I'm supposed to catch that courier flight to Saigon. You know...to go on my Rn'R."

"That shouldn't be a problem."

"Where are you going?" asked the right-seat pilot.

Waverly, the crewchief, answered for him: "Can you believe, sir, he's going to Hawaii, to get married—"

"Married. How old are you, Vaughn?"

"Almost twenty, sir."

A pair of chuckles sounded from the cockpit seats. "Is there any way we can talk you out of it?"

"No way, sir. My girl—Cindy's her name—we've known each other since before we could walk. Her father has the farm right next to ours."

A sigh. "Even in the midst of this bullshit, life does go on. Congratulations. We wish you luck."

"Thank you, sir."

From their vantage point on top the fortress Slater, Huddleston, and Sparky, who was manning the portable radio, watched as the two Cobras made their initial runs on the south treeline. They dove and fired and the resulting shock waves made them shiver. Gray smoke blossomed out and upward. Traces of the smoke drifted toward them and their eyes watered from the cordite carried in the air. During the softening-up process neither ship reported receiving return fire, nor did they see anything during their pullouts that Charlie was massed everywhere below.

"Eight One, this is Two Six, give us a minute now to get into position. Go ahead and start your descent."

"This is Eight One, that's a rog."

For a full minute the radios were silent. The three men atop the fortress watched as the two Cobras now positioned themselves to the west, above the medevac helicopter. Then, very faintly, they heard:

"Dustoff Eight...go ah...and proceed inbound."

"This...Eight One, roger. We...about...sec...out."

Sparky adjusted the radio, while Huddleston, standing next to Kip, peered through a set of binoculars at the south treeline. The captain shook his head. "Something's not right," he said, lowering the glasses.

"What's the matter?"

The team OIC lifted the glasses again. "Charlie should have returned some kind of fire, just for shits and grins, especially on the wing ship. I don't think the command post is where it was when you guys came in."

"Do you think we should call off the extraction?" Slater said.

Huddleston lowered the glasses. He nodded. "Yeah...I think so." Huddleston took the handset from Sparky. "Dustoff Eight One, Perking Ambush Six. Over."

There was no answer. Huddleston tried again. Still no answer. Slater took a sudden deep breath. Sparky checked the radio again. "Damnit."

"What's the matter?"

"I think the battery just went tits up. Hold on, I'll be right back."

"Hurry, for crissake."

To his right, Slater could now hear the sound of the medevac ship, its rotor-blades wop-wopping loudly in the hollow cluster of the Banyan trees directly to their southwest; the two Cobras thrumming overhead added to the clatter. It was then that Slater wished to God Almighty, when they so sorely needed the element of surprise, that a damn helicopter didn't sound like a Saturday-afternoon stampede down the main street of some cowpoke town. Then he heard machine-gun fire. In that instant, Sparky appeared in the doorway out of breath, carrying a fresh battery. He grabbed at the radio, but Huddleston held him off. Their ears perked, they heard very faintly through the dying radio:

"We're hit—we're...ta...hits...!"

With their attention riveted to the right, they saw, through the trees, Dustoff Eight One bank hard right and then...*KAWHUMMP!...KAWHUMMP!*...as the lead Cobra fired. "Jesus Christ! What the hell's going on—?" Slater yelled.

"*Damnit!* I knew it," Huddleston cried. "Charlie changed his location during the night—"

The Sky Soldiers

The medic was slumped forward, blood pumping in gushes from his carotid artery. Horrified, Waverly tried to stop the bleeding but couldn't. "Vaughn! Vaughn! Oh God…no…no…help me—*help me!*"

The ship was now in a hard climb. "You gotta hurry, sir—" Waverly cried to the two pilots up front.

"We're trying—we're trying!"

Waverly's hands were awash in blood; his fatigues were covered by it, his face smeared with it. The crewchief tried to reposition himself, but his hands slipped on the floor's blood-slick surface. The whole left side of Vaughn's neck was a gnarled mass of flesh; it felt to Waverly like he was handling a piece of raw meat. After several more minutes of fruitless effort, Waverly saw Vaughn's eyes glaze over, taking on a blank look. "Hurry, sir—please hurry!"

The ship began to shake. The wind whistled past like ninety.

The left-seat pilot looked back. "Keep trying!"

"I-I think he's gone…!"

"Damnit! You can't stop trying!"

* * *

BARRY WAS SPONGING JUSTEN'S FOREHEAD when Slater entered the high-ceilinged command-post room. The aircraft commander's face was even gaunter than the last time he had seen him, less than an hour before. At that time the medic had given Derek another shot of penicillin. "I'm out of penicillin," Barry had told him.

Slater kneeled by Barry's side. "What's his temperature now?"

"I've got it down to a hundred and two."

"I think you're doing a good job."

Barry said, "Not good enough."

Slater glanced at his watch. It was after seven. Two hours ago, just before dusk, they had moved the command post back into the fortress. Sparky had set the radio up in the corner nearest the door, while Barry had placed Derek in the opposite corner, away from the flow of foot traffic. In another corner, Morgan and Huddleston discussed the diminishing stock of ammunition. Conrad ran a rag over his M-60, applying oil around the cocking mechanism as he did. Finch and Lundsford had a game of checkers going at a small table next to a kerosene lantern that supplied a feeble light throughout the room. Once in a while the flame flickered, causing shadows to dance an exotic rhythm on the walls. Slater looked around him. He was among armed and haggard men held captive inside a cave-like room, while the enemy roamed outside, waiting for the right moment to attack. The scene reminded him of the movie *El Dorado*, starring John Wayne and Robert Mitchum. And then he remembered the theme song, lyrics he must have listened to thirty times during the long flight to Vietnam, over the jetliner's multi-channel music and entertainment system:

> *"Through sunshine and shadow*
> *from darkness till noon...*
> *Over mountains that reach*
> *from the sky to the moon*
> *A man with a dream that will never*
> *let go, keeps searching*
> *To find El Dorado..."*

Slater felt someone touch his shoulder. He had been sitting, leaning against the wall next to Justen's prone body, his legs up, his head against his knees. He looked up. Barry said, "Those cots on the second level are okay to use. Take your crewchief with you. You both look bushed."

Slater nodded then yawned. "Yeah, that sounds pretty good. What about you? When do you sleep?"

"I can sleep standing up." Barry leaned against the wall and slid down. "I was a med-student once."

"You didn't finish?"

"No, but not because I didn't want to," Barry said, drawing a deep breath. "Midway through school I decided to take a break, so I dropped out for a semester. When I did, Uncle Sam sent me a draft notice. I didn't fight it. I enlisted so I could be guaranteed a slot as a medic. That was easy. They needed medics worse than they needed doctors. I spent my first tour with the First Cav Division, when they first came over in 'Sixty-five. I was in the Ia Drang battle." Barry's eyes took on a distant look.

Slater had heard about the 1st Cavalry Division's first blood bath. "It was that bad, huh?"

Barry's eyes remained fixed. "Worse than bad. We were slaughtered like sheep. Men were dying in my arms. There were too many to take care of at one time. By morning, myself and two other guys were all that was left of an entire company not hurt. The rest were either dead or dying. I had run out of first-aid supplies within twenty minutes of the first shots fired."

Abruptly, Barry stood. "Sir, there's been something—Ah, forget it. Go get some sleep. I guarantee you'll know the minute anything happens."

An hour later, unable to sleep, Slater got up and went outside. He found Barry leaning against the fortress wall, his head hung down, a cigarette dangling limp between his lips. Slater said, "You...okay?"

Slowly, Barry looked up. It was then that Slater smelled the distinct odor of burning hay, the scent of marijuana.

The Sky Soldiers

Barry took the smoldering joint from between his lips and offered it to him. Slater said, "Under more favorable circumstances I might partake, but now doesn't seem the right time."

Barry nodded. "I agree. But sometimes I do this to round off the edges. Morgan and Lundsford have their booze. I've got this."

"A while ago you wanted to tell me something. What was it?"

"Nothing. It's not important." Barry's eyes had a glazed-over look.

"Go ahead. I want to know."

"Okay. The truth?" Barry's voice sounded steady.

"Yes."

"With all due respect, sir," the medic began, "I get the impression that this war at one time...was not living up to your expectations. I suspect now it is. I've seen the way you carry your carbine. When the sun is just right, you like to see your shadow against the ground. You admire what you see. So far...am I right?"

Embarrassed, Slater said, "Pretty much."

"I see you keeping a journal. Are you into writing?"

"I want to write a book someday."

"This war then is...grist for the mill?"

Slater cracked a slight smile. "You could say that."

"Try this on for size then." Barry's voice was low and even. "Mr. Justen isn't going to make it."

"What do you mean?"

"I mean, if we don't get him out of here soon, he's going to die. That bullet—it's got to be taken out."

Slater asked, "Could you operate?"

"I'd kill him if I did. Besides, he wouldn't survive post-op. He needs a real surgeon and a hospital."

"But the medevac tried to get in—"

"I know. It was too bad what happened."

"So what do you suggest?"

"Your friend, the pilot who likes to shoot...?"

"Leo?"

"He's got guts. I've already talked to Huddleston. With four gunships as cover, I'll bet he could make it in—and out."

"You think so, huh?"

"But would he do it?" Barry said.

"I-I wouldn't ask him..."

"Then I will—"

Slater peered deep into Barry's bloodshot eyes. He felt the muscles in his back rippling up and down his spine. His pupils narrowed. Leo would do anything I asked, he thought, even die to save me, or Justen, or any pilot or crewmember of the 121st. It was the way he, all of them, from earliest childhood, had been programmed, even trained: that in any war no American (or group of U.S. servicemen) should be left to survive or die alone. But it would bear heavily on his conscience if he asked Leo now to risk his life to attempt a rescue that could only end in failure. He would live and Leo would be dead, and another name would be added to an already long list of men fighting in a war that no one had, as yet, been able to clearly define. Justen, on the verge of death, might die before night's end. And the shame of his dying would be beyond words—the man had volunteered twice to remain near a brother who may or may not be a POW in the U Minh. Disgustedly, Slater shook his head. The war, he had now come to believe, was like a vicious cancer, feeding voraciously, needing ever more bodies and dismembered limbs to grow and keep living. He gritted his teeth and spoke: "Goddamn you to hell…"

Chapter 42

THE FIRST EXPLOSIONS SHOCKED THEM out of a deep sleep. Slater groped in the darkness for his carbine and felt Conrad scrambling out of his cot. "Quick—to the roof!"

The two men jostled each other going up the narrow staircase. Once on top, the chief positioned his M-60, aiming it south; Kip readied the ammunition.

*CRRUMMP!....CRRUMMP!...*Small chunks of steel zinged past; some chipped the tower wall directly above their heads. "It looks like they're trying for the ship—"

The shelling increased. Between explosions they heard machine-gun fire coming from somewhere north of the compound. Tracers streaked overhead and they found themselves crouched below the parapet. Another burst of gunfire. This time chips of stone fell down around them. The two men flattened themselves against the roof floor, which was covered with a fine powdery dust; immediately they started a paroxysm of coughing. There were more flashes, more explosions.

Then the explosions ceased. In its place there came an increase in the rattle of rifle- and machine-gun fire, the bullets zinging nearby. Slater crawled to the north parapet. He eased the top of his head above the wall and looked quickly in the direction he heard shots. Several rounds slashed past his head off to his left. He ducked. "Man, this infantry shit's for the birds!"

Hunkered low, Conrad sidled next to him. "Do you think this is it?"

"Hell—I thought two nights ago was it."

They heard a loud voice coming from below the south wall of the fortress, sharp commands given in Vietnamese. Next they heard the boom of one of the howitzers; the second cannon discharged a second later. Barely able to hear himself think, Slater shouted to Conrad: "What the hell are they shooting at? That makes six friggin' shells left!" They knew immediately that the rounds had landed in the southern rice fields.

"The assholes," Conrad admonished. "They're gooks, dinks, slopes. They do it because they're stupid—!"

Slater cringed. Conrad sounded so much like Leo it was frightening. After several more minutes of seemingly random firing, quiet calm came over the compound. Slater and Conrad crept back to the south wall and peered toward open paddies. An illumination round, fired from a mortar tube east of the compound a few seconds before, was making a quick descent to earth. Conrad's hands readied his M-60. Then, wide-eyed, the two men stared at three dark forms running from left to right a hundred meters to their front.

"Could that be Charlie...?"

"That's a big ten four!" Conrad immediately began firing. Tracers skipped outward like so many racing fireflies. The noise of the gun coupled with the muzzle flashes blanked their view of the targets. Conrad paused for a second to get his bearings, then resumed firing, keeping the hammer down. After a moment, the barrel took on a dusky glow. In another second the light from the flare was gone.

"Stop!" Slater called.

Conrad halted firing. "Why?—what's the matter?"

"The barrel. Look, it's glowing!"

"Jesus…no shit. Hey—did we get them?"

"I don't know. It's too dark to tell."

They perceived no movement. Everywhere was quiet. "I'll bet we got them." Conrad said, his expression eager, smug, determined. *You sonsabitches…show your asses again and I'll blow your shit to Kingdom Come!*

The two men scanned to their front for several minutes, each wishing to see once more this elusive foe upon which they so desperately wanted to vent their anger. In a moment, Slater relaxed. He slapped the little hard-muscled crewchief on the back. "I'll bet you got them. We'll see when morning comes."

* * *

JOURNAL ENTRY, 9 FEBRUARY 1968, Tieu Can

1400 hours. Leo came by an hour ago. His doorgunners had extra ammunition, so they really gave Charlie hell. Leo tossed out five grenades. If I asked, he'd be in here, even without gunship cover.

Conrad and I blasted away at three human forms last night. But this morning, looking through binoculars at where they might—should—have fallen, we saw nothing. Was it our imaginations?

At noon, right after lunch, while most of us had laid down somewhere to nap, Charlie decided to rattle our cages with gunfire. The sounds this time came from the southeast. Conrad and I scrambled for the fortress roof, where I am right now writing this. The shooting persisted for several minutes, then tapered off; finally it ceased.

The lighting was dim. At first he sensed only vague impressions; human shapes, high walls, voices sometimes near, sometimes far away; he sensed dampness, hot and cold, a burning sensation. He felt his chest on fire, his lungs pained and inflamed; his head throbbed. As he laid there, he sensed his body heavy, lead-like. At one point he tried to open his eyes, but his eyelids felt like they were glued shut. His mouth felt parched, his lips dry, rough, cracked. He was thirsty, dreadfully thirsty. He went in and out of delirium, watching the same scene play again and again in his mind. He no longer had any concept of time. How long had he been there? Minutes?...Hours?...Days? ...Weeks? When finally he did open his eyes, everything was a blur, as though he was enveloped in a haze, a faint blue haze. He thought he heard a voice, a woman's voice, soft and gentle and warm. And then a cry erupted from his parched lips. *"Val...No...no...you can't quit. You can't give up—!"*

Justen's sudden outcry startled them awake. Barry, seated nearby, reached over and gently eased the wounded pilot back down. Slater, his skin crawling with gooseflesh, stared wide-eyed at Derek's emaciated figure. Huddleston approached. "How's it going?"

"He's hallucinating," Barry said. "A bad, bad sign." The medic turned; he looked up at Slater.

"What's his temperature?" Kip asked.

"A hundred four point five. And I've run completely out of alcohol."

Slater stared for a moment at Justen's prostrate form. Derek's gaunt face had the color of death. Kip turned; he went and stood over his space on the floor by the wall. They had received a report less than an hour ago that a battalion of VC was amassing for an attack. The word had come from province headquarters. Slater, running a hand over his growth of whiskers, had asked Captain Huddleston: "How do they know things like that?"

The senior district advisor shook his head. "We've heard this before and there was nothing. This time...well you just never know. All we can do is wait."

Each man retreated into his own thoughts.

Slater, having not had a decent night's sleep since the Tet offensive began, now leaned against the bare, damp wall. He slid slowly downward until he sat on the floor. He held the carbine upright between his legs, his fingers joined around the barrel. He fixed his stare at the top of the barrel, at the raised sight. After a moment, he focused his gaze on the far wall, at the dancing shadows of men and combat equipment made by the flickering light of the lantern. He put his head down until his chin touched his chest. He thought of Justen, on the verge of death.

> *"The winds become bitter,*
> *the sky turns to gray.*
> *His body grows weary,*
> *he can't find his way...*
> *But he'll never turn back though*
> *he's lost in the snow,*
> *For he has to find El Dorado..."*

In the beginning, yes, it was all a game, action, adventure, and even an element of romance. But it had worn thin. Their days had been spiked by sudden bursts of gunfire—innocuous yet nerve-wracking gunfire; their nights, by explosions that had them clawing the walls, scrambling for cover, cowering in corners. He had said his peace so many times he was certain God was beginning to turn a deaf ear. He had filled his journal with nonsensical drivel, yearnings for love, life, for peace and home and happiness...

* * *

EYES WATCHED AS THE THREE MEN went slowly by. Each man carried a weapon and several bandoleers of ammunition, and each glanced back and forth between the faces of the townspeople and the way ahead. Every few yards they had to side-step large chunks of building, some of the pieces charred by the fires. As they went along, Slater gaped at portions of buildings where shrapnel had penetrated walls and doors and had shattered windows. They met an old, whisker-faced man hobbling toward them; they stepped aside and let him pass between them. A small group of children paralleled their course, making their way along the sidewalk on the other side of the pockmarked street. Two RF/PF soldiers, seated at a sidewalk café, tipped their heads and smiled in recognition at Huddleston and Lunsford as they went by. Huddleston nodded courteously; Lunsford's face remained passive. He had seventeen days to go before his scheduled departure back to the United States—back to "the World."

They came to the end of the street and found themselves behind a partially destroyed wall. Huddleston set his rifle aside and took his binoculars and looked in the direction of the southern canal. Lunsford, carrying the "blooper," an M-79 grenade-launcher, broke open the chamber and loaded a shell. He leaned it against his hip, pointed in the direction of the canal.

Huddleston lowered the glasses. He handed them to Slater. "You want to take a look?"

"Sure." Slater placed his carbine against the wall next to Huddleston's. Through the glasses he saw the brown water of the canal, the clusters of banana trees along the bank, the coconut palms, a mass of thick low vegetation, and several thatched huts, abandoned by all outward signs. A faint trace of smoke, however, drifted upward on the backside of the huts. Slater squinted a little longer to confirm it. "I see smoke," he declared, lowering the glasses.

Huddleston took the glasses. "Probably a cooking fire." He then nodded to Lunsford, who lifted the blooper, judged the range to the huts to be about two hundred fifty meters, and adjusted the sight. The sergeant next placed the butt of the weapon close to this right shoulder and took aim. Huddleston raised the glasses. "Fire." Lunsford discharged the weapon, a quick kickback into his shoulder. The sound it made was a dull *thunk!* a flat sound against the backdrop of buildings around them.

The Sky Soldiers

A puff of gray smoke. The noise from the explosion hit them a second later. Huddleston lowered the glasses. "Give yourself another twenty-five meters," he said to Lunsford.

Lunsford quickly adjusted the sight. He loaded, aimed and fired again. Huddleston studied the situation for a moment. He lowered the glasses. "Good shot. Now, let's sit back and see what we stir up."

Slater pulled a pack of cigarettes out, took one and lit it. The decision to reconnoiter the south canal came after they discovered no trace of the enemy near the Banyan trees southwest of the compound, where the gunfire had come from the day before, which broke off the medevac attempt. (They had also learned yesterday that the two Cobras had escorted Dustoff Eight One back to Soc Trang, where the medic was pronounced DOA, dead on arrival.) Huddleston had asked Slater if he wanted to go along; Slater decided quickly that he did. He got his carbine, making sure he was amply stocked with ammunition, and was given Barry's steel helmet to wear. It was right after three o'clock when they left the compound. As they went through the compound's large wooden gate, Slater felt an unfamiliar knot deep in the pit of his stomach. This would be his first ever infantry-like combat patrol. He was in unfamiliar territory and knew it. But whatever lay ahead he also knew he could count on Huddleston or Lunsford to direct his actions to the benefit of the patrol.

They waited three minutes. Huddleston no longer saw any smoke drifting upward. What he did see was one man in a sampan, hugging the east bank, trying to slip away. "We stirred up a listening post. We've got a man on the run—in a sampan."

Quickly Lunsford raised the blooper, aimed in the general direction of the huts, and fired. He loaded again and stood ready for further instructions. "Lift it up and move slightly right," Huddleston told him.

Lunsford adjusted his aim and fired again. Huddleston had his glasses raised. The explosion this time caused the target to disappear. "I think you got him," Huddleston said, still looking through the binoculars. The smoke took a moment to clear. "I don't see anything."

Slater asked to have a look. The captain handed him the binoculars. Kip saw movement south of the huts, on the canal. It was the sampan. Straining harder to see, Kip saw someone groping the sides of the narrow boat, struggling to get in. The small canoe-like boat jostled. "Sir, have a look," he said, handing the binoculars back to Huddleston. "I see someone—he's still alive."

Looking, Huddleston nodded. He motioned for Lunsford to fire again. Even without the glasses, Slater saw the round make a direct hit. Huddleston described what he saw. "The sampan is upside down...It's now tilted upward...It's sinking..."

The three men grinned at each other. Huddleston and Slater picked up their rifles. They began to move back toward the compound.

Abe Morgan, the team NCOIC, met them as they came through the compound gate. The black master sergeant handed his team leader a piece of paper. Huddleston read the decoded message.

He turned to Slater. "It's from our headquarters. Helicopters coming in tomorrow at around ten hundred hours. Going to try and get the whole lot of you out. I hope it's not too late for Mr. Justen."

Lunsford spoke up. "Sir, do you think—"

Huddleston waved him short. "You're better off waiting until most of this shit blows over." The captain regarded Lunsford sympathetically. "Besides, why risk it this close to DEROS? When the time is right, we'll get you on a chopper—don't worry."

Lunsford slacked his shoulders. "Yessir..."

* * *

HE HAD BEEN SITTING AT THE TABLE for the past half-hour, watching her. She wore a white blouse and blue peasant skirt, well washed and plain. Her brown feet were adorned by sandals with straps that wrapped around a pair of fine-sculptured legs. It was an hour past dusk. *Well, it's now or never. Nothing ventured...Nothing gained.*

He stood. Her dark eyes widened as he approached from across the small café. "May I sit down?" She hesitated, then nodded. "My name is Keith," he said, pulling out the chair.

She replied with marked hesitance. "I am...Avayla."

He offered his hand. Again she hesitated. She glanced toward the café entrance. Before her was a glass of water and an empty soup bowl. She lifted the glass and took a drink.

"Are you expecting someone?" he asked.

"Perhaps...my father."

The first disconsolate chord. "Your father?...Do you live around here?"

"No."

"Visiting?"

"No."

"Are you on vacation?"

"We sell handmade jewelry," she countered. "My father is asleep. We have a small camper. He snores very loudly. And he drinks...much too much wine."

He nodded. "I see..."

"Tomorrow we are going north," she added. "My father says Buena Vista and Leadville. From there we might go to Glenwood Springs. He says if we get that far, we will come back by way of Grand Junction through Pueblo."

"Making the rounds, are you?"

"Making...the rounds?" Her face held a puzzled look.

"You know, going from place to place..."

She nodded. "Oh, yes, that is what we are doing, 'making the rounds.'"

"Are you sure you don't mind me sitting here? I can go if you like."

Her mouth twitched; then her eyes softened. "No...I don't mind. Please...stay."

"Where are you from?"

"Kansas."

"Hey, that's where I'm from. Where at in Kansas?"

"It is a place near Wichita...You have heard of El Dorado?"

"Oh yeah, I'm not far from you. I was born and raised in Hutchinson. What a coincidence."

"I know that word...'coincidence.' Doesn't it mean that...that we are from nearly the same place...and here we are together...far from that place?"

He smiled. "Yes, that's it exactly." And then he paused, groping for something further to say. After a moment: "Do you travel with your father often?"

"No...this year is the first. It is a gift, a graduation present. When I go back home, I start work."

"Oh? Doing what?"

"My uncle owns a restaurant. I'm to be a hostess."

"What about college?"

"There is no money."

"Yeah, I hear that." He asked a few more questions. He learned that she had just turned eighteen, that she had four brothers and four sisters, and that she was the second oldest sibling. She mentioned that she had just completed high school the week before and for a graduation present was invited to go on this trip. She had never been away from home. He learned more about her father, about his jewelry-making business, about his drinking, where their camper was parked (on the edge of town, about three blocks away). Her father, she told him, liked to drink cheap wine. "My uncle..." she said, "the one with the restaurant...he has big plans for me."

"Big plans? Like what?" Her large, doe-like eyes enthralled him.

"He wants to open another restaurant. At that one, I will be a waitress. I will make good tips."

"That's great." Eyes. Windows to the soul. And then he began to talk about himself. He told her he was going into his second year of college, about his ambitions to write, how he wanted to live in a small mountain town, perhaps be the editor of a weekly newspaper. He also mentioned how he wanted to build a log cabin equipped with a pot-bellied stove. It would have several shelves with lots of books. He said he would have a dog, perhaps a Border collie or German shepherd, for a companion.

"And what about a woman?" she said.

Victor R. Beaver

"Oh, yeah, that too." He explained how he imagined finding just the right woman, someone quiet who loved to read. He wanted someone who didn't mind being alone in nature, who was strong and independent, but who also had a softness to her, someone who would care about him as he would care about her. He tried to have that faraway look as he spoke, yet he also wanted to gaze into her eyes to discern her reaction. When he did manage to notice how she took in what he was saying, he saw an eagerness for him to continue, perhaps a sign that she might be willing to share his dream. He asked:

"Back home, do you have a boyfriend?"

She tilted her head. "Maybe..."

"Maybe? Isn't it either yes or no?"

She hesitated, "Perhaps..."

She took his wrist and looked at his watch. "It is growing late. I must go."

"Would you like for me to walk you to your camper?"

She shook her head. "Oh no...you can't."

"Why not? I won't harm you...really, I won't."

"It's my father. If he should see us."

"It sounds to me, from what you've said, that he's out for the night."

"But if he was to wake up."

"I doubt that he will. All that wine...?"

When she stood, he stood too. She looked at him, smiled. She began moving toward the door and the cash register. She paid her ticket. He then followed her out into the cool clear night.

They walked along the sidewalk, westward, toward the craggy range of snow-capped peaks that seemed but a short distance away. The range was outlined clearly, a ragged definition against the night sky. "Do you know what it means, 'Sangre de Cristo?'" she asked.

"No...I don't."

"It is Spanish meaning 'Blood of Christ.' I went to the library today. There is a story about a priest who was killed by Indians. Apparently, his dying words were meant to describe the way the snow drapes down the mountain sides, when the sun is just right, as if they were bleeding."

He followed the outline of her hand. "Yeah...come to think of it, even as dark as it is, it does look like they're 'bleeding.'"

She said, "I think they are a most beautiful mountain range."

He nodded agreement, then saw that she was shivering. He took off his jacket and draped it over her shoulders. As they continued walking, she pointed toward her father's camper, nothing more than a dark shape with the mountain range as a backdrop. She folded her arms and moved closer to him. He smelled her scent; it was of the earth, slightly pungent; she also smelled of wood smoke; he remembered that she had told him in the café that when they cooked, it was over a campfire. They continued past an old stone building that had once been the jail.

He saw the iron bars that guarded the windows. The little building seemed no larger than a postage stamp. Once at the edge of town, they looked up. Overhead they saw the band of light that was the Milky Way; and the stars, thousands of them, like diamonds adorning a black-blue canvas. Both stood very still.

"Do you know that you are very beautiful?" he said.

"I am?"

"Yes, very much so."

"Well, then, you are very handsome."

He smiled. "Thanks, I needed that."

"But you are."

"Maybe...I don't know."

"And...do you have a girlfriend in Kansas?"

"There are a couple of girls I date," he said. Then he added: "But nothing serious."

"You are not in love with them?"

He shook his head. "Oh no, it's nothing like that."

"I have never been in love," she said.

He nodded. "You're young...that's—"

"I have never made love...either." She said this last with a sort of profound bluntness, which caught him off guard.

"I see. Yes, well...that's interesting—"

"Didn't you say you were staying in a cabin?"

He nodded. "Yes...we went right past it. You can see it from here." He shifted and pointed.

She turned and looked toward it. He remained rooted in place. His heart raced. She extended her hand. "Come, show me how you live."

They started walking. "What about your father?"

"Like you said, he won't waken till morning. Besides, soon enough I will be listening to his snoring. To me he sounds like an old bear."

They were in front of the door. He unlocked it and went in. Slowly, she entered behind him.

It was a one-room cabin barely big enough for two people to turn around in. It was furnished with a bed, a nightstand and lamp, and a small dresser. The only other source of light was a 40-watt bulb that hung down from a wooden ceiling and cast a yellowish glow. There were two tiny add-ons side-by-side: one that was the bathroom, the other the kitchen. Overall, it was very cozy and warm.

She removed his jacket from her shoulders and laid it on the bed. He remained block-still as she went and peeked into the bathroom; she then ventured to the enclave that was the kitchen, within which was a combination appliance: sink, stove, and refrigerator. The nightstand, he told her, doubled as the kitchen table. She went and looked behind a curtained window, then came to the bed and placed the palm of her hand flat against its heavily quilted softness. Next, she examined the books he had been reading, the ones placed on the floor by the bed. She picked up the top one and looked at the cover. "What is this?...'The Fountainhead.'"

"It's about an architect, someone who wishes to build his own way. Mostly, it's about integrity."

"'Integrity?'"

"The word means an adherence to a code of moral, artistic, or other values. This is my fourth reading of it."

"You have read this book four times—?"

"When I like a book, or the message it gives me, I read it more than once."

She smiled. "'Integrity'...I like that word."

"So do I."

Her eyes widened. "What time is it?"

He checked his watch. "Nearly ten o'clock."

"Ayiee, mama mia—*I have to go!*" She bolted for the door. Before he knew it, she had it open and was gone, out into the black-blue night. He caught a glimpse of her figure running in the direction of her father's camper. "Good night," he called after her. She turned and waved.

He sighed and closed the door. He sat on the edge of the bed and stared at the floor. The room still held her scent. An instant later, he saw in his mind's eye reaching out and taking her and gently kissing her soft, full lips. And then leaning her back on the bed and lying next to her. He had no idea how long he sat there with the image of holding her and caressing her, but he soon grew weary and he laid back still clothed on the bed and let his mind drift over what it might have been like to have made love to her.

After a while he heard a soft rapping at the door. Feeling drowsy, he sat up and went to the door and opened it. He stepped back as Avayla entered. She closed the door behind her, making certain it was locked. She went to the window and smoothed the curtain fast against it. She then sat on the edge of the bed. She invited him to sit next to her. "Are you afraid?" she asked.

"I-I don't know."

"I am not afraid."

She took his right hand and put it on the top button of her blouse. He noted that his hand, his whole body, was trembling. He fumbled with the buttons and she helped him. She was wearing a very thin bra and when he undid the clasp, her lovely, well-developed breasts burst forth like a pair of roses to sunlight. Next she helped him with his shirt. His chest exposed, she smoothed her hand over his skin and whispered, "You are so very very white..."

"Avayla...please."

She stopped. "Yes?"

"But you're a—"

"Virgin...So?" She stood and slowly began to lower her skirt.

"But...why me?"

With her skirt on the floor at her feet, she placed her hands on her hips and canted her head. He drank in the sight of her mons pubis, evident through white silken panties; he breathed deep. He noticed her breasts rising and falling rhythmically. She said:

"Because you are a kind person, a gentle person. You are without bravado and because afterwards I will never see you again. Besides, there is no man back home that I want to have me for the first time. Where I live, in my culture, men brag of conquests, of machismo, of scoring...A woman does not have a chance for love, of being made love to, for the simple sake of love. She has no chance to offer her flower like a precious gift."

His eyes widened. "I see..."

She dropped her arms; she moved closer to him. "You don't...want...this gift?"

"Oh yes...yes, I do...Avayla, you are so lovely...so very very lovely..."

> *"My daddy once told me what*
> *a man ought to be...*
> *There is much more to life*
> *than the things we can see...*
> *And the godliest mortal you*
> *ever will know...is the*
> *one with the dream of*
> *El Dorado..."*

"Mr. Slater..."

He opened his eyes. "Yes...?"

Conrad's face looked anxious. "It's Mr. Justen. He's awake. He's asking for you."

Chapter 43

SLATER PONDERED JUSTEN'S EMACIATED form. The man looked feeble, delicate, as if the slightest blow could disintegrate him. His skin appeared pithy; his lips were cracked and dry. If he didn't know any better, Kip would say Derek was being deliberately starved to death: he had the appearance of a concentration camp victim.

Half dazed, his eyes encircled by dark rings, Justen peered back. Groping for Slater's hand, he tried to sit up. Then he tried to speak, but out of his mouth there came only silence. Slater leaned closer. After a moment of intense effort, Justen relaxed and closed his eyes; he had suddenly lost all compulsion to talk. Kip looked toward Barry. The medic shook his head, motioning for Slater to join him off to the side.

Barry said, "I can't believe he's still alive. Any other man would have been long dead by now."

"Can he make it till tomorrow?"

"I don't know. This past half-hour is the first time he's shown any real signs of consciousness."

Slater pondered his next question. "If worse came to worse, could you operate?"

"I don't know—perhaps. But damnit, I'd have to be certain he would die otherwise."

"Well, is he or is he not going to die if we don't get him out of here?"

Barry glanced toward the wounded man. He still felt strongly that the bullet was lodged close to Justen's heart. Without X-rays, though, he couldn't be certain. He knew that if he were to go digging around without proper surgical tools, without anesthesia, without a supply of blood, he could very well finish what the bullet was intended to do in the first place: Kill him. "This is ludicrous. I wouldn't have a clue what I was doing—hacking around inside him. He'd be better off waiting it out, no matter how long it took. Christ. If I operated, for sure he would die. Don't you see—?"

Slater felt a strain across his chest. "You listen to me," he hissed; "you've got to be ready to do something—*anything*. The other night you wanted to risk my friend's life to get Justen out. And believe me, Leo would do it. Any of us would. So what are you afraid of? Your life isn't the one hanging on the line."

"You don't understand," said Barry. "I could kill him—"

"Isn't he sentenced to certain death anyway?"

The medic stood braced against the wall. He peered long into Slater's eyes. He thought of his father. The man had been a surgeon, a great one, and *they* destroyed him. They regarded him as God—thought he could do anything—save anybody—that his utterances were unquestionably right—that he was omnis-

The Sky Soldiers

cient, infallible. "Doctors save and they destroy," his father had told him the day he decided to follow in the man's footsteps and go to medical school. "And they pray that they save or heal more than they destroy."

Barry's face was pale, his shoulders folded inward. "Okay, if I have to, I'll try it. But I promise you nothing."

Slater said, "I only ask that you do your best. That's all Justen would ask."

* * *

IT WAS A LITTLE AFTER 2200. THE COMMAND post within the fortress was unusually packed. Major Tu had several of his men around him, near the radio set, awaiting word from the listening posts for the first signs of attack. Kung Fu, Major Tu's all around gopher, always wearing a disarming smile and one of the few Vietnamese who spoke passably good English, stood next to Finch. "Finch, you hand... is much betta, huh?"

Finch lifted his still heavily bandaged right hand. "Yeah, number one. It's in great fucking shape."

Kung Fu nodded. The glitter in his eager eyes danced in step with the lantern's flickering light against the walls. "You hand numba one. VC numba ten. They all 'round town. Big attack. Time to get dinky-dou." And with those words spoken, Kung Fu, for the fourth night in a row, retrieved his long-stemmed pipe, took a chunk of opium from the bag he carried around his waist, and placed it in the deep, dark-colored bowl. Next he lit a match. And then without giving it a second thought, he cleared all the air out of his lungs, put the lighted match over the bowl, and drew slowly on the stem of the pipe. It seemed his lungs had no limit to the size they could expand as he inhaled. He stopped. A pencil-thin curl of smoke escaped the bowl, slowly dissipating as it ascended within the high-ceilinged room. Slater saw that the area around the man's eyes was so filled with pressure that he thought they might burst. Bug-eyed, Kung Fu held the smoke in his lungs for nearly a full minute. And then, in one tremendous burst, he exhaled. Almost instantly his personality changed from that of sharp-edged joviality to happy, smiling lethargy. Slater, as he had on the three nights before when he observed this definite breach of military discipline, rolled his eyes at either Huddleston or Morgan and wondered what this war would be like if everyone, VC and American alike, stopped fighting long enough to gather together and smoke a bowl of good dope....

Slater peered over the parapet. Conrad worked his jaws on a stick of gum. They had been in position for the last several minutes, the M-60 trained to the south. Conrad said, "How the hell does he get away with that shit?"

"Who?...What shit?"

"That gook smoking that crap."

Victor R. Beaver

"Kung Fu?"
"Yeah."
Slater said, "I don't know. Maybe nobody cares what he does. Maybe they all do it."
"That stuff will fry your brains."
"And liquor pickles your liver."
"Sir?"
"Nothing. Try to get some sleep. I'll wake you in a couple of hours."
Slater listened to Conrad's breathing. The chief could fall asleep at the drop of a hat.
Slater glanced about. Everywhere was quiet. He looked up. Stars. Thousands of them, clear and brilliant. *There—a falling star. I wish, I wish, what do I wish? That I had a pizza, a large sausage and pepperoni pizza, mushrooms and onions and black olives. And a pitcher of beer. I wish I was back on campus. The Buckhorn Tavern, The HiFi Club, Dundee's, Willie Chong's Pizza. The Grinder Shoppe. Excellent food...excellent company...excellent tunes—*
He heard a sound. He looked down. It was the gun crew fussing with the two howitzers. *Six shells left. What the hell can these guys do with six shells? And once the shells are gone, what then?* But it had never mattered. The Vietnamese had never fired the damn things at anything he thought even remotely threatening. *Empty rice paddies, for crissake. And now the advisory team was short on food, water, and ammunition—again. And certainly medical supplies.*
Movement. His eyes narrowed. *Am I spooked or what? There's nothing out there. A battalion of VC, poised for the fourth night in a row to attack. Yeah, right...like the four Viet Cong battalions that were supposed to attack Soc Trang the second night of Tet.* He could hear his grandpa now. *"What war are you in, Bub? Vietnam...? Hell, that ain't no war. World War One, Bub...Now there was a war. Millions dead—in the trenches. Millions. A lot of them gassed. Mustard gas. Bad stuff. It killed my brother, your great uncle. Long gone now, buried somewhere in Belgium. Wrote me a letter before he died. Told me not to come over. 'Don't know how much longer I'll be alive,' he said. He knew he was going to be dead...it was just a matter of time..."*
It's all relative, thought Slater. Big war, little war; big guns, little guns. Dead is dead. Who cares how you're killed? Or how long it takes? In France or Belgium, a soldier didn't leave until he was dead or maimed or the war ended. If it took two years, it took two years. If three, then three—or five. Same with the second "big" one. In Korea, there was no yearly rotation, at least none that he knew of. *But lucky us...Vietnam...one year tour of duty. The moment you step off the plane you're counting down to DEROS. How to stay alive for 365 days. But then, what does it matter? If you go home in one piece, a year Stateside they ship your ass right back. War is war and dying is dying...*
Captain Huddleston appeared before him. "Mr. Slater..."

356

The Sky Soldiers

"Yessir."

"How you doing?"

"Okay, sir."

"Quiet?"

The pilot nodded. "All's quiet, sir... 'All Quiet On The Southern Front', sir."

The captain sat down next to him. Out of his pocket he took a folded sheet of paper. He handed it to Kip.

Kip took it. "What's this?"

"Open it."

Kip unfolded it and read. He put the paper down. "Sir, this isn't necessary."

"I know, but you guys deserve something. It isn't much."

The captain was recommending each pilot for a Silver Star and Finch and Conrad each a Bronze Star with V-device (for valor). "You guys really helped out. Who knows where we would be right now if you hadn't risked your necks flying in here. I just wanted you to know that we all appreciate what you've had to put up with."

Kip listened. "Thanks, sir...but you guys, after we leave, will still be here. And more than likely Charlie will still be out there. And for who knows how long?"

"True, but this is our job. This is our assignment."

"And coming in here and re-supplying you wasn't ours...?"

Huddleston raised an eyebrow. "Whatever. Anyway, give this letter to your CO when you get back. I'll try to get something more formal out as soon as I get time to write it."

"Thank you, sir."

Huddleston extended his right hand. "If I don't get a chance later on..." They shook hands. Then the captain moved away from the wall and disappeared down below.

Slater popped his eyes open to bright sunlight. He sat up. Justen's tough little crewchief was next to him, looking over the wall, sipping at a cup of hot coffee. His M-60 leaned against the wall. Breathing deep, Slater took in the aroma of the coffee. He stretched and yawned. Conrad turned his head. "Good morning, sir."

"Morning." His watch read quarter to eight. "Why'd you let me sleep so late?"

"Want a sip?" Conrad handed him the cup.

Slater took it. "Thanks."

"You were sleeping like a baby," Conrad said. "First time since we got here."

Slater nodded. "I can't believe how quiet it was last night."

"No mortars and no VC...just the way I like it."

"Perhaps the quiet before the storm," Slater remarked.

"I sure hope not."

Victor R. Beaver

Sparky appeared in the doorway at the top of the stairs. "Hey—they've upped the time on the extraction. You guys got twenty minutes to get ready. A chopper's coming in from Tra Vinh. I think it's your buddy," he said, looking at Slater.

"Leo?"

"Yeah."

The two men collected their weapons. They followed the radioman down the stone staircase. For the second time Barry readied the sleeping Justen for medevac extraction. Barry said, "He was awake last night long enough for me to give him some soup. I think he's going to make it."

Huddleston came through the door. "We just got word. Four gunships are providing cover. Two Cobras and two regular gunships."

Abe Morgan, fresh-starched fatigues adorning his tall lanky frame, rubbed his chin. "Sir, if you hurry, you've got time for a shave." The sergeant was smiling. The whole time they were there, he tried to get Kip to shave. Slater smiled back. "What?—and have the guys back at Soc Trang miss seeing me looking so grizzly. Not on your life—"

Morgan extended his hand. "Good luck, sir. Stop back by anytime."

"Yeah, well next time don't need us so desperately."

With everything in place for the extraction, Slater watched as the two Cobras pounded the town's east side, making three runs before walking their coverage toward the south canal. Two Viking gunships flew low-level over the south canal, spraying the trees and low-lying vegetation with machine-gun fire. The plan this time called for the recovery ship to approach the landing zone low level from the east, fly directly over the south canal, and hopefully be in the LZ before Charlie could deliver any clear shots. Slater thought it a workable plan for getting in, certainly better than the two times before, but getting out still had him concerned. But he shrugged it off. Like being caught in the curl of a large ocean wave hitting the beach, it was time to sit back, relax, and let everything tumble out, come what may.

The PRC-25 radio crackled. Leo's voice sounded crisp and clear. Sparky handed the handset to an anxious comrade-in-arms. "Hey, Leo—are you in my ship?"

"Affirmative," Leo radioed back. "They assigned me Alfie and your crew. We're two klicks out. See you in about a minute."

"Be careful, Leo."

"Gotcha covered, buddy. Gotcha covered."

Everywhere was pandemonium. The two howitzers fired three shells each in rapid succession, point blank shots aimed at the south canal. The Viking light fire-team then swooped in and peppered not only the south canal, but after a moment, the grove of Banyan trees southwest of the compound. The two Cobras arched out of the sky and sent two more volleys of rockets into the thatched huts on the edge of the canal. The resulting shock waves rolled over the men waiting at the side of the courtyard.

Slater looked east. After a moment, he saw Tiger 098, *Alfie*, bloom into full view. Leo was coming in fast. He saw *Alfie* slow down and then mushroom over the courtyard wall. Leo brought the ship to a high hover; dust and debris flew everywhere. Kip then watched as Leo practically slammed *Alfie* onto the ground.

Alfie was loaded with ammo, 105-artillery shells, and medical supplies, which were quickly dumped onto the courtyard floor. Several Vietnamese soldiers then helped to lift Justen into the ship. Barry made one last assessment of his patient. Derek was barely conscious. Barry then gave all a thumbs-up. Finch and Conrad hurried around to the opposite side and climbed on board. Slater, with his flight helmet and carbine in hand, struggled onto the cabin floor on the left side. He sat on the edge letting his feet dangle outside. Directly over him, and seated, was someone with a Browning automatic rifle, an extra gunner they had picked up at Tra Vinh.

Kip looked right and gave Leo a thumbs-up. Leo nodded and brought in power. Slater glanced toward Huddleston and team sergeant Morgan, who were both watching from the compound gate. Sparky was kneeling near them, ready with the radio. Lunsford and Barry tipped him a casual good-luck salute. Grinning, he hailed them back. Everyone on the ground braced against the powerful rotor downwash.

Leo turned the ship and faced *Alfie* south. Slater felt a strong hand on his shoulder. He looked up and saw Rusty White's smiling face. Slater put his flight helmet on and plugged into the ship's intercom. "Sir. You're sure a sight for sore eyes," his crewchief said.

"You too—!"

Leo alerted the crew. "Okay—this is it. *We're outta here!*"

Slater felt the ship lift higher. *Alfie* strained under its new load. The south perimeter wall looked like a formidable barrier, but a split second later Leo had the ship over it and moving forward. To their left was the south canal and treeline. Leo put the cyclic control stick forward and increased the airspeed. The man with the BAR aimed the weapon at the treeline and pulled the trigger. The sound, directly over Slater's head, shattered his senses. Hot, spent, shell casings pinged around him. One shell casing singed the back of his neck. After a few seconds, Leo banked the ship right and headed due west.

All four gunships fired in concert. The two Cobras plastered the south treeline while the Viking light fire-team sent a stream of bullets into the grove of Banyan trees. Then they disengaged from their targets and chased after *Alfie* to ride shotgun. As the distance between them and the treeline increased, Leo began to ease the ship up to higher altitudes. At one thousand feet and climbing, Slater began to relax. Wind whipped his face and tore at his clothes, and for the first time since he arrived in-country he looked down upon the wide open Delta and felt oddly elated, as if this were his land, his country, his home…and the skies above was where he belonged.

He felt Rusty's hand on his shoulder. "Sir, did you get the news about Lieutenant Christian?"

Slater felt his heart skip a beat. "No…"

"He and Mr. Harper went down. Ten gooks on board. All killed…burned."

He felt a sickening tug at his stomach. "Who was the crew?"

"Pickett was the gunner. Tagmar, the crewchief."

"What happened?"

"No one knows for sure. It was yesterday morning. They were at altitude, about ten klicks north of Soc Trang, coming back from Can Tho. They think maybe a gook grenade accidentally went off."

"Anybody see it?"

"No, sir."

Kip closed his eyes and hung his head. After a moment he heard Leo speak over the intercom:

"We're going to Dong Tam. Taking Justen to the MASH. We'll be there in about ten minutes. Glad to see you, buddy."

Slater smiled. "Same-same to you, Leo. Same-same to you."

> *"So ride, boldly, ride to the*
> *end of the rainbow…*
> *Ride, boldly, ride till you*
> *find El Dorado…"*

The Sky Soldiers

Chapter 44

AT 39,000 FEET, THE LARGE C-141 "Starlifter" transport jet, with its cargo of sick and wounded, thrummed its way steadily eastward.

One of the nurses, an Air Force first lieutenant, a woman in her mid-twenties, had just returned from several of her forward stations. Most of the huge cabin was bathed in darkness, with an occasional dim white light illuminating where a nurse with a flashlight was tending to a patient. The lieutenant took a canter and poured herself a cup of coffee. She eased into her seat next to a second nurse curled up with a blanket draped around her shoulders. The second nurse stirred. "So...how're your guys doing?" she asked.

"Okay, most of them...except that dark-haired one. He's really having a rough time."

"The one with the nightmares?"

"Yeah."

"What's his temp?"

"Right now a hundred and two. It's been higher."

"When was his last morphine infusion?"

She glanced at her watch. "Less than an hour ago."

"Was he with it?"

"Somewhat. It's pretty hard to tell how much, in his condition."

The nurse with the blanket shifted in her seat. "I'll say this...he sure is good-looking."

The nurse with the coffee gazed at her friend. "Good grief, he's emaciated—"

"Put some meat on him and I sure wouldn't kick him out of bed."

"You're pathetic."

"Horny is a better word."

There was a pause. The nurse with the coffee took a sip and laid her head back full against the seat. She closed her eyes. She felt the steady vibration of the big jet at the base of her neck, down along her spine, in her legs. She was so used to the hum of the four jet engines that she wondered when it was that her senses weren't filled with their steady roar. Ten hours to go, she told herself...ten more hours and after that, in two days, we turn around for another flight. That will make three round-trips across the Pacific in seventeen days, to add to my total of nineteen in fewer than four months. She shuddered. Each one-way crossing was a twenty-hour ordeal. There were times when she felt like screaming. *I can't take another trip...not one more trip.*

She stirred at the voice of her friend. "I forgot to ask, we've been so busy...did your leave get approved?"

"No."

Victor R. Beaver

"Well, I guess that rules out my request too. This offensive sure has screwed things up."

"You can say that again."

"Were you planning to see Chad?"

The one with the coffee sighed. She felt a sudden heaviness come over her. She said, "No."

"How come?"

"He broke off the engagement."

"He did?"

"Yeah, right before I left on this trip."

"How come you didn't tell me?"

"I don't know...I just didn't."

"Was there someone else?"

"He said there wasn't. Maybe it's the separations. In six months we've been together twice."

"I'm really sorry to hear that."

"Yeah...I'm sorry too."

* * *

THE SMALL ENCAMPMENT WAS LOCATED somewhere in the upper regions of the U Minh. Built near a narrow, heavily foliated canal, it was a collection of thatched huts and wooden walkways. Near the commandant's quarters, on top a crooked pole, a Viet Cong flag hung limp in the still air, and like the huts around it, was hidden beneath the thick-limbed branches of the surrounding trees.

Jake Cole went slowly into his cage. He sat down on his mat. *Alone...God, I'm alone—for the first time!*

He had just said good-bye to Baker and Reed. Both men were packed in a sampan and then he watched as the guards shoved off. He stayed rooted in place until the *put-put* sound of the sampan's small outboard motor faded away. He knew their guards would eventually run the coast and within a matter of days get them into Cambodia, and finally to Phnom Penh, Cambodia's capital city. From there the two Americans would be released and shipped home. They did it and he was glad for them. How they did it, what they confessed to, what statements they signed to redeem their captors—ultimately what vestige of honor they relinquished—he did not know nor did he care. He was just simply glad. At least they would be able to tell the world he was still alive and hopefully where the camp was. Rescue would be a matter of weeks, perhaps no more than a couple of months. He could hold out for another two months.

Ever since he had become a prisoner, he had been living in the same camps as Baker and Reed, who had been in captivity two years longer. Most of the time the three men were kept apart. Typically, the only time they were allowed to be physically together was to watch propaganda movies. Too, whenever one of them became ill, the others were permitted to give direct aid and comfort. Otherwise, they slipped each other notes and thus were kept informed of one another's general health, state of mind, and the gist of the interrogations they endured. But now his two companions were gone.

For an hour he wallowed inside his cage in self-pity. Near lunchtime two sampans approached. Through the wooden slats that were the bars to his cage, he watched as several guards brought from the sampans a generous supply of green bananas, several chickens and ducks, and a large, heavy sack of rice. One of the guards brought to Jake Cole's tiny kitchen half a stalk of bananas and a pail of rice. Lately, to supplement his diet, he had been catching water snakes in his nets, and rather than let them go back into the water, he kept them and removed their livers and cooked them with the smaller livers taken from the fish he also netted. He was grateful for the bananas, which were a welcome change to his diet.

To shake his doldrums, Jake began his cooking fire. Then he heard to the south of the camp the drone of an O-1 Bird Dog aircraft. Maybe it's the same O-1 he and the others had spotted three days before, reconnoitering the area, perhaps, he fancied, looking for this very encampment. In the past whenever the three Americans saw an aircraft their spirits rose and they imagined freedom to be attainable, if not within the next few days, then at least within the next week. But their hopes were always dashed when no assault force came to liberate them. Lately, though, spotter aircraft had been directing F-100 airstrikes against positions not far from the camp and now Jake found himself equally hoping for and dreading the sound of the little plane's approach.

Neither he nor Baker or Reed had ever figured a way to signal an aircraft without incurring the wrath of Major Hung and the rest of his staff. Nor had they figured a way to signal an approaching aircraft without prematurely calling in a friendly airstrike. The key, of course, was to be able to signal, escape, and then signal again that they were Americans loose from their captors.

But escape, they had learned early, was next to impossible. During the day they were watched over like a hawk; at night they were locked in leg-irons and then locked inside their separate wooden cages, there to ride out the night battling hopelessness, hellish nightmares, and the thousands of mosquitoes that swarmed over them constantly. Several months before Jake had asked that they each be issued a mosquito net for protection, which to their surprise they were given, and which became a double-edged sword. Now whenever the cadre became frustrated with them during interrogations, they would discover their nets removed from their cages to be "repaired," not to be returned for several days. Or even weeks.

"Chimp," the name they had given one of the guards because his pockmarked face resembled that of a chimpanzee, called for him to cease making his cooking fire. Jake looked up and noticed that several of the guards and the rest of the camp cadre were gathering their weapons and were just now crossing the small footbridge that spanned the canal. With Chimp behind him, he was goaded across the bridge. They walked behind the others who followed a path that led them north, away from where the O-1 was now circling some distance to their south.

Encouraged to move faster, Jake, long without anything substantial in his diet, groped along as fast as he could.

After several minutes of travel, they came to a series of unused bunkers. As the rest of the cadre hunkered near their bunkers, Chimp ordered Jake to stop and get inside the nearest one.

The guard, remaining outside, kept one eye on his prisoner and the other skyward. Whenever Jake tried to look outside, the point of the little man's rifle met him, aimed at his forehead. Shortly, Jake heard the scream of jets and then explosions. He felt the ground shudder beneath him and thought the explosions awfully close to their camp.

He counted three bombing runs. Between explosions, he heard the droning of the O-1 Bird Dog as it circled to the east. He also heard rifle fire. True to form, in this sanctuary of sanctuaries, the Viet Cong always tried to shoot the little spotter aircraft down.

After twenty minutes, the O-1 was gone and so were the two jets. Chimp hustled Jake back to the compound.

Gratefully, he found their camp intact. Jake could tell by the smoke that drifted skyward that the three bombing runs had hit two kilometers farther south. He wondered if the location held any American POWs. It was maddening to think that they would strike at a position without first knowing it empty of prisoners. But how would they get information like that?

Understandably, during the two years he'd been a prisoner, he knew nothing of home: of Valerie, of his two children, or of his half-brother Derek. He knew nothing of the progress of the war. Which side had the edge? Was Derek a pilot? And if so, where was he stationed? Certainly, Derek's first tour, if he had been sent directly to Vietnam after graduation from flight training, was over and he was somewhere back in the United States.

Jake was no longer able to easily conjure Valerie's image. The harder he tried, the more difficult it was to do and he became more and more despondent. What *was* the shape of her face? the color of her hair? her eyes? What was her smile like? What did her body look like? What did it *feel* like? Was she tall? short? or somewhere between? How did she laugh? Did she still love him? *Did she know anything about him, whether or not he was even alive?* It was so maddening.

Dusk came and Chimp prodded Jake into his cage. The slightly built guard grinned as he secured his prisoner's leg-irons and then locked the cage. Speaking a mixture of pidgin English and Vietnamese, Chimp said:

"You friends gone. What you feel like, Co?"

"Like shit," Jake replied.

"You sad?"

"Sure, asshole, wouldn't you be?" Jake replied.

"What is this 'asshole?'" the guard asked.

Smiling, Jake said, "It's what you are, you cheap little two-bit prick," and laughed.

The guard, sensing only good-natured humor, laughed too.

When the guard was gone, Jake huddled under his mosquito net and put his head down on his knees. Dusk and dawn, the two times of the day he hated most. Dawn was always a prelude to hours upon hours of consciousness and survival. Even with the proximity of the other Americans, each waking hour was interminably long. And the nights—God how he hated the nights. They were endless nightmares.

As he sat there, listening to the incessant droning of mosquitoes around his head, he fought with all his might not to cry. Eventually, though, he gave in. His body convulsed. A torrent of tears spilled forth, worse than during the first months of his captivity. The full realization that neither of his American companions were in their own cages nearby, finally hit him.

I'm alone! Truly, truly alone!

Now that Baker and Reed were gone there was no one to watch out for him, to give him encouragement, to tell him to hang on...to endure no matter how long.

There was no one to care for him when he got sick. That was the worst part: the sickness! the bone-aching sickness that made captivity so unbearable. And now his support was gone. *Oh God...help me...help me...HELP ME!*

After a while, he laid down. He whimpered. He loathed wakefulness, yet he feared sleep more. Eventually, exhaustion overcame him.

His sleep was fitful, restless...

The early light of dawn had not yet invaded the night. He peered into the darkness and felt an intermingling of his body juices, a wondrous kind of churning. Something strange was happening. A strong feeling of joy began to overtake him. Feeling had become form...a physical form.

But how?...What was it?

There was no answer. None needed to be given. The form or the feeling signaled for him to be still. And then, after a moment, he felt the form envelop him, as if it were inside him, caressing his heart, even more, caressing his very soul. He felt drawn deep into its presence. And then he felt a love pour forth that was beyond any he had ever known, unfathomable, incomprehensible, yet all-encompassing. He closed his eyes. For a long moment, he luxuriated, swooned, in ecstatic rapture. Wave after wave of this God-sent feeling engulfed him. Someone was actually here with him. He felt marvelous, fabulous—No! it was beyond words. *Beyond description!*

Victor R. Beaver

It was a woman, this he clearly felt. And he could not think for one minute how it was possible...*Who was she?*

Like a babe in her arms, he snuggled closer, and she loved him...she just loved him...

Oh my darling...Oh my beautiful darling. The words seem to come from deep within...*I am here my darling...*

But how? Instead, she quieted him with her continued warmth. Her loving energy radiated. His eyes were open and he was now certain it wasn't a dream. And then slowly, ever so slowly, he became aware of dark shapes; they had been there all along. He kept his eyes open. Yes, they were the dark shapes that made up his bleak, hopeless world.

It must have been the sound of his voice, an upthrusting primordial cry that roused him. He blinked and moved his eyes and saw the darkness that still enveloped him. His arms were outstretched, groping, his fingers taut and curved. He was laying on his side and he felt the damp cool air. And the smell, musty, rotting vegetation. His mosquito net had come off him, his body exposed to the mosquitoes' incessant bloodthirsty buzzing. All of it, his "nothing" life, his existence at its most basic level. And then, fully conscious, he felt the fierce pounding of his heart, his need for air coming in gasps.

The camp was astir at the first full thrust of dawn. Jake gripped the bars of his cage as he watched Chimp, with a wide yawn on his face, amble toward him. The guard unlocked the door and then stooped to unlock the leg-irons.

"Hey."

Chimp looked up. Jake's face and arms were swollen.

"Ask me if I'm sad."

The guard regarded him strangely. "You sad, Co?"

"No, I'm not sad. But I am sick to death—of you, this place and these god-*damned* mosquitoes!"

Chimp grinned. "You friends, they free. You could be free. You stupid."

Jake sneered at the man. "Go to hell."

Chimp retreated to the guard hut.

Through swollen eyes, Jake watched as his hands started his cooking fire. He went to the canal. As he lifted the pail filled with water, he stopped. For a moment he held the pail still. He gazed at it, remembered the "visitation" that had been real but not real. An "ethereal" visitation. Whatever it was, whoever it was, he still felt its presence. His gooseflesh rose. He shook his head. Sunlight streaked through the trees. He stood and then for a long moment stared at his cage.

He walked back to his fire. He added rice and put the pail over the fire. His glance kept going back to the cage. Someone had been inside the cage with him—or at least someone's spirit. But whose spirit?

You're flipping out. Stop it. Stop it!
The rice was ready. He ate.
The sun warmed him.
Strangely, on his second day without the company of Baker and Reed, he didn't feel quite so alone....

Victor R. Beaver

Chapter 45

AFTER SLATER, CONRAD AND FINCH returned to Soc Trang, the 121st, along with her sister companies, began a regimen of flying that would last well into the next month. The offensive had watered down ARVN forces over the entire country. As a result, on February 13, the South Vietnamese government announced that it was mobilizing sixty-five thousand troops.

To assemble and organize these troops was not an overnight process. When they were finally grouped and ready for duty, the process to get them properly located was not a quick and easy task either. When those forces slated for duty in the Mekong Delta were assembled, it fell upon the four assault companies to ferry them into place. Fresh troops gathered at My Tho were airlifted to Chau Phu (Chau Doc), on the Cambodian border. Troops grouped at Vi Thanh were sent to re-enforce the 21st ARVN Division at Bac Lieu and Ca Mau. A battalion of ARVN assembled at Phu Vinh (Tra Vinh) was flown to Vinh Long and Can Tho.

Because of the need to disperse so many men at once (over abnormally long distances), it was not uncommon for several formations of helicopters, of seven or eight ships apiece, to be doing duty all over the Delta. Unfortunately, because the formations were small, it took twice and three times the number of trips to ferry a battalion of men. In many instances this required that pilots and crews begin their day well before dawn, to not finish until long after dusk.

Understandably, the high number of flying hours exacted its toll on both man and machine. Aircraft went into routine inspection a mere three days after release from their last. Hangar mechanics, who for many months before the offensive were able to stagger major aircraft inspections, now performed 100-hour PEs (periodic inspections) on five and six aircraft at a time. Flight crews, exhausted from a grueling sixteen-hour day, eight to ten hours of it spent flying—and in formation no less—landed at night, parked their aircraft, ate a can of cold C-rations, grabbed a quick smoke, performed a once-over of aircraft and guns, and fell asleep on the hard floor of their ship. Or curled against a revetment wall. Or inside the dank confines of a perimeter bunker. Though sleep usually came easy, their periods of rest were interrupted constantly by the din that was the machinery of war: of landing and departing aircraft, by maintenance personnel performing engine run-up checks, by trigger-happy perimeter guards firing their weapons mostly at ghost-like shadows, by the ARVN howitzer battery pumping out H&I fire, and particularly by Viet Cong mortar attacks that wrenched them from an otherwise restless sleep.

One day, after troops had boarded at Can Tho, several pilots watched (in a quasi-mental daze) as the second ship behind Lead lifted to a hover. It moved sideways for some unknown reason, turned and drifted over a shallow pond, and settled gently into the water. The ship rolled left and the rotorblades made contact with the water. In a few seconds, which seemed to last an eternity to those watching, the aircraft lay on its side, a beaten heap. They learned later that the four ARVN seated with their legs dangling out the left side, were pinned between the aircraft and the shallow bottom of the pond and were drowned.

Kip Slater never believed he could hate flying so much. Actually, he never believed he would ever hate flying at all. He had just spent each day for the last two weeks flying in the right seat, in command, desperately fighting sleep. To compound this, his sense of responsibility as an aircraft commander prevented he doze while his peter-pilot operated the controls. Though other ACs (only a few) were able to do so, Slater could not allow himself, no matter how warranted, the briefest nap. Yet he was so exhausted he wanted to scream, to open the door, unbuckle, leap out and free-fall to oblivion. Every molecule in his body ached at the thought of one more ferry trip to Ca Mau...and back to Bac Lieu...and then back to Ca Mau.

To solve this problem, he wrangled from one of the enlisted crewmen a pornographic paperback so explicit that, as he read it and his co-pilot flew, his mind and his body vibrated with tension and excitement. It was precisely the stimulation he needed to keep awake and alert while they flew in formation. And when it came his turn at the controls, with his body at a fever pitch, his mind conjured delightedly the word images he had just perused, anxious again for another stint of *not* being at the controls.

* * *

RANDALL, TANNAH, AND SLATER, SUMMONED by Major Neely, waited quietly in the company orderly room. Major Maes, the executive officer, motioned for them to rise. "The commander will see you now."

They stood at attention in front of Neely's desk. Maes remained behind them, near the door. The three warrant officers saluted. Neely returned their salutes, then stood and moved from behind his desk around to the back of his men. His footsteps creaked on the wooden floor. He stopped next to Slater and peered at the right side of Slater's mouth. "You gentlemen are aware of my 'no moustache' policy?"

"Yes, sir," they each said quietly.

"But I can see quite plainly that the three of you have a problem with it."

There was silence.

"Do each of you have a problem with it?"

Slater turned his head slightly. "Sir—what's wrong with growing a moustache?" After he spoke, Kip felt the tips of his ears turn red.

Victor R. Beaver

Slater felt Neely's glare penetrate deep into his skull. For the first time, Slater felt a true hatred for the man, whose concern for appearance was all consuming. Neely's requirement for stiff military bearing from his subordinates, particularly in lieu of the dangers the men faced each day, was irrational, supercilious behavior. He wanted to shove a fist down Neely's throat, and would have gladly done so had there been a way without being brought up on charges afterwards. It was no idle talk that Neely, during the offensive, was stuffing his headbonnet full of feathers, to later cash in for his silver oak-leaf cluster. The epitome of Neely's career ambitions became clear during the recent Awards and Decorations ceremony, when both he and Slote, along with others who more rightly deserved their awards, received the medals one put the other in for. Two members of Westmoreland's general staff had come down for the ceremonies, and on the morning of their arrival, Neely had his executive officer running about insuring that no pilot needed a haircut, that the enlisted men wore the proper headgear.

Neely said, "Mr. Slater, the right or wrong of my policies is not for you, or anybody, to question. As your commander, it is my prerogative to set whatever standards I deem appropriate—"

"—and no moustaches is one of them," Slater blurted.

"Precisely."

"Well, whatever you say, sir."

"*Mister* Slater—" Neely stopped abruptly. He moved back behind his desk and leaned forward, his fists bare-knuckled against the top of the desk.

Neely's eyes focused on Slater's pupils like two laser beams. The errant warrant officer bored back with equal intensity. Then Neely straightened, turned his head and addressed Tannah and Randall. "You two—get those moustaches off and report back here in twenty minutes."

The two men framed a weak "yessir," saluted, turned and exited. Neely directed Maes out of the room and asked that he close the door.

They were alone. Neely sat down at his desk. He kept Slater standing at attention. From his desk drawer, Neely produced a two-page, typed report. He handled the report with delicate care. He perused the report for a moment, then said, "I don't like your attitude, Mr. Slater."

"Yes, sir."

Neely looked up. "Five days under fire and you think you're quite the combat soldier, don't you?"

"No, sir, I do not."

"Do you know what I have here, Mr. Slater?" Neely said, indicating the report he held between his fingers.

"No, sir."

"It came this morning. It's from Lieutenant Colonel Johnson, senior advisor for Vinh Binh Province, dictated by Captain Huddleston. A very fine letter of recommendation, for you and Mr. Justen and his crew."

"Yessir."

"Until it came, I was considering issuing you a letter of reprimand, along with Mr. Tannah and Mr. Randall, both of whom will still receive one." Slater's ears perked. Though he didn't consider himself a career man, neither did he want to be labeled a misfit. His intent—now derailed—was to grow a damn moustache. *What the hell was wrong with that—?* "However," Neely continued, "I'm reconsidering. After you get that moustache shaved—and you will shave it off—you will report back to me for inspection. You are now the new 'Awards and Decorations' officer, thanks, unfortunately, to the death of Lieutenant Christian. For the action at Tieu Can you will write, for yourself and the others, four recommendations. For Mr. Justen, a Silver Star; for you, the Distinguished Flying Cross with V-device for valor; for the crew, two Bronze Stars also with V-device. In the interim, you will report to me daily. You will be clean-shaved, your fatigues pressed, your boots shined. And your hair will be cut exactly like mine"—Neely waved a hand over his half-inch crop with white sidewalls—"and I am *not* assigning you an assistant. You will be completely on your own. And I expect results. Do you have any questions?"

Slater took a deep breath. He had always hated his duties as Christian's assistant. Writing the narratives for medals was such bullshit. Now the entire can of worms was his baby. "No, sir, no questions."

"Fine. You're dismissed."

Two hours later, Kip stormed into Leo's room. He slammed his pencil down on the notepad he carried, which cartwheeled across the room.

Leo looked up. "What's the matter now?"

Slater picked the pencil up, and holding it like a dart, this time shot it across the room. He shook his head. "I can't do it; I can't write those narratives—"

"Why not?"

"I can't pretend. I can't write a narrative that makes me and the rest sound like we took on a whole battalion of VC, barehanded. In the first place, we were stupid for going in there without gunship support. Secondly, once we were on the ground, Justen was completely out of it. And I didn't do anything more than keep my head down. Same with Conrad and Finch. What did we do that was so goddamned heroic—?"

* * *

IT WASN'T UNTIL THE MIDDLE OF MARCH that the men at the airfield were allowed to go downtown. Kip and Leo, dressed in civilians clothes, eased themselves in the seat behind the cyclo driver. "Let's get this crate going, Papa-san," Leo said.

The little Vietnamese driver, a thin, wiry man whose age was impossible to discern, nodded with a wide grin that bared two silver-capped front teeth. He started his motorcycle and put it into gear. As they sped along, the two pilots looked for telltale signs of the bombing runs committed by the F-100 Supersabres during the early hours of Tet. Strangely, except the occasional charred remains of clusters of hootches, plainly caught in a crossfire, most of the debris they expected to see was cleared out.

They looked ahead. On the left was the courtyard where less than two months before the two pilots, and Mangrum and Pickett, had played foosball. Tannah asked the driver to reduce his speed. As they crept along, the two men gaped at the destruction wrought by several large bombs. The Banyan tree that had gracefully overshadowed the tennis court was a shattered hulk, most of its branches snapped like so many twigs. The bulk of the tree was slumped directly over the tennis court, with the net completely flattened. The little cement blockhouse, where next to it had stood the foosball game board, was intact, though it was surrounded by several large branches. They saw that the game board was gone.

The little driver looked back at his passengers and showed with his hand and arm how the jets had swooped down and dropped their bombs near the little park. Both men shuddered as the driver increased his speed and went on.

Once inside the city they saw more evidence of the bombing. The driver wove his way past several shattered buildings, until they came to MACV province headquarters.

The compound was pockmarked with hundreds of bullet holes and places where VC B-40 rounds had exploded. Two uniformed Vietnamese soldiers stood guard at the building's entrance under a heavily sandbagged hut; the guards eyed the two men curiously. The two pilots got out of the seat and paid the driver. Leo followed Slater past the wreckage of the MACV compound until they came to the entrance of the courtyard where Kim's apartment was located. (The day before Kip had told Leo about Kim and his arrangement with the woman.) What they saw rooted both men in place. The courtyard and the building that housed her tiny enclave were nearly shattered beyond recognition. Slater did see the twisted metal that was the wrought-iron staircase that led to Kim's apartment amid a portion of crumbled wall.

Kip and Leo advanced slowly. A woman and three men, dressed in dark cotton clothing, with slippers on their feet and bandanas tied across their foreheads, were clearing debris away from a small building intact nearby.

Slater went toward the woman, who looked at him with flat staring eyes. "You speak English?" he asked.

The woman frowned, puzzled. "Do you know Kim Thi An, the woman who lived up there?" Slater said, motioning toward where the second floor and the apartment would have been. The woman twisted her face. The men stopped to watch.

The woman shrugged. "No bic..." she said. (I don't understand.)

The Sky Soldiers

"Dumb cunt," Leo said under his breath.

"Shut up, Leo."

Kip pointed to the twisted staircase. He made a motion of climbing the stairs. "The woman who lived there..." he said, his frustration beginning to mount.

One of the men began a quick exchange with the woman. The woman looked at Kip. "She die...she die."

"She what?" Kip said, not sure if what he heard were words in Vietnamese or English. He turned toward Leo.

Leo said, " I think she's saying she's dead."

Kip turned and faced the woman. "Are you saying the woman Kim Thi An is dead?"

Quickly the woman nodded. "She die."

Kip turned toward the man who had spoken to the woman. "You speak English?"

The man nodded. "Tee-tee." Which meant a little bit.

"The woman who lived up there," Slater said, "what happened?"

"She die," spoke the man, whose mouth revealed several gaps of missing teeth.

"Yes—she die! How? How did she die? Was it the bombs?" Kip gestured a bombing run with his hand.

The man nodded.

"Oh my God...the bombs."

"Come on, let's go," said Leo. "She was just a gook—a whore."

Slater swung around. "God damn you, Leo! What the hell do you have against these people—?" Kip's eyes narrowed. The veins in his neck bulged out. For the first time ever his look penetrated deep into Leo's soul. "What is it, Leo? What makes you so hateful toward these people? Where's your compassion?"

For a moment, Leo Tannah glowered back. Finally he said, "Look, let's be cool. We're buddies...right? Buddies? Why don't I meet you back at the airfield?"

"Where are you going?"

"To the...aah nowhere. I just want to be alone."

"Okay, but be careful. Don't forget the curfew."

"Don't worry about me. I can take care of myself."

"So good of you to come, Leo," Mother Caruso said, inviting him in. He followed her through the several buildings making up the orphanage, to her small office. He saw that the number of the children had increased two-fold. "I can understand why you haven't been around lately," she said. "The Viet Cong have been keeping everyone very busy."

Leo said, "My co-pilot was killed during a combat insertion into Vinh Long. There was a memorial service for him and another guy. Do you remember Robin Henry?"

"Oh, yes. He was one of the ones who distributed the candy on Christmas Day." Her eyes widened. "Is he also dead?"

Leo nodded. Mother Caruso made a sign of the cross. "Oh my..."

Leo took out a pack of cigarettes. "Do you mind if I smoke?"

"Go ahead. But it's bad for your health, you know."

Leo gave the nun a weak smile then lit the cigarette. He sat in a chair in front of her desk; the desk was strewn with papers. He thrummed his fingers against his leg. His right foot tapped nervously on the cement floor.

"You have something on your mind, Leo. What is it?"

In his mind's eye, he saw the Viet Cong soldier lying in the tall grasses, his body in a tight fold, shivering with fear against the powerful rotor downwash. He remembered the feel of his .45-caliber pistol when it went off, the jerk it made each time he fired until it was empty and the chamber locked open, ready for a fresh clip. He remembered how he watched the smoke curling from the end of the barrel; and then smelling the lingering cordite. And above all, he remembered the tingling sensation throughout his body, as a sought-after answer had finally revealed itself: Could he personally kill an enemy? That he could gave him a quiet satisfaction, but the tingling in his body startled and baffled him. He thought about the killings later and then rationalized, for his peace of mind, that by shooting the two Viet Cong soldiers, he had derailed a whole series of events. His mind even fancied that he might have saved his own life. Or the life of someone near to him. Like Slater.

"No...not really."

"Are you sure, Leo? You cannot hide from God. You know that, don't you, Leo?"

"I know-I know..." Leo choked suddenly.

She walked him back to the main entrance. She placed her hand on his arm. "Your heart is good, Leo...but you, in this war...I truly fear for your soul."

Chapter 46

THE UNVEILING HAPPENED ON A Friday afternoon. Seymore P. Cutter stood with his back to the main latrine wall that was covered by a large bed sheet held in place by duct tape. In front of him, standing shoulder to shoulder, were all the members of Flight Alpha One. He cleared his throat:

"Attention...please." He turned his gaze toward Mr. Drakeman, their tac officer. "Sir, the members of Flight Alpha One, Class 67-15, do hereby present to the staff of Third Warrant Officer Candidate Company our conception of primary helicopter flight training at Fort Wolters, Texas." Then, with Sandy Adamson at the other end of the sheet, Seymore reached up and pulled the sheet off the wall.

Chief Warrant Officer Drakeman and Captain Manley, the executive officer, studied the richly detailed mural that covered the wall from top to bottom, left to right. Alpha One's artist, Tom Adkins, had managed to show every phase of flight training, from their first day at the flight line to their solo session and dunking in the motel swimming pool. Cross-country navigation, the phase of training they were now in, showed a haphazardly strung-out group of TH-55s meandering over the Texas landscape, zigzagging like a flight of bumblebees; this fostered several chuckles. It was the TH-55 rocket attack on the train, however, that made the two officers laugh outright.

Adkins then directed everyone's attention to the shitter-stall doors. On each was a highly detailed painting of a helicopter: an AH-1G Cobra in an attack dive, a Huey B-model gunship providing close-in combat support over a treeline, a D-model Huey "slick," filled with troops, struggling out of an LZ, and, of course, the TH-55A, in the process of bouncing down a stagefield lane after an autorotation.

* * *

FINALLY, THEY BECAME SENIOR CANDIDATES—the top dogs on the block. Each member of Class 67-15 removed the plain orange tab on their left breast pocket and replaced it with one that had a black stripe down the middle. What remained were four weeks of academics and flight training, before phase graduation and their departure for Fort Rucker, Alabama, or the newly opened Hunter-Stewart, Georgia, flight-training complex.

That first week Willie was appointed candidate battalion commanding officer; Ned Symington assumed the duties of battalion sergeant major. Sandy Adamson wore the double diamonds of battalion executive officer, an honor he found considerably less unsettling than his stint as a platoon leader during the first week of preflight. Willie Cottrell was the only candidate in the entire candi-

Victor R. Beaver

date corps who outranked him. For one solid week the young warrant officer candidate walked around the flight-line barracks smug as a peacock on parade.

On the third day of his newfound status, Senior Candidate Seymore P. Cutter spied a batch of junior candidates fresh from preflight. They were the new members of 1st WOC Company, the Red Hats, whose cadre were the notorious bad guys on the block. He sidled over to them. They stood in formation stiff as boards. As he neared, not a soul stirred, not a man breathed so much as a molecule of air.

With his back to the 1st WOC Company billets, Cutter stepped in front of the first candidate. With the meanest look he could muster, Seymore eyeballed the junior candidate from stem to stern. The junior candidate stared back. Finally the man blinked. "Down and give me ten," Seymore ordered. The man dropped. Seymore stepped to the next candidate. Standing a good five inches taller, the next junior candidate's stare went clean over the top of Seymore's head. "Where are you from, Candidate Butler?" Seymore said. The man's nametag was right at eye-level.

The candidate dropped his gaze to answer. "Indiana, sir."

"Wrong. It's 'Sir, Candidate Butler, I'm from Indiana, sir.' Drop and give me ten." Down went the second candidate. As Cutter stepped in front of the third man, unknown to him there appeared at the main entranceway of one of the company barracks a tac officer known all over the battalion as "Ivan the Terrible." He was a short, compact man, built solid as a tank, with large frowning eyebrows and a perfectly round head completely void of hair. To any candidate who ever had the misfortune of being in his presence, he appeared all the more fearsome due to the large gap between his two top front teeth: truly a "Middle Ages" executioner of the first order.

CW2 Ivan stole silently behind the unsuspecting senior candidate. With four junior candidates now pumping against asphalt, Seymore went to the next candidate. "How tall are you, candidate?" Seymore asked.

"Sir, Candidate Bocher, I'm five-feet-four inches tall, sir!"

"That's the cutoff, isn't it, to be in the flight program?"

"Sir, Candidate Bocher, yes, sir!"

"You don't look that tall, Candidate Bocher."

"Sir, the Army says I am, sir!"

"I'll bet you tippy-toed, didn't you, Candidate Bocher?"

"Sir, Candidate Bocher, no sir, I did not!"

At that moment, Senior Candidate Cutter froze. He felt the shackles rise on the back of his neck. Something was amiss. He surveyed the remaining candidates who continued to stand as stationary as the monuments of Stonehenge. Their faces betrayed nothing; their pupils were mere pinholes, revealing nothing; they appeared almost in a coma. Seymore reached behind his neck and rubbed it.

It's nothing...nothing, he told himself. Ivan moved in closer. Cutter stepped in front of the next candidate. "Hello...candidate," Seymore said, his tone noticeably softer.

"Hello...sir?" the junior candidate replied.

Seymore saw that the man's WOC brass was slightly off center on his left collar. "Candidate, you're brass is a little off kilter."

The man reached up but Seymore quickly cut him off. "No...let me take care of that."

"Yessir," the candidate said, whose eyes triggered not the slightest doubt as to Cutter's undeniable right to be in their midst lording over them. Cutter's hands trembled as he undid the clasps. "You must preflight your uniform as if your life depended on it, candidate."

"Yessir."

Cutter poked his thumb several times with the sharp stubs. Finally the brass was correctly positioned. Cutter then replaced the clasps. He noticed his thumb was bleeding so he took to sucking it, quite conspicuously, without the least regard how it might appear to these men junior to him. Meantime, he felt his stomach rumble and he found himself doubled over to abstain the urge to move his bowels. Suddenly, he did an about face.

"*SO!*—We have the infamous Candidate Cutter!" roared CW2 Ivan.

Cutter's heart leaped into his throat. He stiffened to attention. He tried to salute, but the moment he brought his right arm up his gluteus muscles relaxed and he felt the telltale release in his shorts. "Oh...*shit!*"

The warrant officer loomed larger than life. Cutter saw the man's inflamed eyes, horns growing out from the sides of his forehead, nostrils flaring, front legs stamping at the ground. A hungry, snorting sound issued from his mouth.

"*SIR!*" cried Seymore, "I think I'm having an attack of appendicitis—" And with that exhortation, Seymore bolted from the formation.

Ivan the Terrible turned to his troops. "Heaven help me if any of you ever gets as ditzy as that man—*I'll turn in my wings!*"

* * *

NIGHT CROSS-COUNTRY FLYING COULDN'T have been more difficult had the students been blindfolded and told to read Braille. The city lights of Mineral Wells were easily distinguishable, and Fort Wolters itself provided a wealth of illumination, but to the northwest there was nothing but black. To the west and southwest, small clusters of lights, setting apart individual ranches, were scattered about; however, since the mapmakers rarely charted individual ranches, they couldn't be used as checkpoints by which to guide.

Distances proved to be harder to gauge. A cluster of lights that appeared near at hand could be well over fifty or sixty miles away, as seen through the clear night atmosphere. A person's normal sense of direction, generally easy to determine during the day, considering the time and position of the sun, was completely out of whack at night.

"Can't you see the Big Dipper, Candidate Cutter—which points to the North Star? It's right in front of you—*plain as day.*" It was Seymore's third night cross-country trip and Captain Crandall was all but ready to throw in the towel. "I pity your instrument flight instructor, Candidate Cutter."

"When do I get to do that, sir?" Cutter remarked, plaintively.

Crandall rolled his eyes. "I should be so bold as to wonder..."

At night, a twin-engine chase plane piloted by one of the instructors would fly high overhead watching the string of blinking red beacons as solo students made their way, one behind the other (each spaced usually about a mile apart), from checkpoint to checkpoint. And whenever the lead solo student would turn the wrong way at a checkpoint, or turn too early, with the string following right along behind, it was the chase pilot's job to get on the radio and reorient the misguided herd.

Aside from his talent as an artist, Tom Adkins had his room practically converted into a hobby and crafts shop. His most ambitious project was a rather large-scale model of a TH-55A. It was made of balsa wood, cloth, and put together with glue, tiny nails, and aircraft safety wire. The model's details were so accurate that when it was done, Colonel Eddington, the post commandant, was invited to see it. Impressed by the quality of workmanship, he asked that Adkins donate it for display at post headquarters. But there was only one glitch: as a unit it wouldn't fit through the door of his room. However, by remodeling the rotor-blade attachment configuration (to the rotor head) so that each blade could be removed, Adkins got it out of his room and into the large foyer of the headquarters building.

Their remaining time at Wolters was not without tragedy. In the class behind, an instructor and his student were doing stagefield work when a flawed bolt that holds one of the cyclic-control rods in place, sheared. With no way to control the aircraft left and right, the members of the flight watched horrified as the pair careened to their deaths. The accident caused a grounding of all TH-55s until each similar bolt could be inspected. No further defects were found. This did not, however, offset the wave of student resignations from the flight program.

On a similar note, a student made a ten-dollar bet with a friend that, while solo, he could change from the right seat to the left—*in flight!*

On the day of the mishap, it was arranged that the candidate accepting the bet would see the student in the right seat at takeoff. Another student in another aircraft would fly chase, to insure there were no improprieties.

During flight, the student who had made the bet signaled to the student flying chase that now was the time. Setting maximum friction on the controls, he unbuckled his seatbelt and shoulder harness, and then gingerly shifted his weight across the tiny control console that divided the two seats. Unfortunately, in the process, his right leg hit the right cyclic control stick, which caused the little ship to dive left, out of control. For more than a week, among those candidates who knew of the bet, mum was word, until the student who flew chase confessed all. Naturally, his confession explained to the accident investigation board why the deceased student was displaced from the wreckage by nearly a quarter-mile. On the way down he had fallen out of the ship, and the two, man and machine, had gone their separate ways.

* * *

FINAL PHASE CHECKRIDES. EACH MEMBER of Class 67-15 had a little over a hundred and five flight hours. Those who took their rides early, and got a passing score, looked forward to a trip to Brownwood, Texas, where displayed in a large hangar were several Confederate Air Force World War II relics: bombers, fighters, reconnaissance aircraft. They flew the hour-long flight to Brownwood with their instructors, in formation, usually in a "gaggle" of five or more helicopters.

The last week was hectic. The married men with families in the area had to close out leases, pack, and get wives and children ready to travel. Rose Bowden watched over the younger children while the adults attended to the moving process. Everywhere arrangements were made to accommodate visiting relatives who would be in town for the phase graduation. Cheryl Cochran came to be with Pete, and the couple decided she would leave her job in Oklahoma City and reside in Alabama during her husband's last four months of training.

It was a time when Sandy felt particularly depressed. Long before, he had expected Katie's presence for the ceremonies. So far, none of the letters he had written her had been answered. Frank Bartlett tried to cheer him up, but his despondency only grew worse. The last week at Wolters found him each night at the nearby beer and pizza joint drinking beer and hacking his way through a half-pack of cigarettes.

The auditorium was packed. The post commandant and his staff were on stage, to once again play in the same drama they had done the month before and the month before that, and as they would do many times over in the months to come. Before them were the Blue Hat seniors of 3rd WOC Company. Warrant Officer Candidate Class 67-15 had overcome its first hurdle toward the coveted silver wings of United States Army Aviator. Each man had taken to a machine few thought could be tamed. They had been humbled by it, had experienced heartache and sleepless nights to learn it, but eventually were able to control it. They were not masters of it—not by a long shot. But neither were they any longer in awe of it. Though they had no FAA certificates to prove it—*they were in fact helicopter pilots.*

The barracks were clear; the last trashcan had been emptied. Willie Cottrell called formation:

"Okay, listen up. You folks have got four days to get to Mother Rucker. Drive safe! Have fun! And stay out of jail!"

Sandy and Seymore crammed the last of their baggage into Mark Allen's Impala. Mark had a road map spread out on the hood. "Guess what? If we divert a little farther south, we can hit Panama City Beach on the way in. How about it? Shall we do some partying along the way?"

"Sounds like a plan," Seymore chimed.

Sandy, his face expressionless, said, "What the hell, it doesn't matter to me."

"Hey, come on," Mark said. "Once you get hooked up with one of those beach bunnies, you'll forget all about that girl of yours. Damnit, Sandy, get a grip."

Mark and Seymore each displayed expectant grins. Sandy tried to smile. "Okay-okay, screw it, you're right. Piss on her. Who the hell needs that kind of heartache...?"

"All right. That's the spirit!"

The Sky Soldiers

Chapter 47

DEREK JUSTEN MOVED SLOWLY TOWARD the cab parked at the far end of the Lawton, Oklahoma, airport terminal entrance, his baggage handled by the cab driver who had gone ahead of him and was now loading his suitcase and duffel bag in the trunk. When he finally made it to the cab and was seated in the back, Derek gave the driver Valerie's Fort Sill address.

"You just back from Nam?" the driver asked, easing into his seat.

Justen nodded.

"I been reading in the paper," the man said, as he pulled the cab away from the curb, "that this Tet thing sure stirred up a hornet's nest. Was you in much of the action?"

"Some," Derek replied, glancing toward the man momentarily, noting his inflamed nose and the stale smell of whiskey on his breath.

"You get wounded?"

"Yeah."

"How'd it happen?"

Justen turned and looked out the right window. The driver waited for an answer and when none was forthcoming, mumbled something about how he wished he was back in the service and was over there, he'd kick some butt. The man's ramblings fell on deaf ears. Derek eased back in the seat and thought of Valerie, hoping that when he saw her the past two years had not been too hard on her. As for himself, he felt good. He had just completed his third week of physical rehabilitation. His right leg still felt stiff and his back ached some, but he knew time would take care of that. Within minutes they were on the stretch of highway leading toward post. He gazed at the countryside, at the hills around Lawton and Fort Sill, still covered with a two-inch mantle of hard-packed snow pellets. The temperature hovered in the teens and the roads were icy everywhere. This had prompted him to take a cab instead of phoning Valerie to come to the airport to meet him.

He closed his eyes. It still felt strange to be back in the United States. Had he really been overseas twenty-two months? He remembered, if only vaguely, how his trip home began, nearly five weeks before...

Aside from the several loud discharges from the cannons, there was the tremendous roar and the whirlwind of dust and debris as the helicopter landed in the courtyard. He recalled being jostled on board with tense swiftness. The aircraft lifted. He felt the nose of the helicopter dip forward to pick up speed. Several onboard weapons fired, a shattering sound, after which his mind went blank. He awakened to the sensation of falling, but it was only the helicopter descending to the MASH landing pad at Dong Tam. Once on the ground, there was a flurry of

Victor R. Beaver

activity to get him out of the aircraft cabin. He remembered a large bright light. Then he felt himself going under. Five hours later, pain woke him. He spent two days in post-op, then was flown to Tan Son Nhut, where he was placed on board another aircraft, a medevac transport jet and airlifted to the United States.

    The long flight across the Pacific for most of the men being evacuated was an accumulation of images: of short periods of wakefulness where the thought of actually going home was beyond one's wildest imaginings; of drifting into drug-induced sleep lasting for several hours and more; of dreams pleasant and not so pleasant; of nightmares that had men screaming silently in their sleep, yet upon awakening finding the excursions of their subconscious innocuous compared to the frightening reality they had left behind; of being awakened to have blood pressure and heart rate and temperature checked and recorded, to have IV-lines re-established, to be given whatever their stomachs could handle for nourishment; of being attended to by angels in olive-drab uniforms who went silently about their work, who gave soft-scented comfort unlike anything many of them had known or felt for months. For Derek, it was a long, nightmarish journey, punctuated by moments of bliss (as his caregiver introduced morphine into his IV). He seemed to recall a near constant replay of seeing Jake's image somewhere in a large brightly lit room, close yet far away, beckoning to him, pleading, hurling silent screams at him. And then he would see Jake next to a large smooth boulder, white on a smooth, nearly blinding, white surface. Then Jake would roll the boulder away from him until all Derek saw of his half brother was a tiny dot against the featureless white background. And then he would swoop down with hawk-wings and all that could be seen as he neared the dot was that Jake was gone and the boulder remained. During his more blissful moments, Derek recalled a woman, tired-looking, her long straw-blonde hair disheveled, applying a compress against his forehead. There were times when he felt her body next to his, her breasts, soft and full, against his arm, and sometimes his chest; he recalled trembling. During these times he would look up and see a pair of sad, caring, hazel-colored eyes illuminated by some far-off light. He remembered trying to raise his head, wanting to speak, but his strength was so depleted that he could barely part his lips; she would tell him to relax as she periodically gave him his morphine. After a brief period, she would speak to him, but he never could quite make out her words. Then he was off, drifting, slowly, toward some quiet, peaceful place. And then she would speak to him: "Go to sleep, sugar. You're doing just fine...Go to sleep."

    The C-141 Starlifter transport jet made stops at Hickam Field on Oahu, Hawaii's main island, and one at Travis Air Force Base, outside San Francisco, his original point of departure for Vietnam. And then upon arrival at Denver Stapleton, he felt his first blast of cold air in over twenty-two months, when he was transferred from the plane to a waiting ambulance. The ride from the airport to Fitzsimmons Army Hospital was slow due to snow-packed streets. Though the ambulance's heater was quite adequate, he nonetheless shivered until he was senseless.

At the hospital, an efficient yet taciturn medical team met him and whisked him to his room, where he was undressed, bathed, and put to bed. The nurses and doctors allowed him to sleep for up to eight hours before awakening him to check his vital signs. On the third day following his arrival, he began his physical therapy. It was then that he learned of his temporary reassignment to CONUS (continental United States), permanent assignment orders to be issued pending notification when he would be available for duty.

During his rehabilitation he quickly gained weight and lost that gaunt, pathetic look. At first it was difficult to walk, even using the waist-high parallel bars. But after a week he could cross the length of the large workout room by merely using a cane. By the end of the second week he could go anywhere in the hospital without medical-staff help.

Though in the beginning he tired easily, he nonetheless grew stronger each day, until the doctors declared him fit to go on convalescent leave. He had been in touch with Valerie the moment he could lift a telephone receiver. Initially, she wanted to come and be with him at the hospital, but he told her it would be better if she remained at Fort Sill with the children. He also spent time on the telephone to DA (the Department of the Army) at the Pentagon. Information about Jake remained a big fat zero. Had there been any good news, though, the information would have been anything but recent. Good news could be so quickly dashed by updated bad news.

During his flight from Denver to Lawton, by way of Oklahoma City, he pondered one other aspect of his return to the United States: When would he, when could he, ship back to Vietnam? Or would he be allowed to do so? He was no longer on flight status, according to the flight surgeon at Fitzsimmons, and would not regain that status until his condition improved considerably. There was still much physical therapy he had to go through to regain the proper strength in his muscles, both in his legs and his left shoulder. When he learned of this he began his own workout regimen and vowed that within the next few months, hopefully sooner, he would be back flying again and on orders to return to Vietnam and the Mekong Delta. Two weeks before, he managed to extract a promise from the warrant officer assignment's branch that his next duty station be Fort Rucker, Alabama, where all aviator medical paperwork was sent for evaluation and action.

Deep in thought, Justen didn't notice when the cab stopped. He glanced at the small white duplex located in one of the older Fort Sill post-housing areas. Valerie and the children occupied the right-hand side. Her and Jake's military quarters looked smaller than he remembered, as if it had shrunk in size and had become insignificant. He felt strange, ill at ease. The driver got out and went to the trunk as Derek groped his way out from the passenger side. The driver carried his luggage to the small front porch. Derek handed the man a ten-dollar bill and told him to keep the change.

Justen rang the doorbell.

In a moment he heard footsteps and then the door was unlocked and opened.

Valerie, wearing a heavy cashmere sweater and blue jeans, her blonde hair combed back in a ponytail, stared at him through the screen door, not moving. "Derek...?"

He nodded. "Hi, Val."

The sound of his voice startled her and she practically pushed him back as she hastened to open the screen door.

"Oh, my God, Derek—you look so different. *You're so thin.*"

Gingerly, he made his way into the small living room. He turned and faced her. He handled his cane uneasily in front of her. He frowned and said:

"I'm not really used to this thing. I'm almost embarrassed to walk around with it."

She took a long look at him, then moved closer and cupped his face in her hands. "I've been so worried about you," she said. She reached up and kissed him on the forehead, then stepped back. "How are you?"

"I'm fine...really." He gazed at her for a second. "You look good," he said.

"No, I don't. I look awful. I haven't had a decent night's sleep since I learned you had been wounded. But that's neither here nor there. The question is, How are you doing? How are your wounds?"

"They're nothing. I've been on a pretty stiff rehab program. In a couple of months, I should be good as new."

She glanced outside and saw his luggage. After she helped him get his suitcase and duffel bag inside, he followed her into the kitchen, where she began running water for a pot of coffee. He pulled a chair out at the kitchen table and sat down. He propped the cane against the wall.

She said, "The children are still in school, on a field trip. They went to a museum here on post. I'll be going to get them in a little while. They can't wait to see you."

"How are they doing?" he asked.

"Better than me, that's for sure," she said, sighing heavily. "They're so used to Jake being gone they think it's normal that he's not here. I have to remind them all the time they still have a father and that he needs for them to wonder about him. Just...just like I do."

The coffee began to percolate. She reached over and turned down the heat and for a moment watched the steady throb of water in the little sight glass. "I really shouldn't expect them to act any different. After all, they are just children. They weren't very old when he went over." Her eyes took on a distant look. "I remember the night he left. It was late, right after midnight. He didn't want to wake them, so he went to their beds and one by one cradled them. Neither one stirred. Then he left their rooms. At the door, he held me for the longest time, then finally kissed me gently on the forehead." Derek saw tears come to Valerie's eyes as she spoke. "He didn't even kiss me on the mouth. Maybe he was trying to act like this was just another one of his temporary duty trips." Quizzically, she looked at him. "Derek, was it to make it easier on him?...Or on me?" And then she said, somberly, "Oh, Derek, I wish I knew what to do. I can't even plan my life. I go through each day in a fog. If it wasn't for the children, I swear I'd really be a basket case—"

He stood and went to her. She was crying now and he took her in his arms and held her and caressed her head and smelled the fragrance of her hair and felt the smallness of her lithe frame against his body. He said, "I know it's been hard. I wish I knew what to say. Any day now we should hear something. Honestly, this not knowing can't last forever."

She listened, and as she listened her crying subsided. She found herself leaning against him, the tension in her body easing. She felt his arms enfolding her. After a moment, when she knew that she would be able to maintain her composure, she found herself reluctant to withdraw from him. As she remained within his fold, there stirred within her something very deep and very primitive. At first she was unable to identify it, but when she did, it caused her to recoil from him. When he looked at her with a puzzled frown, she knew he was seeing her face flush. She rushed from the kitchen and went to her bedroom, where she sat on her bed in a mild state of shock at how quickly she had become aroused by him. *No, this did not happen—it never happened.* It took several minutes before she could leave the bedroom and face him. When she returned to the kitchen, she saw that his face betrayed nothing of what she was certain he had seen. Perhaps he was being terribly considerate, but then she thought not. At times, she was in awe of his innocence.

"Are you okay?" he asked, oblivious to her trembling.

"Fine. Just fine. I-I just...suddenly felt overwhelmed."

"Are you sure? You look kind of pale."

"Yes, don't worry about me. Like I said, it's been a long, long time: too much worrying and wondering." There was an awkward moment of silence between them. She wasn't sure what to do next. Then she saw in his face and the condition of his uniform that he must be travel weary. She took him back to Robbie's bedroom, where she said he would be sleeping. She helped him with his luggage and brought him a clean towel and washcloth and told him to make himself at home, she had a few errands to run before going after the children.

That evening, after Robbie and Jill were put to bed, Derek and Valerie stayed up late talking. He spoke of his desire to return overseas as soon as he was well and was back on flying status. She sat in front of him on the couch, her face a

Victor R. Beaver

mixture of curiosity—and horror. "Why, Derek? Haven't you done enough? My God—"

He spoke slowly, evenly, saying there was no way he could remain in the States as long as Jake was in Vietnam, missing in action. "If he's alive, and I feel certain that he is, someone's got to be there."

"But you've already been over there so long," she said, her voice almost a plea. "Haven't you given enough? What more could you do if you went back?"

"I don't know. But that doesn't matter. I can't be back here no matter what."

As he spoke, she listened, wondering, Could his return to Vietnam really make a difference? Somehow she doubted that it would—or could. But he was set on going and she knew that he would not change his mind. But how long would he stay this time? Until he was wounded again, or worse, killed? Innately, she knew that the longer he spent in combat the greater his chances of dying. It wasn't fair that she might lose both of them. And the maddening thing was she wasn't sure she still had Jake!

She diverted her gaze downward, looking at her hands resting on her lap. "Why don't we know something, Derek? What is it that keeps us from knowing? I don't understand. It doesn't make any sense."

He saw the slump in her shoulders. When she looked up he could see the deep hurt in her eyes. He was grateful he hadn't had to face her these past two years. He paused for a moment. What answer could he give that would satisfy her? "Val, they can't report what they don't know. The only thing they know for sure is that he's missing. At least we know he's not a KIA. And I admit," he said, sighing heavily and taking a deep drag on his cigarette, "it would be a slight bit more comforting if we knew he was a POW. At least then we would know for sure he was alive."

It was morning. Valerie lay in bed and yawned deeply. She stretched her arms wide. Her fingers groped, as if trying to bend the shafts of sunlight streaming into her room around her.

She glanced at the clock. She remembered last night she had turned off the alarm. It was Saturday and there was no school, but she awakened as she had always done, as the first rays of sunlight came through her bedroom window, normally a few minutes before the alarm was set to go off.

In the bathroom she splashed water on her face and rubbed vigorously the sleep from her eyes. She toweled her face and then paused for a moment and took a long look at herself. On this morning she saw something different. Typically, her eyes reflected an abundant weariness; today, however, she detected a faint sparkle. She remembered that she had slept the whole night without waking. She had had no unpleasant dreams. She smiled, though the sun hid suddenly behind a cloud.

The Sky Soldiers

She took her robe from the hook on the door and put it on, pulling the cord tight around her waist. She took one last glance in the mirror, patting loose strands of hair into place. She stepped out into the hallway, closing the bedroom door behind her. She peeked into Jill's room, where Jill and Robbie were asleep. Assuring herself that they were still properly covered, she turned and went across the narrow hallway.

She stood at Robbie's bedroom door. It was slightly ajar. All she saw as she looked in was the back of Derek's head, and sensed too that he was still fast asleep. She placed her hand on the doorknob and moved the door more open, to insure, she told herself, that he was okay and perhaps properly covered. And then she saw the scars, dark red and still swollen on his bare back and right leg. She peered at them for a long moment, wondering what it must have felt like to be shot. And then an uncomfortable feeling came over her. She felt a pull in her lower abdomen. What was she doing, staring at him like this? *He was practically naked.* She closed her eyes. "Oh, Derek," she whispered aloud, "what have they done to you?" She kept her eyes closed and when she opened them, he was sitting up, looking at her. She didn't know what to do or say; his gaze left her rooted in place. "I-uh, your door was open," she said. "I was just closing it." He nodded, saying, "I'm a pretty light sleeper." He reached for his cigarettes and lit one. She said, "I'm going to make breakfast. What would you like?" "Coffee, strong and black," he replied. "I can do that," she said, and backed away, closing the door.

She trembled as she prepared the coffee. When she opened the refrigerator door she stood for a long moment not knowing what it was she was searching for, until she saw a carton of eggs and an unopened package of bacon, items she bought yesterday at the commissary in anticipation of his visit. She reached for them and placed them on the kitchen counter. Be calm, she told herself, as she placed the electric skillet on the counter and plugged it in and set the dial. She turned on the radio and hunted for a station she rarely listened to anymore, one that played tunes from recording artists like Percy Faith, The Mystic Moods, Frank Sinatra, and Henry Mancini. She heard one of her favorites, *Moon River.* As she placed the bacon in the skillet, she let the melody wash over her. Soon she found her body swaying, her head lolling gently upon her shoulders. She knew she was smiling; it felt good to smile again. As the bacon began to pop and sizzle, she thought that she should make a fresh container of orange juice. She wanted Derek to smell and taste what home was like again. She had decided last night after she had gone to bed and had lain awake with him out in the living room where she had left him, smoking, sitting on the couch, with only the light over the stove filtering feebly into the living room, that she wanted his stay to be completely restful, a brief respite from the grueling past two months (and longer) he had just endured.

After she made the orange juice, she saw that the bacon was done and forked it onto a paper towel on a plate. She took a half-dozen eggs out of the carton and broke them into a bowl. With a fork she beat them until yoke and egg white were one. And then the thought that Derek was determined to return overseas began to play on her mind, until finally she burst into tears. As she wept, she realized how vulnerable she was, had always been, and now that he was here, his presence became proof that her armor was not ironclad, was, in fact, more fragile that she cared to admit. In the presence of Robbie and Jill, she maintained a good front, a false front, but of the kind her children needed. But whom had she been able to turn to for comfort? No one. *I can't keep this up—* "Derek, how much longer must I go on?" she whispered to herself, through a veil of tears. And then she sensed him standing behind her. She turned. He had emerged from Robbie's bedroom buttoning the front of a blue denim shirt.

"Val? Are you okay?"

In the next instant she found herself in his arms, sobbing. She felt his hands on her back pressing her body into his.

"It's okay, Val...please, it will be all right. I promise." Again his arms enveloped her, she was within the folds of his strong body, and again she felt the same primitive stirrings she did yesterday. She pulled away and dabbed at her eyes with a tissue. She went to the coffeepot and poured him a cup. Derek pulled a chair away from the kitchen table and sat down.

"I'm sorry," she said, trembling. "You're being here...it's...it's done something to—I mean for me..." *To me, for me—Which is it?*

"There's nothing to be sorry for. I wish there was more I could do. Let's try to get through this." He became silent. He didn't know why he said what he said next. "I could go stay in a motel...if you like."

Her eyes grew narrow. She looked at him and saw that he recognized in her that which she had begun to fear most. Reflexively, though, she blurted out: "Oh, no you don't, Derek Patrick Justen." It was then that she threw all caution aside. Her eyes began to glisten and a smile came to her face; and a soft glow permeated her body throughout. The kitchen became brighter as sunlight broke through a split in the clouds; it began pouring forth through the window behind her. "You're staying right here. The children need you. And so do I. And that's final."

Chapter 48

SANDY, MARK, AND SEYMORE DROVE onto Fort Rucker through the Daleville gate. They asked for directions twice and eventually found their new company area. It was situated in an old section of post called Tank Hill, about half a mile from the main candidate billeting area.

Willie Cottrell met them as they drove into the parking lot. He told them that all the original flights were being split up and that he was assigning men to rooms as they came onto post. Mark and Sandy teamed up in a two-man room across the hall from Seymore and Darryl Chancey. Tom Adkins and Frank Bartlett appeared an hour later and became roommates at the opposite end of the barrack.

The isolation of Class 67-15 from the rest of the candidate corps afforded them minimal advantage. The reason became quickly clear: The seniors were too busy preparing for duty in Vietnam to create chaos among the ranks. Perhaps it was because combat loomed so close for everyone that a strong brotherhood prevailed among all candidates, juniors and seniors alike.

They saw other changes. Out went their flight suits (for flying) and in came their fatigues, since pilots in Vietnam wore jungle fatigues just like the ground troops they supported. The seniors, the two classes of upperclassmen next to graduate, had a black felt tab on their pockets and wore on their fatigue caps the same school emblem only on a square-cut, black-felt background.

To compensate for their impending assignment overseas, the married men were allowed to quarter with their families, while the single candidates were required to remain in company barracks. It was only during their last month of training that they could make off-post living arrangements. This meant that for the next three months the unmarried men had to keep their locker displays inspection-ready, their rooms spotlessly clean. It wasn't fair, but that's the way it was.

They spent the first days in-processing, drawing bedding, being briefed on company policies, et cetera. Instead of tac officers, their overseers were tac NCOs (noncommissioned officers), staff sergeants and above. Furthermore, no longer did the candidate chain-of-command change once a week. Former NCOs were made permanent candidate platoon leaders. Right away this caused friction in the ranks. For a four-month period these tin gods could again weld rank with the impunity they thought it deserved. One such "lord and master," a certain Candidate Pardee, strutted the company area like a full-bloomed peacock. During his first week in power he had his men strip the barrack floors of old wax and apply a new coat. He then made them wash all windows, inside and out, scour the latrines, rake up every leaf, twig and pine needle, trim the hedges, and paint the steel hand-rails along the outside stairs going into the old two-story building.

Victor R. Beaver

"What has the sonofabitch got in mind?" Tom Adkins cried. "Graduating as a chief warrant officer ten—!"

They complained to former first sergeant Ned Symington, now the permanent candidate company commander, but all he did was shake his head. "It's his platoon, guys. He can run it anyway he likes—within reason, of course; it's the army way."

Within the first week they took a PT (physical training) test. This meant running, dodging, crawling, jumping, and throwing a make-believe hand grenade for accuracy and distance. Cuts, scrapes, scratches, blood, sweat, tears, blisters, sideaches, shortness of breath, hallucinations, hyperventilation...

"You ought to max this test," Seymore told Sandy, who had the highest score in his basic training company and one of the fastest mile-run times.

"Go fly a kite. I can barely breath in this humidity."

"Better get used to it," said Ron Bowden, the ex-Huey-crewchief. "It's ten times worse in Vietnam."

Just up the street was a one-story building that housed a post exchange, barber shop, dry cleaners, and small snack shop and beer hall. Now that the flights had dispersed, new alliances were formed, and when they gathered in the beer hall in threes and fours, with old friendships blending with the new, Class 67-15 slowly began to take on the character of the rest of the candidate corps: a "one for all and all for one" kind of camaraderie, the only kind to take to war.

* * *

THE VOICE CAME EVENLY OVER THE intercom: "Okay, look at the bank angle index. See it? What does it read? Zero—because the index is directly under the large center tic-mark. At this moment," said the voice, "we are not turning. Notice how the heading gyro remains stationary?"

"Yessir," Sandy Adamson said.

Bates continued: "Also observe the black dot. Notice how it stays right on the artificial horizon, neither above nor below? That's how we keep our altitude."

The two men, student and instructor, were in a TH-13T helicopter at two thousand feet, south of Shell Army Airfield, one of many such airfields around the Fort Rucker training complex. Warren Bates, a heavy-set civilian "contract" instructor with large chubby fingers, had the controls and was demonstrating straight-and-level flight. Sandy had a gray plastic "hood" fitted to his helmet. He could see neither left nor right, and by keeping his head tilted down slightly, he could not see outside the aircraft above the instrument panel. For the past several minutes, with practically all of his peripheral vision gone, Sandy felt like he was continually spinning in an enclosed box.

Before him were several flight instruments. They were designed to tell him one of two things about the attitude of the helicopter with respect to the earth's surface: Whether or not the aircraft (wings or tip-path plane) was level with the horizon, whether or not the nose was pitched up or down (also with respect to the horizon). One instrument, the artificial horizon, a miniature replica of the earth, housed in a metal case and driven by a very sensitive gyro, told him both flight attitudes and was considered the primary flight control instrument. Because the Earth was gone from view (by the hood), it took a giant leap of faith for Sandy to believe the truth of this instrument (as well as others).

"You want to try it?"

"Yessir."

Bates said, "Maintain two thousand feet, sixty knots, and a heading of one eight zero."

"Yessir." Sandy locked his gaze on the artificial horizon. He took hold of the cyclic and collective and put his feet on the anti-torque pedals. At first, the instruments remained stationary, and then he watched as the artificial horizon began to tilt to the right (in its housing), which meant the aircraft was in a turn to the left. (That is, the heading gyro showed a slow rotation.)

"You're in a turn," the IP said. "Don't you see that you're in a turn—?"

Sandy sensed the man's condescending tone; he felt a hot flush come over him. "I...I don't feel it..."

"You're not going to *feel* it necessarily. That's why you have to *see* it on the instruments and react quickly to what you see."

"Yessir." Sandy felt abrupt pressure against the cyclic, as Bates moved the bank angle index (on the artificial horizon) back to a zero indication. During the process, Sandy's body had felt nothing, no sensation of turning. At that moment he felt no kinship either toward Bates, like he had toward Gressing and Crandall. *Damn. I hate this instrument flying already—!*

"Remember," said Bates, "little cyclic corrections done quickly helps maintain the index at zero. This keeps us from having to make big corrections later."

"How much later?"

"A few seconds later, for crying out loud—"

For the next fifteen minutes, Sandy practiced straight-and-level flight. Eventually, he was able to keep the instruments fairly stationary, remaining close to his assigned heading, airspeed, and altitude. "You're doing fair. Lot's of room for improvement, though," Bates told him. "Now let me introduce a straight-ahead descent. We'll descend on a heading of two seven zero, at five hundred feet per minute, to one thousand five hundred feet. First, I'll reduce power and add a little right pedal to counteract the torque effect. I'll keep the horizon bar and the little dot on the horizon bar on the imaginary horizon." In the beginning, Sandy felt the aircraft in a descent, but after the maneuver was in progress he sensed nothing. "Whenever you change power, you've really got to think trim," Bates stated. "If you're not in trim, your inner ear really goes on a tangent: the sensation of tumbling becomes rampant. That's called vertigo, if you haven't already guessed."

Sandy nodded his head. "Yessir...occasionally I've been feeling that...I think."

"That's normal, at least until you get used to the hood."

"Yessir."

Academics constituted the other half of each day. In the classroom they studied programmed text that explained aircraft attitude control. They reviewed page after page of various combinations of instrument indications and were asked to choose among several answers what flight attitude the aircraft was in. Many thought these lessons confused more than they helped, since the displays were not dynamic renditions of the real thing. After a day of classes and practice instrument flying, they returned to the barracks more exhausted than if they had put in eight hours digging ditches.

* * *

EIGHT STUDENTS CROWDED NEAR THE doorway and entered the room. They saw eight large blue wooden rectangular boxes, each slightly curved at the top, on raised platforms, four on either side of the room. Next to each box was a table. On each table was a white sheet of paper covered with pre-printed, criss-crossing lines. Above the paper was a horizontally arranged, multi-hinged arm with a fine-pointed stylus that could move and trace hard-copy lines. As each student went along the aisle, toward an assigned "box," it quickly became apparent that this was not going to be to their liking either: Being seated in the box, shut in, and asked to perform ADF (automatic direction finder) course recognition, interception, and route-following work. The box was the infamous "Blue Canoe" they had all heard about.

Seymore P. Cutter handed his grade folder to a young woman seated at the table next to his assigned cockpit simulator. She stood and greeted him and took his folder and asked that he be seated in the empty chair next to hers.

His mouth agape, Seymore complied.

"My name is Jenny McCoy," she said. "I'll be your instructor."

"I...I...I'm glad to meet you."

"Are you nervous?" she asked, a smile spreading across her face so radiant that Seymore's insides turned instantly to jelly.

"Just a little..."

"Relax...you won't feel a thing."

But he did, because suddenly, Seymore P. Cutter was head-over-heels in love.

For the next several minutes, Jenny McCoy explained the workings of the Blue Canoe. He would be seated in the cockpit, she told him, behind a set of flight controls that loosely resembled the real aircraft. She talked about the paper with the criss-crossing lines. "I'll be giving you air traffic control clearances designed to have you intercept certain courselines. The stylus will trace on the chart how well you set up for that. You'll have to recognize, once you parallel the course, where the course is: to your left or to your right. Then you will fly the appropriate heading to intercept that course at a forty-five-degree angle—just like you've been learning in your programmed text. So far, do you follow?"

"Yes-yes...oh yes, I do..." Seymore replied. His adoring gaze never left her face. She had short wavy brown hair, light brown eyes, a pretty little upturned nose, and a voice that filled the air like a song. He would have "followed" her anywhere.

"You ready to try it?" she said.

"Absolutely."

For some reason, with his head in "a cloud," Seymore was a natural. Jenny McCoy had never in her two years as an instructor seen anyone pick up orientation to the ADF needle so quickly. After an hour, she was certain Seymore had some supernatural insight to the mysteries of instrument flight that had eluded even her. To top it off, his basic aircraft control was extraordinary. "You are doing terrific, Candidate Cutter."

"Aaah...it's nothing, really," Seymore answered over the intercom. He pointed to the RMI (radio magnetic indicator) as if she were in the cockpit with him, looking over his shoulder. "I just imagine I'm the tail of the ADF needle, the center of the RMI card where the needle pivots is the NDB station, and that I am looking down upon myself from above. With my mind's eye, I draw an imaginary line from the card's center to the number or course you ask me to intercept...and from there it's easy."

"That's amazing—I'm really impressed. Keep up the good work."

I would do anything for you, he thought, and then wondered if she was married. "I didn't notice," he said, again over the intercom system, "but are-are you wearing a ring?"

"You mean...am I married?"

"Yeah."

"No, but if you propose to me, you'll be number seventeen. Last month I had twenty-one offers of marriage."

Seymore burst into Mark and Sandy's room. "Mark—I need to borrow your car." Class 67-15 was in the middle of their second week of basic instrument flight training. The two roommates sat at their desks with their program text open, their heads feeling like two blocks of stone as they tried to understand the correct radio procedures that were part and parcel of instrument flying.

"What for?"

"I've got a date."

"With who?" asked Mark.

"My simulator instructor—*Jenny McCoy!*"

"How the hell did you manage that?" Sandy asked, his eyes wide with astonishment.

"She asked me."

"She asked you—?" Sandy's lower lip dropped ten inches.

Mark flipped him the keys. Seymore bolted for the door. "Hey—it needs gas!"

Seymore was already in his room tearing off his fatigues. "I'll fill it up. Thanks!"

Jenny and Seymore sat in the post movie theater, their fingers intertwined. Whenever a tender love scene appeared, Jenny squeezed Seymore's hand and looked adoringly at him in the semi-darkness. The lad's heart was so warm, it felt on the verge of meltdown. Outside, in the warm night air, sweet with the smell of lilac and honeysuckle, Seymore asked, "So, where do you want to go? Do you want to get something to eat?"

"Whatever you want to do, Seymore." Jenny's voice sounded like the call of a mourning dove.

"How about we go get some ice cream?"

At the Dairy Queen, Jenny said, "Your favorite is strawberry, Seymore?"

"Yep...plain ole ordinary everyday strawberry. In a plain ole ordinary everyday cone..."

They were parked near Lake Tholocco, at one of the post recreation areas. A full moon shown brightly overhead. "How'd you get to be a flight instructor?" Seymore asked

Jenny said, "My dad has a flying school in Boise. I've been interested in flying since I was eight. I got my instructor rating in a helicopter when I was twenty. I got this job here at Rucker two years ago. Southern Alabama is like no other place I've been. At night, especially right now in the spring, I feel like I'm being wrapped in a warm wet blanket." She then snuggled closer to him. He smelled the lilac fragrance of her hair. "Do you like it here, Seymore?"

"I love it here."

"I'm glad, Seymore..."

On the third weekend the pair drove to Panama City Beach in Jenny's car. Seymore spread the blanket and erected the large sun umbrella they had bought at one of the many beach stores along the strip. From an ice-cooler he produced a Coke and opened it for her. The white sand and the sun and the sparkle off the water were so bright they had to wear sunglasses to shield the glare.

"Would you put some lotion on my back, Seymore?"

He took the small bottle and opened it while she lay on her stomach and undid her strap. Seymore took a deep breath and began to apply the lotion, spreading it smoothly across the softness of her back. Once in a while Jenny turned her head and peeked up at him, lifting her sunglasses. "Do people tease you about your freckles, Seymore?"

"Aah...not so much anymore."

"I'll never do that, Seymore."

They stayed and watched the sun go down. When finally it dipped below the horizon, it cast off an array of colors so intense that they were dazzled by the spectacle. "That was the loveliest sunset I have ever seen, Seymore." She wrapped her arms around him. "Did you think it was lovely, too?"

He sighed deeply. "I thought it was absolutely beautiful."

* * *

SANDY ADAMSON SLAMMED THE INSTRUMENT flight-training manual on the table. "This crap doesn't make a lick of sense." Mark Allen was seated on his bunk, his hands wrapped around the harmonica he recently bought.

Mark looked up. "You know, I always wanted to learn to play one of these things. How am I doing? Not bad, eh?"

"Are you listening to me?" Sandy exploded.

"Sure."

Sandy slumped in the chair. He looked at Mark. "When I'm in the Blue Canoe, I draw a blank. I look at that ADF needle and the numbers around the RMI card and when I'm given a clearance to intercept some stupid course, I can't see it! What's the matter with me?"

"Hey—you and about three hundred other guys."

"You too?"

"Ditto."

Sandy thumbed toward Seymore and Chancey's room. "I can't understand those two. This shit is a breeze to them—*especially Seymore!* How the hell did he suddenly get to be so brilliant—?"

Mark smiled. "The man's in love. L-O-V-E. Besides, I've been studying him; he's a natural. Wouldn't surprise me, either, if he gets hitched."

"Hitched—? You mean married?"

Mark nodded. "I know the signs. Not only that, she's crazy about him—"

Sandy stared at the floor. Seymore, of all people, had wound up with the cutest girl this side of the Mississippi. It was unbelievable.

Mark began to play a song he had been practicing, a Christy Minstrel's tune...

"Don't cry, Suzanne...don't sigh, Suzanne
Though I'm going away.
Yesterday was Sunday...
Monday is the day.

Victor R. Beaver

*I hear the bugles blowing
calling every man...
I'll be home by early spring,
Don't cry, Suzanne..."*

Chapter 49

THE DAYS THAT FOLLOWED WENT by slowly. Each day Derek made a phone call to the Pentagon, and each day he was informed that nothing new was known of Jake's status or whereabouts. After each call, he wrote a follow-up letter. Long ago Valerie had exhausted her capacity to daily ride herd on her husband's MIA status. She had told Derek that allowing a week to pass before pestering someone (and still not learn anything new) made it much easier to take than the daily declaration of the fact. He agreed, for her sake, that that was probably best. In his own mind, however, just like he had done in Vietnam, he wanted to keep Jake's name from slipping through the cracks. A phone call with a follow-up letter was like using a cattle prod to keep the machinery from ossifying.

Derek became reacquainted with the children. Robbie, seven, had the best recollection of his father and was slow to warm to his uncle. Jill, two years younger, only vaguely remembered her daddy, thus she took to Derek like a long lost playmate. Thereafter, he found himself playing paperdolls, sitting at the small play table being served "tea," and at night his young niece curled up in his lap while he read her bedtime stories from several of her favorite books. Then one day Robbie presented him with a baseball and glove. They went outside and tossed the ball back and forth until darkness and dinner brought them in.

Meanwhile, Valerie watched her children with growing interest. They had become calmer with Derek around. Seeing this caused her to be more and more at peace. Each night her sleep became ever more restful. She enjoyed cooking again, fixing meals that required some thought and care. When she went grocery shopping, she found herself delighted that she could once again buy with the tastes of a man in mind. Jake had always liked steak, or red chili, hot and spicy to the taste. Her brother-in-law's likes weren't any different. She began reading again, books that she had started before Derek arrived but had put down because her mind would wander and she would think of Jake and whether or not he was alive. She went to the beauty parlor and had her hair cut and styled, something she hadn't done in months. She went shopping and bought a new dress. Along with the dress, she splurged and bought a pair of new shoes, new earrings and a necklace. It was a moment of pure frivolousness. She bought wine. During afternoons, she and Derek would share a glass or two. Afterwards, before starting dinner, she would take a hot bath and allow the effects of the water on her skin and the wine to overtake her, putting her even deeper into a state of tranquility. She was fast losing herself in feelings she had not felt for a long time. *It was wonderful...it was delicious...it was...it was—Wrong!* What right did she have to feel this way while her husband rotted in some jungle prison on the other side of

Victor R. Beaver

the world?—if indeed he was a POW. *Jake, my darling...please please forgive me.*

Luckily, her guilt-ridden feelings were short-lived. It had been so long since she had felt anything, except a vague kind of numbness, that even the feeling of guilt was a welcome change. The children had always been her diversion, her excuse for sidestepping her true emotions. Now that Derek was here, and the children preoccupied with someone other than herself, she realized she could step back and evaluate where she had come. She was terribly lonely. A down-deep kind of lonely. And what if they never learned anything? What if Jake stayed missing forever? What then? Wasn't it the lack of knowing, her inability to choose her life's direction based on knowledge that was the true source of her frustration? her loneliness? Yes yes yes—! It was maddening. Missing-in-action. Missing. Missing where?—off the face of the earth! *Why can't he be dead? I could handle that.* Afterwards, she would think, What kind of demented person am I?—to wish my husband was dead!

In spite of it all, she had coped. It was for the children's sake, of course. But she needed fuel—emotional fuel—just like any human being. She needed a safe harbor, away from the storm, though the storm was in her head. She was fast learning that Derek's presence was that safe harbor.

Though Derek's presence was a godsend, after so many months of days that all blended into one, she realized there was also something unsettling about having him around. Even though he wasn't the natural father of her children, whatever he did with them was all so normal—so perfectly acceptable. There was nothing he could not do with them as any real father might. At first this pleased her, but eventually it caused her an odd discomfort. She was still without a man, still without the comforting touch that a man could provide. And because of this she grew emptier of spirit. How difficult it was to be near someone and yet not be able to gather from them that private intimacy she so longed for. As the days passed, the seeds of discontent built, until one evening, late at night, as she lay in bed fully awake, with her mind's eye gathering in the many images she had of Derek together with the children, she realized that they were more blessed by Derek's presence than she would ever be. She burst into tears. "It isn't fair—*it just isn't fair!*" She ceased crying only out of exhaustion. Afterwards, she chided herself for her weakness.

As one day led to another, Derek, too, began to move in a fog of his own. In the beginning, he tolerated the children's attention. Then he began to wish that they would leave him alone. The initial camaraderie had worn off, and he missed being his normal brooding self. It was the only way he knew to guard against the despair he felt about Jake—of not knowing anything—of wondering how long his brother could hold out—wherever he was. He still felt certain Jake was alive somewhere in the U Minh Forest. Was he alone or with others? If alone, his chances of survival were very slim indeed, for he was well aware that it took the misery of some other person to put one's own misery into perspective. He hoped, somewhat ashamedly, that Jake had plenty of company. He knew for a fact that Americans were being held prisoner in the U Minh. In January, Captain Tafoya, the MAT (military advisory team) commander at Thoi Binh, had leaked information to him about sightings of non-oriental men being escorted in sampans by Viet Cong guerillas along the Forest's canals and riverways. He was told they were probably being moved to different camps for security reasons, which meant that the number of camps had to be several. Whether this was good or bad, he didn't know. American-escorted combat excursions into the U Minh had been several during the early years of the war. By late 1966, these excursions dwindled to nothing, perhaps because the fighting in Vietnam had escalated more critically elsewhere. By early 1967, the Americans listed as MIA in the southern portion of the Mekong Delta was known to be about thirty, with ten of those now confirmed as POWs.

It was the last day of his visit. The following morning Derek would leave for Fort Rucker, there to ride out his time until he regained his flying status. That morning, while he was seated at the breakfast table, Valerie had asked if he would like to go out to dinner, perhaps to the officers' club. It would be her treat. She could easily make arrangements for a baby-sitter. She thought it would be pleasant to spend a quiet evening out, just the two of them. Maybe there would be music and they could dance, she told him.

"I don't really have anything to wear," he said.

"Wear your uniform. You look very handsome in it."

"All right."

That evening, when she appeared before him, the sight of her took his breath away. She wore a long, black, low-cut velvet dress with sleeves that covered her long slender arms down to her wrists. As she walked toward him, he could see the slit on the left side that alluringly exposed her leg, nearly to her thigh. Her blonde hair was scooped high on her head in a mass of ringlets. She wore a pair of dazzling earrings that made her look like the goddess he always thought her to be. "Do you like?" she said.

"You are stunning," he said. "I will clearly be the envy of every man at the club."

"Derek...the dress...it's not too...whatever, is it?"

He breathed deep. He knew what she was asking. "Well, it might be a little revealing...but you deserve it, Val."

At the officers' club they ate exquisitely, he a large cut of prime rib, done rare, she a savory dish of chicken cordon bleu. They shared a canter of wine. "I'm afraid that my dancing won't be at all like you remember," he said, directing his attention to the cane leaning against the wall, "but I would be willing to stumble to a few very slow notes." He had risen from his seat and offered his arm.

"Why, sir, I don't mind if I do." She took his arm and he led her onto the dance floor. They were oblivious to the curious stares they generated. They had chosen to dance to a Frank Sinatra song being played by the disc jockey who sat behind a half glassed-in studio of stereo equipment. By the middle of the song, her head was leaning against his chest.

> *"When I was twenty-one...it was*
> *a very good year.*
> *It was a very good year*
> *for city girls who lived*
> *Up the stairs...*
> *With all that perfumed hair*
> *and it came undone*
> *When I was twenty-one..."*

He enfolded her like a child, but she didn't look like a child...or smell like a child...nor in the grasp of his hands and wrapped in his arms did she feel like one. Though there were moments of awkwardness due to his wounds, he swept her across the floor as if they were gliding on a cloud. She snuggled closer to him, her arms were around him caressing the nape of his neck, her lips touching his cheek, building in him a momentum that he suddenly wished had no bounds. And then the longer he held her, the better her body felt, the more the pressure began to build, until, after a while, he heaved a great sigh and said:

"Please, Valerie...we...I...can't...do this."

She looked up and he saw the great welling in her eyes, her smile, half-happy, half-sad, inviting him to hold her and caress her as she was doing to him. He wanted to, the urge to do so was almost overwhelming. She was lovely and soft and giving—*and trusting.*

She said, "Yes...I know-I know."

"God, Val, it isn't right. It just isn't right—"

"I know, darling...I know. Hold me a little longer, Derek, please...just a little longer. What can it hurt?"

> *"But now the days are short...*
> *I'm in the autumn of the year*
> *And now I think of my life*
> *as vintage wine...*
> *From fine old kegs*
> *from the brim to the dregs*

it poured sweet and clear
It was a very good year..."

From the moment they came through the door, they were besieged by pandemonium. The baby-sitter tried to settle the children down, but they kept running around, laughing and screaming.

"What for heaven's sake is it?" Valerie cried.

"You got a call—about fifteen minutes ago!" the young girl answered. "It was from Washington. Some men are right now coming to see you!"

"What for—?"

"It's about your husband, Mrs. Cole. They say he's alive!"

Victor R. Beaver

Chapter 50

ONE DAY SLATER LOOKED IN THE mirror and saw a stranger peering back. He saw the beginnings of deep creases across his forehead and infant "crow's feet" clutching at the corners of his eyes. His eyes particularly were like those of every pilot who spends time in the cockpit, squinting in the bright sun at the horizon and everywhere below. Overall, though, he thought his facial features had become chiseled, like a woodsman's hands that had grown used to the axe. He had come close to death and had seen the dead and the dying. Slater, now the veteran pilot, had a profound sense of his own mortality. He had known stark terror, like the day he averted a mid-air collision with another helicopter. They had been in formation and had been ordered to change the formation. (Munson, his peter-pilot, was flying.) He happened to glance left and saw another helicopter veering toward them. On reflex he slapped the cyclic control stick right causing their helicopter to careen down and to the right. Had he not looked up when he did, he and his crew and the crew of the other helicopter would all be dead.

Kip had seen the same chiseled features on Leo's face. One day, Tannah returned from Moc Hoa with the green skylight above his head shot out. It was the second time his friend happened upon a group of farmers while low leveling across the Plain of Reeds; and it was the second time the "sticks" they were holding had turned suddenly to weapons. Though shaken, Leo shrugged it off. Kip, however, gazed at him and wondered when the day would come when he was told that Tannah was shot down—down in some grove of trees—or down near the Cambodian border—or down along the base of the Seven Mountains—or down within some free-fire zone. "Leo," he asked, "what did you tell Major Maes?"

"That we saw some gooks in a field and when we started to circle back, they opened up."

"While you were at fifteen hundred feet?"

"Sure...at fifteen hundred feet."

The following day, he and Tannah were in formation at two thousand feet, returning from Can Tho. Slater heard Leo report over the radio that he was receiving fire and had his doorgunners start blasting. Lieutenant Oremsby, Tiger Lead, incensed that Leo's gunners were shooting from that high altitude, cried over the radio for the firing to stop.

On the ground, Leo's crewchief inspected their ship for damage, but it was Rusty who found the bullet, in *Alfie,* back in the oil-cooling fan compartment, a single round lodged between two bonded sheets of metal, its momentum skyward all but spent before making contact. It was purely a lucky shot, a desperation shot, which did nothing more than cause a scratch. But where did the rounds from Leo's guns go?...What or whom had they hit?

***

"IT'S THE SAME SHIT AS LAST TIME," Trent Whitaker said to the men gathered around him. They were at the Ca Mau airstrip, north of Nam Can. Phase II of the evacuation of Nam Can was about to begin. "God help whoever goes down."

An hour later saw the first wave of helicopters descend into the Nam Can LZ, followed quickly by the second wave. When the last ship had lifted, one hundred and sixty ARVN were on site to secure the LZ's perimeter and to provide nominal cover for the remaining occupants finally leaving the beleaguered outpost. Nam Can was about to be given over to the Viet Cong—what would be left of it.

This time the trip to Ca Mau through "two-ship country" had them on the edge of their seats. The number of VC flags visible had doubled since the last time they were there. As the slicks neared the outpost, machine-gun and small arm's fire erupted from every quarter. Flanked by a heavy fire team on either side, the pilots and crews of the troop carriers watched breathless as rockets fired and miniguns peppered the route ahead. The doorgunners were allowed to suppress; they fired their swivel-mounted M-60s until the barrels glowed. Half the ships received battle damage. Two lift-helicopter doorgunners received wounds, while one Outlaw pilot was killed after receiving a bullet wound to the head. Only one ship was hit bad enough to be grounded. Abandoning the helicopter in the LZ, the downed crew sought refuge among the ARVN forces at the perimeter's edge, receiving and returning enemy gunfire.

Four AH-1G Cobra gunships orbited overhead, poised to deliver the knockout punch once all troops were gone. Nolan tightened his grip on the handle of the TSU and looked below. "Make sure, if you have to suppress, you keep the pattern in a straight line. Otherwise you're liable to hit friendlies," Hardin warned. "Roger that," Nolan replied.

Before departing Can Tho, Hardin briefed his pilots that all the hours of frustration and boredom the past few weeks flying circles over the Plain of Reeds was about to come to an end. "Today," he said, "we're going to be in what is commonly called a target-rich environment."

Kip Slater sat stiff-backed, his body crammed into the seat as far as it could go. If he could will his body to the size of a pea, he would have gladly done so. Earlier, before departing from Ca Mau, he had noted how the mist hung ghostlike over the elongated body of water next to the airstrip. All the ships, UH-1s, signature of America's first helicopter war, sat silent and dark, their silhouettes appearing like something out of the age of the dinosaur, large, smooth-sloping forms. As he sat there trying to pen his thoughts, a nagging sense of doom crept over him...*this is the day, Slater...this is the day you die...* When he realized he couldn't control his shakes, he moved away from the helicopter to the water's edge. He gazed long and hard at the far bank barely visible through the gray gloom. Several moments later he turned at the sound of footsteps and saw Oakerson appear.

"You got any extra shells?" the gangly warrant officer asked. Slater frowned. Fred almost sounded flippant, cheerful. Normally the eternal pessimist, Fred Oakerson never sounded anything but tense and unsure.

"Yeah...sure, Fred."

As they went toward *Alfie*, Fred asked, "What were you thinking back there?"

"Oh...nothing."

"Whitaker believes Charlie is going to lay low, just like the last time."

"You think so, Fred?" Slater returned.

"Sure." And then he said: "Guess what?—I'm down into the double digits. I marked off day one hundred yesterday. How many days you got?"

Slater paused. They were still several yards from his helicopter. Kip brought out his notebook. He took a moment to calculate. "I have exactly one hundred and eighty-three days." And then: "Hey, I'm right at the halfway point—"

At the aircraft Slater handed over the extra box of .38-caliber ammunition he couldn't fit into his own pockets. "Here, Fred, take all you want."

"Thanks."

As Fred Oakerson turned away, Slater said, "Take care, Fred. I'll be seeing you."

"Yeah, sure. You too."

Martha Slater stood at the open refrigerator, her body still shivering from the dream that had awakened her. She stared at its contents uncertain whether she should choose something cold to drink or heat water to make hot cocoa. After a minute of indecision, while she gave her trembling hands a chance to be still, she closed the door and went to the kitchen table and sat down. A noise behind her caused the gooseflesh to rise over her body. The kitchen light went on.

"Martha...?"

"*Vernon!*—you nearly scared the pee out of me."

Her husband came to the table and sat down. "Are you okay? You look white as a sheet."

His wife's ash-blonde hair hung down in disheveled strands. The dark circles around her eyes gave them a sunken look. He took and held onto her hands. "Tell me—what's the matter?"

Her voice cracked as she spoke. "I-I had a dream. It was about Keith."

Vernon Slater felt the blood drain from his head. "What about...Keith?"

For a long moment she was silent, hesitating to speak, trying to avoid her husband's imploring stare. Then her eyes turned up, a show of terror written across her face. "I dreamt...that...that he died. Oh, my God—*I dreamt that my own son died!"*

"Died?—what do you mean?"

"He's flying...bombs are going off—or something, I don't know. But he doesn't make it out." Martha Slater's eyes filled with tears. "And then in the dream, he's lost, like he doesn't know where he is. Like he's gone *somewhere*—and he's confused."

Vernon Slater took a firmer hold on his wife's hands. "Martha—listen to me. You must listen. It doesn't have to mean anything—"

"But I've never had a dream like that before!"

He got up and took his wife by the arm. He felt her body shaking. "Come, let's go sit on the couch. We'll talk. You've been under a lot of strain lately."

"Yes," she said, "I have. I'm sorry. Now I've got you worried, don't I?"

"It's okay—it's okay. We'll get through this together."

The RF/PF soldiers were lined up in the Nam Can LZ, nine to a helicopter. When the ships landed, crouched bodies moved quickly to get onboard. Everywhere they heard gunfire and rockets exploding. Radios crackled swift messages between the gunships and C&C, and between helicopters in the flight. Fear echoed from each radio transmission. The flight lifted and the ships barely cleared the trees to their front. The flight back to Ca Mau with the evacuees took twenty minutes. (This time, though, they took on extra fuel.) Meanwhile, the security forces prepared for their own hasty departure.

Casualties within the ARVN forces were, so far, two dead and seven wounded. The American crew on the ground had suffered one casualty, a pilot with a bullet wound to the hip. Fred Oakerson's heart thudded madly in his chest as he watched the first wave of helicopters leave RP Tango for the LZ. He glanced over at his co-pilot, Bob Caudle, a soft-spoken twenty-two-year-old from Charleston, South Carolina. The two men were in the same hootch at Soc Trang. They had knocked out the wall that separated their adjacent rooms and were remodeling it with leftover two-by-fours and plywood picked up at R&D. They planned on putting in air-conditioning. Fred reached over and tapped Caudle's shoulder. "Relax, damnit."

"Oh, fuck yeah...*Relax."*

The LZ loomed. Slater saw that the ARVN were hunkered low, ready to dash for the landing helicopters. Whitaker, in the lead ship, began to slow his airspeed. Slater remembered to adjust his pistol holster in front of his groin. As they neared the southern edge of the LZ, he felt the dank air envelope him like a vice. He checked the fuel gauge. Too much fuel. Fuel, the lifeblood of the aircraft. But also their nemesis. A quantity of fuel means weight. Eight hundred pounds of gas combined with high humidity, high air temperature, and nine combat-laden troops eager to hightail it from a hot LZ and what you have is a ship that can't fight (or fly) its way out of a soggy paper bag.

"Lead, your flight is down."

The troops moved quickly to board. Kip saw three of the downed American crew angle toward the rear helicopters, looking for a ship to climb in. They stumbled along with an armful of radios and weapons extracted from their bullet-ridden UH-1. Behind Slater sat eight ARVN soldiers. Two of the downed crewmen approached *Alfie* and with harried looks on their faces, clambered aboard. "Lead, your flight is ready."

"Roger that. We're on the go."

"Red Two taking fire! Three o'clock!"

Rockets blasted the LZ's east side. Gray smoke bloomed upward and outward. Kip felt the resulting shock wave and heard the loud *KRUUMMP!...KRUUMMP!* He saw the lead ships begin to lift and slowly climb above the treetops. Directly ahead, he saw Oakerson's helicopter come to a hover. Tannah's ship, *The Roadrunner*, lifted right behind. "Go, baby...Go, baby, go..." Slater heard himself urging over the intercom as the two ships finally cleared the treetops.

"Our turn," Slater sounded. He knew they would need a clear run at the treeline to achieve the lift necessary to make it over the tops. As he brought *Alfie* to a hover, the LZ ahead erupted in flashing explosions. *WHUUMP!...WHUUMP!...KABOOOM!* The impacts sounded like they had originated inside the cockpit, but the debris that pelted the Plexiglas windshield clearly told them that the rain of earth and steel was occurring outside, like a series of thunderclaps. *WHUUMP!...KABOOM...!*

"The gooks are mortaring the LZ!" Ray Castillo, Slater's peter-pilot, shouted. "Goddamnit to hell—"

More rounds sailed in. Next they saw a fiery explosion. The VC had just scored a direct hit on the previously crippled Warrior helicopter!

The path to their front belched smoke and flame. Slater looked left. Their only way out was the east-west canal that went past the now abandoned Nam Can outpost. Kip Slater radioed his intentions to the orbiting Cobras, whose job now was to escort the last aircraft out of the LZ.

Hardin, watching the trail ship's plight, came back: "We've got your ass covered! Get the hell out of there!"

Other radio traffic came through his headset. At first it was all garbled. Then Slater heard Leo's voice: "Outlaw Six...we've lost a ship! *We've lost a ship!*"

Intent on his own problems, Slater turned the aircraft left and applied the slightest amount of forward cyclic. He heard *Alfie* groan under the load. He glanced at the gauges and saw the N2 and rotor rpm on the decline. "Come on, Alfie...come on. *You can do it...!*" As their speed increased, Kip began to apply more torque pressure to the rotor system; the helicopter began to rise. They were now over the water, however they hadn't gained the height necessary to clear the small wooden footbridge directly to their front that connected the outpost to the landing zone. (Meanwhile, the mortars continued to fly in, impacting at the north end of the LZ.) What to do? Slater turned the aircraft slightly right and added right anti-torque pedal, which translated into a slight increase in power. *Alfie* was now sideslipping toward the footbridge—but they had gained an extra foot of altitude. They were now fifty feet from the bridge and closing. Slater added power and applied a small measure of forward cyclic, to increase their speed. He wanted so desperately to get through ETL (effective translational lift), and into cleaner air so that the helicopter could fly, that his own body language to make it happen began to physically wear him out. As the bridge neared, Slater found himself thinking that if they couldn't rise above the handrail, maybe they could glance off it rather than hook it straight on with the landing gear.

"*Receiving fire!* Two o'clock!" Larkin sounded.

Slater jerked his head right. Larkin's gun began clattering as Kip relayed the information to the Cobras. Barely three seconds later the ground to their right front bloomed with gray smoke.

"Watch out!—*the bridge...!*" Castillo cried.

Slater felt the left side of the ship grind against the handrail, slowing them practically to a standstill. And then the rail snapped and they began descending. Fearing the tailrotor would hit the bridge, Slater applied left cyclic and added more power. The helicopter yawed right, which aggravated the problem. An eternity passed. And then the ground all around them erupted, an explosion and a tremendous flash of light....

"They're not to going to make it," Nolan said, as he took another sight through the TSU.

"Fire to their right," Hardin blasted back. As the AH-1G aircraft commander spoke, he pressed the button and let fly with another two pair of rockets.

On the post-dive pullout, Nolan aimed right and sent a burst of minigun fire at a cluster of hootches where he saw the flashes. The G-forces on the pullout pressed him hard against his seat, making it difficult to continue shooting with any further effectiveness. As they gained altitude, Nolan heard the muffled impact of rockets fired from their wing bird. "Two Six, One Two, the slick is coming up; it's now at your six o'clock."

"Roger that," Hardin said. "Follow them until they're up to altitude. We'll divert to the crash site."

"Roger that."

Slater lifted his head. Slowly he began to assimilate his surroundings. The two men before him began to speak and for a time he wondered if he was in some altered realm, some new and different dimension. The thought crossed his mind that he had died and was waking up *On The Other Side*. And then panic began to overtake him. Neither man standing before him was even remotely familiar. Another moment passed and he became aware of the room he was in. It was cold and stark. In one corner, on top a rolling cart, was a tray filled with delicate, silver-looking instruments. Directly overhead was a large, strange-looking disc held suspended by a mechanically hinged arm. The scent of medicinal alcohol hung heavy in the air. Kip Slater shivered at the stream of cold air blowing across his face.

"Sir...are you okay?"

Slater extended his arms and the two men helped him to be seated upright.

"I...I...don't know. What happened?...Who are you guys?"

"You must have fainted, sir. You're at Soc Trang, in the clinic. I'm Sergeant Taylor. This is Specialist Maldonado."

"Why am I here?"

"We don't know, sir. You sorta just...walked in."

Slater sat back. He still felt groggy, completely out of sorts. He shook his head. "Man—I feel like I've been drugged." He took a deep breath. "Soc Trang? How'd I get back here?"

The two men looked at each other. Taylor said, "Sir, weren't you in that flight of choppers that just came in?"

"I don't know...I guess."

Slater then heard a screen door slam. The sound of Leo's voice brought him to his senses. He turned as Tannah appeared in the doorway. Leo said, "Hey, what's going on?"

"What do you mean...?"

"Didn't you hear me calling you?"

"No. When?"

"As you were leaving operations. I kept talking to you, but you never said anything. How come?"

"I-I don't know."

Leo examined him more closely. "Hey, where have you been, buddy?"

Still slightly dazed, Kip said, "God, Leo—no where that I can remember..."

Then Leo said, "Do you remember that Oakerson's ship went down?"

"What—?"

"I said we lost Oakerson. Everyone onboard was killed."

Slater sat silent. His eyes darted around. His mind whirled, as if trying to catch hold of some notion that kept eluding him. Tears formed in his eyes and his chest began to heave. He began to rock back and forth, his voice suddenly a high-pitched wail. "Oh...God...*Leo!* No...No...*No!*"

Chapter 51

HE HAD BEEN AWAKE FOR SEVERAL minutes when he heard a light tapping at his door and the voice of Specialist Fourth Class Nick Carter, one of his enlisted operations clerks. "Captain Nolan, sir. It's four A.M. You asked me to wake you."

"Yeah, okay...I'm awake. Thanks."

"Yessir."

Nolan listened to Carter's retreating footsteps. Then he sat up, took a cigarette and lit it. He groped in the dark with his feet for his rubber thongs. Taking a towel and his shaving kit, he went out the door of his hootch. He made his way along the wooden walkway to the latrine, a medium-size wooden building two hootches down. Inside the latrine a single light bulb glowed above a row of sinks. He went to one of the sinks, took a final drag on his cigarette, and then snuffed it out in a bucket filled with sand. He then went to one of the shower stalls and took a quick, hot shower. After he toweled himself dry, he returned to the sinks, turned the hot water faucet on, running the water until it became scalding. With his face wet, he smoothed on a thick layer of shaving cream. With painstaking deliberateness, he ran the razor over his face, feeling for any stray patch of whiskers, until everywhere was smooth. Toweling his face dry, he patted on a good dose of Old Spice. After he brushed his teeth, he lit another cigarette, gathered his shaving gear and towel, and this time made his way briskly back to his hootch.

Nolan had always been meticulous about his personal hygiene and dress. He had learned early in his military career the value of cleanliness and smart military bearing. A professional soldier's pride was not only in a job well done, in strictly mission accomplishment, it was also in how he carried himself, how he appeared before his men. Though he never demanded strict military bearing from them, either in mannerism or in dress, he did expect of them the courtesy of acknowledging its value as such. In the chaos of war, a commander's effectiveness depended largely on his previous commitment to training, standardization, a certain amount of pomp and ceremony—and discipline. Without the latter, an individual leader's ability to lead was next to nothing. Its foundation was respect: respect for those lesser in rank and an expectation of the same in return. Of his superiors, he expected nothing less than their best, both in thought and in action. There was nothing he despised more than a self-serving officer who used his men as stepping stones to further his career, and he had known many of them. An officer's first duty was to his men, to lead them by stepping out ahead and setting the pace. He recalled reading accounts of Marine Corps officers in the Pacific during World War II, majors and colonels, who hit the beaches along with their men, who spilled blood and died alongside, and in some instances, in front of them.

Victor R. Beaver

Sadly, in Vietnam, he saw the opposite among members of his own branch of the service, majors and higher in grade, who sat in a helicopter high above the field of battle, out of harm's way. Maybe it was the nature of the war that dictated this. He found it nearly incomprehensible that men were led in combat in this manner.

His jungle fatigues had been laid out neatly the night before by his mama-san who faithfully laundered his clothes and kept his room clean and orderly. He lifted one of his boots and inspected the spit-shine he applied the previous night. It was the one housekeeping chore he preferred to do himself. During those times he would sit quietly and smoke his cigarettes and give thought to the future, to the day when he would retire and go home to the Florida Keys and his father's charter boat business. He looked forward to the peaceful unhurried days out on the water under the sun and blue skies. He longed to walk the sandy beaches, feeling the warm Gulf breeze and to take the salt air into his lungs. He could think of no better way to spend the rest of his life than to fish and watch the glorious Gulf Stream sunsets.

At one point in his career, Nolan thought he should attend night school and get a college degree. Obviously, there was more to learn than what could be gained by leading men on patrol or directing artillery during a firefight. He speculated that he needed more refinement, but then later decided that such refinement would not help him one iota to perform the job he cared most about: that of leading men through enemy infested territory and making certain that his commands given to an artillery unit actually caused the shells to land precisely where he intended. Rather than spend the time in a classroom learning art and literature, subjects he could care less about, he directed his energies learning even more precisely the rudiments of his profession until he could do it in his sleep. Besides, whatever refinement he thought he needed could only come from within. No college education or time spent pouring over the classics or history books could do for him what might not be within him in the first place. He liked the way he was. He hadn't married because he didn't want to change to suit some woman's idea of what he should be like, as he had seen so many married men do. He liked his Jack Daniels and his Marlboros and he liked that he had only himself to be concerned about: he liked his time alone. What woman in her right mind would want to be with him and allow him that? None that he was aware.

After putting on his boots, Nolan stood and lit another cigarette. He gazed at the nightstand next to his cot, at the picture of him and his father and the blue marlin. He took and opened the blue velvet case that held the gold oak-leaf clusters. His eyes studied them for a moment, and then he closed the case. His eyes swept his room. Satisfied that all was in order, he turned and went out the door and strolled easily the short distance to the enlisted mess.

Another of his extra duties, aside from being the future S-3, had been that of messhall officer, which he was now about to relinquish. First Lieutenant Bobby

Daniels, in-country two weeks, would take over that little chore which would then allow him more time in company operations.

The door creaked as he entered; he let it slam behind him. "Atten-hut!" someone called.

"At ease. Carry on."

Several enlisted men were in the chow line; others were already seated at tables. They were the crewchiefs and armament personnel of the company. He walked over to where Lieutenant Daniels was seated next to SFC Spellman, the enlisted mess NCOIC. "Good morning."

"Good morning, sir," Daniels said.

Spellman nodded and voiced a gruff: "Mornin', sir."

"Lieutenant Daniels, glad to see you up so bright and early."

Daniels stretched his lanky frame and yawned. His black hair was still wet from the shower he had hastily taken directly after Nolan had left the latrine. "I'm barely up, sir."

Nolan grinned. "You'll get used to it."

"I'd rather not, sir." Daniels gave Nolan a sheepish grin. "I'd rather be flying."

"Don't worry. You'll get your belly full of that, too." Nolan eyed Sergeant Spellman. The sergeant's beefy frame sat hunched over a mug of coffee. "Has Sergeant Spellman filled you in on any details?"

Spellman's chiseled face glanced up. "Sir, there ain't a goddamn thing that's going to make a lick of sense to anybody this time of the morning. I used to call this early in the morning O'dark thirty. Now it's O'God thirty. In two years I retire. When I do, by God, I ain't risin' till after twelve o'clock noon. And then that's only if I gotta piss—"

Nolan chuckled. "My sentiments exactly." He looked toward Daniels. "Well, it won't take long to explain the books. And then I'll give the reins over to your capable hands."

"Yessir. Oh, and by the way, sir, Major Elroy wanted me to remind you of the party at the club tonight."

Nolan smiled and shook his head. "What is this, some kind of conspiracy? You're the third person to tell me—"

"Yessir, and there may be others. The Old Man says you put in too many hours at the S-3 job. He's invited a couple of the American Red Cross girls to be there, as well as several nurses from the Twenty-ninth Evac." And then Daniels said, "Wild horses couldn't keep me from going—but you've got me scheduled to fly tonight, sir."

"Find a willing replacement and you're off the hook," Nolan replied. "Crap, didn't I just hear you say you'd rather be flying?"

"I was kidding."

"Yeah...right."

Daniels said, "It ought to be fun. You're not married, are you, sir?"
Nolan shuddered. "Bite your tongue—"
"Yessir."

Mike Nolan's responsibilities as the new S-3 had changed little after Captain Dane left. Before taking full charge, he had assumed most of Dane's duties and by the time the captain actually walked out the door, he had put in two full weeks of eighteen-hour days.

His day began at 0400 and often went past midnight. The IV Corps AO comprised nearly twenty-eight thousand square miles. Within this area were sixteen province cities, and within each province were dozens and dozens of district towns, villages, and hamlets. Of these, more than half were home base for some kind of military unit: a Special Forces strike company, a Regional Force/Popular Force (RF/PF) unit, or MACV military advisory team (MAT). The three ARVN divisions in the Mekong Delta commanded the use of one or all four assault helicopter company assets at any given time, to include any other battalion aviation asset considered appropriate for the mission. The 235th Aerial Weapons Company, then, being the only such company in the Delta, was on call for all planned military activities, regardless of unit size, on a priority basis. When no large divisional operations were being conducted, the smaller units sought support from these high-speed, sleek-looking gun platforms, first come, first served. Therefore, requests for either a two-Cobra light or three-Cobra heavy fire-team came at all hours of the day and night.

It was past seven when Nolan finally looked at his watch. He had forgotten to eat lunch and had skipped his first opportunity to attend the evening mess. His stomach rumbled due to all the coffee he had drunk. He glanced at the scheduling board, reviewing once more the missions for that evening. Two AH-1Gs were to be stationed overnight near the Cambodian border, at Chi Lang. Another light fire-team was scheduled to perform Can Tho airfield security, along with a Tiger flareship out of Soc Trang.

The memory of working with the slicks on the final evacuation of Nam Can flashed in his mind. The last lone Tiger slick had left the Nam Can LZ, and was climbing to altitude, when he and Hardin were diverted to support the downed ship. Smoke and flame poured skyward, as if an oil tanker had been hit. One slick, callsign he couldn't remember, kept doing circles around the wreckage, until the pilot was finally ordered (more like threatened with court-martial) to leave. The radio traffic had been horrendous, almost as bad as the day he and his platoon were stranded trying to take Hill 873 near the Laotian border back in April '66. God, that was a day he would never forget. The chaos, the noise, the fear, all was as vivid in his mind as if it had happened yesterday.

Nick Carter interrupted his thoughts. "Sir, maintenance just called and said that Four Four Three won't be ready until later this evening...around ten o'clock. Something about the accumulator."

Nolan glanced up, his gaze quickly diverting to the scheduling board. "Okay, Nick. Uh...go ahead and assign Two Seven Eight. Call back and tell the armorers to install the one-fifty-nine pods."

"Yessir. And, sir, uh...Major Elroy called and said to get your—and these were his exact words—'butt outta there and get ready for the party.'"

"Okay-okay." As Nolan put on his headgear, he said to Carter: "Give me a call if anything comes up. I don't care how minor it is. You got that?"

"Yessir."

"Even if it's for a *damn* hangnail—"

"Yes, sir."

"Oh, come on, Sharon, please...you've not gone to any function that we've been invited to yet. What are you afraid of?"

"I'm not afraid of anything. I don't mind spending all day long with them, but my nights are my only free time."

"Oh, sure, to read."

"Yes, to read. Besides, I don't want to be gazed at as if I was the last woman on earth—or at least the last round-eyed woman on earth—to paraphrase their own saying."

Frieda, thirty-four, and five years Sharon O'Malley's senior, sat before the mirror applying the finishing touches to her makeup. "This is the only chance I ever get to put on a different face and wear real clothes," the older woman said. "All day long I wear these silly jungle fatigues and any makeup I do put on is a mess thirty minutes later in this stifling humidity. At least at a party it's usually too dark to see that my makeup has streaks in it and that my dress is last year's fashion." She paused and gazed at Sharon's reflection in the mirror. "Sometimes, I feel like I might as well be out there in the rice paddies with those guys...or wherever they go to shoot their guns." Frieda sighed. "Look, why don't you go for Ellen's sake. She's been here only two weeks and already I think she's going to crack up. Besides, she's a real—what am I trying to say?—a real case, if you know what I mean."

"No, I don't. What *do* you mean, Frieda? Ellen is a very sweet girl. She has a good heart."

"And a mighty large one at that," Frieda said, giving Sharon a knowing wink. "Frankly, I think her figure could stop a tank; her face could probably put an end to this silly skirmish they call a war. I can understand why she volunteered to come over here."

"Oh, you can, can you—?"

Victor R. Beaver

"Sure, over here she hasn't got any competition. Men oogle over anything that smacks of female...and she is definitely *a lot* of female. Look, I talked to her. She really doesn't want to go unless you go too. Besides, I don't want to go by myself. I'm tired of always going alone. As brazen as you might think I am, seven to one odds is really not my style."

Sharon took a deep breath. Perhaps she should go, for Ellen's sake. Besides, Frieda's litany about her not ever going was so tiresome that by showing up this time the older woman would have to employ a completely new tactic in the future, which she would easily defeat—for awhile. "Okay, I'll go—this time. But I'm not going to make a habit of it."

Frieda turned and gave Sharon a quick wink. "That's a girl. I'll let Ellen know. I just know we're going to have a great time."

"You're going to have a great time, Frieda. You always have a great time. Especially when you've had too much to drink."

Pouting, Frieda said, "I let the drinks loosen me up. Otherwise, I'd have to be selective and over here women my age can't be too selective. Especially if the men are married."

In her room, Sharon O'Malley sat before a fan and allowed the breeze blow full force in her face. Strands of red hair were pasted to her forehead. She really didn't have the energy to get ready for the party. What she really wanted to do, like she did every night, alone, was study the list of books from various publishing companies she intended to buy from, in order to one day stock her own bookstore. It was a dream she had from her earliest memory of her mother, who organized the first library for the town of Milburn, North Dakota. It was during those early growing-up years that she discovered the excitement and adventure that books had to offer. Boys were not foremost on her mind, preferring writing in her journal and reading her favorite authors.

Upon graduation from college, Sharon traveled to Seaside, Oregon, to visit her Aunt Hilga, the trip paid for by her father as a graduation gift. She fell in love with the rugged, untamed Oregon coast and vowed one day to own a bookstore there.

In 1964, with her BA degree in Library Science in hand, Sharon O'Malley chose to become a paid member of the American Red Cross to start her journey of discovery and service to her country. Her first assignment was at Fulda, West Germany, a small town near the East German border where U.S. servicemen were prepared to blunt a Soviet-backed attack across the Fulda Gap. There she found the library section of the small USO dayroom pitifully stocked. Bypassing the usual red-tape to acquire even a rudimentary assortment of books, Sharon O'Malley spent what she would have saved of her first six month's earnings and acquired, above and beyond, those classics she felt the men would have preferred to read had they the mind to say so. Gratefully, she learned she was not far off the mark.

She extended her contract to remain in Fulda twice. But in early 1967, her father's failing health forced her to return to the United States before the second contract extension ran out. In late fall of that year he died and when his affairs were in order, she chose to travel west rather than east, and by early January 1968, she found herself within the confines of Can Tho, U.S. headquarters of the Mekong Delta's IV Corps military might.

Again, she found a dearth of good reading and again, slowly, painstakingly, began to build the library up from scratch. She no doubt had acquired her mother's tenacity to push forward the world's great literary art.

Sharon O'Malley turned the fan from her face and looked in the mirror and decided that, Yes, her face needed a certain livening, a procedure she had long since dismissed as inconsequential, but for the sake of Frieda and Ellen, Why not tonight? She was certain there would be no man present worth more than a slight application of facial powder, the barest amount of color above her eyelids, and a small pressing of lipstick to her lips. Besides, with nearly thirty thousand dollars in savings, plus what she had acquired from her father's modest estate, the likelihood of being derailed from her life dream was, if not completely out of the question, at least highly unlikely. She had been in contact with hundreds of men, many of them young, handsome, and virile, and she found not one to her liking. For awhile she wondered why and then one day understood the reason: Every man who pursued her had acted as though she was the one and only woman for him, had promised her his life, fidelity, and fortune, including a castle of exquisite luxury built in the air. She didn't want a castle built in the air nor did she want children everywhere. She wanted a small bookstore in Seaside, Oregon, where she could serve gourmet coffee amid an atmosphere of quiet browsing and the sound of the ocean outside the door....

After stopping at the wet bar for a drink, Nolan went over to where Major Elroy and Major Riggins, the company executive officer, were standing, made a few comments about what was going on in operations, then quietly, casually drifted to a secluded corner where he could oversee the activities. Music sounded from a jukebox and he watched as several couples danced. Most of the women, he surmised, were nurses from the 29th Evacuation Hospital. He looked toward Elroy and Riggins. An older, attractive woman, in her mid to upper thirties, who had a strong, shapely body, full bosomed, with a narrow waist, had wandered over to them and had them smiling while engaged in conversation. And then across the room Nolan spied two women standing side-by-side, one rather large and not very attractive, the other studious-looking, wearing wire-framed glasses, her red hair pulled tightly back and tied in a bun. She sparked his curiosity only because it looked like she had done her best to be unattractive, even though her slender, youthful figure belied the attempt. Nolan sensed from her body language that she was bored and didn't want to be there any more than he did. An OV-1 Mohawk pilot Mike knew sauntered over to the two women and began a conversation. Strangely, after several minutes, Nolan found himself a little annoyed at the man's apparent self-assuredness and ability to be so glib; next, he felt himself wishing that he could be compelled to just strike up a conversation with any attractive woman he saw without feeling that he might be annoying her or intruding. But it had never been in his character to act impulsively in that manner. To him, it seemed, and indeed he felt it was, a rather phony way of being. And then he became out of sorts, aggravated; he decided to step outside for a breath of fresh air.

He took a cigarette and lit up. He drew the smoke in slowly and exhaled, allowing the smoke to trickle through his nostrils. The night air was damp, musty: the pervasive smell of dying and dead vegetation. After a moment the red-haired woman stepped out through the door. Looking at him, she said, "Are you bored in there, too?"

Nolan turned. He raised an eyebrow and looked her up and down, noting that she was easily two inches taller than him. He smirked. "Bored, tired, you name it."

"Then we have something in common. I find this type of activity pointless and tiresome. Mostly tiresome."

"My CO practically had to order me to be here."

"What would you rather be doing," she asked, "especially over here, when the only entertainment seems to be drinking and then more drinking? Do you like to read?"

Nolan huffed. "It's been ages since I've read a book, for pleasure or any other reason. I can barely plow through the tech manuals I'm responsible for."

"I see. What a shame."

"Are you one of the nurses?" he asked, deciding to try his hand at keeping a conversation going.

"No, I'm with the Red Cross. I run the library section of the dayroom. You might say I'm a matron of books. I believe I inherited the trait from my mother. She was the light and life of the first library in Milburn, North Dakota."

"North Dakota? That's one state I've never been in. My impression is that it is flat and cold."

"It is flat, and an icebox in the winter. I never want to go back."

"No longer home, eh?"

"Not anymore. It had been until my father died late last year. My mother passed away when I was ten. I was an only child," she said.

"Yeah...I was an only child, too. But my father is alive and kicking. He owns a charter boat business, fishing in the Keys. I'm going to help him with the business after I retire."

"Oh? When will that be?"

"In a little less than eight years. That's when I'll have my twenty in."

"Twenty in?"

"Yeah, twenty years active military service and then I can retire at half my base pay. I hope by then to be a major."

"This rank stuff has always been beyond me. What are you now?"

"A captain."

They spoke for several minutes. Nolan learned she had a burning desire to visit Australia, an enthusiasm he shared. He also learned of another of her ambitions, to own a bookstore somewhere on the coast of Oregon. Finally, when the conversation lagged, she stated it was time for her to go, that she had promised her friend Frieda, the woman talking to Elroy and Riggins, that she would come but only stay an hour. Ellen, the other Red Cross girl, would remain. Nolan obligingly offered to walk her to her quarters.

"No thanks. I'm a big girl. I can find my own way."

"Suit yourself."

As she turned to leave, she said, "Come to the library sometime. We've got a real good selection of Mickey Spillaine books. You look like the Mike Hammer type."

Nolan grunted. "Hell, I haven't got time to sleep...much less read."

"Suit yourself. Blessed are the dull and the ignorant."

"What did you say?"

She smirked. "If I offended you, I meant to. I never met a man who couldn't benefit from reading, even for pleasure, and maybe especially so—even if he does it for ten or fifteen minutes a day. Surely, you spend that much time on the john."

"Bullshit."

"And you might even improve your vocabulary."

As she walked away, he thought: Women. Christ, they're always trying to change or fix you. Goddamnit—*I'm not broken!*

It was past midnight when he finally laid down on his bed. He had taken his leave from the party with the excuse that Carter needed him to handle a request for a pair of Cobras to support a small operation southeast of Ha Tien, near the Cement Plant, at daybreak.

As he lay there trying to sleep, he thought of the conversation with the red-haired woman; he realized he didn't know her name, since neither had bothered to make an introduction. *What the hell do you care what her damn name is, anyway? Ten minutes on the john. Ha! I don't even have that, for crissake.*

Victor R. Beaver

Chapter 52

DEREK JUSTEN PARKED HIS FORD FAIRLAINE in a large parking lot behind a long two-story building, got out and opened the trunk. He took his small overnight kit and closed the trunk; he would come back for the heavier stuff later. Still using his cane for support, he went around to the street-side of the building. Going down the narrow walkway, he found Room 138. He inserted the key and unlocked the door. He reached around and turned on the light. For a moment, he stood and looked at his new quarters, his "home" while being stationed at Fort Rucker, Alabama, for God only knew how long. His first thought was how expansive the room was, compared to the one he occupied back at Soc Trang. And the air-conditioning, the glorious air-conditioning.

Justen went in and took note of his new accommodations. More than adequately furnished, it had a TV, desk, dresser, double bed, lamp stand, and small refrigerator—and at long last a private bath. He laid his overnight kit on the bed and went and examined the refrigerator. In it was an assortment of canned soft drinks, beer, wine, and one-ounce bottles of liquor (he would pay for only those drinks he consumed). He withdrew a 7-UP and a tiny bottle of Jim Beam. He took a glass and removed the cellophane wrapping and filled the glass with ice taken from the refrigerator's freezer compartment. He poured in a half-measure of 7-UP and then emptied the Jim Beam over the 7-UP. He stirred, then took a sip and headed for the bed. Justen sat down and removed his shoes. He uncovered the two pillows and propped them against the headboard and laid back. He lifted the glass and examined the mixture of the two liquids. He put the glass to his lips and this time took a long sip. The drink warmed through him and he began to think of Valerie and their last evening together at Fort Sill.

After the baby-sitter had broken the news (and had gone home with her father), Valerie, delirious with relief—and disbelief—began to weep. Fifteen minutes later, two officers, a major and a second lieutenant, both from the post AG's (adjutant general's) office, appeared and gave the details of Jake's present existence. The information had come from two POWs, who had been in the same camp as Jake, then sent to Phnom Penh by motorized sampan for release from captivity. The two men believed their last location to be somewhere in the northern reaches of the U Minh. They reported that Jake Cole was alone, that when they left him he was in good spirits and in reasonably decent health (considering his horrible living conditions and equally horrible diet), and that he had high hopes for his own release. Jake had asked that they relay his love for his wife and children, and to give his regards to a brother named Derek Justen.

Incredulously, Valerie and Derek sat and listened. Next to them Robbie and Jill squirmed on the edge of the couch while remaining quiet as little mice. After the two officers were gone, and the children were finally tucked into bed, Valerie brought out a bottle of champagne she had tucked away in the cabinet. Savoring the good news, they remained talking long into the night.

Though Derek was also elated at the good news, when he and Valerie bid each other good night, a subtle reality began to take shape. The information about Jake was ancient history the moment the two ex-captives had motored out of sight of him. Their last view of Jake, now three months hence, had him standing on the bank of the canal waving them off and telling them "Good luck!" Now what was his status? Was he still alive? Was he still in the Forest? He determined not to voice his concerns to Valerie—not now, not ever.

Again, Derek studied the Beam and Seven. He put the glass to his mouth and downed the rest in one gulp. Now the question was how to get back on flying status so he could be reassigned overseas? He glanced at his watch. An hour ago he had driven onto post, had signed for quarters, and tomorrow morning would report to his new assignment with the training command. He decided quickly that he would worm his way back onto flight status no matter whom he had to bribe or threaten with bodily harm.

As he lay there, with the effects of the alcohol swirling in his head, he began to think of Valerie and their dinner date at the club. He remembered her lips pressed against his lower cheek as they were dancing, her hand caressing the back of his neck, the warmth of her breath soft against his skin, her breathing shallow and inviting. She pressed her body into his and he responded, sighing. All during his visit there had been a tension building between them, one that was both confusing and titillating. He had always liked her—and was undoubtedly attracted to her, ever since Jake had brought her home to meet the family during Christmas of his junior year at West Point. The two had already announced their engagement and had traveled from Princeton, New Jersey, where Valerie was attending school. He was in his second year of college, studying to be a teacher in industrial education. During that Christmas they became close, like brother and sister, which he found at first disconcerting, because she was so warm and receptive toward him; however, later, he set aside the pangs of jealousy he felt toward Jake and became amply comfortable with her loveliness and her warmth. On the evening in question, though, he knew without a doubt that she was grasping for straws and knew also their regrets later had he allowed her feelings, and his feelings, too, to culminate in the only manner they could. Had they made love, there would have been no redemption, for either of them.

A profound weariness came over him. *I am so...damned...tired. So...so...tired.* As he closed his eyes, wishing sleep would quickly overtake him, he suddenly remembered the letter Valerie had given him just before he left. It was still in his pocket, unread. He withdrew it and opened it:

Victor R. Beaver

> *My Dearest Derek,*
> *Words cannot express what I feel right now. In all the world, you have to be the finest, most courageous and honorable man I know. Tonight I would have done anything to make you happy, because you deserved it. And I needed you, Derek, I needed to draw upon your strength to go on. I was depleted of my own. If ever Jake comes home, and I have renewed faith now that he will, I want you to remember that for the rest of my life you will own a part of my heart that no one will ever know. What I say right now takes nothing away from Jake, but I love you, Derek. Please be good to yourself. Please, please return home.*
> *Valerie*

Derek placed the letter on the bed by his side. He felt soothed, comforted—elated. And then in the next instant felt horribly, abysmally alone.

* * *

AT THE END OF TWENTY-FIVE HOURS they took their basic instrument checkrides, to show they could control the aircraft without reference to the ground. For Sandy, it had been the easiest flight examination yet. The training leading to it had not been particularly taxiing, once he got used to the hood. There had been one day, however, when he was asked to perform an ITO (instrument takeoff). The sun flickered on the instrument panel as the rays filtered through the spinning main rotorblades that during the climbout he developed his first case of vertigo (called "flicker" vertigo). Before his instructor took over the controls, he had the small ship pointing vertically toward the ground. "What the hell's the matter with you, boy—?" the chubby-fingered Bates had cried.

A moment later, after Sandy had regained his sense of equilibrium, he told Bates: "It felt like we were going up and backwards, sir. It was so weird."

"You try that shit in the clouds, boy, and it'll be the last we ever hear of you—"

"Yessir."

* * *

"ARMY THREE TWO ZERO, YOU ARE cleared to the Blue Springs NDB, via the one eight zero magnetic course to. Maintain two thousand. Expect approach clearance in zero three minutes." The air traffic controller's voice came through his headset loud and clear.

"This is Army Three Two Zero, roger," Sandy replied. It was his third flight in advanced instruments and he had never in his life been so flustered. He looked at the RMI (radio magnetic indicator) card and saw the circle with the numbers and the tic-marks and the needle with an "arrowhead" at one end, blunted at the other. Both ends of the needle told him exactly what he *needed* to know, to understand where he was in space, if he could just spend a moment or an hour or even a day to understand *how he was supposed to know it.* His time spent in the Blue Canoe had proved equally frustrating. And now here he was in the real aircraft, actually going somewhere, still unable to see outside, yet expected to maneuver the ship toward an unseen destination and perform a tactical instrument approach. For the first time in flight training, Sandy felt like throwing in the towel—giving up—*quitting.* His instructor, a young, quiet CW2 named Ross, back from Vietnam less than four months, sat in the left seat not saying a word.

"I'm going to...parallel the course first. Is that right, sir?" Sandy queried, still unsure of the procedure for recognizing where the course was and how he was to get on that course to the NDB (non-directional beacon), now less than four minutes flight-time away.

"Do what you gotta do," Ross answered, smugly.

Yesterday, and the day before, it had been the same. He had been given instructions by ATC (air traffic control) to intercept a certain course. After turning to the course heading, he couldn't decide whether he was supposed to reference the tail of the needle or the head, to decide where the course was. None of it made any sense. When Ross finally asked him why he wasn't following the procedures outlined in the programmed text, Sandy exclaimed, "I'd do what the damn text said, if I could just understand why I was doing it!"

"Hey, it's your flight training, not mine," Ross came back.

Sandy turned the training helicopter to the heading of 180. The head of the needle was to the left of the heading index, pointing to 120. For a full minute he glared at the head of the ADF needle. And then he remembered that if the needle's head was left of the heading index that was where the course was—to the left. He saw that under the left 45-degree tic-mark on the RMI card was the heading of 135 degrees, the presumed desired heading to fly to intercept the course of 180 at a 45-degree angle. He turned to that heading. Ross spoke, "Slick, it's apparent you can't see it, but you are more than forty-five degrees off course—as we speak. In fact, you are sixty degrees off course. You'll never get to the NDB on a one three five heading. You'll fly right past it."

Okay, thought Sandy, so what the hell heading do I fly, for crissake—? He felt his body tighten, his brain turn to a block of wood. For a long moment, he studied the RMI card and could not see the solution to the problem. *There was no goddamn solution.* As they continued forward, the head of the needle began to move gradually farther to the left of 120, until it pointed to 105 degrees. By this time, not only was there no solution to the problem, there would never be one. He hated instruments, and he hated the man seated next to him, whom he thought not the least bit concerned that his student was screwing up—and was probably rather content that he was. He longed for Gressing's patient willingness to explain; never had he been so well nurtured. With Gressing, and even Captain Crandall, he had been thoroughly spoiled.

It was past eleven. Sandy was at his desk, the light from the lamp throwing off a kind of mesmerizing glow. In the next room he could hear Mark Allen's quiet snoring. Before him were sheets of unlined paper with circles drawn and arrows pointing and a hodge-podge of numbers he had cooked up to understand how to recognize where the NDB course was if the RMI card had failed, had become "fixed," that is, no longer rotated as the aircraft turned. If he couldn't understand how the damn thing was supposed to work when it wasn't broken, how the hell was he expected to do so when it was? he wondered. As he stared at his attempts on paper to uncork the logjam that was inside his head, he suddenly felt the urge to cry. *I'm not going to make it. This is it. I have finally met my limit!*

Feeling utterly miserable, Sandy turned the light out, took his fatigue uniform off, and crawled into bed. In another moment, staring at the dark ceiling above, he felt the tears come. What would his mother say? his father? What would Melissa, his little sister, think, he moaned despondently? Her hero can't figure out the simplest thing! *It is simple, isn't it? But it isn't for me! Why?* Gradually, he felt relief. He remembered that everyone was having the same problem, except Seymore and Chancey, both of whom were sailing through instruments as if riding high on some white cloud. *Seymore! How the hell is he doing it?* And then he shook his head. How the hell did he get tangled up with Jenny McCoy? Man o'man, his friend was *really* riding high.

"Sure, come on over," Pete Cochran said, when Sandy asked the ex-airline pilot to give him some tutoring. "I'll have Cheryl get some hamburger and we'll do up a quick barbecue."

"Thanks. That would be great. This advanced instrument stuff is really kicking my ass. I've just got to understand it—"

Pete and Cheryl had rented a small two-bedroom trailer next to Rose and Ron Bowden, in a mostly run-down trailer court east of Daleville. The two wives had become good friends, and during the day, while their husbands trained, they would get together over coffee and chat, or go visit the other wives, especially the ones with children. Once a week, several of the women would go to the NCO club and share a drink or two and talk of different things, avoiding the topic of Vietnam. "I'll make a salad," Cheryl said to Pete, when her husband mentioned that Sandy was coming over. "Let's try to make him really feel at home. Does he ever say anything about that girl Katie? What a shame about her brother."

After dinner, the two classmates spent an hour drawing on blank sheets of paper with Pete explaining...*head of needle left, course left...head right, course right...turn left or right, depending, to compass heading 45 degrees off from course heading, fly that until head of needle points to the (appropriate) 45-degree tic-mark, at which time you are on course.* "You got that?"

"Yeah...I got it," Sandy sighed. "But can I do it in the air?"

Pete grinned. "When checkride day comes, you'll probably do like the rest—you'll muddle through."

Before leaving, Sandy talked with Cheryl. She asked about Katie and he told her that he had written her many times and had finally got a letter from her just the other day. He explained that Katie (according to her letter) was involved with a peace organization at college and was working hard to keep the guys on campus from being drafted and going to Vietnam. He mentioned to Cheryl that she wished to remain friends, but to keep their relationship on a platonic level. "A platonic level..." spoke Sandy, staring dully at the threadbare carpet on their living room floor. "How can I keep myself at that level when I'm still in love with her?"

"It's got to be hard, Sandy. Maybe it'll change. You never know."

"How?"

"I don't know," Cheryl answered softly. "Don't lose hope."

"Yeah, sure, don't lose hope. It's all I've got left...and not much of that."

* * *

"HOLD ME, SEYMORE, HOLD ME TIGHT," cried Jenny.

The Ferris wheel had finally come to a halt, with the two seated at the very top. Smug and calm, Seymore gripped Jenny close to him. While she kept her eyes closed, he looked bravely about, taking in all of the scenery that was Six Flags Over Georgia. "For someone with a pilot's license, you sure are a 'fraidy cat for heights," he chided.

"It's different, Seymore. I can't explain it. In an airplane or helicopter, I'm belted in, surrounded by the cockpit."

"You're still a 'fraidy cat."

"Not."

"Are."

"That's okay, Seymore. I'll be your 'fraidy cat."

He awakened to the sound of purring and then a slight nuzzling against his check. When his eyes were fully opened, he saw Jenny with her hair tousled, her lips pouting, and her upturned nose like a little button. "Morning..." he sighed.

"Are you going to sleep forever, Seymore?"

"If I can."

"Want me to get you some coffee? They have free coffee in the lobby."

"Sure...but put something on."

"I can't go like this?"
"Only when I buy a deserted island."
"When will that be, Seymore?"
"When I get back from Vietnam. I've decided to have my own charter service. I'm going to hire you to be my Chief Pilot."

Jenny bounced out of bed. "Aye, aye, captain," she said, saluting.

Seymore smiled at what he saw. Her bottom half was bare, and her small top frame was housed inside one of his oversized T-shirts. It had been more than a week since they first made love, in her apartment, and when the two of them were spent, it was the first time in his life he had ever felt so at peace. Never had the world *not* looked so grim, so glum...but warm and wonderful.

"Come here."

She came.

He kissed her. She responded with a quiver and then began to massage him, handling him gently, smoothly, lovingly. "I love you, Jenny," he crooned.

She moved beneath him. Again, gently, she took him, guided him; and then he slipped inside her. She let out a gasp; her eyes grew wide with wonderment. "I love you, too, Seymore...you precious, precious man."

Jenny had driven him to the company area. They were parked in front of the barracks. "I want you to be careful when you're up there flying, Seymore. Always keep your eyes looking out for other aircraft."

"How can I—with that stupid hood on?"

"Peek once in awhile, Seymore. *Peek!*"

She had come to the barracks to take him to Dothan for dinner. "I told my folks about us, Seymore."

"What did they say?"

"They're coming next weekend to meet you."

"Jenny, does this mean—?"

"Yes—it does," she exclaimed. And then, demurely, she asked, "You still want to, don't you, Seymore?"

"Oh, yes, baby, yes yes yes. Jenny, you're going to make a wonderful, wonderful wife."

"I know, because I'll have you, Seymore, as my husband."

The Sky Soldiers

Chapter 53

CAPTAIN SLOTE, STANDING BEFORE the mission planning board, turned as Slater walked into operations. "Mr. Slater, I have just the job for you."
"What is it?"
"How would you like to do a little crop-dusting...say in about an hour?"
"Crop-dusting?"
"Defoliant spraying around the outside of the airfield perimeter."
"Can I defoliate VC Village?"
"Negative."
"Why not? It's the only foliage within three hundred meters of the perimeter."
"No can do."

Journal Entry, 20 April 1968, Soc Trang AAF

Leo and I put in for R&R together. Australia is booked up, but we'll try to get there on standby. The other day I checked the status board and we both have over 800 hours of Vietnam flight time. Alfie got a face-lift. The caption beneath the face now reads "What, Me Worry?"

Four days ago, we caught 3 VC out in the open in a sampan near Go Cong. Doorgunners fired but couldn't hit them from 1,500 feet.

Yesterday, I worked with a Special Forces captain born and raised in Germany. He spoke with a thick German accent. He escorted the Chau Doc province chief to various outposts. He had the little man in a dither, always telling him that the 'chopter pilot' (me) was going to leave him behind if he didn't hurry.

I did C&C for an operation near Mo Cay today. An RF/PF patrol had Charlie on the run. I watched and directed activities from two thousand feet. Alfie took a round in the tailrotor—at two thousand feet!

* * *

ONE DAY, WHILE RETURNING FROM My Tho to Soc Trang, Kip Slater and his crew received an urgent medevac call. They were told to contact an American advisor leading an RF/PF patrol near Ap Long Thanh, a small hamlet twenty-seven kilometers west-northwest of the Tra Vinh airstrip.

As they neared the hamlet, Slater radioed that he had yellow marking smoke.

"Roger that!" a frantic American voice came back. "I've got seven badly wounded men. The area is secure!"

"Roger that."

Victor R. Beaver

After they landed, the three more seriously wounded were rushed aboard first. Kip looked back and saw that they had fist-size holes blown clean through their abdomens. The other four, also appearing badly mauled, were dumped practically on top the first three. Slater saw a terrible agony etched on each man's face, yet none let out the slightest whimper.

The flight to the Tra Vinh airstrip took ten minutes. Kip looked back every few seconds to see how the wounded men were faring, and then he thought that perhaps two of them had died. Directly after liftoff, he radioed ahead and requested an ambulance be standing by. He was told that one would be there upon their arrival.

With the airstrip in sight, Slater added more power and *Alfie* began to shake, rattle and roll. "Mr. Slater. Alfie don't like to go fast!" Rusty cried out.

"Yeah—? Well you're not the one with your guts hanging out—!"

They made a fast descent to the small airstrip, landing less than seventy feet from the ARVN ambulance. Slater got out and urged the three waiting medics forward. When they came upon the scene of blood and mangled torsos and bones, they reared back. Then one of the three braved the wretched mass and checked the pulses of the three that were unconscious. He then directed his two companions to off-load the four that were still conscious. "What about those three?" Slater cried.

"They dead. They dead," the medic said.

"Well, get them the hell off my ship—"

"No can do. You tell we hap seben wounded. Only hap fo!"

"What the fuck difference does that make—?"

Standing there aghast, Slater watched as the four survivors were rushed to the ambulance. The ambulance then roared off. Slater turned and looked at the three dead Vietnamese soldiers lying in puddles of blood on the floor of the ship. He turned toward his gunner. "Ron! Help me get these guys out of here!"

Pilot and gunner grabbed an arm or leg and flopped each body onto the ground. They then dragged them individually to the edge of the dirt strip and plopped them on the grass. Back in his seat, Slater looked at the three men they had left in clumps on the ground. He tried to swallow but the spittle caught halfway down his throat. *You fucking people are fucking amazing—!*

On the way to Soc Trang, Slater kept looking back at the blood smeared over the cabin floor. At the airfield they set down in front of the control tower, where the crash-rescue truck was parked. Keeping the engine running at full throttle, Slater directed the Vietnamese fire-fighting crew to hose down the inside cabin. "It's the blood of your own countrymen!" he shouted. Oblivious to what had been said, they smiled and nodded and sprayed the floor until several hundred gallons of water had been used.

* * *

IN OPERATIONS, SLATER STUDIED THE map before him. On it was drawn a one-hundred-meter-long by seven-hundred-meter-long rectangle, along a straight section of canal, in an area near Long My, less than ten kilometers due north of Vinh Quoi. The person before him, a young, clean-cut Air Force first lieutenant, dressed neatly in jungle fatigues and wearing a cowboy-style olive-drab hat, was pointing his finger south of the rectangle. "I'd like to make our observations from here. We can fly a racetrack pattern parallel to it and get the data I need."

"You really want me to get that close—?" Slater said, noting that the lieutenant was asking that they fly half a kilometer from the target site.

"Sure. Have you ever seen an Arclight?"

"Nope, but I've heard them plenty of times. You mean to tell me that from thirty-three thousand feet not one bomb will hit outside that rectangle?"

"That's what I'm saying."

Slater peered directly into the man's hazel eyes. "This I've got to see."

It would be Slater's first ever observation of a B-52 bomb strike. Even as they spoke, the two ungainly monsters were already more than halfway across the distance that separated Guam, one of several air bases where they were stationed, from their strike point. He had heard the explosions often, both at night and during the day, the dull rumbling impacts that sounded like distant thunder, however with not an anvil cloud anywhere in sight.

Slater checked his watch. "I'll brief the crew. We'll crank in fifteen minutes."

The lieutenant smiled and checked his own watch. "Good. I'll meet you at the aircraft."

Once airborne, Slater headed the ship to the northwest. The TOT, or time on target, as the lieutenant had stated, was set for 1446, exactly. As they flew past Kien Thien, Slater looked out and saw a small hamlet to the north, where he had one day brazenly pointed his carbine out the window and fired at a VC flag hanging limp on a flagpole. The hamlet, ordered abandoned of its occupants by the Vietnamese government, had then been hit with ten 105-artillery shells. He was, on the day he decided to investigate, appalled to find the flagpole still standing and the red, yellow and blue enemy flag still attached to the cord. What possessed him to drop down low-level and do what he did still made him wonder. He was getting as bad as Leo. Afterwards, he cringed at his wanton recklessness. With less than six months remaining to DEROS, the last thing he wanted to develop was a latent death wish.

Speaking over the ICS using a headset, the lieutenant said to Slater: "We're showing up a little too early. Let's not get too close. We don't want to tip our hand."

Slater nodded. He checked his map and then looked ahead. He could just make out the target coordinates. He looked at the ship's clock. It was now 1441, five minutes till show time.

"The bombers are right now crossing the coast," the lieutenant said.

"And good ole Charlie isn't going to see or hear a thing. He won't even know what hit him."

"That's a big ten-four."

"So why the hell are we here?"

"To look for secondary explosions, of course," the lieutenant replied.

Slater nodded. "Of course, why didn't I think of that? We sure as hell aren't here to see if Charlie decides to shoot back."

The lieutenant smiled. "You got that right."

After three minutes, the lieutenant signaled that it was time to get into position. Slater brought the ship closer. He could see trees and heavy brush on both sides of the canal, as likely a Viet Cong hideout as any other location in the Delta. He could see on the north side of the canal where the bomb pattern would start and end. The nearly unseen aircraft would make one pass apiece, each dropping fifty-four thousand pounds (27 tons) of bombs. He knew that the B-52s were accurate, but still found it hard to believe that from thirty-three thousand feet the bombs would remain within the plotted rectangle. He knew, too, that just the force of the concussion alone could scramble a man's brains. A nearness was all it took. He shuddered.

At exactly 1446, Kip Slater saw the first bombs hit. There was a flash, and then around the flash came a wavering, a shimmering, as if he were viewing heat waves radiating from a hot, flat surface. And then there were more flashes, one and two at a time, side-by-side, until after a moment the flashes stopped. Within seconds after the first bombs hit they felt the shock wave and heard the first explosion, followed immediately by more shock waves and more explosions. The helicopter rocked slightly and Slater enhanced his grip on the cyclic control stick. As they flew their racetrack pattern, they looked for the hoped-for secondary explosions, evidence of detonating an ammo supply dump. And then they saw them: new flashes, small secondary explosions, yellow and white smoke blooming up and out. And then they saw a large secondary explosion, indicating the bombs might have hit pay dirt, the mother lode, rockets and mortars and grenades and B-40 ammunition. "Jesus...H...Christ..." Slater heard Ron say over the intercom from his right-side doorgunner position.

Slater looked down and breathed deep. He checked his map. He was astounded. Not one bomb had hit outside the marked set of coordinates.

The lieutenant checked his watch. "Okay, get ready, the second bomber is about to unload."

The smoke began to clear slightly. Slater saw the large craters created by the bombs begin to fill with water. He saw shattered trees and darkened shrub where once there had been lush greenery. Several fires had broken out. So far they had seen no movement, no sign of human activity. The second run went like the first, but seemed half as long in duration. They noted only one small secondary.

When the last shock wave had passed and the sound of the last muffled explosion was gone, and the big bombers, still barely seen, were turning back toward Guam, they stared in mute shock as two men clad in black pajamas paddled hurriedly in a sampan from the gutted treeline, out into the middle of the canal. Their steering appeared erratic, cockeyed. "I see it...but I don't believe it..." Slater whispered. "Can it be true?"

Slater then heard the voice of the clean-cut Air Force first lieutenant, his words calmly spoken: "Have your right doorgunner open up."

Slater gathered his wits and ordered Ron to shoot. For nearly a full minute, tracers sped earthward. The bullets sliced innocuously into the brown water around the two men, who had managed to get to the far shore and disappear among the vegetation. Ron then peppered the vegetation.

Finally, Slater ordered Ron to cease firing.

"What for?" asked the lieutenant.

"We can't see them. Besides if they have half a brain left to remember what they just went through, this will be a day they'll never forget." And then Slater said, "I know I sure as hell won't!"

Chapter 54

SPEC FOUR NICK CARTER RUSHED INTO the orderly room. "Sir!—I just got word that one of our ships went down."

Mike Nolan, talking to Major Elroy, turned. "What?—Who?"

Carter, nearly out of breath, said, "Didn't get that, sir. It's either Captain Hardin and Lieutenant Daniels, or Mr. Thomas and Lieutenant Aster."

"They're up in the Seven Mountains region," Nolan stated, looking at Elroy.

"What happened?"

"Shot down!"

"Oh, Christ..."

In operations Nolan got quickly on the phone to the cav squadron at Vinh Long. After explaining the situation, he said, "What do you have going on around the Seven Mountains?"

"We've got an ops three klicks east of Cai Cai, right at the border," said a tired-sounding voice at the other end. "Charlie Troop and a half-platoon of Blues."

"Any way you can get in touch with them?"

"Sure."

"Could you divert them to the following coordinates?"

"I'll try. Go ahead and give them to me."

Five minutes later, Major Elroy and his XO, were standing in the door to operations, flight gear in hand. "What's up?" Elroy asked.

"I think I've got support from the cav at Vinh Long," Nolan stated. "They say Charlie Troop may be able to divert their Blues. They're east of Cai Cai." Nolan pointed to the location on the large ops map. "I've also alerted Dustoff."

"Good going," Elroy said. "Major Riggins and I are going to take the H-model. Keep us informed."

"Yessir."

When the two officers were gone, Nolan went to the coffee pot and filled his cup. Which ship had gone down? How did they get hit? Were the men dead or alive? Questions questions questions.

He had flown more than a few missions with Hardin, now a captain, who had less than sixty days to go. He had become better acquainted with Bobby Daniels, who impressed him with his youth and energy. Mr. Thomas was a second-tour warrant officer, a steady-handed, methodical Cobra pilot. He had met Lieutenant Aster a week ago, the newest member of the company. Several weeks before, Aster's wife had given birth to twin boys. He dreaded this part of the job, waiting and wondering. Someone back in the States would soon be receiving bad news, of that he was almost certain.

The Sky Soldiers

He lit a cigarette and drew the smoke in slowly. He stared at the far wall. In his mind's eye he saw black smoke and boiling flame shooting skyward on the west side of one of the granite nodules. He recalled how a month ago the ARVN were in heavy contact. The Viet Cong were dug-in in deep caves, halfway up the mountainside. A CH-47 Chinook helicopter, with a sling-load of napalm in fifty-five gallon drums, hovering high above the caves, let go of the load. Thomas had to time his dive just right to have his rockets hit a second after the barrels made contact with the mountainside. After the smoke cleared and the flames had died down, the ARVN checked the caves and found thirty charred bodies, grotesque-looking in their final agonies of death. He could only imagine a Cobra loaded with ordnance and fuel on high-speed impact with the earth displaying the same explosive scene.

Nolan and Carter had been waiting an hour when the FM radio crackled. Nolan went and lifted the handset. "This is Sun Devil Three, go ahead."

"Roger, Three. This is Sun Devil Six. Inbound your location. ETE ten minutes," spoke Major Elroy.

"Roger, Six. Give me a sit-rep."

"Four Four Six down. Both frontseat and backseat are Kilo India Alpha. I'll give you more later."

Chills shot through Nolan as he glanced at the scheduling board. Thomas and Aster were dead.

The bottle of Jack Daniels was stowed on a bookshelf in his room that held but one book: His thumbed-through and marked-over AH-1G "dash ten" operator's manual. Next to it was a small glass. Nolan took the bottle and glass and poured himself a shot. He put the glass to his lips and in one quick motion bolted the liquid down.

Nolan went to his bunk and sat down. He stared glumly at the floor, at the pattern in the rug that lay next to his bed. His boots were off. He saw the point of his stockinged-feet visible beyond the edge of the rug. Earlier, there had been a memorial service for Thomas and Aster that had been attended by every man in the company. They were the unit's first combat-related deaths and everyone was gravely shaken.

He poured himself another shot. He tilted his head back and swallowed. This time the liquid fell like molten lead. His stomach rebelled and he choked back the urge to vomit. In a moment, though, Nolan felt the warm, stinging feeling he sought. He thought of the two pilots. Two more men added to an already long list. What was it all for? What in Christ was this war really for? There were times, few that they were, when he *really* wanted to know. Worse, what possessed these men to be here—to put themselves in position to die such a violent death?

Victor R. Beaver

He thought of himself. How would he go home? Like Thomas or Aster, burned beyond recognition, a hunk of charred torso? He peered into his now empty glass as though it were a crystal ball. *God—how* will *I return?* For a moment the question mesmerized him. He exhaled air in a burst, then poured another shot and bolted it down.

* * *

MIKE NOLAN HESITATED, THEN OPENED the door and entered. He took a couple of steps and stopped. Before him were two sets of book-filled shelves against the far wall. He gazed at them for a moment before diverting his eyes right, toward the room's only desk, tucked in the far corner. The desk, at the moment, was unoccupied. He looked left. He saw three reading tables and around each four steel-framed chairs; adorning the tabletops were several magazines all neatly arranged. In the far corner to his left he saw two sofa chairs placed near each other at a slight angle. Between the two chairs was a tall-standing floor lamp. Seated in the left sofa chair was an enlisted man, wearing dark, horn-rimmed glasses. The man was thumbing the pages of a large hardback book. Nolan saw that he and the enlisted man were the room's only occupants, at least for the moment.

Nolan went toward the left bookshelf. His eyes quickly scanned the titles. When he came to the Western section, he took down a Louis L'Amour book, *Bendigo Shafter*, and opened it. He read a few lines, then replaced the book on the shelf.

"Captain Nolan. What a delightful surprise."

Startled, Mike looked up. At first he thought it strange that she should be wearing a set of jungle fatigues. But then he noted quickly that she didn't look half bad in them, perhaps a little baggy around the waist, where the fatigue jacket hung down outside over the top of the fatigue pants, but around the hips and across her chest she filled them out quite nicely. Her red hair was tied back exactly as he remembered at the party three weeks before. Her eyes, too, were the same iridescent blue that seemed to shift color dependent on the angle they were seen from. "How do you know my name? I don't recall that we were ever introduced."

Sharon O'Malley pointed toward his right breast pocket. "Your nametag. It spells N-O-L-A-N. Remember, I'm a librarian. Being able to read is one of my job qualifications."

"I see."

"Have you come to check out our store of books? If so, considering your type, I still recommend Mickey Spillaine. Fine detective reading. Slightly intricate, but I think you can handle it."

He looked toward the book he had just replaced. He took it down. She extended her hand and he gave it to her. She looked at the cover. "Louis L'Amour. Also excellent reading. Not quite so sophisticated as some Western authors I might recommend, but at your level, this would be a good start."

"My level?"

She smiled. "Forgive me. I'm merely, how you say, paraphrasing what you told me, that you don't ever read for pleasure. If you're going to start, my job as a librarian is not to add too much fuel to the fire. We want the fire to build gradually. Not let it go out prematurely."

As she spoke, he looked at the small indent in her throat, just below her chin. He saw, too, trickles of sweat along the base of her neck, and a few strands of hair pasted to her cheek. He found himself also watching the rise and fall of her chest. He said, "No. We don't want the fire to go out...prematurely."

Still holding the book, she studied him for a moment. He's not the least bit suave or cultured, she thought, like most of the men (officers mainly) she'd met at Can Tho, those who made the effort to get to know her, hoping she would submit to dinner. He's tough, she decided; he's not mean, he's just not tender. Crazily, she thought of how a steak can be rare, medium, or well done. He seemed the medium-well type. "So, why are you here?"

"I was thinking...they do a mean steak sandwich at the officers' club. Maybe you'd like to have lunch with me."

She blinked her eyes. "How uncanny. You know, I was just thinking about...Oh, never mind."

"About what?"

"Nothing-nothing."

"Well, how about it?"

She looked at her watch. It was a little past twelve. Ellen wouldn't be back for another hour. "I'm sorry, but I really can't go right now. At one o'clock I might."

"No dice," he said. "I've got to be back at one."

As he turned to go, he stopped. "You know, I don't know your name. What is it, anyway?"

"You asked me to lunch without first knowing my name? What does that mean?"

"Beats me. So what is it?"

She offered her hand. "My name is Sharon. Sharon O'Malley. And your first name is—?"

"Mike," he answered. He took her hand and shook it, noting how soft yet strong it felt in his grasp.

"Aah, as in Mike Hammer. Private Eye."

"Whatever."

"Can I take a 'raincheck' on the lunch?"

"Sure. How about tomorrow?"

"Oh, I'm sorry, tomorrow is out too. I have a meeting in Saigon."

At first he felt a twinge of disappointment, and then immediate relief. "Tough luck, I guess. Well, it was nice to meet you...Sharon."

"Same to you...Mike."

He nodded. As he again turned toward the door, she said, "Wouldn't you like to check out a book?"

"No, I haven't got the time."

"Some other day, perhaps?"

"Perhaps."

After he was gone, Sharon O'Malley took the L'Amour book she had been holding and went to the window behind her desk and placed it on the ledge, out of the way of the other books that crowded there for space. She looked out the window. She saw him retreating down the narrow street upon which the library and dayroom sat. She thought his walk like a strut, but surely an unconscious strut, for he was not the type to call attention to himself. There was really nothing patently dynamic about him; he was not good-looking, nor was he very tall. In fact it struck her that she was taller than him. But in his presence, why did she feel him towering over her? At one point during his visit, as she studied him, she thought him to be a throwback from some other age. In some ways, he reminded her of the men who lived near Milburn, the ranchers and farmers. They weren't very cerebral, either. From them a grunt was a Yes, a groan or a moan a No. The difference, of course, was that Mike Nolan had seen so many more of the earth's places, while the men of Milburn, North Dakota, had seen little to none. Milburn, North Dakota. Disappointingly, there had been so little of the greater, more intricate world out on the flat open spaces where she had once lived, the very reason she didn't want to return.

But to know where you finally want to be, is to also have been where you didn't. At that moment, she was glad she hadn't been able to go with him to lunch. Right now was not the time to retreat, to step back. Her future was at stake. A dream that doesn't come to fruition...is a life that isn't lived. She resolved then and there that if he was to show up and ask her to lunch again, she would tell him no. And neither would there be the inevitable 'whatever' afterwards. *Whatever?...Whatever what? Oh, how the hell would I know—?*

At the scheduling board in operations, Nolan began grease-penciling in the names of men and equipment needed the next two days to support an operation being conducted by the 9th Infantry Division based at Dong Tam, the only major American combat infantry force in the Mekong Delta. It had been nearly two weeks since his last front-seat flight. As he finished marking his name next to Hardin's, Major Elroy entered operations. "What's your name doing up there?"

Nolan turned. "Sir?"

"Take your name off. You're my operations officer. From now on, any flying you do has to be cleared with me."

"Sir—?"

Elroy held up his hand. "Captain Nolan, I want no argument. I'll decide under what conditions you can fly." Elroy took out a cigarette and lit it. "I hadn't discussed it with you yet, but I was going to move Lieutenant Aster in here as your assistant. It's too late now, of course. And by the way, keep this under your hat, but we may be in store for some swapping—an 'infusion.' Our Vinh Long cav squadron is going to need some old blood so that the whole damn outfit doesn't rotate back to the States at once."

"Yessir—but, sir, about my flying," Nolan countered, "I wish you'd reconsider. I can't be stuck here behind this counter all the time. I'm about ready to go buggy—"

Elroy grunted. "You should have my job. This last week has been unnerving as hell. Have you ever written a letter of condolence to someone's wife, who, of all people, just had twins—?" The major shook his head. "I never want to do that again."

Chapter 55

THE THREE WARRANT OFFICER CANDIDATES arrived late on Saturday afternoon and found a vacancy on South Rampart, in an old seedy hotel just off Canal Street. When they got to their room they found it to be a large, high-ceilinged suite stuffed with old furniture and one large double bed. They flipped to see who got the bed. Tom Adkins won the toss. "It doesn't matter," Mark Allen said. "Who's going to sleep? We're here to party!" And with that said he withdrew a whole fifth of Yukon Jack (sipping whiskey) from his overnight bag, took a swig, and passed it on.

"Boy, that's some *smooooth* shit," Tom Adkins said.

Sandy Adamson took a small sip. He grinned. "I like it—" and tipped the bottle again.

"Hey, don't drink it all."

"Okay. Let's count coin," Adkins said. "How much money you guys got? I count fifty-six and change."

Sandy said, "I have forty-five."

"And I've got a measly thirty-seven," Mark offered.

"Shit, that outta be enough."

This was the weekend the three classmates had decided to investigate New Orleans. Seymore, much to their amusement, had more important matters to attend to. Sandy had left his friend in a near complete state of panic. Jenny's parents were coming in from Idaho to meet the young man who had finally won their daughter's heart. Sandy wished he could have remained behind, a little mouse in Seymore's shirt pocket. He wanted to see their expressions when they met Howdy Doody's nearly exact look-alike.

With showers done (and several slugs apiece of Yukon Jack in their bellies), the trio decided it was time to hit The Quarter. "Why don't we walk?" Sandy suggested.

"Nah, let's drive," Mark said.

"But it's only a couple of blocks—"

"I'd rather drive. Relax, goddamnit—I know what I'm doing."

"Okay, what the hell." They packed themselves into Mark's Impala and drove across Canal Street into the French Quarter.

For twenty minutes they criss-crossed The Quarter looking for a place to park. "Here's one," said Mark, barely squeezing the Impala between two Volkswagen Beetles. They were on Conti Street (a point of fact they knew not at all), between Burgandy Street and one beginning with an R (a point of fact they were only vaguely aware).

Sandy said, "I don't think so. It says No Parking. See the sign?"

Mark glanced up through the windshield and then looked at Tom Adkins. "Piss on it. How many cars have we seen parked the same way? Besides, I'm sure the cops have better things to do than walk around checking on cars. All they'd do anyway is give us a ticket. How much can that be? Pennies, I'll bet."

Tom nodded. "Yeah...screw it."

"Okay," Sandy said. "But don't say I didn't warn you."

"Lighten up, Adamson, damn you, or I'll box your ears. Christ on a crutch, what a worry-wart."

They got out. Mark looked left, then right. Two doors down he found what he thought was a distinguishing landmark, a long-established tobacco shop, older than the first coming of Christ. Later, at four or five in the morning, he didn't want to be stumbling around looking for his car. At that time of the morning all the streets in the French Quarter looked alike, especially in the inebriated state he expected to be in.

As they began to walk, Sandy looked back and asked:

"What street was that?" But his question fell on deaf ears. A minute later, he forgot he even asked a question. "Wow—do I feel loose."

"Hey, you just wait...we haven't even begun to get loose—"

They met the crowd. For the next two hours they wandered up and down Bourbon Street, stopping at practically every corner bar to listen to a band. Sandy was enthralled. It was a completely happy kind of music and the sweating band players were all hard-working crowd pleasers. They ordered Hurricanes, a drink made with dark rum, red passion-fruit punch and lemon juice, and served in tall glasses. After several such drinks (at two dollars a shot) they were feeling no pain. They ate bouillabaisse at the Vieux Carre, crabmeat soup at Delmonico's, and whenever they could, Tom and Mark slurped down oysters on the half-shell. "Yuk—how can you guys stand to eat that crap?" Sandy asked.

"What's the matter?" Mark replied. "I thought you wanted to experience life in the raw. Well, this is as raw as it gets."

"That's just it—*it's raw.*"

"Cripes—what a puss."

Another hour passed. After wandering from street to street, Sandy blurted:

"Hotdamn! I can't remember when I've had such a friggin' good time."

"Hey, my friend, the night is still young," stated Allen.

By two in the morning, the three student pilots couldn't steer a straight course. They had gone into every bar, every porn shop, every restaurant and café, and they even got snookered into three transvestite haunts. "But they all look so beautiful!" Sandy had wailed, after he was cut loose from one of the most gorgeous "creatures" he had ever seen.

At two-thirty, Mark suggested they go to an out of the way place he knew the locals went, a place called The Port of Call, on Esplanade Avenue.

"How do we get there?" Adkins asked.

Mark looked one way and then the other. "First of all," he slurred, "where the hell are we?"

"I don't know."

Sandy was standing next to a street sign. He looked up. He attempted to get his eyes in focus but the harder he tried, the worse it got. "Oh...Lordy Lordy Lordy, would Katie have a fit if she saw me now." And then he wailed:

"I miss my Katie—!"

Mark looked at Adkins. "How's your head?"

"Terrible," he moaned. "Lessh go home..."

"I vote we go to bed," Sandy said, teeter-tottering on the brink of cerebral disaster.

"Me too," Adkins said.

"You weenies," Mark Allen growled. "Damn! What a bunch of party poopers."

"Where's your car?" Adkins said. "I need to shit down."

"I'll find it," Sandy blurted. "Where's the Big Dipper?"

As they had learned at Fort Wolters, planning a cross-country trip was very simple (hardly complicated). One must have a destination and one must decide, using a map, the best path to get there.

Well, they had no map. About all they really knew was that they were somewhere in the French Quarter (how could they be otherwise?). Their destination, they thought, was somewhere on the other side of Bourbon Street, not far from Canal Street. So even their destination was vague. To boot, though they finally saw that they were at one of the corners of St. Phillip and Royal, this tidbit had little value: after nearly five hours of drinking all streets had become one megastreet and all went in the same direction: that (no this) way.

"It's between Burgandy," Sandy said. "And...and Rump...something..."

Mark said, "Burgandy is a long street, slick. And there isn't any street called Rump-something. But, what the hell—it doesn't matter. I know exactly how to get there."

And so they began. On St. Phillip they walked until they came to the French market. "This is all wrong."

"Which way now?"

"How about this way?" They walked down Decatur, past streets named Ursuline, Gov. Nicholls, Barracks, until they came to a wide boulevard with trees running down the middle. "Is this Canal Street?"

"I think so but there's no sign."

"Which way now?"

"Rimpole...Rumpor..." Sandy's brain was now completely fixated on the Rs.

"Let's try to the right."

They walked and weaved until they came to a cemetery. "This isn't Canal Street."

"It could have been."

Eventually they got back on Decatur. "I'm going to be sick. My head is spinning."

They turned right. They went until they got to Royal. "This is Royal."

"How do you know?"

"I'm reading the sign."

"I thought Bourbon Street was one over from Royal?"

"It is."

"Well, we should have crossed it about eight blocks back."

"Eight blocks—that doesn't make any goddamn sense."

"Romper...Rangpole..."

"Christ—my head hurts. What the hell time is it?"

"Screw the time—we've got to find where we parked."

"This is St. Phillip."

"Damn, this is where we started—!"

"True."

"Well, when we started, which way did we go?"

"I can't remember."

They studied the situation. "If we go this way and don't see Bourbon Street in one block, we turn around and go back."

"Right."

"Rankle...Rample..."

One block down they found Chartres. "Let's turn around." They did, but they turned a quarter-turn too much. They walked two blocks. "Gov. Nicholls Street?"

"This is not Bourbon Street!"

"Shit. Now which way do we go?"

"Let's go this way." They did, one block.

"How many times have we been on this street?"

"Three or four."

"Which way now?"

"Let's go that way."

Two blocks. "Royal Street."

"Again—?"

"Well, at least we're getting somewhere."

"We are? Had we stayed in one spot to begin with, we'd be getting somewhere—for godsakes."

"Rimpit...Roncali...Remmington..."

"Shouldn't we ask somebody?"

"No way," Mark said. "Only queers are out at this time of the morning."

Like the blind leading the blind, they crossed Bourbon Street, but they didn't notice it. They were at the far end, near Esplanade. They came to: "Dauphine? This is a new one."

"I'll bet it's this way."

Mark counted five blocks. "Where the hell is Bourbon Street?"

"This is Orleans Street."

"Now which way?"

"That way."

They went one block. "Hey, Burgandy Street!"

"It's not Bourbon Street," said Mark.

"So what? I remember Burgandy!" Adkins exclaimed.

"Me too," Sandy stammered.

"Yeah...and...and something else...starts with an R."

"Yeah, me too..."

"Okay, you smart asses, which way?"

"This way."

At three thirty-six in the morning, they came to Conti. "Is this getting familiar?"

"No."

"Bull, this is it. There's the tobacco store—"

"I've seen three such tobacco shops and they all look the same."

On Conti they spotted the lights of a wrecker. "Look at that shit. Some poor sucker is getting his car towed away."

"What's the make?"

"I can't see it. Too many flashing lights."

The wrecker moved off. They stared at each other. "Let's go one more time."

Sandy slumped down on the curb. He felt like death warmed over, like a bad day at Eagle Rock, like a rotten egg. Like shit.

Adkins rubbed his head over and over. His eyes were bloodshot. "I need a drink."

They looked up Conti one way and then the other. No red and white Impala. "Where the hell is it—?"

"I don't know.'

"Let's check down the next street."

"Rambo...Rimpet..."

Burgandy to Bienville. "Here's a tobacco store. But it looks just like the other one." No car. Bienville to Dauphine to Conti. "This is the street we parked on, I swear it," Mark cried.

Burgandy to St. Louis and then to Toulouse. Down Toulouse to Dauphine. Dauphine to St. Louis. Up St. Louis. "It's not here, either. This is maddening. Where the hell's my car—?"

"I don't know."

"It couldn't have disappeared—could it?"

"Hey, they shoot horses, don't they?"

They ran the circuit again. No Impala. "Well, I'll be go to hell. I swear we parked it right here. Under this sign."

"Yeah—the No Parking sign."

"But there aren't any cars at the other No Parking signs—"

"That's because they've probably been towed away!"

"Randy...Randolf...Rampilke..."

They sat down on the curb. "How the hell are we gonna get back to Rucker? We don't have a car—"

"Can we go to the hotel now? I'm beat."

"What time is it?"

"Not quite six."

"When's daylight?"

"Soon. Let's try again." Burgandy, Conti, Dauphine, Bienville, Burgandy, Conti, Dauphine, St. Louis, Burgandy, Conti. It was an hour later. "Shit. This is maddening! Where the hell's my goddamn car—?"

"I don't know—*I don't know!*"

"Rudolf...Reindeer..."

At seven, they stumbled into the hotel room. Sandy fell onto the bed, passed out. "Look at us," cried Mark. "We should be at Pat O'Briens! Sipping Bloody Marys and Mint Juleps!"

Mark dialed the number. "Sixth Precinct, how can I help you?" said a woman's voice.

"I'd like to report a stolen vehicle."

"Okay, sir, could you give me your name."

"Mark Allen. United States Army."

There was a pause. He heard paper shuffling in the background. Mark said, "Excuse me, but don't you want to know what make it is? what year? the license-plate number?"

"No, sir. We have all that."

"You do—?"

"Of course. 'Sixty-five Chevrolet Impala. White top, red body. Delaware license plate RIH-367."

"Oh, God—where'd you find it? What condition is it in?"

"It's in fine condition, sir. It's been impounded. For illegal parking. To get it back you'll have to pay a forty-dollar impoundment fee plus twenty-five dollars towing charges. All in all, sixty-five dollars, sir."

"Sandy, wake up."

Sandy rolled his eyes. "Wha-what...?"

"Hey, we found the car—we need some money. How much you got?"

"...tween Burgandy and Rampar...stilt...skin," Sandy mumbled.

"What's he saying?"

"Nothing. He's out of it." They rifled through his pants and found that between the three of them they had sixty-eight dollars and seventeen cents. The trio went to the station and paid the fees. Mark said, "Well, at least I've got a gas card."

As they were leaving, Adkins stopped. "Wait a minute." He turned and went back to the sergeant on duty. "Where'd you tow the car from—exactly?"

The police sergeant read the report. "From exactly under a No Parking sign?"

"No, I mean where?—from between what streets?"

"On Conti, between Burgandy and Ram—"

"—*part!* I got it! I got it!" Sandy suddenly blurted. "It's between Burgandy and Rampart!"

"Shut up!"

"What time was it towed away?"

"At three thirty-seven this morning."

Wide-eyed, Adkins and Mark gaped at each other. *"CRAP! We watched them tow it away!"*

Chapter 56

"**A**RMY FOUR SEVEN TWO, IF NO transmissions are received for one minute in the pattern or five seconds on final, attempt contact on emergency frequency and proceed VFR. If unable, execute the Copter NDB Three Six Zero approach."

Sandy Adamson hastily scribbled what he could of the lost communications instructions, then hunted through the small booklet that contained NAVAID approaches pertinent to the Fort Rucker training area for the (lost commo) back-up approach. "Did you pick up on the 'attempt contact on emergency frequency and proceed VFR?'" said Ross, his instructor, seated in the left seat of the TH-13T helicopter.

"Sir...ah, not really."

"What is the emergency UHF frequency, anyway?"

Sandy tried to think what it was, attempting to employ the memory crutch he had learned a week ago, but at the moment it escaped him.

"Never mind," Ross said. "Take the controls. The controller's about to turn you onto base leg."

"Yessir." Sandy dropped the booklet at his feet as he went for the controls. After a moment of struggling, he managed to pick it up. He was certain that Ross thought him an ignoramus, completely unfit to be attending military flight training. "I've got the aircraft," he said.

"You've got the aircraft, eh? Is that the proper announcement for transferring the controls of the aircraft? When are you going to get it right?" Ross's degrading tone filled Sandy with a sordid uneasiness.

Sandy tried to be calm. He had learned early that Ross was more concerned with how things were said or how they appeared, than whether he understood what his student was doing and why. So often at the table when Sandy asked him to explain what the air traffic controller meant by what he said, Ross would state, "That's just the way it is—just do it."

"Army Four Seven Two, turn left heading one three zero."

Sandy banked the helicopter left. "This is Army Four Seven Two, roger, turning left to heading one three zero."

"Army Four Seven Two, what are you're intentions after this approach?"

Ross answered for Sandy. "Request vectors for an ASR approach to Knox Field."

"Roger. In the event of a missed approach, climb straight ahead to two thousand feet, turn left heading two seven zero, vectors for the ASR Three Three Zero approach to Knox Field."

"This is Four Seven Two, roger."

Victor R. Beaver

As they flew, Sandy heard the voices of other classmates talking to air traffic control. Pete Cochran always sounded so professional, having spent nearly four years with Delta Airlines. Even Seymore, with his sometimes high-pitched voice, came back over the radio like he knew what he was doing, which apparently he did. It was common knowledge that Seymore would go for his standard instrument rating rather than settle for the half-baked "tac ticket" most of them would walk away from flight school with. Sandy was proud of Seymore, but wished he knew his friend's secret. To go from class dunce to prime student aviator was no small feat in the current "get'em through and get'em to Vietnam" school atmosphere.

"Army Four Seven Two, turn left heading three six zero, contact final controller on frequency three six six point four."

"This is Army Four Seven Two, roger."

Ross switched frequencies. Sandy reported to the GCA (ground controlled approach) final controller on a discrete frequency. He was now one-on-one with an air traffic controller who sat before a radar screen showing their aircraft *only* (typically) flying toward the airfield. During this final phase of the instrument approach procedure, Sandy would hear no other radio traffic. He felt as though he was inside a cocoon. The final controller's voice came over the radio evenly, every five seconds or less. "On course...On glide path. On course, now going above glide path. Adjust rate of descent." Sandy eased down on the power. "Now on glide path...Going slightly left of course, turn right heading zero zero five."

Halfway down on the descent profile, the controller interrupted the approach. "Army Four Seven Two, we need you to abandon the approach. Proceed VFR to Hanchey. Suggest heading three three zero. How copy?"

Ross touched Sandy's arm to indicate that he would answer the radio. "This is Four Seven Two, roger. What's the problem?"

"All instrument aircraft are being diverted to home stations. That's all I'm allowed to say."

"This is Four Seven Two, roger."

In the briefing room, Sandy met others in his class, noting they had concerned looks on their faces. It was Mark, though, who came and took him aside. "There's been an accident," he whispered.

Sandy's blood suddenly ran cold. "Who—?"

"They're not saying." Then Mark blurted, "It was a fucking mid-air!"

"You're shittin' me—"

"I swear to God."

"Where's Seymore?"

"I don't know—"

"Shit."

Jenny McCoy walked through the door of her apartment and laid her keys on the table. The stereo, turned low, was playing an old Dean Martin song she loved. She went to the stereo and adjusted the volume.

> *"Everybody loves somebody sometime*
> *everybody falls in love somehow...*
> *Something in your kiss just told me,*
> *that sometime is now..."*

In a state of euphoria, Jenny danced around the room in the arms of her imaginary lover. Her parent's visit had been glorious, she thought. *They loved him!—They love him!* On the way to the airport, from which she had just returned, she couldn't get over how much her mother thought Seymore was so darling and sensitive. Her father, slow to warm to the freckle-faced lad, found himself laughing like he had never done before. Throughout the visit Jenny could see her father's pride: His youngest of three daughters, at age twenty-five, was finally going to be married. And now, Jenny, whirling about the room, never felt happier. Even the day she first soloed an airplane couldn't compare. On that day at the hangar, her mother didn't even try to hide her gloom, saying to her father right in front of her: "James, she can out-perform any man in this town. Who is going to want to marry an upstart woman? She'll be an old maid as I go to my grave—!" To which her father responded with his arm firmly around Jenny's shoulder: "Hush, your daughter here is one day going to take over this air service I spent forty years building. She'll have no dearth of young men trying to get into her britches, with the money she'll be making—"

After the song ended, Jenny turned the stereo off and turned the TV on. She frowned as she heard *"...collision occurred at approximately two twenty-seven this afternoon. As you can see behind me, firemen have just begun to control the fire at this particular crash site. There are apparently no survivors of either aircraft...Names are being withheld, pending notification of next of kin."*

Jenny's heart beat faster than it had ever done. Breathless, she watched as the firemen, in the background behind the TV announcer, began to put away their hoses.

She checked her watch. It was now twenty minutes after three. The accident had occurred a little less than an hour ago, before she had let her parents off at the airport. She grabbed her purse and dashed out the door. The drive to post, she would later recall, was a complete blur. The worst of all possible flying disasters. A mid-air collision! *Oh God, please don't let it be him.* By the time she turned onto Tank Hill Road, she was on the verge of tears. *With over six hundred students now going through instrument training, what are the odds that it was him?* Damn little, she thought, as she went past the large single-story building that housed the barbershop, cleaners, snack bar and little beer hall. *But still...but still—*

She took a deep breath and turned into the barracks's parking lot. She stopped the car near a gathering of candidates. Her hands shook as she opened the door.

She saw Mark and Sandy standing alone, their faces pale, their expressions solemn. A huge lump formed in her throat. She went to them. "Who was it?"

"I'm sorry, Jenny...but we're not allowed to say—"

"Was it Seymore?"

"Who?—Seymore? No...No, Jenny, no—"

She felt the blood leave her head as if a floodgate had suddenly opened. When she came to, she found herself flat on the ground, with several faces peering down at her. Someone had his fatigue hat off and was fanning over her head. She felt a pair of hands gently cup her face. She focused her eyes. She saw Seymore staring back at her. "Jenny, Jenny, are you okay?"

"Seymore...?"

"Baby, what happened? Why are you here?"

Drowsily, she said, "The...news, Seymore...I heard the news..."

Cheryl Cochran watched curiously as two military cars pulled slowly into the hard-dirt parking lot. She had been doing the dishes when she happened to look up and saw through the kitchen window the two cars coming down the road that led to their trailer court. The cars stopped and two pairs of occupants, all in dress uniform, got out. She saw one pair step up to the Bowden's door. And then she heard footsteps mounting onto her porch. There came a knock at the door. She opened it.

"Mrs. Cochran?"

"Yes?"

"Is your husband Warrant Officer Candidate Peter Mathew Cochran?"

"Yes..."

"Ma'am, I'm sorry, but I'm afraid we have some very bad news."

It was a warm, beautiful southern Alabama spring day, a day meant for frolic and play; but there was no gaiety in the hearts of the men and women and children who filed into the little post chapel. Chaplains' assistants quietly ushered those who came and when the chapel was full, the chaplain, a small, gray-haired man, looked up and gave the sign of the cross. Sandy Adamson, with a sadness in his soul heavier than he had ever known, listened to the man speak. Across the aisle he watched Rose Bowden and Cheryl Cochran, both wearing black, seated next to each other. Their arms were locked together and Sandy thought he had never seen two women braver. What is it, he wondered, that creates that kind of strength, that kind of mental calm these women were having to display? At the moment, there was nothing on this earth Sandy wanted to know more. Unlike his classmates, he had been unable to go and be with Rose or Cheryl the evening the sad news broke. He went the following day, very reluctantly. He found Cheryl to be exceptionally gracious and calm. She welcomed him with a smile yet he could see in her eyes the pain that was deep in her soul. Rose took him in her arms and, holding him, cried. And then he cried. In the chapel, all of the old flight was there and a portion of the rest of the class: Willie, Ned Symington, Chancey, Zeigler, Adkins, Mayberry, Bartlett, Cottondale, Mark, Jenny, Seymore, and more...

When the service was over, they filed out into the bright spring sunlight. Sandy looked toward Seymore and Jenny, arm-in-arm, and in them he saw a new dawn. And then he remembered the chaplain's words: *"For everything there is a season. A time to laugh, a time to cry; a time to be born, a time to die..."*

And with those words spoken, to Pete Cochran and Ron Bowden, they had bid their final farewell....

Victor R. Beaver

Chapter 57

THE FLIGHT SURGEON, A YOUNG Negro captain, held the stethoscope against Justen's back, just below the left shoulder blade. "Breath deep."

Justen complied.

"Again, but hold it."

Derek filled his lungs and this time held his breath. In a mirror on the wall he watched the captain's facial expression, which had not changed from a perpetual frown the moment the examination began. The doctor next probed his back, gently, asking him how it felt. "Fine," he replied.

"Any soreness?"

"No."

"How's your rehab going?" the captain asked, now examining Justen's right leg and upper thigh.

"Real good."

"You're still having some difficulty with movement in your left arm, though, aren't you?"

"Some...but it isn't anything I can't live with."

The doctor spent another five minutes observing Derek stand and bend and move his upper torso and right leg in different ways. In addition to his three times a week attendance at the rehabilitation center, Derek, for the past month, had also been going to the gymnasium, grappling with the weights and various workout machines.

"I'd give it at least another month, maybe even two," the captain said. "You've made damn good progress, all things considered, but I'd have my butt in a sling if I put you back on flight status right now." The flight surgeon studied Justen for a moment. "Funny, but most guys would kill to have your condition. Anything to keep from going back to Vietnam."

Back in his room Derek made two phone calls. He spoke for several minutes to a chief warrant officer (W4) who handled aviation warrant officer assignments, asking how soon he could get orders back to Vietnam once he regained his flight status. The second phone call was to a major, one of the personnel in the casualties branch. He requested any new information about Jake that he could pass on to Valerie, to whom he spoke every other night. One of his great curiosities, as well as Valerie's, was why it took so long to get word that Jake was a POW. The major explained, with much assuming, that because Jake refused to answer written questions and sign documents that held content contrary to America's purpose in Vietnam, and contrary to the Geneva Convention, his captors also refused to release information about his status to the International Red Cross. It all fit. Jake had probably been led away from the crash site fully aware that if his body wasn't found, the Army would naturally presume him a captive and report accordingly: what more did he need to do to support the fact? In his wildest imaginings, Jake probably couldn't fathom that anything else would have been assumed.

Derek spent the rest of the day at Lowe Field, where the Huey contact and tactics divisions were located. His job ever since he arrived had been to "fly a desk." He worked with the combat skills and development team, producing changes to the POI, program of instruction, "re-inventing the wheel..." as one warrant officer he worked with liked to put it. Derek had little to no contact with the students going through flight training. It was just as well. He had never intended to stay at Fort Rucker, anyway. Besides, he would probably want to teach them tricks of flying the school would never tolerate. *"...I'd give it at least another month, maybe even two,"* the Negro captain had told him.

Another two months. It sounded like a lifetime.

* * *

KIP SLATER AND LEO TANNAH GRABBED their luggage and made their way toward the back of the CH-47 heavy-lift helicopter. They stepped off the ramp and with the huge tandem-set blades whirling overhead, moved quickly to the edge of the runway. They set their bags down and watched as the mammoth helicopter rose effortlessly straight up to a one-thousand-foot hover.

"Christ—would I love to have the power of one of those babies in a hot LZ," Leo exclaimed, now watching the Chinook roll forward to pick up speed.

"I'd settle for one of those damn H-models the cav squadron at Vinh Long has."

"Screw that noise. Let me get my hands on one of their Cobras—"

The two men picked up their bags and went toward the hootch. They entered and met Mac in the hallway. "Hey, guys, how was Rn'R? Did you get to Australia?"

"Nah," said Kip. "We had to settle for Hawaii."

Leo opened his hootch door and invited Mac in. Slater put his luggage in his room. *A whole week of Rn'R done with before it seemed it even began!* At Honolulu, when they stepped off the plane, they were immediately herded into an assembly area specifically designed for men coming into the Islands for R&R and were met by dozens of women looking to meet their husbands. He heard the utter glee when both husband and wife linked together, and saw the frantic dismay on the faces of those women whose husbands had not yet appeared. Some, he later learned, had been waiting for several days. Slater could think of a dozen reasons why a man might not be stepping off the plane, killed in action being one of them. Lord, pity those women who find that to be the case, he remembered thinking.

Victor R. Beaver

In Leo's room, Kip sat down and was handed a beer. Again, Mac asked anxiously how it went.

"We stayed in the Royal Hawaiian," Leo said. "The second night there we met three Pan Am secretaries out of New York. One of them had already linked up with this army captain, pilot-type, who flew with the One O First. The one I liked was kinda pretty but real standoffish. I couldn't get her warmed up at all. The oldest of the three, can you believe, hooks Slater. I named her 'Mrs. Robinson.' Which reminds me, we got to see a movie called 'The Graduate,' with Dustin Hoffman and Anne Bancroft. Two days later, on the flight back to Honolulu after visiting Kauai, quiet Romeo here has 'Mrs. Robinson,' who must have been in her mid-thirties, all over him like hot butter."

"Shut up, Leo."

"It's true, isn't it?"

"Yeah...sure."

He had never in his life been seduced, but Slater had been deliciously so, by overt, unmitigated action. When it was over, he tried to think how he had done it: whatever the damn formula, he wanted it to happen again—!

* * *

ASIDE FROM HIS DUTIES AS AWARDS and Decorations officer, Kip had been asked by Neely to submit articles to the *Delta Devil*, a bi-monthly magazine intended to promote *espirit de corps* among units in the Mekong Delta. It was a task to which Slater happily obliged. Of course, any article he wrote would have to be approved by Neely, and because the chance of getting in print was excellent, Kip took it upon himself to write accordingly. One article that appeared had to do with Monty the Python. Its twelve-foot length, coiled in a cage outside the hootch, had been an attraction for as long as he had been there. One day, a small pig, bought to settle a bet, supplemented Monty's daily ration of mice, rats, and other tasty vermin. Could Monty take the pig whole in his mouth? Without so much as a burp Monty ingested the entire pig, and for a long time afterwards was as swollen as the pocketbooks of the men who had placed their bets on the snake.

Also during that time, the first real serious chain letter Slater had ever seen began floating around, to which the entire 121st Assault Helicopter Company was a party. Thousands of dollars were at stake, all tied up in U.S. Savings Bonds, at a cost of seventy dollars a whack. Neely, because this wasn't the way God intended for man to earn his bread and keep, called upon the same God and the Adjutant General's office to halt this blasphemous "misuse" of American funds. Logically, the money was there—it would have worked—but fear ruled out.

He was in his room when Slater heard the first impacts. He barged out of the hootch and into the dark night and sprinted across the runway as the siren began its ear-piercing wail.

CRUUMMP!...WHUUMP! Slater skidded to a halt in front of the ship. He looked about for the rest of his flareship crew. "Where's everyone—?"

Munson, his peter-pilot, having arrived a moment before, said, "Shit—I don't know."

WHUUMMP!.....WHUUMP!

Stymied, Slater thought for a moment. "Do you think you can drop the flares?"

"What—?"

"They should already be set. Get in the back. We can't wait!"

As Slater tore around to the right cockpit door, the gunships were just coming to full power and in another moment would be scooting forward for takeoff. Without bothering to strap in, Slater flicked the battery switch on and pulled the ignition trigger.

CRUUMP!...WHUUMMP!

"Hurry," Munson hollered.

Slater brought the throttle to full rpm and slid the helicopter forward from its revetment. "Tower, this is the flareship, ready for take-off."

"Roger. Cleared for take-off. Aim east. The flashes are coming from that direction."

"Ten-four."

Slater brought the ship to a quick high hover and banked right. During the climb to three thousand feet, he instructed Munson how to ready the flares for discharge. Seated on the right side of the cabin area, Munson struggled with the silver-looking canisters trying desperately to calm his trembling fingers. At three thousand feet, directly over the gunships floating above the treetops, Slater called for the first flare to be heaved. It went out and in a moment the earth below was brightly lit. "Good going. Good going!"

"I can't see what the hell I'm doing!" Munson cried.

"Get another one ready!"

Munson heaved the second one out as the first ended its million-candlepower burn. Again, a small circle of the earth became brightly lit.

After a minute, a voice came from one of the gunships below. "We need one more, slick."

"Roger that," Slater replied.

And then to the back: "Heave another one out—!"

Without any light to see by, Munson struggled, again, to feel for the right mechanism to set, to send the canister on its lighted journey earthward. All of a sudden, Slater heard an explosion and was simultaneously surrounded by a bright light. Instantly he knew what had happened. The mechanism that triggered the flare parachute to be discharged from the canister had gone off! The blood drained from his face. *Nobody lives through this—Nobody! I've just been killed!*

Slater keyed his mic: "Munson! You ass! I'm too young to die!"

"Hell!—*so am I!*"

Almost the instant it happened, Munson had managed to rid the ship of the deadly canister, but then watched in horror as the parachute wrapped itself around the right-hand M-60 gun mount. Slater instinctively reduced power and began a fast plummet for earth. Jerking his head rearward, he saw that the flare was burning brightly back near the right-side synchronized elevator. As they descended, Slater could think only of keeping the fierce burning power of the flare from touching the ship. To do this he jammed in right anti-torque pedal, which he hoped would cause the helicopter to sideslip enough to have the flare canted—and streamlined—away from the tailboom. Lord of all Lords—*it worked!*

"Can you cut it away—?" Slater yelled, referring to the nylon cords of the parachute.

"I can't reach it!—Besides, I don't have a knife!"

From two thousand feet now and descending, Slater gratefully saw themselves laterally within five hundred meters of the airfield, flying parallel to the runway on the east side. Below he could see the bright explosions of mortars still impacting and debated whether or not to land on the runway. But he had no other choice—

"The second we land get that chute off!"

"Roger that!" Munson replied.

At one thousand feet and near the end of the runway, Slater banked the ship hard right. He had no idea now how close the flare was to the sync elevator and tailboom, but at this point felt his mortality had been extended—at least long enough to get the helicopter on the ground. The runway lights were now directly before them. All the while the bright light from the burning canister had dutifully followed them down. When they were within five hundred feet of the ground Slater checked quickly to see where, if any, the mortars were landing. He saw an occasional explosion off to their left. At two hundred feet he sensed the light dimming behind them, and at one hundred feet the light from the canister had fizzled out. Quickly, he turned on the landing light and saw close to a dozen brand new four-inch-deep craters in the runway, chunks of asphalt scattered everywhere.

Slater brought the helicopter to a hover and then slid the ship onto terra firma. *Earth!*

As Munson worked to unravel the main body of the parachute from the gun mount, Slater opened the door and quickly got out to inspect the right side of the ship where the canister had dangled. To his amazement, he could find no visible damage. He glanced down. What was left of the canister lay smoldering at his feet.

The Sky Soldiers

He heard a mortar round impact at the approach end of Runway Zero Two. "Let's get the hell back up there—"

"Are you crazy—?" Munson shouted.

They took off but during the climb-out saw the gunships returning. Slater banked the ship right and followed them back in.

"God," Leo said. "I thought you were a goner. You should have seen it—you were one bright ball of light—!"

"Very good job, Mr. Slater," Neely had told him later. "I expect to see your narrative for a Bronze Star, for both you and Mr. Munson."

"For what, sir?...Saving our own damn lives—?"

"Yes, Mister Slater."

Victor R. Beaver

Chapter 58

ONE OF SHARON O'MALLEY'S SERVICES with the 29th Evacuation Hospital at Can Tho was to distribute reading material to the sick and wounded. It was gratifying to see how the books and magazines she had chosen with such care enhanced the men's recovery. One day during her rounds, she saw someone familiar standing next to a young man in bed to whom she had delivered a book four days ago.

"Captain Nolan, I declare, you are a man of many uniforms."

Mike Nolan turned. A smile traced across his face. "What are you doing here?"

"One of my routines. The man can't come to the book, so I take the book to the man." She smiled at the young man in bed. "Specialist Craig, I finally got the other book you wanted." She moved the cart she used to transport the books on next to his bed. She withdrew a paperback copy and began to hand it to him. On impulse Nolan intercepted the book; he checked the title: *War and Peace.* "Pretty highbrow stuff," he said, smiling, handing the book on. "It's too thick. He won't be here *that* long."

"Specialist Craig," Sharon said, "is a speed reader, though I don't recommend that people read fast. They should read a good book slowly, savor every word. After all, words do make the world go around. And right now the world is spinning out of control. Don't you agree, Captain Nolan?"

Mike frowned at the sudden, out-of-place implication of Sharon's statement. "Sort of—I guess."

And then he looked toward Craig. Spec Five Craig was another enlisted man who worked in operations, who had come to the hospital with a case of dysentery. He said to him: "The doc says you should be okay in a couple of days. But go ahead and take your time."

"Thank you, sir."

After a few minutes, Sharon and Mike left Craig alone and began walking side-by-side down the aisle. Mike offered to push the cart of books. "It's refreshing to see compassion in a man in uniform," she said. "So often I see just the opposite."

Nolan looked at her, puzzled. "You mean my pushing this cart of books?"

"No-no, I mean that young man back there. You were very considerate of him."

They came to two lounge chairs halfway down a long corridor. He invited her to sit down. He said, as he stooped down and rested his hands on his right knee, "Miss O'Malley, why do you find that so...so out of character? You don't take me to be one of those ticket-punching career men with only his hide and his next promotion to think about, do you? Because if you—"

Sharon O'Malley laid her hand lightly on his forearm. He felt something stir inside as his eyes swept over her slender fingers and delicately polished nails. She reached toward the cart and withdrew a book. It was the Louis L'Amour book *Bendigo Shafter.* She opened it. "Do you mind if I read something to you?"

Frowning, he said, "No, go ahead." And then he listened to the sound of her voice, soft and even:

"Sometimes I think if it were not for books I could not live, I'd be so lonely. But I can take a book out of that trunk, and it is just like talking to an old friend, and I imagine them as they were, bent over their desks or tables, trying to put what they thought into words."

She said, "I know that what I just read may be off the subject, but I can't help thinking that between the two there is some kind of connection."

"There may very well be," Nolan replied. "I wouldn't know." He sat down in the chair next to hers, fixing his gaze straight ahead.

As they sat silent, Sharon began to speculate: *What is there about him? He really isn't any different than the other officers I've met. They are all men of purpose, doing their jobs, whatever the job happened to be, from day to day, everyday. He was in charge of something, a person who coordinated the activities of men and the helicopters they flew or worked on. It was plain that he loved his work, he was at it umpteen hours a day. He was also a pilot, yet didn't spend any time talking about it like the others.* Sharon turned her head slightly to look at him; she sensed his preoccupation. Perhaps he, like all the other career soldiers she had known, actively did seek ways to "...get his ticket punched," contrary to what he had just said. But then again, maybe not. She was curious why he wasn't trying to impress her with his combat exploits. Or was it her? Suddenly, an image flashed in her mind of them together in bed. She had no idea how or why it came, but the image lingered and she found herself tingling inside. She realized she was wet—*as she sat there looking at him.* And then she remembered the horse her father bought her for her thirteenth birthday. She had named it Old Spirit. Every afternoon after school she would put a saddle on him and go for a ride. Oh the freedom she felt as the wind whipped through her hair. And there was always that tingling sensation she felt as the lower part of her body rubbed against the saddle horn. And then one day she had Old Spirit stretched out on a dead run. She felt a new level of ecstasy that she later described in her diary "...sent me reeling." She remembered how frightened she was at how good it felt. How could anything feel that good? she wondered—*riding a horse!* It was several weeks before she rode Old Spirit again. Abruptly, she glanced at her watch; she stood. "I must be going. It's almost noon."

Quickly, Mike stood and reached for her arm. "How about that lunch?"

Instantly her mind formed the word No, but it was the way he looked at her—she felt her heart skip a beat—that caused her to blurt, "Oh, why not? I haven't got anything better to do."

"Good," Mike said, taking the handle of the cart. "Is there a place we can keep these books while you're gone?"

She nodded and led him to a small closet where she stored the cart.

They sat in the back part of the officers' club, away from the crowd. True to his word, the steak sandwich tasted delicious. She ate like she was famished. As she sat there in his company, she felt a comfort level she didn't expect. He spoke freely about his father, the fishing boat, the open waters of the Gulf, the soft breezes, the sunsets that seemed to last for hours. She found him to be worldly and wise and sometimes even poetic, in a rough sort of way. He had his dreams, just like she did...far off dreams that he knew would someday come true...if he was patient...like she had been patient...building up her reserve of cash as down payment for her store. "So, you want to live in Oregon, on the coast, and have a bookstore...?" he reiterated.

"Yes," she said. "My mother had the same dream, for herself that is, before she died. Only she was going to have it in Milburn. I'll bet there weren't more than twenty people in all those empty spaces that would have patronized it. The public library she helped to create was more than adequate. Plus the books were free to read."

"But why Oregon? Why not somewhere south, where it's warm—and sunny?"

"Oregon's not always cold. In fact, the summers are relatively dry and very lovely. Besides, in the wintertime I don't mind the cold or the drizzle. It makes me want to cuddle up with a good book, next to a warm fire. And I love rugged coastlines." She paused; in her mind's eye she saw pounding surf and white-foam waters. Again, she felt a wave of sensual pleasure pass through her. "I love to watch the waves crashing against the rocks. Nature is quite the sculptor, don't you think?"

He was not accustomed to speaking to a woman as he was with her. If he had to gauge her extraordinariness, it would have to be her earnestness about life that he found so refreshing. And she minced no words getting her point across. He remembered from their first meeting that she practically accused him of being ignorant! Though he claimed no over-abundance of intelligence, he knew himself to be quick-minded when he had to be. He found, too, that he'd rather think a problem through than react simply to be reacting. It was the one aspect to officer candidate school that disturbed him most, having to react without thought. He said, "Nature also designed the Florida Keys. To me, they are the most beautiful chain of islands in the world, strung together like pearls. Besides, it's home. I wouldn't live anywhere else. I look forward to the calm. Maybe it's because my life in the military has never really been calm."

She eyed him for a moment and saw for the first time a man who had probably seen too much violence and death. "Of course, it's a place you want to go back to. And by then you'll deserve to be there, as I'm sure you do even right now. I decided to live close to the shore so that I could look out and wonder what strange and wonderful places are beyond the horizon. Like books and knowledge. Every time I open a book, I'm curious what new ideas and images lie between its pages, as if the horizon were right at my fingertips." She stopped. He was gazing at her and it felt as if he was mentally undressing her. Abruptly she said, "I do believe—if given the choice between having a house full of children or one of books—I'd rather have the books." Her eyes grew wide as she realized her choice of words. "Oh my gosh, please don't get me wrong—I love children. I-I just never think of myself as ever having any..."

Mike tilted his head slightly. "Don't apologize. Frankly, I feel the same way. Somehow I believe fate has ordained me for bachelorhood. I could never do the two-car garage and slipper routine."

"You've...never been engaged?" she asked.

"Never. Not even close."

"I see."

In his room, Nolan took the framed picture of him and his father and went before the mirror that hung on the wall next to the table that served as a desk. The resemblance was remarkable: in the deep-set eyes, the nose short and slightly flattened, the strong jaw line, the cleft chin, all square facial features, as if a block of wood had been placed on their shoulders and chiseled into shape, yet retaining the original shape of the wood. Perhaps the reason he had not met the right woman was because he never thought himself to be very attractive. He wasn't, not really, certainly not in the classic sense. And then he wondered, What is a woman attracted to when she finds the right man? He had often seen attractive women, even beautiful women, with plain-looking men. And then it hit him. *Sharon O'Malley was attracted to him!* But why? What had he done? *Damnit, the last thing I need to find, especially in Vietnam, is a woman—!*

Victor R. Beaver

Chapter 59

SANDY ADAMSON OPENED THE RIGHT cockpit door, stepped up, and gingerly fitted himself into the seat. He placed his feet on the anti-torque pedals and right away noticed how far apart they were compared to those in the TH-55A and TH-13T helicopters. The pilot handgrip on top the cyclic control stick had three buttons and a tiny "Chinese hat" and a trigger switch. He was told that the handgrip was more or less the same as on the more sophisticated fighter aircraft that both the Navy and the Air Force flew. To his left, the collective pitch-control lever also housed several switches and other features he couldn't imagine ever using, much less remember what they were for. The entire instrument panel stretched up and down in front of him, and across to his left, out of his direct line of sight. Immediately he noted there was no way to see all the gauges at once. Between the two pilot seats was the center console, a bank of switches and knobs and dials that were in quantity—and complexity—triple to what he had ever experienced. Above his head, to the left, the overhead console had other dials and switches and a bank of circuit breaker "pop-out" buttons that for a moment held him spellbound. Sandy Adamson was seated in a UH-1 helicopter, nicknamed "The Huey," the workhorse of the Vietnam War, and in spite of this long awaited moment, the young student aviator felt suddenly completely overwhelmed.

In the rear cabin area sat Seymore, Mark Allen, and Tom Adkins, completing the ratio of four students per instructor. Now, instead of each student flying alone with an IP (the previous two trainers were strictly two-seater aircraft), other classmates would be seated in the large cabin area behind as an audience, until it came their turn at the controls. The Friday before they had all taken their advanced instrument checkrides. Though most had passed, many still had no clue what they had learned or what they were really supposed to know. Exception: Seymore P. Cutter and Darryl Chancey. They got the two highest scores in the class.

In the evening, they came with flashlights to Lowe Field and found an empty aircraft and drilled each other in the Huey cockpit pre-start and start procedures. As one student followed the checklist, the other would try and recite the procedures from memory.

"Seat and pedals adjust....Shoulder harness and seatbelt fasten and tighten...AC circuit breakers check in...Magnetic compass deviation card current..."

During the day, they came into the crowded briefing room, sat before their gods—the flight instructors—and were drilled in emergency procedures and aircraft limitations. They were then led like lambs out to the flight line. In the beginning, it took them thirty minutes of stumbling recitation to have the aircraft up and running. At the end of three weeks, however, they had it down to about five.

Enthralled by the wonderful wizardry in front of him, Mark Allen did not see that during three trips in the traffic pattern he had taken off with the transmission oil pressure gauge reading zero, yet had announced before every lift off: "All gauges in the green." And he also failed to interpret the signal the four of them had cooked up whenever any of them saw the instructor pull a circuit breaker that commanded any particular instrument (the act of which was designed to test a student's observational powers and attention to detail).

"Why didn't you signal me—?" Allen cried, after they got on the bus to return to the barracks. He had received a pink gradeslip for failure to note a malfunction in the cockpit.

"WE DID!"

"Candidate Adamson, recite the 'main generator failure' emergency procedure."

"Yessir. Ah...Reset the master caution light. Check to see that the standby generator has picked up the load. If it hasn't, try to reset the main generator."

"What if the standby generator still doesn't pick up the electrical load? What would you check?"

"I'd...I'd turn the battery switch off. Maybe the battery voltage is too high."

"Okay, that's not bad."

In academics they were asshole-deep learning aircraft systems. How they longed for the simplicity of the Mattel Messerschmitt (the TH-55A). Many of them had difficulty understanding how turbine power, or the flow of hot gasses through chambers in the engine, could eventually turn the UH-1 transmission system. Sandy in particular was befuddled and managed, along with two dozen others, to fail the power train written examination, thereby sacrificing a weekend to study for the remedial test.

Now that they had a reasonably accurate fuel gauge, it was incumbent on each of them to do a fuel check: pounds per hour burned, time Zulu (Greenwich Mean Time) to fuel burn out, and time Zulu to reach 20-minute "VFR" fuel reserve. "Why can't we just wait until the twenty-minute low fuel caution light comes on?" asked Seymore.

"The point, Candidate Cutter, is to know beforehand when the light will come on—*so that you can already be on the ground!"*

* * *

THE WOC LOUNGE WAS LOCATED IN the middle of the main candidate billeting area. Sandy frequented it often, drinking beer, singing songs, soaking up the camaraderie like a dry sponge. "Any of you guys got a girlfriend?" he blurted.

"Sure, man," replied one candidate, barely able to stand. "We're gonna be married. You gotta girlfriend?"

Sandy whipped out his billfold. He withdrew a dilapidated picture of Katie, one he had thumbed and gazed at until the edges were frayed. "This is my girl!" he stammered. "Her name is Katie...Katie Lee Williams. We're s'posed to get married on graduation...Ain't she beautiful?"

"Let me have a look at her," exclaimed a beefy-armed candidate, who grabbed the picture and started to google-eye it.

Sandy grabbed back. "Give it to me, you sombitch—"

"Hey, you can't talk to me that way."

"I just did, you asshole—"

The first punch knocked Sandy back against the wall. Dazed, he blinked and just barely saw the second punch coming, which breezed past his face. "Hey, what's this shit?" he grumbled.

The next swing caught Sandy on the right side of his mouth. He stumbled back and fell on a table filled with pitchers of beer. He felt a huge splash of liquid spill over him. Globs of submarine sandwich landed on his face. Lying on the floor, he heard shouts, and chairs and tables being overturned, and feet stamping around him. He reached up and felt his eye swelling and the taste of blood around his mouth. He got to his knees and began hunting the floor for Katie's picture. Someone stepped on his hand and he felt his knuckles crack. He reared up screaming. Then he saw the candidate who had grabbed at Katie's photo. Sandy lunged forward and slammed into him; both men plunged to the floor. After a minute of thrashing, flailing his arms wildly, Sandy felt a pair of strong hands grab him and lift him bodily upward. "What the hell you doing, slick? You want to get kicked out of flight school—?"

Struggling, Sandy turned and glared at Mark Allen. "Leave me alone...!"

"The hell I will," Allen said, shoving Sandy through the door, out into the hot night air. The stronger candidate struggled to keep Sandy's arms pinned behind him. "Get a hold of yourself, damnit. Or do you want me to break your arm—?"

"Go ahead, break it, see if I care. Break'em both. I don't even care if I live or die—"

Mark guided the drunken hysterical lad toward his car. He opened the door. "Get in, before the goddamn MPs get here."

"Fuck the MPs. Fuck'em all. I'll fight them too—!"

Mark jammed Sandy into the front seat. "Save your fighting for Vietnam—!"

Lying half prone on the front seat, Sandy began to sob. "Yeah...yeah, save me...for Vietnam. Keep me in one piece...for...Vietnam..."

"Who started it?" said Major Braver, the company commander, handling the MP's report that was on his desk.

Sandy, his right eye swollen, his jaw hurting so badly he wanted to vomit, looked sideways at the major. He and Mark Allen stood 'at ease' in the CO's office, which was next to the company orderly room. "The other guy, sir," Sandy replied. "He grabbed a picture of my girl I was showing some other guy. I grabbed back."

"Is this true?" the major said, looking toward Allen.

"Yessir."

"Okay-okay. I'll handle it," Major Braver said, looking now toward Sandy. "But another incident like this and out the door you go. Is that understood?"

"Yessir. I mean, sir, Candidate Adamson, yes, sir."

* * *

"KATIE, DEAR, YOU'RE GOING TO BE late for class," her mother called from downstairs.

"Yes, Mother...I'm coming."

When she appeared, her mother handed her a light windbreaker and told her that the day was windy and cool, and would she just this once wear something decent outside. "You go out without the least thought of catching a cold. What does Jerry say? Doesn't he even care?"

"Of course, he cares, Mother. I wish you and Dad would quit picking on him—"

Katie's mother sighed. What was this world coming to? The young men she kept bringing home from college made her wish she and Charles had just simply put their foot down. At least Jerry tried to wear clean clothes, and his hair wasn't that long. The others, though, had been slovenly and unshaven. What were they trying to prove? She faced her daughter. "Now about tomorrow. Tell me again where you're going?"

"To Boulder, Mother. CU is having another peace rally. It should last until Sunday."

"You're going to stay until Sunday?"

"Yes. I explained all that yesterday—"

"With who?"

"A bunch of us, Mother. We'll all be together. At the Holiday Inn."

"Not all in the same bed, I hope—"

"Oh, Mother!"

It was after dinner. Harriet Williams was seated on the couch. She looked toward her husband, who had his head between the pages of the newspaper. "Charles?"

Charles Williams bent the page he was reading and looked up. "Yes?"

"I don't like it."

"Don't like what?"

"Katie going up to Boulder. From what I hear, the police may have to do something out of the ordinary to keep the kids under control."

"Oh? And why wasn't I told about this?"

"I did tell you. You weren't listening...as usual."

"I listen, damnit. What do you want me to do? She's hell bent on going—"

"Well, does she have to spend the night—?"

"Frankly, I'd rather she do that than drive back late," her husband said.

"Do you think she's doing those drugs?"

"What—?"

"Drugs, Charles. All the college kids are doing it. Do you think Katie would dare try?"

"Not if she knows what's good for her. Why are you asking that?"

"Oh...no reason. But I swear, the guys she brings home...they all seem spaced out on something. Even Jerry admitted he's tried it."

"Tried what?"

"That marijuana."

Charles Williams put the newspaper down. He shot a stern look at his wife. "You tell Katie that if she even thinks about smoking that stuff, she's had it."

"You tell her."

"Me—? You're the one she listens to. I can't talk to her."

"Well—have you ever tried?"

Suddenly, Charles Williams stood and went into the kitchen. He took down a glass and got himself some water. His wife came into the kitchen. "Another letter came today," she said.

"From Sandy?"

"Yes."

"Does she ever write back?"

"I don't know. I don't think so."

Her husband took a drink and then looked toward the ceiling. "He's a good boy...has a good head on his shoulders. Good values."

"I feel sorry for him."

"Why?"

"I don't know," she said. "I just do. He should be close to graduating from his flight training. Sometime in July, I think."

"What happened between them?" Charles Williams asked.

"You mean between him and Katie?"

He nodded.

Harriet Williams sighed. It was the first time her husband had ever outwardly wondered about their daughter's breakup with Sandy. "It was Brad's death."

"Well, I figured that...but why?"

"She was afraid to get too close."

The Sky Soldiers

"That's bunk. Lot's of people are close—and under worse conditions. Remember how it was with us?"

"Yes, I do. I'll admit to you right now that it was pretty awful. Whenever you left to be with your unit, I thought I'd never see you again."

"I never knew that."

Harriet Williams looked down. Her husband reached out and with his hand lifted her face. He saw that tears had come to her eyes. He took her and held her. "I think Katie's ruined something good between them," he said, stroking the back of her head.

Harriet Williams pulled away. "How would you know?"

"I don't know," he said. "But I agree with you on one thing. She'd better not come to me and ask me to bless her marriage to any of those creepy peaceniks she keeps bringing home for me to meet. I don't even like that Jerry guy. He's so full of himself—spouting all that political hogwash about the war. He especially gives me the creeps."

"Well, what will you do?"

"I'll laugh in her face."

"You will not."

"Watch me."

"Charles—sometimes you are so exasperating."

"I am not."

"Yes, you are—!"

Victor R. Beaver

Chapter 60

KIP SLATER TWEAKED THE DIAL on the ADF receiver until he got a clear signal. He adjusted the volume and listened to the announcer's voice as it came across the Armed Forces radio station: *"...Robert F. Kennedy, democratic senator from Massachusetts, brother of the late John F. Kennedy, today was shot after making a statement announcing his victory in California's Democratic presidential primary..."*

Shocked, as he had been when he learned, in the same manner, of the murder of Dr. Martin Luther King Jr., Slater sat back in his seat and gazed through the aircraft windshield. Ahead he saw rain clouds building, and below them the young tender green of the newly planted rice fields. On the horizon, as clear as spring rain on a windowpane, he saw the dark nodules that were the Seven Mountains region. He glanced from left to right and back to the left, wondering what was going on in the United States that required men to take a gun and end a life? And how was it any different than what was happening in Vietnam? Have the enemies of barbarism become the barbarians? Or had they always been so? He shook his head and for a moment felt ashamed to be an American.

They had been shut down for nearly half an hour at Sa Dec, waiting for Sergeant O'Brien to come with the load for Ap Tan Phong. When the burley sergeant finally drove up in his jeep, they saw seated next to him a red-faced MACV major carrying a carbine, a bandoleer of ammunition, and a PRC-25 field radio. Leaping from the jeep, the major asked, "How fast can you get this thing going?"

Opening the right cockpit door, Slater said, "Hell, sir, in less than a minute—"

"Good. I've got a patrol that has three VC on the run. Let's *git!*"

Slater quickly seated himself, flicked the battery switch on, set the throttle, and turned the main fuel on. He pulled the ignition trigger switch. Lieutenant Leahy, his peter-pilot, new in-country, a long-legged, quiet-mannered twenty-four-year-old from Galveston, Texas, had just buckled up as the N1 (gas producer) was going through 25 percent. "Take over the start while I strap in," Slater told him.

"Roger that."

As Slater buckled his shoulder harness and seatbelt, he thought, What the hell is the big goddamn hurry? What are we going to do from two thousand feet that can't take the extra minute we normally use to get off the ground? Suddenly, he felt like a pawn, overused and unimportant; he felt violated, like a girl who had given in to the persistence of her fumbling boyfriend; he felt ragged and worn, the way it was with a hangover after a long period of sobriety.

After they were airborne, they headed west. Within minutes they were over the target site, a rice field two thousand meters long by five hundred meters wide.

The Sky Soldiers

In the middle of the field they spied three pajama-clad figures spread out and running, angling toward the west treeline. Larkin, in the right doorgunner's seat, had his machine gun up, poised to fire. The red-faced major spoke quickly in the PRC-25 radio handset to the ARVN patrol on the ground; a second later he motioned for Larkin to begin firing. The major watched the tracers streak earthward. The enemy continued angling toward the treeline. After a minute of firing, the major growled, "Damnit! You're not leading your shots! Lead your shots!"

"We're too high!" Larkin replied.

The major crawled forward and motioned for Slater to descend. Angrily, Kip complied. Larkin continued firing during the descent. Slater leveled off at fifteen hundred feet. Meantime, Larkin kept missing the running figures. "Get lower!" the major shouted again to Slater.

"I can only go as low as one thousand feet—*Sir!* Company SOP!" he lied.

Slater leveled the aircraft at one thousand feet. I'm not going one foot lower, he declared to himself. He looked to the right and saw the three Viet Cong still on the run, changing their course every few seconds to confuse their tormentors. Larkin's gun jammed. "We're moving too fast!" the gunner cried. "Have Mr. Slater slow down!"

The major relayed the request. Kip reduced the airspeed to seventy knots.

By now, the patrol had caught up with two of the enemy, who were barely stumbling forward, their tired legs no longer able to carry them along. The third Viet Cong, ahead of the other two by about a hundred meters, had also run out of steam. Slater flew *Alfie* in a wide right-hand orbit while Larkin cleared his machine gun and reloaded. Meanwhile, the major had his carbine poked out the open cabin door and was occasionally firing shots at the lone pajama-clad figure now lying prone against a dike. In a moment, Ron announced that he was ready. "If you can get lower, sir," he said over the intercom, "I know I can plaster that sonofabitch!"

Without hesitation, Slater reduced power and brought the ship lower. He saw the lone, exhausted enemy soldier stand and begin trundling forward again, his speed barely a quarter of what it had been. They were now three hundred feet above the ground, with the helicopter aimed directly toward him. Larkin fired. Bullets skipped just ahead and to the left of the fleeing man. The major repositioned himself on the cabin floor to shoot forward of the cockpit area; he let go a burst of gunfire. The Viet Cong stumbled and fell. As they flew past, they saw the man crouching behind the paddy dike, his legs drawn into the fetal position, his hands and arms covering his head. "Come around again!" the major yelled.

Slater banked the ship hard left. He rolled out and saw that the man was still huddled against the dike. Slater angled the helicopter slightly left to allow the MACV advisor and his gunner to have a clear shot. Larkin fired and this time the rounds hit their mark. The major also fired, bullets spewing water in short geysers near the now prone-positioned body. Flying past this time, they saw the body was spread out, face down. Shocked by what he saw, shocked more by what he felt, a combination of utter disdain and sympathy (but sympathy for whom?), Slater jerked the cyclic back, and, adding power, quickly brought *Alfie* to two thousand feet altitude.

They returned to Sa Dec and shut down. Everyone gathered around Sergeant O'Brien who listened to the major speak with praise for what they had done. Ron Larkin beamed and so did Rusty White, who never really liked it when they had to shoot their M-60s. Lieutenant Leahy's face glowed. He congratulated Kip over and over for the way he handled the flight controls.

They were back at Soc Trang. Slater burst into Leo's room. "Hey—Leo, guess what?"

"What?"

"We finally got us a confirmed kill—!"

"When?—Where?"

"This afternoon. Near Sa Dec. Out in the middle of the paddies. Larkin got him."

"All right—*you did it!*"

Later that night, as he tried to sleep, with the image of the Viet Cong lying dead in the rice paddy, Slater wondered if they couldn't have landed and simply captured the man, like the patrol had done when they caught up with the other two. *Why didn't I do that? Why? I'm turning out to be just like Leo—and I don't want that!*

Still unable to sleep, Slater got up and turned the light on. He took the book he had been reading, given to him by Jeff Mangrum. He opened to the marked page. It was *The Rubaiyat of Omar Khayyam:*

"The Moving Finger writes; and, having writ, Moves on: nor will they Piety nor Wit Shall lure it back to cancel half a line, Nor all thy Tears wash out a Word of it."

* * *

FINALLY, ON JUNE 18, CLASS 67-15 reached the home stretch. Yet many of them were too tired to notice or care. They took their UH-1 transition checkrides, had passed and sighed. Even reaching senior status the month before had little affect on them. What remained were four weeks of tactics training: low-level navigation using topographical maps, mock combat assaults in multi-ship formation, sling-loading barrels filled with cement. And then one day they were allowed to take a UH-1 helicopter, two students per ship, and spend the day going wherever they wished in the training area. As each day passed, the whole reason

The Sky Soldiers

they endured nine months of blood, sweat, tears—and tragedy—loomed like never before. Next stop, after a thirty-day leave, was Vietnam.

It was during this last month that they received their overseas combat assignments. Sandy Adamson and Mark Allen drew the same unit, the 7th Squadron, 1st Air Cavalry, in the Mekong Delta; Seymore P. Cutter, by his outstanding overall checkride scores, managed a Chinook transition before reporting to his unit at Can Tho; Tom Adkins, Frank Bartlett, and Willie Cottrell all drew duty with the 3rd Brigade of the 82nd Airborne Division, currently based in the Hue-Phu Bai area; while all the rest were scattered throughout Vietnam, from Da Nang to Saigon.

The paperwork to shuttle them from enlisted status to that of warrant officer, in preparation for graduation, also numbed them. Everyday there was some "essential" form they had to fill out or sign. They also learned their new military serial numbers, which had been on their assignment orders. Sandy hastily scribbled his number on a piece of paper and slipped it into his billfold, proof, he felt, that he was one step from being a fully ordained Army aviator. They went to the tailors and ordered their graduation-ball dress blues, had the dark green piping sewn on their Class A dress greens, and bought all the necessary rank and insignia accoutrements to adorn their uniforms. They made hotel and motel reservations in anticipation of visiting parents, friends, and relatives. Sandy wrote once more to Katie, asking that she have a change of heart and attend graduation. He received this reply:

Dear Sandy,

Thank you for inviting me to your graduation. I appreciate it. I know that you've always had your heart set on my coming, but I'm afraid I must, out of conscience, decline. I admire your bravery, your resolve to do what you have done by going through flight school and to move on. I know that you cannot see that we, as a nation, do not belong in Vietnam. I fear for you, Sandy, not only for your life, which you might lose over there, but also for what it will do to your humanity. Someday I know you will see I am right. You have a good heart, Sandy, and I still love you for it. But right now I think it is misplaced. I want to always be your friend, no matter what happens. Again, please forgive me for not coming. I too must be brave.

Sincerely yours,
Katie

They spent their last training week at a place called Tac-X, twenty miles southwest of the Fort Rucker main post complex. Shaped like a large kidney bean, it was a heliport base camp drawn and quartered out of the woods. Hidden in the trees were the billets, similar to the kind of housing they would find in Vietnam. Built around these quarters were outdoor latrines and shower facilities, a separate messhall, orderly room, supply room, maintenance sheds and work areas, and an armament room from which they drew .38-caliber pistols (no bullets) and from which the enlisted doorgunners, also in training, drew their M-60s. During the day they reacted to impromptu missions, flew sorties with troops onboard, and listened for the crackle of machine-gun and small-arms fire they were briefed would occur at random, blanks fired by soldiers tasked to make the landings into the LZs as real as possible.

Seymore, Sandy, Willie Cottrell, and Mark Allen had drawn cots next to each other. It was their second night at the Tac-X base camp and Sandy was just beginning to doze.

KABOOM!...BOOM!.....KABOOM!

Startled half out of his wits, Sandy shot straight out of his cot, turned and cracked heads with Seymore. He saw flashes and heard more explosions, sharp and hollow sounding. He and Seymore and Mark, along with several other classmates, scrambled outside. *KABOOOM!*

Shivering, crouching low in their undershorts, they heard other explosions, now farther away. After a few seconds everyone began to squirm around in the dark trying to find a place to hide. "What the hell is going on—?" yelled Seymore.

KABOOM!

"It's a simulated mortar attack, you flakes," Willie responded. The ex-Special Forces veteran yawned deeply and took his time to light a cigarette. He had meandered out of the building, bothering first to put on his pants and gather his cigarettes and lighter. He stood next to the crouching trio, content to let them shiver by his side.

"Did you know they were going to do this—?" Mark Allen cried.

"Not really. But it figures, don't you think?" Just then a siren sounded. Other figures appeared, their instructors, who called out the names of their students and admonished them for not seeking better cover. "Get your goddamn clothes on!" they shouted. "We've got to get to the aircraft!"

"Was that in the plan?" someone called out.

"Plan? What plan? There ain't no fucking plan. And it's going to be the same goddamn way in Vietnam!"

One last exercise remained: E&E, Escape and Evasion. In separate groups of seven to eight candidates, they were taken to different locations and lectured on how to survive in a jungle setting, should they become shot down. Before dark they were given a chicken, a few vegetables and spices, a quantity of water and a stew pot to cook in. They were shown how to start a cook-fire and keep it going. Because he had always been entranced by the idea of cooking meat over an open fire, like he had seen done so many times in movies about the Old West, Sandy convinced the members of his group to roast the chicken rather than brew it along

The Sky Soldiers

with the vegetables in the pot of water. The group was downgraded for this. Making soup out of the chicken and vegetables, they were told, would have afforded them the greatest amount of nutrition.

After dark they were given a topographical map, a compass, and two flashlights and told where they were and where they had to "evade" to. However, along the way the group Sandy was in was "captured" and taken to a make-believe POW compound, where they endured a fair amount of very serious petty harassment by American enlisted men dressed in make-believe enemy uniforms. After an hour, Mark and Sandy saw an opportunity to jump the compound fence and "escape." They found themselves wandering about in the dark without flashlight or map now, and only their rain ponchos to keep out the nighttime chill. By three in the morning, having not the slightest clue where they were, the two curled up in a shallow gully just off a dirt road and waited for the first light of dawn and the deuce-and-a-half trucks to come by and take them to the barracks.

* * *

HE WAS SEATED IN ELROY'S OFFICE when the CO arrived. "Remain as you were," Elroy said, as Nolan began to rise.

"What's going on, sir?"

"Well, it depends on how you look at it. It's either good news or bad," Elroy stated, drawing his chair out from behind his desk.

"Just give it to me straight, sir. The anticipation is killing me."

"Okay," began Elroy, "this is the straight poop. I know how badly you'd like to get back into the field and have a platoon of your own again. Well, I've got just the assignment for you."

"You do?"

"I've got to swap an officer and four warrants with the cav squadron at Vinh Long. Remember, I told you about the infusion…?"

"Yessir, I remember."

"Mike, I don't want to lose you. You've done a helluva job here as my S-3, but I think you'd be happier elsewhere. And it might even be better for your career. So here's the story. Major Rameriz is a good friend of mine. He's got Charlie Troop and needs a Blue Platoon leader. And this is just between you and me, but he's got an ops officer captain-type he wants to get rid of. Something about a personality conflict. Since I've got to give up one RLO and the warrants, I figured I might as well trade tit for tat in the RLO category. Rameriz gets his Blue and I get a replacement operations man, someone I don't have to break in. But I'm leaving it up to you. Do you want to go?"

Nolan breathed deep. "Yes, sir, I do."

Elroy smiled. "I thought so. I didn't even think you'd take a deep breath."

Victor R. Beaver

Nolan walked into the library. He saw Sharon seated at her desk. She looked just as pretty today, he thought, as she did last night in the moonlight, along the path they walked when he escorted her back to her room. He greeted her.

"Michael. What are you doing here? Is it lunchtime already? I haven't even checked my watch."

"No-no. I'm early." He came and stood at her desk. He looked down as she looked up. He handed her *Sackett's Land*, a Louis L'Amour book he had checked out two days before. It was his third reading of this particular book, after reading several other L'Amour titles. She took it from him slowly. "It was good," he said. "And again, I'm glad you read that one passage to me a while back."

"You're welcome..." Sharon O'Malley said, eyeing him curiously. Something was the matter, she could tell in his manner of speaking. She had decided a week and a half ago that his moods were as easy to read as an open book. She said, "I thought that particular passage appropriate...especially with regard to your career—and your being over here..."

He nodded. "I agree." It was now two weeks since he had come to the library and she had lifted the book from the shelf and read to him the passage she had selected. It was also the start of something he knew was inevitable, like the daily rising of the sun. On that day she had said, "Do you mind if I read something to you? Believe me, I mean nothing by it...except that I see you in it." "Sure, go ahead," he replied, "but it can't be long. I've got a staff meeting in ten minutes." "Oh, it's not long at all." She opened the book and began:

> "A man needs heroes. He needs to believe in strength, nobility, and courage. Otherwise we become sheep to be herded to the slaughterhouse of death. I believe this. I am a soldier. I try to fight for the right cause. Sometimes it is hard to know.
>
> But I do not sit back and sneer in cowardice at those with the courage to fight. The blood of good men makes the earth rich, as it is here. When I die sword in hand, I hope someone lives to sing of it. I live my life so when death comes I may die well. I ask no more."

When she was done Mike Nolan took the book and reached for her hand. He held it delicately, bent down and kissed it. "I want to read this book," he said.

"Of course," she said, as she sensed the red of her face match the red of her hair. "I-I can let you check it out now."

"Fine."

He finished it the first time that night. On the following day, he returned it and checked out another and read the second one that evening. He re-read *Sackett's Land* and then went to other titles. All the while he allowed himself to see her, to speak to her, and slowly, steadily, to feel the feelings he felt for her.

"So, what brings you here this early? Are we to have an extra long lunch hour?"

"No, I'm afraid lunch is out," he said. "I have to go to personnel."

"Oh? What for?"

"Sharon, I'm...being transferred. I'm leaving tomorrow."

The jolt she felt could not have been more pronounced had she been kicked in her lower stomach. "You're being...transferred." Her response came out more a statement than a question.

"Yes, I'm being given my own platoon, like I mentioned I had with the One Seventy-third. Only this time I'll also be in charge of a section of lift pilots and crewmembers. I'm going to Vinh Long."

"I see..."

"I'm sorry."

"Oh, that's quite all right. What do you have to be sorry for? I'm very glad for you."

"Yeah...I figured you would be."

Sharon stood and extended her hand. Bravely, she said, "Captain Michael Nolan, it has been a pleasure, and in the beginning, very interesting. I apologize if I embarrassed or hurt you. I never really meant to."

"You didn't. Actually, you made me think—about a lot of things. I even sort of like to read now." For a long moment he held onto her hand. "Look, Sharon, I'm kind of sorry about leaving. I had the chance to stay but this opportunity was too good to pass up. I've enjoyed your company. We had some very nice talks."

"Well, I enjoyed your company, too," she said, taking her hand gently from his. "Maybe you'll fly in sometime. We can have lunch or something."

"Yeah, I'd like that."

"So would I ," she said.

"Well, I've got to go."

"Good-bye, Michael."

"Good-bye."

"Good luck to you."

"Thanks."

Victor R. Beaver

Chapter 61

"I, EDWARD SANDERS ADAMSON, do solemnly swear..." Class 67-15 was standing at attention in the auditorium, their right hands raised, their voices stating for all to hear the oath of office accepting their warrant officer commissions. "...and that I will defend the Constitution of the United States of America against all enemies, foreign and domestic, so help me God." They lowered their hands.

Tom Adkins elbowed Sandy and whispered, "It should read, 'defend against all enemies, real and imagined.'"

Sandy jabbed back. "Shush...quiet."

"Sorry."

They moved outside into bright sunlight. With family and friends gathered around, they had their pictures taken while a loved one pinned on their new brown and gold W1 warrant officer bars.

They went back inside. The moment they had really been waiting for had finally come. The man at the podium, Major General Ogden, the Fort Rucker post commander, tapped at the microphone. "Ladies and gentlemen, family members, friends, I want to extend my deep-felt appreciation for your attendance. I know it means a lot to these men seated before you, who have overcome a fair number of hurdles to be here today.

"As the post commander, and commandant of the United States Army Aviation School, though I am involved in this type of ceremony once a month, it always thrills me to see the faces behind the person who is about to receive his reward for the effort he has shown. Believe me, as an old fixed-wing driver, who a couple of years back got his chance to be checked out in a helicopter, I know what I mean when I say, 'That damn thing wasn't meant to fly—'" A thread of laughter rippled throughout the auditorium. "My instructor was a cranky CW4, an old curmudgeon like myself, and boy let me tell you, me and him had some real go-arounds on how that aircraft was supposed to be flown. He always won, of course." Another thread of laugher.

"Well, enough of that," the general said. "Today is the day these men have been waiting for, so I'd better quit fooling around or I'll never hear the end of it.

"Nine months ago these men began at Fort Wolters, went through the preflight phase, then afterwards started their flight training. I never did fly the 'fifty-five' or the 'twenty-three', but from what I've been told, getting a hold of either one is like trying to wrestle an alligator: just when you have a good clamp on the jaws, the tail whips around to get you. Anyway, once they got past the solo stage, they had to do a fair amount of practice to pass their first checkride. They had to demonstrate their ability to do the basic maneuvers: land, take off, hover, and do an autorotation. After that they were taught how to land in these tiny, enclosed

The Sky Soldiers

locations called confined areas, and then on these raised areas called pinnacles. They learned how to do cross-country navigation using a clock and the whiskey compass. They then left Fort Wolters, came here, and we make them put this silly hood on to block their vision outside the aircraft. We asked them to control the helicopter and navigate without visual reference to the ground. I swear, there were times when I knew we were asking too much of them. Finally they jump into the Huey, by comparison a Cadillac to what they had previously flown. And now we have before us this person ready to go to Vietnam. At least we here at the school hope and pray that he is ready. I'm sure you do too.

"A lot of money has been spent on their training, a lot of hard-earned tax dollars. I hope to high heaven you feel, after today, and especially after the graduation ball tonight, which by the way is being held for the first time in our new Fort Rucker officers' club, that this country got its money's worth." The general paused and looked toward his adjutant. "Let's hand over the diplomas so these guys can get their wings pinned on."

* * *

"SEYMORE, WILL YOU QUIT FIDGETING!" Sandy exclaimed. "I can't get these things put back on with you squirming like some Tasmanian devil. Why didn't you do this before?"

Seymore, with beads of sweat forming on his forehead, and his dress blues feeling unbearably warm, was about to jump out of his skin. "I couldn't find them!"

"*Gawd*—not two hours a brand new Army aviator and you lose your wings! Where *did* you find them—?"

"In one of the sinks in the latrine. Earlier, I was looking at them in the mirror, with them pinned on, and the clasps must have come loose!"

"There." Sandy backed away. Seymore was about ready to collapse. The two men were in Seymore's room. Seymore and Jenny's wedding was due to start in less than thirty minutes and the beleaguered, freckle-faced lad was OBE, overbecome by events. "You look...dashing."

"Really?"

"Well, as dashing as anyone can look in this idiotic southern Alabama humidity." Sandy gazed for a moment at his friend. Shaking his head, he remembered the first time he saw Seymore, there at the café bus stop right after crossing the Texas State line. Sandy extended his hand. "Thanks, Seymore."

"What for?"

"For asking me to be your best man."

"Hey, anytime. I'm sorry I couldn't return the favor."

"Yeah...me too." Just then Katie's image flashed across his mind. How resplendent she would have looked today.

Seymore reached out and placed his hand on Sandy's shoulder. "Maybe someday."

"Yeah...maybe someday."

The little chapel was filled to capacity. Sandy, standing next to Seymore, glanced back and caught sight of Willie Cottrell and his wife, Loree, and around them more than a dozen members of the old Flight Alpha One. The organist pressed a few preparatory notes, and then began playing the wedding march. In the next instant, Jenny came walking down the aisle holding her father's arm. She was wearing a flowing gown of white silk organza adorned with seed pearls fashioned as lilies of the valley. A veil of Chantilly lace surrounded her radiant face. She carried a cascading bouquet of lilies of the valley, violets, and baby's breath, completing a vision of loveliness that took Sandy's breath away. When Jenny reached Seymore, her father kissed her, then stepped back and took his place next to his wife.

"Ladies and gentlemen," the chaplain began, "we are gathered here in the sight of God to join these two young people in the bonds of Holy Matrimony. If there is anyone among you who thinks these two people should not be wed, please speak now or forever hold your peace."

As Sandy listened, he felt a rise of emotion so strong he wanted to weep. The chaplain spoke for several minutes about the sacred responsibilities of marriage and then said, "Do you, Seymore, take Jenny to be your lawfully wedded wife, to cherish and to hold, for richer or for poorer, through sickness and in health, till death do you part?"

"I-I do."

"Do you, Jenny, take Seymore to be your lawfully wedded husband, to honor and obey, (at the word "obey" Seymore glanced quickly at Jenny and gave her a wink; she replied with a swift sidekick to his leg), for richer or for poorer, through sickness and in health, till death do you part?"

Softly, Jenny said, "I do."

"The rings please." Sandy, holding tightly to Jenny's ring, brought his hand up and presented it to Seymore. The chaplain said, "Seymore, repeat after me. With this ring, I thee wed and pledge my love for all time."

His voice barely a squeak, Seymore said, "With this ring, I-I thee wed and pledge my love for-for all time." Trembling, he slipped the ring on Jenny's finger.

Jenny took Seymore's ring and held his hand. The chaplain said, "Jenny, repeat after me. With this ring, I thee wed and pledge my love for all time."

Her eyes gazing adoringly at Seymore, she said, "Seymore, with this ring, I thee wed and pledge my love for all time." As Jenny spoke, Sandy listened, and her voice came across radiating such love and warmth and comfort for his friend that his insides melted.

The Sky Soldiers

The chaplain, smiling, nodded. "By the power vested in me, I now pronounce you man and wife. Seymore, you may kiss the bride."

Gently, Seymore raised the lace covering Jenny's face and tenderly kissed his bride. They turned and faced their guests. Everyone was standing and smiling and crying. The organist played the song *Never, My Love* as they walked down the aisle. Emerging outside they saw standing before them on either side of the sidewalk leading to the limousine, two rows of classmates in dress blues, their swords drawn, their blades touching, forming a pointed arch under which they were about to walk. Those in the church gathered outside ready to throw handfuls of rice once the pair began toward the car.

At the car, Seymore held the door open for Jenny, who turned and tossed her bouquet toward the outstretched hands of several of her friends. Then they got in and ceremoniously drove away.

* * *

FROM THE VERY START, THE MEN ENTERED the brand new officers' club facility as if coming upon hallowed ground. Everywhere there was polish and glitter and the smell of newness and the carpets plush and clean and the water fountain sparkling just so and the mirrors reflecting brightly the splendor that was to be their night. Into these sacred halls the men escorted their mothers, fathers, dates, wives, lovers, friends. They filed through the entrance hallway and met the general's staff and their ladies, both sides nodding politely, everyone presenting their most gracious behavior befitting the occasion. Sandy and Mark came in together, accompanied by Mark's mother and Sandy's parents. Seymore, Jenny, and her parents followed close behind. And there were others, to include the officer class that had performed parallel flight training and had also received their graduation diplomas and silver aviator wings that same morning. After the dinner, and the smoking lamp was lit, and the sound of the band kicked in, Sandy knew that tonight would be one he would never ever forget. Were he to pick a scene from any movie that was representative of what he saw: the women in their formal gowns, the men wearing proudly their dress blue uniforms, the tables lit with candlelight, and the music in the background playing a variety of raucous tunes, he would have chosen the celebration ball in the John Wayne movie *She Wore A Yellow Ribbon* that he had enjoyed several years ago.

He was going to a cavalry squadron in the Mekong Delta and the pure thought of it sent thrills up and down his spine—!

By ten o'clock the band began playing slow-song requests. One of Sandy and Katie's favorites began playing and the young new pilot stood and extended his hand toward Jenny. He looked at Seymore: "May I ask Jenny to dance?"

Seymore nodded graciously. "Sure."

Victor R. Beaver

> *"Oh, my love, my darling...*
> *I've hungered for your touch*
> *A long lonely time..."*

Sandy guided Jenny to the dance floor and put his hand around her slender waist. "Jenny, you look absolutely ravishing, if you'll pardon my choice of words." She was wearing a pale green, figure-hugging mandarin gown of satin brocade; the slit at the left side of the skirt revealed a shapely leg.

"Thank you. You look very handsome. All of you do."

"I can tell you that Seymore is one happy guy. I'm real glad you and him got together."

"That's nice of you to say, Sandy. He really thinks a lot of you. You're the best friend he's ever had, did you know that?"

"Yeah, I know. We've been through quite a lot together."

As Jenny spoke and explained her feelings for Seymore, Sandy could see the glitter in her eyes, almost the same golden-flecked glitter Katie had had for him when they were together. For a moment, Sandy thought he was seeing Katie, but then he shivered and was back in the moment.

"I'm sorry, are you okay?" Jenny asked.

"Yeah...I'm fine."

"Sandy, Seymore told me all about Katie."

"Now how did you know I was thinking about her?"

"Who else would you be thinking about, looking at me the way you just did?"

He smiled. "You are very, very perceptive."

"I'm sorry that Katie's not here. I know it meant a lot to you that she come."

"Yeah, well...win a few, lose a few."

"Sandy, that's not how you really feel."

"You're right. But you know I don't believe we're ever going to be together again. Too much water under the bridge...I guess."

Jenny sighed. "I wish I had the answer for you, Sandy. I don't."

"How does a woman fall out of love, Jenny?" Sandy felt a sudden rise of emotion. "I remember when we would walk down the halls at school and we would be holding hands and out of the blue she would squeeze mine and say, 'Oh, Sandy, I love you so much.' And I would feel on top of the world. Here I had this precious person who loved me. And now...I have no one."

"You'll have someone someday, Sandy," Jenny said, looking up at him. "It may even be Katie. You never know."

"I wonder if it's not too late. I wonder what's going to happen?"

"You mean...in Vietnam?"

"Yeah."

"*Sandy—!*" Jenny's voice suddenly became strong with conviction. "You are coming back. You get that through your thick head. You and Seymore both are coming back—"

"How can you be so sure—?"

"I *can* because I have to be. To think otherwise is to believe we don't have control over our own destinies. You have control, Sandy—do you hear me?"

"Yeah, sure, I hear you, but I'm scared, Jenny, really scared."

The song ended and the two stopped and stood still. "I'm scared, too, Sandy. I'm scared for Seymore. But right now we have each other and together we'll see it through. I can't speak for Katie, I don't know what she's been through, I can only imagine. But you should see her before you go. It's absolutely necessary that you do that. You can't go to Vietnam wondering. Katie has to face you, Sandy. You at least deserve that. Can you do it?"

He sighed. "I think easier said than done, Jenny."

"Maybe so, but you must."

As he guided her back to the table, Sandy said, "Thanks, Jenny."

"For what?"

"For caring like you do."

"Okay, you guys, gather around," said Willie Cottrell, trying to herd the flight together one last time. The lights over the dance floor were just beginning to come on. "This is it. When next we meet, one or two at a time, we'll be in 'Nam, scattered hither and yon. And remember General Grundy. I was a damn grunt. Believe me, you don't know what the sight and sound of a helicopter does to the man on the ground." Cottrell went around and shook everyone's hand.

"See ya, you old-timer," Sandy said.

"Good luck to you, kid. You're not a quitter—and that's good."

Sandy saw Frank Bartlett. He went over and extended his hand. "Till we meet again, Frank. It's been great rapping with you. I've got your address."

"Good, let's keep in touch."

And then the band struck up the last song: *She Wore A Yellow Ribbon.* Somehow it seemed appropriate. Sandy remembered the first day they reported to Fort Wolters. His mind's eye saw a column of men in blue on horseback, dust rising about them. And then he recalled the preamble to the song *Winged Soldiers Are We:*

> "*I am an American fighting man, an Army aviator serving with the forces that make our country free. I will never forget my duty, my men, my honor...I will trust in my God, my country and my ship.*"

Victor R. Beaver

The Sky Soldiers

A Saga of Men in War

Part Three

Derek Justen

War Is The Province of Danger, And Courage Above All Things Is The First Quality of A Warrior

COURAGE is of two kinds: First, physical courage, or courage in the presence of danger to the person; and next, moral courage, or courage before responsibility, whether it be before the judgment seat of external authority or of the inner power, the conscience. We only speak here of the first.

Courage before danger to the person, again, is of two kinds. First it may be indifference to danger, whether it proceeds from the organism of the individual, contempt of death of habit. In any of these kinds it is to be regarded as a permanent condition.

Secondly, courage may proceed from positive motives, such as personal pride, patriotism, enthusiasm of any kind. In this case courage is not so much a normal condition as an impulse. We may conceive that the two kinds act differently. The first kind is more certain, because it has become second nature, never forsakes the man; the second often leads him farther. In the first there is more of firmness, in the second boldness. The first leaves the judgment clearer, the second raises its power at times, but often bewilders it. The two combined make up the perfect kind of courage.

From Ernest Hemingway's anthology *Men At War*

The Sky Soldiers

Chapter 62

"WELL, LEO, I GUESS THIS IS IT," said Kip Slater, as he took one last look at his room. Except for the presence of the mattress, the room was almost exactly as he found it nearly nine months before.

Leo, standing next to him in the doorway, said, "You're lucky. You didn't have near the shit to take to the pad as I did." Leo's stereo equipment and souvenir collection had filled three small wooden crates and was right now loaded in the helicopter that was to head them north to Vinh Long.

Just then Mac appeared in the hallway. Approaching the two pilots, the ex-flight-school classmate said, "You guys 'bout ready to go?"

"Roger that," Slater said, extending his hand. "Old Neely sure knows to get rid of his riff-raff, his non-consorts."

"Bullshit. The Tigers are losing two highly experienced ACs. He's a frickin' idiot."

"Well, he got what he was after while he was here, that's for damn sure," Slater replied. Neely, in three weeks, was being transferred to battalion headquarters, his promotion to lieutenant colonel an assured formality. Two months later, Slater would meet the ex-commanding officer of the Soc Trang Tigers seated in a jeep on a side street near the officers' club at Can Tho. One could cut the forced cordiality between the two men with a knife.

"Well, good luck," said Mac. "Stop in when you get a chance."

Leo said, "Next time I see you, Mac, I expect you to be in the right seat of that gunship—"

"Crap on that. With less than a hundred days, I could be flying a desk and it wouldn't bother me." Because Mac and Leo had arrived in Vietnam on the same day, October 18, Mac told Leo he expected to see him on that freedom bird home. Laughing, Leo said, "Wild horses couldn't keep me in this asshole country one minute longer than I have to. Don't worry about me—"

Inside the cabin of the helicopter, with both men belted in and their backs flush against the transmission bulkhead, Leo and Kip felt the old Dog-model Huey rise from the pad. As the ship hovered forward, Slater gave a half-hearted salute to Slote's Piece of Shit Turquoise Shack. "Adios, Soc Trang... You were a good home while you lasted."

The climb to two thousand feet took several minutes. Slater leaned back; he felt the rush of air through the cabin. It had been a week since he and Leo were informed they had been "infused" into Charlie Troop, 7th Squadron, 1st Air Cavalry at Vinh Long. Both pilots could only surmise that they had been chosen because twice they had challenged Neely's no-moustache policy. Besides, Leo had done next to nothing to convince any of the enlisted men to buy U.S. Savings Bonds, his extra duty while with the 121st. And on more than one occasion Slater had had run-ins with Neely concerning his duties as Awards and Decorations officer. They were warrant officer pilots! To dilly-dink around with paperwork was not the warrant officer style! But still, to be sent off like errant children—the idea of it just didn't sit well in Slater's craw. He liked Soc Trang, and he liked flying with the 121st; he knew he would miss the Tiger camaraderie most of all.

Several days before, Kip had also said good-bye to Rusty and Ron, his crew-chief and gunner. Since both crewmen were leaving Vietnam within the week, all three bid farewell to *Alfie*, who did nothing more than return his toothy, *What, Me Worry?* grin. (Unfortunately, two weeks later *Alfie* would be a wreaked heap; and a gunner would be killed, as *Alfie* is crash-landed, with Oremsby at the controls, at an LZ not far from Soc Trang.)

Slater and Tannah unloaded their gear from the three-quarter-ton truck. The enlisted man that had picked them up at the Vinh Long transient pad had stopped in front of a wooden, tin-roofed building fortified with sandbags on all sides. Encircling the building just below the eave of the roof were screened-in windows. The two pilots opened the screen door of their new quarters and went in. They found themselves in a corner of the building used as a gathering place for its inhabitants. "Well, what have we heah?" spoke a long-legged, thin-shouldered man in T-shirt and undershorts. The man, sipping a beer, was seated on a metal folding chair, his feet propped on top a wooden, medium-size rolled-cable holder tilted on its side, used now as a table.

"Fresh meat?" remarked a black warrant officer sporting a neatly trimmed, pencil-thin moustache. He stood off to one side, leaning against an outside wall.

"Well, blow me down, a couple of FNGs," said a bushy-browed warrant officer with an equally bushy moustache, also seated on a metal folding chair at the same make-shift table.

"FNGs my ass!" Leo exclaimed. "How long you turkeys been over here?"

"We came over on the boat," said the T-shirt. "Got here the end of February." The man stood and extended his hand. "The name's LeDeux. Robert E. LeDeux. From Baton Rouge, Louisiana. At your service, suhs." He took a deep bow then motioned toward the black warrant officer. "And may ah introduce my man-servant, Russell Thomas, better known as RT." Suddenly LeDeux blurted, "Hey, boy! Brang me another Mint Julep! And be quick about it!"

"Yessuh, massa, yessuh...right away, suh! Please don't hit po Jim *no mo!*"

Suppressing the urge to laugh, Kip and Leo looked for a place to dump their baggage. Behind them the door opened and a shaved-headed first lieutenant walked in. "You guys just come in from Soc Trang?"

"That's a roger."

"Well, I'm Lieutenant Briscoe. I'll be your section leader. Have you met everyone?"

The bushy moustache rose. "I haven't introduced myself. I'm William Koehler. Call me Buddy." Koehler spoke with a clipped Maine accent. "I didn't catch the names," he said, looking first at Tannah and then Slater. Leo extended his hand. "I'm Leo Tannah. This is Keith Slater. Kip for short." Everyone shook hands all around.

"There are three vacant cubicles," Briscoe told Leo and Kip, "so take your pick. We've got another infusion coming in later today, from the Knights, just down the road from us. A guy named Ashcroft. It looks like the lift section is going to be overloaded with aircraft commanders, after we issue AC orders." Briscoe spoke with a business-like, matter-of-fact attitude. He told them there was some paper-shuffling they had to do in the orderly room, later, after they were settled in. Leo brought in his stereo equipment and began to set up his reel-to-reel. Slater opened his duffel bag and suitcase and began hanging his uniforms and the few civilian clothes he owned. The cubicle was smaller than his room at Soc Trang and far less private. Within the half-hour, Leo had his reel-to-reel playing.

*"We gotta get out of this place,
If it's the last thing we ever do..."*

They met another lift pilot, a warrant officer pilot from Wichita Falls, Texas, nicknamed Cowboy. At four o'clock, Ashcroft, the infusion from the Knights, the 114th Assault Helicopter Company, appeared, packed and ready to move in. He was a thin-faced, stoop-shouldered twenty-year-old who reminded Kip of little Westy Harper, the gum-smacking Arkansasan killed right before his rescue from Tieu Can. Ashcroft had a cigarette hanging insolently out of the corner of his mouth. With sixty-seven days left in-country, he immediately became the resident short-timer, beating Leo and Kip's DEROS dates by some thirty days.

Kip, his cubicle all set for his remaining three months in Vietnam, went to the corner gathering area. He stood watching as Buddy lackadaisically shuffled a deck of cards. "Around here," the Maine accent said, "we play lots of Solitaire and Hearts. We don't do near the amount of flying we heard you guys in the assault companies do, so be prepared to slow to a snail's pace."

"In fact," said RT, "there are times, I swear, when we go so slow we have to speed up to stop."

"What's Briscoe like?" Slater asked.

"He's a fucking peacock," Cowboy answered.

"Yeah, he used to be in the Scouts, until he got wounded," said Buddy. "When he returned from the hospital, they put him in charge of the lift section." Koehler continued to shuffle the cards. "He hasn't got enough common sense to fill a teacup."

"Don't be surprised if he collars one of you new guys to be his *personal* aircraft commander," LeDeux said.

Cowboy spoke. "He hasn't yet been able to get through an AC checkride. But then, he hasn't got dick-squat for flying time over here. Maybe a hundred hours in the OH-6 before he got wounded. And then not more than twenty hours total in the H-model since he's been in the section."

"I flew with him one time after he joined us," Buddy said. "He didn't listen to a goddamn thing I said. *I* was the AC and he acted like *he* was in charge."

Kip smiled. "He sounds almost amusing," and then wondered how he would handle the man should he be asked to fly as pilot-in-command.

They ate dinner in the messhall, a large screened-in wooden building set next to the orderly room. After chow, Kip and Leo decided to scout their new surroundings. The squadron had been formed during spring last year at Fort Knox, Kentucky, trained for six months, and then shipped en mass to Vietnam, arriving in February. True to the spirit of the cavalry, the Stetson, adorned with gold tassels and crossed sabers, was authorized headgear, though not everyone wore one or even had one. As they walked on sidewalks made of wood, passing by wooden hootches that served as living quarters, each with several small banana-tree clusters around them as adornment, they began to meet the other pilots in the troop. One pilot in particular caught their eye. Kip and Leo both looked at each other and grinned. The man they saw coming toward them had to be Errol Flynn's exact look-alike, if ever there was one. He had a moustache with the ends so long they curled into one great circle, fixed in place by moustache wax. They stopped in front of the man, a first lieutenant with clear, sparkling blue eyes. Leo asked, "What platoon are you in?"

"The gun platoon."

"The CO doesn't care that your moustache looks like that?"

"Who...Rameriz? Hell no. Are you guys a part of the new infusion?"

"Yeah."

"Welcome. My name's Emery, Malcom Emery," he said, extending his hand. "I'm in charge of one of the gun sections. We're going to have a couple of openings pretty soon. Have you ever seen the inside of a Cobra?"

"No," Leo replied, suddenly glancing at Kip, a gleam in his eye so unmistakable that Kip shuddered.

"Well, come on. I've got to get my map from the ship."

As they walked along, they caught a whiff of something burning. "What the hell's that smell?" And then they saw the source. An enlisted man was standing by three 55-gallon oil drums cut to one-third their original size. From each black smoke poured skyward.

"Shit. And JP-4. That joker there used to be one of my armorers. I got rid of his ass, a real dopehead. One day he lit a joint right in front of me. Rather than send him to Long Binh Jail, where he'd be totally useless, Rameriz figured he could be the troop shit-burner." From where they stood they saw that the man had a crop of unruly silver-blonde hair held somewhat in check by a red bandana. Several necklaces of beads dangled down around his neck. His fatigue pants were filthy with grease and dirt, and he was shirtless.

When they got to the flight line, less than two hundred meters from the main billeting area, they saw the Cobras. Each was housed in a protective revetment. When they came to the third Cobra parked in its revetment, Emery stepped up, opened the rear cockpit canopy door, retrieved his map and stepped down. Nodding toward Leo, the section leader said, "Go on, take a look. Get in if you like."

Leo stepped up and for a moment gazed at the narrow cockpit and the mass of gauges and switches on the instrument panel. He lifted himself farther and settled into the seat. He took a firm grip on the cyclic and out of habit reached out and adjusted the altimeter. For several minutes he had the lieutenant describe where all the armament switches were and explain the Cobra's several gun configurations, ammo capacities, effective firing ranges, and rates of fire. From down below, Kip watched as Leo listened intently. "Come on, Leo...let's not get any bright ideas."

Once the two friends were alone, Leo said, "That damn thing carries enough firepower to destroy an entire village—!"

Back at the hootch, they met two more lift pilots, one of them a chief warrant officer (W2) who had just come in from a training flight. "This is Mr. Montgomery, one of our stan pilots," Briscoe told them. "He'll give you your AC checkouts tomorrow." Standing next to Montgomery was a husky, blonde-haired warrant officer, perhaps the best looking man Kip had ever seen, introduced as John Sampson.

LeDeux stood and sidled next to Sampson. "You gotta watch out for this one," he said. "When Samp gets a few drinks in him, he's the biggest damn baby I ever saw. But I can understand why. With a face like his, he's probably got women pining for him from coast to coast, nawth to south."

Later they learned that Sampson, twenty-eight, had been in the Navy, and while serving did quite a bit of commercial air traveling. For some reason, God only knew why "...the stewardesses always gave me their phone numbers. I didn't do a damn thing, I swear," he said to them.

It was eight o'clock. "Okay, everybody," LeDeux sounded, grabbing the deck of cards, "let's get it together. Hearts for points. Nickel a point. And boy!" he exclaimed, looking at RT, "brang me another Mint Julep!"

"Yessa, massa...yessa! Please don't hit Jim no mo'!"

* * *

STAFF SERGEANT TYRONE FABIUS ATWATER stood before the small shelf he had built and gazed at the more than four dozen titles in his collection.

Victor R. Beaver

They ranged from D.H. Lawrence's *Lady Chatterly's Lover* to Herman Melville's *Moby Dick*, from Ayn Rand's *Atlas Shrugged* to Victor Hugo's *Les Miserables*. He had read them all twice, several of them three times. Though he was never a serious student of classical literature while in college, his main thrust being to make enough money working three part-time jobs (in order to remain in school) to finally earn a bachelor's degree in psychology, he nonetheless developed a thirst for such readings when he discovered after he graduated that his degree and a quarter got him, a black man, a hot cup of coffee and another dead-end job at the local Dairy Queen. With a wife and two children, and a third on the way, Tyrone Fabius Atwater knew he had to do better. In less than six months he discovered how: by joining the army.

Within a year and a half he made buck sergeant. He got his next stripe by asking clearly and directly of his commanding officer: "Sir, I've got to have me a max ER. I've got to make more money to feed my babies. What do I have to do *exactly* to get that kind of efficiency report?" His platoon leader, a man whom he soon learned he could trust, mapped out his every step. Five months later he was promoted. Afterwards, Tyrone Fabius Atwater had the right formula for getting ahead in the service and in the process found the time to develop his second passion: Reading, which included major historical and philosophical works.

He began his first Vietnam tour, in late 1965, as a spec four RTO (radiotelephone operator) with the 1st Cavalry Division. Within five months after his arrival he was wounded and sent back to the United States. He spent two months healing a punctured right lung and several cracked ribs. Afterwards, he was assigned to Fort Leonardwood, Missouri, as a drill instructor, which was where he gained his buck sergeant stripes. A year later he volunteered to be reassigned to Vietnam. He wound up at Pleiku, in the 4th Infantry Division, as a squad leader. Directly after his promotion to staff sergeant, he saw that his next promotion wouldn't come as quickly in the unit he was in, so he volunteered to be infused into Charlie Troop, 7th of the 1st, there to fill the Blue Platoon NCOIC slot. He had been at Vinh Long now two months awaiting, along with the rest, the arrival of their new platoon leader.

As Atwater perused the books on the shelf, he wondered what the new captain was like. His only information was that the man had come up through the ranks, had received his commission through Infantry OCS, and was anxious to have his own platoon. *A captain anxious to have his own platoon! Jesus—where had the man been?* Already he sounded like some deadbeat RLO, fallen desperately behind. Great. There goes my chance at my next stripe, Atwater thought. *Well, you have to take the bad with the good. Let's just hope you don't have to spoon-feed him in front of the men.*

"Man o'man, Sarge, you sure got to have some smarts to read that stuff," said Vinny, the platoon RTO, standing in the doorway of Atwater's private room, looking in.

The Sky Soldiers

Atwater turned. "Vincenzo, get the hell out of here. You and that damn infernal comment of yours. I'm about to kick your ass—"

"Hey, no offense, Sarge," Vinny said. The little RTO stood bare-chested, displaying a series of upper-body muscles that were stretched taut over a wiry frame.

"Where's Childs?" Atwater asked.

"Doc?...He's checking over his stock, like you told him."

"Good. What about the machine gunners, especially Chico and Big George? Are they cleaning those 'sixty' bandoleers? I swear, why can't those two keep them in the damn ammo cans, instead of parading around like a couple of Mexican banditos. They've got to keep the dirt and rust off those links."

"We don't hardly ever shoot the M-60s, Sarge. What's the big deal?"

"That's exactly the big deal, you moron. When we do have to use the ammo, sure as hell that dirt and rust will cause a jam."

Atwater, standing six-feet-two, looked down at Vincenzo, nearly a whole head shorter. The RTO's face was as clean of whiskers as a baby's bottom. "How old are you *really*, Vincenzo?"

"You know, Sarge. Army records don't lie. I'm nineteen."

"Oh bullcrap."

Vinny quickly whipped out his billfold. "See my ID. Nine-fucking-teen—"

"You're no older than my oldest daughter. She's fifteen. Your recruiter must have been pretty goddamn desperate."

Just then, Patterson, Third Squad leader, appeared. Patterson said, after glancing at his watch: "Any word on when the new captain's going to be in?"

"Today. Sometime today. That's all I know," Atwater replied.

"Everyone's on pins and needles," Patterson said, running his hand through a bristle of light brown hair.

"What for? Do you think he's going to eat them alive? He puts his trousers on same way we all do—one damn leg at a time."

"Maybe it's because he's a captain. First and second lieutenants are easy to handle. But a captain—in charge of a measly platoon—he's either right on top of things or so damned far out in left field it isn't funny."

"Well, which do you think he is, Patterson?"

"I vote he's a dickhead," Vinny interrupted.

"What are we voting on?" asked Clarence Douglas Brave Water Hermosa, appearing suddenly behind Vincenzo.

"Jesus Christ—" Atwater exclaimed. "What is this—Grand Central Station?"

"Me always interested in White Man talk," Brave Water retorted. Hermosa was one of the platoon's eleven bravos (infantry MOS, military occupational specialty), a Navajo born and raised on the Navajo Nation Indian reservation, near Farmington, New Mexico. Bravo Water grabbed Vincenzo around the neck and said, "What did you do with my cigarettes, you little shit—?"

Victor R. Beaver

Struggling to breathe, Vincenzo reached back and smacked his assailant on top the head. The Indian let go and backed off. The RTO faced the Indian. "I didn't do nothing with your cigarettes! It ain't my fucking day to watch your goddamn cigarettes!"

At the exchange, more laughable than serious, Atwater and Patterson shook their heads. "At ease, goddamnit," Atwater said. "I swear, everyone's as stir crazy as a bunch of cons. The captain's going to have a fit when he sees the kind of platoon he's inheriting."

"I still say he's gonna be a dick, just like the last asshole we had. Thank God they sent his ass home." Vinny turned toward the Navajo. He swiftly motioned his right fist into Clarence's mid-section, coming up short of an actual punch.

"Dago White Man best watch his friggin' step." Brave Water gave the Italian RTO a piercing look.

"Anytime, asshole, anytime. I thought you Nava-hoos was supposed to be blanket weavers, not fighters."

Patterson said, "I vote he's a drinkin' man, a lifer, and the first chance he gets, he's outta here, especially if he's a pilot, which no doubt he is."

"No bets," the platoon NCOIC said. "All I care about is, Will he keep us out of unnecessary shit?"

"Yeah, like the Old Man," Vinny remarked. "For a Mexican, he's all right. He don't take crap off anyone."

"All right, you eightballs, out of here," Atwater ordered. After Brave Water and Vinny were gone, Atwater motioned for Patterson to sit down. "How's Chico doing?"

"Okay," Patterson said.

Atwater shook his head. "Next time we go out, I'm holding you responsible for his actions. I will not tolerate anymore mutilations. Is that clear?"

"Jesus, man, he's only done it once—so far as I know."

"Yeah, but once is too goddamn many times already."

"Okay-okay. You've made your point. I'll watch him. But what do you want me to do if I see him at it again—shoot him?"

"No, I—"

"Just remember, man, them little VC pricks have done it to us—maybe not in this unit but in others."

"All right. Forget it," Atwater recanted. "Damn—sometimes I wonder what the hell is going on over here."

"Yeah...you and me both, Sarge. You and me both..."

The Sky Soldiers

Chapter 63

MAJOR SALVADOR FRANCISCO RAMERIZ stared obliquely at the top of his desk. He touched his lips with his right index finger and gently pressed it to the glassed-over solitary picture of his wife, Prescilla Rosato Rameriz. Next to her picture, in a separate frame, was a photo of his children, three sons and two daughters. Their ages ranged from fourteen years down to three and a half. For a moment his eyes went back and forth between the two photos, until they settled on the one of his wife.

He was indeed a very fortunate man. When he had the chance to leave the home of his parents, in Monterrey, Mexico, at the age of fourteen, and go north, he did not hesitate. In fact his parents practically shoved him out of their little adobe house. There was no longer any room for him in either of the two beds his seven sisters and brothers shared. Besides, he being the oldest, it was time he went out into the world to make it on his own.

With two companions, Salvador Francisco Rameriz crossed the Rio Grande west of Laredo. They made their way slowly through Texas and across New Mexico until they reached Colorado. There they found fieldwork in the fertile San Luis Valley, at a place called San Acacio, located twenty-five miles south and east of Alamosa. Though life for young Salvador was hard, especially being so far from home, he knew it was easier than had he remained in Old Mexico. He gained his U.S. citizenship after a year, by a method he never thereafter discussed, and in the same month married the woman Prescilla Rosato Cordova, three years his senior, who bore him two sons in two years and a daughter a year later. After the birth of his third child, he found himself in the same predicament as before: too many bodies and not enough bed, there being only one bed in the small two-room field quarters he and his young family shared. So off he went again, this time into the United States Army.

He spent his first overseas tour in Germany, as an MP guard in Berlin at Checkpoint Charlie. He came home once a year for a month at Christmas time. After three years, he returned to the United States and immediately applied for officer candidate school and attended Transportation OCS. With no war to fight and no way to rise quickly in rank, Second Lieutenant Salvador Francisco Rameriz chose to return to Germany, where he commanded a motor pool that consistently turned out a 100-percent availability of vehicles. He did this by working day and night, side-by-side with his men, foraging for parts, to include having them locally machined. After being promoted to first lieutenant, he volunteered for another overseas assignment, this time in Korea, as a quick way to gain rank. He ran another motor pool with the same outstanding results. By now, Vietnam was fast becoming a household word, but instead of volunteering to go there, he saw something he wanted to do more: Attend helicopter flight training, even though he had been advised that to serve as a commissioned officer in aviation would be the death knell of his military career. His third son was born while he attended flight school. Finally, Prescilla Rosato Rameriz gave birth to his last child, a second daughter, a mite of a thing whom he adored almost more than his other children combined (though he would never admit this to himself, much less to the other members of his family).

He spent his first combat aviation tour with the 1st Brigade of the 101st Airborne Division, the Screaming Eagles, where he was assigned as maintenance officer. A 90-percent availability of aircraft was superior, yet Captain Salvador Francisco Rameriz had an unheard of 97-percent availability. How he did it, for the most part, mum was the word. But he had a way of working the books, without sacrificing safety (along with begging, borrowing, and stealing), to create the numbers he knew his commanders liked. Before returning to the United States, he was promoted to major and simultaneously given his next assignment: command of Charlie Troop, of the re-designated 7th Squadron, 1st Air Cavalry, at Fort Knox, Kentucky.

Rameriz sat forward. He reached out and took the picture of his wife. "You have been a fine, fine woman," he said aloud. "After this tour...I come home. And I will build the house you have always wanted, near San Luis." (San Luis, Colorado, was where her parents lived. They were growing old and she wanted the house to be big enough for them to live in, along with her and her children, and all the grandchildren she hoped to someday have.) He placed his wife's picture back on the desk and took up the one of his children. He gazed first at his two oldest sons. The fourteen-year-old was already as tall as he was. His thirteen-year-old, he learned, had already been in the pants of the neighbor girl (of the same age) across the street from where they lived at Fort Knox. His twelve-year-old daughter, just beginning puberty, was still very homely, but this did not diminish the pride he had in her, for he knew that some flowers took longer to bloom than others. His third son, Felipe, recently turned five, already had ambitions to join the service and be a pilot. And Celia Maria Rosita, his three-and-a-half-year-old, his precious treasure, well, she would just have to wait to sit on her daddy's lap. "Can you wait until after February?" he asked the child in the picture. He nodded and said, "I'm sure you can, little one...but can I?"

He placed the picture of his children back on the desk. He looked up. On the wall opposite his desk was a status board. Listed were Charlie Troop's monthly tally of Viet Cong killed and those taken prisoner. The tally under VC KIA outnumbered VC POW ten-to-one. His commanders now wanted body count. And body count he intended to give them. To date, Charlie Troop's tally was running about twenty percent ahead of the other troops in the squadron.

Salvador Francisco Rameriz heard the screen door to the orderly room creak open. Through the open door of his office he saw just the man he had been waiting for. He stood and went into the outer office. "Captain Nolan."

Mike Nolan stiffened slightly. "Yessir."

"You made it. Come into my office."

"Yessir."

Rameriz directed him to take a seat, then went to a pot of coffee heating on an electric warming plate, on a small table near his desk. "Major Elroy phoned me right away after your decision. It pleased me that you didn't hesitate. You made a good decision. Coffee?"

"Yessir."

Rameriz, holding the pot, took up a cup and began to pour. "Cream?... Sugar?"

"Straight black, sir."

"My last Blue Platoon leader came down sick about a month ago, some kind of bad intestinal problem. They had to evacuate him to the States. Since then, Staff Sergeant Atwater has been in charge. Damn good man. He's Negro. Nothing wrong there, eh?"

"Not a thing, sir."

"Good. The Blues have quite mixture. Like a melting pot, if you know what I mean. Good kids, most of them."

Nolan nodded. "Yessir, I understand. Shouldn't be a problem."

"How do you feel about working for a Hispanic?" Rameriz was now seated at his desk. Nolan saw that his new commanding officer was extremely good-looking, with short curly black hair and teeth as white as polished pearl. He wore a full, evenly trimmed moustache.

"Sir, I've never had a problem with race or national origin before; I don't intend to start now. As far as I'm concerned, a man does his job, he gets no flak from me, commanding officer or otherwise. Are you expecting a problem, sir?"

"No. But I must warn you. The kind of troop I run, you may find a little strange at times."

"How's that, sir?"

"I come from Old Mexico. Family is important to me. This troop is my immediate family now. I take care of my family. I don't take any shit from anybody, I don't care what his rank: Bird colonel or four stars. You fuck with my family, I fuck back. Which means that from time to time when I give an order you might not understand what I'm intending until, perhaps, later. You'll have to bear with me."

Mike Nolan grinned. "Sir, a lot of orders given in the heat of battle sometimes don't make sense, especially to the man on the ground. That's the military."

Rameriz wagged his finger. "No, that may be military elsewhere, but it won't cut it here. The orders I give really do make sense, because the safety of my men is always my top priority. Remember, the military is mission oriented; I'm family oriented. There's a big, big difference."

Victor R. Beaver

Again Nolan grinned. Rameriz sat back. "Here are your standing orders. Number one: shoot first, ask questions later. Number two: don't dick around with your men—*my men.*"

Nolan took a deep breath. He heard clearly the two criteria, but at the moment, wasn't sure of either of Rameriz's intended meanings. "Well, sir, may I speak bluntly?"

"Go ahead. Always speak bluntly to me. I'm hard of hearing otherwise."

"I don't intend to 'dick' around with 'the' men, though they may at times believe I am doing just that. And as far as protecting them, I won't expose them to any danger or risk I'm not willing to take myself."

Rameriz leaned forward. For a long moment the two men peered at each other. Then Major Rameriz cracked the slightest smile, the gleam of white teeth showing through. He rose. Nolan rose too. Extending his hand, Major Salvador Francisco Rameriz said:

"I think we have an understanding, Captain Nolan. Welcome to Charlie Troop. Get with your platoon as soon as you're settled in."

Nolan took the major's hand. "Yessir. Thank you, sir. I intend to do just that."

Mike Nolan placed the picture of him and his father on the small stand next to his bunk. He opened the blue velvet case containing the gold oak-leaf clusters. For a long moment he gazed at them. He was certain he would make major, now more than ever. He had too much active duty time left before reaching twenty years not to, and now this present opportunity at command would cinch it.

After he replaced the blue velvet case on the stand next to the picture, he stood and checked himself in the mirror. Then he went outside and walked down the company street; he turned and entered the platoon hootch. Earlier, he had instructed Lieutenant Briscoe to have the lift section, which included all pilots, crewchiefs, and gunners, to assemble behind the messhall at 1300 hours so he could address the entire platoon at once.

"Atten-hut!"

"At ease. Sergeant Atwater, gather all the squads and meet me behind the messhall in ten minutes."

"Yessir—"

Nolan stood before his men. The enlisted personnel were seated on the ground while the pilots stood behind them. He took a minute to survey faces, all fifty-seven. Then he began:

"For those who don't know me, I'm Captain Nolan, your new platoon leader. For starters, I checked your records, so there isn't much I don't know about each and everyone of you, including the officers. As you know, a Blue Platoon is typically commanded by a captain, who normally remains with the aviation assets during an operation, while a second or first lieutenant, infantry-type, is on the ground with the grunts. Well, fortunately or unfortunately, however you want to look at it, Lieutenant Briscoe is not a member of the infantry branch—but I am. Therefore I make this immediate change. I'll be going out with the eleven bravos, while Lieutenant Briscoe commands the air assets. I'll still be in charge overall, but frankly I believe I can do a better job by being on the ground. So far are there any questions?" There were none.

"It is my understanding that an aero-rifle platoon is a kind of bastard platoon in an air cavalry troop. While Cn'C and the Cobras and Scouts are out doing their thing, we remain behind ready to react to whatever they find—or, sad to say, if an aircraft goes down. I'm well aware that you haven't seen much action. The Scouts have been racking up most of the kills. I wish I knew how long this would last. But I can't. The Army's mission changes constantly. Who knows when we may be called upon to give more than accustomed. Therefore, I want to prepare everyone for an eventuality that may or may not come. I do this because my life and your life are otherwise at risk. So far now are there any questions?" One person raised his hand. "State your name and your question?" Nolan said.

"Vincenzo, sir. Anthony Vincenzo, platoon RTO. Sir, does this mean that we have to play army, and spit-shine our boots, and be *strac*, and all that neat shit?" Several smiles broke out, along with a few chuckles. Vincenzo beamed, glad that he had had the nerve to speak first.

"Specialist Vincenzo, you're from Queens," Nolan said. "You live right near Bushwick Park. I was there once, several years back. The whole Queens-Brooklyn area reminded me of a former combat zone, where house-to-house fighting had taken place. After which the activity to clean up was in full swing." Nolan remembered a drive down Flushing Avenue. Never had he seen such a beehive of humanity, worse than any disturbed anthill, the trash that lay about, the hustling, the graffiti, the utter disrepair of the buildings. The place apparently had a soul but there wasn't a thing glossy about it, at least not what he had seen. Then: "No, Specialist Vincenzo. It doesn't mean that at all. Within reason, of course, and mainly for hygiene-sake, I could care less what you look like, so long as you don't look or act like a bunch of goddamn pirates.

"But here's what it does mean," Nolan said, this time changing his stance, spreading his feet apart, and placing his hands on his hips. "You're going to train, and train thoroughly. There will be something new everyday. I want you people in classes, with the expert in any particular subject doing the teaching. We're going to find out who the experts are and draw on their knowledge and experiences. We're going to do PT, daily. We're going to push ourselves. Why? I'll tell you. Because I intend to see everyone of you leave here in one piece—alive and healthy. Not one of you is going to die or get wounded because there was something we could have done to prevent it. War is chaos. How do we fight chaos? By training hard and standardizing our actions. This does not preclude inventiveness.

But inventiveness for the sake of it—forget it. It has to have a reason. Am I understood?"

Slater raised his hand. "How does this affect the pilots? What can we do? A helicopter is a helicopter. You tell us where to take you and we take you there."

"Good point. Here's what I intend. I don't want the grunts carrying any more than they have to: weapons, a good variety, beaucoup ammunition and grenades, and plenty of water. Anything else we need, the slicks will bring to us. Since I'll be on the ground, I'll be in the best position to determine what more we need at any particular time."

Nolan then drew a line in the dirt with the heel of his boot. "Okay. Who here wants to challenge all that I've said? Anyone? If so, take a step across this line and we'll find us a place to settle who's the goddamn boss."

For a moment everyone was still. Then one of the assistant machine-gunners stood and stepped across the line. Nolan looked up. Staring at the giant before him, he read the man's nametag: *KOWALINSKI*, the big farm boy from Wahoo, Nebraska, nicknamed Big George.

Big George said, "Sir, I got my old man's farm I want to go home to. You tell me what to do, sir, and I'll do it. Put her there, sir." The giant extended his hand. Mike took it.

"Fine." He looked around. "It's settled." Nolan glanced toward his black NCOIC. "Sergeant Atwater, let's you, me and the squad leaders have us a meeting."

"Yes, sir—!"

Chapter 64

SANDY ADAMSON, WEARING HIS SUMMER khaki uniform and brand new silver Army aviator wings, stepped to the door. He hesitated, and then rang the doorbell. The door opened.

"Yes?"

He removed his saucer hat. "Hello, Mrs. Williams. Is Katie here?"

"Sandy...?"

"Yes, Mrs. Williams."

"Good gosh, look at you. I barely recognized you—"

"Yes, ma'am," he said, running his hand through his hair. "I've got most of my hair back."

"Certainly, that must be it. The last time we saw you...it was much shorter."

"Is Katie here, Mrs. Williams?" he asked again.

Mrs. Williams hesitated. "No. She's not. She's out...with a friend. But you can come in. I don't expect her until later tonight, though."

"That's okay, ma'am. I'll...I'll just come back tomorrow."

"Well...whatever you like. But if you could, call first, Sandy—that would be good, too."

"Harriet! Who's at the door?"

Mrs. Williams turned. "It's Sandy, Charles!"

Just then Katie's father appeared. "Hey, Sandy! How are you? I see you finally made it. You really look great!" Sandy stood a little straighter; he thrust his chest forward. Charles Williams shook the young pilot's hand.

"Yes, sir, I sure did. Graduated a week ago. Drove home with my folks. We stopped to visit some relatives in Iowa. We got in late last night. I thought I'd drop by to see if Katie was home. I guess she's not."

"No, she and Jerr—" Harriet Williams nudged her husband's arm. "Uh—she's out, gone with some friends...to Denver, I believe. Harriet, didn't she mention the planetarium? Great place. Have you ever been there, Sandy?"

"Once, sir. As a matter of fact, Katie and I went together."

"Yes...well, she should be back sometime this evening, probably around midnight."

After Sandy left, Katie's father said, "He really looks good." And then he shook his head. "Gosh, it's hard to believe he's a helicopter pilot."

"Yes, but where he's going is not good," Harriet Williams said. "I'll bet his parents are fit to be tied."

"Yeah, well...I guess it wasn't any different for us when Brad left." The two stood silent for a moment. Earlier, right after breakfast, they had watched Katie leave for the cemetery to put flowers on Brad's grave. She did this once a month, on the anniversary date of his death. Thinking of this, Harriet said:

Victor R. Beaver

"Charles, do you think Katie will ever get over what happened to Brad?"

"Of course. Someday...anyway," he said.

"And what about Sandy? I can't help but think there's still something between them, something she hasn't let go. But she's been so involved with this peace movement. Have you noticed she's begun to wear those strange clothes, all loose fitting—nothing that matches? And her hair? It's so long and she always ties a headband around it. She used to dress so nice."

"Just a phase—just a phase," Charles Williams said. "They've got to have their say, these college kids."

"Well, that's sure a switch," his wife said. "Last month you were knocking her friends. Now they're okay."

"Well, maybe if this peace movement had been going on sooner and stronger, the war wouldn't have escalated at all. And then maybe Brad—" Charles Williams cut himself short. "I don't know. Something's got to give. That idiotic war can't last forever. Maybe these kids *can* end it. Who knows? We'll see what happens if Nixon gets in."

Harriet Williams shook her head. "I hope it's over before something bad happens to Sandy. I'm really afraid for him. He'll try to be right in the middle of it, he's that kind of person."

Charles Williams sighed. "Yeah, you're right. He'll want to be right smack in the thick of it."

Sandy drove south along the interstate, going nowhere in particular. He kept rethinking the scene at Katie's house. Her father had almost blurted out the name of the person she was with, some guy's name, he was certain. He had seen out of the corner of his eye Mrs. Williams nudge her husband, who then quickly changed what he was about to say. He felt sick. All his heart-rending dreams about her were true! Katie no longer loved him. All they had shared, all they had meant to each other, now seemed as if it never happened. How? How do you become so close to someone, only to have it suddenly be so different? What went wrong? He thought their love was special—that nothing could come between them. How does a person fall *out* of love? His love for Katie had not diminished: In fact it had grown stronger, deeper. But how can love grow deeper without nourishment? That didn't make sense either. His nightly dreams were full of contradictions. They showed Katie still caring for him, but whenever he tried to get close to her, to recapture the intensity of the emotions they once shared, she cooled and pushed him away. It was maddening. He was grateful for flight school, for it had kept him too busy during the day to dwell on the hurt he felt. He knew he had to face her, to have her tell him once and for all where he really stood.

Sandy telephoned the following day. Again, Katie was not at home. He asked that she return his call. He waited until past midnight and there was no call. That night he avoided sleep until he could no longer stay awake, finally dozing just before dawn. He had another dream about Katie, one that had him crying out to her how much he loved her, tears streaming down his face, bawling like a baby. In the dream she just stood there and watched him with a kind of forced detachment, caring for him yet remaining apart from him. He awakened trembling.

On the morning of the third day, without calling first, he went to her home. Katie opened the door. Behind her stood a tall, bearded young man, dressed in a plain white cotton shirt and bell-bottom jeans. For a moment she just stared at him. "Oh...Hi...Mom told me you were in."

Sandy's heart was in his throat. Katie looked so different. Her auburn hair had grown long and she was wearing it frizzed out, held in check by a beaded headband. He saw in her eyes and in the slant of her mouth a look of scorn, affection, and impatience. "Why didn't you return my calls?" he asked.

"I...uh..."

The young man behind her shifted to Katie's side. She turned slightly. Giving Sandy a forced smile, she said, "Jerry, this is Sandy Adamson. Remember I told you about him?"

Jerry put his arm across Katie's shoulder. "Yeah, I remember." The three endured an awkward moment of silence. And then Jerry said, "I understand you just went through chopper school?"

Sandy nodded. "Yeah, I did."

"So, you're going right over to 'Nam, eh—do your share of killing?"

Sandy tensed at Jerry's apparent accusation, his outright condescending tone. "Yes. I report to Oakland, California—in two weeks." He was looking directly at Katie as he spoke, trying to remain calm. He detected a glimmer of concern. His looked at the golden flecks in her eyes and his whole being shivered for her. He said, "Katie and I would like to have a moment alone?"

Jerry glanced at Katie. "Sure. Screw it. I don't care."

Katie looked furtively at her friend. "I'll just be a minute."

Sandy led Katie away from the front steps. They stopped halfway between the porch and the curb, where Sandy had parked his parent's car. She gazed at him. "Are you doing okay, Sandy?"

"Yeah, fine."

"Sandy, I was going to call...really I was."

"When?"

"I...I don't know."

"Like never? Were you just going to let me leave without saying anything? Huh?" His voice now had a sharp edge to it. He wished he could wipe from his mind the image of Jerry's hand on Katie's shoulder.

"No. I wasn't going to do that."

Suddenly: "Katie, I still love you. What happened to us—?"

"Oh, Sandy," she said, "I don't know—I wish I knew."

Victor R. Beaver

In that moment he reached out and took her and pressed his lips firmly to hers. There was no tenderness; it was a kiss of desperation, meant to re-establish ownership, and to exorcise all his helpless, hapless dreams about her in an instant.

He withdrew. Katie's lips had felt soft and yielding, yet her arms had remained limp by her side.

Sandy Adamson let go and backed away, the sickness he felt in the pit of his stomach worse than before. He turned and went quickly to the car. He opened the door and stopped. Katie remained rooted in place, the expression on her face uncertain, frightened, bewildered. And then he cried, "Good-bye, Katie—*good-bye!* I won't ever bother you again!"

"*Sandy...!*"

He got in and drove away.

* * *

SLATER AND HIS CREW WERE SHUT down at Hotel Three, at the Tan Son Nhut air base. Kip had his feet propped against the open right cockpit door. It had been nearly three weeks since he and Leo had taken their H-model checkrides. As it had proved time and again, the H-model Huey, with the more powerful L-13 engine, could easily lift eight fully equipped American infantrymen with hardly a whimper. Kip still found it difficult to believe: a troop-carrying utility helicopter that could do the job it was intended!

He was penning an entry in his journal when he felt a strong slap against his boot.

"You still writing in that goddamn thing?" said a familiar voice.

Startled, Slater looked up. "Justen! What the hell you doing here—?"

"Same old shit."

"Man, the last time I saw you, the angels were nipping at your heels—*bigtime!* I swear you looked like death warmed over when we dropped you off at Dong Tam. How the hell are you?"

"Fine," Justen said, taking Slater's hand. "You look good yourself. I came over when I saw the crossed sabers on the front of the ship. You going anywhere near Vinh Long? If so, have you got room for three passengers and all their baggage?"

"Vinh Long's exactly where we're heading. Why there?"

"My new assignment. The cav squadron. Same as those two wobbly ones," Justen said, indicating the two new warrant officer aviators standing next to the terminal building, out of the sun.

"No shit. That's the squadron I'm in. Leo and I got assigned to it last month. We got infused into Charlie Troop. Go tell'em they've got a ride."

"All right. I appreciate it."

The Sky Soldiers

Mark Allen and Sandy Adamson quickly hoisted their duffel bags. With the crewchief and gunner toting the rest of their gear, the four made their way to the helicopter. Following close behind, Justen carried a tightly packed duffel bag along with a bag filled with his Vietnam clothing issue.

They situated themselves in the back cabin area and buckled in. Sandy glanced at the interior of the ship. He watched as the right-seat pilot quickly went through the start procedures. In just a little over a minute the engine was at full flight rpm and they were lifting. This was it: the flight that would take them to their first combat unit. Sandy looked toward Allen, who gave him a thumbs-up. Flight school was now ancient history. Sandy wondered about the rest of the class, how their thirty-day leaves at home had transpired. Once past the fringes of Saigon, he sat back and watched the two pilots up front. The left-seat pilot, a guy named Sampson, was an extremely good-looking warrant officer, curly blonde hair, an easy-going manner coupled with a disarming smile. The one in the right seat, named Slater, looked seasoned, old before his time. Puzzled, he and Mark had noticed that Slater was very familiar with CW2 Justen, whom the two had met at Travis Air Force Base and who sat by them completely silent during the long flight over. Justen seemed ancient. Sandy was now among pilots, not instructors, with hundreds and hundreds of combat flying hours, still in the game. These were the guys from whom he now needed to learn. What tricks of the trade did they possess? Whatever they were, they were probably hard learned and hard won, all designed to beat the enemy, survive, and return safely home....

Victor R. Beaver

Chapter 65

SANDY ADAMSON TILTED HIS HEAD back. He felt the heat of the sun through closed eyelids. He opened his eyes and squinted. The sun was so bright it made the sky one great white haze. He looked toward the horizon; he saw the air shimmering, undulating; it was a sea of air, motionless yet flowing. This sea of scorching air undulated across the Plain of Reeds. It felt so hot that it was a wonder the incessant drone of the insects had not been stilled.

Sandy turned his gaze toward a group of children seated at the edge of the Moc Hoa airstrip. Normally exuberant, full of chatter and playful curiosity, they too sat silent, immobilized by the sun's rays, now at its zenith, as they watched the helicopter crews lounge with equal lassitude near their aircraft.

"What are you thinking?"

The young warrant officer turned at the voice of Kip Slater. Slater was lying on the floor of the cabin of the helicopter. He had taken off his fatigue shirt and had rolled it up and had his head on it, while his feet were propped against the back of the left cockpit seat. "This heat," Sandy said. "It reminds me of this one summer I spent on my uncle's farm in Iowa. It was August and we were waiting to bring in the wheat. It was so hot that everyone just limped around like wet dish rags. Is it this way all the time? Gee—I wish we'd fly."

Slater, hardly able to rouse himself, peered at the new pilot who had been in the unit now barely a week. Everything about him was still Stateside fresh: his haircut, his stance, his manner of speaking. His uniform and boots issued at Camp Alpha and the patches he had sewn on, still held their newness. Slater could even see the months of flight training on the young man's face, the furtive, hesitant curiosities. Slater liked him. There was something familiar about him, as if he were looking at himself when he first came into the country ten months ago. There was the same innocence, the same curiosity, and even the same appearance. He remembered the adage: *"There is nothing more constant than change."* Then thought: *"And nothing more constant than repetition, either."*

Slater said, "We will. Even I can't stand this sitting around. I'm down to sixty-nine days and a wake-up. Time has slowed to a crawl for me. I'm sapped. Every time I start to read, I fall asleep." When he and Leo came into the squadron, Kip noted the sharp contrast between the cav and the assault companies. Most of the flying was done by the Scouts and Cobras, with a C&C ship in the immediate vicinity to coordinate the action as well as watch over the Loaches (LOHs, light observation helicopters, or Scouts) as they hovered a few feet about the ground hunting for Charlie. With the Snakes orbiting overhead, poised to strike the moment the Loaches made contact, Slater saw that this was the more effective way to look for the elusive Viet Cong in the Mekong Delta. But he hated this languishing. However, when the slicks were asked to crank and take

The Sky Soldiers

the Blues out to investigate what the Scouts had found, Slater found himself equally unmotivated to fly. It was an interruption of a pattern he liked: lounging, dozing, reading, not to mention lolling in the security he felt at the reduced exposure of activities related to combat.

Sandy Adamson wandered over to Buddy and RT's ship, where Buddy, Cowboy, Montgomery, and LeDeux had a game of Heart's going. He stood and watched for a short while, then heard the sound of helicopters approaching. The troop commander's aircraft along with the Scouts and Cobras were on their way in to refuel. They landed and a fuel truck came and topped off their tanks. He had investigated the OH-6A Cayuse helicopter several days ago, talked to one of the pilots and his gunner, saw the little decals that looked like a head with a bamboo hat practically covering both men's helmets. "What are those for?" he asked.

"Kills," the pilot answered. "Every time we waste a gook, we stick one on."

"Waste?"

"Yeah...you know: shoot, kill, blow away."

"Is he shooting at you?"

"If he ever did or was...he won't anymore."

When Sandy told Mark about this, Mark's eyes lit up. "No shit? They just blow'em away? They don't take any prisoners?"

"Damn few..."

Leo came to Kip's aircraft and leaned against the edge of the cabin deck. "What's up, Leo?"

"You got a cigarette?"

Kip flipped Leo his pack. Leo took one and lit it. He flipped the pack back. "Keep it," Kip said.

"They're yours," Leo said.

"Bullshit, you smoke half of them. When are you going to start buying your own again?"

"When you quit."

"In my next life."

Leo took a drag. "I've been thinking...talking...you know, to Lieutenant Emery."

"What about, Leo?" Kip already knew the answer.

"Getting into the Cobras."

"How? You'd have to extend."

Leo turned. "Yeah. I've been thinking about that too."

"Are you serious—?" said Kip.

"Kip, let's do it together—" Leo suddenly blurted.

"Leo—no way. I've got sixty-nine days and a wake-up. Sixty-nine days and I'm out of here, *back to the World—*"

"Listen," said Leo, now drawing in close. "You could get into the Scouts. I'd be above you. Whenever you take fire, I'll roll in. We'd be a team—"

"Oh sure, here's how that goes, 'From the burning Loach, the target is'—Na, it ain't gonna happen."

"Whatever. But this shit, sitting around everyday, really sucks. Kip, we could spend our free thirty days in Australia. We'll go there at the end of our extension." Leo's eyes saw it all. "And your book. You'd have all the material you need to write it. Come on, let's do it. What do you say?"

Kip canted his head. For a moment he peered at Leo. "You're really serious...aren't you?"

"I've already talked to Rameriz. If I extend, they send me to Vung Tau for the Cobra transition. And with my time over here, I could be an AC by the first of January."

Slater began to think. Extending, especially if Leo did it too, really didn't sound that bad. The Delta, at least compared to the rest of Vietnam, was still relatively benign. Helicopters weren't falling out of the sky like flies, like they sometimes did farther north, in the 1st Cavalry Division or the 101st. Besides, ever since he dropped into the double-digits, his double-digit fidgets were getting worse. To extend, therefore, would cancel that—for the time being. It was crazy, a sort of no-win situation: let the countdown to DEROS continue and suffer the nerves. Or extend and suffer the nerves later. Maybe by then he'd be too tired to care...At least he hoped to be alive to be too tired to care.

"Let me think about it. I'll let you know in a couple of days."

"Sergeant Atwater, what's that you're reading?" Nolan had glanced over to where the platoon sergeant was sitting, under the tailboom of the lead Huey, out of direct sunlight. Unlike the rest of the men, most of who were lazing their time away, Atwater savored his every free moment (when they lagered—stood by waiting to lift) with his nose stuck between the pages of a book. Nolan, in spite of how much he enjoyed the L'Amour books he had recently bought, couldn't muster the energy to concentrate on reading like the sergeant could.

Atwater shifted the book slightly and glanced at the front cover. "'The Oxbow Incident,' sir, by Walter Van Tilburg Clark. My second reading."

"Is it a Western?"

"To some extent, yes, sir. Actually, it's about a lynching, men taking the law into their own hands: judge, jury, and hangman. It's considered a classic. If you're interested in reading it, sir, I won't tell you anything more about it."

During the past month Nolan had come to like and admire the sergeant, not only for his leadership abilities, his discipline, but his intellect, which seemed out of place in his current profession. There were many times when Nolan thought Atwater should be teaching, perhaps in a university, some subject like history or philosophy. Gratefully, the man's degree in psychology had been a considerable advantage. Atwater had a way of dealing with the men that kept their self-esteem intact. He was a great motivator, without acting like the toe of his boot up someone's ass was the way to get the job done. The military needed intelligent men: intelligence was the precursor of individual initiative. Besides, you can't have the ignorant leading the relatively educated, which was how he viewed the intellectual qualities of most of the men. In spite of how they tried to appear otherwise, most of them were bright, quick-witted. They tried to hide this though under a mask of bravado, which he knew to be a cover for hidden fears, either of dying, or of being severely maimed; or worse, of being revealed a coward in the face of danger.

"Have you ever thought of going to OCS, Sergeant?" Nolan asked.

Atwater said, "Gave it some thought, sir, then dismissed it. After this tour, I'm going to ETS, get the heck out. I've been gone long enough from my family. I also want to go back to college and get my master's degree. It's about time I got serious what my education can do for me. Don't get me wrong, sir, I like the army. It's been good to me and my family, but I want more. I didn't realize this until just recently. Like the good Reverend King, God rest his soul, I've got to face my fears head on and do it peaceably. I think his death, more than any other, has made me realize that. Right now, most white people consider Martin Luther King Junior a kind of rabble-rouser, a misfit. Well, a misfit he might have been, but he was an educated man. I'm not as much into religion as he was, don't have a whole lot of use for it, personally, but I believe that each of us can do good in the world if we're calm with those around us. You can be tolerant without giving in or appeasing. It's a matter of self-confidence. Or better still, having a boat-load of self esteem."

Nolan listened. He remembered the conversation he had with Dave Grange that day in Savannah, in the little out-of-the-way lounge they went to. Something about "keeping the wolves at bay."

"Why did you come to Vietnam?" Nolan asked the sergeant.

"Sir?"

"What are your reasons for being here?"

Atwater drew his head back, tilted it, then frowned. "Pardon me, sir. But are you really asking me that?"

For a moment Nolan pondered the sergeant's puzzlement. Why *had* he posed the question the way he did? Maybe it was because Sharon had asked him the same question one day that almost ended in heated argument, when he tried, in vain, to explain how he perceived the Army's required necessity to fight in Vietnam. "No-no, I want to know your *personal* reasons for being here?" she said, rephrasing the question.

"Why are *you* here, Miss O'Malley?" he quickly replied.

His answer caught her off guard. "I uh...came to help...the men."

"What for?—Money?"

"Yes...somewhat for money."

Victor R. Beaver

"Listen, you were the one who read the passage from 'Sackett's Land' to me, something about trying to fight for the right cause. I admit that today it is hard to know what the right cause is. I wish I knew positively."

She sighed. "I'm sorry," she said. "It was presumptuous of me. I should have examined my own motives first. It wasn't a fair question."

Peering at her, he tried again. "Simply, I'm a military man and a military man follows orders. I'm here because my country ordered me here. I volunteered to be in the army, which ultimately means I may be sent to unpleasant places."

"Like Vietnam—"

"Yes, Vietnam—"

"—to fight in an undeclared war."

"Damnit, Miss O'Malley, I'm not a politician. War—anywhere, anytime, declared or otherwise—is crappy business. But it isn't for a soldier to decide the political correctness of its country's duly elected leaders. I didn't start this shindig—"

"But you always told me you like to take responsibility for your actions."

"I have. I have a responsibility to follow orders—"

She saw that the heat had risen in him to a greater level and knew to back off. "Look, I didn't mean to upset you," she said. "I think the point of my question had to do with what reading is all about."

"In what way?" he asked, again wishing to be calm in her presence.

She smiled, yet felt smaller due to his original defensiveness. "I'd like to think that our purpose in reading is to learn, to educate ourselves of the thoughts and opinions of others. How else do we form our worldview? We can't be everywhere at once, so we must learn from those who have been to places we have not been or cannot go. We must learn from the experiences of others for the same reason."

Nolan looked toward his platoon sergeant. "Sergeant Atwater, I retract my question."

"No, sir, that's all right. I'll answer...as best I can." The sergeant took a moment to reflect. Then he began:

"For everything, there is its opposite. Or so it seems. Day and night. White and black. Peace and war. Right and wrong. Life and death. Yin and Yang, to borrow a term from Zen Buddhism. But between the two extremes is a lot of gray. The gray is the glue that binds. Within the realm of human events, I call this gray the will, or freedom of choice. A better way to put this is: I'm here because at the moment this is where I *choose* to be. If I really didn't want to be here, *I mean really didn't want to,* I'd be gone yesterday. Don't let anyone fool you, sir. Every one of us has a choice. Those in the United States who fled to Canada to avoid the draft, did what they chose to do. If they are still in Canada, they've chosen to remain there. Had they not fled, this place—here, Vietnam—is likely where they'd be. Well, this is where we are—you and I—by choice. Some of us by in-action, by not avoiding the draft, legally or otherwise. Sir, it's the only thing that makes sense. I'm here because, at the moment, my being here allows me to gain some advantage suitable to me, whatever that happens to be. If you ask any of the men: Vincenzo, Childs, Patterson, why they're here, they'd give all kinds of answers, from 'I was drafted' to 'I joined.' Inaction or action, they exercised a choice. Or ask the dude who burns the shit everyday, the one with the hair and the beads and the headband. He got here by not fighting the draft or fleeing to Canada. Now that he's here, he don't want to be here. He's gone, maybe not physically, but his head sure is gone. All he's waiting for is his DEROS date and that freedom bird home. At the end of World War Two, practically the whole German nation—minus that small percentage that knew what was going on and got out, or who tried to, or who died in the attempt—claimed their innocence by saying they had no choice. Yet they followed Hitler almost literally to the gates of hell. What, their hands were tied behind their backs? their sense of right and wrong suspended completely?—every one of them? Give me a break. They and the Japanese people were the most willfully led people on the face of the earth. Sir, if history one day proves that we Americans shouldn't have been here, let no one be duped into thinking, you or I or anyone else who came, that we didn't have the choice."

Victor R. Beaver

Chapter 66

DEREK JUSTEN LET HIS FEET DANGLE out the left side of the LOH. They hung just above the tip of the six circular-mounted minigun barrels mounted below the level of the left cockpit door of the OH-6A Cayuse helicopter. He wore a chest protector and on his lap sat a CAR-15 automatic rifle. Sipping slowly at a can of Coke, he gazed at the five lift-section Hueys parked along the east edge of the Moc Hoa airstrip. The fuel truck had just topped off the helicopter he and Lieutenant Scott had been flying in and had moved on to the next ship.

It was his second day in the Loach and already he found the scout platoon's manner of flying unlike anything he had ever done. It was slow, exhausting, dangerous work. Though they had been on the hunt since early that morning, scouting several waterways in the Plain of Reeds, they found no new traces of Viet Cong movement, no sampans loaded with munitions or supplies—though the potential was there, without a doubt.

The day he came into the unit Justen heard there were two openings in the platoon. He went to Captain Kubiak, the scout platoon leader, and said he wanted in.

Kubiak told him to talk to the Old Man. "Rameriz picks them personally."

Justen met with Rameriz the next day.

"Why?"

"Sir?"

"Why do you want to be in the Scouts? That's a young man's game. Do you have a death wish?"

"No, sir."

"I could use you as my Huey stan pilot. Montgomery will be leaving in another month."

Justen drew a deep breath. "Sir...I've...my brother, he's a POW somewhere down around Ca Mau, probably in the U Minh." It was the first time Derek had ever spoken about Jake to gain an advantage. When he was done, Derek stood still, waiting.

"No," Rameriz said. "Right away I don't want you. I don't want some guy out there with an axe to grind. You'd be a loose cannon, especially if we ever operate around Ca Mau. I wouldn't be able to control you."

Derek stiffened. "That's crap, sir. I'm a professional soldier. I'm not asking for one goddamn favor. If I can't cut it, you can get rid of me—"

Rameriz's eyes widened. He leaned back in his chair, the tips of his fingers pressed against one another. He gazed at the dark-haired, olive-skinned chief warrant officer for a full minute. He liked the way Justen stood his ground. It was exactly what he wanted in his scout pilots. Plus, there was that mixture of tension and calm about him too that he liked. What the hell, he thought. The man deserves at least a try. The troop commander nodded his head. "Okay. But here are my conditions. I tell you to waste somebody, you do it. No second guesses. You hesitate once and you're out. I have yet to lose a scout pilot. I don't intend to start with you. Do you read?"

"Loud and clear, sir."

"Good. Get with Lieutenant Scott. He can start your orientation tomorrow."

The next day Justen flew in the left seat with Scott, the troop OH-6 standardization pilot. They followed a winding narrow riverway that coursed through the western edge of the Plain of Reeds, three scout helicopters scooting quickly across the ground. When they came to their first suspicious trail, Rameriz, in the C&C ship high above, told them to follow it. When he saw them get close to a large cluster of low-lying vegetation, he told them to back off. They skirted the edge of the cluster to draw fire, but there was none. This was the pattern all day. Later that evening, Scott reported to Rameriz: "He's really steady on the controls. I didn't see any nervousness."

"Good...but the real test is yet to come," the major said.

Just then Scott appeared map in hand. "Okay, we might have something. This is your big chance." Scott laid the map on Derek's lap. He pointed to a canal intersection situated near the Cambodian border, twenty-five kilometers northwest of Moc Hoa. "An OV-1 Mohawk took some pictures last night. Several sampans appeared in the photos. We get to check the area out."

The lieutenant got into his right-seat position. As Justen was buckling in, Scott flicked the battery on and the fuel boost pump switch. He checked the throttle to OFF. He yelled clear and pressed the ignition "trigger" button on the collective-pitch control lever. The high whining sound of the engine pierced the surrounding air. At fifteen-percent N1, Scott cracked the throttle open, going past the spring stop; the engine blasted on. He watched the TOT (turbine outlet temperature) rise. When the N1 reached 59 percent, Scott released the button. Four main rotorblades turned swiftly overhead.

When everyone was ready, the three Loaches lifted and sped west low-level while the Cobras and the C&C ship climbed high and followed. The pack continued west for several minutes. Finally, they came to a north-south canal. Scott and Justen were in the lead scout aircraft. Scott turned the ship and began to parallel the canal on the east side. He swerved the ship left and right slightly as he flew. Justen held tightly to the CAR-15. He moved his eyes from left to right. With the weapon off safe, he was poised to fire. After three minutes, they saw a cluster of low-lying trees appearing at their ten o'clock. Derek fixed his gaze on them. Speaking of the tree cluster, Scott told Derek: "A month ago we found beaucoup rice, medical supplies, and B-40 ammunition. The guns got two secondaries. I zapped three gooks with my minigun. Jonathan Hart, also known as Chicken Man, got four with his."

They skirted the cluster wide to the right. After another minute they came to a point where the canal took a turn to the northwest.

"One Five, this is Six," spoke Rameriz over the VHF radio."

"Go ahead, Six," Scott replied over the UHF radio.

"Fly heading three five zero. I can see the intersection. It's five klicks to your eleven o'clock."

"Roger, Six."

Scott began speaking to his wingmen. "One Two and One Three, this is One Five, how's it going? Chat with me."

"A-okay, One Five. We gotcha covered."

"Betcha Charlie's got our little cluster restocked."

"No way. He's not that stupid."

"Give it another week."

As the Scouts got closer to the intersection, Rameriz told them to slow down. Scott brought the airspeed back. Derek's grip on the little short-barreled CAR-15 rifle tightened.

To their left front, about two hundred meters away, was a clump of tall grass, high enough to hide a small sampan against the bank. "Sometimes, when the wind is just right, I can smell'em," Scott declared. "I've been told it's the nuc muom, that putrid sauce shit they put on everything they eat. They say it secretes out through the pores of their skin."

Derek glanced up through the left skylight. The two Cobras were orbiting directly overhead at two thousand feet. Rameriz's Huey was at fifteen hundred feet, off to one side.

Scott brought the OH-6A forward, aimed toward the tall sawgrass. They were less than twenty feet above the ground, moving along at thirty knots. Suddenly something caught his eye and he bent the ship left. "A footpath," he said over the UHF radio. He began now to converse over the air, speaking so that Rameriz, the gunships, and his wingmen could hear what he was seeing. He spoke a steady stream, "...maybe a day old, heading slightly north by northwest...going toward the canal...looks like it's bending now to the right...a couple of meters...changing course again..."

Meantime, Derek kept his gaze on the cluster of grasses still to their left front. He looked for any kind of movement, a change in the color of the vegetation. He perked his nose to catch a scent, but if any out-of-the-ordinary smells were there, the exhausted fuel flowing forward from the tailpipe masked them.

Scott continued to follow the trail, barely visible through the sawgrass. Gradually, Derek began to feel an uneasiness creep over him, something in the way the cluster of taller grasses was bent. He took a split second to insure the CAR-15 was off safe. Then it happened. An automatic weapon opened up. Instantly Scott bent the ship right. "One Five taking fire! Ten o'clock!" As the

The Sky Soldiers

three Loaches made their escape to the right, the lead Cobra rolled in and fired two pairs of rockets. *KAWHUMMP!...KAWHUMMP!*

The impacts were dead on. Like a suddenly appearing dark cloud, smoke enveloped the target area. *KAWHUMMP!...KAWHUMMP!* The second Cobra had just fired. Again the ground erupted. Grass and clods of dirt and water spread out and up and then rained down everywhere. As the two Cobras made their post-dive pullouts, the Scouts moved in to protect. Scott maneuvered their ship left and fired the OH-6's electrically operated minigun. The barrels rotated and lead flew forward at the rate of four thousand rounds per minute.

"Back out of there—" Rameriz commanded, speaking over the radio. "Come to the right. Plenty of clear area."

All three Loaches diverted right. Derek kept the barrel of his rifle pointed at the target area. When the first enemy shots were fired, he heard several rounds chink against the left side of the ship. Without giving it a second thought, he had the CAR-15 sending return fire.

"Keep your eyes moving," Scott told him. "Every place now is a potential target."

"Roger that," Derek replied, trying to divide his attention between what was going on outside the aircraft and reading the ship's gauges inside.

Sensing Derek's concerns, Scott said, "No warning lights—yet."

Just then Derek happened to glance right. A small wooden fixture stood in another cluster of tall grasses, a footbridge. Beyond it was a small hootch, built low to the ground and partially camouflaged. Suddenly, Derek felt as if they had just stumbled onto a hornet's nest.

As Scott brought the ship farther to the right, Derek saw two men, both wearing black pajamas. They appeared to the left of the hootch and began to step quickly away. He couldn't make out whether they were armed or not. They slipped away hidden in the grasses almost as suddenly as they appeared. "Two gooks," he declared.

"Roger that—I just now saw'em," said Scott.

Scott spoke to Rameriz over the radio: "We've got a couple of guys to our nine o'clock. They've disappeared in the grasses. I think they're making their way west."

"Roger," Rameriz replied. "Take a wide turn to the north. If you see them again—shoot."

"Roger that, Six."

Scott picked up speed and raced north like he was told. Derek now looked for the two men with intensity, beyond anything he had ever known. Within the next several seconds he would come face to face with a truth: would he be able to gun down the retreating men? Or balk and ruin permanently his chance to be in the Scouts? He hoped it would be a case of kill or be killed. He prayed that it would.

As they came upon a thin ribbon of water, no wider than three feet at its best, Derek saw movement in the grasses to their immediate front. He caught a glimpse of something brown, some kind of wooden structure that appeared to be gliding. Scott saw it too and brought the ship slightly right, again to give Derek the best angle to shoot.

And then Derek saw them, two men, one behind the other, seated in a sampan, their hands free of any weapons, their eyes wide, their faces taut. "Waste'em!" Scott ordered.

Moments later, Derek would realize the only reason he pulled the trigger was because he saw the dark trace of a rifle barrel against the background of the grasses. When his shots went off, they were aimed first at the barrel and then at the two men in the sampan, who had quickly grabbed for their weapons.

The two men launched backwards as the CAR-15 rounds hit them full force in their chests. The third Viet Cong, whom Derek had spied behind the partially hidden gun barrel, upon further investigation, was laid sprawled in the grasses. Derek saw that the complete right side of the man's head had been blown away. After a thorough search for others, the Scouts moved out of the way to allow the Cobras to destroy the sampan and any possible caches. Then Scott gave control of the ship over to Derek, who led the pack back to Moc Hoa to rearm and refuel.

"How did you know the third guy was there?" asked Scott.

"I saw his rifle barrel," Derek replied.

"I never saw it. That was good shooting. For a split second, I thought you would choke. You're in scout platoon as far as I'm concerned."

"Thanks."

The Sky Soldiers

Chapter 67

LEO TANNAH EXTENDED HIS HAND. "Keep the home fires burning, buddy. I'll be back in no time."

"Okay, Leo," Kip said. "You be careful."

With suitcase in hand, Leo turned and went toward the waiting helicopter. The pilot increased the engine rpm as Leo climbed aboard. In a moment the ship lifted and when it was a mere speck in the sky, Kip retreated to the hootch. He pulled a light blue plastic carrying case from under his cot, laid it on top an ammo crate, and opened it. He took the electrical cord, plugged it in, and turned the machine on. His brand new Smith-Corona electric typewriter, sent for several weeks ago, had just arrived. It gave off a slight humming sound. He inserted a clean sheet of paper.

Journal Entry, 2 September 1968, Vinh Long AAF

Well, Leo is off to Vung Tau for the Cobra transition, which lasts four weeks. I can't believe we did it. We extended! Our new DEROS dates are now the latter part of April 1969. I can't help feeling that we've made a huge mistake...

"Okay, boys, the game is five-card stud, jacks or better to open," Buddy said, dealing out the cards.

"What's the ante?"

"Nickel."

"Hey, boy, brang me anotha Mint Julep!"

"Hey, honkie, I'm on break," RT said. "Get your own goddamn Mint Julep!"

"Tsk...tsk, a man just can't find good help anymore."

"I open with a dime," Cowboy said, tossing the MPC down on the table.

"The man opens with a dime."

"Here's your dime and I'm kicking in a nickel," LeDeux said.

"How many?"

"Give me three."

Slater eyed his cards. He had a pair of tens, queen high. "I'll take two."

Buddy dealt. "So, your friend Tannah is going to be a Cobra jock. What, we don't bathe often enough around here to suit him?"

Slater shook his head and took a sip of beer. "Leo has always wanted to be in the guns, ever since we got to Soc Trang."

"I'll tell ya," Cowboy said, "he's one crazy SOB, pardon my saying so. I flew with him and he lobbed a whole box of grenades at this one hootch about

Victor R. Beaver

fifteen klicks east of the airfield. You should have seen him. His eyes were wild—"

Slater nodded. "Okay, who's the bet to?"

"Back to Robert E. Lee-Deux."

"How about a quarter?"

"Man, what do you got?"

"Gotta kick in a quarter to find out."

"Slater, did Briscoe nail you to be his right-hand man?"

"Yeah."

"Have fun."

"I fold."

"If he tries that 'I'm in charge of the aircraft' shit with me," Slater said, "I'll tell him to take a hike."

"Talk's cheap."

Just then the door opened. Mark Allen walked in holding a *Playboy* magazine with the centerfold exposed.

"That shit will cause you to go blind."

"I wouldn't mind being blind if I could check her out by Braille."

"Man, she has a fine pair of legs," John Sampson said, looking over Allen's shoulder.

"You a leg man, too?"

"Samp's a boob man and a hip man and a leg man," Buddy said. "Show'em the picture of that stewardess in the swimsuit—the one who writes to you all the time."

"Hey, where's Adamson? He said he wanted to play."

"The kid's at the movies again. They're showing another John Wayne thriller."

"Hey, don't knock the Duke," Cowboy said.

"Did you see him in that Green Beret thing? What a joke. Fuckin' army propaganda."

"Win a few, lose a few."

"My favorite's still 'The Searchers,' with Jeffery Hunter and Natalie Wood."

"Is anybody playing cards or are we gonna talk?"

"I call."

"Three jacks."

"Beats me."

"Full house."

"And that's all you bet—?"

"Got to keep it friendly," Slater said. "I played poker at a college frat house one night. Lost my shirt. It started off nickels and dimes and escalated after that. In two hours, I was out over a hundred and fifty bucks."

"Were you drunk?"

The Sky Soldiers

"Of course."

"The key is not to drink while you play."

"Tell me about it."

RT asked, "What do you put in that notebook of yours?"

"Personal stuff."

"You going to write a book?"

"Maybe...someday."

"Well, you don't have to go far to find characters. This hootch is full of them."

"Yeah, but they got to be believable."

"What, we ain't believable?"

"You're too believable."

"Bullshit—"

"I'll tell you what ain't believable. It's them scout pilots. Chicken Man's got over a seventy decals on his helmet. Scott has at least fifty. I wonder how they sleep at night."

"They don't. Have you ever been in their hootch? They got a pair of black lights. And some lava lamps. It looks like a damn opium den in there. I wouldn't doubt they get doped up every night."

"Give me mah Mint Julep," LeDeux sounded.

"To each their own."

"Slater, what's your poison?"

"Beer and wine."

"You ever smoke dope?"

"A couple of times. Back at Soc Trang. I had to cut it out. I was getting to like it just a little too much."

Buddy said, "I didn't know you and Tannah knew Justen. He's about the quietest guy I ever met."

Slater nodded. "Yeah, but that's only half of it. He's got a brother who's a POW. Justen thinks he's somewhere in the U Minh."

"No shit?"

"No shit."

"I've heard that the place probably has a dozen, maybe two dozen, POWs down there. Wouldn't that be something to go looking for them?"

"Hey, don't be surprised if we do just that," Buddy remarked.

"That's a big ten-four. We're cav. And if you ain't cav, you ain't shit."

"That's if you're in the First Cav Division, you dipshit. Not in this rinky-dink squadron," LeDeux said.

"Hey, you can knock the squadron all you want, but I think our Mexican commander, bless his pea-picking heart, is going to get *his* butt in hot water and we're gonna find *our* butts in some far-off place like the U Minh—mark my words."

"I don't think so," said Slater. "The U Minh is a pretty vast area, and it's loaded with Charlie. It'll take something larger than a cav troop or squadron to handle."

"That's a big ten-four."

* * *

THE TWO MEN SALUTED. RAMERIZ returned the salutes. "Be at ease, gentlemen."

Sandy Adamson and Mark Allen relaxed. Captain Kubiak had told them to report to the CO's office a half-hour earlier. On the way to the orderly room, Mark Allen said:

"They've got an opening in the Scouts. I'll bet that's what this is all about."

"The Scouts?" Sandy said. "Do you want to do that?"

"Hell, yeah. Don't you?"

"I don't know. It sounds pretty risky."

"Maybe so, but right now it sure would beat the slicks. We hardly fly at all."

Sandy agreed. They had been in the unit three weeks and had flown fewer hours each week than in flight school. The days were beginning to drag and they had barely begun their DEROS countdown.

"The reason I called you two in," the major began, "is because I need a volunteer to be a scout pilot. Lieutenant Scott has been watching both of you." Sandy and Mark both glanced at each other. "Now before either of you raises a hand, I want to tell you that just because you volunteer doesn't mean you have to stay with it. It isn't for everyone. Second, the flying is dangerous, very dangerous. A scout pilot's longevity can be very short, given the right circumstances. And it isn't that glamorous. You put in a lot of hours out there in the AO. Some days we don't find diddlysquat. Third, and most important, gentlemen, you'll be expected to kill, sometimes face-to-face. I can't put it any plainer than that. It's kill or be killed. When you find Charlie, you can't turn your back on him. You do it one time and it could be your last. So far, are there any questions?" Neither man said a word.

"Okay, who wants to volunteer?"

Immediately Mark Allen raised his hand. Major Rameriz looked toward Sandy Adamson. "Go and wait in the orderly room."

"Yessir."

Sandy stepped out of the room and closed the door. He waited several minutes and then Allen appeared. The two men began walking down the company street. "So, what did the Old Man say?"

Mark looked toward Sandy. "He...uh...asked me not to tell you."

"How come?"

"I...uh, it's hard to say. I might let you know later."

"What's the big damn secret?" Sandy blurted.

"Nothing. Will you let me alone—"

Sandy watched Allen during the days that followed, asking each day how his training was going. He looked for clues to questions in his mind about flying in the Scouts that puzzled him. Allen, however, remained true to his word he had given to the commanding officer. Mark was exuberant about scout flying. He told Sandy that the first chance he got he should join the platoon. "Man, it is a fucking kick in the ass to be out there. I've got that little CAR-15 rifle in my hands and we're hovering right above the ground—" The day before the Scouts had discovered a large cache of rice, weapons, and medical supplies. Mark related how he and Scott stayed back while the guns wiped it out with a dozen rockets. "I ain't worried about Charlie," he said. "Our firepower is awesome and he knows it."

One day, Allen took his OH-6A checkride and became a full-fledged scout pilot. He now flew with an enlisted crewchief/gunner seated behind him in the back on the right-hand side with an M-60 machine gun. Meantime, Sandy, in the lift section, continued to fly as peter-pilot. They went daily to Moc Hoa and sat, waiting for something to happen that would cause the slicks to launch. He became more and more bored. This was not the war he thought he would be fighting. Occasionally, they lifted the Blues into LZs, usually near thick treelines that needed men on the ground to recon more thoroughly. But those times were rare. The day Allen got his first confirmed kill was the day Sandy stood in awe of his ex-classmate. "I blew him away so fast with that minigun, he was dead before he hit the ground," Mark had told him.

"How did you see him? Was he shooting at you?"

"He was running away. Rameriz told me to plug him. I got him in the back.'

"In the back?"

"Yeah, where else would I have got him?"

* * *

"I HATE SPENDING THE NIGHT OUT there," Kowalinski, the big Nebraska farm boy said. Big George was lifting several cans of machine-gun ammo in the back of the helicopter.

"How come, Big George?" said Chico, looking sideways at his assistant machine-gunner. "Don't you want to catch Charlie in a sampan and blast him? Think of it like a camping trip."

"It's the snakes, Chico. I hate snakes. It makes me shiver just to think about them."

"Fuck the snakes. It's them fuckin' ants, and especially them leeches, I hate." The little Puerto Rican ran his hand over the barrel of his M-60. "But if we blast Charlie, it will be worth it. Don't you think, Big George?"

"Yeah...yeah."

Victor R. Beaver

Atwater eyed the men as they prepared to be airlifted. It was late afternoon, with the sun now sinking slowly toward the horizon. He looked toward Captain Nolan, Blue. He smiled. Already the man had picked up the nickname most members of any aero-rifle platoon gave their platoon leader. Captain Nolan was putting on his LBE (load bearing equipment) straps. Festooned on the straps were several grenades, two colored smoke bombs, and a flashlight with red lens cover. Hung on his web belt around his waist were two canteens, two ammo pouches, and small field dressing pouch. His fanny pack contained a rain poncho, extra flashlight batteries, and a plastic container of bug juice. His watchband was caught on the upper portion of the left shoulder strap and Atwater went over to help. "Thanks, Sergeant. Guess I forgot to hang my watch where I normally did—fastened to these LBE straps."

"No problem, Blue." As Nolan was shifting the weight of the load and buckling up, Atwater said, "You sure you want to go out like this, sir? Nighttime is pretty spooky."

Nolan grinned. "You hang tight here, Sergeant. Believe me, this is no big deal. I doubt if we even see anything."

"Now, sir, that sounds like famous last words."

"Well, then, knock on wood."

"Yessir," Atwater replied, smiling.

In another minute, they heard the lead Huey start up. Directly afterwards, the two Cobras began their start sequence. Atwater accompanied Vincenzo, the RTO, Brave Water, and two other riflemen, along with Nolan, to the lead ship. "Keep the men entertained, Sergeant. I want Second Squad to tear into that 'prick' twenty-five field radio and see why that damn battery can't keep dry."

"Not much we can do about it out here, Blue."

"Have them look at it anyway. I want these guys to be smarter than their equipment."

In a couple of minutes, the three Hueys along with their cover birds lifted. In each slick were five infantrymen. They flew west. Their objective was a two-kilometer length of canal along which ran a heavy treeline. They would set up along the canal's west edge at the north end to monitor any boat traffic that came along during the night. In the third ship was Sergeant Patterson, Third Squad leader. With him were Childs, the medic, and three others. One of them, a squat twenty-two-year-old named Fields, from Augusta, Georgia, held tightly to a case which housed the mission's most essential piece of equipment, other than weapons and ammunition. It was the AN/PVS-2 Starlight image intensifying scope, a night-seeing device that could be mounted on an M-16 rifle. With it a scene in starlight, which appeared black to the unaided eye, could be viewed as if it were daylight through the image intensifier. Though it couldn't work in total darkness, it nonetheless allowed limited contrasts to be magnified up to sixty thousand times, giving the viewer at least a grainy picture to see movement by.

The Sky Soldiers

Slater, flying as aircraft commander, sat in the right seat of the lead ship. Briscoe, in the left seat, acting as peter-pilot (though he was in charge overall of the flight), was at the controls. Slater peered ahead, his right hand raised to shield the glare of the sun, which sat directly above the horizon. He directed Briscoe to turn the aircraft slightly to the right. Abruptly, Briscoe banked right and rolled to wings level. "Come a little more to the right. The sun's still right in my eyes."

"This should be good enough," Briscoe said.

"Lieutenant, if you don't turn a little more to the right, I won't be able to see where we're going at all."

"I calculated a two-eight-three-degree heading for thirteen point five minutes," Briscoe said. "We'll get lost if we deviate too much from that heading."

For the past three days, it had been Briscoe challenging, Slater defending. Slater was getting fed up. "Come right to heading two nine zero. That way I can tell where we are on the map. If we do get lost, every one of these goddamn canals are all going to look alike. Right now, I know exactly where we are. Fly that heading until I tell you to do otherwise. Comprehende, sir?"

Grudgingly, Briscoe complied. He was now aggravated with Slater's tone. "We'll talk about this later."

"Whatever you say, sir—"

Along the way, they made a diversionary landing four kilometers east of their objective, then took off with the Blues still onboard. The sun was now three degrees above the horizon.

Nolan looked toward Vincenzo. The spunky radio operator returned a smile full of polished white teeth. Nolan felt the ship bank left and start a descent. Out the right cabin side Nolan caught a glimpse of one of the Cobras angling along in step with the slicks. He didn't miss flying at all, like he thought he might. It had come upon him recently that flying really wasn't his sport. Being with the men on the ground, that was his thing.

The three ships touched down and the men jumped out and moved swiftly to the treeline. The slicks lifted and a moment later were out of sight. Nolan dispersed the men quickly once he had a chance to check the terrain and vegetation. He positioned Fields, with the Starlight scope, and four others between Patterson's men on the right, with he, Vincenzo, Brave Water, Chico and Big George on the left. Then he directed a rifleman named Hoyt where to place the two Claymore mines they had carried and how to run the electrical detonating cords. Finally, with Vincenzo fast by his side, Nolan grabbed for the radio handset and spoke to the lead Cobra. "Three Three, this is Two Six. We're in the treeline now, all set for the night."

"Roger, Two Six. We're heading back. Give a holler if you need us."

"Roger that. Will do. Two Six. Out."

By the time everyone was settled, it was pitch black. The moon, after it rose at midnight, would provide Fields with an abundance of ambient light. Now, sharpness of detail was practically non-existent; later, with a gibbous moon, contrasts would be more distinct.

Nolan leaned back. He heard Big George and Chico on his right stir slightly. "Quiet," he hissed.

"Yessir."

To his left, he heard Vincenzo's steady breathing. Brave Water's stomach rumbled. "Sorry, Blue," the Indian whispered. "I didn't eat anything before we came out."

An hour passed. Nolan checked the luminous dials on his watch. It was barely past nine o'clock. The first hours were always the hardest, though they went by the quickest. Nolan knew that everyone's anxiety level was up, but would wane dramatically as the night wore on; and then time would slow to a snail's pace. He whispered to Vincenzo that he was going to sleep. "Wake me at midnight."

"Yes, sir, Blue."

Nolan closed his eyes. He knew that if any traffic came along at all, it would probably be after midnight, when the moon gave off enough light to travel by without having to use artificial light. He wanted to be awake then to keep his men alert. After a moment he began to doze. He slept until something startled him awake. Vinny had clicked the handset to report in. "This is Two Six Alpha...Two Six Alpha. All okay."

Vincenzo looked toward him. "Sorry, sir."

"It's all right." Nolan glanced at his watch. He had been asleep for nearly an hour. He remembered he had dreamt about Sharon O'Malley. At the moment he couldn't recall any details, but the dream had been pleasant and this pleasantness lingered causing him to smile. He thought about her now. So far, they had exchanged two letters apiece. Hers were about the library, her visits to the hospital, her trouble getting funds to expand her number of books. His letters were about the men, the training program he had established for them, and about Sergeant Atwater, whom he knew she would one day like to meet. Though they had been apart now for over a month, he found himself still wondering about her, about what they had in common, if anything. They had such diverse ambitions, to be fulfilled at opposite ends of the United States. Though he found her attractive, in a bookish way, he couldn't quite see himself with her. Since he seldom thought of his appearance where women were concerned, he couldn't quite fathom how she perceived him. She was taller than him and wondered if this bothered her. It had never bothered him. When he left Can Tho, he did so with a certain relief. He didn't need nor want the complication of a woman. At least so he believed. Since he'd been at Vinh Long, though, he often found himself wondering how their friendship would have gone had he remained at Can Tho. By now he had reconciled it a moot point. Though, as the crow flies, Vinh Long and Can Tho were a mere seventeen miles apart, they might as well be hundreds of miles apart for all the time and effort it would take to be together on any consistent basis. In the next instant he realized that he missed her and felt a strong urge to talk to her, to hear her voice. He decided he would call her at the next opportunity.

At midnight, Vincenzo nudged him awake. Nolan adjusted his eyes and peered through the vegetation at the surface of the canal. The moon had just appeared above the eastern horizon. "Nothing, yet, eh?"

"Not a whisper, sir."

"Good."

Nolan could now distinguish outlines. He passed the word that everyone should be still. He looked to see how well the men had applied the camouflage paint to their faces. There was not one hint of white. He knew Atwater had assured himself the thoroughness of this particular task.

Brave Water took over RTO duties while Vincenzo slept. Another hour passed. The moon rose higher.

Fields traded off looking though the Starlight scope with a rifleman named Benny Espinoza, a Hispanic from Santa Fe, New Mexico. Benny scoped the canal for half an hour before tiring at seeing no movement. He spoke softly to Hoyt. "How come we haven't seen anything?"

"Because we just haven't," Hoyt said. "What do you think, the VC are out at night everywhere? That's physically impossible." Hoyt dropped his head in the crook of his arm and sighed. He thought of what it would be like to be in the Scouts, as a gunner, but dismissed it since their quota was full. (Plus, he wasn't crewchief qualified.) *Now there was where the action was, by god—*

Five minutes passed. Suddenly, Benny reached over and put his hand on Hoyt's arm. "Hey, I think I see something."

Hoyt immediately raised his head; he placed his hand on the remote control that detonated the left-hand Claymore. "Where?"

"On the other side of the canal."

Espinoza peered intently through the scope. Whatever he had seen had disappeared in the brush. Hoyt, in the meantime, woke Fields, who was instantly alert. "Did you tell Blue?" he asked.

"The captain? Not yet."

Fields said, "Let me look." Benny gave the weapon with the Starlight scope over. "What do you think it was?"

"I don't know. To me it was just movement."

"Maybe it was some kind of animal."

"It could have been."

Fields scanned across the canal for several minutes. "It must have been an animal. Go to sleep. I'll watch for a while. It's going to be light soon."

The moon stood straight up when the eastern skies began to lighten. Nolan checked his watch. Pickup time would be in another hour. He yawned.

"Pssst...pssst, sir."

Nolan peered over at Fields. "What is it?"

"Look."

Nolan turned his head and glanced across the canal. Grazing on the other side were two South Indian hog deer. Built low to the ground, they had a bushy tail, and appeared heavier than the deer found in North America. Calm and graceful, they fed without the slightest regard to the men with automatic weapons on the opposite side. He wished he had a camera. They almost looked like they belonged in a Walt Disney movie, their eyes seemed so human-like and innocent. Nolan roused Vinny, who perched himself instantly on one arm, his M-16 poised ready to fire. "Bambis," Nolan whispered.

"Wow, no shit. It looks just like him. Or her. Was Bambi a him or her?"

Nolan said, "Hell, I don't think I ever knew."

At six thirty, the lift ships came. Slater and Briscoe, in the lead ship, landed to a canister of dying purple smoke that had been set out by Brave Water.

At Moc Hoa, Atwater greeted his captain. "See anything, sir?"

"Bambi...two Bambis."

"Sir?"

"A couple of deer. Grazing." Nolan began to unbuckle his web gear. "Let the men get something to eat. I'm beginning to think I might be getting too old for this...this camping out. Give me a soft bed anyday."

"Yes, sir. I can understand that. That's why I wasn't going to insist you let me go."

"I'll remember that next time, Sergeant."

"Yessir. I'm sure you will."

The Sky Soldiers

Chapter 68

THE WORD SPREAD LIKE WILDFIRE. One of the Scouts had gone down. In the process of organizing the men, Nolan caught Atwater returning from the PX.

"What's up, Blue?"

"We've got a Scout down, in dense trees south of Cai Nhum. I've got the co-ordinates. Briscoe is getting the pilots together. Keep it under your hat, but I think we've got a couple of KIAs."

"Who went down?"

"I don't know. I don't know any names. Could be one of the new guys...Justen or somebody."

"I'll get the squad leaders assembled."

"Yeah, and make sure everyone's got plenty of ammo. I think it's going to be hot."

At the flight line LeDeux, RT, Cowboy, Sampson, Buddy, Adamson and the other pilots were strapping in. The crewchiefs and gunners hastily donned their chest protectors. Slater opened the right cockpit door of his ship and noticed that Briscoe had placed his helmet and chickenplate in the right seat. Slater took Briscoe's equipment and tossed it in the left seat. Briscoe appeared a moment later.

"I'm sitting in the right seat," Briscoe said.

"No you're not. I'm the AC and I sit in the right seat."

"Look, all the other ACs sit in the left seat, so you will too. Besides, I hate flying in the left seat."

"Listen, you prick, all the other ACs are sitting in the *wrong* seat."

Briscoe watched as the errant warrant officer continued to strap in. "Did you hear me, *Mister* Slater?"

"Loud and clear. Now get in your goddamn seat or I'll start this aircraft and take off without you—Sir."

Briscoe's ears turned red. He went around to the left door, opened it, and threw his operational map at the instrument panel. He got in. Slater yelled "clear" and pulled the ignition trigger switch.

It took less than ten minutes to get to Cai Nhum, a small district town seventeen kilometers southeast of Vinh Long. From fifteen hundred feet up they could see smoke coming from a location two klicks south of Cai Nhum. They spied Rameriz's C&C ship and four Cobras circling overhead. Looking below Nolan caught a glimpse of one of the Scouts working not far from the smoke. And then he saw a second LOH behind the first.

"I've got you in sight, Two Six," Rameriz said over the radio to his Blue Platoon leader. "Orbit Charlie November. Right now I've got an ARVN patrol caught right smack in the middle of this."

"Roger that, Six," Nolan replied.

When the flight arrived over Cai Nhum, Slater told Briscoe to start a left turn. "Come to a heading of two seven zero."

Briscoe banked the ship hard left. Immediately, Slater looked back and saw the men on the left side leaning back as far as they could inside the cabin, a look of fear etched across their faces. "You know, Lieutenant Briscoe, that if one of these guys falls out because you banked too steep, I'm going to have a hard time explaining it to the CO."

"Why you?"

"Because *I'm* responsible for your goddamn actions—!"

"I don't think so—"

"You'd better think so. Now, I'm only going to tell you this once. You make your turns shallow. If you don't, you can find someone else to be your damn AC. But I'm afraid you've used them all up."

"You can't talk to me like that."

"Billy Boy, I just did."

Rameriz's voice came over the radio: "Two Six, this is Six. I'm going to have you land to a square open field. It'll be on the right side of the canal that leads almost due south out of Charlie November. The slicks should make their approach from the south. I'm going to have one of the Scouts throw out smoke. Land right to that smoke."

"Roger that, Six."

"After landing, you'll proceed due north. The treeline you'll be going to will be less than two hundred meters from point of touchdown. How copy?"

"Good copy, Six."

During their approach to the LZ, a pair of Cobras provided cover. Slater, on the controls, brought the flight low and slow to a dying smoke canister.

As the helicopter came closer to the ground, Nolan readied himself to jump. With the Huey still three feet up, he watched Vinny leap out first. And then he saw the others exit from the cabin. Nolan felt the landing gear touch and then his feet were on the ground. As the lead ship lifted, Nolan looked back and saw the rest of the platoon exiting from their ships. Spying Atwater twenty meters back, he ordered the men to fan out and move forward. With Vinny at his side, Nolan moved briskly toward the treeline. Up ahead the remaining two Loaches were cutting back and forth in front of them, scouting the vegetation and terrain below.

"Two Six, this is One Eight, how copy?" Derek said over the radio.

"Loud and clear, One Eight. Can you give me something better to guide on?"

"Roger that," Derek replied. "I'm the left bird. Directly ahead is a small pagoda. Can you see it?"

"Affirmative."

"On the other side and to the left are several tall coconut trees and then some lower brush. Seventy meters to the north of the coconut trees is where One Three went down."

"Okay, good copy. Have you been taking any fire?"

"Affirmative. North of the crash site, where the ARVN patrol is in contact."

The Blues skirted the pagoda on the right side. When they were directly abeam it, Nolan broke his platoon up, sending First Squad to the left and Third Squad down the middle. He fanned the other two squads out to the right. (On their left flank would be the two LOHs.) They heard sporadic gunfire to the north. "One Eight, Two Six, what's the enemy strength?"

"The patrol says a platoon."

"I don't want to get into any accidental firefights with friendlies," Nolan said.

"Roger that. Six has been in contact with their advisor. He says they'll try to stay put."

"Good. Keep me informed of their situation."

"No problem there, Two Six."

Nolan halted the platoon behind a dike that ran in a gentle curve in front of the treeline. He directed Atwater to spread the left squad out and move wide right of the tall coconut palms. Nolan prepared the right two squads for their assault on the main treeline. He looked right and told Chico not to fire at anything unless he was sure of his target. "Those guys could be out of the ship, dazed. Don't want to blow away our own folks."

"Roger that, sir."

With everyone ready, they moved into the dense foliage. No one could see more than a couple of yards ahead. They guided on the rising smoke forty meters to their front, the still smoldering brush surrounding the downed ship. After fifteen minutes of hacking through the thick growth, they saw a small clearing and then the wreckage. Atwater ordered the squads to disperse and set up a defensive perimeter. Nolan knelt next to Vinny and spoke on the radio: "Sandpiper Six, this is Two Six. We're at the crash site."

"Roger. Give me a report ASAP," said Rameriz.

"Roger that."

From fifteen meters away, Nolan took a moment to evaluate what he saw. The aircraft appeared to be lying on its left side, tangled in the charred remains of trees and undergrowth. The fuselage was almost completely gutted by the post-crash fire. Sunlight poured in through the opening of the double canopy that had been created when the small ship went down. It illuminated the crash site like a spotlight. He ordered Brave Water and Fields to flank him as he and Vinny moved in closer. It was hard to distinguish the features of the fuselage. And then Nolan got next to what he believed was the forward portion of the aircraft. He saw the charred body of the pilot. Behind it and to the right were the remains of the gunner. Fields immediately turned and dropped to his knees. Vinny's eyes grew wide with horror. Cautiously Nolan moved in closer. The sight was more gruesome than he had ever seen.

Atwater came and stood at Nolan's side. "Which pilot was it?" he asked.

"I don't know. I'm not familiar with names or callsigns."

Hoyt edged forward and saw something familiar on the pilot's helmet. It was a red heart painted on the left side that had not been charred by the post-crash fire. "It's Chicken Man. His gunner was Andy Coons. I knew Coons real well."

Atwater found a broken tree branch and wrestled it into a short stick to poke at the bodies. After a moment, he could see Coons's ID tags tied in his bootlaces. He took his pocketknife and cut it free. Nolan did the same with the pilot. With both ID tags secured in his pocket, Nolan had Atwater arrange to free the bodies from the wreckage while he spoke into the PRC-25 radio handset. "Sandpiper Six, this is Two Six."

"Go ahead."

"Both men are Kilo India Alpha. Burned bad. We'll have them out in another fifteen minutes. I should have them at the PZ in half an hour."

"Roger that."

The men began the grisly task of extracting the two bodies. Explosions sounded to the north. Nolan again took the handset. "One Eight, this is Two Six. Now what's happening?"

Derek came quickly back on the radio. "The ARVN patrol is receiving mortar fire. I've also informed Six that me and One Two are low on fuel."

"Roger that...Break, Sandpiper Six, this is Two Six."

"Go ahead."

"Give us another five minutes and we'll be heading for the PZ."

"Roger. The American advisor also says that Charlie is breaking contact. He reports the VC are moving in your direction."

Nolan looked up. He could see one of the Cobras through the tops of the trees in an attack dive. The explosions came at them through the dense growth as a series of muffled *whummpfs!* Nolan directed the men to be ready to pull out.

"That shit's getting close!" Atwater cried, as the Cobras slammed in more rockets.

With the two bodies encased in black body bags, they began to egress south from the crash site. As Atwater led the men away, Nolan remained a part of the rear guard.

The lead squads stumbled and hacked their way back through the undergrowth until they finally reached open ground.

Childs, the medic, heard gunfire close to the rear and turned. He saw Brave Water, Benny Espinoza, Big George, Chico and Nolan coming quickly forward. And then there was an explosion. The ground shook and he saw several bodies hurling at him. Brave Water landed in a clump at his feet. Stunned, the Navajo sat up, shook his head, and then dazedly searched the ground for his weapon. Childs saw Espinoza with blood over the right side of his face. As he ran forward to help, he saw Nolan struggling to get up, his face grimacing with pain. Big George and Chico were dazed but unhurt. They had set the machine gun up and were returning fire to the rear. After quickly applying a compress to Espinoza's wound, Childs next went to his captain.

Nolan tried to speak but Childs told him to relax and be still. Childs turned Nolan onto his right side and saw blood. Shrapnel had hit him in the leg and the buttock. As he was cutting away Nolan's fatigue pants, Vinny came and kneeled by his side. "*Jesus*—is he all right?"

Nolan blinked incomprehensibly at his radio operator. In another instant, two more men appeared and were kneeling with rifles pointed outward to provide protection. Childs worked quickly to cover Nolan's wounds and in a minute had him ready to be moved. With Chico and Big George laying down covering fire, Childs, Brave Water, and Vinny and two others helped Nolan and Benny Espinoza to the edge of the trees. Once in the open, the men went quickly to the east side of the pagoda, where Atwater had set up another defensive position. Grabbing Vinny's handset, Atwater radioed that the guns could plaster the crash site. The Cobras dove and expended their ordnance with a vengeance.

* * *

SHARON O'MALLEY WENT SLOWLY down the file of beds rolling her cart of books before her. She stopped at each bed, offering the men the opportunity to peruse her selection. As she neared the end of the large room, she saw a man laying on his left side with his back to her. She paused. She noted there was something oddly familiar with the shape of his head and the cut and color of his hair. As she came closer, the man turned. She gasped:

"Oh, my God..."

The man lifted his head. "I was wondering...when you'd get here."

"Michael—what?...Are you all right? What happened?" In the next instant, she was at his side, looking down.

"Took some...mortar shrapnel..." he said, his voice sounding drowsy from the painkiller he had been given.

Her heart pounded madly as she came around to his other side. She sat down on the chair next to the bed. "Wh-when did this happen?"

"Yesterday...about noon...got operated on a little later...so I was told."

"Where?"

"Cai Nhum. Not far from—"

"No, I mean where were you hurt?—what part of your body?"

"My...right leg...and my butt."

He saw shock in her face and then suddenly tears.

Feebly, he reached over and touched a tear. "What's this?"

"Oh my God...I can't think. *Let me think—*" She took his hand. At least he was okay. He was alive, though she had no idea how serious his wounds were, or what complications could arise, now or later. As she sat before him, she felt a mixture of care, concern, wonderment and sympathy.

He said, "It's not that bad...I should be out of here...in a couple of weeks." As she sat there crying, she held his hand next to her face. She moved the back of his hand up and down over her cheek. He watched the look in her face transform from fear and puzzlement to a wondering glow. Her eyes became softer, her mouth, her lips took the shape of a Valentine heart. "I've been...thinking about you," he said.

"I've done a lot of thinking about you too," she replied.

"You have?...How?"

"I don't know. I've missed you."

Nolan's heart skipped a beat. "I've missed you too."

"Oh, Michael, I've been so worried about you. You can't imagine—"

He frowned. "Well, I guess where I am and what I do isn't the safest job in the world." And then she let go of his hand and reached up and placed her hands tenderly on his cheeks. "I...I think I've—"

Quickly, he interrupted her. "Helluva place...to start...a romance, don't you think?" He glanced about the hospital ward filled with sick and wounded men.

With the backside of her hand, she tried to void her face of tears. She smiled. "Good a place as any."

He took her hands and gave the tips of her fingers a light kiss. In spite of his drugged state, his body felt suddenly wonderfully alive. "You realize...we've just let the cows...out of the barn."

She began to pout. "Michael, can't you come up with something better than that."

"Sorry. I guess I've read too many L'Amour books."

And then she smiled. "Don't be sorry. I was just kidding."

"I've never been...in love before," he said. "If this is what it feels like, I like it—a lot."

Sharon O'Malley nodded. "I'm in love with you, too." She looked around and then bent forward and kissed him tenderly on the lips. "There," she said, "I guess it's sealed."

"Roped...took down...and tied."

Sharon nudged him gently on the head. "Oh, you."

Chapter 69

SANDY ADAMSON STOOD IN FRONT of the orderly room. He studied the two M-16 rifles with their bayonets attached and stuck in the ground. Two scorched flight helmets sat perched on the rifle butts. Charlie Troop had held memorial services early that morning for WO1 Jonathan Hart and SP/5 Andy Coons, the two Scout crewmen killed near Cai Nhum. Though he knew neither man personally, Sandy still felt sorrow at the troop's first combat losses.

He turned and went into the orderly room. "Top, I'd like to see Major Rameriz."

The first sergeant looked up. His eyes narrowed as he momentarily examined the young warrant officer. "What about?—Sir."

"It's uh...personal."

"Okay, sir."

Sandy stood before the troop commander. "What can I do for you, son?"

"Sir, I'd like to volunteer for Scouts."

The major nodded. "I see."

"I can do the job, sir—I know I can."

"You think so, eh?"

"Yes, sir."

Rameriz opened his desk drawer and withdrew three photos. He laid them each on the desk picture-side up, facing the young pilot. Sandy glanced down. "Pick them up. Take a good look."

Sandy reached for the first photo. "That one," Rameriz said, "is a picture of a ten-year-old boy shot in the chest, right after he threw a grenade at a jeep in a convoy." The boy lay in a heap in a pool of blood.

He looked at the second photo. Laid out in a neat row were the bodies of several Vietnamese, he presumed to be Viet Cong. "Of the eight dead you see in that picture," Rameriz said, "three are women. They were caught in sampans early in the morning, just south of the Cambodian border. Our Scouts did the killing. The sampans were loaded with weapons and ammunition. In one sampan was an adapted American fifty-caliber machine gun on a Soviet-made anti-aircraft tripod complete with Soviet AA machine-gun sight."

The third photo turned Sandy's stomach upside down. It was a picture of a man lying in a patch of reeds—minus his head. "That," the major went on, "is what the rapid fire of a minigun can do to a person at close range. He made the mistake of thinking he could out-duel Warrant Officer Hart: Chicken Man."

Sandy laid the last photo down. Now he understood why Mark couldn't speak of his conversation with Rameriz the day the CO asked for a volunteer.

Rameriz gazed hard into Sandy's eyes. "I show these pictures because I want you to know what it's going to be like out there." Then the Hispanic commander

Victor R. Beaver

breathed deep. "Son, I make no bones about it. We're in the killing business. Hunt them, find them—and kill them. Because if we don't, they'll kill us, sooner or later. I'd rather it be them than us. Do you understand?—Do you agree?"

"Yessir," Sandy said, nodding, the image of the headless man still implanted in his mind.

Rameriz continued: "I know what you've been told about me, that I am out to count bodies. This is true." Rameriz motioned for the young warrant officer to turn and look at the tally-board behind him on the wall. "I keep a count. Everyday. Right now, Charlie Troop is running about twenty percent ahead of the other troops. Son, I want to keep it that way. Those numbers make me happy for this reason: It means, at least to me, that my men will have a better chance of going home. Since the goddamn politicians have decided this to be a limited war, we have to win it at our level—to insure our own survival. And the only way I know to do that is to shoot the bastards first. For the basic combat soldier, Mr. Adamson, in any war—past, present, and future—survival is the name of the game."

From the time of his arrival, Sandy had been billeted separate from the rest of the lift section. Now, with Mark Allen's help, he made the permanent move into the Scout hootch. He found the center of the hootch, the gathering room, for some reason to be very limited on lighting. And then he saw that each window was covered to block out the sun. Two soft-glowing blacklights hung on opposite walls and provided the room's main feeble source of light. After his eyes adjusted, Sandy saw in the center of the room a table with its legs shortened and around it seven or eight beanbag pillows. On the walls hung a variety of captured memorabilia: two VC flags, a 7.62mm Soviet Model 44 Mosin Nagant bolt-action carbine, several NVA canteens, medical and ammunition pouches, and two personal letters scribbled in Vietnamese. Lying about were personal weapons, grenades, smoke canisters, ammunition, knives, and flight helmets. The whole scene reminded Sandy of a medieval dungeon or torture chamber, where the tools of his new trade were all laid out, waiting to be used. A TV, refrigerator, and two makeshift bookshelves in separate corners looked so out of place against this paraphernalia that it suddenly made him grin. And then a cold chill ran through him as he thought of Chicken Man and the way he died. *Oh my God, have I just signed my own death warrant—?*

Allen showed Sandy to Chicken Man's vacant room. It was a six-by-six cubbyhole barely big enough for a cot and a place to hang his clothes. Allen said, "Kinda eerie, moving into a dead man's room, uh?"

"Yeah." Sandy felt the gooseflesh once again prickle his skin. He dug into his duffel bag. A small wooden crate provided his only other article of furniture. He used it to arrange his OD underwear, books, letter writing materials, and toilet gear. In the process of moving the crate, he found a strange-looking object on the floor...a small metal "smoking" pipe that emitted a strong, pungent odor.

"They partake," Mark said, standing in the doorway. "It ain't bad. Takes away the edge."

"What do you mean?"

"Dope. It mellows everyone out. Better than booze."

"Does Lieutenant Scott know?"

"Roger that. He's does it too."

Later that evening, Scott took him aside and told him his training would begin the following day. "Anytime you want to quit," he said, "you can—no hard feelings and no black mark on your record. Rameriz's policy."

"Yeah, I know. Thanks."

"Get a good night's sleep. We'll be lifting at first light."

The next day the troop operated out of Chi Lang. They supported a Special Forces's A-team patrol near the base of the easternmost nodule in the Seven Mountains region. Long a Viet Cong stronghold, the mountains and surrounding landscape reminded Sandy of movie scenes shot in southern Arizona. As he flew with Lieutenant Scott, it was not hard to imagine being part of a troop of mounted cavalrymen in search of Apaches among the Dragoon Mountains. On that day, as in the historical past, Charlie Troop's hunt was unsuccessful. Victor Charlie, wherever his location around the base of the granite outcroppings, was an equally elusive foe.

* * *

THE SCREEN DOOR OPENED AND SLAMMED. "Hey, where the hell is everybody?"

"Leo—!"

Kip, seated at his typewriter, came to the door. It was early afternoon. The two slapped each other on the back. "How'd your training go?"

"It was great. What are you doing here?"

"Cooling my heels," Kip said.

"What for?"

"Briscoe and I got into it yesterday. I'd been warning him about rolling the throttle off after the cool down, sitting on the slick PSP, with his feet off the pedals. Yesterday he did it and we nearly trashed the helicopter. I was writing in the logbook, not paying any attention, when suddenly the whole fuselage rotated. I caught it just before the sync elevator hit the revetment. I cussed him out bad."

"No shit? Are you in trouble?"

"Just a little. Rameriz called me in and had me apologize to the asshole for calling him a dumbshit-prick in front of the crewchief and gunner."

Slater brought Leo up to date on the loss of Chicken Man and Coons. "What happened?"

"He was taking fire," Slater said. "And then Justen saw him dip his tailrotor into the trees. He lost control from about seventy-five feet up."

"That's too bad."

* * *

SHARON O'MALLEY MADE HER NORMAL visits to the hospital in the afternoon. Afterwards, she sat at Nolan's bedside until it was time for his bandages to be changed. She brought him more Louis L'Amour books to read, which he did later in the evening, after she left from her second visit at dinnertime. "You know," he said, "I'm going to be so savvy, you won't know what to do with me. When are you going to bring me something really serious, though, to read?"

"You mean...like a classic?"

"Na, not one of them...but something I have to think about. I'm ready for it. What do you say?"

"I'm sorry I never brought you anything more serious. I just...didn't think you'd be interested."

"Bring me something you've read that you liked. I want to know what makes you tick."

"Michael, that's really sweet of you."

"Na, not really. Look, we started pretty shaky. Then we became reasonably good friends. And now, well...now I want to get to really know you."

On the following day, Nolan was told he had to get used to walking. The first two days a member of the hospital staff helped him around the hospital grounds. Then Sharon asked to take over the rehabilitation duties. In bright sunlight, he managed two trips around the wide veranda before the stifling humidity tired him. Sharon helped him sit down. "Thank you."

"My pleasure, sir."

He fumbled for his cigarettes. She took the pack and lit one for him. "You smoke like a train," she said.

"No, I smoke like a chimney."

"What's the difference?"

"A train is moving. Right now I'm sitting still...like a house."

She laughed. "Where'd you get your sense of humor? I never thought you had one."

"Not from my father, I can tell you that."

"What's he like, your dad?"

"Old. Old before his time. He raised me alone from when I was ten."

"Do you write to him?"

"About once a month, to let him know I'm still alive and kicking. He writes back telling me he and the boat are still puttering along."

"Do you miss him?"

"Sometimes."

"Oh?"

"When he starts to tell me his 'war' stories in the merchant marines, I can't stand him. I hope when I have children I don't bore them with stuff like that."

"Children?"

"Yeah...children." He frowned. Had he really said that? Children? He looked at her. She looked away. "What's the matter?"

Tears had begun to form. "I...I never thought you'd be interested in that sort of thing. You have your dad...the boat—your plans."

"Yeah, I know. And you have your plans. The bookstore in Oregon, remember?"

"I've been thinking about that." She canted her head. Her eyes had suddenly turned colors, from light hazel to a soft yellowish green. "Really, I could have my bookstore anywhere. It doesn't have to be in Oregon."

"But I thought you liked that kind of coastline—rugged, with the waves always crashing."

"They don't have to be crashing. They can be gentle."

He listened to her and felt his love for her grow even stronger. "What about the Keys? Could you live there?"

"I could try."

"I'd be out on the boat all day."

"That's okay. I'd have my bookstore."

"What if children came along?" he asked.

"What if they did?"

Nolan looked at her. A lump formed in his throat. "Did we—"

"—just propose to each other?" Sharon finished.

"Yeah."

"I think so."

"That's what I thought," Mike said.

It was his last night at Can Tho. Nolan had escorted Sharon to the club for dinner. Unlike usual, everything seemed glittery and soft and elegant. The candles on the tables flickered in step with the music that filtered throughout the club. He was dressed in a fresh pair of jungle fatigues, she in a white print dress that exposed her shoulders and the fine swell of her breasts. He ordered wine, something he had never done. The waiter, a squat Vietnamese man dressed in white, poured the light pink liquid as if entertaining royalty. She said, "How did you do it?"

"Do what?"

"Change the whole atmosphere of the club? Normally it's so loud...so raucous."

"Raucous? That's a helluva word."

"Well...?"

"Can you believe, one night a month, the club manager, a captain I know, really tries to make this place more than a packed house of stir-crazy officers. If any of them are lucky enough to have a special woman, this is the night to bring her. We're lucky." And then his face revealed a wry smile. "I bribed my friend to let tonight be that night."

"Michael, you forever astound me."

He raised his glass. "Then let this be a toast to forever. You and me."

Their glasses clinked. "This is simply perfect," she said.

After dinner they sat and luxuriated in front of each other. They listened to the jukebox playing soft, mellow tunes by Frank Sinatra, Tony Bennett, Dean Martin. Nolan rose and offered his hand. "Would you care to dance?"

Rising, she said, "Are you sure you can?"

"Why not? The only thing that aches right now is my butt, which means I'd prefer to stand—at least right now. And I don't plan on dancing fast enough to land on *it*."

He took her in his arms and he felt his pulse quicken. He drew her close to him. He felt the firmness of her breasts pressed against his chest. The delicious scent of her hair sent a quiver through his body and he knew there was no turning back. And he knew she knew it too.

> *"Wise men say...only fools rush in*
> *But I can't help falling in love with you...*
> *Shall I stay*
> *Would it be a sin...*
> *If I can't help falling in love with you.*
> *Like a river flows, surely to the sea,*
> *darling so it goes,*
> *some things are meant to be..."*

They held hands as he guided her back to the table. He helped her be seated. As he was sitting down, Nolan reached into his pocket. "I guess this is as good a time as any," he said, handing her a small velvet jewelry case. Sharon's eyes widened as she opened the case. The diamond sparkled, it seemed, in step with the dancing candlelight that also reflected from her eyes. "Oh, Michael, it's so absolutely beautiful..."

"Well, let's try it on for size." He took the ring and reached for her hand. "Sharon, will you marry me? I promise to behave as best I can, if you'll help me. A good-size two-by-four ought to do." Then he slipped the ring on her finger.

She looked at the ring for the longest time. Her words came almost haltingly. "My heart is-is racing so fast, I-I can't believe it. I will marry you. And I do love you so. We'll do just fine." And then she said, "It fits perfect."

They were in her room. She lit a candle. He took her in his arms. She snuggled close to him, sighing. "Michael...I-I don't know how to say this, but I've never...been with a man before. I...I don't know what to do."

He looked at her and frowned. "Never...?" Shyly, she shook her head. He smiled. "We'll go slow, there's no hurry. Frankly, I'm not all that experienced myself. A couple of gals several years back..."

"I don't want to disappoint you."

"Don't worry, baby, nothing you could do...or not do would disappoint me." And then he said, "We could wait...if you like."

She closed her eyes. When she opened them, he saw that they seemed sad. "No...I don't want to wait." And then she began to unbutton his fatigue shirt. He helped to take it off. She lifted his T-shirt and smoothed her hands over his chest. He cupped her face with his hands and kissed her, a soft whispering kiss. She trembled. He let go.

She nodded for him to go to her bed. He did. "Michael, turn around, please."

"Sharon—"

"I don't want you to see me...not yet."

He did as she asked. She went into the bathroom. He went to the bed and took off his fatigue pants; he placed them over a chair. A moment later he lay between the sheets. She reappeared, a towel wrapped around her. She approached the bed holding the towel firmly to her breasts. She slipped into bed next to him. She lay on her side. The light from the candle was behind him. He propped himself on an elbow. Gently, he tried to urge the towel down from around her chest. She resisted. And then she let go. The towel fell open. He saw the loveliness of her breasts, two beautiful globes of white around a pair of dark aureoles. Then he viewed the gentle swell of her hips and the shapeliness of her legs. Finally, he focused on the soft patch of hair that formed the V between her thighs. For the longest moment he drank in the sight of her. "Am I beautiful...do you still want me?" she asked.

"More than ever."

She snuggled closer to him, her lips brushing against his neck. He began to move his right hand over her hip, down along her thigh. His hand trailed sensuously back and forth. She lifted her head and gently kissed his forehead, his nose, and then his mouth. He felt her breasts against his chest. Her breathing became labored. She lifted her leg over his and rubbed her pelvis against him. Her right hand went down and touched him. Her hand retreated. She now lay on her back. His left hand brushed the V of hair. She parted her legs slightly, invitingly. He kissed the base of her breasts. He brushed her nipples softly with his lips. She arched her back. He rose above her. They were face to face. He trailed his kisses softly over her forehead, then down along the bridge of her nose, past her lips. He paused and looked at her. Her eyes were closed and her lips were murmuring *"...I love you...I love you...I love you..."*

Afterwards, as they lay wrapped in each other's arms, he felt a shudder pass through her. "Are you cold?" he asked.

"Yes. No. I don't know. Suddenly I just felt this chill."

He covered her with the sheet. "Is that better?"

She nodded. She lay there staring at the ceiling. She felt his hand over her stomach, massaging, gently. "Michael?"

"What?"

"How much danger are you in out there?"

Her question blindsided him. For a split second he just stared at her. "Look, damnit...Sharon, baby, how do you want me to answer that?"

"Truthfully. Please, Michael...I have to know—"

"Truthfully?"

"Yes."

"I could be killed—what do you want me to say?"

"But you won't—because you'll always be careful."

"Yes...yes, baby, you know I'll be careful."

"That's all I need to know."

For a long moment there was silence. Both were afraid to speak. He felt her body trembling. He took and held her. "You're shivering...how come?"

"I don't know. I think it's because I'm so happy. Hold me, Michael—hold me close. Please, *please* don't ever leave me."

He snuggled her closer, holding her tight, rubbing his hand briskly over the small of her back. "Hey, don't worry. You'll never lose me—never."

"I want to believe you, Michael—really I do."

"Go to sleep," he said, "I'll...I'll watch over your soul."

She sighed, suddenly calm. "Sometimes you say the most beautiful things."

"I'm trying, baby, I'm really trying."

Chapter 70

JOHN SAMPSON SAT ON THE EDGE OF HIS bunk, a letter in one hand and a photo in the other. He was blubbering like a baby. Kip Slater stood in the doorway; he heard a Glen Campbell song playing, coming from John's stereo.

"By the time I get to Phoenix
she'll be risin'.
She'll find the note I left
hangin' on her door..."

LeDeux sidled next to Slater. "Like I said, Samp gets into some of the godawfulest crying spells. That's a picture of Pam, one of the stewardesses he got tangled up with."

Kip stooped low in front of the bawling ex-navy enlisted man. The tears poured down Sampson's cheeks. Slater reeled back. "Phew!—he's also drunk! Samp, what's the matter, why these alligator tears? Talk to me, pal." Sampson held a picture of a lovely, blonde-haired woman with a gorgeous figure in a bikini swimsuit.

John shoved the letter toward him. "She wrote...the sweetest letter to me...!" he wailed.

"By the time I make Oklahoma
she'll be sleepin'.
She'll turn softly
and call my name out loud..."

"They all write the sweetest letters to you," RT exclaimed, now at LeDeux's side. "For a honkie, you got more damn women chasing after your dick than any black dude I know—"

"Silence." LeDeux gave RT a curt look. "Did you get the stables cleaned? And what about mah Mint Julep?"

"Pam's from Phoenix," Sampson cried. "We were tight, real tight. She wanted to get married...but Barbara wanted to get married too. I-I didn't know which one to do...!"

"Do? Barbara? Where's she from?"

"Tulsa...!"

"Oh, Lordy," Slater mumbled. "I wish I had your problems..."

Everyday it rained, usually a cloudburst that would last for several minutes, then stop. One day everyone decided to take a shower. (Why waste the water?)

Victor R. Beaver

Kip, Cowboy, Buddy, LeDeux, and RT grabbed their soap and ran outside. The rain pelted down and avalanched off the corrugated roofs of the hootches. Then they dove into the overflowing ditches and came out looking like creatures from the Black Lagoon.

* * *

JOURNAL ENTRY, 26 SEPTEMBER 1968, Chi Lang

The Blues are preparing a 235th Cobra for extraction. Engine failure. The pilots autorotated to a spot five klicks west of here, in open rice paddy south of Hill 899, part of the Seven Mountains region. A Chinook will sling it out. Very fortunate we were in the area when it went down.

Seated on the floor of the cabin of his helicopter, Kip Slater watched as the C-123 made its approach from the west. The Chi Lang airstrip was not more than two thousand feet long. It mystified him how the Air Force could put the monster cargo airplane down on such a short runway—and a dirt strip at that. On final approach, the large two-engine plane dipped and slipped and careened toward the earth like a charging bull. Its approach angle looked like the beast was taking a nosedive for the ground. At the last second, though, Kip watched the plane's nose come up and the back wheels touch down. Reverse thrust, a tremendous roar, and the plane was taxing slowly along the ground.

At the airstrip, the Scouts were parked apart from the slicks. Sandy Adamson kneeled and began stirring his C-ration can of beans and franks perched on top the fluttering JP-4 fire. Mark Allen, leaning against the side of Scott's OH-6, watched. "So far, how do you like it?" he asked.

Sandy looked up. "What, the training? It's all right."

For the past several days the troop had been working the mountains and had found several caches of supplies and ammunition, but no Charlie. On the terrain around the base of the mountains they encountered Vietnamese peasants, usually old men and a few women who ignored them as they hovered past. None of them presented a direct threat. Sandy had practiced firing his CAR-15 rifle at trees and bushes and clumps of grass, on the move and while at a stationary hover. He had yet to fire at a human being, nor had they been shot at. He was beginning to wonder if being in the Scouts was all that it was cooked up to be.

Sandy tested a frank and decided the food was hot enough. He took a bite and then heard the Chinook approaching. He and Mark Allen watched as the heavy-lift helicopter, with the crippled Cobra extending underneath by several nylon straps, came over the airstrip and began to hover down. After another minute, the Cobra was on the ground and the straps were released and the big ship hovered off to the side and set down.

When it was shut down, Allen said, "Let's go take a look inside."

"Okay, let me tell Scott."

As they approached the CH-47, they saw somebody with freckles and red hair coming down the back ramp. "Seymore!"

"Hey, guys!"

Within seconds, the three friends were pumping handshakes and hugging and slapping each other on the back. "Was that you bringing in that Cobra? I can't believe it."

"Don't get too thrilled. I'm just a peter-pilot. It'll probably take my whole tour to make AC. That thing is one complex aircraft. Tandem rotors, two engines, a combining gearbox."

"I'd hate to fly that beast," Mark said. "It looks like a damn mid-air collision all by itself." To fly, the massive front and back blades had to mesh at just the right moment, much like an electric or hand-crank food mixer. Mark shivered at the engineering complexity involved.

"Boy, ain't that the truth," Seymore said. "If that combining gearbox goes out and those blades get out of sync, they tell me the best thing to do is sit on the cyclic."

"How come?"

"So it'll be up my ass when they find me in the crash!"

"You at Can Tho?"

"Yep, got there a week ago. How's the cav?"

"Great," Mark said. "Me and Sandy got ourselves in the Scouts."

"No shit—?"

"Roger that."

"How's Jenny?" Sandy asked.

"Oh crap. I forgot to tell you. She's gonna have a baby—!"

"Goddamn—you're kidding. Just think—*another Seymore!*"

"It's gonna be a girl—!"

* * *

"CLEAN YOUR GEAR, CLEAN YOUR weapon, clean your ammo, practice this, practice that. Fuck! What's it all for? So we can look *strac* for Charlie? Bullshit—"

"Can it, Vinny—" Patterson said.

"You can it, Sarge. Out in the AO all we do is sit around, we wait, maybe we lift, maybe we don't. I'm going nuts."

"And don't forget, before chow we get to take the PT test."

"Oh, Jesus...a PT test. Here? In Vietnam—?"

"Once a year. And tomorrow we get to re-qualify with our M-16s."

"Yeah, right, I can dig that. 'Cause we never fire'em. We have to re-qualify—!"

The men sat in a large cluster outside the hootch, on the ground, cleaning and checking their equipment, a regimen Nolan insisted they perform once a week. In the beginning, everyone took heartily to Nolan's structure of leadership. They thought it would kill the boredom; they thought it might even get them out in the field more often where time had a way of passing quickly.

"Have any of you noticed ever since Blue got back from the hospital he's been out of it...like on some kind of cloud nine?" said Childs, the medic.

"Yeah, I noticed," Fields said.

"You'd think he met a broad," Vinny piped in.

"Here?—in Vietnam? What broad? A slope?" Brave Water said.

"Fuck no. A round-eyed woman. They got'em here, you dickhead," Chico stated.

"I've never seen one," Brave Water said.

"What about the nurses and them donut dollies?" Hoyt said.

"Them?"

"Yeah, them."

"Oh, yeah, I forgot," the Navajo said.

"But they're always scooped up by the docs and the pilots," Fields remarked. "None of us can touch one—"

"Who wants to touch'em?" Vinny said. "Me, I just want to bounce on their bones!"

"Hey, show some respect."

"Mind your own damn business, Hoyt. A guy's entitled to his own admonitions."

"What's ammonition?" Big George asked. "Is it like bullets?"

"No. Ad-monition. It comes from the word-book I've been studying," Vinny said. "It means declaration, assertion."

Patterson, an English major in college, said, "Admonition doesn't mean that."

"Well, what the fuck does it mean?"

"It means caution, warning...Jesus, do you study with your eyes *crossed—?*"

Just then, Atwater appeared. Chico said, "Hey, Sarge, when's Espinoza getting back?" It had been three weeks since Chicken Man went down. Espinoza had suffered a wound around his right eye during the explosion that had also wounded Nolan. He had been sent to Japan when it appeared the wound was worse than originally thought.

"He's not."

"How come?"

"He's going home. He lost his eye."

"What—?" Child's cried. "It wasn't that bad—I swear it."

"It must have been worse than you thought. Sorry."
"I...I did the best I could..." he proclaimed.
"Hey," Vinny said, "you ain't God."
"Damn, the wound wasn't that bad..."

Captain Merryman, the troop executive officer, dressed neatly in pressed fatigues and wearing his black Stetson cavalry hat, called the men to attention. He turned: "Sir, all present or accounted for, sir."

"Stand at—EASE," Major Rameriz called.

Kip Slater and Leo Tannah in formation along with the rest of the troop placed their feet apart and pressed their hands firmly against the small of their backs. Rameriz said, "Mr. Keith Slater and Mr. Leo Tannah, step forward." The two pilots came to attention and marched to the front of the troop. The troop commander spoke:

"Let it be known by all men present that the following individuals have been promoted to the reserve warrant officer rank of chief warrant officer W2. Warrant Officer W1 Keith Perry Slater and Warrant Officer W1 Leo Martin Tannah." Rameriz pinned a set of metal W2 bars over the cloth W1 bars on Kip's collar. Kip saluted. Rameriz extended his hand. "Congratulations, Mr. Slater."

"Thank you, sir."

Rameriz did the same for Leo. "Congratulations, Mr. Tannah."

"Yes, sir."

Rameriz said, "We have a tradition in this troop when someone is promoted." The major turned. He motioned forward the enlisted man standing off to the side holding two tall glasses filled with a dark brown liquid. Rameriz took the two glasses. He handed Slater and Tannah each a glass. "You must drink this without stopping."

The two new chief warrant officers put the glasses to their noses. *Booze!* But it smelled almost sweet. They tasted it. *Brandy!* They looked at each other and grinned.

"Bottoms up, boys!"

When they were done, their heads were reeling. The major said, "Okay, there's beer, music, and plenty of chow in the barbecue area. Let the festivities begin!"

Victor R. Beaver

Chapter 71

IT WAS AFTER THE EVENING MESS. Sandy sat on his cot writing a letter home. He pondered what to say, what not to say. It was difficult. There was so much he wanted his parents to know, but he dare not tell all.

> Dear Mom and Dad,
> How are you? I am fine. As I mentioned in my last letter, I've met some really great guys. Of course, Mark is here and we keep each other company. It's nice to be with an ex-flight-school classmate. He keeps me up when I'm feeling blue.
> Major Rameriz, our commanding officer, is one cool guy. I found out the other day he was born in Old Mexico. He came to the United States to find work and eventually joined the Army. Everyone really likes and respects him. A while back he got into it with a full bird colonel who wanted to use the troop to do something stupid, so I was told. Rameriz told him to go fly a kite. I guess he doesn't take any junk off anyone. That's really good for us.
> One of our scouts went down in heavy trees about three weeks ago. Both the pilot and gunner were killed. They were the first deaths in the troop. It really bummed everyone out. Rameriz needed a volunteer so that's what I did. I'm now a scout pilot, or at least training to be one. Now before you get real worried, it isn't that dangerous, especially here in the Mekong Delta. Besides, Major Rameriz is real cautious and he tries real hard not to let us get into anything we can't handle. The gunships fly directly overhead. The Viet Cong won't try anything with those guys ready to blast them to Kingdom Come. I should be finished with my training in a week. I've met my gunner and he's an OK guy. They call him Roach. I can't figure out why. The other gunners are Wolfman, Smiley, and Grumpy...

Sandy sniffed at the air. He smelled the same strange odor coming from the central gathering room as he had on the two previous evenings, the odor of burning hay. Lieutenant McCloud, another pilot in Scott's scout section, had his tape player on. Sandy recognized a Doors' album coming over the speakers. He decided tonight to investigate.

Sandy gazed down at the men on the floor on beanbag pillows around the short-legged table. Scott looked up and smiled. He gestured for his new pilot to grab a pillow and join in. "Take a load off," he said. The section leader then took the pipe Mark Allen had handed him and put it to his lips. Scott took a long, deep drag. He kept the smoke in for several seconds and then slowly let the smoke out. He then handed the pipe to Roach seated next to him. Watching, Sandy said, "Sure, what the hell…why not."

The Sky Soldiers

> *"You know that it would be untrue,*
> *you know that I would be a liar...*
> *If I was to say to you,*
> *Girl we couldn't get much higher—*
> *Come on, baby, light my fire..."*

The scene reminded Sandy of a movie from his childhood. The setting, he recalled, was in Damascus or Baghdad or somewhere similar. Everyone before him appeared drowsy, mellow. Mark nodded toward him as he sat down. Mark's face had a knowing grin, a grin that said that all was right with the world. As the music played, Mark swayed back and forth, his head tilting and rolling. When the pipe came to Sandy, he took it, looked at it, and passed it on. Roach said, "Come on, sir. You need this. It's okay. Everyone is cool."

"I-I don't know if I should."

"Don't goad him," Lieutenant McCloud said. McCloud took a sip of wine and offered Sandy his glass. "Here, try this. It'll make you mellow too."

"Thanks." Sandy took a drink and handed the glass back. He got up and found an unused mug. He returned and poured from the gallon jug on the floor next to McCloud. After several minutes of sipping, he saw Grumpy light a rolled cigarette that had been among the clutter of smoking paraphernalia that was spread across the table. The gunner took a drag and then reached across and offered the cigarette to the young warrant officer. Sandy took the smoldering joint and put it gingerly to his lips. He took a short drag and coughed the smoke out immediately.

"Take it in real slow and gentle," Roach said. Scott nodded and then closed his eyes. Sandy got an immediate impression that everyone was in the middle of a tropical lagoon, floating on beach rafts in calm water. There was blue sky overhead and just enough of a breeze to rustle the trees. After several more tries with the burning cigarette, Sandy began to feel his body take on a lumbering heaviness. Slowly, gradually, his body descended, as if it were collapsing in on itself. He looked at Allen and gazed at Mark's ID tags dangling from his neck. A beaded chain, like little BBs strung together, little silver pearls...dogtags...around a man's neck. He frowned. Then smiled. *We wear dogtags... Are we dogs?...Dogs flying helicopters?...Cool...Cool.* He lifted his own set of ID tags and peered at them. Name: *Adamson, Edward S.* Serial number: *W3157487.* Religious preference: *Lutheran.* Blood type: *A+.* Tags. Tag. Hide and seek. *I play hide and seek with Charlie. One...Two...Three...ready or not, here I come...*

> *"Riders on the storm,*
> *riders on the storm...*

Victor R. Beaver

> *Into this house we're born...*
> *into this world we're thrown*
> *Like a dog without a bone,*
> *an actor out on loan...*
> *Riders on the storm..."*

Sandy shook his head. He breathed deep and exhaled. He peered at his watch. It seemed as if he had been sitting there for ages, but only a few minutes had passed since he entered the room. He glanced at Mark and then at Roach and then at the others. *Oh fuck...these are my comrades...my brothers in arms. We share the same dangers...Wow!...that's really heavy, man...heavy...heavy... heavy...*

He began to think. Bells went off in his head. He looked back. Into his past, which was ancient history now. Another place, another time. Who was he now? He thought about Katie and the day he asked her to go to Homecoming with him. Where was his mind then? It wasn't on joining the army—or flying a helicopter—or being in Vietnam. When did all that occur? Why did he do it? It was the *National Geographic.* They had run an article depicting members of the United States Special Forces caught between revolting montagnards (mountain people) and the South Vietnamese government. It was an old *National Geographic* issue. The dedication and professionalism of the U.S. Army Green Berets had impressed him.

He stood. Swaying slightly, he went to his room. He saw the unfinished letter on his cot. He reread it and thought how silly it sounded, how simple. There was truth in it and yet there was so much truth missing. *If Mom and Dad could see me now, they would blow a gasket. They would really blow a gasket—*

* * *

THEY HAD BEEN ON THE MOVE FOR an hour, flying along the base of Hill 899. Sandy guided the ship cautiously forward. His eyes scanned quickly between the instrument panel and the vegetation below. He was getting more and more used to hovering directly above the treetops, his eyes looking everywhere at once. He still had mild attacks of panic whenever he detected potential signs of Charlie: a footpath out of nowhere, a deserted, very well camouflaged hootch, an indent in the rocks that could hide a squad of Viet Cong. But his growing confidence had now made these feelings short-lived.

The troop had been operating in the Seven Mountains region for a little over two weeks now. Though he and Scott had yet to come face to face with an enemy soldier, Sandy knew that hidden deep within scores of caves were caches of food, medical supplies, ammunition, and weapons, enough to support most of the upper region of the Mekong Delta.

Lieutenant Scott, seated in the left seat, gripped the short-barreled CAR-15 rifle. Sandy was now spending his final days of training at the controls of the OH-6, dividing his attention between flying and observing. Scott told him to come left. "Let's get away from these trees."

Sandy brought the ship left, his gaze now on open ground about three hundred meters across. In the middle of the field was a cluster of rocks, some of them boulder-size. Sandy spoke to their wingman: "One Nine, this is One Five Alpha, check that outcropping to my two o'clock."

"Roger that," Mark Allen radioed back, angling his Loach toward the rocks. The mid-afternoon sun glanced through a cloud-filled sky. There was more shadow than spots of sunlight. The wind kicked up in furtive bursts of quickly spent energy. And then the cloud directly above them spilled gushes of water.

The two helicopters slowed their forward motion. Sandy looked right, through the open cockpit doorway. The four-foot-high, eight- or nine-rock outcropping of granite was now less than seventy meters away. Continuing to regard it with suspicion, Sandy hovered toward the rock cluster as if it were a safe harbor to drop anchor. "Whenever you least expect to find Charlie, that's when you will," Scott had told him time and again. "And they're always exactly where you expect them to be—and then some." As a precaution, Sandy checked to make sure the minigun was still armed.

Suddenly, the downpour ceased, replaced now by a steady drizzle. Sandy continued toward the outcropping of rocks. He saw movement. A face popped up and then quickly disappeared. "One Five Alpha has something in the rocks!"

Rameriz and the Cobras, to avoid the rain shower, had maneuvered slightly to the east. They were now at their three o'clock position. "Roger. We have you in sight," Rameriz's steady voice answered back.

Scott told Sandy to swing wide right. Sandy obeyed. Scott said, "Be ready to fire."

The words coursed through the young warrant officer like a thunderclap. His shackles rose and his heart rate quickened. He brought the ship closer. Suddenly, the face, and now the body, dressed in black, burst into flight. Sandy gave chase. "One Nine, One Five Alpha, cover the rocks," Sandy called.

"Roger that—"

The running figure had stumbled and was now scrambling on all fours. Sandy sensed desperation beyond mere survival in the figure's movement. A dark face looked back, the eyes crazed with fear. But more, they seemed to declare, *Chase me! Chase me!* "Could this be a trap?" Sandy asked.

"If it is, it won't be for long—" Scott declared.

Sandy maneuvered the Loach to within twenty meters of the fleeing figure, now beginning to tire. It fell, stared back, her body half slumped on the ground. "It's a woman!" Sandy cried.

Victor R. Beaver

During the scramble, the woman's hair, apparently tied back, had unraveled. "She's got something clutched to her stomach," Sandy said.

"Roger that. *Blast her.*"

Sandy brought the Loach to a steady hover. He aimed the ship and the minigun directly at the woman, his finger poised to squeeze the trigger. Hesitating, he gazed at the woman's face. Instead of panic or fear, he sensed brazen determination: *Shoot me. Kill me. Do it. Do It!* Sandy glanced left. Scott raised his rifle and fired. The rounds hit the ground to the woman's left.

"What are you doing—?"

"I told you to blast her!"

The woman got up and began scrambling again. Meantime, One Nine maneuvered around the rocks. He saw something hidden in one of the crevices, a dark bundle. "She left something behind," Mark radioed. "Whatever it is, it's wrapped and squirming."

"Roger that," Rameriz replied.

As Sandy resumed the chase, the woman turned and raised her hand. "She's got a grenade. Shoot her!" Scott ordered, trying desperately to get his young protégé to commit to the ultimate act in combat.

For one brief instant, the words "shoot her" slammed into Sandy's chest like a sledgehammer. He pressed the trigger. The minigun barrels rotated and fired. The rounds kicked innocuously to the left and front of her feet. "Goddamnit! You've got to aim better than that!" Scott cried. Time stood still. Sandy focused his eyes on the dark object the woman clutched over her head, poised to let fly. It was jagged and much too large for her tiny fist. "It's a rock!" he cried.

"Waste her, goddamnit!"

"She's holding a rock—"

"Hot *damn!* You're right!"

Sandy, his heart nearly in his throat, backed the helicopter off.

Rameriz, in the C&C Huey, made his approach to the south side of the granite outcropping. As the ship touched down, Hoyt and Brave Water jumped out. With rifles at the ready, they went to the woman. She had surrendered and had been driven back to the rocks. They frisked her and checked the dark bundle she held in her arms and escorted her and the squirming bundle to the aircraft. As they helped her board, the bundle let out a loud wail. The two Blues peaked inside the bundle. Peering at them were a pair of dark wide little eyes. As they helped the woman be seated and buckled in, she opened her blouse and put the baby's mouth to a breast. Contented, she gave the two riflemen a weak smile and began to rock back and forth on the seat.

* * *

SERGEANT ATWATER RUSHED UP TO HIM. "Sir, we've got us a situation—"

"What is it?" Nolan asked. A moment before he had heard a single rifle shot. Thinking it came from the perimeter, fired by a trigger-happy guard, he dismissed it.

"Cunningham just shot himself in the foot—!"

"What—?"

"Yessir. Childs is right now bandaging him up. It looks bad. We need to get him to Dong Tam."

"Self-inflicted?"

"I think so, sir."

"*Crap*—Okay, I'll have Lieutenant Briscoe get a Huey ready."

Kip Slater grabbed his flight helmet. John Sampson followed close behind. "What's up?"

"One of the Blues blew his foot off," Kip said.

"On purpose?"

"That's the word."

"What for?"

"To go home early—Christ, how the hell would I know?"

Kip did a quick turn around the ship. Sampson got in the left cockpit side and strapped in. As Kip opened his door, he saw a crowd of soldiers approach. They were carrying a man on a stretcher with his right foot heavily bandaged. Childs walked hurriedly alongside. Nolan and Atwater accompanied the throng. Nolan went to the ship's right side. "Do you mind if I get some stick-time?" he asked Slater.

"No, sir, not at all."

"I may be a little rusty, but I'm sure you can handle whatever shenanigans I try to pull."

"No problem, sir."

As Cunningham was being placed aboard, Sampson unstrapped and Mike Nolan climbed into the left seat. They were airborne in two minutes.

"You still got the touch, sir," Slater told his blue platoon leader.

"Thanks. It's been awhile. This is the first time since tactics at Rucker that I've flown in the left seat. I remember my stick buddy and I deciding to take a detour down along the coast. We were way out of the AO."

Slater chuckled. "So, you did that too, huh, sir?"

"Damn, that sand was so white and the water so clean and blue. Panama City Beach wouldn't be a bad place to honeymoon, either."

"I heard you were getting married, sir."

"Roger that. Sharon and I are going to Australia for Christmas. We're going to the Great Barrier Reef. Tie the knot at a resort there."

"That's great, sir. Good luck to you."

Victor R. Beaver

"Thanks."

Mike put the envelope to his nose and smiled. It had her scent. He went to his room and opened it.

My dearest Michael,

It was good to get your letter. I'm so sorry to hear that one of your men decided to do such a dreadful thing. He must have been pretty desperate. I know you wish you could have seen it coming, but unfortunately you can't foresee everything. Some things are not meant to be known, thank goodness. How horrible life would be if we knew ahead of time all the bad that was to happen to us or to those around us.

I talked to Frieda yesterday and she sees no reason why I can't take that week off at Christmas. Australia is going to be simply wonderful. What a great place to be married and have a honeymoon.

How coincidental, too, that my contract will expire in January, as your tour is completed. We couldn't have planned things better had we tried.

Well, keep a brave heart, my dearest. I look forward to your next visit, whenever that will be. I'm always waiting on pins and needles to see you. Oh, I almost forgot, how did you like "To Kill A Mockingbird," or have you read it yet?

Yours Forever,
Sharon

Nolan set the letter aside. He glance at the calendar on the wall above his bed. He reached up and marked off today's date. It was October 10. He had just dropped into the double digits. Ninety-nine days to go. He felt wonderfully, marvelously at peace.

Chapter 72

JAKE COLE'S EYES FLUTTERED OPEN. He squinted for a moment through the bamboo bars of his cage, at the shafts of sunlight splicing through the trees. He sat up.

Another dawn.

He had just spent his second night in a row fighting the swarms of mosquitoes in frenzied gyrations, hallucinating and lapsing in and out of consciousness till the morning hours. Two days ago, as punishment for refusing to state in writing repentance for America's involvement in the war, the guards had taken his mosquito net and clothes, under the guise that they intended to wash his clothes and replace the net with a new one.

He felt his body covered with welts, his eyes mere slits in a swollen face. He reached down and adjusted the ring of iron around his thin raw ankles.

Chimp appeared and stooped to unlock his cage. The guard reeled at the foul smell surrounding the prisoner. Several times during the night Jake's diarrhea had forced him to evacuate his bowels without the benefit of his nuc muom pot to go in; the guards had surreptitiously confiscated that too.

Chimp, waving his hand in front of his face, took the key he kept on a chain around his neck, reached down and unlocked the leg irons. "How feel dis morning, Co?"

"Fine, you two-bit jerk," Jake Cole replied. "Number one—"

Chimp nodded, grinned. "Numba one? You look numba ten."

The guard ambled away. Jake emerged from his cage. He went gingerly along the log walkway to the edge of the small wooden platform that hung over the canal. As he stood relieving himself, he contemplated the condition of his cage, the filth, the smell, symbolizing the abject misery of his existence—his pathetic existence.

Jake was back in his cage. He examined his body. The infection on his legs and arms itched unbearably. He wore only a pair of ragged brown shorts, so filthy and worn that they seemed to rip at the slightest touch. Exhausted, he lay back, making a feeble attempt to avoid his own excrement; he slumbered. An hour later he woke feeling weaker, more miserable than before.

Chimp appeared again. "Why you no cook you rice? You no hungry?"

"I'll eat when I feel like it."

He sat up. He had to wash, to clean himself of the filth on his skin. He took his pail and the small bar of soap he hoarded. He went to the edge of the water a few paces upstream from where he had gone to the toilet and, leaving his pail on the bank, plunged in, splashing the water over his skin. He took the soap and made a feeble amount of lather with which to wash. The lye stung the welts and the infected sores on his skin. It took every ounce of effort not to scream.

Victor R. Beaver

When he was through, he filled the pail with water and walked past the long meeting hut where he saw inside the other guards seated and chatting at the long table upon which they took their meals. He saw Major Hung, the camp commander, seated at his own table, watching him. "Fuck you," he mumbled, "and all your relatives—" Hung, hearing the greeting, nodded and smiled.

Jake barely had the energy to clean the inside of his cage. When he was through, it was time to check his fishnets. He was glad it wasn't raining, which meant fewer mosquitoes to contend with.

He walked along the path to the south of the camp where his nets were located. Though his every move was (probably) observed, it still mystified him the relative freedom he was given to do the simple chores necessary to maintain his own survival. He checked his first string: bare. The second and third series of strings and nets offered several small fish. As he gathered these into his pail, he looked downstream and wondered how simple it would be to duck under water and swim away. The thought had crossed his mind hundreds of times. But where would he go? He had no idea where he was. How would he stay hidden? If he was recaptured, how would he be treated? Suddenly, his wife's image came to his mind. She appeared so clear, so real, that he wanted to cry. How was she doing? How were Robbie and Jill? Were they okay? Or had something bad happened that he dreaded ever to know? And where was his brother? Was Derek in Vietnam? Jake felt his condition so hopeless that he no longer knew where he fit in the world. His every waking moment was so focused on his personal survival that there was no room for even the luxury of memories. He knew nothing of the outside world, except what he was told. And he knew that what he was told were mostly lies, insults to his intelligence. His discussions with Major Hung bordered on the inane, the ludicrous. He was told that during the "Tet Populous Uprising," the United States had lost eighty thousand men, that nearly thirty combat battalions had been wiped out. He was told the American people were finally fed up with the butchering and the bombing done by its forces to a peace-loving nation. He was informed that American artillery and the "indiscriminate" bombing of North Vietnam had killed more civilians than were lost during all the allied bombing raids over Germany—all a mass of intricate (yet obvious) contradictions. Without another American in the camp to compare his will to resist, Jake knew his defense against the National Liberation Front's psychological onslaught was fast eroding. How much longer could he hold out? How often had he been told that the Front's lenient policy toward repenting prisoners was the key to his release, these faint glimmerings of repatriation only to be dashed by Major Hung's insistence that he write and sign a paper he felt in his heart were lies?...

"Your country will not punish you," Major Hung had told him. "The American people will not permit your military to react to your honest attempt to repent of your sins and the sins of your military against the Vietnamese people. They are only too aware of its government's corrupt policies!"

"Go to hell. I'm not signing shit—" he would cry.

But he would go back to his cage and wonder, What *was* the sense of his resistance? Where was it getting him? If what Major Hung had said about America's resistance to the war was true, why should he die in this mosquito-infested swamp for a cause his country no longer believed in?

As he continued to peer downstream, his vision of Valerie now gone, he thought, Why escape? *They would find me and drag me back and I would have to put up with twice the mental anguish and physical pain I now endure, as punishment. I'll never get out alive—NEVER.* As these thoughts washed over him, his memory of last night came to him so vividly that his body automatically recoiled. He could see the clouds of mosquitoes swarming over him, actually "feel" their stingers penetrate his skin. Writhing uncontrollably, Jake Cole fell back against the mud embankment upon which he stood and cried:

"I can't do this. I can't take one more second of this existence—I won't!"

* * *

JUSTEN SHIFTED UNEASILY IN HIS SEAT. The footpath they were following trailed into low-lying trees near a shear rock wall halfway up the mountainside. Several clusters of dense vegetation guarded the base of the wall, while next to it stood an abandoned thatched hut. Yesterday, his gunner, Rick Kalbach, had caught sight of the hut from about a kilometer away. It was then that Rameriz ordered the Scouts to abandon their hunt and return immediately to Chi Lang.

"But Six, I think we're onto something here," Justen had said.

"I repeat, break it off. Do as I say—" Rameriz radioed back.

When he and Kalbach returned to the airstrip, and had parked and shut down, Derek watched as Major Rameriz confronted the American lieutenant colonel in charge of the small operation in which they had been requested to participate. Derek motioned for Kalbach to get out of earshot and join the Blues seated off to the side of the airstrip near the lift ships.

"Sir, this is bullshit," Derek heard Rameriz say. "There's no way I can protect my Scouts if we make the approach that way."

The American light colonel, a senior advisor with the 9th ARVN Division, drew to his full five-foot-seven-inch height. "Major, I'm not asking, I'm telling. We've got to come in that way to keep the ARVN from being ambushed. All I want your scout ships to do is recon by fire. If they take shots, I want them to move out of the way—"

"If they take fire, goddamnit, how's that any different than the ARVN getting ambushed? Do you know how hard it is to replace one of those ships? Not to mention the cost to replace a pilot and gunner—"

Victor R. Beaver

"Major, these troops aren't any more expendable. But yours have mobility. If I get them mired down up there, you'll pay more hell helping to move them off that damn mountain!"

Rameriz drew back. "That's for damn sure, colonel. We go up there, get bogged down, lose a lot of men, and those little VC pricks are money ahead by our losses—at barely a dime's worth of cost to them!"

The colonel puffed out his chest. "I want you to come up with a solution, Major—ASAP."

Rameriz gritted his teeth. "Yes, sir."

He gathered his pilots. "I want everyone in on this. I want input," Rameriz said, kneeling in front of them. "We've been screwing around this mountain for three weeks now. We've been sniped at but Charlie is buried so deep, the Cobras can't hit back. It's a good idea to get these ARVN shits finally involved here, especially in force, but you know as well as I do that when the first shot is fired, they're not going to move one inch and they're going to cry like hell to get out of there."

"What about the Blues, sir?" said Leo Tannah. "Couldn't we insert them around one of those high points, and then they could infiltrate down, reconnoiter from above?"

Rameriz peered at Tannah for a moment, then turned his gaze toward Nolan. "I don't like it. Too risky, especially when Charlie can see every move we make. Besides, wherever the Blues maneuver, if *they* get stuck, how will we get *them* out?"

Nolan said, "We could go in at night, sir. We could stay put above them and use flares and the Starlight scopes to pick them out and mark their position. If we don't see anything during the night, we might be able to see their cooking fires early in the morning. At least then the ARVN would know where to concentrate their assaults."

Rameriz listened, nodding his head. "That might work. But damnit, these mountains are one big bunker complex." Rameriz was silent. He said, "Okay, but first we need to know exactly were to put you. We also need to know where to pick you up should anyone need to be medevaced."

Justen raised his hand. "Sir, Kalbach and I spotted a pretty good location. It looked big enough for at least three ships. It's right next to an abandoned hootch. In fact, it wouldn't be a bad place to secure just for that reason alone. And let the ARVN secure it. They could sit there till doomsday."

Rameriz presented the plan to the colonel. "I want that damn location scouted first," the little colonel said.

"I'll have my ships out at first light."

"And by the way, Major, I'll not tolerate another outburst of insubordination. I've heard about you. You're getting quite a reputation. Your colonel is going to hear about this."

"Sir, you can do whatever you feel your rank entitles you to. On the other hand, as troop commander, it's my responsibility to watch out for my men. And I'll do *that* however *I* see fit—"

With the hut now plainly in sight, Justen keyed his mic: "Six, this is One Eight, we're at the LZ. The ground is uneven and smaller than it looked yesterday. There are several large boulders in the area. They could give us tailrotor problems. Suggest we reconsider."

"Roger that," Rameriz replied. "I see a possible alternative about three hundred meters farther south. Suggest a one nine zero heading to start. You and One Seven will be going over the next ridgeline. Keep your speed up."

"Roger that."

Sandy Adamson, callsign Sandpiper One Seven, alone with Roach, his gunner, picked up his speed. They followed Justen and Kalbach away from the rock wall. There had been VC signs, new signs, fresh tracks, maybe a day old. As they skirted away from the area, Sandy spied several prime ambush sites above the trail. He wondered how close they had just come to having the hell knocked out of them.

"Pretty spooky shit, uh, sir?" said Roach.

"Roger that."

Roach held firmly to his M-60. Both pilot and gunner had become close friends ever since Sandy was let loose on his own. Whenever they spent the night at Vinh Long, about four nights a week now, McCloud, Scott, Roach, Wolfman, Grumpy, Smiley, Allen and Sandy would break out the bowls and the rolled cigarettes. Though he had felt a special kinship toward his classmates in flight school, Sandy felt a much closer camaraderie with the pilots and gunners in Scott's scout section. The reel-to-reel would play, the flames from the candles they lit would waver and dance in sync with the music, everyone would listen to the light and feel the sounds, and they would explore the depths of their minds, their souls, as if they had come upon some fabulous treasure.

As the two LOHs crossed the ridge, Justen saw the alternate LZ Rameriz was directing them to. It was an oval-shaped open space fifty meters long by twenty meters wide, three hundred feet from the top of the mountain. Bordered by low foliage on the west and south, it dropped steeply to the east. A footpath went through the foliage before disappearing near a cluster of rocks.

The LZ had a dangerous fifteen-degree slope to it. Even the most experienced lift pilot would find it difficult to negotiate. Justen considered negating it as a possible landing site when Rameriz came on the radio. "One Eight, how does that south side look?"

"Give me a second, Six."

Justen guided his aircraft along the downslope side. Sandy, close behind, kept his eyes darting back and forth between the trees to the west and Derek's ship. He remained on the high side of the slope. "One Seven, One Eight...cover the upslope side of the trees," Derek said.

"I'm doing just that," Sandy answered.

A ten-knot wind swept up the mountainside. The moving air tumbled over a pair of downslope boulders, causing the two egg-shaped helicopters to buffet and bob like corks in a pan of agitated water. Sandy found himself struggling to maintain tailrotor control. The needle on the TOT (turbine outlet temperature) gauge hovered right below the red line.

The treeline opened up with AK-47 fire. Sandy watched as Derek broke left and veered downslope. "Taking fire!"

Sandy looked up and saw flashes at a higher part of the rock cliffs, just above the proposed LZ. "The fire is coming from above the LZ, southwest side," he called over the radio.

Quicker then he could count to five, the rocks above the LZ exploded. Fist-size chunks of rock showered down on the two helicopters. The trees to Sandy's front opened up. Roach fired his M-60. Spent shell casings pinged and ricocheted off the right side of the helicopter. Following Derek's lead, Sandy peeled left and cried: "The trees! The trees!"

Leo Tannah, in the front seat of the second Cobra, looked through the TSU (telescopic sighting unit). He held the reticule on the target, steadied himself, and then fired. A stream of tracers sped forward, saturating the treeline. The rounds glanced off nearby rock sending jagged pieces of lead flying off at odd angles. One ricocheting round split a grove across the Plexiglas windshield of Sandy's aircraft. It careened across the top portion of the instrument panel and exited out the left side of the ship.

Derek aimed his ship toward a cluster of boulders downslope from the LZ. Sandy, the front of his windshield a splintered, hazed surface, followed close behind. Derek then banked his ship left and took a position two hundred meters east of the ambush site. "One Seven, One Eight, are you doing all right?"

"Roger that," Sandy answered quickly. "My windshield's a mess. Otherwise we're okay."

Rameriz came over the radio. "Okay you two low birds, get the hell out of there," he ordered. And then he told the Cobras to saturate the area with rockets and 40mm.

As Derek and Sandy flew eastward and gained altitude, the guns dove and fired until both ships announced thirty-percent ordnance remaining. Meantime, the standby Red "gun" team, which had been told to launch several minutes before, was just now coming into view.

After the second pair of Cobras had blasted the area, Rameriz ordered his men back to Chi Lang.

"That mountain is a hotbed, Colonel," Rameriz told the senior MACV advisor. "It's suicidal to try to do anything more up there. It'll take more than your measly two companies of ARVN to even get a foothold. And I'm sure as hell not going to risk my troop playing games on a chunk of rock you're going to abandon when the day is through. It's not worth it—"

"Is that your final say, Major?"

"Yes, sir."

Chapter 73

"DAMNIT, SAL, WHAT THE HELL is going on—?" blasted Lieutenant Colonel Meador, the squadron commander. "This is the third time I've been called on the carpet because you can't work with some outside element." The colonel, taller than Rameriz by several inches, leaned forward on his desk. He had wavy, salt-and-pepper hair, combed neatly back. The squadron CO usually presented a fatherly demeanor to his troop commanders but right now his ears were perked back and red.

"Sir, with all due respect," Rameriz defended, "that MACV light colonel had no more idea what to do with us than the man in the moon. We're not a lift company, we're recon. If the ARVN want to charge into those outcroppings in force, more power to them. But do it with the One Fourteenth or the One Seventy-fifth. Charlie is so well hidden in those mountains, it will take six months to find a quarter of the caves they occupy and then forever to clean them out. At a loss—I might add—that can't even be fathomed."

"That may be true, but you can't just up and bring your troop back here without getting a release."

"Sir, I'm not going to risk the lives of my men in those mountains for you, or MACV, or any other damn advisor colonel. To accomplish what? *Nothing!* I still can't believe you pulled us out of Moc Hoa. At least when we worked the Plain of Reeds we had Charlie on the run. Working those damn mountains, we're just pissing in the wind—"

The colonel peered hard at his troop commander. "You and I both know why I got you out of Moc Hoa. One more incident with Colonel Bell and he'd have had your ass. That last was the clincher—!"

"Sir, I explained that Cambode mercenary thing. We caught those two little shits red-handed—in cahoots with Charlie!"

"Yes, but there are better ways to handle it. You shouldn't have brought them back hog-tied, parading past the other mercenaries. That really pissed him off."

"He should have been thankful I didn't have them shot and their bodies dumped at his feet!"

"Jesus Christ. Sit down, Sal—sit down. This isn't getting us anywhere."

"Yes, sir."

"Listen, as of this moment, I'm pulling you out of the Seven Mountains region. I'm giving Faraday's Bravo Troop that AO now."

"Good luck to him," Rameriz responded. "Believe me, he's going to need it..."

"And I'm assigning your troop the Mo Cay AO."

At the location name, Rameriz slumped in his seat. His men had operated around Mo Cay several months back and found the civilian population so intermingled with the Viet Cong there was no way to distinguish between the two. At least in the Plain of Reeds, normally uninhabited by anybody but the VC, usually floating supplies and ammunition south into the Delta on sampans, the war was cut and dry. Trying to penetrate the Seven Mountains and find Charlie, Rameriz soon discovered, though the stronghold was saturated with their presence, was no easier to do than one or two mosquitoes trying to get at its next victim through a screened-in porch. Mo Cay, on the other hand, was a horse of an altogether different color. The Viet Cong could use women and children to hide behind and there wouldn't be a thing they could do.

"The mission is search and detain," Lieutenant Colonel Meador stated, as an afterthought.

"What—?"

"With the Riverine Brigade of the American Ninth Infantry."

"Oh, God..."

"Can I depend on you, Sal?"

"Sir...?"

"Your men are going to have to practice some real restraint. The rules of engagement are going to be very strict."

"How so?"

"No one can shoot unless fired upon. This is real serious, Sal. You've got some pretty trigger-happy scout crews."

"Sir, they don't engage anybody unless I tell them to. You know that—"

"Yes. *You're* going to have to practice restraint," the colonel said. He looked plaintively at Rameriz. "Don't let me down, Sal. One more incident, especially with a senior officer, and I'll have to relieve you of your command. Am I clear on that point?"

Rameriz grimaced. "Yes, sir."

* * *

CHARLIE TROOP WAS GATHERED IN the back briefing room, a mixture of pilots and the Blue Platoon NCOIC, and squad leaders. The air was tense; cigarette smoke swirled and a buzz of rumors flew from everyone's lips. When Rameriz entered, everyone came to attention. The commanding officer went to the podium. "Be seated, gentlemen."

They took their seats.

"To quell any rumors, yes, I'm still the CO. And no, we will not be going back to the Seven Mountains." Rameriz waited for the "thank Gods" and the "all rights" to die down. "Tomorrow, however, we begin Operation Brave Shield, within the Mo Cay AO." A dull rumble of complaints coursed through the room. "It should last two weeks. We will be a small part of a rather extensive operation. Gentlemen, the purpose of this operation is to completely disrupt the enemy's infrastructure in the area. As you may know, the VC do a lot of tax collecting from the locals along the major rivers and inland along the canals. It's one of the ways they finance their war efforts." Rameriz turned and indicated to the spec four standing behind him to lift the large sheet of paper that covered the battle plan and flip it over. Looking at the first sheet, Rameriz, pointer in hand, said, "We are going to combine forces with two battalions of the Ninth Infantry Division, from the Riverine Brigade." Rameriz aimed the pointer. "They will make their penetrations inland along the Song Ham Luong, this river here that runs south of Ben Tre and north and east of the AO. Our mission, along with their air cavalry unit, Delta Troop, Third Squadron, Fifth Cav, will be to provide recon support in advance of the flotilla, as they move inland along the canals, and the infantry as they advance on land. Navy Seawolf gunships will provide immediate air support over the flotilla. Three battalions of the ARVN Seventh Division will be staged at Ben Tre as a reactionary force should the flotilla run into anything heavy. The One Twenty-first and the One Seventy-fifth assault helicopter companies will be their lift element.

"Brave Shield is a search and detain mission. The two American battalions, along with a Vietnamese marine battalion, will sweep through and round up the villagers, who will be taken to strategic points and questioned. The higher ups are hoping that they'll be frightened enough—or brave enough—or pissed enough to point out where Charlie is—or who he is. Three days ago they dropped a load of leaflets over the area—Chieu Hoi stuff plus a bunch of other crap. Frankly, that aggravates the piss out of me. The thinking is that if we can let everyone know we're coming—and why—the villagers won't panic. But that means Charlie could scatter the hell outta there, which to me defeats the whole frickin' mission." The men looked at each other and shook their heads. "The sweep will be followed up by a bunch of doctors and nurses and other such goody two-shoes who will offer medical examinations, medicine, farming tools, advice, et cetera, to the farmers and villagers. It all sounds like a crock to me, but who knows, maybe some good will come of this happy bullshit."

Rameriz paused. He stood gaunt before his men, his wavy black hair and dark skin shiny in the bright light of the room; he drew a deep breath. "And now for the real crap. My orders are that we can't engage Charlie unless we can see the whites of his eyes. We have to see him aiming at us and firing before we can shoot." A sudden uproar filled the room. "Quiet down—damnit. Now hear me out. Delta Troop will be working with the larger element, almost directly north of Mo Cay. We'll be with the smaller contingent of the flotilla, coming down this river right here, before it takes this U-turn and heads northwest toward Mo Cay. It's my understanding that fewer farmers are in this area. The vegetation will be thicker, but that may be to our advantage."

"And also to Charlie's advantage," someone in the back said.

Rameriz nodded, then smiled. "Let them little shits start something. You low-bird pilots, if you radio that you can see the whites of their eyes, I'll let the Cobras shred them with their seventeen-pounders. How does that sound? If I walk out of this rat-trap of a country with just my skivvies, so be it—"

Leo Tannah stood. "Sir, I think I speak for every man here. You show us the gates of hell and we'll follow. Let's do it—!"

"At first flash of Eden...
we race down to the sea.
Standing there
On freedom's shore
Waiting for the sun...
Waiting for the sun, waiting
For the sun..."

Nolan appeared at Atwater's door. The sergeant was at the desk he had built with discarded rocket crates, a three-ring binder open before him. Atwater looked up. "Yessir, what can I do for you?"

"At twenty thirty hours, I want a meeting with the squad leaders."

Atwater rose, closing the binder. "Yes, sir."

"By the way, what were you reading?"

"I was just glancing through the unit history. Did you know that the Seventh Squadron, First Air Cavalry goes back to January Eighteen Thirty-four, when it was first formed as G Company, United States Regiment of Dragoons at Jefferson Barracks, Missouri?"

"No, I didn't."

"It was later renamed the First Regiment of Dragoons. And then in Eighteen Sixty-one, it was again re-designated, as G Company, First Cavalry. And then of course, it was reactivated last year in April at Fort Knox with its present designation. Probably all lineages of all cavalry units operating in Vietnam go back that far. I traced my own heritage once and found that I had a great-great-grandfather who fought with the Tenth Cavalry Regiment in the Indian wars. He was a buffalo soldier. He saw action in west Texas, in most of New Mexico, and a little in Arizona. He was stationed at a place called Saint Angelia, later named San Angelo." Atwater paused for a moment. "Interesting the Major telling us this afternoon our troop callsign is changed to Comanche. I often wondered how many Comanches my ancestor tangled with back in his day. I'll bet he was scared to death. Did you know that the Comanche Indian breed was by far the most sadistic? Somewhere along the way they got the name 'Children of the Devil.' They took great pleasure torturing their victims. In fact it was the women's job to keep the victim conscious and alive as long as possible to endure more and more torture." Atwater shuddered. "God help us if we ever find one of our own tortured like that here. I think the men would go bananas."

Mike nodded. "I guess it would be our job, then, to see that that didn't happen, wouldn't it, Sergeant?"

"Yessir."

They were in the center room, all seated around the table on the beanbag pillows. Roach and Smiley took out their plastic bags filled with the dried grass. Lieutenant McCloud had bought a water-bong in Honolulu during his R&R. He brought it out and poured a small amount of water from a canteen into the cylinder. Roach took it and filled the bowl with marijuana. He lit it, inhaled deeply, then let the smoke out slowly. He passed the bong to McCloud. By the time it got to Sandy, the young warrant officer's body was tingling with excitement. He took a drag and then passed the bong onto Scott, whose face, Sandy noticed, had taken on a kind of rubbery look.

"To everything
Turn turn turn...
There is a season
Turn turn turn...
And a time to every purpose
Under heaven..."

It was the next day. "Vinny, is that a picture of your girlfriend?" asked Childs, the medic.

The RTO looked up. "Yeah, she just sent it to me." Vinny then opened the letter it came with and began to reread it. "It says here she's not getting along with her old man, so she's gonna get an apartment with a girlfriend. She says her dad really threw a fit. He cried and shouted at her and told her she couldn't leave. But she says she's gonna do it anyway, right after Thanksgiving. Wow!...Can you believe it's already Thanksgiving? Pretty soon it'll be Christmas. Fuck—do you realize, we've been here almost a year—"

Childs nodded. "It seems to me like we've been here forever. Sometimes, I really get scared. Do you get scared, Vinny?"

"What for? What the hell is there to be scared about? We been in this platoon ever since it started. Who have we lost? No one...except Espinoza. He went home with his million-dollar wound."

"But he lost an eye, Vinny—"

"Better an eye than his life. I'd rather give up these legs than my life."

"Me, I'd rather die," Childs said. "Who wants a pair of stumps for legs?"

Vinny looked closely at Childs. "They make those...uh...pratheeses, don't they, Doc? What's wrong with them?"

"You mean a prosthesis?"

"Yeah, that's what I mean," Vinny replied. "They ain't the real thing, but better than nothing. Shit, I ain't worried about none of that. Blue will watch out for us, and so will the Old Man. Even this fucking little Mo Cay thing doesn't scare me. This is a big operation. I bet Charlie's made tracks clean out of the area. What do you want to bet? Ten bucks? A hundred?"

"I don't make bets like that," Childs stated.

"How come?"

"Because sure as shit something bad will happen."

"Aw, crap...you're just superstitious."

Victor R. Beaver

Chapter 74

*"In the early mornin' rain
with a dollar in my hand
And an aching in my heart,
and my pockets full of sand
I'm a long way from home
and I miss my loved one so..."*

OPERATION BRAVE SHIELD BEGAN early on the morning of November 12. Before first light, seventy-six boats of River Assault Squadrons 9 and 11 broke from their mobile riverine base on the Song My Tho, at Dong Tam, and proceeded westbound until they came to the junction of the Song Ham Luong. The flotilla was a mixture of ATCs (armored troop carriers), monitors, two refuelers, three CCBs (command and communications boats), and the minesweeping ASPBs (assault support patrol boats). At the Ham Luong River the three river assault divisions took a U-turn and chugged eastward until they came to their first maneuver objective, a narrow riverway that would lead the first element directly to Mo Cay. (A fourth river assault division remained behind to provide security for River Support Squadron 7, the mobile riverine base.)

At 0934 hours, thirteen ATCs, three monitors, and eight ASPBs of River Assault Division 91 broke from the main element and began their drive along a narrow watercourse away from the main tributary. Each ATC was heavily armed and heavily armored. Aside from its boat crew of seven, each armored troop carrier had on board approximately thirty-five 9th Division infantrymen (approximately a platoon), with their assorted M-16s, LAWs, M-79 grenade launchers, and M-60 machine guns. The heavily armored monitors, the battleships of the river assault squadrons, were each armed with one Navy-type 81mm mortar, one 40mm and one 20mm automatic cannon, two .50-caliber machine guns, and two Mk.18 grenade launchers. Leading the way were the ASPBs, the riverine minesweeper and destroyer element of the flotilla. Each of these boats were heavily armored and equipped with a mine countermeasures chain drag. The ASPBs special exhaust systems, which exhaust underwater, made these boats quieter than the other river assault craft.

The remaining two river assault squadrons continued southeastward, until the ATCs of River Assault Division 92 found their attack stations and drove their bows onto the muddy banks on the south side of the Song Ham Luong. The last of the flotilla then continued their trek along the Song Ham Luong until River Assault Division 111 came to the southern tributary, a narrower watercourse that led to Mo Cay from the southeast. At 1020 hours, the Vietnamese marine battalion was airlifted into two LZ locations south of Mo Cay, a large triangle of land dense with vegetation but short on farmers and villagers.

By 1229, all forces were in place. At exactly 1300, the command was given to begin the sweep.

Painstakingly, methodically, using the barest of coercion, the people were gathered in groups of twos and threes and more, and made to assemble in detainment areas surrounded by concertina wire. There they were quartered and fed, medically examined and treated for whatever ailments that could be quickly administered, and then questioned. Higher headquarter MACV personnel and other officials were on hand to insure that all proprieties were met. Infantrymen surrounded each detainment area. As the internal workings of the operation took place, the soldiers, armed and tense, guarded the periphery, unfamiliar with how an operation of this type should be conducted. They were neither on the offensive nor were they in the proper defensive posture.

By late afternoon, over seven hundred villagers and farmers had been detained and questioned. Before the sun went down, the men set up their night defensive positions and either camped near the villages or back onboard the ATCs. They spent the night under a halo of descending flares and the sound of helicopters patrolling overhead. During the night not one shot was fired.

The following morning, before daylight, the teams were up and moving again. There were an estimated thirteen thousand Vietnamese peasants in the area to be rounded up and detained, of which one-third was likely to be either Viet Cong or Viet Cong sympathizers. All young men between the ages of seventeen and thirty were to be tagged for possible duty in the ARVN forces. Group political lectures told the true purpose of the National Liberation Front and how they were linked to the aspirations of North Vietnam. The villagers listened passively, as was their custom to do, in the same manner they listened to the Viet Cong spout the evils of the South Vietnam government and its link to the United States.

Operation Brave Shield was the first major step toward Vietnamization of the war in the Mekong Delta (to allow the ARVN to take over more of the ground combat role from the American 9th Infantry Division stationed in the Delta), a fact few were aware. To them it was just another operation, albeit a strange one, with an unfamiliar political overtone. Though each grunt was on guard for the slightest hostile act, they eventually relaxed when they saw how willingly the people accepted the relatively non-hostile urgings of this large assembly of forces. Most of the people had never seen a doctor or nurse. But the gentleness of these caring individuals, all combined with the distribution of food and farming implements and the kindness of their own countrymen (of the Vietnamese marine battalion), quelled any doubts that these forces were here on a mission of good will. It was later determined that the leaflets dropped several days before the operation had had their effect. By the end of the second day nearly one hundred Viet Cong had been repatriated. The former enemy told tales of hardship in remote places, of estrangement from their families, of political indoctrination they no longer believed in. They were also eager to gain the small amount of money promised them for switching sides. By the middle of the third day, more than three dozen Viet Cong tax collectors were identified and taken into custody. These individuals were led with hands tied behind their backs and ropes around their necks, to pick-up zones for helicopter transportation to My Tho, where they were interned and further questioned, to eventually be transported to the large POW camp at Vinh Loi (Bac Lieu), southwest of Soc Trang Army Airfield.

* * *

IT WAS THE LIFT SECTION'S FOURTH day at the Ben Tre airstrip, parked at the edge of the dirt and gravel runway. So far their only flight had occurred two days before when Slater and RT in one ship and Buddy and Sampson in another brought a crew of reporters from CBS News to cover the operation. The reporters had left yesterday morning, one reporter declaring that the brigade's sweep through the area was hardly titillating. "There's no action, no fighting, nobody's dying—*this isn't news."*

"Hey, Mr. Slater. Here's a picture of my son you said you wanted to see," said Chico, the Puerto Rican machine gunner, as he approached Kip's helicopter.

Slater laid his journal down and took the photo. Big George Kowalinsky, Chico's assistant machine-gunner, seated on the ground several steps away, was looking on, grinning. His steel pot rested back on his massive head. "Man, he is one cute little kid," Kip said. "Is that your wife holding him?"

"Nah...that's my sister. My wife died. She got hit by a car."

"Oh, God, I'm really sorry. Where did it happen? Was it in Puerto Rico?"

"Nah...at Fort Bragg. I saw the motherfucker who did it. He was fucking drunk. I almost killed him. I would've if they hadn't dragged me off him."

Slater grimaced. "That must have been tough, huh?"

Chico smiled. "Tougher on the other guy. That motherfucker is still in jail. When he gets out, I'm going to kill him. They'll never find the body when I get done with it."

Slater eyed the wire-thin Puerto Rican with suspicion. He said, "You're really serious, aren't you?"

"Fuckin' eh, sir." Chico pulled out a switchblade knife; the blade flashed in the sunlight. "I'm going to slice that motherfucker from one end to the other. First thing I'm going to do is cut off his dick and balls and stuff them in his mouth. After that, it's gonna be one slice at a time, until he ain't even good shark meat."

Appalled at what he was hearing, Slater said, "Why are you telling me this?"

"Hey, I thought you wanted to know...so you could put it in your book."

Big George said, "Sir, you shoulda seen what he did to this one gook we killed back in May. Chico wanted to cut his head off, but Sergeant Patterson stopped him. Instead, he just whacked off his ears."

"Hey, yeah, sir. You want to see'em?" Chico grabbed for the leather pouch he had tied to a cord looped around his neck. He opened the pouch and pulled something out that looked like a dried mushroom, dark and shriveled. He handed it to Slater, who bent away.

"That's an ear?"

"Fuckin' eh. You wanna see the other one?"

"No-no...I don't think so."

"Something is happenin' here.
Stop, what's that sound?
Look what's going round
And round..."

Embarrassed, Sharon O'Malley took the small box wrapped in brown paper from the young spec four at the post office window and went hurriedly to her room. Making sure the door was locked, she took the box to her bed, sat down and began to unwrap it. Her anticipation at seeing its contents caused tingles to run up and down her spine. It was the first time she had ever ordered anything like it and the feeling she experienced was electric. Carefully, she lifted the lid; her eyes widened with excitement. She smoothed her hands carefully over the silken material, then held it up to examine it closer. It was a cloudy black, half-length, see-through negligee, with narrow, spaghetti-like shoulder straps. Accompanying it was a pair of see-through bikini panties. She had ordered it several weeks ago from a Frederick's of Hollywood catalog Frieda had given her, hoping to have it before Michael's visit on Thanksgiving Day.

She stood and went to her mirror and held it to her chest. She frowned at the ridiculous contrast, the negligee held over her fatigue shirt and pants she wore everyday. She removed her shirt and then her T-shirt. She undid her bra and this time held the article against the swell of her breasts. She smiled. Michael will be pleased, she thought, very, very pleased.

* * *

"COMANCHE SIX, THIS IS ONE EIGHT. It looks deserted. Not a soul in sight." Justen released his mic switch. He glanced quickly at his ARM switch to make sure he was "hot." "Everything looks real quiet," he added.

"Roger that, One Eight," Rameriz replied.

Justen brought the LOH around toward the road that led into the small village. From the outskirts of the hamlet, he had seen no activity, no movement, no

Victor R. Beaver

children playing, not even a dog loose. "I'll be coming in from the east, Six. Break, One Seven, One Eight, cover my left side. Keep an eye on that one hootch that's partially burned. Should be at my ten o'clock."

Sandy Adamson turned his ship left and keyed his mic: "That's a rog, One Eight. I see some chickens. Right now that's all I've got."

Roach, looking out the right side, had his M-60 trained on the deserted hootch. "God, this is weird, sir," the gunner said. "Where would they be?"

"Beats me," Sandy said, now spying a small pig rooting near a bush. "One Eight, I've got a pig now in sight. Munching on something in the bushes."

It was nearing ten o'clock in the morning. Since daylight, the Scouts had been out in advance of the ASPBs, the CCB, the three monitors, and thirteen ATCs, reconnoitering both sides of the river as the small flotilla moved slowly northward. When they came to the junction where the right fork went toward Mo Cay and the left aimed westward toward Ap An Loc, a small village less than three kilometers from the Song Co Chien, Rameriz and his pilots were asked to divert due south to a remote hamlet north of Huong My. Huong My was a district town that housed a MACV advisory team. Earlier, the team had received an intelligence report that said a heavily armed enemy element, perhaps a platoon, was camped near the remote hamlet.

As the two scouts came in closer, Sandy caught a whiff of something burning or burnt, like meat on a barbecue grill, void of any special flavoring though. "Smells like a leftover cooking fire," Sandy said. The young warrant officer felt shivers course up and down his spine. "Why would they suddenly be gone?"

"Beats me, sir," Roach replied, "but this shit is getting spookier by the minute."

"Six, One Eight, we've got a dead gook here," Justen called. "Looks like a young kid." Derek had just cleared a small cluster of hootches. On the other side, Rick Kalbach, his gunner, had spied the upper portion of a body positioned half outside a darkened doorway. The rotor downwash had lifted a banana frond that had been covering it and exposed was a small boy whose chest had been riddled with bullets. Kalbach checked quickly about and saw a pair of legs sticking out from a line of bushes near another cluster of hootches. "Shit, sir, look at that—"

"Six, One Eight, scramble the Blues. I think we have a situation here."

"What's up, One Eight?" Rameriz's voice came back sounding tense.

"I'm not sure, but we've got another body here."

Sandy brought his ship closer to where he had seen the pig rooting in the bushes, which moments before had run off, zigzagging in all directions. Next to the bushes was another hut that had been burned. The rotor downwash from his ship blew back the brush and exposed the charred remains of still another body. Sandy's eyes widened. The LOH was at a ten-foot hover, almost directly over the body. He saw that it was mangled and torn apart at the stomach, the entrails spilling out in a coagulated mess. "Jesus," he breathed, "that damn pig was having himself *a meal!*"

Justen brought the slicks into an open area south of the hamlet. As the Blues deployed, Justen and Adamson scouted the periphery of the village from east to north. Chico and Big George moved quickly to the nearest cluster of trees and set up a defensive position to cover the rest of the platoon. Crouching low, Nolan and Vincenzo set up ten meters away. Atwater directed Patterson, and Hattaway, Fourth Squad leader, to angle their squads to the right. Then he told Gomez to deploy his First Squad to the left. Nolan took the handset and pressed the key: "Comanche Six, this is Two Six. We're in position."

"Roger that. Go in there slow and easy. Back out if you take fire."

"This is Two Six, roger that."

Hoyt nudged Fields in the ribs and pointed. "That's gotta be that damn pig they were talking about. Eating a person...!"

Childs felt the heft of his medical bag and crossed himself. He took his St. Christopher out and pressed it to his lips.

Nolan took one last moment to survey the village, then gave the signal to move out. Everyone rose."

"Spread out, you guys," Atwater called. "You're not a bunch of damn rookies."

Fields and Hoyt came to the first hootch and looked inside. It was empty, except for a few clay pots, a single straw mat covering a dirt floor, a wooden table built low to the ground, and a few articles of clothing hanging on a line strung across the room. Childs looked ahead and saw several chickens in a pen, pecking calmly at the ground. Brave Water gazed occasionally upward, searching for signs of snipers hidden in the trees.

They came across the first body and stared in horror at the sight of it. Burned beyond recognition, the body lay at a grotesque angle, its mouth open in a silent scream. Two of the men turned away and vomited. Nolan stared at the body, still partially clothed, trying to discern its sex. There was no way to tell. He glanced at the men and wondered what they were thinking. Each man's face was a mixture of horror and revulsion—and anger, bordering on revenge.

They advanced slowly through the middle of the village, checking each hootch as they did. They found the small boy, previously uncovered of debris by Justen's rotor downwash, whose small chest was covered with blood. Automatically, Childs stooped to check for a pulse. Hoyt and Brave Water poked their rifles through a window and saw a pair of candles next to a crucifix. The candles and the crucifix had been dumped on the floor. Atwater came next to Nolan. "You want to know what I think, Blue?"

"I know exactly," Nolan said. "The VC are going to try and spread the word that we did this. They've probably got a couple of hostages to validate their point."

At the far side of the village was a thick grove of trees and a footpath leading into it. Hoyt, at point, stooped down and examined a dark red spot on the ground; leading away from it was a set of heel marks. "What do you have?" Nolan asked, as he approached.

"Blood, sir. It looks like they're dragging a body."

Nolan signaled Vinny for the handset. "Six, this is Two Six. I've got a trail of blood going into the woods. Except the five dead we've seen, the rest of the village is deserted."

"Okay, Two Six. Go ahead and follow the trail. Stop after twenty-five meters. Remember, one shot fired, back out and I'll let the Cobras at'em."

"Roger that, Six."

Nolan signaled for Hoyt to proceed. He turned to Atwater. "Fan the other two squads out. Tell Patterson to keep his squad here, as back up."

"Aye aye, Captain."

Nolan grinned. "Going navy on me are you, Sergeant?"

Grim-faced, Atwater said, "A momentary loss of control, Blue. It's times like these I wished I'd have joined the navy. Damn, they don't do crap like this."

"What, and miss out on all this fun?" Nolan said sarcastically.

"Yeah, right, sir."

Hoyt inched his way forward. He examined every leaf, every twig, every vine. The footpath went straight for ten meters and then curved slightly left. When he got to the curve, he halted. Ahead, he saw the brush trampled. The Viet Cong would never be that careless, he thought. He turned to Fields, whose face was wreathed in sweat. "Pass the word back to Blue," he whispered. "Tell him the brush looks like a herd of buffalo went beyond this point."

Nolan heard the report. He frowned. Were they being led into an ambush? It was impossible to tell. Vinny gazed upward through the trees and saw one of the Loaches pass overhead. "Sir, maybe the Scouts can see something."

Nolan shook his head. "Too thick." He took the handset again. "One Eight, Two Six, could you move off to the east a little. I think we may find the villagers hidden in here. I don't want to spook them."

"Roger that, Two Six. Will do. Be careful."

Nolan signaled for Hoyt to go five meters farther and stop. He then directed Chico and Big George to move forward. "Before you fire, try to identify your target," he hissed.

Chico nodded.

Hoyt was now on his belly, low-crawling forward. He could hear the two flanking squads moving cautiously forward to his right and left rear. Then they stopped. The silence was deafening.

The Sky Soldiers

He waited. Gradually, the riflemen heard a strange sound, as if someone were whimpering. And then he recognized the sound of a baby crying. He turned again to Fields. "Tell Blue I think the rest of the village is just ahead."

Nolan came forward. He knelt by Hoyt's side, who was now on his knees. "I think the whole shootin' match is in that thicket," Hoyt whispered, pointing. Nolan listened. He heard a voice, a woman's voice, very soft, very low. "Yeah, I think you're right." Vinny was next to him. "Go back and get Atwater. We'll see how good his Vietnamese is."

Atwater crouched next to Nolan, producing a Vietnamese phrase book he carried in his pocket. For the past two months the Blue Platoon NCOIC had been studying the language, practicing on the mama-san who cleaned his hootch room. Nolan said, "Can you tell them to come out, that they won't be harmed?"

"Yes, sir, I'll try. Let me study this for a minute. I could say the right words but they come out the opposite of what I intend." Atwater rummaged quickly through the booklet. When he found an approximation to what he wanted to say, he called out in Vietnamese. "Come out. You will not be harmed!"

They waited in silence. The black platoon sergeant tried again. He spoke his words more gently. "We are Americans. We will not harm you. Please come out."

Still no response from the thicket. They heard a baby squeal and then a woman's voice trying to hush it. "Sir, I don't think there's any danger my going in there," Atwater said.

"You're probably right, but I rather you not take the chance."

Atwater shifted his rifle. "Let me try, Blue. I've been practicing a couple of phrases that might work, especially if they can actually see me speaking."

Nolan stared at Atwater, who had a calm reposed look about him. The sergeant grinned. "Hey...no one lives forever."

"Okay, but I want Chico and Big George right behind you."

The trio edged forward into the thicket. Branches snapped and limbs whipped at their faces. After a couple of minutes, they saw a small clearing. Chico and Big George quickly dropped to their knees behind Atwater. They heard voices and a rustling sound coming from the bushes beyond the clearing. The sergeant turned and handed his rifle to the big Nebraska farm boy. "What—are you crazy, Sarge?" Chico sounded.

"If they were going to hurt us, they'd have done it by now," Atwater replied.

Atwater referred to his Vietnamese phrase book. He spoke: "You can come out. We are here to help you." And then he added in English: "VC number ten. VC number ten."

Slowly a woman stood, coming into full view, followed by an older man. Chico had his M-60 trained right at her chest. Kowalinsky had the belted ammunition ready to feed. Atwater stepped forward, showing he had no weapon. The

569

old man stepped in front of the woman and bowed. Atwater bowed in return. "As you can see, I am unarmed," he said.

Atwater turned slightly; he spoke softly to Chico and Big George: "You guys move back, get out of sight, but keep me covered."

The sergeant went forward, closer to the middle of the clearing. His eyes widened as he saw several more individuals emerge from hiding, mostly women and a few small children. Two of the women carried babies. Atwater spoke a few more words; gradually the rest of the villagers appeared. The woman who had shown herself first came forward and motioned for Atwater to follow her to the spot in the bushes where she had been hiding. What he saw sickened him. It was another old man, covered with blood and barely breathing. Next to him, her back against a tree, was a young girl, not more than eleven or twelve. Her right arm, what was left of it, was heavily bandaged in torn clothing material. He bent over the old man, who stared back at him feebly. The man coughed and blood appeared at his mouth. Atwater reached toward the girl. She leaned back. Her brown skin appeared pale. "Come, I must get you help," he said in Vietnamese.

Atwater carried the girl into the clearing, then advanced into the thick vegetation where Chico and Big George had relocated.. "Chico, get Childs. This girl's in shock." And then he said, "Kowalinski, follow this woman. There's an old man back there. Bring him out. He's been shot."

Standing to one side, Nolan watched the villagers file past behind Atwater. Once inside the village, the women quickly dispersed to their own huts. Soon there was a terrible wailing as they found the dead. Childs went and quickly checked the old man where Big George had laid him down gently in the shade of a banana tree. "He's dead," the medic declared to Nolan.

Childs then began to administer to the girl, whose right arm had been ripped off by gunfire. Brave Water, standing nearby, gagged at the sight of the bloody stump of her right arm. With all the courage she could muster, the girl tried to smile. Atwater was next to her and she reached up and touched his face. Her large doe-like eyes made the hearts of the men in the platoon suddenly melt.

Atwater left her side and went and sat down next to a wooden fence several paces away. He leaned back. He took out his canteen and undid the cap. Nolan, off to one side, looked at his platoon sergeant. Tears had formed in the black man's eyes. "I have a daughter her age," he said. "With her in my arms, it felt like I was carrying my own child...Oh, God, how I miss my kids—"

"I'm sure you do," Nolan said, glancing back at the girl. Atwater raised the canteen to his mouth. A single shot rang out. Within a split second every man was flat on the ground. Rifles trained outward in all directions. Nolan had his .45-caliber Colt automatic out. "Somebody—from what direction?"

"Can't tell!" Fields cried.

Nolan looked quickly toward Atwater who was still leaning against the fence. "Get down!" he called.

The Sky Soldiers

Just then Chico spotted a single flash. "There!" he cried, as the second gunshot rang out, coming from high up in the trees. In the next instant Chico's M-60 was pointed upward and firing. A dozen rounds exploded where he saw the shots come from. With arms and legs flailing, a body dressed in black pajamas fell earthward. It made a loud thumping sound as it hit the ground. "Everyone—stay low!" Nolan commanded. He looked back toward Atwater. "God *damnit,* Sergeant, I said get *down!"*

Nolan canted his head. "Sergeant...what's the—Oh, shit! Childs, get over here!"

The medic scrambled to where Atwater was sitting. He saw a small spot of blood near the middle of his chest, to the left of the sternum. Frantically, Childs felt for a pulse. He said, "Come on, Sarge...Come on!" The black man's upper torso slumped sideways.

Looking on, Nolan felt as if his heart was beating in his throat. He grabbed at Atwater's wrist. "Come on, Sergeant, quit playing, goddamnit. Wake up. Wake up." Nolan by now had grabbed the man's shirt collar. "You can't do this. You *can't—!"*

Fields, and then Hoyt, scrambled to Nolan's side. They took hold of him. "Sir—"

Childs got in Nolan's face. "Sir...it's no use. He got it right through the heart. He's dead—"

A wave of nausea came over him and then Nolan felt faint. Struggling to stand, he turned in time to see Chico get up and charge the base of the trees where the sniper had fallen. "Aiiyyeeee...you motherfucker! *You cocksucking sonofabitch!"* The machine gunner fired his M-60; shots went off in all directions; behind him trailed the belted 7.62 ammunition.

This burst of frenzied action was like a sharp slap in the face. Nolan's attention was now acutely focused on Big George's machine gunner. "Chico!" he yelled. "Cease fire! *Cease fire!"*

The man had gone completely berserk. He halted in front of the prostrate body. He aimed downward and fired short, angry bursts. The platoon watched as the body shifted and bobbed with each round that when in.

"Cease fire!" Nolan yelled again.

Chico stopped. All of a sudden he turned and ran frantically toward one of the villagers, a woman lying prone on the ground. Beside her was a small child. He pointed his weapon at the woman's forehead. "You did this!" he screamed. "You VC! You VC!"

The woman came quickly to her knees, her hands out, pleading: "No VC! No VC! No VC!"

"CHICO!" Nolan had his .45 up and leveled at the Puerto Rican. "Put your gun down!"

"The whole village is VC!"

Victor R. Beaver

Nolan held the .45 steady. "I said put your weapon down, Chico—*Now!*"

Nolan advanced forward. The rest of the platoon and the villagers remained like statues; not a body stirred. Nolan saw that Chico's body was shaking. "Put your M-60 down, Chico...Do it now or I swear to God, I'll shoot you—I'll kill you."

Chico turned. The machine gunner brought his weapon to the level of Nolan's stomach. "They killed him," he sobbed. "They killed him...!"

"No—*they* didn't. The man who did is dead. You got him, Chico. Now lay your weapon down. Chico, do it now—*or I shoot.*"

Nolan reset his grip on the cocked pistol. The barrel was leveled at Chico's forehead. Nolan moved in closer. "Put the gun down, Chico. Don't make me kill you. I will." Nolan took another step. The barrel of Chico's M-60 was now pressed into his abdomen. At the same time Chico's eyes were crossed as he stared at the black hole of Nolan's pistol barrel.

"I could blow you away, Captain," Chico said.

"I know you could. But you won't."

Nolan pressed the barrel of his pistol into Chico's forehead. With his left hand, he slowly moved Chico's M-60 away from his stomach. Chico's shoulders went slack. He slumped to the ground, still gripping his M-60.

Brave Water and Sergeant Patterson came quickly forward. "Take his weapon," Nolan said. "Have Childs give him some morphine."

"Yes, sir."

Nolan stooped down. He tried to comfort the woman, but she pushed him away. "No VC! No VC!" she cried. He went over to Atwater's body. Vinny handed him the handset. "Comanche Six, this is Comanche Two Six. We need a security force at this location, ASAP. My men are ready for extraction. Aside from the original body count of friendlies, we have one Uniform Sierra KIA and one enemy KIA. And one very badly wounded Vietnamese girl."

"Roger that, Two Six."

The Sky Soldiers

Chapter 75

MIKE NOLAN STEADIED HIS HAND. He lifted the pen and put the point to the blank sheet of paper before him. He paused for a moment, then began to write.

Dear Mrs. Atwater,

It pains me deeply to have to write this letter. I was your husband's platoon leader. I hope that what I say doesn't sound trite in light of the news you are having to bear right now, but I found your husband to be one of the finest men I've ever known. I had profound trust in his abilities as a soldier and in his qualities as a leader. On the day he died, he demonstrated the utmost bravery when he coaxed a group of Vietnamese villagers from their hiding place after the Viet Cong had overrun their hamlet. I always knew his humanity to be extraordinary. On this particular day, he proved it beyond question. He carried a badly wounded Vietnamese girl out of the jungle to be given urgent medical attention. His comment to me as he handed the girl over to our medic was that she reminded him of his own young daughter. He had tears in his eyes when he said he missed his children. I am grateful to say that he died instantly and without pain. You and his children were the last thoughts on his mind. If there is anything I can do, please don't hesitate to ask. I took it upon on myself to see that his personal belongings were gathered and boxed appropriately. You should be receiving them soon. I wish I could do more.

Sincerely,
Michael T. Nolan, Captain
Commanding

Nolan laid the pen down. He took and read the letter slowly, wondering how anyone could bear the kind of news he had the misfortune now to deliver. He knew that if he could change places with Atwater right now, he would. It didn't seem fair. Why some are destined to die so much sooner than others, others who had so much less to give to the world. Or maybe that was the key: the best do so much in such a short time that their brief interlude on Earth is all that is necessary in the grand cosmic design. They touch the lives of those around them—and then—and then....What? We are left behind, he thought, to ponder what more they could have done. But maybe it isn't up to them anymore. The torch is passed. And the human race must carry on.

Victor R. Beaver

* * *

"ADAMSON," LIEUTENANT SCOTT CALLED.

"Yessir...?"

"I've got a three-day Rn'R to Vung Tau open, if you want it."

"Sure, that sounds great. When?"

"You'll be leaving this afternoon. A maintenance bird is heading that way at 1300 hours."

"Okay, sir. I'll be ready."

Sandy quickly put together a bag of clothing and his shaving kit. Mark Allen, standing at his door, said, "You want to take some 'shit' with you?"

Sandy shook his head. "Nah. I'm getting kind of burned out on it. I need a vacation to get my head clear."

"Suit yourself."

"Thanks anyway."

"One other thing. Don't go falling in love with the first skirt that comes along. I understand Vung Tau is loaded with attractive Vietnamese women, most of them prostitutes."

"Don't worry. I'm not that far gone."

The Vung Tau shoreline stretched for nearly six miles in a long gentle curve to the northeast. The white sands and the calm blue waters reminded Sandy of his several trips to Panama City Beach while he was at Fort Rucker. He had met a girl there who was seventeen and staying with her parents in one of the rental cottages on the shore. Her name was Michelle Bannister. She had soft curly brown hair, a playful smile, and a cute diminutive figure that reminded him of Katie. With her parents hovering nearby, they spent the day talking, playing Frisbee, and building sandcastles. These moments were interspersed out on the warm sparkling water, her floating on a beach raft, he hanging onto the sides. He thought of her now as he gazed out at the placid waters of the South China Sea.

She was from Georgia and had given him her address, but he'd never written her. Now he wondered why. He remembered how playful she was and he liked that. It contrasted sharply with his serious side. Before he met her, he didn't realize how emotionally aged he had grown. Since his decision to join the army and go to flight school, he had undertaken no activity that didn't require his utmost concentration. In one brief stroke he had leaped far beyond his boyhood.

"Hi, GI, you want buy Coke?"

Sandy glanced up. Standing in front of him were two young Vietnamese boys. He smiled.

"Dey velly ice-cold. One dolla," the smaller of the two said, extending his hand.

"One dollar, are you kidding? That's outrageous—"

The Sky Soldiers

"Sebenty-bive cents. You want buy?"

"Fifty cents and not a nickel more."

"Hokay." The taller one brought a bottle out from a cloth bag. Swiftly he lifted the cap with a bottle opener. Sandy retrieved a wad of crumpled MPC from his shirt lying by his side.

"I don't have any Vietnamese money," he said.

"MPC hokay," said the smaller boy, his hand still extended.

Sandy took the bottle. It was wet but it wasn't ice-cold. It was barely a degree below lukewarm but he took a drink and thanked them anyway.

They ambled off to their next victims, a group of U.S. servicemen lounging on large beach towels several yards away. As the two approached, one of the servicemen threw a handful of sand at them. The boys skirted quickly away, then turned and taunted the men. One of the men got up and chased them farther down the beach. "What did you do that for?" Sandy called over to them.

"What's it to you—?"

"They didn't do any harm."

"Mind your own damn business."

Sandy felt the heat rise in his chest. He looked away, out toward the water. Screw it, he thought. What the hell do I care? They're just gooks. And then he frowned. *Did I say that? I didn't mean it. Or did I? Boy, I guess I've changed.* He lay back on his towel and closed his eyes. The hot sun beat down. Again, he thought of Michelle. I should write her, he thought. What harm would it do? He remembered that she liked him. She told him she was very proud of the men who had joined the service and who were willing to go to Vietnam. He had delighted listening to her, not only for the words she spoke, so different from Katie's, but her southern accent became quickly endearing. He remembered, too, that she had asked him what he intended to do after he got out of the army. "I don't really know," he replied.

"You want to fly, don't you?"

"Oh, yeah, I want it to be my life career. I'm hoping I can do it somewhere overseas, like South America or Africa. I'd like to see the whole world, get to all the continents, if I can. My dad was in the service. We got to see a lot of places, but I want to see more."

"That's great," she said. "I want to see more of the world, too."

"What do you want to do?" he asked.

"I'm going to nursing school after I get my college prerequisites out of the way. I'll be able to go most anywhere with a RN certificate. I've been thinking about joining the Peace Corps. Maybe you could do that as a helicopter pilot. Maybe we could even be together."

Sandy smiled. "Yeah, that would neat."

"I want to help people," she said. "There is so much poverty in the world, so much sickness and suffering. After the Peace Corps, I'd want to settle down. Get married, have children. How about you? Do you have a girl back home?"

"I did," Sandy said, wondering how much he should reveal about Katie, wondering, too, if he should disclose that he still cared for her. "We broke up last Christmas."

"That's too bad. Was it another guy?"

"No." He explained the circumstances of Brad's death and how it had affected Katie. He told Michelle he was still puzzled by their breakup.

"Maybe you'll get back together," she said. "You never know. She could change."

"I doubt it."

Sandy gazed into Michelle's eyes. He read deep sympathy and caring. He asked, "How about you? Do you have a boyfriend?"

"No. Most of the guys at my high school aren't worth two cents. They're all trying to figure out ways to avoid the draft. One boy I know talked his girlfriend into getting pregnant—*so they could get married.* Don't you think that's sick? As far as I know, they're not drafting married men with children, especially guys barely out of high school."

Sandy nodded. "Yeah, gosh, that's really sad. I would have never done that."

By three in the afternoon, Michelle's parents signaled that it was time to come in and prepare for their trip home. "I like you, Sandy. You have a good heart and a good head on your shoulders. You'll go far, I just know it."

"I wish it wasn't Sunday," he told her.

"Me too. I think it would have been fun to go on a date." She took a pen and paper from her beach bag and wrote down her address. "Write to me, Sandy. I promise I'll write back, even if—and especially if—you're in Vietnam."

"Okay, sure," he said, taking the folded paper. "Maybe I will."

"Good-bye, Sandy, and good luck to you."

"Yeah, thanks. Same to you, Michelle."

He opened his eyes and saw a fishing boat, on the horizon, trolling. Suddenly he had a feeling of déja vu, a feeling of being transported back to that moment on the beach with the girl named Michelle. "Hey, GI, you want notha ice-cold Coke?"

Sandy turned. It was the two Vietnamese boys again. "Sure, how much this time?"

"Same-same as befo. Bipty cents," the smaller one said.

"I'll give you seventy-five. That last Coke was number one. You boys are number one."

They giggled excitedly. "Hokay. You numba one GI." The taller one uncapped the bottle. As he handed the lukewarm drink to the naive American sol-

The Sky Soldiers

dier, he said, "You want numba one boom-boom, GI? We get you good woman, velly cheap. Numba one, numba one."

Sandy grinned. "No thanks. I think I'll pass. Now run along."

"Hokay, GI. But you be very sorry."

"Yeah, I probably will."

When he got back to his hotel room, Sandy took a long shower. The water felt cool against his skin. It soothed him. Again, the image of Michelle came to his mind. He remembered that she wore a navy-blue one-piece bathing suit that accentuated nicely her thighs. His body tingled as he recalled the swell of her breasts and the points of her nipples beneath the fabric. He remembered, too, that it was difficult to keep his eyes from periodically probing the V between her thighs, which appeared as a finally shaped mound. There were times when he couldn't rise from where he sat on the sand for fear of revealing his desire for her. She would be in college now, he thought, probably hooked up with some guy who had her same ambitions. He knew that joining the Peace Corps was one avenue men of draft age took to avoid military service, or at least forestall it. Surely she would have found someone who wanted also to be in the Peace Corps, but who was able to convince her that his purpose in joining was more noble than merely to avoid the draft.

He turned the water off and toweled himself vigorously and went and lay down naked on the bed. He stared at the high ceiling. A fan turned slowly overhead. He wondered what it would be like to be with Michelle. She had a sensuous, almost frivolous, quality about her, he remembered, quite unlike Katie's slightly more severe, more reserved manner, a manner she undoubtedly inherited from her New England-born mother. Yet there was that day after he got home for the Christmas holidays, and Brad's funeral, which still baffled him. Katie had become transformed, a moment in time when her sexuality ruled. He grew strong and tender thinking of that moment. Within minutes, fantasizing between that moment with Katie and how he imagined it would be with Michelle, Sandy exploded in a grand fury of emotion. As he lay there spent, he knew also that the past several days, of hovering exposed above the trees, hunting for the elusive Charlie, had worn him thin. Slowly, surely, he began to realize...*I'm not going to make it through this. I'm going to die here, and I don't want to die here. I need a reason to live—a reason to survive.* He felt the welling in his chest and the tears began to form. *Please, God...Please ...Please...Please...*

Victor R. Beaver

Chapter 76

IT WAS AFTER DARK. THE SHOWERS were going full bore. Hot steam leaked out through every crack and crevice, poured out through both the front and back doors.

> *"Oiyee adoree, don't spit*
> *On the flooree,*
> *Use the cuspidoree*
> *What you think it's foree..."*

"Oh, God, Samp, shut up! My ears! My ears!" Buddy cried.

"What, you don't like my singing?"

"Sir, that is not singing," LeDeux stated. "That is a bull pissing on a flat rock."

"Worse. You sound like a cow in heat!" In spite of their laments, Sampson kept bellowing out notes, his deep baritone voice voiding the steaming shower room of all other sounds. Earlier, he had received a letter from Pam, the stewardess who flew out of Phoenix, saying she would be in Hawaii the weekend before Christmas. Would he care to join her there?

KA...BOOM! KABOOM!

"What the hell—?!"

"Incoming!...Incoming!"

In a split second, the shower stalls were evacuated. Naked as jaybirds, the trio charged toward the nearest bunker and dove in. *KABOOOM!* "Those are the weirdest explosions I ever heard," said Kip, out of the darkness.

"What, they're not mortars...?" someone said.

"I don't think so. It sounded more like a huge flashbulb going off."

"Yeah, come to think of it...that's exactly what it sounded like. Besides, I don't hear the siren going off."

They ventured outside.

"Relax, everybody," Rameriz said, coming out of his hootch. "That was an OV-1 Mohawk, taking pictures."

"Damn, did he have to do it right on top of us? I about slipped and broke my neck!" RT cried.

"Be grateful he's doing it at all," Rameriz said. "Charlie may be up to something. We're taking pictures of the areas surrounding the perimeter for later comparison."

* * *

"I'LL TELL YOU WHAT," COWBOY SAID, "these cooks can run my chuckwagon any day. This damn turkey and these mash potatoes are the best I've ever eaten."

LeDeux reached for the salt and pepper. "I'll tell you all something better, though. We had us a Nigra cook who did up the best black-eyed peas I ever ate. She made cornbread with sugar in it. I'd slap me a dollop of butter on my hunk and it was like eating a piece of heaven, I swear to the All Mighty."

"About every other year we'd have ham for Thanksgiving," Tannah said. "My mother would put a glaze over it so thick it was like eating candy."

Sampson put a sliver of cranberry on his bite of turkey. "You know, I was just thinking. Too bad about Atwater. Man, he was in the wrong place at the wrong time."

"When it's your time...it's your time. That's my philosophy," Buddy remarked.

LeDeux said, "Me, I want to be ninety-five when I die—"

"And shot by a jealous husband. Yeah yeah yeah. When you going to change that tune?"

"What about Chico?" Slater asked. "Has anyone heard?"

"They're shipping him back to the States. I always thought he was one for the nuthouse, especially after he tried to whack that VC's head off."

Rameriz opened the telegram marked urgent and read. It had come late that afternoon.

> *To Captain Michael Thomas Nolan. Stop. Your father has had a stroke. Stop. Left side partially paralyzed. Stop. Request you take special leave to come home. Stop. Aunt Lil. Stop.*

"Get a call through to Can Tho," Rameriz said to his orderly room clerk. "We need to get in touch with Captain Nolan. It's urgent."

"Yessir."

"Wasn't that a great Thanksgiving dinner?" Sharon said, opening the door to her room.

"You bet. And I'm stuffed." Nolan sat down in a wicker chair. "Do you have any kind of liqueur, something sweet? That sounds about what I'd like to have right now."

"Yes," Sharon called from the bathroom. "It's in the cabinet above my desk. Some Cream de Menthe."

"What are you doing?"

"Nothing. Pour me a drink, too. I'll be out in a minute."

Victor R. Beaver

He found the bottle of green liqueur and two glasses and poured a small amount in each. He sat back down in the chair and lifted his glass to the light. "I've been thinking about our trip to Australia," he called out.

"What about it?"

"I've always wanted to visit Alice Springs, in the Outback. Ever since I read that book you gave me by Nevil Shute, the one called 'The Legacy.'"

"Wasn't that a good book?"

"It was great. Very moving. I'm glad you suggested it. You've got me on quite a reading program."

"Shute's books really have a moral to them, very subtle though. Two others I really liked that he wrote are 'No Highway' and 'Trustee From The Toolroom,'" Sharon said. "I've got them for you to take back with you."

As he thought of *The Legacy,* he thought too about Atwater and the kind of man he was. There had been something almost saintly about him. He had poise and grace and dignity, character traits he seldom found combined all in one person. He made a silent vow to go see Atwater's family one day, after he and Sharon had settled in the States.

He stood and went to her bed and proceeded to take his clothes off. He turned the bed down and got under the covers.

"Michael?"

"What?"

"Light the candle that's on the table next to the bed, please."

"Okay."

When she appeared, he thought he was seeing a vision of an angel. She seemed to float before him as if on a cloud. There was a kind of halo around her head and he had to take a second look to reassure himself that it was his imagination. "Oh...my God...you...look dynamite."

"Dynamite...?" she said demurely. "Well, I suppose we are going to create a few fireworks." She turned to one side and then the other to give him a full view. "Kind of risqué, but I thought, why wait until Christmas to give you this gift. How do you like the way I'm wrapped?"

Nolan took a deep breath. "Better than any Christmas present I've ever received, you can bet on that."

She got under the covers and snuggled in his arms. "Michael, I want to say this to you, Darling, and I mean it with my whole heart and soul. For some reason, don't ask me why, I thought I would never be with a man. Maybe it wasn't in my sights. But that's all changed now. You are my love and my life, from now until forever. Whatever you want...whatever you need...whatever you desire...I want you to come to me to receive it. Do you promise that you will never want because of something I could have given you?" He had turned his head. As he was listening to her, tears had formed. "Look at me, Darling."

"I...I can't..."

580

"The loss of your platoon sergeant has been hard on you, hasn't it?"
"Yes."
She enfolded him in her arms and held him, placing his head against the swell of her breasts. She cradled his head with one hand and ran her fingers lightly across the back of his head, stroking him, comforting him. "It's okay, my darling, it's okay. Wherever he is, he's certainly in a better place...You do you believe that, don't you?"

Mike slowly nodded his head. After a few moments, he felt the tension ease from his body, to be replaced by a tension of another kind. It hadn't occur to him until recently that in the throes of making love, particularly in the absolute delicious anticipation of it, how the world surrounding him could all be made to disappear at once, as if the only universe he occupied was the one that contained just him and the one he loved. Suddenly, he felt utterly secure, totally at peace. He had never known the world could be so bright in the middle of so much gloom. Atwater was gone, gone as if he had never existed, but he had existed; and Nolan knew he would never forget the one man he could have easily called his brother.

Sharon turned his head toward her. Tenderly, she kissed his eyes and also the trail of tears that went down the side of his face. Her lips went down to his neck and he felt the surge of tingles up and down his spine. She trailed her kisses down and across his chest, back and forth, back and forth. "Sharon...Sharon...you are so lovely...so incredible...I love you."

"I love you, too, Michael. I can't wait to be your wife."

They had just dropped off to sleep when there came a light knocking on the door. "Sharon, are you in there?" came the voice from outside.

Sharon gathered her robe. "Yes, who is it?"

"It's me, Frieda."

Sharon moved the door slightly ajar. "What's the matter?"

"I really hate to disturb you, but...is Michael there with you?"

"Yes—"

"He's supposed to call his base. It's very urgent, something about his father."

"Oh...okay. Thank you, Frieda."

Sharon closed the door. Michael was up and getting dressed. In the library, across the breezeway from her room, Sharon listened as Michael spoke on the phone. "...thank you, sir. I appreciate it. I'll be right there." He put the receiver down. "My father's had a stroke. My CO has arranged for me to take emergency leave."

"Is it bad?"

"Yes, pretty bad. Damn, I really hate to leave. I'm so sorry, Sharon."

"Don't apologize, sweetheart. Go. I'll be here waiting when you get back."

"I'll probably be gone a week. I really wanted you to meet him."

"Don't worry. Unless he's worse than you've been told, I'll meet him."

He took her in his arms. He held her tight, tighter than he had ever done. "Darling, don't worry about me," she said, when he had loosened his hold on her. "You do what you have to do. I feel bad for you."

Nolan strode to the waiting helicopter. He climbed aboard, looked back and waved. As it lifted, Sharon cried out, *"Come back, my love, please come back soon—"*

* * *

IT WAS NEARING TEN O'CLOCK IN THE evening. The nurse, a woman in her early thirties, dressed in an aquamarine smock and white pants, led Nolan down the narrow hospital corridor. "He should be sleeping now," she said. "I gave him a sedative fifteen minutes ago."

"That's okay. I just want to see him."

"He's not doing too bad, all things considered," she remarked. "But I'm afraid his days out on the water may be over. What a shame."

The nurse came to his father's room and quietly opened the door. "Mr. Nolan, I can't believe you're not asleep yet," she said, going to him and adjusting his pillow. "You have a visitor." His father turned and looked up.

"Hi, Pop. How're you doing?"

"Mi-Michael?"

"Yeah, it's me, Pop. Lay back now...that's good."

"How...how did you get...here?" his father asked.

He lifted his hand and Michael took it. The nurse scooted a chair toward him and he sat down. "I'll be back at the nurse's station if you need me," she said. "Just push this little button."

"Okay, thanks."

He could tell that his father's eyes were heavy, fighting sleep. "I left Saigon yesterday morning, Pop. Got to Travis Air Force Base—that's in California—this morning. I caught the first direct flight I could. They didn't have anything leaving for Miami until the afternoon."

"The...boat, Son. I didn't moor it...very good," his father said feebly.

"That's okay, Pop. I talked to Ben. He said she's tied up good and everything's been stowed." Ben Murphy was the owner of the small marina where the *Laura Lee* was berthed. "Are you comfortable? Can I get you anything?"

"Wa...water..."

"Sure, Pop." Nolan reached for the pitcher on the hospital bed table that was just above his father's lower legs. He helped his father to sit up. Michael placed the glass next to his lips; the old man's right arm shook as he tried to put his hand next to his son's.

"Thanks...I get so damn dry."

As Nolan sat there watching his father's eyelids droop lower and lower, he pondered Aunt Lil's proposal to have her brother come to Toledo to live with her, where she maintained a small two-story home on a modest pension. There was nothing else to do, Mike concluded sadly. His father had taken his last trip on the *Laura Lee*. Between the two of them there had been so much promise. And now it had all come to an end. He continued to hold onto his father's hand. "Is she pretty?" the older man asked, still fighting sleep.

"Who?...You mean Sharon?"

"Yeah."

"Yes, Pop. At least I think so."

"I still...want to...to meet her."

"You will, Pop. Sometime this coming January, I'll be bringing her home. She wants to meet you too."

"You'll be...married then?"

"Yes. We're going to Australia. We'll be married over the Christmas holidays. It's...the way we planned it, Pop."

His father tightened his grip. "What, Pop?"

"Do...you have a...picture of her?"

"No...no I don't." Nolan sighed. At that moment he realized it was one of his great regrets, that neither he nor Sharon owned a camera, thus they had no pictures of any of their times together. "I'll send one when I get back, Pop, I promise."

"That's good...that's good." His father paused for a minute. "Do you still have that picture...of you and me in front of the Laura Lee, with the—"

"Blue marlin. You bet, Pop. I keep it right at my bed, like I told you I always would."

The old man nodded. He closed his eyes. After a few minutes, Michael saw the old man's chest rising and lowering rhythmically, fast asleep finally.

* * *

THE CAB DRIVER SPOKE LITTLE AS he watched the windshield wipers work furiously to stay the giant snowflakes. The lake-effect snow off Lake Erie had already blanketed most of northern Ohio and the weather system was making its way eastward into Pennsylvania. "Been a while since we've had this kind of donnybrook," he said, turning to his occupants in the back.

Mike nodded. He glanced at his father seated next to him, bundled in a heavy coat, with a scarf around his neck, and wearing leather gloves and a tan felt hat. "How's it going, Pop?"

"I can't remember the last time I saw so much snow," his father said glumly.

"Yeah, me either. Do you think you can get used to it?"

"Maybe...I don't know. I doubt it."

"I'm sorry, Pop."

"That's okay. My time has come. What I had couldn't last forever."

"No, I guess not."

The driver switched on the radio. *"...several major installations were hit. Sources say that over seventy-five rockets landed at the Da Nang air base, in I Corps, destroying four CH-53 helicopters and seven F-4 Phantom jets. Other news, intelligence reports state that North Vietnamese troops within the demilitarized zone have prompted U.S. and ARVN forces to enter the buffer zone with the intent of driving the enemy back from its advanced positions. Advisors to the President state that he should resume bombing raids over Hanoi."*

After several more minutes of maneuvering on the white, snow-packed streets, they pulled in front of his aunt's house, a square two-story building made of rose-red brick with small white leaded bay windows and a Greek porch over the front door. While the cab driver worked to get the luggage, Nolan guided his father gingerly along the snowcapped sidewalk to the front steps and helped him onto the porch. "I remember once doing the same for you," his father said quietly, "taking you by the hand. It was snowing to beat the band, I remember."

"I was four or five, wasn't I?"

"Something like that."

His aunt, a little stoop-shouldered woman in her late seventies, ushered them in. After giving her brother a quick visual examination, assuring herself that he was not a total invalid, and her nephew a cursory look hinting at affection, she turned and, shuffling ahead of them, led them into a high-ceilinged kitchen. After a few minutes she had them both comfortable at the kitchen table. "I'm brewing some tea, or I can make coffee. I've got eggnog, too, if you prefer," she said, her voice sounding on the edge of impatience.

"You got any rum?" her brother asked.

"Not a drop."

"It's going to be fun living around here," he grumbled.

"No more pirating for you, little brother. I also run a tight ship. You step out of line I'll make you walk the plank—"

His father smiled which raised Nolan's spirits slightly for having to bring him to this dreary place so far from the Florida Keys. "This summer," his aunt said, "you can bring your new wife here, Michael, and we'll go boating on Lake Erie. It's rather picturesque...maybe not like Florida, but—"

"Thanks, Aunt Lil."

It was the following day. Michael was scheduled to leave. As he waited for the cab to take him to the airport, the news on TV caught his eye and he stood riveted to the set. *"A Saigon military spokesman for Operation Samurai Sword, as it is being dubbed by Pentagon officials, says that an allied force of nearly four thousand men using riverine armored troop carriers and river patrol boats and helicopters have begun to enter the extreme southern tip of the Ca Mau Pen-*

insula. They will also attempt to eradicate the Viet Cong from a long-held sanctuary called the U Minh, a large forest of mangrove to the north and west of Ca Mau City."

"Sonofabitch," Nolan stated aloud, watching more of the news tape. He saw several cav helicopters landing at the Ca Mau airstrip. "That's my damn unit!"

Just then the doorbell rang. Nolan stood. He bent down and put his arms around his father. "That's the cab, Pop. I guess I'll be going. I'm sorry...for everything."

His father grabbed his hand. Michael saw that the old man had tears in his eyes. "Watch out for yourself, Son. About the business...and the boat...it's all yours. Consider it a...wedding gift. Good luck...and be happy."

"Yeah, sure, Pop. You too. I'll be seeing you soon."

"Good-bye, Son."

"Good-bye, Pop."

Chapter 77

VALERIE COLE SAT IN FRONT OF THE TV, her eyes fixed on the newscaster, a lump forming in her throat. She was barely breathing. She had been doing the dishes when she caught a glimpse of the newscast. She had then come quickly into the living room to catch the rest of what was being said. When the clip was over, she found the dishtowel she was holding wound tight around her hands.

"What's the matter, Mommy?" Jill asked. "Why are you crying?"

"Dear...I just am. There was some good new about where Daddy might be...and it just made me cry."

"Is he coming home? Is he-is he?" the child stammered happily.

"No-no, dear, nothing like that...at least not yet." Valerie took her daughter and held her on her lap. "But don't worry. Someday that will happen and you'll get to see him."

"I want to see him now. Do you think he'll remember me?"

"Oh, yes, darling, yes he will. I bet he's thinking about you right now."

"I'll bet he's not thinking of Robbie!"

"Jill, how dare you say that—"

"But, Mommy, Robbie pinched me—hard!"

"What for?"

"I don't know. I told him his room was a mess."

"Listen, young lady, that's my job to tell him his room is a mess, not yours—"

"He has his things everywhere. I found one of his dirty socks under my bed."

Later that evening, as she was tucking the children into bed, her son asked, "When's Dad coming home?"

"I don't know, Robbie. I wish I could tell you. It's hard, isn't it, darling, to wait and wait and wait?"

"Are you going to tell on me when he gets back?"

"Tell on you?"

"All the bad things I did? I'll bet you have lots to tell. I guess I'm a bad person, huh?"

Valerie sighed. "Robbie, listen to me. You're not a bad person. Sometimes you do bad things, like put bubblegum in your sister's hair, or you don't take out the trash when I ask, but that doesn't make you bad. Besides, Daddy loves you no matter what. You're not automatically good and you're not automatically bad, but you have to strive to be good."

"Will you tell him that I tried to be good?" her son said.

"Oh, yes, darling, of course I will."

"Mom, are you afraid that Dad will never come home?"

The Sky Soldiers

"Sometimes."

"When will we know if he's not going to be back?"

"I don't know. But I heard on the news today that the Army is going to try harder to look for him. I hate to make any promises, but maybe sometime soon we'll know more about where he is and when he might be coming home."

Her son suddenly jumped out of bed. He went to his closet. "What are you doing?" she said.

"Uncle Derek gave me something to keep. He said if I take good care of them, and make sure they're always shiny, that my dad will come home someday."

"Well, goodness, what is it?"

He emerged from the closet with an old cigar box. "I've got them in here." He came and handed her the box, opening it as he did. Gleaming back at her were a set of Army aviator wings and a graduation ring.

"You said Uncle Derek gave these to you?"

"Yes. They're his. He got them when he graduated from helicopter school. He asked me to keep them safe for him. Aren't they shiny?"

She took the wings and turned them over and then back again. "You've done a beautiful job, Robbie." She replaced the wings as her son lifted the ring. She had never seen it before. He handed it to her and she gazed at the blue stone. On one side of the stone was a miniature replica of a set of Army aviator wings; on the other was the school emblem; embossed underneath the emblem were the words "Above the Best." She looked at the inside of the ring. The initials *DPJ* had been engraved there. Suddenly, she clutched the ring tightly to her chest. She looked away.

"What's the matter, Mom? Why are you crying?" the boy said, reaching and touching her arm.

She took a moment to speak. "I guess...because your Uncle Derek has been trying...so hard to find your father. And it's taking him so long."

"Yeah, I know," Robbie said. "He's brave. He's my hero."

Valerie reached up and patted her son's head. "Mine too, dear. Your Uncle Derek is my hero, too."

* * *

HE SAT WITH HIS BACK STRAIGHT AGAINST the nylon seat. He was a passenger among thirty other men in the large CH-47 helicopter, which now lifted into flight and began its roll forward to pick up speed. The Chinook was bound for Can Tho, and from there he would catch another flight to Vinh Long, after his visit with Sharon. During the week and a half he'd been gone time had stood still. The grueling nineteen-hour flight to the States, the formalities of settling his father's affairs, the trip to Toledo, and then the equally long flight back

Victor R. Beaver

had taken its toll. Mike Nolan felt exhausted. He had got precious little sleep during the return trip and knew from what he had seen and heard on the news there would be little chance to catch up.

He had been dozing when the helicopter banked hard right and woke him up. Nolan turned and looked out the window. Can Tho. He quickly got his bearings: There was the control tower, the long line of revetments that protected the Cobras of the 235th, there was his old hootch, and operations where he had spent so much of his time, and then he saw next to it several buildings that appeared to have been flattened, as if by a bad storm, with debris still scattered about. And then he saw the officers' club and a portion of it destroyed. The man next to him, a young spec five, said, "VC rockets took out several hootches near the main hangar down there. A buddy of mine got killed."

As the helicopter rolled to an attitude level with the horizon, Mike said, "How many came in?"

"Five one twenty-two-millimeter rockets, they said, and about fifty mortar rounds. I was on Rn'R. Another buddy said the mortars came in so fast he couldn't count them."

Nolan felt his stomach muscles tighten. He looked out the window and tried to get a glimpse of the library and dayroom, next to Sharon's room, but the ship was out of position. "How many casualties?"

"Seven killed and thirty-two wounded."

Nolan took a deep breath. He felt his heart racing. He wanted to ask about the library and dayroom but dared not. In a moment the aircraft came to a high hover and began to settle downward. When it was finally on the ground, the crewchief extended the back ramp and the men unbuckled and began to move out of the ship with their luggage.

Nolan stepped from the ship, immediately shielding his eyes from the bright glare of the sun. He could feel his legs shaking as he tried to quell the rising terror within him. *Everything's going to be all right...everything's going to be just fine.* Calmly, he walked over to K Street, past the air traffic control tower, past the airfield operations hootch, past the officers' club. He turned and went two more blocks, to the street the library and dayroom sat on. He stared at what was left of the library, which now gaped back at him as a pile of splintered rubble. His heart throbbed now in his throat. He went slowly down the street and came to where the front door had been. He stopped. Several enlisted men were still sifting through the rubble, trying to salvage whatever books they could find not damaged by the blast. He saw that several cardboard boxes had already been filled. For some reason this lifted his spirits; each book retrieved from the debris, he fantasized momentarily, meant...meant...meant—What? He looked to his left. Sharon's room, still somewhat connected by the breezeway, stood intact. Gazing at it, Nolan took his first deep breath in several minutes. He relaxed. "How's it going, guys?"

One of the enlisted men looked up, hesitated, and then managed a weak salute. Nolan returned it casually. "Kind of a mess, uh?" Nolan said.

"Yessir," the man said, and then diverted his attention to the task at hand.

Nolan stooped down and picked up the remains of a shredded book that had been tossed aside. "Was anybody hurt here?"

"Uh...yessir. The uh...woman who ran the library."

Michael's heart stopped. "Oh?...How is she?"

"I-I don't know, sir. They had to evacuate her and several other people—I think, that is."

"Michael..."

He turned. It was Frieda, Sharon's co-worker. The pallor in her face, the look in her eyes, made the blood drain from his head. Suddenly he felt faint. Frieda said, "Would you...come with me?"

"Is she—?"

Frieda nodded. For the longest moment he just stood and stared at her. And then his legs buckled. Later, long afterwards, he would remember a primordial scream that had emanated from deep within his being, as if his soul had been wrenched from his gut.

Nolan came to consciousness in a sun-filled room; he found himself covered by a clean white linen sheet. He blinked several times to catch his bearings, but nothing around him seemed even remotely familiar. A woman in jungle fatigues, a stethoscope draped around her neck, passed in front of his bed, smiled, and kept on moving. The man in the bed next to his looked over at him and bid him good morning. "Who are you?" Nolan asked.

"The name's Miller. And you?"

Nolan frowned. I uh...I'm not sure. Where am I?"

"The Twenty-ninth Evac. Can Tho. Don't you know?"

Nolan glanced around until he came to recognize some of the features of his surroundings, now coming back to him from his stay back in October, after he was wounded. Down the hall he saw a woman coming toward him. He recognized the gait, the form of the body, the shape, color and cut of the hair. She was pushing a cart. He smiled. He waved. He mouthed a name. "Sharon...?" When the woman came closer, he saw that her features had somehow changed completely, and the cart she pushed filled with a varying assortment of hospital instruments. And then the reality hit him. He clutched the side of the bed, gasping, as if the breath had been knocked completely out of him. Suddenly he felt his chest in a vice-like grip. And then he broke down heaving.

* * *

"SIT DOWN, CAPTAIN NOLAN. PLEASE."

"Yessir."

Victor R. Beaver

Major Salvador Francisco Rameriz reached over and offered Nolan a cigarette. Michael declined.

"We...uh tried to get in touch with you, but had no way of doing so," the major said.

"That's okay, sir. I understand."

"I'm really sorry."

"Yes, sir." And then softly: "So am I..."

"Are you going to be all right?"

"Yes, sir...I'll be just fine."

Major Rameriz reached back and took from a wooden stand near his chair a jumble of papers and laid them on his desk. "We're moving the troop to Ca Mau," he said. "We've got to start the process tomorrow. Can I depend on you to follow through at your end?"

"Yes, sir. Of course...you can, sir."

"We haven't got much time, less than seven days to be there and operational."

"I understand, sir."

"Look, Mike..." Rameriz said, trying now to cut through the glare of sorrow that clouded over the man like an ugly veil, "...I wish I could help. Damn do I wish I could help. I'm in a tight spot. The whole troop is. You need some time alone, but I'm afraid I can't give—"

"Sir," Nolan interrupted. "I'm going to be fine. I'm a soldier, sir...Remember?"

Rameriz nodded. "Yes...yes, you are."

Nolan stood. Lethargically, he raised his arm and saluted. "May I go now, sir? I've got to attend to my men."

Rameriz half-heartedly returned the salute. "Yes. Go ahead."

Nolan turned and went toward the door.

"Mike."

Nolan stopped, still facing the door. "Yes, sir?"

"If you need someone to talk to..."

Slowly, Nolan nodded his head. "I'll remember that, sir. Thank you, sir." Then he went out the door.

In his room, Nolan wept, not knowing how he was going to go on. In the past two days there had not been one moment when he didn't think of her. At night, to get to sleep, he drank, but would awaken early to a room full of darkness. He wept then, too, uncontrollably, like a frightened child. In daylight, in front of the men, he represented the epitome of stoicism. He gave orders, quietly, methodically. His Blues moved silently about him.

He had learned later from Frieda, when he could listen, that Sharon had been working late, sorting through a new shipment of books in the back room, when the first rockets hit. The main part of the library had taken a direct hit and a large chunk of shrapnel had gone through the wall and had slashed into her back. When the medics found her, they determined that she had been knocked unconscious and had bled to death. They said she had a copy of Robert Louis Stevenson poems clutched to her chest. Frieda had given him the book. He picked it up and opened it to the page Sharon had placed a bookmark, the last words on earth she must have been reading.

> "We uncommiserate pass into the night
> From the loud banquet, and departing leave
> A tremor in men's memories, faint and sweet
> And frail as music. Features of our face,
> The tones of the voice, the touch of the loved hand,
> Perish and vanish, one by one, from earth:
> Meanwhile, in the hall of song, the multitude
> Applauds the new performer. One, perchance,
> One ultimate survivor lingers on,
> And smiles, and to his ancient heart recalls
> The long forgotten. Ere the morrow die,
> He too, returning, though the curtain comes,
> And the new age forgets us and moves on."

* * *

SANDY ADAMSON TOOK THE ENVELOPE and saw the delicate handwriting. He glanced at the return address and his heart took a leap. It smelled of perfume, the kind he remembered her wearing the morning they met on the beach. Quickly, he opened it.

Dear Sandy,
  I received your letter this morning and felt compelled to return the same right away. What a delight to hear from you. I've often thought about you and wondered how you were doing. I can't even imagine the danger you're in. I hope you are doing everything you can to be safe. In the past, I used to pray for all our servicemen fighting in Vietnam, but now that I know for certain you are there, I will say a special prayer just for you.
  It must be very difficult to be so far from home. Are you eating okay? Do you get to sleep in a bed or a foxhole? I've always wondered why they call it that. Is it because you share it with a fox, like a foxy lady? Ha Ha.
  If you have time to write again, please do. I'd love to hear from you.
                                            Sincerely yours,
                                            Michelle

Victor R. Beaver

Chapter 78

THE MOVE TO CA MAU AND BE operational took the better part of six days. A compound was built north of the oblong-shaped lake, on the side opposite the dirt and gravel airstrip. During the build-up process, Rameriz directed the TOC (tactical operations center) to be placed in the middle of the new camp, along with the messhall, orderly room, and supply. On the periphery the men erected a maze of GP-medium tents as living quarters. Showers, shaving stations, and shitters went up; nothing, however, as elaborate as what they had at Vinh Long. Guard bunkers sprouted around the perimeter, to be manned day and night. C-123s flew in hundreds of cases of rockets, M-79 rounds, and rifle- and machine-gun ammunition; these were stored in large CONEX containers, tucked safely away from the main compound. Near the shore Army construction engineers erected revetments, enough to protect at least half the aircraft. They a built a small, tin-roofed hangar where the mechanics and armorers could perform minor aircraft and armament maintenance. Chinook helicopters sling-loaded in two dozen fuel bladders, large black rubberized containers filled with JP-4. While all this was going on, a U.S. Army 155-artillery battery was moved in and positioned south of the runway at the east end. On the morning of the third day, the artillerymen began to register their guns. After this was done, the cannons went off around the clock, H&I (harassment and interdiction) fire, in the beginning aimed to the south. Later, when it was determined where the VC actually where in the U Minh Forest, north and west of Ca Mau, and with a large measure of concern for the safety of any POWs, H&I fire would be directed there, too. Occasionally, they conducted a FAC-requested fire mission. Each time one of the guns fired, Derek Justen cringed in his boots, wondering where the shells were impacting.

After the Tet offensive that spring, after the Viet Cong took over the Nam Can outpost and the area was abandoned by the Saigon government, an operation's order was issued in November for U.S. Navy Swift boats to penetrate the lower Ca Mau Peninsula, there to begin regular raids along the rivers and canals. The Viet Cong answered this threat by building bunkers and other fortifications along the rivers. Dozens of barricades also went across the more important waterways to stem the easy access of the Swift boats. Then, a week before Charlie Troop's move to Ca Mau, elements of River Assault Squadron 11 made an open sea transit from Rach Gia, a coastal city north of inland Ca Mau, to the Song Qua Lon, the river that runs past Nam Can. In a matter of days the task force demolished the solidly constructed barricades and followed up by establishing Navy Nam Can, a base near the old city from which Navy SEALs and the Mobile Riverine Force could operate. By December 12, all forces were in place. The allied plan to retake the peninsula and to eradicate the Viet Cong from the U Minh Forest was ready to begin.

Scott gathered his scout pilots and gunners. The swarthy lieutenant had dark circles around his eyes from lack of sleep, as did most of his men. "Here's the skinny. We're going into a new mode of operation, just like the real cav up north: we're going to operate in two-ship, hunter-killer teams. A single Cobra as the high bird and a Loach as the low bird. We're also going to get rid of the minigun." Scott paused to let this bit of news sink in. Everyone's face held a deadpan look. "I'm giving you crewchief-gunners the option of staying in the rear, behind the pilot, with your M-60s, or move up front with an M-16 or CAR-15. From now on the Scouts will operate with a third man onboard. Now I know what you're thinking: why change horses in mid-stream? Guys, I'll put it to you like the Old Man did to me. South of Dam Doi, especially in the vicinity of Nam Can, the VC are thick as flies. You're likely to come under fire by any person you see. And it's going to be worse if we penetrate the U Minh. Since to aim the minigun we have to turn the aircraft toward the target, getting rid of it and having a gunner slash observer up front will give us another pair of eyes and a greater arc of fire. It would be nice to keep the minigun, but with the third man, plus all the ammo you both will be stocked with, the system plus its own ammo supply are just too much weight to carry."

"Are we going to get any training on this new way of operating?" Mark Allen asked.

Scott nodded. "You'll be given two days to get your shit together, as a team in the cockpit, and with the high bird. I'll arrange a training schedule and post it tonight. When we start getting our daily combat assignments, we're likely to have three and four 'pink teams' out at a time. If you're not aware of it, that's what they call the combination of a single Cobra and a low bird. Red for guns and white for scouts make pink. Also, the gunner in the back is called 'the torque.' I guess because when he fires his M-60 the aircraft wants to twist the opposite way the bullets are going. I never thought of it that way, but it makes sense."

Scott took a deep breath. "The Major will no longer be in everyone's hip pocket like he's been in the past. He'll be out in the AO, he told me, to monitor some of our activities. Mostly, though, we'll be on our own. In some instances, recon by fire will be the order of the day. Are there any questions?"

Sandy raised his hand. "Where will we get the other gunner?"

"I've asked for volunteers from the rest of the troop, mainly the Blue Platoon. We need six; so far I've got thirteen. I'll make my selections tonight. Are there anymore questions?" There were none. "Okay, guys. Get some rest. And lay off the shit for a while. Tomorrow—and from here on—we're going to be busier than a band of Indians at a massacre. We wanted a target-rich environment, by God, we're going to have one."

Victor R. Beaver

* * *

"CAN YOU BELIEVE IT?" LEO TANNAH said, seated on his cot in the gun platoon tent. "We lost Oakerson and his crew back in May evacuating Nam Can. Now the Navy waltzes in and has a damn operational base down there. What gives—?"

Kip Slater's face turned a bright crimson. "Damnit, Leo, don't ask me shit like that!"

Earlier, Slater and John Sampson, along with LeDeux and RT, received word from Briscoe that they would be flying "two-ship" to Nam Can, to work with one of the SEAL teams. At first, the thought of flying these quick-strike teams anywhere paralyzed Slater. But then he remembered their reputation while operating in the Rung Sat Special Zone, south of Saigon, and a nearly unbelievable story of their tenacity and valor that occurred during Tet. Two SEALs were sent to recon the Cambodian border near the Seven Mountains region in February. Dressed in black pajamas, and carrying weapons that could not identify them as Americans, they passed themselves off to the local inhabitants as Russian advisors. They verified the presence of several hundred enemy soldiers in camps around the region, and of numerous caches of food, weapons, ammunition, and other supplies.

Leo handed Kip his camera. "Take some pictures of those guys for me, will you?"

"Leo, I'm not going down there to sightsee."

"Are you scared?"

"Yes, damnit."

Kip met John Sampson at the ship. "Are you ready?" he asked the good-looking ex-navy enlisted man.

"Sure."

"The hell you are. Stuff your pockets with everything you can think of."

"How come?"

"Samp, goddamnit, where we're going, we may never come back."

"Are you serious?"

"As a heart attack."

"Oh, fuck..."

At eight o'clock that morning, Derek Justen met his new machine gunner, a man named Hoyt, from the Blue Platoon. Standing off to one side, he watched as Kalbach showed Hoyt around the OH-6, pointing out where he would sit, how he would have to fire his M-60, what to do in case of an emergency. Justen then started the helicopter and the three men flew to a safe area northeast of Ca Mau, where he placed the aircraft in various flight attitudes to see how the new man reacted.

On the ground, Hoyt said, "Man, sir, that was fucking great. Do we fly like that all the time?"

"Pretty much."

Kalbach showed Hoyt how to refuel the aircraft. When this task was done, Justen called his two gunners together. He took a cigarette and lit it. "I'm going to tell you how it's going to be out there," he began. "Around Nam Can we're not going to have any trouble finding Charlie. Nor will we if we get into the U Minh. But there are still civilians out there, fishermen and woodcutters, doing their thing away from their villages, who could care less who's running the damn government. We don't want to hurt or kill them if we can help it." Justen shrugged. "We probably will anyway. When I consider the conditions appropriate, I'll give you guys blanket permission to fire. Otherwise, consider yourselves on 'safe,' which means you ask me first for permission to shoot. I personally want to see your target. Is that understood?" Both men nodded. "Also, in this part of the Delta there are an estimated three dozen American POWs. After two and three and four years of captivity, I doubt they're going to look a whole lot different than their captors, at least at first sight. We've got to make damn sure we don't zap one of them." Justen paused for a second. He glowered at them. "I swear to God, I'll kill whichever one of you who does."

Hoyt's eyes widened. "Sir—are you serious?"

Calmly, Derek said, "Yes, I am."

"But what if we shoot somebody because we couldn't tell the difference—?"

"You have to know the difference—do you hear me? *You have to know the difference—*"

"Yes, sir."

* * *

THE FLIGHT TO NAM CAN TOOK LESS than twenty minutes. Slater led his two-ship formation at two thousand feet altitude, out of effective range of most small-arms fire. With Sampson at the controls, Slater gazed down at the terrain. Before him lay a region of thick mangrove swamps, barren mud flats, and winding rivers. It seemed a place of desolation, of strangulation—of death.

Five minutes out from Nam Cam, Kip felt the same dread he did during his last extraction from the Nam Can LZ, in May. The knot in his stomach tightened and a cold sweat broke out on his brow. And then he saw it. *The whole riverine task force!* The *Benewah,* the flotilla's command and control flagship, sat anchored in the middle of the Song Qua Lon, near Old Nam Can City, surrounded by her sister ships and dozens and dozens of smaller ATCs, monitors, and ASPBs. He recognized the *Colleton,* another barracks ship, which also housed the hospital facilities for both Navy and Army 9th Division, 2nd Brigade personnel. Alongside the *Askari,* the repair ship for the Mobile Riverine Force, Slater saw two Ammi pontoons and several armored troop carriers. Among these larger ships, as a member of River Support Squadron 7, was one support LST assigned as a storage ship, with enough space to keep a ten-day supply of ammunition and C-rations, a ten-day emergency backup of dry cargo, and that portion of the basic army troop support load (primarily ammunition and weapon spares) which could not be carried on the *Benewah*, the *Colleton*, or one of the non-self-propelled APLs.

The entire show of force brought shivers up and down Kip's spine, mostly shivers of pride. During practically his whole tour in the Mekong Delta he had dealt mainly with the ARVN, and never once in all the time he airlifted them into LZs, or picked them out of the field, did he feel any real camaraderie toward them. For this lack of kinship, though, Kip and his fellow pilots didn't have to airlift their own countrymen into combat, which would have made their tour with the Delta's assault companies that much harder to bear—and probably to survive.

Patrol boats ran orbits on all four sides of the flotilla, providing the riverine base's main defense perimeter. As added security, on both shores near the flotilla, were an armed force of men: local South Vietnamese "Biet Hai" Rangers on one bank, Kit Carson scouts (former VC who had defected and worked on missions against their ex-comrades) on the other. Sampson declared to Slater over the intercom: "Man, what the hell were you worried about? Our whole damn navy is here."

As they flew over the *Benewah*, the two pilots saw the large, square, white helicopter landing pad built on the deck of the self-propelled barracks ship. A seaman on the deck waved and Sampson waved back.

Slater relaxed. He pulled out a pack of cigarettes, took one and lit up. Easing back in his seat, he told Sampson to circle the *Benewah*. He spoke to LeDeux on the radio. "Comanche Two Two, this is Two Seven. Let's come up the contact frequency and see what's going on."

"Roger that," LeDeux answered.

"Dark Shadow Three Seven Alpha, this is Comanche Two Seven. We're the two UH-1s overhead. Where do you want us?"

"Roger, Comanche Two Seven, this is Dark Shadow Three Seven Alpha. We want you to land one helicopter at a time. I'll have the first ship land, load and then lift. Then we'll take the second helicopter. Make your approach from north to south. Have the pilot who is *not* flying put his arm out the window. The landing guide will focus on the *other* pilot to get you in."

"Roger that," Kip replied.

While LeDeux and RT remained at altitude, Slater told Sampson to set up a left-hand traffic pattern letdown. On final approach, Slater stuck his arm out the right cockpit window, which signaled to the landing guide that Sampson was at the controls.

The Sky Soldiers

Once on the pad, three men dressed in Tiger fatigues, their faces painted, wearing boonie hats or headbands, and carrying a varying assortment of weapons, clambered onboard. One of them, a sharp-featured, clean-shaven man, with fierce blazing eyes, held onto a map encased in plastic. He grabbed Slater's shoulder and pointed at a location on the map encircled by grease pencil. "We're going here!" he shouted.

"Oh yeah?" Slater shouted back. "And then what?"

"We'll let you know!"

"Do we need gunship cover?"

"What for—?"

Slater rolled his eyes. "Oh, Christ...No reason I can think of!"

"Then let's get the hell out of here!"

To his right, Slater saw three more SEALs, armed and waiting. He took the controls. "Two Two, this Two Seven, we're lifting. Looks like you'll have three more of these guys to pick up."

"Roger that."

"We'll be orbiting until you come up."

"Ten-four," LeDeux answered. "What's the scoop?"

"Top Secret. I hope your life insurance is paid up."

After the two ships rejoined, Slater handed control of the aircraft back over to Sampson. He then compared his smaller scale operational map with the one he had been given. He told Sampson to take up a 145-degree heading to start.

"Roger that. Where are we going?"

"Hell, I don't know—out in the middle of nowhere—a swampy area less that two klicks from the shore."

Sampson glanced back at the three vacant-faced U.S. Navy SEALs. One of them carried a shotgun, "choked" to throw 4-buck wide when fired, a nice horizontal spray of buckshot. The other two carried M63s, the Stoner, a diverse weapon that could be converted into an assault rifle, a sub-machine gun, or when mounted on a tripod, a light or medium machine gun. Turning his gaze forward, he said, "I knew one of those guys at Pensacola. I swear to God, this is no shit, he slept on seashells spread out on the floor—barebacked."

"What for?"

"I didn't ask."

After several minutes they were over the coordinates marked on the map. "What do you see, anything?" Slater asked Sampson.

"Nothing but flat marsh."

The one who had given up the map, grabbed again at Slater's shoulder and pointed downward. "Land there!"

"There?—I don't see anything!"

"You can't!"

"Oh—"

"Two Two, this is Two Seven. This dude in the back wants me to make an approach right below us. What are your guys saying?"

"Not a damn word. They're just looking out the side, two of them hanging out like they're going to jump."

"But they don't have any parachutes—"

"Hell, I know that," LeDeux replied.

A flash of light caught Slater's eye. "Did you just see a signal mirror flash?"

"Yeah, I did," said Sampson.

The lead SEAL in the back motioned for them to descend. "Let's get down there!"

Slater directed Sampson to make his approach from the west, to have a clear approach path in. When they came to within a hundred feet of the ground, three uniformed men emerged from their camouflage cover. As Sampson brought the ship to within a few feet of the ground, the trio slogged their way forward through the marsh, their weapons leveled at two Viet Cong prisoners wearing black short-sleeved shirts and black shorts. The POWs had their hands tied behind their backs.

"We're getting out here!" shouted the lead SEAL, the one who had furnished the map. "Take these guys that are coming back to the ship!"

"What about our other aircraft?"

"They should be getting their instructions now!"

"Okay, roger that!"

The crew being recovered shoved the two prisoners into the back cabin and then got onboard, taking up positions on the floor around them. "Damn, I've never seen a live VC before," Sampson said.

"You and a lot of others."

"They look scrawny and underfed."

"They are scrawny and underfed, but they bite like hell—"

They were given the signal to go. "I've got the controls," Slater said.

"You've got'em."

"Two Two, this is Two Seven, we're coming up."

"Roger that. We've been directed to another set of coordinates. Where are you headed?"

"Back to the Benewah."

"Roger that, we'll see you there."

"Be careful."

"Ten-four."

Sampson turned and stared at the group behind him. Of the two Viet Cong prisoners, he could see only the backs of their heads, so he tried to read the faces of the Navy SEALs, who sat stone-faced in their wet Tiger fatigues, their weapons cradled casually in their arms. He motioned one of them, a man with a double chin and spiked hair, to come forward. "What's with these guys?"

"Gun runners!"

"What are you going to do with them?"

"Interrogate them!"

"What if they don't talk?"

The man with the double chin smiled. "They'll talk!"

Sampson nodded. "I'd hate to be in their shoes!"

The SEAL grinned and said, "So would I!"

They were directed again to make their approach from north to south, onto the helicopter pad of the *Benewah*. "You can also shut down, Two Seven," came the voice of the controller.

"This is Two Seven, roger."

When they touched down, the SEALs leaped out and quickly herded their prisoners toward a set of ladders leading down into the folds of the ship. Curious, Slater said, "I wonder if they have a dungeon, a place where they torture them?"

"I don't want to know."

After the blades were tied down, Slater and his crew were directed to follow a business-like lieutenant j.g. "Are you guys hungry? How about some steaks? We've also got crab, lobster, shrimp—you name it. Or you can have both: surf and turf. Your choice."

Slater's crewchief, a buck-toothed nineteen-year-old named Banks, said, "Sir, if you all don't mind, I'd just as soon have a hamburger."

Sampson rolled his eyes. "The Navy goes first cabin and you don't take advantage? Lordy Lordy, boy, I'm going to have to teach you—"

They wound their way through several narrow passageways, down a flight of steel stairs, until they came to the eating area. They were invited to sit at a long table with the edges built up to contain whatever was on the table during rough seas. "So," Slater said, looking at the lieutenant, "what's the plan for you guys? How soon will you be in the U Minh?"

The navy officer shrugged. "If we never go there, it'll be too soon for me."

After they had eaten, the lieutenant led them back through the maze of passageways, to their helicopter. On the return flight to Ca Mau, Sampson said:

"Is the U Minh really that bad?"

Slater paused for a second; he gazed out toward the horizon; he said, tonelessly, as if contemplating his own mortality:

"They call it the Forest of Darkness. I have a feeling that Charlie Troop is soon going to find out why..."

Victor R. Beaver

Chapter 79

"THREE ONE, ONE EIGHT, I'VE GOT several bunkers here. Also, a path leading toward the south."

With one eye on Justen's ship below, Leo, in the front seat of the high bird, quickly checked his map. He wrote down a series of numbers on a pad of paper he kept by his side. It was the fifth spot report of significance that morning in less than an hour. He keyed his mic: "Roger that, I've got the coordinates."

"Also," spoke Justen, "I've got some footprints here. Can't be more than a day old."

WO1 Daniel Cavanaugh, the aircraft commander, in the back seat behind Leo, said, "Are you going to follow them?" From Laredo, Texas, Cavanaugh spoke with a distinct drawl, his voice sounding slightly leaden.

"Affirmative."

Leo watched as Justen banked the OH-6 to the right. It turned to level and then began to skim toward a narrow channel that bordered a crescent-shaped lagoon. Once over the lagoon, Leo could see Justen's rotor downwash leave ripples on the water's surface. Justen banked left. He was now over a tidal flat. "You've got a heavy concentration of trees ahead of you," Leo said.

"Roger that."

Leo glanced up and to the right, into the little mirror above his head. Dan Cavanaugh's long, hollow-cheeked face was half hidden behind his sunvisor. "What do you think?"

"Let's be ready," Cavanaugh said.

"I was born ready," Leo answered.

Leo watched as Justen's ship came closer to the trees. Then it began a slow clockwise turn. He could see Hoyt, Justen's new machine gunner, seated in the back seat on the right-hand side. From two thousand feet up, Leo could just barely make out the barrel of Hoyt's M-60, pointed outward toward the trees.

Hoyt spoke over the intercom: "Sir, can we have blanket permission to fire?"

It was their third day together in the AO and the first time the issue had come up. Justen leveled his eyes at the tangle of trees and shrubs, still some thirty meters to their right front. He glanced at Kalbach to his left. The man had his M-16 pointed toward a cluster of nipa palms directly out the left door. In his left hand, the front-seat gunner held a red smoke grenade. The pin was pulled, ready to toss at the first sight or sound of gunfire. "Yes, you have permission...Just remember what I told you."

"Yes, sir, I will."

Leo, up high, tapped his right index finger lightly on the trigger of the TSU. He felt simultaneously calm, tense, and excited. Everywhere below was a true hunter's paradise, one large free-fire zone, where the slightest provocation gave him the authority to unleash the Cobra's devastating firepower. On their first day working the AO, Justen, in the low bird, had discovered an abandoned Viet Cong encampment. It was located less than eight miles from Nam Can, at the junction of two narrow rivers, an intricate maze of elevated wooden walkways linking several thatched huts built on stilts. Tangled structures of vines, tree branches, and roots constituted storage and protective bunkers. These, Justen and his crew had found, were empty. There were, however, strewn about the camp, remnants of cookware and bits and pieces of discarded clothing, damp and laying in the mud. On the outside of one hut there had hung by a leather strap a long forgotten food pouch, which flew off into the trees as Derek hovered overhead. Seeing no sign of life, he had moved his ship to one side and directed Leo and Cavanaugh to blow the camp up. After three diving runs, the camp was a shattered and twisted pile of smoking rubble.

Today, they were five kilometers north of Nam Can, on the west side of a narrow winding river. Justen brought the OH-6 closer to the trees. "The tracks continue along the edge of the trees here," he radioed.

"Roger that," Cavanaugh replied. "Watch yourself now."

Hoyt was looking almost straight down. He saw a small area of sandy ground covered with broad, leafy vegetation. He thought he detected movement under the vegetation, but quickly dismissed it as airflow from the downwash of the rotorblades causing the leaves to rise slightly. As Justen guided the ship in a gentle arc to the right, Hoyt saw another, more extensive patch of vegetation, the leaves broader and higher above the ground. "Sir, come a little more to the right."

"What do you see?"

Hoyt said, "I can't really tell. A patch of darkness; could be the opening to a bunker."

"Okay, I see it."

"I've got gooks!" Kalbach cried. In the next instant the sound of his M-16 ripped the air. As he fired, he flipped the smoke grenade out and red smoke began to mushroom up and out.

Leo saw the tracers from Kalbach's gun first, then the outpouring of red smoke. "They're taking fire—"

"One Eight—what's up? Talk to me," Cavanaugh radioed.

"We're taking fire!"

"Get out then! *Get out!*"

Justen saw tracers flying in all directions. For an instant, he couldn't decide which way to go: left, right, forward or back. Although the initial burst of enemy gunfire had been intense, they took no hits. He heard Hoyt's M-60 rattle behind him. The rear gunner's tracers zipped into the patch of darkness. "We're breaking left," Justen radioed to his high bird.

"Roger that, One Eight. Get out of there—"

Justen aimed the ship away from the trees. Kalbach quickly reloaded his M-16 with a fresh clip of ammunition. "I stitched one of them," he said. "Right in the face."

"How many did you see?"

"Six or seven—at least."

"One Eight, remain well clear of the trees." Cavanaugh's normally leaden voice came over the radio now at a higher pitch. Over the intercom he said:

"Leo, after I fire, hit that left cluster of trees with the chunker."

"Roger that."

Cavanaugh rolled into a dive. He pointed the nose of the Cobra at the eastern edge of the trees. Through the front center section of the cockpit, he could see the top of Leo's helmet. Above Leo's helmet, he saw the marking smoke through the red crosshairs reflected off the thin piece of glass that made up the rocket sight. He aimed and fired. Two pairs of rockets *swished!* forward. In an instant he saw their flight path; he made a slight adjustment, then fired three pairs in rapid succession.

From less than seventy-five meters away, Justen and Kalbach watched as the target area became engulfed in gray smoke. Then, to add to the din and spectacle, they saw the area peppered with 40mm grenade rounds.

As Cavanaugh continued the dive, Justen saw a slow steady stream of large green tracers suddenly arc upward. "You're taking fifty-caliber fire!" he radioed. "Pull out! *Pull out!* Go to your right!"

Leo, hearing the report, flattened himself in his armor-plated seat. "You don't tangle with a fifty-caliber anti-aircraft weapon," Lieutenant Emery had warned him one day. "You'll lose every time—"

Cavanaugh banked hard right and began the pullout. The resulting G-forces pressed the two pilots into their seats. Justen saw the tracers arc higher. The Cobra was almost directly over the enemy position. Justen maneuvered his Loach toward the dreaded weapon, hoping to get behind it. Meantime, Leo looked left and saw another string of tracers coming at them with a flatter trajectory. "Dan, we've got another fifty, at our nine o'clock. We're in a crossfire!"

"Shit!"

Leo then heard one of the massive bullets slam into the ship, a loud chunk, almost like a small explosion. And then he heard a cry from the back:

"Tannah!...Oh God, Tannah, I'm hit!"

Leo felt the ship lurch right. He grabbed the front-seat controls and quickly put his feet on the anti-torque pedals. "I've got the controls!"

"Tannah!...my right arm...*it's gone!*"

"What?...Gone?"

As Leo began to wrench the ship from the deadly chaos below, he heard Cavanaugh's voice coming back at him over the intercom:

"Tannah, I'm bleeding—I can't stop it...!"

The Sky Soldiers

"Hold on! Hold on! I'll find a place to land!"

When Justen received Tannah's report that Cavanaugh had been hit, the condition of his arm, he turned his ship and raced westward in front of the gunship. "There's an open area just ahead," Derek radioed to Leo.

"Give me a heading."

"Follow me."

"Where are you? I can't see you!" Leo cried.

"Kalbach, get another smoke. Pull the pin and hold it," Justen ordered.

"Roger that."

Kalbach did as he was told. Soon a trail of red smoke poured rearward, out from the cockpit. "Do you see our red smoke?" Justen radioed to Leo.

"Yeah-yeah, I've got you now."

Justen approached the open area and began to circle it wide to the right. "Is the area dry?" Leo asked.

"I can't tell," Justen replied. And then: "No—it isn't."

"It doesn't matter. Call and scramble the Blues—"

"I already did."

Leo saw an open stretch of river ahead, and on the far side of it the proposed landing site. "I've got the site now."

Again, Cavanaugh keyed his (floor) microphone switch. His voice was weak, and getting weaker. "Tannah...I...can't stop...the bleeding..."

"Hang on, damnit. Hang on. We'll be on the ground in a second." Leo glanced quickly into the little mirror. He saw Cavanaugh's head slumped to the right.

Leo brought the Cobra to the left of the LZ and banked sharply right. He looked down and saw low shrub and a few nipa palms on the north edge. He saw Justen's ship circling the LZ in a right-hand orbit. The surface of the LZ appeared to be muddy with a few pools of water. Once they were one the ground, he knew the skids would be completely stuck. *Fuck it. Cavanaugh is dying!*

"The area's clear," he heard Justen report.

"We're coming in."

"Tannah...I...I..."

Leo Tannah made a spiraling approach to the LZ. Coming to a high hover, he swung the tailboom right and set the Cobra quickly on the ground, in what felt like deep mud. He struggled to unbuckled his seatbelt and open the canopy. He got out and began to slog through water and mud, his boots getting stuck with every step, around to the right side of the ship. He fell forward. His hands felt the slick, gooey undersurface. "Cavanaugh! Hang on. I'll make it! I'll make it!"

Leo felt his heart pounding in his chest. His face was now covered with mud. His hands were inches from the landing gear. He grabbed the rear crosstube and pulled himself up. He looked up. The inside of the back cockpit was completely splattered with blood.

Victor R. Beaver

Leo struggled to reach the rear-canopy doorlatch. He touched the handle but his hands slipped as he tried to undo the latch. Finally with the door open, he gaped at Cavanaugh's right arm, severed just above the elbow. A stretched piece of flesh kept the arm attached to the stump; the nearly severed appendage lay in Cavanaugh's lap. Leo jerked Cavanaugh's helmet off. "Cavanaugh, wake up!" he shouted over the high whine of the engine. "Wake up! Wake up!"

The aircraft commander opened his eyes slightly. Then they closed. Tannah grabbed the stump and squeezed. Blood mixed with chocolate brown mud. Cavanaugh's head was now slumped forward. Derek had brought his ship to a hover less than twenty meters away. Leo signaled for him to come forward. He motioned for one of the gunners to leap out and help. Derek then maneuvered his ship around to the right side of the Cobra. Kalbach unbuckled and with the ship at a three-foot hover, jumped out. While Leo was trying desperately to do something for Cavanaugh—anything—Kalbach slugged his way to the Cobra. He climbed up to Leo's side and looked in. The gooseflesh rose all over his body as he looked at the bloody mess made by the .50-caliber impact. Leo's hands gripped Cavanaugh's stump. Kalbach shook his head. And then he glanced at Leo's face. He saw a pair of terror stricken eyes. He shuddered.

* * *

JAKE COLE OPENED HIS EYES; INSTANTLY he was aware he had been dreaming. He realized he had been reciting something, perhaps a poem learned long ago and forgotten. He blinked his eyes several times and suddenly the words came to him and he spoke, clear and resonant: *"Through birth and life, be calm, be still and carry on. The spirit of man is moving. Your salvation, your brothers are close at hand. Darkness is receding. Freedom!—Glorious freedom!"*

Jake had awakened lying on his back. He rolled onto his side and peered out through the wooden bars of his cage, out at the pre-dawn darkness. He began to think: For the past several days there had been an undefined agitation among the guards. Instead of their usual languishing, there was a heightened sharpness to their movements, and to the commands they gave him. He had noted that gestures or looks of apology always succeeded these commands. Something was in the wind, but what it was, he couldn't be certain, except that they had begun to pay closer attention to his eating habits and his health. Major Hung still spoke to him about America's role in Vietnam, how the "imperialists" had devastated the countryside, how the anger of the people had been growing steadily until one day there would a fierce uprising. There had been several hints, too, about his release, yet he was told he still needed to get his "words" right before being allowed to speak in front of the Central Committee. There were times when he felt the advent of going home so near that he wanted to rip his cage apart, to kick, scream

The Sky Soldiers

and shout. What more could they want from him? *I've already given three years of my life—!*

Twice in the past several days he had caught glimpses of spotter aircraft, in the distance, up high, receding from his field of view. This was not so unusual, except that both times Major Hung and his guards had shown a greater than normal awareness of their presence. And then the day before, while he was preparing his food, he was told to put his cooking fire out. He was given, instead, as retribution perhaps, some of the fish and rice his guards had already prepared.

"What?—why are you doing this?" he asked.

"Yo food lack essential nutritious ingredients, Co," offered Chimp, speaking almost like a real human being.

"...And I suppose yours does?"

Chimp frowned and said, "Eat!"

Last night Jake was invited to sit before Major Hung. The major, his lips everted, pouty, and his velvet brown eyes squinting, said:

"The Committee has asked me to speak again of your release. As you know, without your proper repentance, I cannot recommend that you be repatriated with your countrymen. I must know that you have learned all your lessons well."

Major Hung leaned back. For a long moment he studied his prisoner. "At this time, too, I cannot guarantee your safe passage among the people. I have been warned that the sight of any American has caused whole villages to rise against the Saigon puppet masters."

Jake listened and nodded, wishing at times he could reach over and wring the major's scrawny little chicken neck. "I would like to discuss my health," Jake said, as calmly as he could. And then his voice became more authoritative: "My severe case of dysentery does not allow me to retain what little nutrition my body does take in. I need some medicine—"

The major winced. He took a deep breath, then spoke in a swift, harsh tone to one of the guards seated outside on the wooden outer porch. "Piglet," the guard who reminded Jake of a small pig, with its upturned snout and beady little eyes, rose quickly and entered the room. He bowed. Major Hung spoke abruptly in Vietnamese. Piglet bowed again and left the room. "I have summoned the doctor," he said. "He will bring medicine."

Jake inclined his head. "Thank you." Several weeks before, "Dr. Kildare," a kind of roving camp physician, whom he knew was visiting their camp right now, had given him a series of tablets from an outdated package of medicines. They slowed his stools but the blood and mucous remained. Later, he received several injections of streptomycin, which only eliminated the symptoms and did not provide a cure.

"It is the leniency of the Front that you should be grateful," the major said, now tapping his fingers on the table. "We must go over your statements again. They are very important if you wish to meet the approval of the Committee."

Victor R. Beaver

Later, after the doctor had examined him and had given him some wild concoction to "plug him up," the major allowed him to return to his cage for the night. As Jake was leaving, Major Hung said:

"In the morning, after you have had time to review your thoughts, we will see what more can be done for you. It is the policy of the Front to insure all prisoners are in good health before they are released."

Jake glanced up through the wooden bars of his cage. The full moon had gone from its zenith now halfway toward the horizon. He didn't have a watch, of course, but it must be about three A.M., he decided. Two years before, on a hoarded scrap of paper, he drew out the phases of the moon and where it appeared above the horizon and thus deciphered the approximate time of day or night these appearances represented. There were many other mental diversions he employed to keep from going insane. He calculated, for instance, every penny he must have earned while in captivity, which included all pay increases for one reason or another. Methodically, he planned how every dollar was to be spent when he returned. Of course, Valerie would have used a good portion of it to maintain their home and provide for the children. Still, with him not spending a cent due to his confinement, there would have to be a substantial amount left over. For Robbie, he decided on a remote-controlled airplane; he imagined in every detail how it would be on the day he and his son took it to fly from the small asphalt airstrip south of the Fort Sill main post complex. For his daughter, Jill, who he believed might now be heavily into Barbie dolls, he would buy one of the those large Barbie dream homes, with the miniature furniture and lamps and rugs and the tiny dishes and forks and spoons to be placed on the dining room table, along with dozens and dozens of articles of clothing for the dolls. For Valerie, he saw himself laying down fifteen hundred dollars cash for the diamond necklace and matching earrings he had once seen at Ballas Jewelers on Fourteenth Street, in downtown Lawton. For himself, he wanted a Corvette. He fancied himself on a tour of the country with Valerie for a couple of months, much the same way Buzz and Todd did on the TV show *Route 66*. Possessing practically nothing, except his ceramic eating bowl, chopsticks, mosquito net, and sleeping mat, and the few articles of clothing he wore, these futuristic purchasing ambitions contrived to keep his mind occupied, as a starving man contrives the sumptuous meals he intends to eat and the gallons and gallons of liquids he intends to consume once he crosses the desert and reaches civilization.

Jake leaned back and noted that the moon had traveled about fifteen degrees, which would put the time at about four o'clock.

Lately, too, he had begun to think seriously about escape. But now that Major Hung was hinting strongly at his release, he wondered if he shouldn't forego these thoughts and concentrate on the ways that he could win the Committee's approval without compromising his principles. He was mulling this over when he finally drifted back to sleep.

"Chung bi di!"

Jake jerked upright. Though the skies to the east were lighter, the sun had not yet reached the horizon, after which its rays would split through the low shrubs and ferns that surrounded the base of the coconut trees lining the canal. In the half dawn of light, he fixed his gaze on Chimp's ugly stare. "What is it?"

"Chung bi di!"—prepare to go!

"Where?"

Instead of answering, Chimp opened the cage and undid his leg irons and ordered him to turn around. Jake struggled to his knees, turning his back slightly to the pugnacious guard. Chimp then tied a black cloth around his head to cover his eyes. "Where are you taking me?"

"No can tell. *Mau di!*"

"All right...Jesus. I'm moving—I'm moving."

Chimp and Piglet helped him into one of the long, narrow boats the soldiers kept tied near the bank, secured by a lock and chain. Chimp ordered him to lie down. He was then covered with a captured American rain poncho. "Keep still! No noise!"

As he felt the boat slip from shore, Jake heard the sound of a helicopter, still some distance away, approaching the area of the camp. He heard the voices of the other guards as they moved their boats from shore. After a few minutes, the boat he was in stopped. He felt branches and leaves brush over him, one branch gouging his back. He tried to move it but Chimp jabbed him several times with the point of his rifle. He sensed the tension in the air around him as the helicopter came closer. He heard Major Hung speak sharply to one of his guards. He knew enough Vietnamese to understand that one of the soldiers had brought his weapon up, as if to fire. The major had quickly remanded him to be still.

The heavy wop-wop sound was now practically overhead. The urge to stand, to wave and shout, became so great that he knew positively that in the next instant he would do it—*all caution aside!* His stirrings caused Chimp to poke him again with his rifle barrel.

"Get that damn thing out of my back, you asshole—" he cried. Suddenly, he threw the poncho back from his head. Chimp drew the rifle up and Jake found himself staring down the dark hole of the barrel. He saw Chimp's eyes bulging, his teeth bared, a crooked smile across his face. The steady drumbeat of the helicopter receded and Jake Cole slumped down. He began to sob.

Victor R. Beaver

Chapter 80

MAJOR SALVADOR FRANCISCO RAMERIZ checked the ship's clock. It was several minutes before dawn. He looked out ahead of his UH-1 C&C helicopter, through the Plexiglas windshield. Before him was a great flooded forest, the U Minh, called *The Forest of Darkness*. Known geographically as a place thick with tangled roots above murky, mosquito-infested waters, and inhabited by creeping, crawling, slithering things, large and small, deadly and otherwise, it was also known tactically as a place where hanging vines could trap a squad like a spider's web; where sticky-thick, chocolate-brown mud could immobilize and make useless as a fighting force a platoon, a company, a battalion of infantrymen; a place where water-filled passageways choked with reeds became impassable to an armored troop carrier (ATC) or the heavily armed monitor; and where interlacing canals and riverways twisted and turned into dead ends leading nowhere and everywhere. The Americans had their own names for it: *Forest of Mystery, Forest of Treachery, Forest of Death.* Comprising over fifteen hundred square miles, it was the Viet Cong's largest in-country sanctuary, and the day before it became Charlie Troop's new AO, area of operation.

Rameriz breathed deep. He turned his head right. In the same instant the sun's rays split over the horizon. He squinted at the sudden sharp daggers of light. Looking down, he saw the still shadowless depths below. A patch of vaporous mist hung among the treetops. Gradually, slowly, the sun lifted clear of the horizon and began to glow a bright yellowish orange. Within the hour it would begin to burn off the fog and make visible (to some degree) the Forest's darkly kept secrets.

After several more minutes, with the chill in his bones receding, Rameriz looked at his map and then at the terrain ahead. To his immediate left was the Gulf of Thailand. Along the coast, winding its way north, he saw a string of river patrol boats, minesweeping craft, and a pair of monitors, followed by armored troop carriers, salvage vessels, and a command and control boat.

Enemy reaction to the Navy's unwanted presence on the Song Qua Lon near Nam Can had taken the form of increased mining and ambush of Swift boat patrols. A vigorous "psywar" campaign had also been mounted. Banners raised along the waterways read: *"Americans and Vietnamese Soldiers Who Come Here Will Die,"* and *"We Kill Imperialist Americans."* Leaflets floated on tiny wooden rafts to the ships of the riverine support base urged an end to the "U.S. aggressive war" and threatened to "blow the American navy out of the water," to which the Army's 2nd Brigade commander retorted: "Let their skinny little asses try!"

The people of Nam Can were warned by the VC to stay away from the base. Gradually, however, when it became evident that the Navy was there to stay, visitors came in increasing numbers. They were treated to hot meals, small gifts, and services that included sampan motor repair and the grinding of woodcutter's axes. Medical treatment was also provided, and eventually this service was expanded upon the arrival of a Vietnamese hospital ship.

And now the allied plan to branch north had begun. The still formidable Forest, with its several hidden Main Force and Local Force units, including an NVA support company, was about to feel the sting of both the Vietnamese and United States brown water navies.

Rameriz told Captain Carrell, the troop operations officer, to turn the aircraft slightly right. "I want to overfly Thoi Binh. From there we'll go due north. After that we'll head south along the coast, check out those navy boats. How are you feeling?"

Carrell turned his head. "Fine. How about you, sir?"

"Better. Especially after everyone got their operational maps prepared."

"Yessir, I think everyone was pretty shocked."

Rameriz nodded. The day following Cavanaugh's memorial service he had called all his pilots and crews in for a briefing at noon. Everyone was seated on the gray metal folding chairs under the large operations briefing tent, smoking, each man quiet, tense. Rolls of maps were handed out and the men unfolded them on the plywood floor. The first thing that leaped out at them was the name at the top of everyone's map: *U Minh.* Afterwards, there was a flurry of activity as each pilot copied from a main operational map placed on a tripod stand, the numbered operational checkpoints to be used to adjust artillery fire and to give spot reports. As the men made their marks, there was little to none of the lighthearted banter that usually took place among them. Rameriz told them then, almost as an afterthought: "We're no longer up against irregular forces, gentlemen. Consider yourselves in the big league dealing with hardcore Main Force battalion-size units."

* * *

LEO ANGLED TOWARD THE LAKE THAT paralleled the Ca Mau airstrip. Kip hung back a couple of steps, wondering what was bothering him. "Leo, how'd your AC checkride go?"

"It went fine."

"What's the matter, Leo?"

"Kip, can...can we talk?"

"Sure, what's up?"

"We've been buddies a long time."

At first, Kip was puzzled. "Since before flight school." And then: "Hell, Leo, we even went through basic training together."

"Kip, what I'm going to tell you, I don't want you to think I'm chicken."

"Leo, what are you talking about?"

Leo Tannah stopped at the water's edge. He pulled out a cigarette, lit it and stooped down. He plucked a blade of grass and began to snap it apart. "I'm afraid, Kip. I'm afraid of dying."

Kneeling, Kip said, softly, "Leo...we're all afraid of dying."

"Yeah, but I'm real scared. The past two nights...I-I haven't been able to sleep. I lay on my cot and toss and turn. I shake and I perspire real badly. I dread flying."

"You mean...because of what happened to Cavanaugh?"

Leo nodded.

Kip touched Leo's shoulder. "Cavanaugh died because he couldn't stop the bleeding. Justen told me you wasted no time getting the aircraft on the ground. Leo, you did all you could."

"Yeah...I know...but there's more, Kip."

"What, Leo? What is it?"

"I can't figure out anymore what the hell we're doing here. What's it all for? So we can pull out and let the ARVN give this country over to Charlie? They're not going to fight. They're used to us doing their fighting for them. Do you realize, Kip, if anymore of us die over here, it'll all be for nothing. It pisses me off and scares me. I don't want to die in this country. I'm done fighting. I wish now I never got into the Cobras—"

"But, Leo, you've always wanted to be in the guns. You couldn't wait to do it."

"But now I don't want to do it," Leo hissed. "I don't want to be an AC. I should have flunked my checkride—"

"Leo, that wouldn't have been like you—not at all. The troop needs good Cobra ACs." Again, Kip touched Leo's shoulder. "Listen to me, Leo, you're going to be all right. You're a good pilot. Do you hear me? You're a damn good pilot. You're going to get through it—"

"I don't know, Kip...*I just don't know—*"

* * *

A DARK SHADOW FILLED THE OPENING of his tent. Nolan glanced up. Sergeant Patterson, the new platoon NCOIC, held a perplexed look. "Sir, I hate to disturb you."

"What is it, Sergeant?"

"Well, sir, it's about Specialist Fields."

"What about him?"

"For the past couple of days he's been acting kind of strange, real remote. I don't know what to make of it."

"Is he having family problems back home, an illness or something?"

The Sky Soldiers

"No, sir, none that I'm aware. He's grown real distant. He doesn't joke around like he used to. I try to talk to him and he tells me to fuck off."

"He does, does he? Well, have him report to me right away."

Spec Four Fields entered the tent and reported. "Be at ease," Nolan said. Looking at Fields, the Blue Platoon leader saw a long, pale, joyless face. "Sergeant Patterson tells me you have a problem. What's up?"

Fields slacked his shoulders, then shrugged. He said nothing.

"Look, I want to know what's going on and I want to know now. This is a goddamn shitty time to be acting up. What the hell's the matter? Why can't you speak?"

Fields gazed at his platoon leader. Stammering, he said, "Sir, I...well, I-I sometimes have these dreams...you know like something bad is going to happen. I-I really can't explain it. I wish I could."

"Have you had them before—that is, before now?"

"Yes, sir."

"When—what was it about?"

Fields hesitated. "It was the...the night before Sergeant Atwater got killed."

"What was the dream like?"

"Sir—" Fields blurted. "He got shot just the way my dream was—in practically every detail!"

"Are you serious—?"

"Absolutely, sir."

"So you've had another dream, is that it?"

"Yessir...it's-it's been...repetitive."

"What is it about?"

"Well, sir, we're on a helicopter crew recovery operation...in the U Minh."

"A crew went down?—Who?"

"I-I can't remember that part, sir. But then we go in to get them out and there's this...this explosion—"

"And then what?"

Fields paused, his eyes growing wider. "I-I can't tell you, sir."

"Why not?"

"I'd really rather not say, sir. Please don't make me—"

The gooseflesh had risen all over Nolan's body. He gazed hard at the worn-looking man before him. "Were you one of them?"

Slowly, Fields moved his head up and down. "Yes...yessir. At least...I think I was."

Nolan took a deep breath. He had known of these premonitions, when a man believes his time has come. There were times, after Sharon's death, that he was certain she had known something dreadful was going to happen—but he thought it had something to do with him—*never her!* The very thought of it chilled him to the bone. This dream stuff, though, was new to him. Nolan was silent while he collected his thoughts. Then: "Listen to me. The Blues have spent a lot of time kicking back. So far, we've only had one serious casualty and that was Atwater. And now we're about to go into the U Minh. It's natural to have doubts. There's a real chance, if we have to react to a helicopter down, that something bad can happen, especially in that swampy, godforsaken place." Nolan looked down. He said, "Crap, even I have second thoughts sometimes. But then I get over them. It's the body's way of preparing for action. If we weren't keyed up, none of us would react the way we were trained. We'd be stunned by the first shots fired." Nolan went to his desk, a small OD-colored folding table. He picked up a piece of paper. "The lift section needs a replacement doorgunner. I was going to ask for a volunteer. Do you want to transfer to the lift section in that position?"

Fields took the paper. He fingered it with trepidation. "Yes, sir, I do want to transfer. Thank you. I appreciate it."

"Keep this between you and me, would you?"

"Yessir, I will, sir."

"Another thing. Keep your dreams to yourself."

"Yessir...I understand, sir."

"You're dismissed."

Nolan was alone. He looked down at the trampled grass that was his floor. He lifted his head and looked at the map spread out on top of his cot. For a long time he gazed at it, at the grease-markings on the plastic overlay. For years the Forest had been immune to any kind of massive military action, which meant its occupants should now be thoroughly entrenched. And because it was known that American POWs were being held there, the usual preparation for an invasion could not be employed for fear of killing or wounding them by friendly artillery and aerial gunnery fire. He sighed heavily and whispered aloud: "Damn. We'll be like bumblebees attacking through solid armor."

* * *

Dear Derek,

It's been nearly a month since your last letter and so I'm worried as to whether or not you're okay. I've been following the news and wondering if you're involved in that part of the Mekong Delta where they might be looking for the POWs. Oh God, are we that close that Jake might soon be free? It's been three years, Derek. Three years! I'm so afraid of what he'll be like, how I'm going to react when I see him. Will Robbie and Jill accept him? They sense that something is going to happen soon. There is a strange expectant air in these oftentimes-desolate living quarters.

Are you doing okay? I never told you this but I had the strangest feeling when you left to go back to Vietnam. I thought, What if I never saw either you

The Sky Soldiers

got permission to engage anyone suspicious. This time the VC will probably be wearing some kind of formal uniform. Rameriz reminded us to 'shoot first and ask questions later.' I agree with that."

"What about this POW thing? We still gotta watch out for those guys if we see'em."

Sandy nodded. "I doubt we will. The Forest is awful goddamn big. They'll more than likely be under wraps if the VC hear or see us coming, so that we can't recognize what we're looking at. Remember, it's our ass if we hesitate."

"Yessir."

Baca blew out a big bubble and let it pop. Sandy said, "Spit that damn gum out. The last time you had that shit all over the microphone of your flight helmet."

"Yessir."

Sandy checked his watch. The skies to the east were showing more and more light. After a quick preflight, he examined Baca's store of M-60 ammunition. "You got plenty of grenades?"

"Yessir, about a dozen."

"Get another dozen."

"Yes, sir."

Sandy glanced toward the lake that paralleled the airstrip. He went to the water's edge, near a small cluster of reeds. A mist rose from the placid surface, eerie-like, reminding him of a Sherlock Holmes book he had once read, *The Hound of the Baskervilles*. He stooped down. He plucked a blade of grass, examined it, then tossed it aside. *You're nervous, scared—what of it? You're not the only one, so deal with it.* He looked down at his right foot; he saw his second set of ID tags, secured by the laces of his boot. The first set, taped together, was around his neck. He drew them out. Katie's class ring was gone! And then he remembered, he had placed it in his shaving kit. He wondered what she was doing, whether she ever thought of him. He doubted it. Wasn't their love over? And then there was Michelle. She believed in him, at least so he thought. Where did she fit in the grand scheme of things? How could she mean anything to him?—he didn't even know her. They had never even kissed, though while they were together on the beach that one Sunday he wanted to lavish kisses all over her tender young body.

Suddenly, angrily, he stood. *You don't need anyone to believe in you to make it. You have yourself!* He reached for his .38. He opened the cylinder, saw six bullets, then snapped it shut. Last night he had made sure he was well stocked with ammunition, all slots filled on his pistol belt. At Vinh Long he remembered standing before a mirror in the latrine. With the pistol belt on he looked like a gunslinger out of the Old West. He wore it like John Wayne, The Duke. He put the .38 back in the holster. He turned. Several of the crewchiefs from the lift section were beginning to untie the blades. His watch read a quarter to seven. Still

Victor R. Beaver

fifteen minutes to crank. The fog would probably keep them grounded, though, for another hour.

He went back to his ship. Baca had returned with the other dozen grenades. Roach sat idly by, a cigarette dangling from his mouth, the smoke drifting lazily upward, without the slightest waver. Sandy asked for a cigarette. Roach reached in his pocket and gave him one. Roach offered his lighter. Sandy lit the cigarette, drew the smoke in, and coughed the smoke out. He tried again. "You're not nervous, are you, sir?"

"A little."

"Yeah, me too."

At twenty-three past seven, the men could see blue sky above. The fog began to quickly dissipate. Sandy looked at his crew. He shrugged. "You ready?"

"Yessir."

He got in and buckled up. Roach stood as fireguard while Baca got onboard in the back. Sandy turned the battery and main fuel on, set the throttle, and called, "Clear."

Roach whirled his right hand above his head.

"Comin' hot."

Sandy pressed the button on the collective control lever and listened to the N1 turbine whine. At fifteen-percent N1, he cracked the throttle open and watched the TOT quickly rise. Soon he had the radios going, flicked on by the master avionics switch. He donned his flight helmet. Over the radios he heard several commo checks going. "One Seven is up on Fox," said Sandy.

"This is Three Three, got you loud and clear," replied Franklin, aircraft commander of his high bird.

"Roger that. I'm ready to hover."

"Give us another second."

At half-past seven, Franklin's Pink Team lifted, with Sandy taking off low-level in the lead. "Come up to altitude, One Seven."

"Roger that," Sandy replied.

They flew west for five kilometers, until they came to the Song On Doc, the river that ran in a gentle curve to the village at the mouth of the river with the same name. They passed south of Quan Long City, a small village that hugged the banks of the Song On Doc. Looking down they saw several small fishing boats in the middle of the river traveling in their direction. The faces of the occupants in the boats turned their attention skyward and for a second Sandy felt compelled to wave. He decided against it. This is not a friendly excursion we're on, he thought.

"One Seven, come up thirty-nine point six Foxmike."

"This is One Seven, roger."

On the new frequency, Sandy called, "Three Three, One Seven, how copy?"

"Loud and clear. I'll wait another zero five to make contact."

"Roger that." They passed Xam Rach Cu, another small village, which sat on the north side of the river. West of the village Sandy saw a large area of rice fields. The fields were covered in water. The water's surface looked glassy in the early morning light.

"One Seven, Three Three, you guys ready for a real turkey shoot?" WO1 Franklin asked.

Roach, hearing Franklin's radio transmission, gave Sandy a quick thumbs up. Baca, over the intercom, blurted: "That's affirmative, sir."

"This is One Seven, my observer gives me a thumbs up and my torque says a-ffirm."

At twenty kilometers out Franklin gave a radio call to the flotilla. "Roving Anchor Six Bravo, this is Comanche Three Three, how copy?"

"This is Six Bravo, got you Lima Charlie...loud and clear. What's your location? Over."

"We're about two zero klicks out. ETE one zero mikes."

"Roger that. We're on the north side of the river, just coming up on the first canal. We'll be holding until you arrive."

"This is Three Three, roger that."

The low and high bird worked both the VHF and UHF radios for communication between them. Sandy would talked to Franklin and Channing on VHF and listen to them come back on UHF. That way each could communicate instantaneously with the other. "Stay high until we get Six Bravo in sight," Franklin said.

"Roger that," Sandy replied.

"Sir," Baca said, speaking from behind him, "I need to test-fire my gun."

"Okay, go ahead and give it a couple of short bursts in the water. It's clear." Sandy spoke to Franklin and Channing: "My torque is going to test-fire his M-60."

"Roger that."

"I'll cream that log floating to our two o'clock," Baca said.

"Ten bucks says you better frickin' hit it," Sandy stated.

The blast of Baca's M-60 sounded like a hammer hitting wood. The first rounds sped downward and ripped the water to the left of the floating log. Several rounds of the second burst, though, hit their mark square on. "He's got the formula," Channing, Franklin's front-seat pilot, radioed.

"I bribe'em good," Sandy replied.

In the distance they could see the advance elements of the riverine assault division, the minesweeping ASPBs, followed by the armored troops carriers and a pair of monitors. "Six Bravo, Comanche Three Three, we've got you in sight."

"Roger, we also have you in sight."

"One Seven, go ahead and start your descent," Franklin radioed to his low bird. "Cut across the trees and let me know how well you can see downward. It may be a little too early."

"Roger that." Sandy kicked in right pedal and whipped the cyclic over, forcing the OH-6 into a tight right-hand descending turn, the scout technique for coming out of altitude. Soon Sandy and his crew were at treetop level, parallel to the edge of the river. Next he began a slowdown, until the airspeed indicator registered sixty knots. Ahead of them, the minesweepers loomed larger and larger. Sandy looked down into the trees to see what kind of definitions he could make out. The sun was still too low to see anything except dark shadows below the tops of the trees.

"How's it looking?" Franklin asked.

"Still pretty dark," Sandy said. "I'd give it another ten to fifteen minutes."

"It's your call."

"Let me get back up to altitude. I'd like to get a better look at the lay of the land."

Sandy added power and put the cyclic forward. In a moment, he brought the cyclic back and did a cyclic climb, topping out at two thousand feet, level with his high bird. "Watch out, you'll get a nose bleed up here," Channing said.

"I wish that's all I had to worry about."

"I hear you."

Sandy looked north. What he saw reminded him of pictures he had seen of the Florida Everglades. Before him lay a large cypress swamp with the gnarled roots of trees writhing down in the brackish waters. He could see tattered moss trailing down from the branches and tropical flowers blossoming in the gloom. He saw a thin ribbon of water cutting through the swamp, one of the canals the flotilla had been tasked to probe. He looked right and saw that the sun had now risen higher, with its light cutting through pink-white stratocumulus clouds off in the distance. "I've seen enough, let's get this show on the road."

Channing watched as Sandy descended in another spiraling right-hand turn. Soon it became difficult to distinguish the OD color of One Seven's ship from the swamp green below. He held his map open along with a notepad to jot down spot reports as they came. "Can you see him all right?" Franklin asked.

"Yeah, I've got him okay now."

"Boy, this place looks spookier than down around Nam Can," Franklin said.

Channing glanced into the little mirror that allowed the two pilots to maintain eye contact. "Damn, no shit."

"Don't be looking at me," Franklin said. "Keep your eyes pinned on One Seven."

"We've got a sampan down here," Sandy said, his voice suddenly sounding excited.

"Okay, check it out."

The Sky Soldiers

"And people, too, in some kind of uniform—"

Through Sandy's keyed microphone, the two high bird pilots heard Baca's M-60 firing. Franklin had armed the Cobra's weapons system immediately after leaving Ca Mau. He took a quick glance to make sure the "armed" light was on.

Sandy radioed: "They had AK-47 assault rifles leveled—ready to shoot. My torque plastered two of them. A third is somewhere in the water swimming around."

"What was in the sampan?" Franklin called.

"Crates of something. I couldn't tell."

"Okay, try to find the other gook. I'll let Six Bravo know."

"Roger that."

Sandy banked the ship hard left. "Roach, keep your eye on the east bank."

"Roger that."

In another moment, Sandy had the ship aimed perpendicular to the canal. Roach cried, "I see him! He's right near the bank!"

"Get him!"

Roach's M-16 opened up and Sandy watched several tracers skip toward the lone figure struggling in a tangle of vines. Just then Baca's M-60 opened up and Sandy jerked his head right. "A gook popped out of that hut back there," Baca stated.

"Did you zap him?"

"Bigger than shit."

Roach's victim lay face down in the water, the blue-green water surrounding the body turning a reddish purple. "Three Three, we've got a real nest down here. We're outta here if you want to make a run."

"Roger, rolling in hot."

"Hey—give me a chance to get out."

"Not to worry, little buddy, they don't call me Dead-eye Franklin for nothing."

Sandy tore right and gunned his Loach hard away from the target area. Several loud *whuumpfs!* sounded behind him and he felt the aftershock from Franklin's impacting seventeen-pounders. He pulled the nose up and then banked left to cover the Cobra's pullout. Clouds of gray smoke drifted upward. "Not even a measly secondary," Channing radioed.

"Are you going to try again?" Sandy asked.

The words had barely left his mouth when an explosion bloomed in front of him. "Holy Jesus Christ...!"

"The mother lode."

Through smoke and spewing flames, Sandy saw Franklin's ship lifting skyward. "Score one for our side."

"Let's get the hell out of here," Franklin enjoined. "I think we might have been hit by shrapnel on our underside. So far no warning lights."

"Not a bad morning's work already," Channing chimed in.

The two helicopters were now back up to altitude. Sandy brought his ship up close to Franklin's Cobra and examined the underside. "I see a couple of spots, like indents, maybe even slashes. Nothing large. Right behind the left rear crosstube."

"Okay," Franklin said. "We need to head back and refuel and rearm anyway."

As Channing radioed Six Bravo their intentions, Sandy had a chance to relax. He turned on the ADF receiver and tuned to the Armed Forces radio station, AFVN. An orchestra version of *Ghost Riders in the Sky* was playing and suddenly he felt elated. *Damn. We got those bastards good!* He was on top of the world. His world.

As they made their approach to the Ca Mau airstrip, Sandy could see Mark standing outside his ship while Wolfman, his left-seat gunner, refueled their aircraft. Mark waved and Sandy pressed lightly on the anti-torque pedals to wiggle the Loach's tailboom from side to side as a greeting. After they were shut down, Sandy went over to Mark. "How'd it go with you guys?" Sandy asked.

Mark's face was beaming. "My gunners got six gooks. My high bird got four secondaries—"

"We got four confirmed and one large secondary," said Sandy.

"All right."

"Is Justen back yet?"

"He came and left already. He doesn't screw around."

"No shit—"

"Is this all right?—Or is this all right?" Mark sounded aloud.

"We're on a roll now, that's for sure."

Sandy then looked around. He saw the Blues scattered about, some checking over their weapons, others catching up on sleep. Franklin came over to him and said that Channing was in the TOC giving the after-action report. "We're going to get some coffee. Be ready to lift in thirty minutes."

"Okay. How's your ship?"

"A couple of slashes, just like you said. Nothing to get alarmed about."

Within an hour they rejoined Six Bravo and the flotilla, however the remainder of the day was anti-climatic. Sandy and his crew found several abandoned huts but no sign of the enemy. That evening, though, the entire troop buzzed with conversation. Everyone had a war story to tell. Aside from blowing apart several bunkers and killing four Viet Cong caught in the open, Justen's Pink Team had also chased down several water buffalo. Scott told his men. "Today, we caught them napping. Tomorrow, we're probably really going to get into the shit."

The Sky Soldiers

Chapter 82

IT WAS 5:20 A.M. THEY SAT ACROSS from each other at one of the tables in the mess tent. "You look beat," Sandy said. Mark's eyes had that hollowed-out look.

Mark nodded. He took a sip of his coffee and then a bite of burnt toast. "Four straight days flying over that damned forest...yeah, I could take a break."

"Me too."

Mark shook his head. "God, I don't know how many more close calls I can take. That one round that came through the windshield missed me by less than an inch—"

Sandy nodded. "You were lucky."

Suddenly, Mark shivered.

"What's the matter?"

"I don't know, I just suddenly felt...weird, you know...like somebody just walked over a grave...that kind of thing."

Sandy's eyes widened. Shivers coursed through his body. For the past two nights he had dreamt about Katie, but he kept appearing before her in the dream as if he were some kind of disembodied spirit. Whenever he tried to talk to her she acted like he wasn't there, going about her business happy and content. He would wake up in a sweat, shivering and cold.

Mark checked his watch then stood. "Well...I guess it's time for the briefing."

Sandy took hold of Mark's arm. "You won't forget to do what I asked, you know...with the ring?"

Mark gave Sandy a deadpan look. Unblinking, he gazed at Sandy's cloth wings sewn on his jungle fatigue shirt above the left pocket. "While we were going through flight school, did you ever think it would be like this?"

"No...I didn't," Sandy whispered. "Except maybe Bowden and Cottrell, I don't think any of us did."

A smirk formed on Mark's face. "And now Nixon gets himself elected promising to shit-can the war. What's the point of fighting now?"

"Beats me," Sandy said, softly.

"Well, if you find out, let me know."

"Yeah, sure."

Mark Allen keyed his radio. "Comanche Three Niner and Two Seven, this is One Nine on Fox. Have you guys got your rpms up?"

Leo Tannah responded, "This is Three Niner, give us another one zero."

"This is Two Seven, we're still waiting for one of the Blues," Kip Slater said.

"Roger that. We'll be picking up to a hover. I want to see if they fixed that blade that was out of track."

"Could you hold a second, sir?" said Wolfman to Mark Allen.

"What for?"

"I gotta take another shit—"

"Jesus, how many times is that?"

"It'll be number five. Sorry. I think my nerves are shot."

"Well hurry."

"Three Niner, One Nine, my front-seat gunner decided to take another crap. I'm still going to test-hover this bird."

Mark had repositioned the ship to its original parking spot when Wolfman returned. Displaying a sheepish grin, the gunner re-strapped himself in. Mark twisted the throttle full open. He picked the Loach up to a hover and led his two high birds onto the Ca Mau airstrip, accelerating as he moved forward. As the three helicopters gained altitude, Mark glanced toward the rising sun and saw that it was full above the horizon. He spoke into the intercom: "Pap, in another minute I'll let you test-fire your sixty."

"Roger that, sir," acknowledged Joe "Pap" Harris, seated behind Mark on the right rear seat. Harris, age thirty-one, recently promoted to staff sergeant, was the oldest member of the Scouts and the platoon NCOIC. He was thin, stoop-shouldered, and had stringy, pre-mature, iron gray hair. When Mark first met Pap he thought the man looked like a concentration camp victim, with his deep-socket eyes, thin nose and Adam's apple that bobbed up and down in front of his thin neck when he spoke. Today, Pap was taking the place of Mark's normally assigned torque, who had come down with a case of severe chills and a high fever.

Slater keyed his mic: "One Nine, this is Two Seven, I checked with artillery and they have a fire mission. We need to remain well east of the river."

"This is One Nine, roger that," Mark replied.

Kip glanced toward RT, his black peter-pilot. "I got a question for you."

"So shoot."

"How come it doesn't bother you that LeDeux talks to you the way he does, with that Mint Julep stuff?"

"Sometimes it bothers me, but I know he doesn't mean anything by it. I've known him since we were little boys. You're going to laugh at this, but until a year ago my mother was his family's maid in Baton Rouge. His father is a big-shot lawyer. They own this huge house, I mean it's big—twenty rooms. After school, I'd come over and we'd play basketball together, on the court his dad had built especially for him."

"So now here you are pilots in the same unit."

"Yeah, can you dig it? He could've avoided military service if he'd have wanted, but he didn't. I joined right after he did."

After three minutes, Slater radioed to Allen that he could now overfly the river.

"Roger that, coming back left."

"One Nine, this Three Niner," said Tannah, "I've got a visual on the boats. They're about ten klicks to your twelve o'clock."

Mark glanced ahead and saw the string of ATCs, ASPBs, and two monitors heading north on the Song On Doc. "I've got'em. Are you going to give them a call?"

"Affirmative," Tannah replied. "Come up thirty-two five on Fox."

"Switching."

"One Lima Alpha, this is Comanche Three Niner."

"This is One Lima Alpha, go ahead. Over."

"Roger, flight of three, ten klicks to your south. How close are you to Checkpoint Tango Bravo?"

"It's just now to our right. We've got the left fork of the river in sight. Over."

"Roger that. Give us another couple of minutes."

"Take your time. We've been reconning the west shore by fire. So far, nothing."

Slater glanced up for a second and then down at his map. Thoi Binh, Checkpoint Tango Bravo, was just ahead. Beyond it, less than a kilometer, the river angled toward the northwest. Before that the Kinh Song Trem, a tributary canal which flowed into the Song On Doc, took off to the northeast, an arrow-straight shot for nearly thirty kilometers. The convoy of boats, however, would maneuver up the left fork, called the Song Trem Trem. Their mission today was to scout a maze of interlacing canals that connected to the Song Trem Trem at forty-five-degree angles. Kip thought it would take real concentration to distinguish one canal from another.

After Pap test-fired his M-60 into the river, Mark radioed that he was coming out of altitude.

"Gotcha covered, One Nine," Leo radioed back.

Pap cradled his M-60 and began to scan through the trees below. Wolfman, in the left front seat, gripped his M-16 and switched it to automatic. He held a red smoke grenade ready to toss. "Keep an extra sharp eye," Mark said.

"Sir, do you ever wonder what it would be like flying over here, with no war going on, stoned?"

Mark nodded. "I've given it a thought or two."

"Wouldn't it be fucking groovy? I mean, wow, it'd be outta sight. Really, this country is pretty far out. I think I'd like to come back someday when this shit's over. Be a tourist." Wolfman grinned inwardly. "Yeah, I can dig it...I can really dig it."

Mark said, "You'd better start digging what we're looking for: Sir Charles."

"Yeah, right...Sir Charles: Chas. Rhymes with jazz."

Victor R. Beaver

> *"Leaving on a jet plane,*
> *I don't know when I'll be back again.*
> *Oh, Babe, I hate to go..."*

They skimmed above Thoi Binh. The most forward elements of the boat convoy were just ahead. Glancing down, Mark thought the village deserted, but then caught sight of a woman carrying water in a clay pot on top her head. He saw a dog trailing behind at her bare feet.

Mark banked the ship slightly left and followed the bend in the river that became the Song Trem Trem. He slowed the OH-6 and soon they were at forty-five knots airspeed. Mark guided the little egg-shaped helicopter over the Song Trem Trem until they came to the first canal intersection, one which led off to the northeast.

At first, Slater, looking down, saw there wasn't much cover—for either the VC or the low bird. Mark flew his Loach until he came to another canal intersection, this time a short canal which led off to the northwest, until it intersected yet another canal that led to the northeast. The maze below was almost dizzying. At this point in the mission, Mark followed where his nose led him, whatever looked suspicious. Now he was over dense growth, nipa palms and low shrubs that grew along both sides of the canal. Slater saw the low bird begin to circle the same spot. He grew tense when he heard Mark's radio report. "I've got a trail running along the north edge of this canal here, lot's of footprints, fresh as hell. Looks like maybe somebody decided to stash something."

Tannah checked the pair-firing selection of his rockets. He took a quick reassuring glance at the red caution light indicating the status of his weapons. "Watch yourself now, One Nine."

"Roger that."

Slater glanced behind him. Three members of the Blue Platoon were seated on the floor, their weapons held across their laps. He looked back at Fields, his new doorgunner, seated in the right doorgunner well, who had recently transferred from the Blue Platoon. "Fields, you doing okay back there?"

"Real fine, sir," Fields said. "Sure is nice to know I don't have to get out with these guys, in all that mud and water, if something happens."

"I hear you," Slater replied. "We, in the lift section, try to fight the war the clean way."

"Yes, sir."

"Taking fire! Taking fire! We're hit—we're going down!"

Quickly, Slater glanced down. Mark's LOH had rolled right then began to wallow erratically, its tail wagging briskly like an eager puppy. "Can you make the open area to your right, less than fifty meters away?" Leo Tannah radioed.

The Sky Soldiers

"I don't know—I can't control it. It's got a helluva vibration—like maybe the flight controls have been hit!"

Suddenly, Slater saw Mark's aircraft pitch down and roll inverted. It hit and then tore through several nipa palms. He saw chunks of helicopter and rotorblades flying off at odd angles along with pieces of tree branches. The helicopter righted itself before slamming into the ground. And then it exploded in a fireball of red and black flames.

"Jesus," RT cried. *"Jesus...!"*

Leo quickly called Comanche operations. "Low bird down. Scramble the Blues. Scramble scramble!"

"Roger Three Niner, scramble the Blues—"

Slater banked his ship hard right and began a steep descent toward Mark's burning ship. "Shit, who could live through that—?" Slater said aloud, as he guided his Huey past the column of black smoke and flames roiling out of the crash site.

"I see Pap," cried Fields. "He's off to the side—with his sixty."

"Is he hurt, wounded—?"

"I don't know, I can't tell."

Slater glanced left. He saw the open area Leo mentioned, about forty meters from the burning Loach. He banked hard left and reduced speed. "We'll land there," he told his crew. "We've got to see if we can get to Pap."

"What the hell are you doing, Kip?" cried Tannah, frantically deciding whether or not to dive and fire.

"What does it look like? Pap may be alive. We're going to try and get to him. Keep us covered."

"Roger that."

Dead branches and leaves blew everywhere as Slater brought his ship to a hover. The Blues bailed out as the Huey came within five feet of the ground. Fields then watched Childs, Brave Water with the portable radio, and Miller, who had been promoted to squad leader after Patterson became platoon NCOIC, dash toward a cluster of trees that blocked their path to the burning Loach. Slogging forward through ankle deep mud and occasional puddles of water, Miller laid down a volley of covering fire to his right. Fields unstrapped and pulled his M-60 from its mount. "Where the hell are you going?" cried Slater.

"Sir, they might need extra covering fire," the gunner stated.

"Shit—"

RT then watched as Slater began to unstrap himself from his right-seat position. Slater said, "You and the crewchief stay here."

"What are *you* going to do—?"

"Damned if I know."

Slater grabbed his carbine and began to slug his way behind Fields through the mud. He had only gone a few yards when he heard AK-47 fire, a coarse, staccato-like, ripping sound. Crouching low, Kip made his way to Fields's side. Fields rose up and laid down a heavy stream of fire toward the edge of the trees. They saw a black-clad figure pitched back spread-eagle and disappear into the tree-cluster. It became quiet. Everyone stayed still for several seconds, then Miller gave the signal to move ahead.

"What the hell you doing here, sir?" said Miller, as Slater came to his side.

"I haven't got a clue."

Once inside the cluster of nipa palms, they saw what Mark and his crew had stumbled onto. It was a Viet Cong camp with all the trimmings: tables, chairs, several hastily dowsed cooking fires, pots of steaming rice, weapons and ammunition everywhere. Childs had to disassemble himself from clothes drying on a line. Just then gunfire erupted from a location on the other side of the burning OH-6. Everyone ducked. "Could that be Pap firing?" Slater asked.

"That ain't no M-60, sir," Miller said, now taking the radio handset and handing it to Slater. "Call Three Niner and tell him to put some fire north of the crash site."

Slater nodded and took the handset. He pressed the button. "Hey, Leo."

"Yeah, that you, Kip?"

"Ten-four, good buddy. We hear gunfire north of Mark's aircraft. Put some rockets in that area."

"Roger that. Is anyone alive?"

"We don't know—yet."

Three pairs of rockets exploded north of the crash site. "How's that?"

Slater asked Miller what he thought. The squad leader nodded eagerly and formed a circle with his thumb and forefinger. "That was good, Leo. Watch us now, we're going to try and get to the ship. Pap's off to the side. He may still be alive."

"Roger that. And by the way—you are one dumb shit—!"

Slater pressed the handset. "Thanks, I needed that."

The five men moved forward cautiously toward the now smoldering LOH. As they edged closer, they felt the remnants of the once intense heat that had been generated during the post-crash fire. Childs pointed to his right, then ripped forward. Pap was lying in a prone position with his machine pointed outward, away from the OH-6. Crouching low, Kip came to Childs' side. The medic shook his head. "Pap's dead, sir. A broken neck."

Fields, Miller, and Brave Water maneuvered around to the cockpit end of the low bird. What they saw made them physically weak. Mark Allen and Wolfman were still strapped into their seats, burned beyond recognition.

As Tannah circled overhead, Slater began to hear the sound of approaching aircraft. "I'm going back to the helicopter," he said. "Those guys are going to need our ship out of there to be able to land."

Chapter 81

HE WAS AWAKENED BY A LIGHT SHINING on his face. "Mr. Adamson, sir, it's time to get up."

"Oh, okay...yeah."

"The mess tent's already made coffee," the CQ runner said.

Sandy checked his watch: 0530. He swung his legs to the hard-packed ground and got up. He retrieved his shaving kit and towel and went out into the night. The air had a raw, bleak feel to it. He looked up. A thousand stars were visible which gave him little comfort, until he spied the Pleiades, an exploding cluster of some three hundred stars, of which half a dozen were actually visible to the naked eye. They were his good-luck stars. He had entrusted them to Katie one evening while they were dating. "I discovered them when my family and I were living in Hawaii," he had told her. "They are my gift to you, my diamonds in the night."

Standing off by itself, the shaving station was a drum filled with water built high on a steel frame over two wash basins built within a waist-high two-by-four wood scaffolding. A narrow wooden walkway led to a steel-grated platform upon which the men could stand while they performed their shaving chores. A low-wattage bulb hanging over the basins provided the only source of light. Sandy flung his towel over the right-hand post and opened his kit. He looked at his image in the mirror over the right-hand basin.

"How's it going?" the person to his left said.

"Fine." Sandy glanced at Kip Slater.

"Big day, uh?"

"Yeah." Sandy splashed cold water on his face, then filled his hand with shaving foam.

Kip toweled the last of the shaving soap off his face. He grabbed his kit and turned. "Don't get in over your head out there."

Sandy gave the older pilot a weak grin. "Easier said than done, don't you think?"

"Probably."

Sandy asked, "How are you handling this?"

"Same as everybody, I try not to think about it."

"I don't think I slept more than two hours last night, if that," the younger pilot said.

"Me either." Kip laid his hand on Sandy's shoulder. "I'll see you at the briefing."

Sandy nodded. "I hope it's short, sweet and to the point."

"Don't worry, it will be."

A line had already formed in the mess tent in front of the coffeepot. Sandy grabbed a cup and got behind one of the gunpilots. The smell of bacon filled the air. At the table he tried to read the faces of those around him. Conversation seemed at an all-time low. He took a sip of his coffee and noticed that his hand was shaking. Mark Allen sat down in front of him and began to wolf down a plateful of scrambled eggs. "How can you eat?" he asked.

"Hey, they say that breakfast is the most important meal of the day. You'd better have something more than just coffee."

"I'm not hungry. My stomach feels queasy."

Tannah grabbed Slater by the sleeve, nearly tipping over his coffee. Kip turned. "Leo, you up?"

"Up and ready, bud, up and ready."

"You feeling better, uh?"

"Lot's better," Leo said, rubbing his hands together. "Let's bring it on—"

"Who's your front-seat pilot?"

"Roxbury."

"Aah...Spider Man."

"You're telling me. I still don't know how he fits in the gunner's seat. He's all arms and legs."

In the briefing tent Captain Carrell, the troop S-3, clipboard in hand, began reading off assignments. He stood before a blow-up map of the U Minh Forest. "Mr. Franklin and Lieutenant Channing, your Pink Team will fly to Song On Doc, at the mouth of the river here. Your low bird will be Mr. Adamson. You guys will be working with River Assault Division Ninety-one. Lieutenant Emery and Mr. Devrie, your Pink Team will rendezvous with River Assault Division One Twelve near Thoi Binh. Mr. Justen will be your low bird. Mr. Allen will be the low bird with a Purple Team, Mr. Tannah and Mr. Roxbury along with Mr. Slater and Mr. Sampson. You guys will be working independently, starting in from this junction right here, called Checkpoint Bravo. Mark that down." As the other assignments were read and checked off, Sandy began to ease back in his seat. He knew by looking at the map that his team would be working the southern fringes of the U Minh, near a Special Forces A-team camp. Any Main Force units would probably be farther north. "Okay," Carrell said finally, "the weather should be good, after the morning fog burns off, then maybe a rain shower later this afternoon. Pay attention to callsigns and frequencies. This is already a cluster, we don't want to make it more so."

Sandy met Roach at the ship, along with Gabriel Baca, Sandy's new M-60 man, a slightly built Hispanic with velvet brown eyes and a short, brush-like haircut. Baca smacked at a wad of bubblegum, his way of keeping calm. "So what's the story, sir?" Roach said.

"The story is, we go to the coast and work with part of the flotilla. They're going to be probing a few canals." Sandy held his map open, pointing. "We've

The Sky Soldiers

Sandy Adamson stood at the edge of the airstrip and watched the three lift ships approach Ca Mau from the north. He stood still, his body tense, his breathing shallow. The knowledge of what he was about to see made his whole body sick with dread. When the ships landed, he moved slowly toward the lead slick. Then stopped. Two Blues had jumped out from the cabin and were turning to assist in the unloading. Sandy saw them begin to handle the three bodies enclosed in black rubber body bags. Seymore, who had flown in earlier with a sling-load of artillery shells, came and stood by his side. The two ex-classmates eyed each other. They shook their heads then watched as the Blues carried the dead men to a tent on the other side of the compound.

Following close behind, Sandy felt the pressure in his chest mount, until he thought he would explode. "God, just this morning I was talking to him. Just this morning—!"

Seymore put his hand on Sandy's shoulder. Sandy stopped and turned. "Why was it him, Seymore? It was supposed to be me. I was supposed to die first."

Seymore stared incredulously at his friend. "What? What do you mean?—Die first." he exclaimed. "What the hell kind of talk is that—?"

Sandy, his eyes filled with tears, his body shivering as if he had been suddenly overcome by cold, said, "Don't you understand? It's the way I always pictured it. Mark was supposed to write a letter about me to Katie—!"

"You're crazy. Where did you come up with this? Is this some more of your hero bullshit—?"

Sobbing, Sandy turned and stormed back toward the airstrip. Catching him from behind, Seymore grabbed Sandy and threw him to the ground. Fuming, he said, "You piss me off! Mark is dead and all you can think about is yourself. How you want to be the big hero and die a hero's death. Do you know how many times I had to listen to that crap while were where going through flight school—?" His eyes blinking, Sandy gazed at Seymore as if he were seeing him for the first time. Seymore continued: "I'm sick of it, do you hear? Sick of it! Katie is out of your life forever and you can't let go. You want to change places with Mark? How? He's the one who's dead!"

Sandy's hands groped forward. "Seymore, I-I'm sorry, you're right. Jesus, you're so right! I-I didn't care...if I lived or died. It-it was like...I wanted to show Katie—by being killed—that she couldn't do what she did to me. Holy Christ, how stupid!"

Seymore knelt by Sandy's heaving body. He said, "It's okay...it's okay. You'll get through this. We both will. Come on, get up."

Seymore helped Sandy to the scout tent. He laid his sobbing friend on his cot. "Take it easy now," Seymore said. Sandy gripped Seymore's hand. Seymore tightened his own grip. "You just hang on...as long as you want."

Teary-eyed, Sandy said, "I'll be all right, Seymore. Thanks." And then he asked: "What do you hear...from Jenny? How far along is she?"

"Six months."

"Damn—where has the time gone?"

"You're telling me." Seymore reached in his back pocket and withdrew his billfold. "Get a load of this picture. Look at that belly."

He noticed that Jenny had gained weight nowhere else but her mid-section. Smiling, Sandy said, "It's gonna be a boy, don't you think?"

"I don't care what it is, as long as he or she looks like her—and not *me.*"

"What a stroke of luck when you found her, huh?"

Seymore said, "Don't worry, someday you'll find somebody—I promise."

"You think so?"

"Sure. Besides, you asked me to be the best man at your wedding, remember?"

Sandy nodded. "Yeah, you're right. I-I guess I forgot."

Standing, Seymore said, "Look, I've got to go. Tell Mark's mother—hell, I don't know—tell her whatever."

"Yeah, I understand. This fucking war sucks. *Damn*—this war sucks."

Seymore took Sandy's hand. "You hang in there. You've got plenty to live for."

"You're right. Thanks for reminding me."

"Take care, you hear?"

"I will."

"Adios, my friend."

"Yeah, you too, Seymore. Be careful."

"Roger that."

* * *

"WHAT THE HELL KIND OF GIZMO CONTRAPTION is that?" LeDeux said.

"I don't know but they'd better not ask me to fly it," Cowboy said, now walking toward the Huey gunship that had just landed and was now shutting down.

"Man, that ship's got to have one helluva forward center of gravity," Slater commented, noting the two large separate circular periscopes integrated with a large rounded rectangular casing attached to the front of the ship, just below the radio-compartment access door.

Buddy and RT strode forward together, both eyeing a long black three-inch diameter hose, or tube, extending from the right periscope into the left cockpit area through the lower cockpit windshield. It appeared to be somehow connected to the telescopic sighting unit used by the left-seat pilot to fire the miniguns mounted on either side of the ship. "Another goddamn toy the Army needs to fight the war with, I'll bet," Buddy said.

The Sky Soldiers

"Yeah, and I'll bet somebody's making a killing off the stock the manufacturer in the States is issuing right now."

Others had started to gather around the aircraft, curious about its mission and what it was doing at Ca Mau. When the rotorblades came to a complete stop, they stepped up to the open door of the left cockpit. The left-seat pilot had just removed his helmet. He gave them a sidelong look and put on his fatigue cap. They saw the large 1st Cavalry Division patch sewn on the upper left sleeve of his jungle fatigue shirt. "What the hell are you guys doing down here?" Tannah asked.

The left-seat pilot, a boyish-looking warrant officer, gave them a slight grin. The right-seat pilot, a first lieutenant with wide-set eyes and wavy light brown hair, said to them from across the center console: "We can't talk too much about it right now. At least not until we've had a chance to brief your CO."

"Top Secret, eh?" RT said.

"Sorta."

"Figures. Well, put me down for a dozen, though I don't know if I'm going to last long enough in this troop to draw my retirement. However, this does look like a good investment."

The lieutenant smiled. "I'll trade places with you any day. Where we're based, we got NVA coming out our ears."

"Well, at least they wear fucking uniforms. Half the time down here we don't know who to shoot at."

"INFANT, eh?" said Rameriz, standing in his tent, looking weary and depressed. "What the hell does that stand for?"

"Iroquois Night Fighter and Night Tracker, sir," the wavy-haired lieutenant said. "We're part of a New Equipment Introductory Team, NEIT, based at Lai Khe. It's an ambient light-gathering system designed to see at night, much like the Starlight scope. The system is slaved to the ship's weapons system. Whatever the gunner looks at through the right periscope, the crosshairs in the recticle are matched to the aim of the two miniguns. Should the right-seat pilot wish to fire at what he sees through his television monitor, those images that come in through the left periscope, he punches a button on the control panel and the crosshairs on the screen become slaved to match the aim of the rocket tubes. A third television monitor is in the cabin area. One of your men could ride along as an observer, if you wish."

"Well, I'll tell you what," Rameriz said. "You're welcome to play with that thing all you want; but you're not to fire at anything unless you clear it with me first."

"Yes, sir. But why, sir? Whatever we see may not be around when permission is finally given to engage."

631

Victor R. Beaver

"Yes, lieutenant, I understand that, but we've still got American POWs being held in the U Minh. I can't allow you to jeopardize their lives by shooting at just any target you see. My men have been told they must make damn sure who they're firing at. It's hard enough to identify a target during daylight. It's impossible at night. Can that damn thing distinguish between an American and a gook at night?"

"Well, no sir...but if we take fire—"

"Lieutenant, my conditions are as I stated. Take them or leave them."

Galloway sighed. "Yes, sir. I guess it's your AO, sir."

"You damn right it is."

tended? Trembling, he said, "In what way have I shown you that I have repented? Tell me. I have said nothing. I have done nothing. I have signed nothing. What have you got—?"

Major Hung's eyes grew wide, unsure what to say next. And then he leaned forward. "It is the Committee's decision! There is to be no more discussion! You must pack your things at once—"

Jake's mind was reeling. For the past three weeks he had been planning his escape, to leave when the moon was waning, three nights after it had reached full-moon status. He had figured a way to make it look like his leg-irons were locked, by slipping a piece of wood into the socket where the clasps came together. It was a trick that he had already tried two nights before and it worked. He had been working feverishly for two weeks to weaken the hinges that held the door of his cage in place and now it was on the verge of collapse (appearing to the guards, however, like nothing was amiss). He had been hoarding rice, practically one grain at a time, hiding it in a hole he had dug under his sleeping mat.

All this had been prompted by the increase in O-1 Bird Dog and helicopter activity. And farther north, for the first time ever, he heard the distinct rumble of several B-52 strikes. Whatever was going on, he knew it was only a matter of time before either the bombs hit their camp or the camp was discovered. His face was so darkly tanned and his body so emaciated and his clothing so like that of his captors, that even in spite of his dark scraggly face, any pilot who spotted him would probably assumed him to be a VC—and shoot. It was time to get out.

But to be released. Was he hearing Major Hung correctly? Or was this just another trick, a means to screw with his mind? to get him to thinking that going home was possible...if only one final condition was met: signing a document or making a statement while being photographed? And if he refused, what then? Would he be executed, as being of no further use as a propaganda tool?

He was shuttled back to his cage. Chimp and Piglet hovered over him as he began to slowly gather his meager belongings. He turned and glared at them. "Leave me alone. Give me a little time—"

The two guards looked at one another, shrugged, and moved away.

Jake dug under his sleeping mat and brought out his small supply of rice that he had been keeping in a small cloth pouch. Wherever they were taking him, he would make his break at the first opportunity...even if it meant being shot and killed. *I don't care anymore...I just don't goddamn care.*

Justen, along with Slater and Sampson, who would be flying chase, met with the INFANT crew an hour before sundown. With a map of the AO laid out on a table, Lieutenant Galloway, on Justen's suggestion, plotted his first search pattern. It was in the same area Mark Allen and his crew had been shot down, however a little farther north and west. For as long as he had been in Vietnam, Justen had always felt a strong pull toward that section of the U Minh, like ferrous metal drawn to a magnet. Lately, though, he had noted that whenever he flew over or near the area, the attraction was stronger than ever. Though he couldn't logically explain it, and there were many times when he thought that what he felt was nothing more than hocus-pocus, they had to start somewhere—why not there?

It was well past dark when they finally cranked. Justen sat in the back, his flight helmet on, in front of a 13-inch television monitor that glowed an unearthly green. Up front, the two pilots had their own 7-inch TV monitors to look at, with the left-seat pilot having the additional advantage of being able to see outside through a rather large fiber optics bundle (leading to the right periscope), all slaved to the miniguns via the TSU (telescopic sighting unit). A control panel was set in the center console.

"Tomorrow night I'd like to sit in the left front seat," Justen said over the intercom.

Galloway said, "Yeah, sure. Tonight should give you a pretty good idea how we operate. By the way, the Major said you'd be the only one flying with us for the next several nights. Any special reason?"

"No...no special reason."

"I was thinking maybe some of the other pilots would like to take a turn. The lieutenant colonel in charge of this project also has the responsibility of 'selling' this system. The more who see it the merrier."

Justen said nothing.

"Well," Galloway said, looking back at Justen and the two doorgunners, "is everybody ready?"

"Ready left, sir."

"Ready on the right."

"Comanche Two Seven, this Night Bird One, we'll be lifting in one zero."

Kip Slater spoke evenly into the microphone. "This is Two Seven, roger. We're right behind you."

They took off north into pitch-blackness. The INFANT ship leveled off at one thousand feet, while Slater continued his climb to fifteen hundred. Slater looked below. The INFANT helicopter was blacked out, while his aircraft maintained minimum lighting: no red rotating beacon, the red and green navigation lights on dim.

Through the television monitor Derek watched the terrain pass below, a strange panorama of varying shades of green and white blended into a constantly changing scene. Sensing Justen's disappointment in the quality of the picture, which was very grainy, Galloway said, "The moon comes up in about twenty minutes—pretty close to ten o'clock. When it gets full above the horizon, we should see everything a lot clearer."

"Would it help if we got lower?" Justen said.

"Some, but right now I want to make sure we get to the right area. When we flew out of Lai Khe, we had the advantage of working with radar to plot our loca-ion. Here we have to use dead reckoning. We'll also keep track of where we are by using these TV monitors to recognize the canal system as it's plotted on the map."

Their first dead-reckoning checkpoint was a small village named Xom Ngon. When they calculated they were over it, all they could see, due to poor ambient lighting, was a slight variation in the way the trees normally looked. Nothing out of the ordinary gave them any real clues to distinguish this location from any other they had passed over. "I've got a canal running diagonally to the northeast," Justen said.

"Yeah, I've got it too," Galloway responded.

Justen spoke to the left-seat pilot, a warrant officer named Mattingly: "What do you see through that TSU?"

"Not a damn thing. We need some moonlight, bad."

At exactly 2204, Slater looked east and saw the first peek of the moon above the horizon. The two ships had been in nearly constant radio contact with each other, companions in an intriguing—yet deadly—endeavor, which at this point only hinted at great possibilities. Slater could easily visualize Justen glued to the TV monitor, all his hopes now focused on what the low-light level system might reveal. Slater felt the gooseflesh rise all over his body as he contemplated the likelihood of finding Derek's half-brother.

With the moon now full above the horizon, Slater radioed, "Are you guys seeing better now?"

"Lot's better," Galloway came back. "Too bad we couldn't have started with a waxing moon. From here on, each night we fly the moon comes up later in the evening and there's less of it."

They spent the next half-hour zigzagging back and forth within the coordinates they had plotted, trying to catch a glimpse of something, anything, to whet their appetites for more. They didn't even have the boats of the Navy flotilla to spot since they had moved farther up the Song Trem Trem, to the district town of Kien An. Bright points of light came at them almost constantly, appearing on the monitors as green "tracers" streaking at them from the front. When Derek first saw this, he reported: "We're taking fire—"

"Those are flying insects," Galloway immediately explained. "The first time I saw those on my TV monitor, I thought bullets were coming right at my crotch. Scared the shit out of me—"

Another fifteen minutes passed. Still they saw nothing out of the ordinary, no glaring evidence of any VC camps, no sampans on the narrow channels of water, no movement of any kind. The VC were their usual masters at camouflage. Finally Galloway tapped at the glass over the fuel gauge. "We need to get back. We'll take off the next time at one o'clock. The moon will be a lot higher then."

There was no way to get a backward glance at what they were leaving: the two periscope lenses pointed only forward. As they departed, Derek felt a tug in his gut greater than he had ever known before. When they had lifted from Ca Mau, he had had such high expectations. Now he felt only dread. To look for Jake was worse than trying to find a needle in a haystack. First you had to find the right haystack in a field of haystacks!

At dawn, after two more sorties into the same area without seeing any hard evidence of Charlie, even with a bright gibbous moon, Derek went despondently to his cot and lay down. For the first time ever, he felt the fruitlessness of his quest. He felt exhausted, less from being physically tired than from fully realizing the sheer magnitude of his task. Yes, Jake by far had it much worse. And there was no doubt that Valerie, at the opposite extreme, had to endure a different kind of torment. But he had nothing tangible to cling to, no hope of freedom, no expectation of seeing a spouse finally come home. What drove him was an undying conviction that he could never rest until Jake was found—dead or alive. After that, then what? He had no wife, no children, no house or place anywhere to call his own. It was then, too, that he realized just how dreadfully lonely he was, how much he yearned to have a woman, a lover, a companion to go to when his quest was done.

In the faint light of dawn, Derek put his hands over his eyes and wept, shedding at last an accumulation of over thirty-six months of tears.

Chapter 83

DEREK JUSTEN WENT BRISKLY INTO Rameriz's tent. He saluted. "Sir, I'd like to go up with that INFANT ship tonight."

Rameriz looked into Justen's ocean blue eyes. "I was wondering when you'd show up, ever since that Lieutenant Galloway told me it had an observer monitor in the back. Well, you can't go."

"What? Why not—?"

"Because I don't want you seeing where you think your brother might be and then going off half-cocked the next day looking for him. I won't have it."

Derek felt the heat rise in his chest. "Then damnit, sir, what the hell is the purpose of that ship around here at night for anyway—goddamn nothing?"

Rameriz roared back. "Mr. Justen. You don't run this outfit—I do. And I will not tolerate insubordination. Do I make myself perfectly clear?"

"Yes, sir. I understand that, sir. But this is the perfect piece of equipment to go hunting Charlie at night. I know the odds are slim to none that we'll find my brother specifically, but Christ Almighty, sir, I've got to at least try—"

Before Justen came into his tent, Rameriz had steeled himself against the man's resolute nature. But something in the chief warrant officer's pleading eyes made him ponder the request. Of all his scout pilots, Derek had proven himself to be the most effective, uncovering caches of weapons and food as if he were a born bloodhound. He always managed to avoid getting in too deep with the Viet Cong, knowing that the Cobras could do a better job of blasting their asses apart than he could with his gunners. His spot reports were the most accurate, the most methodically given, and he was always so perfectly calm. Several crewmen had commented to him that Justen had nerves of steel. And then it hit him. What better person to have onboard than someone with a vested interest that the INFANT crew *not* engage a target without permission, for fear they might hit his brother. "Okay. You can go. But let me tell you something. Whatever you see, you mark it down and then get the hell out of there, fast. Remember, according to what we've been told, those jokers have orders to kill any POW on the slightest provocation."

"Sir, you got to know I understand that—"

Rameriz nodded. He softened and said, "Yeah, I know, I know." As Justen turned to go, he took hold of Justen's arm. "Listen, I feel for you. Your brother's been on my mind ever since you told me about him. I've...never forgotten."

Derek bent his head down. "I appreciate that, sir."

Rameriz pondered his next statement. "Something else I want you to know and for godsake, you can't breathe a word of it to anyone...but because of your brother I asked to come down here. None of the other troops commanders were willing to commit to this assignment...mainly due to the goddamn moving and the logistics involved."

Justen suddenly became glassy-eyed. He diverted his attention to the corner of the tent where Rameriz had several of his fatigue uniforms hanging on a wire. The welling of gratitude within him was suddenly more than he could bear. In all the months he had been in Vietnam, he had never felt a kinship to anyone. For the first time since hearing the news about Jake's MIA status, Derek Justen had to quell the urge to cry.

He had been repairing one of his fishing nets when Chimp appeared. *"Mau di!* You must come!"

"What the hell for?" Jake Cole said, turning his head away and glancing toward his fishing line attached to a makeshift bobber floating on the surface of the canal.

Chimp brought his foot up and gave Jake a swift kick to his left side. He told Jake that Major Hung wished to see him. *"Mau di!"*

Jake's left arm swung out just as Chimp stepped back. "You little piece of shit. The next time you kick me, I swear, I'll kill you—"

Within the next instant, Piglet and another guard whom he nicknamed "Spitball", because he was always hawking and spitting, surrounded Jake. "All right...all right, damnit. Let me get my line in," he said, reaching for the bamboo pole he had setting a few feet away.

"No more fish!" yelled Chimp, who then motioned for the two guards to grab him.

Jake shoved them away. "I can get up by myself, goddamnit—"

Jake stood slouched before Major Hung, who sat in front of him smoking a foul-smelling European cigarette. He watched as the man put the cigarette to his mouth and take a deep drag, letting the smoke filter outward slowly through his nostrils as he exhaled. "The Committee has been reconsidering your case. It looks very favorable that you should be released. What you think of that?"

Jake blinked. "What...?"

"You have shown considerable repentance. That visit among the people two weeks ago to show you the truth about how the people are suffering with your American forces here, went very well. The Front now wishes to show its leniency toward you."

Jake gazed at Major Hung in rapt disbelief. "What?"

"Do you not understand? You are to be released." Major Hung smiled, showing his crooked, tobacco-stained teeth. "Are you not—"

"Released! Repentance!" Jake's body suddenly stiffened. What kind of concoction had they cooked up to show that he now favored their side? what documents? what photos? what had they rearranged? What had he said on tape during his many interrogations that could be construed to mean other than what he in-

The Sky Soldiers

Chapter 84

THE FOLLOWING TWO NIGHTS IT RAINED. And each night Justen sat on his cot and listened to the raindrops pelt the top and sides of the tent. Belligerently he cursed each raindrop, and the sum of all raindrops, because even divided by a thousand they added up to more than all the seconds they could have spent flying. On the afternoon of December 24, the skies began to clear. By early evening the clouds were completely gone. But there was to be no flying that night...

"O little town of Bethlehem
How still we see thee lie
Above thy deep and dreamless sleep
The silent stars go by..."

Leo Tannah, whispering softly, began: "Forgive me, Father, I have sinned. It has been eight months since my last confession. I have failed to observe the Sabbath, especially during those times when I could. Many times I have taken the Lord's name in vain. I have committed many killings, too many now to mention. And lately, Father, I have begun to doubt my own reasons for being here. I mean, if Nixon is eventually going to pull us out, why must we continue to go out day after day after day? Maybe you can help me on that...I-I don't like what I've become...just an instrument in the hands of those who don't even know me, yet who expect me to go on flying and fighting..."

Tannah stepped into the lift section tent. He saw that Slater was alone. He approached Kip's cot.

Kip looked up. "What's the matter, Leo? You don't look so good."

Leo's face was blanched, the look in his eyes troubled, pained. His lip's quivered as he spoke. "I-I just went to confession." Leo then sat down on Slater's cot. "Kip, would you do something for me?"

"Sure, Leo, what?"

"Would you go with me to that Catholic Church on the far side of the MACV compound? The chaplain told me they have a real nice midnight Mass."

"Leo...I'm not Catholic."

"That won't matter."

Gently, Kip said, "But, Leo...it's a Vietnamese church. You've never liked these people."

"Kip...did you ever stop to think that...maybe I didn't mean it?"

"Leo...I always wanted to think you didn't mean it."

Victor R. Beaver

> *"Yet in the dark night shineth*
> *The everlasting light*
> *The hopes and fears of all the years*
> *Are met in thee tonight..."*

Sandy Adamson gazed at the return address. The lump in his throat grew larger as he made his way back to his tent. He opened the letter and brought it under the light. Curiously, he noted that there were places where the ink was smeared.

Dear Sandy,

I hope this letter doesn't come as too great a shock. Your mother was kind enough to give me your address, so I thought I should write. Sandy, you don't know how many letters I've started to you and never sent. When Brad died, it hurt me so bad that I never knew how to say what I meant and in the process I know I hurt you deeply. I have never forgotten you, Sandy. After Brad's funeral, I wanted to forget you, to believe that you never even existed, because I didn't want ever to go through with you what I did with Brad.

As you know, it's been a year since we got word that Brad was killed and I can honestly say the memory of that day when our pastor and those two men came to the door still haunts me. But now I realize that what I have done to you is far worse than Brad dying. We all have to die someday. Some of us, of course, will do so sooner than others. The reason I decided to write you now is because of what the pastor of our church said last Sunday. It just made so much sense. He said, "You can't forsake the living for the dead. To do so is to die within." Pretty profound, don't you think?

Anyway, I know that you have probably forgotten me and maybe even found yourself another girl. If you have, I'm glad for you and I'm glad for her. Can you forgive me, Sandy, for the way I treated you? I am so sorry, that even as I write this, my tears are falling on the page and making a mess of the ink. If you can't forgive me, I'll try to understand.

Sincerely yours,
Katie

Patterson, the Blue Platoon NCOIC, went ahead of Vinny as the two men wound their way through the maze of tents into officer country. When they came to the one they wanted, they stepped to the opening and peeked in. "Captain Nolan, sir?"

"Yes?"

"Would you like to come with us?"

"What's this all about, Sergeant? Is it another problem with one of the men?"

"No, sir. You'll see," Patterson answered.

They made their way to the platoon tent. The night air was still. As they went they heard a radio playing from somewhere.

"Silent night, Holy night
All is calm, All is bright..."

Patterson parted the tent flap and Nolan stepped in. Most of the men were seated on their cots, drinking beer, playing cards, talking. "Atten-hut...!" Childs, the medic, sounded.

"Be at ease," Nolan said. He saw Patterson disappear out the other end of the tent.

Spec Four Hoyt stood. Tottering slightly, he said, "How you doing, Blue? Nice you could join our little party."

"I'm doing fine. And I can see that none of you is feeling any pain." He looked toward Brave Water and Big George, seated next to each other on a pair of ammo crates.

Fields went to a bucket of ice that sat in the middle of the tent. He retrieved a can of beer. He opened it and handed it to Nolan.

"Thanks."

"Thank you, sir."

"For what?"

"You know, sir."

"Oh, yeah, I...I forgot. How are you liking it in the lift section?"

"It's the greatest, sir. Couldn't be better."

Just then Patterson reappeared. He was carrying a paper bag. "Okay, everybody, listen up." The men quieted down. They gathered around. Patterson stood before his captain. "Sir, on behalf of the men of the Blue Platoon, I would like to present you with this gift." Patterson handed Nolan the bag. "Sorry we couldn't wrap it with real gift paper, sir, but we think you'll like it anyway."

Nolan took the paper bag. He reached in and withdrew its content. It was a half-gallon bottle of Jack Daniels. He gazed at the bottle, turning it from side to side. "What the hell—?"

Vinny said, "Jack's your favorite, isn't it, sir?"

"You bet it is."

Patterson said, "The men—well, we all pitched in, sir. We hope it's okay."

Nolan looked around at his men. He saw mostly a group of somber faces, trying to break into a smile. Childs came forward. "Sir, we, uh, know...you've been having a...pretty rough time. We also know that...well Christmas was supposed to be when—"

"I was to get married."

"Yessir."

Victor R. Beaver

The space beneath the tent grew silent. Taking a deep breath, Nolan returned his gaze at the bottle. He waited for a moment and then said, "Well...this is a very nice gift. I-I...don't know how I can repay you."

"Repay us, sir?" Patterson said. "Sir, you don't have to do that. This is just our way of showing you that we think you're a pretty damn good platoon leader. Lot's better than many of us figured."

Nolan looked thoughtfully at the bottle and then into the eyes of his men. He unscrewed the cap, took a whiff of the liquid, raised the bottle and said:

"Here's to a damn fine bunch of men. You're professionals, everyone of you." Nolan then put the bottle to his lips. He took a swig and passed it on. Each man did the same, murmured a few words, then took a swig. By the time they were done, more than half of the bottle was gone.

Gingerly, Nolan took the bottle and replaced the cap. He felt a constriction in his throat. He turned. "I...uh, if you guys don't mind...I'd like to be alone..."

"Sure, Blue," Childs said. "We understand. Merry Christmas."

"Yeah. Same to you..."

"'Round yon Virgin Mother and Child
Holy infant so tender and mild
Sleep in heavenly peace..."

In his tent Nolan sat down and studied the bottle, feeling lonely and depressed. A tear formed. He wiped it away and then unscrewed the cap. He took a long, slow sip. This time the liquid warmed through him like a slow fire. He replaced the cap and put the bottle on the wooden stand next to his cot. He looked at the picture he had always kept next to wherever he slept, the one of him and his father and the blue marlin. For a long moment he gazed at the *Laura Lee* in the background, the boat upon which he and his father had planned to spend so many days out on the water in. He took the blue velvet case that held the gold oak-leaf clusters, opened it, looked at them for a moment, and then slowly closed the lid. He replaced the case next to another picture on the stand, one that he had recently put there. It was a childhood picture of a little girl in pigtails, cuddling a kitten she had been given on her twelfth birthday, according to the writing on the back. It was a girlhood picture of Sharon, one that Frieda had found and had given to him after she had cleared Sharon's room of her personal belongings, a room completely intact, the same room Sharon would have been in had she not been working late. *Sharon...Sharon...Sharon, baby, why that night? Why couldn't you have just been too tired and gone to bed? You'd still be alive...*

Then for the fourth time that day Captain Michael Thomas Nolan buried his face in his hands and cried.

"Sleep in heavenly peace..."

Leo squinted at the paper held under the dim light in the middle of the tent. His lips moved as he repeated silently the words he read. Kip opened the tent flap and walked in.

"How's it going, Leo?"

"It's okay. You still want to go with me to Mass?"

"Sure." Kip glanced at the paper in Leo's hand. "What's that you're reading?"

Leo handed him the paper. Kip read:

> *"Everyday a new picture is painted and framed,*
> *Held up for half an hour,*
> *In such lights as the great Artist chooses,*
> *And then withdrawn, and the curtain falls.*
> *And the sun goes down,*
> *And the long afterglow gives light.*
> *And then the damask curtains glow along the Western window*
> *And now the first star is lit,*
> *And I go home."*

Kip shuddered and handed the slip of paper back. "Leo...this is by Thoreau. Why are you reading it?"

"I-I don't know. It's something I found in my billfold. I remember now my mother giving it to me as I was leaving home to come here." Ashen-faced, Leo said:

"I want to go home, Kip. I'm sorry to God I extended. Why did we do it? Why...?"

Kip looked at his friend. He shook his head, a lump suddenly forming in his throat. "I don't know, Leo...I don't know."

At midnight, Kip and Leo edged their way into the small crowded church. Several parishioners, seeing the Americans enter, bowed politely and stepped aside. An organ played somewhere in the background. As the two men nudged forward a young woman holding a baby turned and looked at them. The baby squirmed and the woman accidentally let go of a ragged piece of dark cloth. Leo bent and picked it up. He handed it to her. The woman, her face appearing grave, took it and turned back around.

The two men looked to the front. The priest, an elderly man with graying hair and soft twinkling eyes, his hands extended, began chanting. "He's now saying the First Eucharistic prayer," Leo whispered.

"How do you know? He's speaking Vietnamese."

"Because all over the world, in every Catholic Church, Christmas Mass is performed the same."

"Oh...I see."

One of the assistants began to ring a set of bells. As Leo turned his attention back to the priest, Kip studied his friend out of the corner of his eye. Leo seemed calm, at peace.

"O Holy night, The stars
Are brightly shining
It is the night of
the dear Saviour's birth..."

When it came time for communion, Leo moved forward along with the rest and took the bread and wine. As he watched Leo return, Kip felt a warm comradeship toward him. "Leo...you doing okay?"

"Sure, why do you ask it like that?"

"Oh...no reason. I'm just glad to see you feeling okay."

"I'm feeling fine, really I am."

Slater nodded. "That's good. I'm glad."

Chapter 85

IT WAS MID-AFTERNOON. THE COOKS in the mess tent had just finished serving Christmas dinner. First Lieutenant Malcolm Emery walked into the gun platoon tent. He tacked a sheet of paper to one of the middle tent posts. "I've got the assignments here for tomorrow. Two Pink Teams are going up."

Leo sidled next to the lieutenant. He examined the paper. "Hey, you haven't even got me on standby—what gives?"

"Too many hours. You need a break."

"Hey, give someone else a break, I'd rather be flying."

"No dice."

"Well, at least put me on standby—*for crissake.*"

"Look, Tannah, why can't you just give it a rest once in awhile—?"

"Ah shit. Flying just makes the time in this asshole country go by faster."

Emery peered into Leo's face. Tannah's eyes had that lost puppy dog look. "Okay, I'll put you on standby. Will that make you happy?"

Leo shrugged. "Yeah, sure...you bet."

Derek Justen shined his flashlight ahead as he went quickly toward the flight line. He glanced up occasionally, checking the night sky. It was brightly lit with stars. He met Lieutenant Galloway, Warrant Officer Mattingly, and the rest of the INFANT crew at the ship. "Sorry, I'm late...I was just finishing up a letter."

"That's okay," Galloway said. "We finally got the searchlight system above the miniguns to work. It'll help to see better, even before the moon comes up."

"Good. I'm ready."

Derek strapped into the left seat while Galloway went through the start procedures. Meantime, Mattingly, who would now be seated in the back, behind the observer monitor, showed him how to work the telescopic sighting unit and what buttons to push on the control panel mounted on the center console that were a part of the image-intensifying INFANT system.

When the helicopter was ready to hover, Galloway made his call. "Comanche Two Seven, this is Night Bird One, we're ready to hover."

"This is Two Seven, roger that. We're up to rpm," Slater replied.

Like they did the first night, they navigated toward Xom Ngon. As they flew on a northwesterly heading from Ca Mau, Derek looked through the TSU, panning the right periscope back and forth, up and down, trying to distinguish between natural vegetation and any kind of camouflage cover. To his disgust, he found the picture still too grainy to make any kind of distinction between the two. Looking through the TSU over Derek's shoulder, Mattingly saw that the searchlight was out again. "Damn. There must be an electrical short somewhere."

"We'll just have to wait again for the moon," Galloway responded.

From Xom Ngon, they turned west, flew for five minutes, then turned due north. They flew for one minute then turned due east.

"What we need to do," Justen said, "is to run these canals up one and down another. Forget this east-west, school-book, search-pattern crap. Charlie's either going to be right on the canal or slightly offset from it."

Galloway nodded. "Yeah, I agree. Let's do it that way."

They flew for an hour. They saw nothing, no movement on the canals, no evidence of any structures or hootches. Galloway checked the fuel gauge. "Sorry but it's time to head back.

"When did you figure the moon to rise tonight?"

"A little after one," Galloway said. "It'll also be less than half. It really won't do us much good until past two or so."

After refueling, Slater went over to Derek, who was standing alone by the lake, smoking. "Can't see anything, uh?"

Derek took a drag, then disgustedly tossed a half-smoked cigarette into the water. "Nothing. Unless there's some kind of movement or maybe a light, we aren't able to see shit—"

"What about when the moon comes up?"

Derek looked to the east. He could see a low band of clouds beginning to form. "I don't know. We may be out of luck there too."

The team waited until half past two before the second lift-off. By then the moon was fifteen degrees above the horizon. The band of clouds to the east had become more prominent. Over the search area, Derek peered through the TSU until his eyes became watery. Still, he saw nothing more than trees, water, and low-lying brush. At 3:45 A.M., they headed back to Ca Mau.

After they landed, and the blades were tied down, Derek took his helmet and went to Galloway standing off to the side. "Listen, I appreciate your patience with me. I'm going to try and catch a couple hours of sleep. I've got myself scheduled to fly at daybreak."

"Sure, no problem. Me and Mattingly and the rest will give it one more try tonight."

"Okay. Good."

They had been in the air an hour and fifteen minutes when Galloway tapped at the fuel gauge. "We need to get back," he said to Mattingly.

"Damn," the co-pilot said. "I wish when we refueled we could put a full load on. I'm getting a good view now. Everything is really clear." (The added weight of the INFANT system, along with all the armament and ammunition, precluded filling the fuel tank to its maximum capacity.) The clouds to the east, instead of blanking out the moon, had thinned and then disappeared.

Galloway keyed his mic: "Comanche Two Seven, this is Night Bird One. We'll be heading back."

"Roger that," Slater replied, tiredly.

The Sky Soldiers

Mattingly said, "Let's fly along that south river on the way back, the one that goes by Xom Ngon, however the hell you say it."

"Roger that."

Galloway banked the ship right and rolled out on a southeasterly heading. "There's the river."

Mattingly panned ahead and then brought the periscope view directly to their front. He swept both sides of the river and then suddenly held the TSU still. "I see something."

"What—?"

"A sampan—*with someone in it!*"

"Are you serious?"

"Unslew your monitor. Look."

"Goddamn, *you're right.*"

"There's a gook—standing and waving."

"No shit, Sherlock."

"It looks like he's alone." And then Mattingly said, "But why is he waving...?"

"Fuck, maybe he's a POW—and escaped POW!"

"Christ, you could be right."

As they flew over the target, Galloway keyed the radio. He tried to sound calm. "Two Seven, Night Bird One, we've got a sampan right below us. We'll be turning back around."

"Roger that."

Galloway banked the ship hard right. When finally he rolled to a level attitude, they were flying perpendicular to the river. "Look straight ahead now," Galloway said.

"Roger that."

"What do you see—anything?"

"I'm looking—I'm looking."

"Pan quickly left and right."

"I am."

"Do you see the sampan? Do you even see the river?"

"No—yes! Crap! We just crossed it."

"Damn!" Galloway banked hard left. He rolled out on a northwesterly heading, parallel to the river. Mattingly looked at the fuel gauge; he pushed the 20-minute low-fuel test-light button. "Any minute and we're going to get us a low-fuel light."

Galloway banked the ship hard left again. They rolled out heading directly down river. "Pan straight ahead."

"I am-I am."

"See anything?"

"Nothing—shit."

"I know this is where we saw it."

"Yeah, me too."

The master caution light illuminated. Galloway looked down at the segment panel light on the center console. "There it is—the twenty-minute light. We've got to head back."

Mattingly checked his map and circled where they were with a grease pencil.

"Night Bird One, this is Comanche Two Seven. What did you see?" asked Slater.

Galloway keyed his mic: "A sampan for sure...and we think we spotted someone standing and waving at us...But hell, that couldn't be—"

"Someone waving—?" Slater replied, incredulously.

"That's affirmative."

Someone standing...and waving! Slater felt the gooseflesh rise over his body like it had never done before. *Christ! What if it was Justen's brother? What if it was—?* "We need to head back," Slater blurted over the radio.

"You're telling us. We've got a twenty-minute light—" Galloway responded.

The two helicopters raced back to Ca Mau. Slater could barely contain himself. He looked east just as the sun's rays peeked over the horizon.

Slater called the troop tactical operations center. "Comanche Control, this is Two Seven."

"Go, Two Seven."

"We're inbound your location, be there in zero five. Is Mr. Justen, Comanche One Eight, there?"

"Negative, he's gone out to his aircraft."

"Roger that."

As they made their approach to the Ca Mau airstrip, Slater saw three lone figures making their way toward the Scout parking area. He recognized Justen's tall sloping form with Hoyt and Kalbach a step behind, their weapons in hand.

When they landed, Slater went quickly to the INFANT bird. He practically wrenched Mattingly out of his seat. "Hurry, you've got to tell Mr. Justen what you saw."

Stunned, Justen listened, carefully plotting the coordinates on his map. He turned to Kalbach. "Untie the blades. We're cranking right now—"

"But...what about our high bird?"

"They'll catch up. Get moving, damnit."

Major Rameriz had just entered the TOC when Derek announced over the radio he was lifting. Rameriz, recognizing the callsign, glanced at his watch. "Where the hell is he going? Lift-off isn't for another half-hour."

Before the specialist on duty could answer, Slater and Galloway stormed into the tent. Breathless, Slater said, "Sir, the INFANT bird saw someone in a sampan—he was alone and he was waving." Slater grabbed Galloway's map and

The Sky Soldiers

hoved it at the troop commander. (On the way to the TOC, Slater had told Galloway about Derek's brother.)

Rameriz took the map, checked it, and then blurted, "Damnit! I knew he would do this—the first hair-brained thing he saw!"

"But, sir, he wasn't with us when we spotted the sampan," Galloway stated.

"He wasn't—?"

"No, sir. Mr. Mattingly and I both saw the man waving. It was like he was frantically trying to get our attention."

"Are you sure?"

"Absolutely."

Rameriz wheeled around. He shot out orders to have the Blues on standby. He told Slater to go back to his ship and wait. "Have my crew ready to go," Rameriz shouted as he was leaving the tent.

The OH-6 shuddered as Justen raced his ship north at the red-line limits. Feeling the wind tear at their pant legs, Kalbach and Hoyt gripped their weapons and scanned ahead and below. "Sir, do we have blanket permission to fire?" Hoyt asked.

"Negative. I repeat negative. You do not," Justen stated emphatically. "We'll be looking for an American POW."

"Are you serious—?"

"Absolutely."

They flew past Khai Quang, a small hamlet that sat on the same river the coordinates were plotted. "Keep a look out now," Justen said. "Tell me anything you see—*anything.*"

"Roger that, sir."

As they neared the exact location of the coordinates, they heard Franklin, the AC of their high bird, come over the radio. "Comanche One Eight, this is Three Three, where are you?"

"From Checkpoint Tango Bravo, fly heading three zero zero for approximately twelve klicks," Derek answered.

"Roger that, we're now five klicks south of Tango Bravo."

Justen then said, "Three Three, do not fire at anything unless I tell you exactly where. How copy?"

"Roger that, good copy. Oh, and by the way, Two Seven briefed us before we lifted. Good hunting and good luck, Derek."

"Roger that, and thanks."

"Sir—*I see a sampan!*—two o'clock!" Hoyt cried.

Derek looked right. There it was among the reeds, firm against the bank, partially hidden under the overhanging branches of several trees. Derek slowed the ship and began a right-hand orbit. Hoyt scanned from his front to the rear of the ship. Derek looked toward the right front. They did three orbits and saw no one around or near the empty boat. The high bird called. "One Eight, Three Three I've got you in sight."

"Roger that, we've got an abandoned sampan here. No sign of anything else."

Derek then began to widen his orbit. "Sir," said Hoyt, "I've got a hootch Three o'clock. And another. Shit—and bunkers!"

Just then they heard shots coming from the left. Kalbach fired his M-16. "Do you see what you're shooting at—?" Derek exclaimed.

"A couple of gooks. Ten o'clock! They had rifles!"

Derek heard Franklin come over the radio. "One Eight, Three Three, we've got a lone man moving rather quickly in an open area to your left rear, on the south side of the river."

"Roger that, we're coming left. We received fire from our left. Cover that north bank," Derek radioed back.

"Roger that."

Derek turned the Loach hard left and gained altitude to clear the trees on the south side of the river. When they got to the other side they saw a flat marshy area. A lone man in black pajamas was struggling to gain headway toward a cluster of low trees fifty meters to his front. Derek put the cyclic forward and added power to gain speed. "Kalbach, cover him. Try to get a good look at his face."

"Roger that."

A burst of AK-47 fire erupted from a small cluster of nipa palms to their right front. "Receiving fire, sir!" Hoyt called out.

"Shoot back!"

Tracers from Hoyt's M-60 ripped forward. Derek heard Rameriz's voice come over the radio, stating he was due south of Thoi Binh, inbound. As One Eight flew past the figure in black, Kalbach turned and saw a man with a thin scraggly-looking face staring back, groping forward on his hands and knees in the murky water. "I can't tell what he is," Kalbach sounded.

Derek pulled back hard on the cyclic. He leveled off and aimed the ship right at the man. And then his eyes widened. *Oh my God...Oh my God! Jake?* Kalbach quickly glanced right. "Sir, what are we stopping for? He's a gook!"

"Gooks don't have growth on their faces like that," Derek said. "Look at his eyes. He's an American!" By now the man had his arms outstretched, his fingers taut, willing the ship to come to him.

"Jesus!...You're right!"

Derek keyed his mic: "Six, One Eight. We've got an American down here—"

"Roger that," Rameriz replied. "Are you still taking fire?"

No one onboard the LOH saw the three Viet Cong rise from their bunker on the edge of the treeline to the left and empty their rifles into the cockpit. The bullets ripped through the windshield and shattered the instrument panel, sending shards of metal flying everywhere. Derek felt an immediate burning sensation in the left side of his chest, then everything went blank. The ship pitched nose up then slammed onto its left side. Pieces of rotorblades flew off, sending sharp missiles zinging through the air.

"Sergeant Patterson!"
"Yessir!"
"Where's Vinny?" Nolan said, buckling on his web gear.
"He's coming."
Nolan grabbed for his rifle. "Did he get that extra battery for the radio?"
"Yessir."
"Good. Let's go. This is going to be one helluva show—"

Sandy Adamson quickly strapped in, turned the battery switch on, and set the throttle. "Clear—"
"Clear," Roach called out.
As Sandy pressed the starter, Gabriel Baca, shouldering his M-60, ran up and hopped in the right side. "What's up?"
"One Eight's down," Roach said. "Kalbach's wounded bad. Hoyt's okay."

Lieutenant Emery ran forward across the compound. He looked back. "Roxbury—"
"Yo..."
"Did they fix that arming-light problem?"
"I think so. I just left them and they were gathering up their tools."
"Okay—good."
"Lieutenant, watch out—the hole!"
Emery pitched backward, twisting his body violently as he fell. Roxbury raced up. He knelt down. "My leg," Emery said, "Jesus, I think it's broken, God—*fuck!*—it hurts."
"What'll we do?"
"I-I can't fly...We've got to get out there. Get Tannah. He's on standby—"
"Roger that."
"Hurry!"

Slater and the rest of the lift section had their rotors turning when the Blues appeared and clambered aboard. Lieutenant Briscoe announced an immediate pitch pull. As they were climbing out, Slater, in the trail position, looked back to see Leo racing for Emery's gunship. "What the hell's he doing? I thought Emery was primary," Kip said aloud over the intercom.
"What was that?" Cowboy said.
"Nothing...nothing."

Rameriz gazed down at the battle raging below. "Three Three, this is Six. Hit that west treeline again."

"Roger that, Six."

Sampson, Rameriz's assigned co-pilot for the day, watched as Franklin's ship made another dive. The rockets exploded and Sampson saw dirt and shattered trees fly up less than a hundred meters from Justen's downed OH-6. "Shouldn't we be do something, sir?"

"Hang on, we're about to." Rameriz keyed his radio. "Two Six, this is Six, what's your ETE?"

Briscoe turned around and gave Nolan six fingers. Nolan, listening on his headset, keyed the radio: "We're zero six out."

"Okay. Here's the story. There's heavy fire coming from the west treeline. I've got three live guys on the ground. One of them we think is an escaped American POW. He's out of sight of Justen's crew, who are both pinned down near the ship. The POW, we believe, is hiding in the thicket of trees to the east of the downed bird. Plan to come in from the south. You'll be setting up a screen with your men while I slip in behind and try to find him."

"Roger that, Six. Good copy."

Rameriz added: "Be careful. Hoyt radioed, before they had to turn the aircraft battery off, that they overflew a large camp—heavily bunkered. Hoyt also said they'd been hearing lots of AK-47 fire."

When they were less than three minutes from the LZ, Slater happened to glance right. He saw Tannah, in Emery's Cobra, gliding by. The two men waved at each other. "Three Niner, this Two Seven. What happened to Emery?"

Tannah keyed his mic: "He fell in a hole, broke his leg. I'm it, bud."

"Roger that. Watch yourself, Leo."

"Don't worry about me. Break, Comanche Six, this is Three Niner. Give me a sit-rep."

Rameriz briefed Leo as he did Captain Nolan, but added: "I want you to cover Briscoe's flight going into the LZ. I'll be slipping in right behind him."

"Good copy," Leo replied.

Lieutenant Briscoe now guided his flight of four Hueys toward the LZ, letting down quickly as he did. Slater looked ahead. He saw Derek's Loach lying on its side. He still found it hard to believe that Justen was dead. *He can't be...He just can't be!"* Then Briscoe briefed his flight. "After the Blues are off, everybody do a one-eighty and leave the way we came in. Two Seven, you'll take up the lead."

"This is Two Seven, roger that," Kip said.

As the flight touched down, Rameriz brought his Huey in behind Slater's ship and began to maneuver around the east treeline, hunting frantically for the American. "I've got him, sir," Sampson said over the intercom. "There he is!"

Rameriz saw the man groping toward them, his face gaunt, his eyes wild with fear and anticipation. "Reynolds—get out and help him," Rameriz said to his right-side doorgunner.

"On my way, sir—"

Reynolds, six-feet-two, weighing over two hundred pounds, leaped out and slogged his way toward the struggling man. After a moment, he grabbed him by the shirt and felt a bony arm. Reynolds reached down and lifted him into his arms and carried him handily back to the ship. The gunner then laid him carefully on the cabin floor and resumed his position behind his M-60. "You in, Reynolds?" Rameriz asked.

"Let's haul ass, sir!" Reynolds said. And then he said, "Man, that guy is nothing but skin and bone, Major."

"I wouldn't doubt that. Find out who he is."

"Yes, sir, I'll try. But he's bawling like a baby."

Bullets whizzed overhead. Nolan looked left. He pointed toward the west treeline. "Sergeant Patterson, have your machine gunner direct his fire more to the right—"

"Yessir."

"Vinny, get over here!"

Vincenzo, crouching low, came to his captain's side. "Sir, I can't get this radio to work."

"Did you change the battery?"

"Yes, sir. That didn't help. We're shit out of luck—"

"Here's why it won't work," Nolan said, quickly examining the radio pack on Vinny's back. "The damn thing took a round."

"God, no shit!"

Nolan looked toward the downed low bird. Suddenly he had an idea. "Patterson, move Second Squad ten meters to the left, toward that clump of brush. We're taking fire now from that other side!"

"Yessir!"

Nolan glanced at Vinny. "Where's Childs?"

"Over by Hoyt and Kalbach. Kalbach's arm is real bad."

Franklin, orbiting overhead, continued to key his mic: "Two Six, Three Three, answer me, damnit. Answer me. We need to know where to fire!"

Nolan jerked his head up. He heard the unmistakable sound of a mortar round leave its tube. "Patterson! Mortars! Mortars!" He turned to Vinny. "Cover me. I'm going over to the Loach. I'm going to use the ship's radio."

Vincenzo grabbed Nolan's arm. "You can't, sir. The VC's got to be using it to zero in!"

Nolan shoved the RTO back. "Get out of my way. *We've got to re-establish commo!*"

Sandy Adamson looked ahead. He had Derek's downed low bird in sight and a lone figure running toward it. A quick glance and he saw where the rest of the Blues were dispersed. They were in two loose clusters, ten to fifteen meters apart north of the downed ship. "Three Three, this is One Seven. What do you want me to do?"

Franklin keyed his mic: "One Seven, we don't have commo with anyone down there. See if you can find out where we need to direct our fire."

"Roger that. I'll be in position in about zero three," Sandy said.

"Three Three, this is Three Niner. Look—they're getting mortared—" Lee said.

"Goddamnit—!"

Tannah looked down and to his right. "I've got one of their sites. I'm rolling in."

Ignoring the shelling, Nolan gazed for a moment at Justen's blood-smeared body, still strapped inside the shattered cockpit. He found Hoyt's flight helmet, discarded on the ground, and put it on. He reached across and flicked the battery switch on. He found the master avionics switch and turned it on. Immediately he heard radio chatter. He keyed the switch on the cyclic control stick. "Three Three, this is Two Six, how copy?"

"Loud and clear now. What the hell's going on down there?"

"A real shindig, that's for damn sure—" Nolan answered. "Listen, we're getting mortared from the north."

"Roger that. We've been plastering the camp across the river. It's a real hornets nest down there."

"I've got three Blues wounded. Hoyt's okay. Kalbach's in bad shape. We need a medevac." Then Nolan said, "I want my men out of here—ASAP. Where's Comanche Six?"

"He's taking the American back to Ca Mau. The man's in real bad shape."

The shelling had tapered off. Nolan glanced south. He saw a single Loach approaching low-level. The radio crackled. "Two Six, this is One Seven," Sandy said. "Are you at the downed ship?"

"Affirmative," Nolan said. "What I need for you to do is cover my guys as we pull back."

"Will do," Sandy replied.

Nolan turned his head. He heard a whistle and then an explosion. There was a flash and then he felt himself spinning like a man caught in a whirlpool. He felt himself bashed to the ground. Dazed, his ears ringing, he struggled to sit upright and gaped at the brackish water around him turning red.

Vinny, lying several yards away, felt something strike him in the head. He rolled over. *It was a man's leg!*

Vinny scrambled over to his captain. "Blue!"

The Sky Soldiers

"For godsake, Vincenzo, get down!" Nolan said, as he struggled to tie a tourniquet around the stump. "Go tell Sergeant Patterson to start pulling back. Get ready for extraction!"

The RTO knelt down. "But...but, Blue, your leg...your face...!"

"Do as you're told!"

Vincenzo turned around. "Medic! Medic!"

Rameriz spoke over the intercom. "Reynolds, has he told you who he is yet?"

"Yessir, finally, sir—"

"Well, who is he?"

"Pfizer, sir. Sergeant Rick Pfizer. Been a POW since early 'sixty-four. Said he was on a Special Forces A-team operation with a bunch of CIDG folks. Got surrounded by a battalion of VC, near Tan Phu. They ran out of ammunition and he and two other Americans got themselves captured."

"Are you sure?"

"That's what he said, sir."

"Holy, Holy Mother of Christ..."

Kip Slater watched as Big George and Brave Water carried Captain Nolan toward the ship. The captain's right leg was gone above the knee, heavily bandaged with several battle dressings. His head was also bandaged and his right arm hung limp by his side. Slater saw Fields, his right doorgunner, leap out of the ship to give assistance, his face streaming with tears.

"I knew it, sir," Fields cried. He turned to Childs. "This is how it was in my dreams—"

Nolan lifted his head slightly, then it slumped down. "Get back, you jerk!" Childs shouted.

"But I knew this was going to happen!" Fields screamed.

"You don't know shit—now get out of the way!"

Sandy Adamson brought his ship near the west treeline. Roach saw flashes and then heard a tremendous ripping roar. "A fifty-caliber!"

"We're taking fire," Sandy cried over the radio. To our nine o'clock! It's a fifty!"

The huge anti-aircraft rounds ripped into the ship, hardly slowing as they exited out the other side. Sandy felt his left hand suddenly sling back. He gaped down at what was left of the collective control lever. He heard Roach cry out over the intercom:

"I-I'm hit—Oh, God, *I'm hit—!*"

Regaining his composure, Sandy grabbed the shattered collective pitch-control lever and jammed the cyclic control stick hard right. He heard rockets from Tannah's ship impact behind him. AK-47 fire raked the left side of the ship and Sandy saw Roach slump forward in his shoulder harness. Blood was splattered everywhere on the inside of the windshield. Sandy looked out the right door and guided the ship south, away from the deadly treeline. Behind him, he heard Gab's M-60 firing. He caught a quick glimpse of the four lift ships climbing to altitude. He felt another .50-caliber round hit on the right side, jolting the ship hard to the left. Another burst of gunfire. He felt a sharp stinging sensation on his neck. Horrified, he saw blood squirting out in front of his chest. He put his left hand up, felt his neck, and then pulled his hand away. *It was smeared with blood!* He heard a voice calling him...quiet-like...in the distance...as if speaking from inside a tomb. He barely recognized Franklin's voice. "One Seven...this is Three Three...I'm right behind you...I've got you covered...get out...get out..." Sandy's thumb fumbled to press the radio-talk switch; he was struck by a sudden wave of nausea. Glancing upward he saw Tannah's Cobra silhouetted against the pale blue sky on a post-dive pullout. "Damn...those guys...are good...good..." he heard himself mumbling.

Franklin spoke to Leo over the radio. "Three Niner, Three Three, let's get the hell out of here—"

"I'm going to make one more run. Punch off my load."

"Negative, Three Niner. Break it off—break it off!"

Kip Slater, listening, said, "Leo, do like he says—*break it off!*"

"No problem, Kip, no problem. Take care, buddy..."

Tannah dove. He lined up the crosshairs, checked his trim, pressed the button. Nothing. He recycled the arming switch. He pressed the button. *Swoosh!...Swoosh!* The final two pairs of rockets sped forward. Roxbury, up front, spoke:

"Receiving fire. From nine o'clock—" Two .50-caliber rounds slammed into the left side of the ship. The ship began to pitch back and roll inverted. Leo tried to correct with cyclic-control input. No response. He put the cyclic forward. Still no response. "I've lost control," he cried. Roxbury grabbed for his cyclic. He moved it left. Nothing. The ship was now upside down. Horrified, the two men felt the aircraft plunge earthward. The last thing either pilot saw before impact, looking upward through their separate cockpit canopies, was an instant vision of blue sky, the thin line of the horizon, and then green earth.

Meanwhile, Slater watched as Leo's ship careened toward the ground inverted. He saw the Cobra hit and explode. *"Leo—!"*

Sandy Adamson felt his body growing weaker. His head fell back. He jerked awake. *Got to make it...back...to make it...back—Katie!...I love you...got to...make it...back...to my Katie—* He felt dizzy. He tried to focus his eyes. He sensed his breathing becoming shallower and shallower. He looked at Roach slumped forward in his seat. The whole front of the man's face was practically gone. "Gab...Gab..." he called to his gunner in the back. "Can you...hear me, Gab?" He knew that his lips had formed the words, but couldn't tell whether they became actual sounds over the intercom. Occasionally, dimly, he heard a voice. It was an urging voice telling him to turn left, then right, or to bring the nose of the helicopter up. *Katie...Katie...where are you...my darling...darling...Katie...?*

Sandy gazed ahead of the ship. The landscape swam before his eyes. He saw the dirt strip. "Ca Mau...Ca Mau...is that you?" He saw the three 155-howitzers. He banked slightly right and saw that he was lined up on the airstrip. He reduced power. His head slumped down. "Shoot me down...you sonsabitches...I-I dare you..."

"Sir, wake up," Gab shouted over the intercom.

Sandy jerked his head up. The ground was coming right at them. He reared back on the cyclic. The ship wavered erratically. The Loach rolled left. He moved the cyclic right. *Got to land this thing...got to get...to my Katie. Katie...Katie...Katie...I love you, Katie...*

"Pull back, sir!"

Sandy opened his eyes. The ship had again pitched nose down. Again, he heaved back on the cyclic. He felt the right rear skid hit; the sudden jolt awakened him nearly to full consciousness. *"Katie...!"* He pushed the shattered collective full down. The helicopter jostled and then slid forward on the dirt strip a few feet before coming to a full stop. Sandy Adamson lifted his head slightly, then his body slumped forward.

Captain Merryman, the troop executive officer, was seated on the passenger side of a jeep stopped next to the aircraft parking area. He watched as the OH-6 made its approach to the far end of the runway, passing over the artillery battery; then it wobbled crazily as it came closer to the ground and landed. He saw it remain stationary, the rotorblades continuing to spin at full rpm. Merryman looked toward Spec Four Howard, the driver. "What's with him? Why doesn't he hover down here and park?"

"I don't know, sir."

Suddenly, Merryman said, "Quick. Let's make tracks down there—"

The jeep skidded to a halt as Gabriel Baca unbuckled himself from the ship. The machine gunner stumbled around to the left side of the helicopter. He fell to the ground when he saw what was left of Roach's head. Merryman leaped out of the jeep and went to the right side of the ship. He reached over and turned the fuel switch off. He lifted Sandy's head. "Is he dead?" asked the driver.

Grim-faced, Merryman felt for a pulse. After several seconds, his expression still looked grim. "I don't know—I can't really tell. Go get a medic."

Victor R. Beaver

Chapter 86

KEITH SLATER LET THE LID DOWN on his suitcase and pushed in the latches. He checked around his cot. Underneath the cot he had stowed his flight helmet and rifle and armored chestplate and duffel bag filled with his uniforms and other personal belongings. He glanced at John Sampson standing a few feet away. He extended his hand. "Samp, you take care. I want to see your ugly face when I get back."

Sampson extended his own hand and nodded. "How long will you be gone?"

"A couple of weeks."

"Do you get any leave after the funeral?"

"Yeah...seven days."

In Rameriz's tent, Slater stood with his orders in hand. "So, you all set to go?" the commanding officer said.

"Yessir."

"I don't envy you. I had that body escort duty once. Luckily, I didn't know the guy." Rameriz turned; he picked up a small case lying on his desk and opened it. Slater saw a shining metallic star attached to a red, white and blue ribbon. "I put Mr. Tannah in for the Silver Star." Kip reached out and felt the raised relief of the medal. He withdrew his hand and Rameriz closed the case. "Take this with you...give it to his parents or something."

"Yessir."

Rameriz extended his hand. "Well, son, have a good trip. And give it some more thought about accepting that 'postcard' direct commission to first lieutenant. You'll be in charge of the lift section, if you do?"

"Thank you, sir. I'll...I'll really give it some thought." Slater looked at Rameriz. He saw the man's soft dark eyes, the wavy, jet-black hair with streaks of gray, the neatly trimmed moustache above a classically shaped upper lip. "Sir, do you mind if I say something?"

"No...go ahead."

"Well, sir, I have never met a commanding officer I've respected and admired more than you. If our army could have more men like you in charge, more guys would be willing to stay in."

The two aviators gazed at each other. A moment of silence passed as Rameriz thought of the men in his troop, of his family of men. "Well...I'll tell you," he said; "I've got some goddamn fine troops here." A moistness came to his eyes, his eyes suddenly puffy, as he thought, too, of those he had lost: CW2 Justen, Captain Nolan, Spec Four Dillard (Roach), Spec Five Halyard (Wolfman), Staff Sergeant Joe "Pap" Harris, Warrant Officers Adamson, Allen, Cavenaugh, and Roxbury. And CW2 Leo Tannah. And then: "If we never do another

The Sky Soldiers

decent thing over here, at least we repatriated one American from that damned forest."

Slater nodded. "Yes, sir, at least we did that..."

As Slater turned to go, Rameriz said, "Oh, I almost forgot." From a drawer in his desk, Rameriz withdrew a manila envelope and handed it to Slater. "I'd like for you to stop at Can Tho and deliver this to the hospital."

"What is it?"

"Letters for Mr. Adamson."

"Okay, I'll do that."

"Tell him I'll be up tomorrow to see him." Rameriz pointed toward another small case on his desk. "I've got to give him his Purple Heart. I also put him in for a DFC with V-device."

"That's good, sir. He deserves it."

"Yeah." Rameriz shook his head. "By all rights, that young man should be dead."

"Yessir."

Carrying the manila envelope, Slater went down the long row of beds until he found the right one. "Hey, how you doing?"

Sandy Adamson turned. He looked up and gave a week smile of recognition. He strained to raise his head. Kip saw that the young pilot's neck was still heavily bandaged. Sandy tried to speak but all he could manage was a slight mumble. "That's okay. You don't have to say anything." Kip handed him the envelope. "The CO wanted me to deliver these letters to you. He also said he'd be by tomorrow to award your Purple Heart."

Sandy nodded and said, very faintly, "Where...you...going?"

"Back to the States, for Leo's funeral. His folks asked that I be his 'official' body escort."

Sandy winced; then he said, "How's...Captain...Nolan...?"

Kip shrugged. "I don't know. The last we heard he was on his way to Japan. You remember he lost his right leg and the use of his right arm, don't you?"

Sandy nodded. "I...vaguely...remember..."

"His face also got pretty mangled. I'm the one who airlifted him out." Kip further related how the riverine forces came in and fought for two days and nights before demolishing the camp and routing the enemy. "When all was said and done," Kip said, "they decided that Derek stumbled onto a Viet Cong Main Force battalion plus a support company of NVA."

Sandy sighed heavily and sank his head down into the pillow. He closed his eyes. When he reopened them, he asked:

"What...about...the POW...?"

"He should already be back in the States with his family. He was to leave right after New Year's Day."

Sandy strained to raise his head again. "It's too bad..."

"What?"

"That it wasn't...Justen's brother..."

Kip nodded. "Yeah, it's too bad." There was a moment of silence between them.

Sandy said, "Do you think...Justen...believed it *was* his brother?"

The older pilot shook his head. Softly, Kip said, "I don't know. I hope to God he did..."

"Yeah...me too."

"There was something else, " Kip said. "Food for thought, I guess."

"What?"

"The man was on the verge of being released, so he had been told, but he refused to sign a certain document condemning America's involvement in the war; it would have been a gesture to condone his captors. He just couldn't bring himself to do it. Then on Christmas Day, late in the evening, he escapes."

At first Sandy frowned. And then his eyes grew wide with astonishment. "Oh my God...oh my God—"

Kip's eyes took on a distant look. "Yeah...I know exactly what you're thinking. How different it all might have been had he signed."

Sandy's eyes narrowed. "I...wouldn't have...signed," he said, trying now to struggle to his elbows.

"You know," Kip replied, "I don't think I would have either...but I don't know why. For the life of me, I can't think why—"

Sandy said, "Do you think...it might have something...to do with...integrity...?"

The older pilot shook his head. "I don't know—I would hope that it would—but I don't know. God, the lives that were lost—"

Sandy reached over and touched Kip's arm. Kip's eyes had a glazed-over look. "Good luck...to you," Sandy said, "whatever you...decide."

"'Decide...?'"

"Yeah...if you decide...whether or not...to come back."

"I'll be back," Kip whispered.

"Maybe...you won't..."

After Slater was gone, Sandy opened the manila envelope. There was a card from his sister Melissa, which he opened and read, and then a letter from his mother, filled with dread for his health and safety. Two other letters were from ex-high-school classmates. The last letter was from Katie.

Dear Sandy,

I got the news from your mother that you were wounded. My heart plunged when she told me. I cried for over an hour, and then when I could finally hold a pen steady, I decided to write.

I love you, Sandy. I love you, I love you, I love you! Do you hear me? I want you to come home to me. I want to have what we once had. I want to be married to you, if you'll have me. I want to have your children and I want us to grow old together. Is it too late, Sandy? Please, please tell me that it isn't. My tears are streaming down my face and getting the ink all smeary again. Your last letter was so nice. I knew when I read it there was some hope for me. And now I'm pouring out my heart and soul to you...

Sandy laid the letter down. He tried to call for a nurse but the wound on his neck forced him to keep his voice barely at a whisper. When a nurse finally did walk by, he signaled for her to approach. She saw tears streaming down his face. He gripped her arm. "What's the matter—?" the nurse asked, her face now looking grave with concern.

"I...I'm...going to be...married—" Sandy finally said.

"Well, good for you, Mr. Adamson. Who's the lucky girl?"

Sandy shoved the letter toward her. "Her name...is Katie...Katie Lee Williams—"

* * *

THEY HAD BEEN IN THE DESCENT profile for more than ten minutes passing through several tendrils of clouds when the jetliner broke out in the clear and the captain of the World Airways Boeing 707 came over the PA system. "We are now coming into the San Francisco Bay area. For those seated on the left, the Golden Gate Bridge is just ahead...It looks, too, like the morning fog has finally cleared..." The captain paused for a moment. And then he said:

"Guys, may I be the first to welcome you home. We are now officially over the territorial waters of the United States of America—"

A loud round of applause erupted throughout the cabin. There were cheers and whistles, backslaps and handshakes, as one hundred and sixty-two passengers, all men who, for the better part of three hundred and sixty-five days, doubted this day would ever come, finally felt the culmination of their long journey home.

"Where to soldier?" the cab driver said.

"Oakland Army Depot," Slater replied.

"You just get in from 'Nam?"

"Yes."

Victor R. Beaver

"How was it over there?"

"It sucked."

"I hear that. What do you think about Nixon gonna pull everybody out and end the war?"

"It's too late," Kip murmured.

Kip, still in the same jungle fatigue uniform he had on when he left Ca Mau, met the lieutenant in charge of the escort detachment. He checked Kip's orders and then rifled through a file of papers. "Here it is. CW2 Leo M. Tannah. He's scheduled to leave at six thirty-seven P.M., tonight. On United Flight Five One Six. Nonstop to Pittsburgh." And then he said, eyeing Kip's uniform more closely: "Looks like you're going to need a whole new outfit: dress greens, saucer cap, low quarters, belt, the works."

"How do I get all that stuff? I've only got fifty bucks on me—in MPC."

The lieutenant pulled out a special form, entered some information from Kip's orders, and handed it to him. "Here take this and go to Room One Fifteen. As you go out my office, take a right. It's three doors down on the left. They'll fix you up with a uniform. It's where they prepare and clothe the deceased before final shipment home. Shoes, brass, and ribbons all can be bought at the PX. It's open twenty-four hours a day." The lieutenant looked at Kip's face, suddenly turned pale. "What's the matter? Don't you feel well?"

"Yeah, yeah...It was just...a long flight."

Slater opened the door to Room 115 and went in. The lieutenant had told him that he would be entering an outer office that had access to a much larger room on the opposite side. As he closed the door behind him, the office took on a kind of hushed silence, Straight ahead was a desk. Against the right wall were three chairs and against the left a row of file cabinets. Beyond and to the right of the desk was a gray metal door with the words *AUTHORIZED PERSONNEL ONLY* stenciled on it. He was just beginning to sit down when a tall, stoop-shouldered man appeared, entering through the gray metal door. Wearing a white smock, gray pants, and rubber gloves, he peered at Kip through a pair of dark, horn-rimmed eyeglasses. Kip quickly handed over the form the lieutenant had given him.

The man looked at the form. "Sure, we can fix you up. If you'll just come with me..." The man invited Kip to precede him through the gray metal door.

It was a clean, bright, high-ceilinged room, with three long windows spaced evenly apart near the ceiling of each wall. In the room he saw several men also dressed in white smock, gray pants, and wearing rubber gloves. They glanced up as he entered. Each man stood alone at a table. Kip's eyes widened as he saw lying on each table the body of a man, the bare chest exposed, the lower part of the body covered by a clean white sheet. As he was led across the room, Kip happened to pause and glance at the head of one of bodies. Its face had a chalky made-over appearance, the way a woman's face looks when it has had too much rouge applied. Its eyes were closed, its lips pressed shut, its nostrils a study in stillness. The man working on him turned and smiled at Slater. As if giving a progress report, he said:

"I had a little trouble with his mouth, but I think he looks real good. Don't you?"

Slater nodded, then resumed walking. The man leading him said, "Your orders say you'll be escorting a chief warrant officer named Leo Tannah?" Kip nodded again, his mind's eye still riveted to the sight of the dead body resting on the table. "Well, you're in luck. We've got him all set to go."

"You do?"

"Oh yeah. Of course, his remains are non-viewable so there wasn't much we had to do."

"Where is he?"

The man motioned with his head toward an open doorway. "He's in there."

"May I...go in?"

"Sure."

As they went into the room, Kip's eyes went immediately to an aluminum shipping casket poised on top a stainless steel gurney. The man leading him stopped, turned, then stepped aside.

For a long moment Kip stood fixed in one spot. He stared, tilting his head slightly, his eyes narrowing. After a minute, after his breathing had become shallow and steady, it dawned on him that he had nothing momentous to say, nothing that Leo might want to hear should his spirit...his energy...be lingering somewhere nearby. He reached in his pocket and withdrew the Silver Star Rameriz had given him. His eyes fixed on the casket, Kip said, "You don't have to do this now...but would you place this medal somewhere inside after I leave? If you could, maybe on his chest..."

"Sure, no problem." The man reached for the medal and asked, puzzled:

"Do you know him?"

Slater looked at the man as if seeing him for the first time. He moved his eyes over the white smock, the gray pants, the rubber-gloved hands. It was the man's uniform, the uniform of his grisly trade. He was a mortician, employed by the United States government, a man who "processed" bodies "produced" by the war to be shipped home. He wanted to reach out and strangle him, to scream at him that this was not just another body—not just another hunk of burned flesh. *This is Leo...Leo was my friend! We flew together! We drank together and got stoned together! He got shot down! Do you hear me? He got killed helping to rescue an American POW! And now he's dead! Do you hear what I'm saying? Do you care? Does anybody here care—?* Slater stepped back, his eyes now refocusing on the casket. He said, softly:

"Yeah...I knew him. We were buddies..."

Victor R. Beaver

The western skies were showing the very last rays of sunlight. With a folded American flag under his right arm, Slater stood on the concrete surface of the loading ramp and watched the loading crew drive forward bearing Leo's casket. When the vehicle, designed to raise heavy objects up until level with the cargo opening of the plane, had stopped, Kip stepped forward and asked that one of the men help him spread the flag to cover the casket. A young man, eighteen, his face expressionless, complied. Kip handed him one end and the two carefully unfolded the red, white and blue cloth and gently laid it over the casket. After it was secured, Kip stepped back and, choking back tears, slowly raised his right arm; he held the salute for a heartbeat longer than usual and then let his arm come slowly down.

Kip went and stood at the bottom of the stairs that led back into the terminal waiting area. He watched the men raise the casket to the cargo opening. As the casket went into the cargo hold of the plane, he happened to glance to his left. On the concrete surface he saw three white doves stepping about, cooing softly. He peered at them for a moment and then, without apparent cause or reason, they burst into flight. With wings fluttering, Kip saw them fly past the cargo opening and then were gone into the black-blue night.

The cargo door remained open. He turned, glanced at the door at the top of the stairs, then looked back at the plane, at the open cargo door. Kip took a step and then remembered the piece of paper and the poem written by Thoreau. Leo had left it on his cot. He removed his billfold, took out the paper and unfolded it.

> *"...And the long afterglow gives light.*
> *And the damask curtains glow along the*
> *Western window*
> *And now the first star is lit*
> *And I go home..."*

Just then the cargo door closed. Kip saw a lone star twinkling overhead. He said, "Come on, Leo...It's time to go home."

Epilogue

STATE OF THE WAR

"The end of the year 1968 seems to be yet another threshold for a war that has now become the most pervasive concern of most of the world. Some U.S. officials continue to claim that the allied forces are making increasing progress against Communist forces, but few others really believe that the war is going to be decided on the battlefield. As it happens, the Tet offensive of the early weeks of 1968 is in fact something of a military defeat for the Communists (and unbeknownst to the rest of the world, the North Vietnamese leaders have been engaged in debates—and recriminations—over the strategy and tactics that are proving to be so costly in manpower). But the Tet offensive has such an impact on Americans that it leads President Johnson to stop complying with the requests of the military chiefs to have infinite amounts of men and material. It also leads Johnson effectively to not seeking another term, and in turn to the tumultuous summer of 1968 that climaxes at the Chicago Democratic Convention. The election is won by Richard Nixon, and there is a general sense that he had both a plan and a mandate to bring the war quickly to an end. Since January 1961, some 31,000 U.S. servicemen have died in Vietnam—14,314 in 1968 alone—and some 200,000 U.S. personnel have been wounded. During 1968, 20,482 South Vietnamese military personnel were killed in combat as were 978 other allied military personnel. Allied estimates of Viet Cong and North Vietnamese military deaths are 35,774 for the year 1968, while a total of some 439,000 Communists are claimed to have been killed since January 1961. Even if these figures represent inflated 'body counts,' there is no denying that hundreds of thousands of Vietnamese, civilians as well as military, Southern as well as Northern, have been killed in the war. Little wonder that as President Johnson ends the year with only a few weeks left in office, he is reported to be 'haunted' by the war."

The Vietnam War Almanac
World Almanac Publications
New York, New York, 1985

Author Info

Victor R. Beaver began flying in 1967, when he attended the U.S. Army Aviation School during the height of the Vietnam War. He spent fourteen months in Vietnam in the late 1960s, after which he was released from active duty and received an honorable discharge in 1971. He began work on *The Sky Soldiers* in March 1976, finally completing the manuscript in May 1996. He then began the long and grueling process of perfecting his work. He is currently employed by Rocky Mountain Helicopters as an emergency medical service helicopter pilot at St. Joseph, Missouri.

As mentioned, *The Sky Soldiers* pretends to be neither history nor an exact personal account of his experiences in Vietnam and elsewhere. As in every common experience, the war became one thing to one person and an entirely different thing to another. But to all who participated, whether as soldier on duty in Vietnam or as war protestor in the United States, no better words can sum up the author's feelings toward America's less than auspicious involvement in Vietnam—to this day—than by quoting General Harold K. Johnson, Army chief of staff from 1964 to 1969, when a colleague asked:

> "If you had to do your life over, what would you do differently?" Johnson replied, "I remember the day I was ready to go over to the Oval Office and give my four stars to the president and tell him, 'You have refused to tell the country they cannot fight a war without mobilization; you have required me to send men into battle with little hope of their ultimate victory; and you have forced us in the military to violate almost every one of the principles of war. Therefore I resign and will hold a press conference after I walk out your door.'" With anguish on his face, [Johnson] concluded, "I made the typical mistake of believing I could do more for my country and for the Army if I stayed in than if I got out. And now I am going to my grave with that burden of lapse of moral courage on my back." (*Historical Atlas of the Vietnam War*, Houghton Mifflin Company, New York, New York, 1995)

or Jake again? What would my life be like then? To lose both of you would do me in. I don't know if I could bear it.

I want to tell you something else. I hope you don't mind. Two weeks ago I met this very lovely lady who works on post, a very beautiful woman. She's a divorcee with two very well behaved daughters. So far we've had several long talks over coffee and I showed her your picture. I have a feeling that if you and her were to meet you'd get along just fine. It's something to keep in mind when you get back. I know you must be terribly lonely, and she's the kind of person who doesn't go out with just anyone.

Forgive me. I'm not into matchmaking, but you never know. Please write soon. Derek, I need to hear from you, please.

Sincerely yours,
Valerie

P.S. Robbie and Jill send their love.

Valerie Cole's hands trembled as she opened Derek's return letter.

Dear Val,

I'm sorry that I've been so neglectful. It may be because I don't want to say anything that could get false hopes up. Yes, I am a part of the force that is working the Ca Mau Peninsula where I believe Jake is being held. We haven't been specifically tasked, though, to look for POWs. That's not to say that we couldn't stumble onto a POW camp. However, I must caution you that the odds of doing so are very remote. Stumbling onto the one Jake is being held at would then be even more remote. The U Minh Forest is very large. Jake could be anywhere. He could also be somewhere completely different. Heaven help me, I know this can't be very comforting to you. I will tell you this: If Jake is anywhere to be found and I am in the position to locate him, I will, you know I will. That's the only promise I can make. Take care and give my love to the kids.

Derek

The letter fell at her feet. Valerie Cole lay down on her bed and wept. There cannot be a God, she thought. No God would allow this kind of misery among His children.

* * *

MARK ALLEN CAME INTO THE SCOUT platoon tent and flopped down on his cot. "Did you get your will written?"

Sandy nodded. "How about you?"

Victor R. Beaver

"Yeah, I just gave it to the First Sergeant. I'm not leaving much, just my Impala to my mom. She'll probably just get rid of it." Allen glanced at the sheet of paper in front of his friend. "What are you doing now?"

"Writing a letter."

"Are you still after that high school sweetheart?"

"No," Sandy said softly. "This is to someone else."

"You never give up, do you?"

Sandy shrugged. He said, "Mark, would you do something for me?"

"Sure."

Sandy took his ID tag chain from around his neck. He undid the chain and slipped a girl's ring into the palm of his hand. "This is Katie's class ring. I never gave it back. I'm putting it inside my shaving kit. If something happens to me, would you send it to this address." He handed Mark a folded slip of paper with Katie's address.

"Sure...if that's what you want."

Sandy went back to his letter. After a few minutes, he was done.

Dear Michelle,

I hesitated writing to you again because I feared that if I say what I feel I will frighten you away. Looking back on the way I dealt with Katie, my old girlfriend, the harder I fought to keep her, the more distant she became, until finally we broke up altogether.

I remember the day you and I spent on the beach and how comfortable it was. We laughed and played and got along the way I always imagined two people should. For just a day, we were friends, there was nothing serious between us and it felt uplifting and free. Did you feel the same way?

Thank you for the picture. We look pretty good together, don't you think? How's college? Are you dating anyone? If you are, I'll bet he is a real nice person, because you're a real nice person.

No, I don't sleep in a foxhole. Right now I live in a tent, at a place called Ca Mau, near a very bad place called the U Minh Forest. They told us yesterday that we are going to start flying in there to look for the Viet Cong. We may even run across a POW camp where Americans are being held. But we have to very careful, because we've also been told that the VC will kill any prisoner who tries to escape or has the potential of being rescued. Also, if an American has been a prisoner long, he may look just like the Viet Cong. God help us if we accidentally shoot one of our own.

Well, I have to go. I want to be well rested before my first flight in the U Minh.

Sincerely yours,
Sandy